VICTORIAN
FAIRY TALES

Victorian Fairy Tales

Edited with an Introduction and Notes by
MICHAEL NEWTON

UNIVERSITY PRESS

Great Clarendon Street, Oxford, OX2 6DP,
United Kingdom

Oxford University Press is a department of the University of Oxford.
It furthers the University's objective of excellence in research, scholarship,
and education by publishing worldwide. Oxford is a registered trade mark of
Oxford University Press in the UK and in certain other countries

Selection and editorial material © Michael Newton 2015

Although every effort has been made to trace and contact the copyright holder for
Laurence Housman prior to publication, we have been unsuccessful. If notified,
we will be pleased to rectify this at the earliest opportunity.

The moral rights of the author have been asserted

First published 2015

Impression: 1

All rights reserved. No part of this publication may be reproduced, stored in
a retrieval system, or transmitted, in any form or by any means, without the
prior permission in writing of Oxford University Press, or as expressly permitted
by law, by licence or under terms agreed with the appropriate reprographics
rights organization. Enquiries concerning reproduction outside the scope of the
above should be sent to the Rights Department, Oxford University Press, at the
address above

You must not circulate this work in any other form
and you must impose this same condition on any acquirer

Published in the United States of America by Oxford University Press
198 Madison Avenue, New York, NY 10016, United States of America

British Library Cataloguing in Publication Data

Data available

Library of Congress Control Number: 2014949669

ISBN 978–0–19–960195–0

Printed in Italy by
L.E.G.O. S.p.A.—Lavis TN

Links to third party websites are provided by Oxford in good faith and
for information only. Oxford disclaims any responsibility for the materials
contained in any third party website referenced in this work.

ACKNOWLEDGEMENTS

My greatest thanks go to my exemplary editor, Judith Luna, for her patience, her diligence, and her insight. Also at Oxford University Press, I would like to express my thanks to Jenni Crosskey and Emily Brand for their support, Rowena Anketell and Peter Gibbs for their inspired scrutiny of the text, and Bob Elliott for his excellent design work. I am grateful to the staff of the British Library, Leiden University Library, and the Bodleian Library, especially the staff of the Imaging Services department. I am indebted to Professor Rolf Bremmer for Old English counsel. My especial thanks go to Jenny Weston and to Jenneka Janzen, for their enormous help.

I thank Lena, as ever, for her support, concern, and warmth. I dedicate this book and all my work in it to the very wonderful Alice and Hannah Newton, who both love fairy tales, but are not, as yet, interested in explanatory notes.

CONTENTS

Introduction	IX
Note on the Texts	XXIX
Select Bibliography	XXXI
A Chronology of the Literary Fairy Tale	XXXVI

PROLOGUE

JAKOB AND WILHELM GRIMM
   Rumpel-Stilts-kin   3

HANS CHRISTIAN ANDERSEN
   The Princess and the Peas   6

VICTORIAN FAIRY TALES

ROBERT SOUTHEY
   The Story of the Three Bears   11

JOHN RUSKIN
   The King of the Golden River   15

WILLIAM MAKEPEACE THACKERAY
   The Rose and the Ring   38

GEORGE MacDONALD
   The Golden Key   115

DINAH MULOCK CRAIK
   The Little Lame Prince and his Travelling Cloak   141

MARY DE MORGAN
   The Wanderings of Arasmon   206

JULIANA HORATIA EWING
   The First Wife's Wedding-Ring   223

OSCAR WILDE
   The Selfish Giant   228

ANDREW LANG
   Prince Prigio   233

FORD MADOX FORD
   The Queen Who Flew   276

LAURENCE HOUSMAN
   The Story of the Herons   327

KENNETH GRAHAME
   The Reluctant Dragon   342

E. NESBIT
   Melisande   366

RUDYARD KIPLING
   Dymchurch Flit   378

Appendix: What is a Fairy Tale?   391
   JOHN RUSKIN
      'Introduction' to *German Popular Tales*   391
   JULIANA HORATIA EWING
      'Preface' to *Old-Fashioned Fairy Tales*   395
   GEORGE MacDONALD
      'The Fantastic Imagination'   397
   LAURENCE HOUSMAN
      'Introduction' to *Gammer Grethel's Fairy Tales*   401

Explanatory Notes   405

INTRODUCTION

In Britain and Ireland during the nineteenth century, writers started creating their own fairy stories, sometimes for children and sometimes also for adults, transforming a form based in the shared telling of tales into self-conscious, authored literary texts. They were also imitating a tradition of collecting and writing down such oral tales, or making up new ones, that had begun centuries before in Italy, had moved to France in the late seventeenth century, and then around the turn of the nineteenth century flourished in the German states. In doing so, those British and Irish writers responded to their own notions of what those original, anonymously invented texts meant, and therefore also to ideas of 'the folk', the fairy, and the child. They experimented with the form to explore political and social concerns, as well as questions of identity, love, and the moral life. Together they built up a body of work that contains some of the most vivid, most astonishing, and most entertaining writing of the century.

Some have decried the literary fairy tale as sentimental, escapist, and kitsch. Though much substandard work was published, in the finest examples there is a lot of tough-mindedness, wit and genuine humour, as well as cognizance of suffering, and traces too of the numinous. The literary fairy story involves the fantastic, a supernatural that is neither eerie nor horrific, but rather is whimsical, playful, or invitingly strange. Condemnations of escapism should further be tempered by the fact that for loathers of industrialism such as John Ruskin or George MacDonald, for women like Dinah Mulock Craik and Mary De Morgan, for gay men like Oscar Wilde or Laurence Housman, there was much in contemporary Victorian life from which one might want to escape. Moreover, far from pure flight from life, such stories are rather a way to expose social tensions and psychological conflicts and to devise their potential solutions.

Critics and writers have frequently presented fairy tales as neglected, spurned, on the point of being lost. Anxiety hovers about them. This fear concerning fairy stories often situates itself as a defence of traditions, of the old cultural and economic ways. The ogre that threatens fairyland is dry rationalism, a tepidly actuarial take on life. At the start of the century, in 1803, the devoutly

Anglican writer Sarah Trimmer (1741–1810) could see fairy tales as injuring children's minds by 'exciting unreasonable and groundless fears'.[1] On the other side of the political spectrum, the radical Mrs Anna Barbauld shared her antipathy. A practical, no-nonsense form of fiction for children was proposed, and the child was supposed to be stranded among the dry, if rational pages of an author like Jane Marcet, a writer of popular scientific texts for children. Such critiques were countered by many over the next hundred years, though for some they retained their force. In particular, the circle of 'the Lake poets' (Samuel Taylor Coleridge, William Wordsworth, and, in far-off London, Charles Lamb) held out against this somewhat exaggerated threat. They would protect the fairy tale from harm, rescue it from neglect. In his 'Preface' to *German Popular Stories* (1823), Edgar Taylor begins by lamenting that 'Popular fictions and traditions are somewhat gone out of fashion; yet most will own them to be associated with the brightest recollections of their youth'.[2] We should grasp that part of the appeal of the Grimms' tales to early nineteenth-century British readers was that they enshrined the free imagination, but did so by recalling native versions of tales they had already listened to in childhood. From the start of the century such stories belonged to nostalgia; they were believed to be despised by others, but beloved and cherished by you.

The defenders of the fairy tale, such as Coleridge, Dickens, Ruskin, Craik, Ewing, and MacDonald, all saw it as a form implicitly moral, but spoilt by overt moralization. Fairy tale stands for all that the Gradgrinds and the Bounderbys of the world would reject; in place of fact, calculation, and the ratio, they propose fancy and mystery; in place of a mathematical and analytical understanding, they offer affection, intuition, and strangeness.

In any case, far from being an endangered species in the nineteenth century, it is noticeable how vital Perrault, d'Aulnoy, Grimm, Andersen, and the *Thousand and One Nights* were to the majority of British and Irish writers. Even so poignantly down-to-earth a text as Elizabeth Gaskell's *Cranford* (1851–3)—let alone Charles Dickens's

---

[1] Quoted in Nicholas Tucker (ed.), *Suitable for Children: Controversies in Children's Literature* (Berkeley and Los Angeles: University of California Press, 1976), 38. Trimmer was, however, not consistently opposed to fairy tales.

[2] Edgar Taylor, 'Preface' to *German Popular Stories*, trans. Taylor (London: C. Baldwyn, 1823), p. iii.

Hard Times (1854)—consistently has recourse to these fables and fairy tales; they were simply part of the shared vocabulary of Victorian culture. If we wish to understand the Victorians, we should read their dreams.

Sources, Inspirations, Origins

Often fairy tales include no actual fairy. Perhaps, as Jack Zipes has suggested, the very term 'fairy tale' misleads us, and it would be better to think of such stories as a *Zaubermärchen*, as a *conte merveilleux*, a tale of wonder and supernatural fantasy.[3]

Nevertheless fairies, those elusive beings, continue to colour our sense of such stories. Like ghost stories, the fairy tale can depend on a sense of ineffable presence, the immaterial materialized in another kind of body, another kind of self. These fairies are not abject as ghosts are, but superior, delicate, better than ourselves. They have been seen variously as nature spirits, dwindled gods, visitors from other worlds; as another race of rational beings besides humans and angels; as the dead; as the merely natural, creatures like any other, resembling the human, but soulless. As these contrasting theories demonstrate, in the Victorian period, fairies—like fairy tales, children's literature, and childhood itself—were objects of contention. In *The Discarded Image*, C. S. Lewis argued that fairies had brought to the coherent and overarching medieval picture of the world an element of elusive mystery; these were creatures who moved easily between categories, sometimes damned spirits, sometimes mirthful and miniature creatures, sometimes high emissaries from another finer, more dangerous world.[4] Though alleviated in most cases by an absence of actual belief, this indeterminacy, this fugitive and uncategorizable quality in the fairies persisted into the nineteenth century. Fairies, like fairy tales, were never one kind of thing, or perhaps were things that might be interpreted in many contrasting, and even contradictory, ways.

If one vital, if indirect, source for the Victorian literary fairy tale was the idea of the fairy, another was the body of classic fairy

---

[3] Jack Zipes, 'Introduction' to Zipes (ed.), *The Oxford Companion to Fairy Tales* (Oxford: Oxford University Press, 2000), p. xvi.

[4] C. S. Lewis, 'The *Longaevi*', in Lewis, *The Discarded Image: An Introduction to Medieval and Renaissance Literature* (Cambridge: Cambridge University Press, 1964), 122–38.

tales, from Giovanni Straparola and Giambattista Basile, through Charles Perrault, Madame d'Aulnoy, Madame de Beaumont, and the *Thousand and One Nights*, to the Grimms and Hans Christian Andersen. In particular, the Grimms' volume vitalized the form. Indeed, it may be, as Caroline Sumpter has suggested, that Grimm in particular became the canonical version of such tales with the 1823 volume, assuming an inviolable status as true origin which extended to Cruikshank's illustrations.[5] The Victorian writers love to refer back to their famous predecessors. Everywhere these stories contentedly expose the fact that they are indebted to other stories, and several of the best fairy stories are also pastiche fairy stories (as in the tales in this volume by Thackeray, Lang, Grahame, and Nesbit). This inherited body of literary fairy tales from Straparola to the Grimms had very probably emerged out of the oral form.[6] The literary fairy tale was therefore both entwined with the 'popular', 'oral' folkloric tale, while being also distinct from it. The popular *Märchen* (or folk fairy tale) was felt to be a different kind of thing from the self-conscious *Kunstmärchen* (an authored and imitative fairy tale), for the latter was curiously doubled, an artful version of supposedly naive folk art.

Oral tradition remains potent in a tale such as 'The Three Bears'. Southey recommends the reading of his tale with a proper emphasis for it 'never fails of effect with that fit audience for which it is designed, if it be told with dramatic spirit, in the manner that our way of printing it may sufficiently indicate, without the aid of musical notation'.[7] He returns to the same thought at the tale's conclusion, visualizing it as having been not just read, but acted out to its child audience.[8]

It may now seem a strange anomaly of literary history that Ford Madox Ford, author of the magnificently jaded *The Good Soldier* (1915), began his career with the writing of fairy tales. Fairy tales were not merely ethereal properties, they were also a business, and afforded to writers a dual market of children and adults, as well as a means to position themselves as a particular kind of writer. Few writers were only fairy-tale writers: Ruskin was a critic; Thackeray

---

[5] Caroline Sumpter, *The Victorian Press and the Fairy Tale* (London: Palgrave Macmillan, 2008), 28.
[6] See Jens Tismar, *Kunstmärchen* (Stuttgart: J. B. Metzler, 1977).
[7] From Robert Southey, *The Doctor* (London: Longman, Rees, Orme, Brown, Green and Longman, 1837), iv. 316–17.
[8] Southey, *The Doctor*. iv. 327–8.

and MacDonald were novelists and editors; Wilde was a man of letters staking a claim for himself as an author in many different fields; Craik was one of the most famous novelists of her day. Many of the writers produced other kinds of fantastic fiction, notably ghost stories, as in the case of E. Nesbit and Kipling. Nonetheless the fairy tale was a recognizable niche product, one that took its place in the book market or in periodicals alongside many other kinds of fiction for children, and for adults. The fairy-tale volume, married as it was to illustration, formed a natural locale for writers who might broadly be described as 'aesthetic' or even 'decadent'.

Literary fairy tales, of course, worked differently from their cousins in the oral tradition. They were authored, manufactured, derivative; yet something of the folk idea clung to them. They may not be authentically primitive, but they were certainly aspiringly primitivist.

In fact the fairy tale is the most eclectic of forms, whose origins are fascinatingly varied, drawing in such native examples of 'the fairy way of writing' as Sir Edmund Spenser's *The Faerie Queene* and William Shakespeare's *A Midsummer Night's Dream* and *The Tempest*, as well as the work of the German Romantics—Novalis, Tieck, Motte Fouqué, and Hoffmann. These sources were mixed, and were themselves potently 'syncretic', relaxedly combining Athens and the English woods, Christendom and fairyland, nobility, mechanicals, and fairy royalty. At a time when anthropologists and folklorists dreamt of purity, the writers borrowed freely from whatever inspired them, giving their tales a glorious hybrid, piebald form.

When, in his essay 'The Fantastic Imagination', George MacDonald asks what is a fairy tale, he answers by pointing to Motte Fouqué's *Undine*—and not to 'The Yellow Dwarf' or 'Sleeping Beauty'. This Germanic connection was not shared by everyone; some of the writers in this volume might be thought of as Francophile rather than Germanophile. Yet in some quarters there was a particular interest in England's sharing a 'Northern antiquity' with the Grimm tales.[9] Some writers, folklorists, and anthropologists were especially impelled to trace back the tales to some envisioned, pure beginning. This place of origin was seen as being variously Celtic, or Saxon or Teutonic. When Charles Boner translated Hans Christian Andersen's stories they were presented as 'the *Danish* story-book'—the product

---

[9] Taylor, 'Preface' to *German Popular Stories*, p. vi.

of a country, and not an author. A taste for a certain kind of fairy story might tell of political allegiances. In aligning themselves as more akin to Perrault or to the Grimms, to the Scandinavians or the Celts, more was at stake than a purely aesthetic choice; an affiliation to a particular image of culture was involved. If the initial influences were French or German, as the century progressed interest sparked up in locally national identities, in Celtic tales or English lore. In this way the collection of oral, popular folk tales could form part of a nationalist project, the establishment of an unsullied identity; such they were to W. B. Yeats and Lady Augusta Gregory, collecting folk tales of the peasantry with an eye to the establishment of a purely national myth.

In the Victorian literary fairy tale, folklore becomes the root of a literary art. Though their primary interest was not artistic, but philological or anthropological, at their best the folklorists were responsive to other things. Men like Sir Walter Scott were touchingly in love with the wonders they researched. The gift that folklorists gave to the writers of literary fairy tales was a path back to a reality, a past that was everywhere open to the marvellous.

This marvellous might have connotations of national identity that linked folklore inextricably to political aims. Now that most critics understand Wilde as a covertly Irish nationalist writer, undermining 'John Bull' through wit and humour that English people failed to get, it is all the more surprising that in his fairy tales he did not ostensibly take the Celtic route followed by Yeats. After all, his father had collected oral folk tales from among the Irish peasantry, and his mother had written such tales herself. As we shall see, it may be that there are indeed references and allusions to Ireland in Wilde's stories. It may also be that all kinds of fairy tale proposed a kind of national self-definition, as many Scots, Welsh, and Irish writers—the romantic, anti-empiricist 'Celtic fringe'—favoured fantasy.

This interest in 'the folk' was just one of the highly contemporary ways in which writers conceived of a state prior to modernity. Although such concerns had been present since the Grimms, in the 1880s and 1890s, thinking on the fairy tale was transformed under the pressure of evolutionary theories, particularly the idea of recapitulation (the belief that the life of the individual re-enacts the story of the race). Edward Clodd's study *Tom Tit Tot: An Essay on Savage Philosophy in Folk Tale* (1898) exemplifies this belief. In his monograph, fairy tales go on to link us to the childhood of the human race in savagery, and to the more childlike, unsophisticated world of the peasant. Moreover, such tales are themselves expressive of atavistic states of mind, relics of an original philosophical understanding of the world. On the principle of analogy—but also with the thought that some kind of shared identity was in fact involved—folklorists, educational theorists, and anthropologists fancied savages, peasants, children, and sometimes women, to be all at the same primitive developmental point, possessing an atavistic mode of mental and imaginative perception. This archaic simplicity, smuggled into the present in the bodies and minds of these modern people could be represented as desirable or despicable. In his 'Preface' to the *Violet Fairy Book* (1901), Andrew Lang writes, 'These stories are as old as anything that man has invented. They are narrated by naked savage women to naked savage children . . . Then learned men collected and printed the country people's stories, and these we have translated, to amuse children. Their tastes remain like the tastes of their naked ancestors, thousands of years ago, and they seem to like fairy tales better than history, poetry, geography, or arithmetic, just as grown-up people like novels better than anything else.'[10] (In this account, primitive women tell the tales; savage children hear them; sophisticated men collect them.) The thought outlined here could be illustrated by dozens of other similar statements.

Now the fairy tale and the fairy itself both appeared as dark survivals. The notion is strongest in the supernatural fiction of Arthur Machen, whose masterpiece 'The White People' (1899), though not a fairy tale as such, succeeds in reinvesting the fairy with an ancient, lingering malevolence. It is there in a more benign form in Kipling's writing, where Puck stands as an ever-present embodiment of the spirit of place, the stories recommending a backwards path into a real England of wonder and enchantment. *Puck of Pook's Hill* is a book of exiles, of people out of place, and in 'Dymchurch Flit' the fairies themselves become the latest such migrants. With urbanization and the decline of the rural economy, the poor of the countryside were on the move, and their new peripatetic lifestyle finds its mirror in this story.

Just as, in relation to race, the fairy tale could seem a trace of a pure historical origin, so the stories themselves and the manner of their

[10] Andrew Lang, 'Preface' to Lang, *The Violet Fairy Book* (London: Longmans and Co., 1901), pp. ix–x.

telling might appear both ancient and timeless. However, it is a paradox quickly grasped that in these 'secondary fairy tales', these literary imitations of a literary response to an anyway historicized oral narrative, the very fact of the tale expresses yearnings for timelessness in the midst of an industrialized modernity. If fairy tales relate to primitive psychology, to savage ideas, we should consider what it means for a sophisticated writer self-consciously to produce one as a literary construction.

Faced with this literary and psychological conundrum, writers responded variously to the challenge. Some fell back on artfulness and whimsy, others sought a Romantic attuning to primitive and fugitive states of mind, to the suprarational self, and to the past (the child, the savage, the rustic) against the modern world.

Certainly the fairy tale shadows the history of technology over the century, and beyond. The form stands as a pre-industrial survival, and therefore an implicit emblem of resistance to modernity; yet fairy tales fitted comfortably into the niches created by each innovation: changes in the printing technology transmuted the literary form, particularly with regard to its relationship to illustration. At the end of the century in particular, with the growing impact of the 'gift-book' and new techniques of colour reproduction (mostly through chromolithography and the three-colour process) the fairy-tale volume became a luxury item. Modern methods of printing and publishing indisputably also made a space in which the literary fairy tale could flourish.[11]

Such sumptuous products inevitably raised questions as to whether or not they were intended for children. In any case, writing on fairy tales inevitably, and perhaps unfortunately, brings in the question of their audience. Are these stories for children or adults or both? As J. R. R. Tolkien explained in his essay 'On Fairy Stories', there is no necessary connection between the child and the fairy tale; although it is vital to our understanding of the form that in the nineteenth century people perceived one. Ideas of the childlike, and of the trust, open-heartedness, and wonder once found in the child, infiltrated critics' and writers' views of the form. For adults, reading fairy tales extended a route back into the childhood they had lost, or retained merely fitfully. Jack Zipes has suggested that writers always had two audiences in mind, the middle-class young and the middle-class adult, and that they had different aims in mind with each of these

---

[11] See Sumpter, *The Victorian Press and the Fairy Tale*.

audiences: with the children, they wished to influence and form; with the grown-ups, they hoped to 'challenge and reform'.[12] These are stories told by adults to children, and as such can only exist through a tacit understanding of what childhood is conceived to be. In both writing and reading such tales, adults dramatize their own wants and dreams, and simultaneously dream themselves back into their own childhood and project themselves out into the childhood of others. Concepts of the child interact with concepts of 'the fairy' and of 'the fairy tale', and these distinct things start to seem allied. The child recapitulated a lost past, and so brought into the world both its own absolute newness and also something archaic, the thoughts and feelings of the human race at its origin. If these stories and their style harked back to a simpler age, this was therefore likewise true of their anticipated audience, of childhood as conceived before and within these stories.

That such stories were good for adults as well as children was a commonplace—as Israel Zangwill remarked of the folklorist Joseph Jacobs, 'his books delighted equally the nursery and the drawing-room'.[13] Thackeray described *The Rose and the Ring* as a story for 'us children'.[14] The gifted fantasy writer Neil Gaiman has spoken of the way in which such stories do not envision an absolute literary divide between children and adults, but rather appeal to the literariness of the child and the childlike in the adult reader. It is with fairy tales that the child makes his or her first discovery of intertextuality; these stories are something known, and loved, and mockable, and quickly understood as working in generic terms, according to accepted rules. The tales in this volume play on the knowledge of the child reader. Thackeray, Lang, and Nesbit, in particular, rely on our knowingness—that we will have guessed most of the plot already, that we are clever, worldly-wise readers and therefore not 'childish', even if we are still children.

This question of the audience raises the suitability of the tales for children. In 1891, a critic wrote of Wilde's latest book of fairy tales: 'Is *A House of Pomegranates* intended for a children's book? We confess that we do not exactly know. The ultra-aestheticism of the pictures

---

[12] Jack Zipes, 'Preface' to Zipes (ed.), *Victorian Fairy Tales: The Revolt of the Fairies and Elves* (New York and London: Routledge, 1987), p. xi.

[13] Quoted in Anne J. Kershen, 'Joseph Jacobs', in *Oxford Dictionary of National Biography* (Oxford: Oxford University Press).

[14] William Makepeace Thackeray, letter to James Hain Friswell, 10 December 1854, in *The Letters and Private Papers of William Makepeace Thackeray*, ed. Gordon Ray (London: Oxford University Press, 1946), iii. 405.

seems unsuitable for children—as also the rather "fleshly" style of Mr. Wilde's writing.'[15] Here knowingness becomes suspect, as such stories are felt to touch on matters of love and sex—questions popularly supposed to be properly absent from children's books, though palpably at the heart of the Victorian fairy tales.

The Stories: Fairyland and the Real World

Fairy tales may be regarded by some as the simplest of all narrative forms. However, they are in fact one of the most experimental of all nineteenth-century genres. After all, these stories, from Ruskin to De Morgan, are what the great twentieth-century Modernists read as children. In particular, they inherit from German Romanticism a mode of narrative that is fragmented, apparently irrational, the organized structure of a tale coming closest to the visionary freedom of dreams. The fairy tale disobeyed aesthetic strictures that demanded a strict realism and adherence to fact in the literary work.

In Robert Southey's 'The Three Bears', language exists as structure and incantation, building the sense of inevitability contained in pattern. It is a story with no real resolution, no consolation. It only establishes a design in which a disruptive outsider breaks into an order (of three). The woman is an intruding rogue, the bears put upon; but her coming is a random event; she's just someone up to no good.

There were other ways to play with storytelling. Fairy stories were often framed within larger narratives, as in Dickens's *Pickwick Papers*, MacDonald's *At the Back of the North Wind*, or the children's novels of Mary Molesworth. In Grahame's *Dream Days*, the frames around the story 'The Reluctant Dragon' multiply, taking in the narrator's tale, the circus-man's yarn, the conventional stories that the Boy reads, the lies told by the villagers, and the feigned performance presented by St George and the dragon. Everyone here is a storyteller, and sometimes a listener to others' stories. The story tells us what does not get into the books (though such information is, of course, present in this one).

If, in Grahame's story, narrative expectations are comically defeated, then the ultimate such expectation in the fairy tale is that the story should end happily. We may wonder if a fairy tale should ever be tragic.

---

[15] From *Pall Mall Gazette*, 30 November 1891, p. 3.

Introduction

The phrase 'a fairy-tale ending' implies a happy one. Yet Andersen, De Morgan, and Wilde all produced moving tales with markedly unhappy conclusions. Thackeray's *The Rose and the Ring* plays with the possibility of tragedy, taking the plot of *Hamlet* and turning it comic.

Such contrasts work too in the very style of the stories, and, at times, in their illustration. Fairy tales could radically mix techniques, as in Oscar Wilde's tales, which sometimes pose a style derived from Andersen against an Orientalist luxuriance. A different contrast animates Thackeray's *The Rose and the Ring*. Thackeray perhaps found his theme in the drawings that inspired his text. There he draws out an intriguing contrast between an art that improves on nature and an art that uglifies it; both are seen as distortions. Within the tale, Tommaso Lorenzo's painting counterfeits a notably enhanced and lying version of its subject (see illustration on p. 57), while Thackeray's art of caricature exposes the grotesque exaggeration of human moral and physical frailty. In his drawings, Thackeray could purvey either a passable version of the fashionably prettified style of the time, or give himself over to the outrageously ridiculous. Sometimes Thackeray's two styles of drawing confront each other in the same picture. By these means, Thackeray wonders over the difference between true and illusory beauty, as expressed in the mystifying effect of the fairy ring. This is a story about the creation of a world through the lens of a style, and the eye of a beholder. The mixture of prettiness and the grotesque manifest here vivifies innumerable fairy paintings, which both show a beautified world yet impress on it the twisted, improbable bodies of the fairies themselves.

Thackeray's approach endorses the knowing artfulness, the position of performance in the fairy-tale tradition. This aspect of the fairy tale was connected to one other of its manifestations and sources—the place of theatre, fairy ballet (such as *La Sylphide*), and, especially, pantomime. In his 'Preface' to his translation of the Grimms' tales, Edgar Taylor makes the link:

Popular fictions and traditions are somewhat gone out of fashion; yet most will own them to be associated with the brightest recollections of their youth. They are, like the Christmas Pantomime, ostensibly brought forth to tickle the palate of the young, but are often received with as keen an appetite by those of graver years.[16]

---

[16] Taylor, 'Preface' to *German Popular Stories*, p. iii.

For this reason, fairy stories, like ghost stories, were strongly connected with Christmas; indeed Dickens's *A Christmas Carol* (1843) may be deemed to have equally forged the association of two kinds of supernatural tale with the season. Thackeray's *The Rose and the Ring* derives from the Twelfth Night characters; and Ruskin's *The King of the Golden River* was also a Christmas book (and, like *The Christmas Carol*, one that celebrated giving over meanness and lack of charity). However, the link between fairy tales and Christmas may have had other, higher connotations, and have as much to do with 'incarnation' and midwinter renewal as with performance and make-up.

During the nineteenth century some writers worried over the potential impiety of the fairy tale, as though the supernatural it offered was contaminated by ancient paganism. Others were happy to use the form, implicitly or explicitly, for Christian purposes. Andersen, MacDonald, and Craik actively Christianize the fairy tale, rendering it the vehicle of a religiously understood sense of mystery; the Christian resonances at the close of Wilde's 'The Selfish Giant' are also salient. MacDonald's novel *Adela Cathcart* enacts this idea, showing its heroine restored to faith in God, in life and love by hearing tales—including fairy tales. It may be that, for some, the very basis of the tales carry religious significances, in so far as they celebrate the world while expressing and transcending our dissatisfaction with it. Here is a world like our own, but also better, more natural; perhaps this is just more escapism, or perhaps part of a human longing for a golden world. Similarly the morality of fairy tales offers a justice for which there is no real equivalent in human life; the humble and good are exalted, the proud and wicked cast down.

It is sometimes argued that the Victorian interest in fairies (as, in a darker vein, with ghosts, spirits, and vampires) represented an attempt to find the sacred in a world disenchanted (in the terms used by the sociologist Max Weber) by industrialism, urbanization, and 'the death of God'. The interest in fairy tales might simply be part of a broader simultaneous re-enchantment of the world, found in the European interest in spiritualism, in parapsychology, in Indian religions, in theosophy, in a renewed commitment to a miraculous Christianity, and, for someone like W. B. Yeats, in a willed desire to believe in the fairies that science would reject. Certainly when Doyle came to write his book about the case of the Cottingley fairies, it was vital to him that the existence of fairies, as evidenced in the photographs taken by two young Yorkshire girls, could demonstrate the existence of a spiritual realm.

How might these concerns play out in the stories themselves, where, as many have noted, fairies often play little or no part? They do so in part by dramatizing questions of belief and credence, in asking us to follow the characters within the stories and so 'awake our faith'. Hence, at its worst, that infamous moment in J. M. Barrie's *Peter Pan*, when the audience are emotionally blackmailed into declaring a belief in fairies. At its best, as in Lang's *Prince Prigio*, we have a story that comprehends the sceptic's position. Tolkien disapproved of the fact that in Lang facetiousness gets entangled in the fable, sarcasm impinging on the sense of wonder. In fact that is the story's strength, one that enables it, through a joke, to affirm faith in love and in the marvellous. Here, in self-forgetting, love lifts you above scepticism.

Whatever the theological implications of the form, nonetheless belief was central to the tales, in so far as they assert fantasy over realism; artifice over naturalism; romance over the real. This set of preferences once made the stories seem unengaged with the social conditions and political conflicts of the time. In fact, of course, these tales themselves offered a way into thinking about the problems of the present and of framing political concerns. Fairy tales engage with modernity, but do so surreptitiously.

As Jack Zipes has argued, in the fairy tale modern industrial society and the pursuit of money and social success are often questioned.[17] Such ideas inspired traditionalists but also social radicals; both impulses (conservatism and radicalism) merge in Ruskin and William Morris. *The King of the Golden River* is, among other things, an ecological fable, contrasting material gold and the real gold of natural things.

Most recent criticism focuses on the literary fairy tale as primarily political, and (in most accounts) hiddenly engaged in subversion, the making of a mirror-space where protests against Victorian culture and morality could be voiced. In such critiques, as in fairy tales themselves, nothing is what it appears to be, and anything might at some point turn into something else. Penetrating insights derived from psychoanalysis and sociology pierce the story; the fantastic text

---

[17] Zipes, 'Introduction' to Zipes (ed.), *Victorian Fairy Tales: The Revolt of the Fairies and Elves*, p. xvi.

becomes a mask designed by its very unreality to lay bare the strictures and constrictions imposed on Victorian social identity. The old belief was that within the surface, in images of something infinitely desirable, were concealed truths too great for telling. The contemporary critical orthodoxy is that this same surface actually delineates tensions and conflicts in the class, imperial, and gender relations of the time. It is the productive tension between these two aspects of these tales, as both psychologically pregnant and perhaps inherently political, that establishes their continuing relevance to us.

The pleasures of these tales were no doubt touched for contemporary writers and readers by such political dreams. Images of the political (on the large or the personal scale) imbue the fairy tale. Even a cursory reading of the tales would show how fascinated they are with ideas of authority, power, and rule. The starkly simplified political worlds of these tales offer satirical but also symbolic representations of power and inheritance. The fairy-tale world is so often a place of kings and queens, princes and princesses, but then so was Britain and most of Europe. The queens and kings in the stories aptly reminded readers of their own heads of state. (After all, Disraeli dubbed Victoria 'the faery'.) Questions of inheritance are central to the literary fairy tale, partly drawing on the oral tradition and partly on Shakespeare (following *Hamlet* and *King John*, uncles get as bad a press as stepmothers). The very grain of the stories can be steeped in politics; these are often tales of rule and misrule. In one sense, fairyland is no utopia; in the mirror of its being, injustice exists there as here. Far from being straightforwardly monarchical, such tales can sometimes show the weariness of ruling; the heroes and heroines are as likely to wish to forgo their royalty, as to try to win it.

It is not hard to find contemporary political concerns manifest in the tales. Written in an Italy partly ruled by Austria and prevented from unifying by Louis Napoleon, Thackeray's *The Rose and the Ring* explores tyranny and the effects of corrupt government (as well as offering patriotic succour during the Crimean War). Craik too offers the creation of a no-place that is also a reflection of here, in a tale that is political and socially conscious. (One critic has suggested that Craik's most popular 'realist' novel, *John Halifax, Gentleman*, was itself 'the fairy-tale of the middle classes'.[18]) Wilde's tales certainly contained

---

[18] Alan Horsman, *The Victorian Novel* (Oxford: Clarendon Press, 1990), 199.

discreet social comment. The presence of the notable socialist Walter Crane as illustrator for his first fairy-tale volume perhaps signals Wilde's own attempt to combine aestheticism and radicalism. This volume, *The Happy Prince and Other Tales*, has its connections to the impoverished East End in the period; that book was published in 1888, the year of the match girls' strike, and symbolically enough Wilde sent a copy to Toynbee Hall (a philanthropic institution in Whitechapel). He examines here the same problems that preoccupied the naturalist novels of the period, but by means of a fable; one reviewer described his second volume of fairy-stories, *The House of Pomegranates*, as 'half-medieval, half-modern Socialist'.[19]

Wilde's tales may have had their own tacit relation to Britain's colonial rule of Ireland. Very likely the history of empire in the period provided a political context against which the apparently ahistorical world of the fairy tale might be understood. (In Thackeray, race would appear to be absent from the tale, but it is there in the pictures, if not in the text, in so far as the servants in Crim Tartary are all black.) Across Ford's fairy country, the shadow of British imperial conquest obliquely falls: 'there is even no talk of opening the country up, which alone shows how difficult it must be to reach' (p. 324). His *The Queen Who Flew* seemed subversive at the time; one reviewer complained that the tale did not end as it should—Eldrida instead choosing poverty and rustic life over royalty and succession.[20] Ford's politics are hard to read; he presented himself as both papist and Tory, but also as someone intrigued by his friends' and acquaintances' Anarchist leanings; there is something of an Anarchist utopia about the farm of Woodward and the country where it stands. However, for all the sympathy for poverty, there are class rigidities here too; the working-class voices are mocked; the norm is the nicely well-spoken upper-middle-class child.

Such stories also offer a space for dreams, for lucid refreshment, for images that startle and astonish and both prompt our yearning and in some small measure satisfy it. No one can wish themselves naive; no reader ought to pretend that fairyland was as simple a place as some

---

[19] Review in the *Saturday Review*, in Karl Beckson (ed.), *Oscar Wilde: The Critical Heritage* (London: Routledge & Kegan Paul, 1970), 115.

[20] See Alison Lurie, 'Ford Madox Ford's Fairy Tales for Children', in Sondra J. Stang (ed.), *The Presence of Ford Madox Ford* (Philadelphia: University of Pennsylvania Press, 1981), 136–7.

Romantics and Victorians longed for it to be. The stories work, it is true, by delight, by the romance of images, the allure of glamour, by humour—all of which feed taste and moral discrimination, and not by explicit or implicit 'messages'.

The writers of the literary fairy tales themselves seem to have been engaged by a sense that the folk tale depicts (and perhaps stems from) a historyless space. The stories take place in time, and not in history—or they happen in a world so remote, geographically or chronologically, that they can be conceived in any way the writer wants. The world of 'time' crosses the path of history.

Fairy tales begin with 'Il était une fois', 'Es war einmal', or 'Once upon a time'. These words signal a uniqueness, the single occasion that this thing happened. The events here are something possible, but highly unusual and indeed unrepeatable. The fairy story tenders a unique event against the endless recurrence of individual human lives and the further background of eternity. The time in which it takes place is a past, a time that is another place and is unreachable. The fairy tale speaks from its historyless time to what is timeless in us. In fairy-tale time the assumption is that the future will resemble the past. The dailiness of history, its repetitions, its movements, laws, and typicalities are alien to the frame of the fairy tale. As we have just seen, most modern critics have wanted to historicize the tales, to return them to a political context. Certainly the literary tales themselves remain solidly Victorian; the ahistorical world they concoct now reads like a mirrored nineteenth-century England. Indeed, on occasion, as in Thackeray or Lang, the perspective shifts and we seem in an alternative version of now. Still, matters of time and history permeate the tales. It appears an open question when Lang's *Prince Prigio* is set. It seems to belong to a remote medieval world (with its talk of Saracens), yet the date on the cheque (itself a pragmatic property in a tale of seven-league boots and magic water) places it firmly in the eighteenth century. Both Thackeray and Lang set their tales not in some inaccessible land, but in recognizably situated (if highly exotic) European countries. Ruskin's valley appears a location to which we might one day travel. Happy anachronisms mark Ford's fairyland, a world where you can both meet the geese who saved the Capitol and have your photograph taken. In *Puck of Pook's Hill*, Kipling's stories take place now and in England, locating the world of fairy within the consciousness of history and of tradition.

Also caught between history and timelessness, personality and character, body and soul, is human identity. Classic fairy tales reveal a situation—and therefore an identity—hitherto concealed: the kitchen-maid is really a princess, the beast really a handsome prince. We think ourselves grand, but we are callous; we think ourselves lowly bodies and unimportant persons, but we are to be touched by the gift of grandeur. The tales let us identify with the inauthentic version and then with the real that the tale discloses. At the centre of such stories is an expectation of identification; the hero or heroine might resemble me, their reward could be mine, and their failings too. We are not merely vicarious participants in such stories, we are watchers of them, perhaps even watchers of ourselves watching; we are outside the tale, for all that we might be absorbed in it, and as such we may scrutinize and reflect.

As W. H. Auden has remarked, humility characterizes the fairy-tale hero or heroine; and if, like Prince Prigio, they are not humble at the tale's beginning, they learn to be so by its end. The reader too might be thought to be invited to share this open-hearted attitude, to forget themselves in the tale, and give themselves over to it. As the narrator in Joseph Conrad's *The Shadow-Line* remarks: 'I was very much like people in fairy tales. Nothing ever astonishes them.'[21] In any case, the surface of identity is mixed up and in flux here, though beneath all appearances lies a settled, ineradicable truth. In MacDonald's 'The Golden Key', the deaths of Mossy and Tangle create a strange dislocation; their deaths seem to alter nothing and their story continues regardless. So it is that in *The Rose and the Ring*, some people are two people, both Betsinda and Rosalba, just as the Princes, usurping kings, and deposed children are doubled, and anyone (by virtue of the ring) can be a beauty or a fright.

Sometimes this play with the nature of identity particularly involves thoughts of gender. While male writers longed to linger in childhood, women authors, oppressed by societal standards and conventions that worked to infantilize women, were more sceptical and more apt to stress the need to grow up and leave the idealized (because passive and powerless) child-state behind. Lamenting the narrow social opportunities permitted to women, Nina Auerbach and U. C. Knoepflmacher have convincingly argued that, 'In theory, at

---

[21] Joseph Conrad, *The Shadow-Line* (Oxford: Oxford University Press, 1985), 40.

any rate, women lived the condition Carroll, MacDonald, and Barrie longed for. If they were good, they never grew up.'[22]

Fantasy offers the possibility of fantasizing gender relations, both exposing injustice in the real world and opening up the possibility of other social models. Often the protagonist is a woman or a girl. Many of the most famous classic stories are tales of girlhood, of Sleeping Beauty, of Snow White, of Cinderella. But these are also markedly passive heroines. The Victorian tales take over this feature of the form, but also transform it, giving us increasingly strong, independent figures, though also still marked by an unfashionable passivity—with its endorsement of patience, of the necessity of relatedness, of holding still. Elaine Showalter has forcefully argued that in Craik's *The Little Lame Prince*, Prince Dolor stands in for the author herself: 'cast out of the happy kingdom by her father's desertion, crippled by her female role, and finally redeemed through self-discipline and imagination'.[23] In a book on Craik, Sally Mitchell concurs, writing: 'The orphaned and helpless Prince Dolor is a projection of the female situation.'[24] As evidenced in her last novels, Craik was passionate about the social and political injustice experienced by women. However, convincing as this is, if *The Little Lame Prince* is about the passive suffering of women, then nonetheless Craik chose to make her central figure a boy and then a man—albeit one whose name and character derive from his mother. Mitchell has also argued that Craik's story aims at the education of the emotions, the creation of 'habits of feeling', a thought that answers the pathos and still beauty of the text, its evident investment both in resignation and in the wonder that resignation discovers, or that exists as its alternative.[25]

Concerns with gender and sexuality, and with desire and love, certainly pervade these tales. One element in the pleasure of fairy paintings was the titillation of a whimsical erotic impulse. Perhaps in part because its audience was more likely to belong to the nursery, the literary fairy tale was more circumspect in this regard. Love and marriage is central to the genre; though desire exists, in matters of sex, it

---

[22] Nina Auerbach and U. C. Knoepflmacher (eds.), *Forbidden Journeys: Fairy Tales and Fantasies by Victorian Women Writers* (Chicago and London: University of Chicago Press, 1992), 1.
[23] Elaine Showalter, 'Dinah Mulock Craik and the Tactics of Sentiment: A Case Study in Victorian Female Authorship', *Feminist Studies*, 2/3 (1975), 8.
[24] Sally Mitchell, *Dinah Mulock Craik* (Boston: Twayne Publishers, 1983), 88.
[25] Mitchell, *Dinah Mulock Craik*, 79–80.

Introduction xxvii

is in most cases strikingly chaste. In *The Little Lame Prince*, 'Prince Dolor' is ostensibly without sexual longings, literally dead from the waist down. He is emotionally linked only to his dead mother. Instead of active erotic longing, he pursues a passive, unthreatening habit of observation.

The manner in which love most arrestingly appears in the stories in this volume is with respect to the making of the self through suffering and through relatedness to others. As Craik's Dolor asserts: 'One cannot make oneself, but one can sometimes help a little in the making of somebody else.' The story is present at the reader's making too, a framing and altering of the self, performed by reading—fostering the capacity to play and the sense of justice. We take part in the making of the Prince, as he twice survives his dead image: once with the wax figure who is buried and once where the godmother replaces him with a 'quantity of moonshine'. (Perhaps there is a trace here of 'moonshine' as a synonym for nonsense.) Later the usurping king is himself laid out like a waxwork; there is a rhyme in the story here, a connection between death and a kind of feigned resurrection.

Love too lies at the heart of *The Rose and the Ring*, the contrast being between genuine love and doting. There is a worry throughout that persons may be interchangeable, one lover taking the place of another, one king on the wrong throne, exchanging one prince to be executed with another. Some of Mary De Morgan's tales (such as 'A Toy Princess' or 'The Windfairies') movingly posit the conflict between a real self—instinctual, passionate, and loving—and a social self—conventional, tamed, and mechanical. In this Romantic way, like many in the genre, her story intrinsically subverts the codes of polite society. The good that it celebrates is courtesy, not politeness, and the real and spontaneous human soul.

Questions of gender and of love inform Ford's *The Queen Who Flew*, presenting the difficulties of a trapped and pampered femininity. It is a tale that consciously takes (as do Ford's other fairy tales) the woman's position. For much of its length, it is apparently anti-romance, with Eldrida resisting numerous apt, if unwanted proposals of marriage. First, men wish to marry her for political reasons, and later fall in love with her by a kind of enchantment. Both prove simply a nuisance. The Queen (no princess, she) flees Narrowlands, a place that is, as its name would suggest, a country of constricted possibilities. It is a violent tale, with beheadings and assaults; the Regent shoves his wife (we assume) into a bear-pit; and evil King Mark is trapped in the tower, and left there until he dies. The tailor similarly proves ready to murder his wife, if that means he can marry Eldrida. Some of the violence of Perrault and Grimm returns here, and is possibly one source of enjoyment for the child audience. There's a note of realism, a sort of angry energy and a vein of wild fantasy in it—as when Eldrida flies up to the sun, and is sent back to the earth by God. There's a touch of magic too, as in the beautiful stillness of the picture of the ploughman at twilight, an earthy presence. And for all its apparent refusal of interest in love, it stands as a kind of parable about affection too.

Housman's tales are often of love and transformation, with partners separated by the human–animal divide, or the division between the moon and the earth. Love between men and women seems possible, but roots itself in an immense difference, in which each must exchange part of their nature with the other. As in Wilde's stories, it is possible to see Housman's fairy tales as coded accounts of homosexual love—another desire that in the 1890s seemed bound up with suffering. Yet here, as everywhere in these tales, there is a sense that we must accept differences, that the world contains many possibilities, many kinds of uniqueness.

There is a famous anecdote, in which Vyvyan Holland, Oscar Wilde's son, recalled that his father cried when he read 'The Selfish Giant'. When asked why, Wilde replied that 'really beautiful things always made him cry'.[26] Tears normally have no place in critical accounts, or even in introductions. Wilde's story, and all the stories in this book, both provide places for thinking and reflection, and simultaneously play upon our feelings and exercise our capacity for compassion. Reading them is a serious delight. They introduce us to an already familiar strangeness, and through the resources of art grant a space to make believe.

[26] Vyvyan Holland, *Son of Oscar Wilde* (New York: Oxford University Press, 1988), 53–4.

NOTE ON THE TEXTS

As far as possible, the copy-texts used in this edition are based on their first appearance in volume form. Original spellings and punctuation have been retained, though single quotation marks have been used in place of double ones; obvious errors have been corrected. Full details of each copy-text used appear in the Explanatory Notes, as well as information about the authors and their careers. Individual notes are signalled with an asterisk in the text. An appendix brings together four classic critical explorations of the fairy tale, by Ruskin, Ewing, MacDonald, and Housman.

I followed a number of principles in selecting the tales for this anthology. In part, stories were chosen because of their representative nature, in order to give the reader a sense of the kinds of literary fairy story that were available in the Victorian period. Stories were similarly picked so that the most influential authors working in the field would be included. However, more than just being typical examples of the genre, each story was also chosen for its aesthetic interest. I have also been guided by my sense of which stories have seemed the most illuminating and complex to other writers and readers. These considerations have meant that I have not shied away from choosing stories that are likely to be already familiar to those engaged with the genre. On the other hand, some of the most interesting tales in the field have not been much anthologized (if ever), and I am very happy to include here Andrew Lang's *Prince Prigio*, Ford Madox Ford's *The Queen Who Flew*, and excellent less-known tales by Mary De Morgan, Juliana Horatia Ewing, and Laurence Housman. The volume ends with Kipling, a Victorian author writing on into the Edwardian period, who, while slightly outside the chronological limits of this volume, nonetheless provides a fitting end to it, with a tale that bids farewell to the fairy tale and to the fairies.

The volume begins with a prologue, featuring two short tales by Grimm and Andersen. These are included as an appetizer to the main feast for several reasons. First, the impact of Edgar Taylor's translation of Grimm and of the several translations of Hans Andersen's work appearing in 1846 cannot be overestimated. This is not to belittle the influence of other fairy-tale writers and collectors, such as

Charles Perrault or Madame d'Aulnoy. However, these are in their origin nineteenth-century books that had a vivifying effect on the Victorian fairy tale. Second, I felt it vital to show that one of the key ways that fairy tales permeated Victorian culture was indeed in the form of translation; the taking in of 'foreign' works and making them central to the English-language imagination was one of the animating forces of the time. Third, George Cruikshank's pictures adorn Taylor's translation, and, when it came to fairies, these images themselves expanded and opened up the Victorian imagination.

The only constraints on inclusion were length (hence the absence of Jean Ingelow's *Mopsa the Fairy*) and that each tale should make sense as an individual story if extracted from the book of which they form a part (hence the absence of anything by Mary Molesworth). While excellent in themselves, Anne Isabella Ritchie's fairy-tale pastiches seemed to me to belong more to an anthology of parodies than of Victorian fairy tales.

Illustration was central to the meaning and the appreciation of many of these tales. When *The King of the Golden River* appeared in 1851, the book's chief selling-point (and the only name to feature on its title page) was not its author, John Ruskin, but its illustrator, Richard Doyle. Thackeray's *The Rose and the Ring* is more a story constructed to make sense of its author's pictures than simply an illustrated book. (After all, the subtitle of *Vanity Fair* was 'Pen and Pencil Sketches of English Society'.) While it has not been possible to reproduce all the original illustrations that accompanied these tales, I hope the selection in this volume will give some indication of their style, quality, and charm.

It became a feature of the fairy-tale book to experiment with typography, layout, font, and printing techniques, so that the actual physical presence and look of the book become an element in the meaning of the tale. These books were aesthetic objects in their own right, formed by the relationship between author, artist, and printer. Some of this can be seen here in the expressive use of typesize in stories such as Southey's 'The Three Bears', and in displayed type in other stories.

SELECT BIBLIOGRAPHY

Anthologies of Victorian Fairy Tales

Auerbach, Nina, and Knoepflmacher, U. C. (eds.), *Forbidden Journeys: Fairy Tales and Fantasies by Victorian Women Writers* (Chicago and London: University of Chicago Press, 1992).

Hearn, Michael Patrick (ed.), *The Victorian Fairy Tale Book* (Edinburgh: Canongate, 1988).

Opie, Iona, and Opie, Peter (eds.), *The Classic Fairy Tales* (Oxford: Oxford University Press, 1974).

Zipes, Jack (ed.), *Victorian Fairy Tales: The Revolt of the Fairies and Elves* (New York and London: Routledge, 1987).

Reference Books

Davidson, Ellis, and Chaudri, Anna (eds.), *A Companion to the Fairy Tale* (Cambridge: D. S. Brewer, 2003).

Zipes, Jack (ed.), *The Oxford Companion to Fairy Tales* (Oxford: Oxford University Press, 2000).

On Fairies

Briggs, Katherine, *The Fairies in English Tradition and Literature* (Chicago: University of Chicago Press, 1967).

Duffy, Maureen, *The Erotic World of Faery* (London: Hodder and Stoughton, 1971).

Silver, Carole, *Strange and Secret Peoples: Fairies and Victorian Consciousness* (Oxford: Oxford University Press, 1999).

The Critical History of the Fairy Tale

Alderson, Brian, *Hans Christian Andersen and His Eventyr in England* (Wormley: Five Owls Press, 1982).

Ben-Amos, Dan, 'Straparola: The Revolution That Was Not', *Journal of American Folklore*, 123 (Fall 2010), 447–96.

Bottigheimer, Ruth, *Fairy Tales: A New History* (Albany, NY: Excelsior, 2009).

Harries, Elizabeth Wanning, *Twice Upon A Time: Women Writers and the History of the Fairy Tale* (Princeton: Princeton University Press, 2001).

Propp, Vladimir, *The Morphology of the Folk Tale* (1928; Austin: University of Texas Press, 2009).

Tatar, Maria, *The Hard Facts of the Grimms' Fairy Tales* (Princeton: Princeton University Press, 1987).

Tatar, Maria, *Off With Their Heads! Fairy Tales and the Culture of Childhood* (Princeton: Princeton University Press, 1992).

Tolkien, J. R. R., 'On Fairy-Stories' (1947), in *The Monsters and the Critics and Other Essays* (London: George Allen & Unwin, 1997), 109–61.

Warner, Maria, *From the Beast to the Blonde: On Fairy Tales and Their Tellers* (London: Chatto and Windus, 1994).

Zipes, Jack, *When Dreams Come True: Classical Fairy Tales and Their Traditions* (New York and London: Routledge, 1999).

—— *The Irresistible Fairy Tale: The Cultural and Social History of a Genre* (Princeton and Oxford: Princeton University Press, 2012).

Biographical Works

Avery, Gillian, *Mrs Ewing*, etc. (London: Bodley Head, 1961).

Briggs, Julia, *A Woman of Passion: The Life of E. Nesbit, 1858–1924* (London: Hutchinson, 1987).

Carrington, Charles, *Rudyard Kipling: His Life and Work* (rev. edn., Harmondsworth: Penguin Books, 1986).

Ellmann, Richard, *Oscar Wilde* (London: Hamish Hamilton, 1987).

Engen, Rodney K., *Laurence Housman* (Stroud: Catalpa Press, 1983).

Green, Peter, *Kenneth Grahame, 1859–1932* (London: John Murray, 1959).

Hilton, Timothy, *John Ruskin: The Early Years* (New Haven and London: Yale University Press, 1985).

Pemberton, Marilyn, *Out of the Shadows: The Life and Works of Mary De Morgan* (Newcastle: Cambridge Scholars, 2012).

Ray, Gordon, *Thackeray: The Age of Wisdom, 1847–1863* (London: Oxford University Press, 1958).

Saunders, Max, *Ford Madox Ford: A Dual Life*, 2 vols. (Oxford and New York: Oxford University Press, 1996).

Storey, Mark, *Robert Southey: A Life* (Oxford: Oxford University Press, 1997).

Triggs, Kathy, *The Stars and the Stillness: A Portrait of George MacDonald* (Cambridge: Lutterworth Press, 1986).

Wullschlager, Jackie, *Hans Christian Andersen: The Life of a Storyteller* (London: Allen Lane, 2000).

Zipes, Jack, *The Brothers Grimm: From Enchanted Forest to Modern World* (2nd edn., London: Palgrave Macmillan, 2003).

Background Works on Children's Literature

Bratton, J. S., *The Impact of Victorian Children's Fiction* (London: Croom Helm, 1981).

Carpenter, Humphrey, *Secret Gardens: A Study of The Golden Age of Children's Literature* (London: George Allen & Unwin, 1985).

Select Bibliography　　　　　　　　　　　　　　xxxiii

Dusinberre, Juliet, *Alice to the Lighthouse: Children's Books and the Radical Experiments in Art* (Basingstoke: Macmillan, 1987).
Reynolds, Kimberly, *Girls Only? Gender and Popular Children's Fiction in Britain, 1880–1910* (Philadelphia: Temple University Press, 1990).
Rose, Jacqueline, *The Case of Peter Pan, or, the Impossibility of Children's Literature* (London: Macmillan, 1984).
Sale, Roger, *Fairy Tales and After: From Snow White to E. B. White* (Cambridge, MA: Harvard University Press, 1978).

Critical Monographs and Essays on Victorian Fairy Tales

Avery, Gillian, 'The Quest for Fairyland', *Quarterly Journal of the Library of Congress*, 38/4 (Fall 1981), 220–7.
Bown, Nicola, *Fairies in Nineteenth-Century Art and Literature* (Cambridge: Cambridge University Press, 2001).
Goldthwaite, John, *The Natural History of Make-Believe* (New York and Oxford: Oxford University Press, 1996).
Hillard, Molly Clark, *Spellbound: The Fairy Tale and the Victorians* (Columbus, OH: Ohio State University Press, 2014).
Knoepflmacher, U. C., *Ventures Into Childland: Victorians, Fairy Tales and Femininity* (Chicago and London: University of Chicago Press, 1998).
Manlove, Colin, *Modern Fantasy: Five Studies* (Cambridge: Cambridge University Press, 1975).
Prickett, Stephen, *Victorian Fantasy* (Sussex: Harvester, 1979).
Sumpter, Caroline, *The Victorian Press and the Fairy Tale* (London: Palgrave Macmillan, 2008).
Talairach-Vielmas, Laurence, 'Beautiful Maidens, Hideous Suitors: Victorian Fairy Tales and the Process of Civilization', *Marvels & Tales*, 24/2 (Detroit: Wayne State University Press, 2010), 272–96.
Wilson, Anita C., 'The Shining Garb of Wonder: The Paradox of Literary Fairy Tales in Mid-Victorian England', *Cahiers victoriens et édouardiens*, 37 (1993), 73–93.

Critical Works on Individual Authors

Filstrup, Jane Merrill, 'Thirst for Enchanted Views in Ruskin's *The King of the Golden River*', *Children's Literature*, 8 (Yale, New Haven: Yale University Press, 1980), 68–79.
Fowler, James, 'The Golden Harp: Mary De Morgan's Centrality in Victorian Fairy-Tale Literature', *Children's Literature*, 33 (2005), 224–36.
Gray, William, *Fantasy, Art and Life: Essays on George MacDonald, Robert Louis Stevenson and Other Fantasy Writers* (Newcastle: Cambridge Scholars Publishing, 2011).
Killeen, Jarlath, *The Fairy Tales of Oscar Wilde* (Aldershot: Ashgate, 2007).

Kotzin, Michael, '"The Selfish Giant" as Literary Fairy Tale', *Studies in Short Fiction*, 16/4 (Fall 1979), 301–9.

Lewis, Lisa A. F., '"References", "Cross-References", and Notions of History in Kipling's *Puck of Pook's Hill* and *Rewards and Fairies*', *English Literature in Transition, 1880–1920*, 50/2 (Greensboro, NC: ELT Press, 2007), 192–209.

Lurie, Alison, 'Ford Madox Ford's Fairy Tales for Children', in Sondra J. Stang (ed.), *The Presence of Ford Madox Ford* (Philadelphia: University of Pennsylvania Press, 1981), 130–42.

McCormack, Jerusha, 'Wilde's Fiction(s)', in Peter Raby (ed.), *The Cambridge Companion to Oscar Wilde* (Cambridge: Cambridge University Press, 1997), 96–117.

Markey, Anne, *Oscar Wilde's Fairy Tales: Origins and Contexts* (Dublin and Portland, OR: Irish Academic Press, 2011).

Misenheimer, Carylyn, 'Southey's "The Three Bears": Irony, Anonymity, and Editorial Ineptitude', *Charles Lamb Bulletin*, 97 (January 1997), 41–2.

Mitchell, Sally, *Dinah Mulock Craik* (Boston: Twayne Publishers, 1983).

Philipoise, Lily, 'The Politics of the Hearth in Victorian Children's Fantasy: Dinah Mulock Craik's *The Little Lame Prince*', *Children's Literature Association Quarterly*, 21/3 (Fall 1996), 133–9.

Raeper, William (ed.), *The Gold Thread: Essays on George MacDonald* (Edinburgh: Edinburgh University Press, 1990).

Scott, Jeremy, 'The Soul of the Eye and the Words on the Page: Ruskin's Literary Vision and *The King of the Golden River*', in Carmen Casaliggi and Paul March-Russell (eds.), *Ruskin in Perspective: Contemporary Essays* (Newcastle upon Tyne: Cambridge Scholars, 2010), 67–79.

Showalter, Elaine, 'Dinah Mulock Craik and the Tactics of Sentiment: A Case Study in Victorian Female Authorship', *Feminist Studies*, 2/3 (1975), 5–23.

Wood, Naomi, 'Creating the Sensual Child: Paterian Aesthetics, Pederasty and Oscar Wilde's Fairy Tales', *Marvels & Tales: Journal of Fairy Tale Studies*, 16/2 (2002), 156–70.

On Victorian Fairy Painting

Martineau, Jane (ed.), *Victorian Fairy Painting* (London: Royal Academy of Arts, 1997).

Wood, Christopher, *Fairies in Victorian Art* (Woodbridge: Antique Collectors' Club, 2000).

Further Reading in Oxford World's Classics

Andersen, Hans, *Fairy Tales*, trans. L. W. Kingsland, introduction by Naomi Lewis.

Select Bibliography

Arabian Nights' Entertainments, ed. Robert L. Mack.
Barrie, J. M., *Peter Pan and Other Plays*, ed. Peter Hollindale.
—— *Peter Pan in Kensington Gardens / Peter and Wendy*, ed. Peter Hollindale.
Carroll, Lewis, *Alice's Adventures in Wonderland* and *Through The Looking-Glass*, ed. Peter Hunt.
Collodi, Carlo, *The Adventures of Pinocchio*, trans. and ed. Ann Lawson Lucas.
Grahame, Kenneth, *The Wind in the Willows*, ed. Peter Hunt.
Hoffmann, E. T. A, *The Golden Pot and Other Tales*, trans. and ed. Ritchie Robertson.
Kingsley, Charles, *The Water-Babies*, ed. Brian Alderson, introduction by Robert Douglas-Fairhurst.
Perrault, Charles, *The Complete Fairy Tales*, trans. and ed. Christopher Betts.
Wilde, Oscar, *The Complete Short Stories*, ed. John Sloan.

A CHRONOLOGY OF THE LITERARY FAIRY TALE

1705–8 Grub Street translation of the *Arabian Nights Entertainments* (*Thousand and One Nights*) (including the tales of 'Aladdin', 'Ali Baba', and 'Sindbad the Sailor').

1721–2 Translation into English of Madame d'Aulnoy, *A Collection of Novels and Tales* (including 'The Yellow Dwarf').

1729 First translation into English of Charles Perrault, *Histories or Tales of Past Times*.

1761 Madame de Beaumont, *The Young Misses Magazine* (the first translation of 'Beauty and the Beast' and 'The Three Wishes' into English).

1774 Birth of Robert Southey.

1803 Sir Walter Scott, 'On the Fairies of Popular Superstition', in *Minstrelsy of the Scottish Border* (1802–3).

1804 Benjamin Tabart starts publishing his series of *Popular Stories* (to 1809), including versions of tales by Madame d'Aulnoy and 'Jack the Giant-Killer'.

1811 Charles Lamb, *Prince Dorus*; birth of William Makepeace Thackeray.

1812 Jakob and Wilhelm Grimm, *Kinder-und Hausmärchen* (in German).

1818 First English translation of Motte Fouqué, *Undine*.

1819 John Keats, 'La Belle Dame Sans Merci'; birth of John Ruskin. Peterloo Massacre.

1820 Birth of Jean Ingelow.

1823 Edgar Taylor's translation of Jakob and Wilhelm Grimm's *German Popular Stories*, with illustrations by George Cruikshank.

1824 Birth of Richard Doyle; birth of George MacDonald.

1825 Thomas Crofton Croker, *Fairy Legends and Traditions of the South of Ireland* (an expanded edition follows in 1828, with illustrations by Daniel Maclise).

1826 Carl Maria von Weber's opera *Oberon* (with libretto by James Robinson Planché) has its premiere at Covent Garden, London; Felix Mendelssohn composes his Overture to *A Midsummer Night's Dream*; birth of Dinah Mulock.

1827 Translation of E. T. A. Hoffmann, *The Golden Pot* (by Thomas Carlyle).

1828 Thomas Keightley, *The Fairy Mythology*.

Chronology

1832 Filippo Taglioni (choreography) and Jean-Madeleine Schneitzhoeffer (music), *La Sylphide*.

1837 Robert Southey, 'The Story of the Three Bears'; birth of Anne Isabella Thackeray Ritchie.

Accession of Victoria.

1839 Catherine Sinclair, *Holiday House* (containing the chapter 'Uncle David's Nonsensical Story about Giants and Fairies').

1841 A. W. Pugin, *The Principles of English Architecture*; John Ruskin writes *The King of the Golden River*; birth of Juliana Horatia Ewing.

Henry Fox Talbot patents his photographic process.

1842 Coal Mines Act forbids the employment of children under the age of 10 and of women in underground coal mines.

1843 Charles Dickens, *A Christmas Carol*; death of Robert Southey.

1844 Birth of Andrew Lang.

1845 James Orchard Halliwell (ed.), *Illustrations of the Fairy Mythology of A Midsummer Night's Dream*.

Famine begins in Ireland (to 1850, the worst year being 1847).

1846 Hans Andersen, *A Danish Story-Book* (trans. Charles Boner); *Danish Fairy Legends and Tales* (trans. Caroline Peachey); *The Nightingale and Other Tales* (trans. Charles Boner); publication of *Household Stories* (first appearance in English of 'Hansel and Gretel'); Edward Lear, *A Book of Nonsense*.

Sir Joseph Noel Paton paints *The Reconciliation of Oberon and Titania*.

1848 First translation into English of Giambattista Basile, *The Pentamerone* (trans. John Edward Taylor, with illustrations by George Cruikshank).

Karl Marx and Friedrich Engels, *The Communist Manifesto*; the Pre-Raphaelite Brotherhood founded.

1850 William Allingham, 'The Fairies'; birth of Mary De Morgan; at Christmas, John Ruskin, *The King of the Golden River*, with illustrations by Richard Doyle.

1851 Dinah Mulock Craik, *Alice Learmont*; Margaret Gatty, *The Fairy Godmothers*.

The Great Exhibition held in London.

1852 Sir William Wilde, *Irish Popular Superstitions*.

1853 George Cruikshank begins publishing his *Fairy Library*, a series of fairy tales rewritten in order to further a temperance message; Charles Dickens, 'Fraud on the Fairies' published in *Household Words*.

Start of the Crimean War.

Chronology

1854 Charles Dickens, *Hard Times*; William Makepeace Thackeray, *The Rose and the Ring*; birth of Oscar Wilde.

1855 Richard Dadd begins painting *The Fairy Feller's Master Stroke* (to 1864).

1856 William Morris, 'The Hollow Land'; Charles Kean's spectacular production of *A Midsummer Night's Dream* at the Princess Theatre, London (with Ellen Terry playing Puck).

End of the Crimean War.

1857 Frances Browne, *Granny's Wonderful Chair and Its Tales of Fairy Times*.

The Indian Mutiny.

1858 George MacDonald, *Phantastes*; birth of Edith Nesbit; John Anster Fitzgerald paints *The Stuff That Dreams Are Made Of*.

Victoria proclaims permanent British rule of India by the Crown (as opposed to the East India Company).

1859 Charles Darwin, *The Origin of Species*; George Dasent, *Popular Tales From the Norse*; Henry Morley, *Fables and Fairy Tales*; birth of Kenneth Grahame.

1860 Alfred Crowquill, 'Heinrich; or, the Love of Gold' (in *Fairy Footsteps*); Henry Morley, *Oberon's Horn*.

William Morris founds Morris, Marshall, Faulkner & Co.

1862 Christina Rossetti, *Goblin Market*.

1863 Charles Kingsley, *The Water Babies* (illustrated by Joseph Noel Paton and Percival Skelton); death of William Makepeace Thackeray.

The underground railway opens in London.

1864 George MacDonald, *Adela Cathcart*.

1865 Lewis Carroll, *Alice's Adventures in Wonderland*; birth of Laurence Housman; birth of Rudyard Kipling.

First Women's Suffrage Committee founded.

1866 First publication of *Aunt Judy's Magazine*, edited by Margaret Gatty.

1867 Lewis Carroll, 'Bruno's Revenge' (published in *Aunt Judy's Magazine*); George MacDonald, *Dealings with the Fairies*; William Morris, *The Life and Death of Jason*.

1868 Charles Dickens, 'The Magic Fishbone' (published in *All the Year Round*); Anne Isabella Ritchie, *Five Old Friends and a Young Prince*; Alexander Strahan founds the journal *Good Words for the Young* (first edited by Norman Macleod, and later by George MacDonald).

Chronology

1869 Jean Ingelow, *Mopsa the Fairy*; John Ruskin, 'Introduction' to *German Popular Tales*.

Founding of Girton College for women in Cambridge.

1870 William Allingham (poems) and Richard Doyle (illustrations), *In Fairyland*; Juliana Horatia Ewing, 'Christmas Crackers', 'Amelia and the Dwarfs', 'Under the Sun' (in *The Brownies and Other Tales*); Edward Burne-Jones paints his first *Briar Rose* sequence (to 1873).

Married Women's Property Act; W. E. Forster's Education Act.

1871 Juliana Horatia Ewing, 'The Ogre Courting' and 'The Little Darner' (published in *Aunt Judy's Magazine*); Edward H. Knatchbull-Hugessen, *Moonshine* (including 'Charlie Among the Elves'); Edward Lear, *Nonsense Songs*; George MacDonald, *At the Back of the North Wind* published in volume form; Christina Rossetti, *Sing Song*.

1872 Lewis Carroll, *Through the Looking-Glass*; George MacDonald, *The Princess and the Goblin*.

1873 Birth of Ford Madox Ford (Ford Hermann Hueffer).

Invention of the typewriter.

1874 Dinah Mulock Craik, *The Little Lame Prince and His Travelling Cloak*; Anne Isabella Ritchie, *Bluebeard's Keys and Other Stories*; Christina Rossetti, *Speaking Likenesses*.

1875 George MacDonald, *The Wise Woman*.

Norman Shaw designs Bedford Park, London's first garden suburb.

1876 Lewis Carroll, *The Hunting of the Snark*.

Queen Victoria named Empress of India; invention of the telephone by Alexander Graham Bell.

1877 Edward Lear, *Laughable Lyrics* (including 'The Dong with a Luminous Nose'); Mary De Morgan, 'A Toy Princess' (in *On a Pincushion and Other Tales*); Pyotr Tchaikovsky composes *Swan Lake*.

Thomas Edison patents the phonograph.

1878 The Folklore Society founded in London (founding members include Andrew Lang, Jessie Weston, and Alfred Nutt).

Founding of Lady Margaret Hall, the first college for women in Oxford.

1879 Mary Molesworth, 'The Brown Bull of Norrowa' (in *The Tapestry Room*).

First electric street lighting in London.

1880 Mary De Morgan, *The Necklace of Princess Fiorimonde*.

1881 W. S. Gilbert (libretto) and Arthur Sullivan (music), *Iolanthe*.

1882 Juliana Horatia Ewing, *Old-Fashioned Fairy Tales* (including 'The Ogre Courting' and 'The First Wife's Wedding Ring').

The Phoenix Park Murders in Ireland; Second Married Women's Property Act.

1883 George MacDonald, *The Princess and Curdie*.

In Chicago, the first skyscraper is built (ten storeys high).

1884 Andrew Lang, *The Princess Nobody*; Andrew Lang, *Custom and Myth*.

Sir Hiram Stevens Maxim invents the machine gun.

1885 Sir Richard Burton's translation of *The Book of a Thousand Nights and a Night* (in sixteen volumes, to 1888); death of Juliana Horatia Ewing.

Criminal Law Amendment Act; among other provisions, it raises the age of consent from 13 to 16, and also recriminalizes sexual contact (or 'gross indecency') between men.

1887 Mary Molesworth, *Four Winds Farm*; Lady Wilde, *Ancient Legends, Mystic Charms and Superstitions of Ireland* (partly based on material gathered by Sir William Wilde); death of Dinah Mulock Craik.

Thomas Edison patents the Kinetoscope.

1888 Andrew Lang, *The Gold of Fairnilee*; Andrew Lang's edition of Charles Perrault; Constance Wilde, *There Was Once: Grandma's Stories*; Oscar Wilde, *The Happy Prince and Other Tales*; W. B. Yeats, *Fairy and Folk Tales of the Irish Peasantry*.

'Bloody Sunday': violence breaks out between police and radical demonstrators in Trafalgar Square.

1889 Lewis Carroll, *Sylvie and Bruno*; Andrew Lang, *Prince Prigio*; Andrew Lang, *The Blue Fairy Book*; W. B. Yeats, *The Wanderings of Oisin*.

1890 Joseph Jacobs, *English Fairy Tales*; Sir James Fraser begins publication of *The Golden Bough* (to 1915).

William Morris founds the Kelmscott Press.

1891 Oscar Wilde, *The House of Pomegranates*.

Death of the Irish politician Charles Stewart Parnell; the Assisted Education Act establishes the right to free elementary schooling.

1892 Ford Madox Ford, *The Brown Owl*; first English translation of Henrik Ibsen, *Peer Gynt*; Joseph Jacobs, *Celtic Fairy Tales*; Mary Molesworth, 'The Summer Princess' (in *The Enchanted Garden*); Pyotr Tchaikovsky, *The Nutcracker* (ballet).

Chronology

1893 Andrew Lang, *Prince Ricardo of Pantouflia*; George MacDonald, 'The Fantastic Imagination'; W. B. Yeats, *The Celtic Twilight*.

1894 Ford Madox Ford, *The Queen Who Flew*; Laurence Housman, *A Farm in Fairyland*; Rudyard Kipling, *The Jungle Book*; William Morris, *The Wood Beyond the World*; death of Christina Rossetti.

1895 Kenneth Grahame, *The Golden Age*; Laurence Housman, *The House of Joy*; Rudyard Kipling, *The Second Jungle Book*; George MacDonald, *Lilith*; Frances MacDonald draws *The Sleeping Princess*.

1896 William Morris, *The Well at the World's End*.

The invention of radio.

1897 W. B. Yeats, *The Secret Rose*.

1898 Edward Clodd, *Tom-Tit-Tot*; Kenneth Grahame, 'The Reluctant Dragon' (in *Dream Days*); Laurence Housman, *The Field of Clover*; Evelyn Sharp, *All the Way to Fairyland*.

1899 Arthur Machen, 'The White People'.

1900 L. Frank Baum, *The Wonderful Wizard of Oz*; Mary De Morgan, *The Windfairies and Other Tales*; E. Nesbit, *The Book of Dragons*; Alfred Nutt, *The Fairy Mythology of Shakespeare*; Evelyn Sharp, *The Other Side of the Sun*; death of John Ruskin; death of Oscar Wilde.

1901 E. Nesbit, 'Melisande' (in *Nine Unlikely Tales for Children*); Georges Méliès's film *Barbe-bleue* (*Bluebeard*).

Death of Queen Victoria; accession of Edward VII.

1902 Rudyard Kipling, *Just So Stories*; E. Nesbit, *Five Children and It*.

1903 The Wright Brothers' first successful powered flight; Ford Motor Company founded.

1904 First performance of J. M. Barrie's *Peter Pan*; E. Nesbit, *The Phoenix and the Carpet*.

1905 Laurence Housman, 'Introduction' to *Gammer Grethel's Fairy Tales*; death of George MacDonald.

Albert Einstein describes the Theory of Relativity.

1906 J. M. Barrie, *Peter Pan in Kensington Gardens* (with illustrations by Arthur Rackham); Rudyard Kipling, *Puck of Pook's Hill*; E. Nesbit, *The Story of the Amulet*; Patrick Pearse rewrites Wilde's 'The Selfish Giant' in Irish as *Ísogán*.

1907 E. Nesbit, *The Enchanted Castle*; death of Mary De Morgan.

1908 Kenneth Grahame, *The Wind in the Willows*.

1910 Lady Augusta Gregory, *Gods and Fighting Men*; Rudyard Kipling, *Rewards and Fairies*; E. Nesbit, *The Magic City*.
1911 J. M. Barrie, *Peter and Wendy*; Evans Wentz, *Fairy Faith in Celtic Countries*.
1912 James Stephens, *The Crock of Gold*; death of Andrew Lang. The sinking of the *Titanic*.
1914 The beginning of the First World War.

PROLOGUE

JAKOB AND WILHELM GRIMM

Rumpel-Stilts-kin

IN a certain kingdom once lived a poor miller who had a very beautiful daughter. She was moreover exceedingly shrewd and clever; and the miller was so vain and proud of her, that he one day told the king of the land that his daughter could spin gold out of straw. Now this king was very fond of money; and when he heard the miller's boast, his avarice was excited, and he ordered the girl to be brought before him. Then he led her to a chamber where there was a great quantity of straw, gave her a spinning-wheel, and said, 'All this must be spun into gold before morning, as you value your life.' It was in vain that the poor maiden declared that she could do no such thing, the chamber was locked and she remained alone.

She sat down in one corner of the room and began to lament over her hard fate, when on a sudden the door opened, and a droll-looking little man hobbled in, and said 'Good morrow to you, my good lass, what are you weeping for?' 'Alas!' answered she, 'I must spin this straw into gold, and I know not how.' 'What will you give me,' said the little man, 'to do it for you?' 'My necklace,' replied the maiden. He took her at her word, and set himself down to the wheel; round about it went merrily, and presently the work was done, and the gold all spun.

When the king came and saw this, he was greatly astonished and pleased; but his heart grew still more greedy of gain, and he shut up the poor miller's daughter again with a fresh task. Then she knew not what to do, and sat down once more to weep; but the little man presently opened the door, and said 'What will you give me to do your task?' 'The ring on my finger,' replied she. So her little friend took the ring, and began to work at the wheel, till by the morning all was finished again.

The king was vastly delighted to see all his glittering treasure; but still he was not satisfied, and took the miller's daughter into a yet larger room, and said, 'All this must be spun to-night; and if you succeed you shall be my queen.' As soon as she was alone the dwarf came in, and said 'What will you give me to spin gold for you this third time?' 'I have nothing left,' said she. 'Then promise me,' said the little man, 'your first little child when you are queen.' 'That may never be,' thought the miller's daughter; and as she knew no other way to get her task done, she promised him what he asked, and he spun once more the whole heap of gold. The king came in the morning, and finding all he wanted, married her, and so the miller's daughter really became queen.

At the birth of her first little child the queen rejoiced very much, and forgot the little man and her promise; but one day he came into her chamber and reminded her of it. Then she grieved sorely at her misfortune, and offered him all the treasures of the kingdom in exchange; but in vain, till at last her tears softened him, and he said 'I will give you three days' grace, and if during that time you tell me my name, you shall keep your child.'

Now the queen lay awake all night, thinking of all the odd names that she had ever heard, and dispatched messengers all over the land to inquire after new ones. The next day the little man came, and she began with Timothy, Benjamin, Jeremiah, and all the names she could remember; but to all of them he said, 'That's not my name.'

The second day she began with all the comical names she could hear of, Bandy-legs, Hunch-back, Crook-shanks, and so on; but the little gentleman still said to every one of them, 'That's not my name.'

The third day one of the messengers came back, and said 'I can hear of no other names; but yesterday, as I was climbing a high hill among the trees of the forest where the fox and the hare bid each other good night, I saw a little hut, and before the hut burnt a fire, and round about the fire a funny little man danced upon one leg, and sang

> "Merrily the feast I'll make,
> To-day I'll brew, to-morrow bake;
> Merrily I'll dance and sing,
> For next day will a stranger bring:
> Little does my lady dream
> Rumpel-Stilts-kin is my name!"'

When the queen heard this, she jumped for joy, and as soon as her little visitor came, and said 'Now, lady, what is my name?' 'Is it John?' asked she. 'No!' 'Is it Tom?' 'No!'

'Can your name be Rumpel-Stilts-kin?'

'Some witch told you that! Some witch told you that!' cried the little man, and dashed his right foot in a rage so deep into the floor, that he was forced to lay hold of it with both hands to pull it out. Then he makes the best of his way off, while every body laughed at him for having had all his trouble for nothing.

HANS CHRISTIAN ANDERSEN

The Princess and the Peas

THERE lived, once upon a time, a Prince, and he wished to marry a Princess, but then she must be really and truly a Princess. So he travelled over the whole world to find one; but there was always something or other to prevent his being successful. Princesses he found in plenty, but he could never make out if they were real Princesses; for sometimes one thing and sometimes another appeared to him to be not quite right about the ladies. So at last he returned home quite cast down; for he wanted very much to have a real Princess for a wife.

One evening, a dreadful storm was gathering; it thundered and lightened, and the rain poured down from heaven in torrents; it was, too, as dark as pitch. Suddenly a loud knocking was heard at the town-gates; and the old King, the Prince's father, went out himself to see who was there.

It was a Princess that stood at the gate; but, Lord bless me! what a figure she was from the rain! The water ran down from her hair, and her dress was dripping wet and stuck quite close to her body. She said she was a real Princess.

'We'll soon see about that,' thought the old Queen Dowager: however, she said not a word, but went into the bed-room, took out all the bedding, and laid three small peas on the bottom of the bedstead. Then she took, first, twenty mattresses, and laid them one upon the other on the three peas, and then she took twenty feather-beds more, and put these again a-top of the mattresses.

This was the bed the Princess was to sleep in.

The next morning she asked her if she had had a good night.

'Oh, no! a horrid night!' said the Princess. 'I was hardly able to close my eyes the whole night! Heaven knows what was in my bed, but there was a something hard under me, and my whole body is black and blue with bruises! I can't tell you what I've suffered!'

Then they knew that the lady they had lodged was a real Princess, since she had felt the three small peas through twenty mattresses and twenty feather beds; for it is quite impossible for anyone but a true Princess to be so tender.

So the Prince married her; for he was now convinced that he had a real Princess for his wife. The three peas were deposited in the Museum, where they are still to be seen; that is to say, if they have not been lost.

Now was not that a lady of exquisite feeling?

VICTORIAN FAIRY TALES

ROBERT SOUTHEY

The Story of the Three Bears

A tale which may content the minds
Of learned men and grave philosophers.*
GASCOYNE

Once upon a time there were Three Bears, who lived together in a house of their own, in a wood. One of them was a Little, Small, Wee Bear; and one was a Middle-sized Bear, and the other was Great, Huge Bear. They had each a pot for their porridge, a little pot for the Little, Small, Wee Bear; and a middle-sized pot for the Middle Bear, and a great pot for the Great, Huge Bear. And they each had a chair to sit in; a little chair for the Little, Small, Wee Bear; and a middle-sized chair for the Middle Bear; and a great chair for the Great, Huge Bear. And they each had a bed to sleep in; a little bed for the Little, Small, Wee Bear; and a middle-sized bed for the Middle Bear; and a great bed for the Great, Huge Bear.

One day, after they had made the porridge for their breakfast, and poured it into their porridge-pots, they walked out into the wood while their porridge was cooling, that they might not burn their mouths, by beginning too soon to eat it. And while they were walking, a little old Woman came to the House. She could not have been a good, honest old Woman; for first she looked in at the window, and then she peeped in at the keyhole; and seeing nobody in the house, she lifted the latch. The door was not fastened, because the Bears were good Bears, who did nobody any harm, and never suspected that any body would harm them. So the little old Woman opened the door, and went in; and well pleased she was when she saw the porridge on the table. If she had been a good little old Woman, she would have waited till the Bears came home, and then, perhaps, they would have asked her to breakfast; for they were good Bears—a little rough or so, as the manner of Bears is, but for all that very good natured and hospitable. But she was an impudent, bad old Woman, and set about helping herself.

So first she tasted the porridge of the Great, Huge Bear, and that was too hot for her; and she said a bad word about that. And then she tasted the porridge of the Middle Bear, and that was too cold for her; and she said a bad word about that, too. And then she went to the porridge of the Little, Small, Wee Bear, and tasted that; and that was neither too hot, nor too cold, but just right; and she liked it so well, that she ate it all up; but the naughty old Woman said a bad word about the little porridge-pot, because it did not hold enough for her.

Then the little old Woman sate down in the chair of the Great Huge Bear, and that was too hard for her. And then she sate down in the chair of the Middle Bear, and that was too soft for her. And then she sate down in the chair of the Little, Small, Wee Bear, and that was neither too hard, nor too soft, but just right. So she seated herself in it, and there she sate till the bottom of the chair came out, and down came hers, plump upon the ground. And the naughty old Woman said a wicked word about that too.

Then the little old Woman went up stairs into the bed-chamber in which the three Bears slept. And first she lay down upon the bed of the Great, Huge Bear; but that was too high at the head for her. And next she lay down upon the bed of the Middle Bear; and that was too high at the foot for her. And then she lay down upon the bed of the Little, Small, Wee Bear; and that was neither too high at the head, nor the foot, but just right. So she covered herself up comfortably, and lay there till she fell fast asleep.

By this time the Three Bears thought their porridge would be cool enough; so they came home to breakfast. Now the little, old Woman had left the spoon of the Great, Huge Bear, standing in his porridge.

'Somebody has been at my porridge!'

said the Great, Huge Bear, in his great, rough, gruff voice. And when the Middle Bear looked at his, he saw that the spoon was standing in it too. They were wooden spoons; if they had been silver ones, the naughty old Woman would have put them in her pocket.

'SOMEBODY HAS BEEN AT MY PORRIDGE!'

said the Middle Bear, in his middle voice.

Then the Little, Small, Wee Bear, looked at his, and there was the spoon in the porridge-pot, but the porridge was all gone.

'Somebody has been at my porridge, and has eaten it all up!'

said the Little, Small, Wee Bear in his little, small, wee voice.

Upon this the Three Bears, seeing that some one had entered their house, and eaten up the Little, Small, Wee Bear's breakfast, began to look about them. Now the little old woman had not put the hard cushion straight when she rose from the chair of the Great, Huge Bear.

'Somebody has been sitting in my chair!'

said the Great, Huge Bear, in his great, rough, gruff voice.

And the little old Woman had squatted down the soft cushion of the Middle Bear.

'SOMEBODY HAS BEEN SITTING IN MY CHAIR!'

said the Middle Bear, in his middle voice.

And you know what the little old Woman had done to the third chair.

'Somebody has been sitting in my chair, and has sate the bottom of it out!'

said the Little, Small, Wee Bear, in his little, small, wee voice.

Then the Three Bears thought it necessary that they should make farther search, so they went up stairs into their bed-chamber. Now the little old Woman had pulled the pillow of the Great, Huge Bear, out of its place.

'Somebody has been lying in my bed!'

said the Great, Huge Bear, in his great, rough, gruff voice.

And the little old Woman has pulled the bolster* of the Middle Bear out of its place.

'SOMEBODY HAS BEEN LYING IN MY BED!'

said the Middle Bear, in his middle voice.

And when the Little, Small, Wee Bear, came to look at his bed, there was the bolster in its place; and the pillow in its place on the bolster; and upon the pillow was the little, old Woman's ugly, dirty head,—which was not in its place, for she had no business there.

'Somebody has been lying in my bed,—and here she is!'

said the Little, Small, Wee Bear, in his little, small, wee voice.

The little old Woman had heard in her sleep the great, rough, gruff voice of the Great, Huge Bear; but she was so fast asleep that it was no more to her than the roaring of wind, or the rumbling of thunder. And she heard the middle voice of the Middle Bear, but it was only as if she had heard some one speaking in a dream. But when she heard the little, small, wee voice of the Little, Small, Wee Bear, it was so sharp, and so shrill, that it awakened her at once. Up she started; and when she saw the Three Bears on one side of the bed, she tumbled herself out at the other, and ran to the window. Now the window was open, because the Bears, like good, tidy Bears, as they were, always opened their bed-chamber window when they got up in the morning. Out the little old Woman jumped; and whether she broke her neck in the fall; or ran into the wood and was lost there; or found her way out of the wood, and was taken up by the constable and sent to the House of Correction* for a vagrant as she was, I cannot tell. But the Three Bears never saw any thing more of her.

JOHN RUSKIN

The King of the Golden River or The Black Brothers
A Tale of Stiria

CHAPTER I
HOW THE AGRICULTURAL SYSTEM OF THE BLACK BROTHERS WAS INTERFERED WITH BY SOUTH-WEST WIND, ESQUIRE

IN a secluded and mountainous part of Stiria,* there was, in old time, a valley of the most surprising and luxuriant fertility. It was surrounded, on all sides, by steep and rocky mountains, rising into peaks, which were always covered with snow, and from which a number of torrents descended in constant cataracts. One of these fell westward, over the face of a crag so high, that, when the sun had set to everything else, and all below was darkness, his beams still shone upon this waterfall, so that it looked like a shower of gold. It was, therefore, called by the people of the neighbourhood, the Golden River. It was strange that none of these streams fell into the valley itself. They all descended on the other side of the mountains, and wound away through broad plains and by populous cities. But the clouds were drawn so constantly to the snowy hills, and rested so softly in the circular hollow, that in time of drought and heat, when all the country round was burnt up, there was still rain in the little valley; and its crops were so heavy, and its hay so high, and its apples so red, and its grapes so blue, and its wine so rich, and its honey so sweet, that it was a marvel to everyone who beheld it, and was commonly called the Treasure Valley.

The whole of this little valley belonged to three brothers, called Schwartz, Hans, and Gluck.* Schwartz and Hans, the two elder brothers, were very ugly men, with over-hanging eyebrows and small dull eyes, which were always half shut, so that you couldn't see into *them*, and always fancied they saw very far into *you*. They lived by farming the Treasure Valley, and very good farmers they were. They killed everything that did not pay for its eating. They shot the blackbirds, because they pecked the fruit; and killed the hedgehogs, lest they should suck the cows; they poisoned the crickets for eating the crumbs in the kitchen; and smothered the cicadas, which used to sing all summer in the lime-trees. They worked their servants without any wages, till they would not work any more, and then quarrelled with them, and turned them out of doors without paying them. It would have been very odd, if with such a farm, and such a system of farming, they hadn't got very rich; and very rich they *did* get. They generally contrived to keep their corn by them till it was very dear, and then sell it for twice its value; they had heaps of gold lying about on their floors, yet it was never known that they had given so much as a penny or a crust in charity; they never went to mass; grumbled perpetually at paying tithes; and were, in a word, of so cruel and grinding a temper, as to receive from all those with whom they had any dealings, the nick-name of the 'Black Brothers.'

The youngest brother, Gluck, was as completely opposed, in both appearance and character, to his seniors as could possibly be imagined or desired. He was not above twelve years old, fair, blue-eyed, and kind in temper to every living thing. He did not, of course, agree particularly well with his brothers, or rather, they did not agree with *him*. He was usually appointed to the honourable office of turnspit, when there was anything to roast, which was not often; for, to do the brothers justice, they were hardly less sparing upon themselves than upon other people. At other times he used to clean the shoes, floors, and sometimes the plates, occasionally getting what was left on them, by way of encouragement, and a wholesome quantity of dry blows, by way of education.

Things went on in this manner for a long time. At last came a very wet summer, and everything went wrong in the country around. The hay had hardly been got in, when the haystacks were floated bodily down to sea by an inundation; the vines were cut to pieces with the hail; the corn was all killed by a black blight; only in the Treasure Valley, as usual, all was safe. As it had rain when there was rain nowhere else, so it had sun when there was sun nowhere else. Everybody came to buy corn at the farm, and went away pouring maledictions upon the Black Brothers. They asked what they liked, and got it, except

The King of the Golden River

from the poor people, who could only beg, and several of whom were starved at their very door, without the slightest regard or notice.

It was drawing towards winter, and very cold weather, when one day the two elder brothers had gone out, with their usual warning to little Gluck, who was left to mind the roast, that he was to let nobody in, and give nothing out. Gluck sat down quite close to the fire, for it was raining very hard, and the kitchen walls were by no means dry or comfortable-looking. He turned and turned, and the roast got nice and brown. 'What a pity,' thought Gluck, 'my brothers never ask anybody to dinner. I'm sure, when they've got such a nice piece of mutton as this, and nobody else has got so much as a dry piece of bread, it would do their hearts good to have somebody to eat it with them.'

Just as he spoke, there came a double knock at the house door, yet heavy and dull, as though the knocker had been tied up—more like a puff than a knock.

'It must be the wind,' said Gluck; 'nobody else would venture to knock double knocks at our door.'

No; it wasn't the wind: there it came again very hard, and what was particularly astounding, the knocker seemed to be in a hurry, and not to be in the least afraid of the consequences. Gluck went to the window, opened it, and put his head out to see who it was.

It was the most extraordinary looking little gentleman he had ever seen in his life. He had a very large nose, slightly brass-coloured; his cheeks were very round, and very red, and might have warranted a supposition that he had been blowing a refractory fire for the last eight-and-forty hours; his eyes twinkled merrily through long silky eyelashes, his moustaches curled twice round like a corkscrew on each side of his mouth, and his hair, of a curious pepper-and-salt colour, descended far over his shoulders. He was about four feet six in height, and wore a conical pointed cap of nearly the same altitude, decorated with a black feather some three feet long.* His doublet was prolonged behind into something resembling a violent exaggeration of what is now termed a 'swallow-tail,'* but was much obscured by the swelling folds of an enormous, black, glossy-looking cloak, which must have been very much too long in calm weather, as the wind, whistling round the old house, carried it clear out from the wearer's shoulders to about four times its own length.

Gluck was so perfectly paralyzed by the singular appearance of his visitor, that he remained fixed without uttering a word, until the old

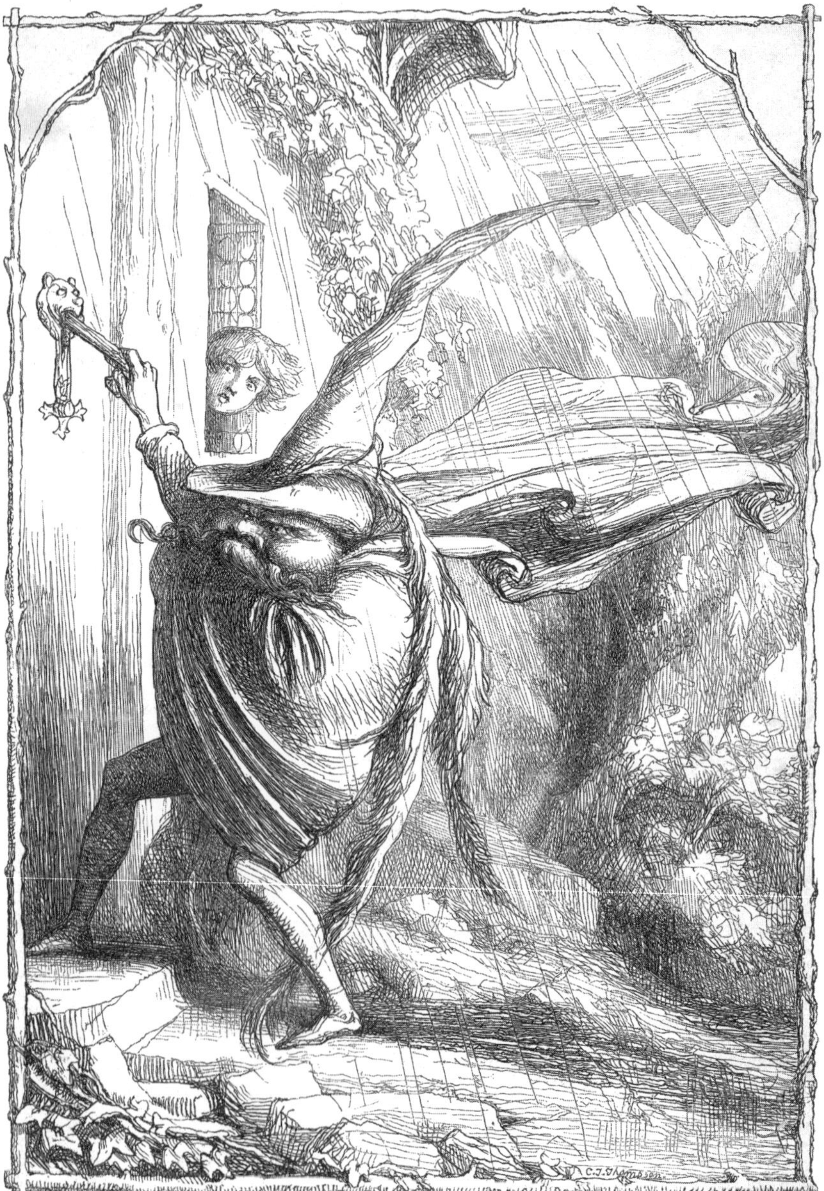

gentleman, having performed another, and a more energetic concerto on the knocker, turned round to look after his fly-away cloak. In so doing, he caught sight of Gluck's little yellow head jammed in the window, with its mouth and eyes very wide open indeed.

'Hollo!' said the little gentleman, 'that's not the way to answer the door: I'm wet, let me in.'

To do the little gentleman justice, he *was* wet. His feather hung down between his legs like a beaten puppy's tail, dripping like an umbrella; and from the ends of his moustaches the water was running into his waistcoat pockets, and out again like a mill stream.

'I beg pardon, sir,' said Gluck, 'I'm very sorry, but I really can't.'

'Can't what?' said the old gentleman.

'I can't let you in, sir,——I can't indeed; my brothers would beat me to death, sir, if I thought of such a thing. What do you want, sir?'

'Want?' said the old gentleman, petulantly. 'I want fire, and shelter; and there's your great fire blazing, crackling, and dancing on the walls with nobody to feel it. Let me in, I say; I only want to warm myself.'

Gluck had had his head, by this time, so long out of the window, that he began to feel it was really unpleasantly cold, and when he turned, and saw the beautiful fire rustling and roaring, and throwing long bright tongues up the chimney, as if it were licking its chops on the savoury smell of the leg of mutton, his heart melted within him that it should be burning away for nothing. 'He does look *very* wet,' said little Gluck; 'I'll just let him in for a quarter of an hour.' Round he went to the door, and opened it; and as the little gentleman walked in, there came a gust of wind through the house, that made the old chimneys totter.

'That's a good boy,' said the little gentleman. 'Never mind your brothers. I'll talk to them.'

'Pray, sir, don't do any such thing,' said Gluck. 'I can't let you stay till they come; they'd be the death of me.'

'Dear me,' said the old gentleman, 'I'm very sorry to hear that. How long may I stay?'

'Only till the mutton's done, sir,' replied Gluck, 'and it's very brown.'

Then the old gentleman walked into the kitchen, and sat himself down on the hob, with the top of his cap accommodated up the chimney, for it was a great deal too high for the roof.

'You'll soon dry there, sir,' said Gluck, and sat down again to turn the mutton. But the old gentleman did *not* dry there, but went on drip, drip, dripping among the cinders, and the fire fizzed and sputtered, and began to look very black, and uncomfortable: never was such a cloak; every fold in it ran like a gutter.

'I beg pardon, sir,' said Gluck, at length, after watching the water spreading in long, quicksilver-like streams over the floor for a quarter of an hour; 'mayn't I take your cloak?'

'No, thank you,' said the old gentleman.

'Your cap, sir?'

'I am all right, thank you,' said the old gentleman rather gruffly.

'But,—sir,—I'm very sorry,' said Gluck, hesitatingly; 'but—really, sir,—you're—putting the fire out.'

'It'll take longer to do the mutton, then,' replied his visitor drily.

Gluck was very much puzzled by the behaviour of his guest; it was such a strange mixture of coolness and humility. He turned away at the string* meditatively for another five minutes.

'That mutton looks very nice,' said the old gentleman at length. 'Can't you give me a little bit?'

'Impossible, sir,' said Gluck.

'I'm very hungry,' continued the old gentleman; 'I've had nothing to eat yesterday, nor to-day. They surely couldn't miss a bit from the knuckle!'

He spoke in so very melancholy a tone, that it quite melted Gluck's heart. 'They promised me one slice to-day, sir,' said he; 'I can give you that, but not a bit more.'

'That's a good boy,' said the old gentleman again.

Then Gluck warmed a plate, and sharpened a knife. 'I don't care if I do get beaten for it,' thought he. Just as he had cut a large slice out of the mutton, there came a tremendous rap at the door. The old gentleman jumped off the hob, as if it had suddenly become inconveniently warm. Gluck fitted the slice into the mutton again, with desperate efforts at exactitude, and ran to open the door.

'What did you keep us waiting in the rain for?' said Schwartz, as he walked in, throwing his umbrella in Gluck's face. 'Ay! what for, indeed, you little vagabond?' said Hans, administering an educational box on the ear, as he followed his brother into the kitchen.

'Bless my soul!' said Schwartz when he opened the door.

'Amen,' said the little gentleman, who had taken his cap off, and was standing in the middle of the kitchen, bowing with the utmost possible velocity.

'Who's that?' said Schwartz, catching up a rolling-pin, and turning to Gluck with a fierce frown.

'I don't know, indeed, brother,' said Gluck in great terror.

'How did he get in?' roared Schwartz.

'My dear brother,' said Gluck, deprecatingly, 'he was so *very* wet!'

The rolling-pin was descending on Gluck's head; but, at the instant, the old gentleman interposed his conical cap, on which it crashed with a shock that shook the water out of it all over the room. What was very odd, the rolling-pin no sooner touched the cap, than it flew out of Schwartz's hand, spinning like a straw in a high wind, and fell into the corner at the further end of the room.

'Who are you, sir?' demanded Schwartz, turning upon him.

'What's your business?' snarled Hans.

'I'm a poor old man, sir,' the little gentleman began very modestly, 'and I saw your fire through the window, and begged shelter for a quarter of an hour.'

'Have the goodness to walk out again, then,' said Schwartz. 'We've quite enough water in our kitchen, without making it a drying-house.'

'It is a cold day to turn an old man out in, sir; look at my grey hairs.' They hung down to his shoulders, as I told you before.

'Ay!' said Hans, 'there are enough of them to keep you warm. Walk!'

'I'm very, very hungry, sir; couldn't you spare me a bit of bread before I go?'

'Bread, indeed!' said Schwartz; 'do you suppose we've nothing to do with our bread, but to give it so such red-nosed fellows as you?'

'Why don't you sell your feather?' said Hans, sneeringly. 'Out with you!'

'A little bit,' said the old gentleman.

'Be off!' said Schwartz.

'Pray, gentlemen——'

'Off, and be hanged!' cried Hans, seizing him by the collar. But he had no sooner touched the old gentleman's collar, than away he went after the rolling-pin, spinning round and round, till he fell into the corner on the top of it. Then Schwartz was very angry, and ran at the old gentleman to turn him out; but he also had hardly touched him, when away he went after Hans and the rolling-pin, and hit his head against the wall as he tumbled into the corner. And so there they lay, all three.

Then the old gentleman spun himself round with velocity in the opposite direction; continued to spin until his long cloak was all wound neatly about him; clapped his cap on his head, very much on one side (for it could not stand upright without going through the ceiling), gave an additional twist to his corkscrew moustaches, and replied with perfect coolness: 'Gentlemen, I wish you a very good morning. At twelve o'clock to-night I'll call again; after such a refusal of hospitality as I have just experienced, you will not be surprised if that visit is the last I ever pay you.'

'If ever I catch you here again,' muttered Schwartz, coming, half-frightened, out of the corner—but, before he could finish his sentence, the old gentleman had shut the house door behind him with a great bang: and there drove past the window, at the same instant, a wreath of ragged cloud, that whirled and rolled down the valley in all manner of shapes; turning over and over in the air, and melting away at last in a gush of rain.

'A very pretty business, indeed, Mr. Gluck!' said Schwartz. 'Dish the mutton, sir. If ever I catch you at such a trick again—bless me, why the mutton's been cut!'

'You promised me one slice, brother, you know,' said Gluck.

'Oh! and you were cutting it hot, I suppose, and going to catch all the gravy. It'll be long before I promise you such a thing again. Leave the room, sir; and have the kindness to wait in the coal-cellar till I call you.'

Gluck left the room, melancholy enough. The brothers ate as much mutton as they could, locked the rest in the cupboard, and proceeded to get very drunk after dinner.

Such a night as it was! Howling wind, and rushing rain, without intermission. The brothers had just sense enough left to put up all the shutters, and double bar the door before they went to bed. They usually slept in the same room. As the clock struck twelve, they were both awakened by a tremendous crash. Their door burst open with a violence that shook the house from top to bottom.

'What's that?' cried Schwartz, starting up in his bed.

'Only I,' said the little gentleman.

The two brothers sat up on their bolster, and stared into the darkness. The room was full of water, and by a misty moonbeam, which found its way through a hole in the shutter, they could see in the midst of it an enormous foam globe, spinning round, and bobbing up and down like a cork, on which, as on a most luxurious cushion, reclined the little old gentleman, cap and all. There was plenty of room for it now, for the roof was off.

'Sorry to incommode you,' said their visitor, ironically. 'I'm afraid your beds are dampish; perhaps you had better go to your brother's room: I've left the ceiling on, there.'

They required no second admonition, but rushed into Gluck's room, wet through, and in an agony of terror.

'You'll find my card on the kitchen table,' the old gentleman called after them. 'Remember, the *last* visit.'

'Pray Heaven it may!' said Schwartz, shuddering. And the foam globe disappeared.

Dawn came at last, and the two brothers looked out of Gluck's little window in the morning. The Treasure Valley was one mass of ruin and desolation. The inundation had swept away trees, crops, and cattle, and left in their stead a waste of red sand and grey mud. The two brothers crept shivering and horror-struck into the kitchen. The water had gutted the whole first floor; corn, money, almost every moveable thing had been swept away, and there was only left a small white card on the kitchen table. On it, in large, breezy, long-legged letters, were engraved the words:—

South West Wind Esquire

CHAPTER II

OF THE PROCEEDINGS OF THE THREE BROTHERS AFTER THE VISIT OF SOUTH-WEST WIND, ESQUIRE; AND HOW LITTLE GLUCK HAD AN INTERVIEW WITH THE KING OF THE GOLDEN RIVER

SOUTH-WEST WIND, Esquire, was as good as his word. After the momentous visit above related, he entered the Treasure Valley no more; and, what was worse, he had so much influence with his relations, the West Winds in general, and used it so effectually, that they all adopted a similar line of conduct. So no rain fell in the valley from one year's end to another. Though everything remained green and flourishing in the plains below, the inheritance of the Three Brothers was a desert. What had once been the richest soil in the kingdom, became a shifting heap of red sand; and the brothers, unable longer to contend with the adverse skies, abandoned their valueless patrimony in despair, to seek some means of gaining a livelihood among the cities and people of the plains. All their money was gone, and they had nothing left but some curious old-fashioned pieces of gold plate, the last remnants of their ill-gotten wealth.

'Suppose we turn goldsmiths?' said Schwartz to Hans, as they entered the large city. 'It is a good knave's trade; we can put a great deal of copper into the gold, without any one's finding it out.'

The thought was agreed to be a very good one; they hired a furnace, and turned goldsmiths. But two slight circumstances affected their trade: the first, that people did not approve of the coppered gold; the second, that the two elder brothers, whenever they had sold anything, used to leave little Gluck to mind the furnace, and go and drink out the money in the ale-house next door. So they melted all their gold, without making money enough to buy more, and were at last reduced to one large drinking mug, which an uncle of his had given to little Gluck, and which he was very fond of, and would not have parted with for the world; though he never drank anything out of it but milk and water. The mug was a very odd mug to look at. The handle was formed of two wreaths of flowing golden hair, so finely spun that it looked more like silk than metal, and these wreaths descended into, and mixed with, a beard and whiskers of the same exquisite workmanship, which surrounded and decorated a very fierce little face, of the reddest gold imaginable, right in the front of the mug, with a pair of eyes in it which seemed to command its whole circumference. It was impossible to drink out of the mug without being subjected to an intense gaze out of the side of those eyes; and Schwartz positively averred, that once, after emptying it, full of Rhenish* seventeen times, he had seen them wink! When it came to the mug's turn to be made into spoons, it half broke poor little Gluck's heart; but the brothers only laughed at him, tossed the mug into the melting-pot, and staggered out to the ale-house: leaving him, as usual, to pour the gold into bars, when it was all ready.

When they were gone, Gluck took a farewell look at his old friend in the melting-pot. The flowing hair was all gone; nothing remained but the red nose, and the sparkling eyes, which looked more malicious than ever. 'And no wonder,' thought Gluck, 'after being treated in that way.' He sauntered disconsolately to the window, and sat himself down to catch the fresh evening air, and escape the hot breath of the furnace. Now this window commanded a direct view of the range of mountains, which, as I told you before, overhung the Treasure Valley, and more especially of the peak from which fell the Golden River. It was just at the close of the day, and when Gluck sat down at the window, he saw the rocks of the mountain tops, all crimson, and purple with the sunset; and there were bright tongues of fiery cloud burning and quivering about them; and the river, brighter than all, fell, in a waving column of pure gold, from precipice to precipice, with the double arch of a broad purple rainbow stretched across it, flushing and fading alternately in the wreaths of spray.

'Ah!' said Gluck aloud, after he had looked at it for a while, 'if that river were really all gold, what a nice thing it would be!'

'No it wouldn't, Gluck,' said a clear metallic voice, close at his ear.

'Bless me! what's that?' exclaimed Gluck, jumping up. There was nobody there. He looked round the room, and under the table, and a great many times behind him, but there was certainly nobody there, and he sat down again at the window. This time he didn't speak, but he couldn't help thinking again that it would be very convenient if the river were really all gold.

'Not at all, my boy,' said the same voice, louder than before.

'Bless me!' said Gluck, 'what *is* that?' He looked again into all the corners and cupboards, and then began turning round, and round, as fast as he could in the middle of the room, thinking there was somebody behind him, when the same voice struck again on his ear. It was singing now very merrily, 'Lala-lira-la;' no words, only a soft running effervescent melody, something like that of a kettle on the boil. Gluck looked out of the window. No, it was certainly in that very room, coming in quicker time, and clearer notes, every moment. 'Lala-lira-la.' All at once it struck Gluck that it sounded louder near the furnace. He ran to the opening, and looked in: yes, he saw right, it seemed to be coming, not only out of the furnace, but out of the pot. He uncovered it, and ran back in a great fright, for the pot was certainly singing! He stood in the farthest corner of the room, with his hands up, and his mouth open, for a minute or two, when the singing stopped, and the voice became clear, and pronunciative.

'Hollo!' said the voice.

Gluck made no answer.

'Hollo, Gluck, my boy,' said the pot again.

Gluck summoned up all his energies, walked straight up to the crucible, drew it out of the furnace, and looked in. The gold was all melted, and its surface as smooth and polished as a river; but instead of reflecting little Gluck's head, as he looked in, he saw meeting his glance from beneath the gold the red nose and sharp eyes of his old friend of the mug, a thousand times redder and sharper than ever he had seen them in his life.

'Come, Gluck, my boy,' said the voice out of the pot again, 'I'm all right; pour me out.'

But Gluck was too much astonished to do anything of the kind.

'Pour me out, I say,' said the voice rather gruffly.

Still Gluck couldn't move.

'*Will* you pour me out?' said the voice passionately, 'I'm too hot.'

By a violent effort, Gluck recovered the use of his limbs, took hold of the crucible, and sloped it so as to pour out the gold. But instead of a liquid stream, there came out, first, a pair of pretty little yellow legs, then some coat tails, then a pair of arms stuck a-kimbo, and, finally, the well-known head of his friend the mug; all which articles, uniting as they rolled out, stood up energetically on the floor, in the shape of a little golden dwarf, about a foot and a half high.

'That's right!' said the dwarf, stretching out first his legs, and then his arms, and then shaking his head up and down, and as far round as it would go, for five minutes, without stopping; apparently with the view of ascertaining if he were quite correctly put together, while

Gluck stood contemplating him in speechless amazement. He was dressed in a slashed doublet of spun gold, so fine in its texture, that the prismatic colours gleamed over it, as if on a surface of mother of pearl; and, over this brilliant doublet, his hair and beard fell full half-way to the ground, in waving curls, so exquisitely delicate, that Gluck could hardly tell where they ended; they seemed to melt into air. The features of his face, however, were by no means finished with the same delicacy; they were rather coarse, slightly inclining to coppery in complexion, and indicative, in expression, of a very pertinacious and intractable disposition in their small proprietor. When the dwarf had finished his self-examination, he turned his small sharp eyes on Gluck, and stared at him deliberately for a minute or two. 'No, it wouldn't, Gluck, my boy,' said the little man.

This was certainly a rather abrupt and unconnected mode of commencing conversation. It might indeed be supposed to refer to the course of Gluck's thoughts, which had first produced the dwarf's observations out of the pot; but whatever it referred to, Gluck had no inclination to dispute the dictum.

'Wouldn't it, sir?' said Gluck, very mildly and submissively indeed.

'No,' said the dwarf, conclusively. 'No, it wouldn't.' And with that, the dwarf pulled his cap hard over his brows, and took two turns, of three feet long, up and down the room, lifting his legs up very high, and setting them down very hard. This pause gave time for Gluck to collect his thoughts a little, and, seeing no great reason to view his diminutive visitor with dread, and feeling his curiosity overcome his amazement, he ventured on a question of peculiar delicacy.

'Pray, sir,' said Gluck, rather hesitatingly, 'were you my mug?'

On which the little man turned sharp round, walked straight up to Gluck, and drew himself up to his full height. 'I,' said the little man, 'am the King of the Golden River.' Whereupon he turned about again, and took two more turns, some six feet long, in order to allow time for the consternation which this announcement produced in his auditor to evaporate. After which, he again walked up to Gluck and stood still, as if expecting some comment on his communication.

Gluck determined to say something at all events. 'I hope your Majesty is very well,' said Gluck.

'Listen!' said the little man, deigning no reply to this polite inquiry. 'I am the King of what you mortals call the Golden River. The shape you saw me in was owing to the malice of a stronger king, from whose enchantments you have this instant freed me. What I have seen of you, and your conduct to your wicked brothers, renders me willing to serve you; therefore, attend to what I tell you. Whoever shall climb to the top of that mountain from which you see the Golden River issue, and shall cast into the stream at its source three drops of holy water, for him, and for him only, shall the river turn to gold. But no one failing in his first, can succeed in a second attempt; and if any one shall cast unholy water into the river, it will overwhelm him, and he will become a black stone.' So saying, the King of the Golden River turned away and deliberately walked into the centre of the hottest flame of the furnace. His figure became red, white, transparent dazzling,—a blaze of intense light,—rose, trembled, and disappeared. The King of the Golden River had evaporated.

'Oh!' cried poor Gluck, running to look up the chimney after him; 'Oh dear, dear, dear me! My mug! my mug! my mug!'

CHAPTER III

HOW MR. HANS SET OFF ON AN EXPEDITION TO THE GOLDEN RIVER, AND HOW HE PROSPERED THEREIN

THE King of the Golden River had hardly made the extraordinary exit related in the last chapter, before Hans and Schwartz came roaring into the house, very savagely drunk. The discovery of the total loss of their last piece of plate had the effect of sobering them up just enough to enable them to stand over Gluck, beating him very steadily for a quarter of an hour; at the expiration of which period they dropped into a couple of chairs, and requested to know what he had got to say for himself. Gluck told them his story, of which, of course, they did not believe a word. They beat him again, till their arms were tired, and staggered to bed. In the morning, however, the steadiness with which he adhered to his story obtained him some degree of credence; the immediate consequence of which was, that the two brothers, after wrangling a long time on the knotty question, which of them should try his fortune first, drew their swords and began fighting. The noise of the fray alarmed the neighbours, who, finding they could not pacify the combatants, sent for the constable.

Hans, on hearing this, contrived to escape, and hid himself; but Schwartz was taken before the magistrate, fined for breaking the peace, and, having drunk out his last penny the evening before, was thrown into prison till he should pay.

When Hans heard this, he was much delighted, and determined to set out immediately for the Golden River. How to get the holy water was the question. He went to the priest; but the priest could not give any holy water to so abandoned a character. So Hans went to vespers* in the evening for the first time in his life, and under pretence of crossing himself, stole a cupful, and returned home in triumph.

Next morning he got up before the sun rose, put the holy water into a strong flask, and two bottles of wine and some meat in a basket, slung them over his back, took his alpine staff in his hand, and set off for the mountains.

On his way out of the town he had to pass the prison, and as he looked in at the windows, whom should he see but Schwartz himself peeping out of the bars, and looking very disconsolate.

'Good morning, brother,' said Hans; 'have you any message for the King of the Golden River?'

Schwartz gnashed his teeth with rage, and shook the bars with all his strength; but Hans only laughed at him, and advising him to make himself comfortable till he came back again, shouldered his basket, shook the bottle of holy water in Schwartz's face till it frothed again, and marched off in the highest spirits in the world.

It was, indeed, a morning that might have made any one happy, even with no Golden River to seek for. Level lines of dewy mist lay stretched along the valley, out of which rose the nasty mountains— their lower cliffs in pale grey shadow, hardly distinguishable from the floating vapour, but gradually ascending till they caught the sunlight, which ran in sharp touches of ruddy colour along the angular crags, and pierced, in long level rays, through their fringes of spear-like pine. Far above, shot up red splintered masses of castellated rock, jagged and shivered into myriads of fantastic forms, with here and there a streak of sunlit snow, traced down their chasms like a line of forked lightning; and, far beyond, and far above all these, fainter than the morning cloud, but purer and changeless, slept, in the blue sky, the utmost peaks of the eternal snow.

The Golden River, which sprang from one of the lower and

snowless elevations, was now nearly in shadow; all but the uppermost jets of spray, which rose like slow smoke above the undulating lines of the cataract, and floated away in feeble wreaths upon the morning wind.

On this object, and on this alone, Hans' eyes and thoughts were fixed; forgetting the distance he had to traverse, he set off at an imprudent rate of walking, which greatly exhausted him before he had scaled the first range of the green and low hills. He was, moreover, surprised, on surmounting them, to find that a large glacier, of whose existence, notwithstanding his previous knowledge of the mountains, he had been absolutely ignorant, lay between him and the source of the Golden River. He entered on it with the boldness of a practised mountaineer; yet he thought that he had never traversed so strange or so dangerous a glacier in his life. The ice was excessively slippery, and out of all its chasms came wild sounds of gushing water; not monotonous or low, but changeful and loud, rising occasionally into drifting passages of wild melody, then breaking off into short melancholy tones, or sudden shrieks, resembling those of human voices in distress or pain. The ice was broken into thousands of confused shapes, but none, Hans thought, like the ordinary forms of splintered ice. There seemed a curious *expression* about all these outlines—a perpetual resemblance to living features, distorted and scornful. Myriads of deceitful shadows, and lurid lights, played and floated about and through the pale blue pinnacles, dazzling and confusing the sight of the traveller; while his ears grew dull and his head giddy with the constant gush and roar of the concealed waters. These painful circumstances increased upon him as he advanced; the ice crashed and yawned into fresh chasms at his feet, tottering spires nodded around him, and fell thundering across his path; and though he had repeatedly faced these dangers on the most terrific glaciers, and in the wildest weather, it was with a new and oppressive feeling of panic terror that he leaped the last chasm, and flung himself, exhausted and shuddering, on the firm turf of the mountain.

He had been compelled to abandon his basket of food, which became a perilous incumbrance on the glacier, and had now no means of refreshing himself but by breaking off and eating some of the pieces of ice. This, however, relieved his thirst; an hour's repose recruited his hardy frame, and with the indomitable spirit of avarice, he resumed his laborious journey.

The King of the Golden River

His way now lay straight up a ridge of bare red rocks, without a blade of grass to ease the foot, or a projecting angle to afford an inch of shade from the south sun. It was past noon, and the rays beat intensely upon the steep path, while the whole atmosphere was motionless, and penetrated with heat. Intense thirst was soon added to the bodily fatigue with which Hans was now afflicted; glance after glance he cast on the flask of water which hung at his belt. 'Three drops are enough,' at last thought he; 'I may, at least, cool my lips with it.'

He opened the flask, and was raising it to his lips, when his eye fell on an object lying on the rock beside him; he thought it moved. It was a small dog, apparently in the last agony of death from thirst. Its tongue was out, its jaws dry, its limbs extended lifelessly, and a swarm of black ants were crawling about its lips and throat. Its eye moved to the bottle which Hans held in his hand. He raised it, drank, spurned the animal with his foot, and passed on. And he did not know how it was, but he thought that a strange shadow had suddenly come across the blue sky.

The path became steeper and more rugged every moment; and the high hill air, instead of refreshing him, seemed to throw his blood into a fever. The noise of the hill cataracts sounded like mockery in his ears; they were all distant, and his thirst increased every moment. Another hour passed, and he again looked down to the flask at his side; it was half empty; but there was much more than three drops in it. He stopped to open it, and again, as he did so, something moved in the path above him. It was a fair child, stretched nearly lifeless on the rock, its breast heaving with thirst, its eyes closed, and its lips parched and burning. Hans eyed it deliberately, drank, and passed on. And a dark grey cloud came over the sun, and long, snake-like shadows crept up along the mountain sides. Hans struggled on. The sun was sinking, but its descent seemed to bring no coolness; the leaden weight of the dead air pressed upon his brow and heart, but the goal was near. He saw the cataract of the Golden River springing from the hill-side, scarcely five hundred feet above him. He paused for a moment to breathe, and sprang on to complete his task.

At this instant a faint cry fell on his ear. He turned, and saw a grey-haired old man extended on the rocks. His eyes were sunk, his features deadly pale, and gathered into an expression of despair. 'Water!' he stretched his arms to Hans, and cried feebly, 'Water! I am dying!'

'I have none,' replied Hans; 'thou hast had thy share of life.' He strode over the prostrate body, and darted on. And a flash of blue lightning rose out of the East, shaped like a sword; it shook thrice over the whole heaven, and left it dark with one heavy, impenetrable shade. The sun was setting; it plunged towards the horizon like a red-hot ball.

The roar of the Golden River rose on Hans' ear. He stood at the brink of the chasm through which it ran. Its waves were filled with the red glory of the sunset: they shook their crests like tongues of fire, and flashes of bloody light gleamed along their foam. Their sound came mightier and mightier on his senses; his brain grew giddy with the prolonged thunder. Shuddering he drew the flask from his girdle, and hurled it into the centre of the torrent. As he did so, an icy chill shot through his limbs: he staggered, shrieked, and fell. The waters closed over his cry. And the moaning of the river rose wildly into the night, as it gushed over

THE BLACK STONE.

CHAPTER IV

HOW MR. SCHWARTZ SET OFF ON AN EXPEDITION TO THE GOLDEN RIVER, AND HOW HE PROSPERED THEREIN

POOR little Gluck waited very anxiously alone in the house for Hans' return. Finding he did not come back, he was terribly frightened, and went and told Schwartz in the prison all that had happened. Then Schwartz was very much pleased, and said that Hans must certainly have been turned into a black stone, and he should have all the gold to himself. But Gluck was very sorry, and cried all night. When he got up in the morning there was no bread in the house, nor any money; so

The King of the Golden River 33

Gluck went and hired himself to another goldsmith, and he worked so hard, and so neatly, and so long every day, that he soon got money enough together to pay his brother's fine, and he went and gave it all to Schwartz, and Schwartz got out of prison. Then Schwartz was quite pleased, and said he should have some of the gold of the river. But Gluck only begged he would go and see what had become of Hans.

Now when Schwartz had heard that Hans had stolen the holy water, he thought to himself that such a procedure might not be considered altogether correct by the King of the Golden River, and determined to manage matters better. So he took some more of Gluck's money, and went to a bad priest, who gave him some holy water very readily for it. Then Schwartz was sure it was all quite right. So Schwartz got up early in the morning before the sun rose, and took some bread and wine in a basket, and put his holy water in a flask, and set off for the mountains. Like his brother, he was much surprised at the sight of the glacier, and had great difficulty in crossing it, even after leaving his basket behind him. The day was cloudless, but not bright; there was a heavy purple haze hanging over the sky, and the hills looked lowering and gloomy. And as Schwartz climbed the steep rock path, the thirst came upon him, as it had upon his brother, until he lifted his flask to his lips to drink. Then he saw the fair child lying near him on the rocks, and it cried to him, and moaned for water.

'Water indeed,' said Schwartz; 'I haven't half enough for myself,' and passed on. And as he went he thought the sunbeams grew more dim, and he saw a low bank of black cloud rising out of the West; and, when he had climbed for another hour the thirst overcame him again, and he would have drunk. Then he saw the old man lying before him on the path, and heard him cry out for water. 'Water, indeed,' said Schwartz, 'I haven't half enough for myself,' and on he went.

Then again the light seemed to fade from before his eyes, and he looked up, and behold, a mist, of the colour of blood, had come over the sun; and the bank of black cloud had risen very high, and its edges were tossing and tumbling like the waves of the angry sea. And they cast long shadows, which flickered over Schwartz's path.

Then Schwartz climbed for another hour, and again his thirst returned; and as he lifted his flask to his lips, he thought he saw his brother Hans lying exhausted on the path before him, and, as he gazed, the figure stretched its arms to him, and cried for water. 'Ha, ha,' laughed Schwartz, 'are you there? remember the prison bars, my boy. Water, indeed! do you suppose I carried it all the way up here for *you?*' And he strode over the figure; yet, as he passed, he thought he saw a strange expression of mockery about its lips. And, when he had gone a few yards farther, he looked back; but the figure was not there.

And a sudden horror came over Schwartz, he knew not why; but the thirst for gold prevailed over his fear, and he rushed on. And the bank of black cloud rose to the zenith, and out of it came bursts of spiry lightning, and waves of darkness seemed to heave and float between their flashes over the whole heavens. And the sky where the sun was setting was all level, and like a lake of blood; and a strong wind came out of that sky, tearing its crimson clouds into fragments, and scattering them far into the darkness. And when Schwartz stood by the brink of the Golden River, its waves were black, like thunder clouds, but their foam was like fire; and the roar of the waters below, and the thunders above, met, as he cast the flask into the stream. And, as he did so, the lightning glared into his eyes, and the earth gave way beneath him, and the waters closed over his cry. And the moaning of the river rose wildly into the night, as it gushed over the

Two Black Stones.

CHAPTER V

HOW LITTLE GLUCK SET OFF ON AN EXPEDITION TO THE GOLDEN RIVER, AND HOW HE PROSPERED THEREIN; WITH OTHER MATTERS OF INTEREST

When Gluck found that Schwartz did not come back he was very sorry, and did not know what to do. He had no money, and was obliged to go and hire himself again to the same goldsmith, who worked him very hard, and gave him very little money. So, after a month or two, Gluck grew tired, and made up his mind to go and try his fortune with the Golden River. 'The little king looked very kind,' thought he. 'I don't think he will turn me into a black stone.' So he went to the priest, and the priest gave him some holy water as soon as he asked for it. Then Gluck took some bread in his basket, and the bottle of water, and set off very early for the mountains.

If the glacier had occasioned a great deal of fatigue to his brothers, it was twenty times worse for him, who was neither so strong nor so practised on the mountains. He had several very bad falls, lost his basket and bread, and was very much frightened at the strange noises under the ice. He lay a long time to rest on the grass, after he had got over, and began to climb the hill just in the hottest part of the day. When he had climbed for an hour, he got dreadfully thirsty, and was going to drink like his brothers, when he saw an old man coming down the path above him, looking very feeble, and leaning on a staff. 'My son,' said the old man, 'I am faint with thirst, give me some of that water.' Then Gluck looked at him, and when he saw that he was pale and weary, he gave him the water; 'Only pray don't drink it all,' said Gluck. But the old man drank a great deal, and gave him back the bottle two-thirds empty. Then he bade him good speed, and Gluck went on again merrily. And the path became easier to his feet, and two or three blades of grass appeared upon it, and some grasshoppers began singing on the bank beside it; and Gluck thought that he had never heard such merry singing.

Then he went on for another hour, and the thirst increased on him so that he thought he should be forced to drink. But, as he raised the flask, he saw a little child lying panting by the roadside, and it cried out piteously for water. Then Gluck struggled with himself, and determined to bear the thirst a little longer; and he put the bottle to the child's lips, and it drank it all but a few drops. Then it smiled on him, and got up, and ran down the hill; and Gluck looked after it, till it became as small as a little star, and then turned and began climbing again. And then there were all kinds of sweet flowers growing on the rocks, bright green moss, with pale pink starry flowers, and soft bellied gentians, more blue than the sky at its deepest, and pure white transparent lilies. And crimson and purple butterflies darted hither and thither, and the sky sent down such pure light, that Gluck had never felt so happy in his life.

Yet, when he had climbed for another hour, his thirst became intolerable again; and, when he looked at his bottle, he saw that there were only five or six drops left in it, and he could not venture to drink. And, as he was hanging the flask to his belt again, he saw a little dog lying on the rocks gasping for breath—just as Hans had seen it on the day of his ascent. And Gluck stopped and looked at it, and then at the Golden River, not five hundred yards above him; and he thought of the dwarf's words, 'that no one could succeed, except in his first attempt'; and he tried to pass the dog, but it whined piteously, and Gluck stopped again. 'Poor beastie,' said Gluck, 'it'll be dead when I come down again, if I don't help it.' Then he looked closer and closer at it, and its eye turned on him so mournfully, that he could not stand it. 'Confound the King and his gold too,' said Gluck; and he opened the flask, and poured all the water into the dog's mouth.

The dog sprang up and stood on its hind legs. Its tail disappeared, its ears became long, longer, silky, golden; its nose became very red, its eyes became very twinkling; in three seconds the dog was gone, and before Gluck stood his old acquaintance, the King of the Golden River.

'Thank you,' said the monarch; 'but don't be frightened, it's all right'; for Gluck showed manifest symptoms of consternation at this unlooked-for reply to his last observation. 'Why didn't you come before,' continued the dwarf, 'instead of sending me those rascally brothers of yours, for me to have the trouble of turning into stones? Very hard stones they make too.'

'Oh dear me!' said Gluck, 'have you really been so cruel?'

'Cruel!' said the dwarf, 'they poured unholy water into my stream: do you suppose I'm going to allow that?'

'Why,' said Gluck, 'I am sure, sir—your majesty, I mean—they got the water out of the church font.'

'Very probably,' replied the dwarf; 'but,' and his countenance grew stern as he spoke, 'the water which has been refused to the cry of the weary and dying, is unholy, though it had been blessed by every saint in heaven; and the water which is found in the vessel of mercy is holy, though it had been defiled with corpses.'

So saying, the dwarf stooped and plucked a lily that grew at his feet. On its white leaves there hung three drops of clear dew. And the dwarf shook them into the flask which Gluck held in his hand. 'Cast these into the river,' he said, 'and descend on the other side of the mountains into the Treasure Valley. And so good speed.'

As he spoke, the figure of the dwarf became indistinct. The playing colours of his robe formed themselves into a prismatic mist of dewy light; he stood for an instant veiled with them as with the belt of a broad rainbow. The colours grew faint, the mist rose into the air; the monarch had evaporated.

And Gluck climbed to the brink of the Golden River, and its waves were as clear as crystal, and as brilliant as the sun. And, when he cast the three drops of dew into the stream, there opened where they fell a small circular whirlpool, into which the waters descended with a musical noise.

Gluck stood watching it for some time, very much disappointed, because not only was the river not turned into gold, but its waters seemed much diminished in quantity. Yet he obeyed his friend the dwarf, and descended the other side of the mountains towards the Treasure Valley; and, as he went, he thought he heard the noise of water working its way under the ground. And, when he came in sight of the Treasure Valley, behold, a river, like the Golden River, was springing from a new cleft in the rocks above it, and was flowing in innumerable streams among the dry heaps of red sand.

And as Gluck gazed, fresh grass sprang beside the new streams, and creeping plants grew, and climbed among the moistening soil. Young flowers opened suddenly along the river sides, as stars leap out when twilight is deepening, and thickets of myrtle, and tendrils of vine, cast lengthening shadows over the valley as they grew. And thus the Treasure Valley became a garden again, and the inheritance which had been lost by cruelty, was regained by love.

And Gluck went, and dwelt in the valley, and the poor were never driven from his door: so that his barns became full of corn, and his house of treasure. And, for him, the river had, according to the dwarf's promise, become a River of Gold.

And, to this day, the inhabitants of the valley point out the place where the three drops of holy water were cast into the stream, and trace the course of the Golden River under the ground, until it emerges in the Treasure Valley. And at the top of the cataract of the Golden River, are still to be seen two BLACK STONES, round which the waters howl mournfully every day at sunset; and these stones are still called by the people of the valley

THE BLACK BROTHERS.

WILLIAM MAKEPEACE THACKERAY

The Rose and the Ring; or, The History of Prince Giglio and Prince Bulbo

A Fire-Side Pantomime for Great and Small Children

PRELUDE

IT happened that the undersigned spent the last Christmas season in a foreign city where there were many English children.*

In that city, if you wanted to give a child's party, you could not even get a magic lantern or buy Twelfth-Night characters*—those funny painted pictures of the King, the Queen, the Lover, the Lady, the Dandy, the Captain, and so on—with which our young ones are wont to recreate themselves at this festive time.

My friend, Miss Bunch, who was governess of a large family, that lived in the *Piano Nobile** of the house inhabited by myself and my young charges (it was the Palazzo Poniatowski at Rome, and Messrs. Spillmann, two of the best pastry-cooks in Christendom, have their shop on the ground-floor)—Miss Bunch, I say, begged me to draw a set of Twelfth-Night characters for the amusement of our young people.

She is a lady of great fancy and droll imagination, and having looked at the characters, she and I composed a history about them, which was recited to the little folks at night, and served as our FIRE-SIDE PANTOMIME.*

Our juvenile audience was amused by the adventures of Giglio and Bulbo, Rosalba and Angelica. I am bound to say the fate of the Hall Porter created a considerable sensation; and the wrath of Countess Gruffanuff was received with extreme pleasure.

If these children are pleased, thought I, why should not others be amused also? In a few days, Dr. Birch's young friends will be expected to re-assemble at Rodwell Regis,* where they will learn everything that is useful, and under the eyes of careful ushers continue the business of their little lives.

But in the meanwhile, and for a brief holyday, let us laugh and be as pleasant as we can. And you elder folks—a little joking and dancing and fooling will do even you no harm. The author wishes you a merry Christmas, and welcomes you to the Fire-side Pantomime.

M. A. Titmarsh.*

December, 1854.

THE ROSE AND THE RING

I

SHOWS HOW THE ROYAL FAMILY SATE DOWN TO BREAKFAST

This is Valoroso XXIV, King of Paflagonia,* seated with his Queen and only child at their royal breakfast-table, and receiving the letter which announces to his Majesty a proposed visit from Prince Bulbo, heir of Padella,* reigning King of Crim Tartary.* Remark the delight upon the monarch's royal features. He is so absorbed in the perusal of the King of Crim Tartary's letter, that he allows his eggs to get cold, and leaves his august muffins untasted.

'What! that wicked, brave, delightful Prince Bulbo!' cries Princess Angelica*—'so handsome, so accomplished, so witty,—the conqueror of Rimbombamento,* where he slew ten thousand giants!'

'Who told you of him, my dear?' asks his Majesty.

'A little bird,' says Angelica.

'Poor Giglio!'* says mamma, pouring out the tea.

'Bother Giglio!' cries Angelica, tossing up her head, which rustled with a thousand curl-papers.

'I wish,' growls the King, 'I wish Giglio was. . . . .'

'Was better? Yes, dear, he is better,' says the Queen. 'Angelica's little maid, Betsinda, told me so when she came to my room this morning with my early tea.'

'You are always drinking tea,' said the Monarch, with a scowl.

'It is better than drinking port, or brandy-and-water,' replies her Majesty.

'Well, well, my dear, I only said you were fond of drinking tea,' said the King of Paflagonia, with an effort as if to command his temper. 'Angelica! I hope you have plenty of new dresses; your milliners' bills are long enough. My dear Queen, you must see and have some parties. I prefer dinners, but of course you will be for balls. Your everlasting blue velvet quite tires me: and my love I should like you to have a new necklace. Order one. Not more than a hundred or a hundred and fifty thousand pounds.'

'And Giglio, dear?' says the Queen.

'GIGLIO MAY GO TO THE—'

'Oh, sir,' screams her Majesty. 'Your own nephew! our late King's only son!'

'Giglio may go to the tailor's, and order the bills to be sent in to Glumboso* to pay. Confound him! I mean bless his dear heart. He need want for nothing; give him a couple of guineas for pocket-money, my dear, and you may as well order yourself bracelets, while you are about the necklaces, Mrs. V.'

Her Majesty, or *Mrs. V.*, as the monarch facetiously called her (for even royalty will have its sport, and this august family were very much attached), embraced her husband, and, twining her arm round her daughter's waist, they quitted the breakfast-room in order to make all things ready for the princely stranger.

When they were gone, the smile that had lighted up the eyes of the *husband* and *father* fled—the pride of the *King* fled—the MAN was alone. Had I the pen of a G. P. R. James,* I would also depict his flashing eye, his distended nostril—his dressing-gown, pocket-handkerchief, and boots. But I need not say I have *not* the pen of that novelist; suffice it to say, Valoroso was alone.

He rushed to the cupboard, seizing from the table one of the many egg-cups with which his princely board was served for the matin meal, drew out a bottle of right Nantz or Cognac,* filled and emptied the cup several times, and laid it down with a hoarse 'Ha, ha, ha! now Valoroso is a man again!'

'But oh!' he went on (still sipping, I am sorry to say,) 'ere I was a king, I needed not this intoxicating draught; once I detested the hot brandy wine, and quaffed no other fount but nature's rill. It dashes not more quickly o'er the rocks, than I did, as, with blunderbuss in hand, I brushed away the early morning dew, and shot the partridge, snipe, or antlered deer! Ah! well may England's dramatist remark, "Uneasy lies the head that wears a crown!"* Why did I steal my nephew's, my young Giglio's—? Steal! said I; no, no, no, not steal, not steal. Let me withdraw that odious expression. I took, and on my manly head I set, the royal crown of Paflagonia; I took, and with my royal arm I wield, the sceptral rod of Paflagonia; I took, and in my outstretched hand I hold, the royal orb of Paflagonia! Could a poor boy, a snivelling, drivelling boy—was in his nurse's arms but yesterday, and cried for sugar-plums and puled for pap—bear up the awful weight of crown, orb, sceptre? gird on the sword my royal fathers wore, and meet in fight the tough Crimean foe?'

And then the monarch went on to argue in his own mind (though we need not say that blank verse* is not argument) that what he had got it was his duty to keep, and that, if at one time he had entertained ideas of a certain restitution, which shall be nameless, the prospect by a *certain marriage* of uniting two crowns and two nations which had been engaged in bloody and expensive wars, as the Paflagonians and Crimeans had been, put the idea of Giglio's restoration to the throne out of the question: nay, were his own brother, King Savio* alive, he would certainly will away the crown from his son in order to bring about such a desirable union.

Thus easily do we deceive ourselves! Thus do we fancy what we wish is right! The King took courage, read the papers, finished his muffins and eggs, and rang the bell for his Prime Minister. The Queen, after thinking whether she should go up and see Giglio, who had been sick, thought 'Not now. Business first; pleasure afterwards. I will go and see dear Giglio this afternoon; and now I will drive to the jeweller's, to look for the necklace and bracelets.' The Princess went up into her own room, and made Betsinda, her maid, bring out all her dresses; and as for Giglio, they forgot him as much as I forget what I had for dinner last Tuesday twelvemonth.

II

HOW KING VALOROSO GOT THE CROWN, AND PRINCE GIGLIO WENT WITHOUT

PAFLAGONIA, ten or twenty thousand years ago, appears to have been one of those kingdoms where the laws of succession were not settled; for when King Savio died, leaving his brother Regent of the kingdom, and guardian of Savio's orphan infant, this unfaithful regent took no sort of regard of the late monarch's will; he had himself proclaimed the sovereign of Paflagonia under the title of King Valoroso XXIV, had a most splendid coronation, and ordered all the nobles of the kingdom to pay him homage. So long as Valoroso gave them plenty of balls at Court, plenty of money, and lucrative places, the Paflagonian nobility did not care who was king; and, as for the people, in those early times, they were equally indifferent. The Prince Giglio, by reason of his tender age at his royal father's death did not feel the loss of his crown and empire. As long as he had plenty of toys and sweet-meats, a holiday five times a week, and a horse and gun to go out shooting when he grew a little older, and, above all, the company of his darling cousin, the King's only child, poor Giglio was perfectly contented; nor did he envy his uncle the royal robes and sceptre, the great hot uncomfortable throne of state, and the enormous cumbersome crown in which that monarch appeared, from morning till night. King Valoroso's portrait has been left to us; and I think you will agree with me that he must have been sometimes *rather tired* of his velvet, and his diamonds, and his ermine, and his grandeur. I shouldn't like to sit in that stifling robe with such a thing as that on my head. No doubt, the Queen must have been lovely in her youth; for, though she grew rather stout in after life, yet her features, as shown in her portrait, are certainly *pleasing*. If she was fond of flattery, scandal, cards, and fine clothes, let us deal gently with her infirmities, which, after all, may be no greater than our own. She was kind to her nephew; and if she had any scruples of conscience about her husband's taking the young Prince's crown, consoled herself by thinking that the King, though a usurper, was a most respectable man, and that at his death Prince Giglio would be restored to his throne, and share it with his cousin, whom she loved so fondly.

The Prime Minister was Glumboso, an old statesman, who most cheerfully swore fidelity to King Valoroso, and in whose hands the monarch left all the affairs of his kingdom. All Valoroso wanted was plenty of money, plenty of hunting, plenty of flattery, and as little trouble as possible. As long as he had his sport, this monarch cared little how his people paid for it: he engaged in some wars and of course, the Paflagonian newspapers announced that he gained prodigious victories: he had statues erected to himself in every city of the empire; and of course his pictures placed everywhere, and in all the print-shops: he was Valoroso the Magnanimous, Valoroso the Victorious, Valoroso the Great, and so forth;—for even in these early times courtiers and people knew how to flatter.

This royal pair had one only child, the Princess Angelica, who, you may be sure, was a paragon in the courtiers' eyes, in her parents', and in her own. It was said she had the longest hair, the largest eyes, the slimmest waist, the smallest foot, and the most lovely complexion of any young lady in the Paflagonian dominions. Her accomplishments were announced to be even superior to her beauty; and governesses used to shame their idle pupils by telling them what Princess Angelica could do. She could play the most difficult pieces of music at sight. She could answer any one of Mangnal's Questions.* She knew every date in the history of Paflagonia and every other country. She knew French, English, Italian, German, Spanish, Hebrew, Greek, Latin, Cappadocian, Samothracian,* Ægean, and Crim Tartar. In a word, she was a most accomplished young creature; and her governess and lady-in-waiting was the severe Countess Gruffanuff.*

Would you not fancy, from this picture, that Gruffanuff must have been a person of the highest birth? She looks so haughty that I should have thought her a Princess at the very least, with a pedigree reaching as far back as the deluge. But this lady was no better born than many other ladies who give themselves airs; and all sensible people laughed at her absurd pretensions: the fact is, she had been maid-servant to the Queen when her Majesty was only Princess, and her husband had been head footman, but after his death or *disappearance*, of which you shall hear presently, this Mrs. Gruffanuff, by flattering, toadying, and wheedling her royal mistress, became a favourite with the Queen (who was rather a weak woman), and her Majesty gave her a title, and made her nursery governess to the Princess.

And now I must tell you about the Princess's learning and accomplishments, for which she had such a wonderful character. Clever Angelica certainly was, but as *idle as possible*. Play at sight, indeed! she could play one or two pieces, and pretend that she had never seen them before; she could answer half-a-dozen Mangnal's Questions; but then you must take care to ask the *right* ones. As for her languages, she had masters in plenty, but I doubt whether she knew more than a few phrases in each, for all her pretence; and as for her embroidery and her drawing, she showed beautiful specimens, it is true, but *who did them?*

This obliges me to tell the truth, and to do so I must go back ever so far, and tell you about the FAIRY BLACKSTICK.

III

TELLS WHO THE FAIRY BLACKSTICK WAS, AND WHO WERE EVER SO MANY GRAND PERSONAGES BESIDES

BETWEEN the kingdoms of Paflagonia and Crim Tartary there lived a mysterious personage, who was known in those countries as the Fairy Blackstick, from the ebony wand or crutch which she carried; on which she rode to the moon sometimes, or upon other excursions of business or pleasure, and with which she performed her wonders.

When she was young, and had been first taught the art of conjuring by the necromancer,* her father, she was always practising her skill, whizzing about from one kingdom to another upon her black stick, and conferring her fairy favours upon this Prince or that. She had scores of royal godchildren; turned numberless wicked people into beasts, birds, millstones, clocks, pumps, bootjacks, umbrellas, or other absurd shapes; and in a word was one of the most active and officious of the whole College of fairies.

But after two or three thousand years of this sport, I suppose Blackstick grew tired of it. Or perhaps she thought, 'What good am I doing by sending this Princess to sleep for a hundred years? by fixing a black pudding on to that booby's nose? by causing diamonds and pearls to drop from one little girl's mouth, and vipers and toads from another's?* I begin to think I do as much harm as good by my performances. I might as well shut my incantations up, and allow things to take their natural course.

'There were my two young goddaughters, King Savio's wife and Duke Padella's wife, I gave them each a present, which was to render them charming in the eyes of their husbands, and secure the affection of those gentlemen as long as they lived. What good did my Rose and my Ring do these two women? None on earth. From having all their whims indulged by their husbands, they became capricious, lazy, ill-humoured, absurdly vain, and leered and languished, and fancied themselves irresistibly beautiful, when they were really quite old and hideous, the ridiculous creatures! They used actually to patronise me when I went to pay them a visit; *me*, the Fairy Blackstick, who knows all the wisdom of the necromancers, and who could have turned them into baboons, and all their diamonds into strings of onions by a single wave of my rod!' So she locked up her books in her cupboard, declined further magical performances, and scarcely used her wand at all except as a cane to walk about with.

So when Duke Padella's lady had a little son (the duke was at that time only one of the principal noblemen in Crim Tartary), Blackstick, although invited to the christening would not so much as attend; but merely sent her compliments and a silver papboat for the baby, which was really not worth a couple of guineas. About the same time the Queen of Paflagonia presented his Majesty with a son and heir; and guns were fired, the capital illuminated, and no end of feasts ordained to celebrate the young Prince's birth. It was thought the fairy, who was asked to be his godmother, would at least have presented him with an invisible jacket, a flying horse, a Fortunatus's purse,* or some other valuable token of her favour; but instead, Blackstick went up to the cradle of the child Giglio, when everybody was admiring him and complimenting his royal papa and mamma, and said, 'My poor child, the best thing I can send you is a little *misfortune*,' and this was all she would utter, to the disgust of Giglio's parents, who died very soon after, when Giglio's uncle took the throne, as we read in Chapter I.

In like manner, when CAVOLFIORE,* King of Crim Tartary, had a christening of his only child, ROSALBA,* the Fairy Blackstick, who had been invited, was not more gracious than in Prince Giglio's case. Whilst everybody was expatiating over the beauty of the darling child, and congratulating its parents, the Fairy Blackstick looked very sadly at the baby and its mother, and said, 'My good woman (for the Fairy was very familiar, and no more minded a Queen than a washerwoman)—my good woman, these people who are following you will be the first to turn against you; and, as for this little lady, the best thing I can wish her is a *little misfortune*.' So she touched Rosalba with her black wand, looked severely at the courtiers, motioned the Queen an adieu with her hand, and sailed slowly up into the air out of the window.

When she was gone, the Court people, who had been awed and silent in her presence, began to speak. 'What an odious Fairy she is (they said) a pretty Fairy, indeed! Why, she went to the King of Paflagonia's christening, and pretended to do all sorts of things for that family; and what has happened—the Prince, her godson, has been turned off his throne by his uncle. Would we allow our sweet Princess to be deprived of her rights by any enemy? Never, never, never, never!'

And they all shouted in a chorus, 'Never, never, never, never!'

Now, I should like to know, and how did these fine courtiers show their fidelity? One of the King Cavolfiore's vassals, the Duke Padella just mentioned, rebelled against the King, who went out to chastise his rebellious subject. 'Any one rebel against our beloved and august monarch!' cried the courtiers; 'any one resist *him*? Pooh! He is invincible, irresistible. He will bring home Padella a prisoner, and tie him to a donkey's tail, and drive him round the town, saying, "This is the way the Great Cavolfiore treats rebels."'

The King went forth to vanquish Padella; and the poor Queen, who was a very timid, anxious creature, grew so frightened and ill, that I am sorry to say she died; leaving injunctions with her ladies to take care of the dear little Rosalba.—Of course they said they would. Of course they vowed they would die rather than any harm should happen to the Princess. At first the 'Crim Tartar Court Journal' stated that the King was obtaining great victories over the audacious rebel: then it was announced that the troops of the infamous Padella were in flight: then it was said that the royal army would soon come up with the enemy, and then—then the news came that King Cavolfiore was vanquished and slain by His Majesty, King Padella the First!

At this news, half the courtiers ran off to pay their duty to the conquering chief, and the other half ran away, laying hands on all the best articles in the palace, and poor little Rosalba was left there quite alone—quite alone; and she toddled from one room to another, crying, 'Countess! Duchess!' (only she said 'Tountess, Duttess,' not being able to speak plain), 'bring me my mutton sop; my Royal Highness hungy! Tountess, Duttess!' And she went from the private apartments into the throne-room, and nobody was there;—and thence into the ball-room, and nobody was there;—and thence into the pages' room, and nobody was there;—and she toddled down the great staircase into the hall, and nobody was there;—and the door was open, and she went into the court, and into the garden, and thence into the wilderness, and thence into the forest where the wild beasts live, and was never heard of any more!

A piece of her torn mantle and one of her shoes were found in the wood in the mouths of two lioness's cubs, whom KING PADELLA and a royal hunting party shot—for he was King now, and reigned over Crim Tartary. 'So the poor little Princess is done for,' said he; 'well, what's done can't be helped. Gentlemen, let us go to luncheon!' And one of the courtiers took up the shoe and put it in his pocket. And there was an end of Rosalba!

IV

HOW BLACKSTICK WAS NOT ASKED TO THE PRINCESS ANGELICA'S CHRISTENING

WHEN the Princess Angelica was born, her parents not only did not ask the Fairy Blackstick to the christening party, but gave orders to their porter absolutely to refuse her if she called. This porter's name was Gruffanuff, and he had been selected for the post by their Royal Highnesses because he was a very tall fierce man, who could say 'Not at home' to a tradesman or an unwelcome visitor with a rudeness which frightened most such persons away. He was the husband of that Countess whose picture we have just seen, and as long as they were together they quarrelled from morning till night. Now this fellow tried his rudeness once too often, as you shall hear. For the Fairy Blackstick coming to call upon the Prince and Princess, who were actually sitting at the open drawing-room window, Gruffanuff not only denied them, but made the most *odious vulgar sign* as he was going to slam the door in the Fairy's face! 'Git away, hold Blackstick!' said he. 'I tell you, Master and Missis ain't at home to you:' and he was, as we have said, *going* to slam the door.

But the Fairy, with her wand, prevented the door being shut; and Gruffanuff came out again in a fury, swearing in the most abominable way, and asking the Fairy 'whether she thought he was going to stay at that there door hall day?'*

'You *are* going to stay at that door all day and all night, and for many a long year,' the Fairy said, very majestically; and Gruffanuff, coming out of the door, straddling before it with his great calves, burst out laughing, and cried, 'Ha, ha, ha! this *is* a good un! Ha—ah—what's this? Let me down—O—o—H'm!' and then he was dumb!

For, as the Fairy waved her wand over him, he felt himself rising off the ground, and fluttering up against the door, and then, as if a screw ran into his stomach, he felt a dreadful pain there, and was pinned to the door; and then his arms flew up over his head; and his legs, after writhing about wildly, twisted under his body; and he felt cold, cold, growing over him, as if he was turning into metal, and he said, 'O—o—H'm!' and could say no more, because he was dumb.

He *was* turned into metal! He was from being *brazen, brass!* He was neither more nor less than a knocker! And there he was, nailed to the door in the blazing summer day, till he burned almost red hot; and there he was nailed to the door all the bitter winter nights, till his brass nose was dropping with icicles. And the postman came and rapped at him, and the vulgarest boy with a letter came and hit him up against the door. And the King and Queen (Princess and Prince they were then) coming home from a walk that evening, the King said, 'Hullo, my dear! you have had a new knocker put on the door. Why, it's rather like our Porter in the face! What has become of that boozy vagabond?' And the housemaid came and scrubbed his nose with sandpaper; and once, when the Princess Angelica's little sister was born, he was tied up in an old kid glove; and, another night, some *larking* young men tried to wrench him off, and put him to the most excruciating agony with a turnscrew. And then the Queen had a fancy to have the colour of the door altered; and the painters dabbed him over the mouth and eyes, and nearly choked him, as they painted him pea-green. I warrant he had leisure to repent of having been rude to the Fairy Blackstick!

As for his wife, she did not miss him; and as he was always guzzling beer at the public house, and notoriously quarrelling with his wife, and in debt to the tradesmen, it was supposed he had run away from all these evils, and emigrated to Australia or America. And when the Prince and Princess chose to become King and Queen, they left their old house, and nobody thought of the Porter any more.

V

HOW PRINCESS ANGELICA TOOK A LITTLE MAID

ONE day, when the Princess Angelica was quite a little girl, she was walking in the garden of the palace, with Mrs. Gruffanuff, the governess, holding a parasol over her head, to keep her sweet complexion from the freckles, and Angelica was carrying a bun, to feed the swans and ducks in the royal pond.

They had not reached the duck-pond, when there came toddling up to them such a funny little girl! She had a great quantity of hair blowing about her chubby little cheeks, and looked as if she had not been washed or combed for ever so long. She wore a ragged bit of a cloak, and had only one shoe on.

'You little wretch, who let you in here?' asked Gruffanuff.

'Dive me dat bun,' said the little girl, 'me vely hungry.'

'Hungry! what is that?' asked Princess Angelica, and gave the child the bun.

'Oh, Princess!' says Gruffanuff, 'how good, how kind, how truly angelical you are! See, your Majesties,' she said to the King and Queen, who now came up, along with their nephew, Prince Giglio, 'how kind the Princess is! She met this little dirty wretch in the garden—I can't tell how she came in here, or why the guards did not shoot her dead at the gate! and the dear darling of a Princess has given her the whole of her bun!'

'I didn't want it,' said Angelica.

'But you are a darling little angel all the same,' says the governess.

'Yes; I know I am,' said Angelica. 'Dirty little girl, don't you think I am very pretty?' Indeed, she had on the finest of little dresses and hats; and, as her hair was carefully curled, she really looked very well.

'Oh, pooty, pooty!' says the little girl, capering about, laughing, and dancing, and munching her bun; and as she ate it she began to sing, 'Oh what fun, to have a plum bun! how I wis it never was done!' At which, and her funny accent, Angelica, Giglio, and the King and Queen began to laugh very merrily.

'I can dance as well as sing,' says the little girl. 'I can dance, and I can sing, and I can do all sorts of ting.' And she ran to a flower-bed, and, pulling a few polyanthuses, rhododendrons, and other flowers, made herself a little wreath, and danced before the King and Queen so drolly and prettily, that everybody was delighted.

'Who was your mother—who were your relations, little girl?' said the Queen.

The little girl said, 'Little lion was my brudder; great big lioness my mudder; neber heard of any udder.' And she capered away on her one shoe, and everybody was exceedingly diverted.

So Angelica said to the Queen, 'Mamma, my parrot flew away yesterday out of its cage, and I don't care any more for any of my toys; and I think this funny little dirty child will amuse me. I will take her home, and give her some of my old frocks.'

'Oh, the generous darling!' says Gruffanuff.

'Which I have worn ever so many times, and am quite tired of,' Angelica went on; 'and she shall be my little maid. Will you come home with me, little dirty girl?'

The child clapped her hands, and said, 'Go home with you—yes! You pooty Princess! Have a nice dinner, and wear a new dress!'

And they all laughed again, and took home the child to the palace, where, when she was washed and combed, and had one of the Princess's frocks given to her, she looked as handsome as Angelica, almost. Not that Angelica ever thought so; for this little lady never imagined that anybody in the world could be as pretty, as good, or as clever as herself. In order that the little girl should not become too proud and conceited, Mrs. Gruffanuff took her old ragged mantle and one shoe, and put them into a glass box, with a card laid upon them, upon which was written, 'These were the old clothes in which little BETSINDA was found, when the great goodness and admirable kindness of her Royal Highness the Princess Angelica received this little outcast.' And the date was added, and the box locked up.

For a while little Betsinda was a great favourite with the Princess, and she danced, and sang, and made her little rhymes, to amuse her mistress. But then the Princess got a monkey, and afterwards a little dog, and afterwards a doll, and did not care for Betsinda any more, who became very melancholy and quiet, and sang no more funny songs, because nobody cared to hear her. And then, as she grew older, she was made a little lady's maid to the Princess; and though she had no wages, she worked and mended, and put Angelica's hair in papers, and was never cross when scolded, and was always eager to please her mistress, and was always up early and to bed late, and at hand when wanted, and in fact became a perfect little maid. So the two girls grew up, and, when the Princess came out, Betsinda was never tired of waiting on her; and made her dresses better than the best milliner, and was useful in a hundred ways. Whilst the Princess was having her masters, Betsinda would sit and watch them; and in this way she picked up a great deal of learning; for she was always awake, though her mistress was not, and listened to the wise professors when Angelica was yawning, or thinking of the next ball. And when the dancing-master came, Betsinda learned along with Angelica; and when the music-master came, she watched him, and practised the Princess's pieces when Angelica was away at balls and parties; and when the drawing-master came, she took note of all he said and did; and the same with French, Italian, and all other languages—she learned them from the teacher who came to Angelica. When the Princess was going out of an evening she would say, 'My good Betsinda, you may as well finish what I have begun.' 'Yes, Miss,' Betsinda would say, and sit down very cheerful, not to *finish* what Angelica had begun, but to *do* it.

For instance, the Princess would begin the head of a warrior, let us say, and when it was begun it was something like this.

But when it was done, the warrior was like this (only handsomer still if possible), and the Princess put her name to the drawing; and the Court and the King and Queen and above all poor Giglio, admired the picture of all things, and said, 'Was there ever a genius like Angelica?' So, I am sorry to say, was it with the Princess's embroidery and other accomplishments; and Angelica actually believed that she did these things herself, and received all the flattery of the Court as if every word of it was true. Thus she began to think that there was no young woman in all the world equal to herself, and that no young man was good enough for her. As for Betsinda, as she heard none of these praises, she was not puffed up by them, and being a most grateful, good-natured girl, she was only too anxious to do everything which might give her mistress pleasure. Now you begin to perceive that Angelica had faults of her own, and was by no means such a wonder of wonders as people represented Her Royal Highness to be.

VI

HOW PRINCE GIGLIO BEHAVED HIMSELF

AND now let us speak about Prince Giglio, the nephew of the reigning monarch of Paflagonia. It has already been stated, in page 42, that as long as he had a smart coat to wear, a good horse to ride, and money in his pocket, or rather to take out of his pocket, for he was very good-natured, my young Prince did not care for the loss of his crown and sceptre, being a thoughtless youth, not much inclined to politics or any kind of learning. So his tutor had a sinecure. Giglio would not learn classics or mathematics, and the Lord Chancellor of Paflagonia, SQUARETOSO,* pulled a very long face because the Prince could not be got to study the Paflagonian laws and constitution; but on the other hand, the King's gamekeepers and huntsmen found the Prince an apt pupil; the dancing-master pronounced that he was a most elegant and assiduous scholar; the First Lord of the Billiard Table gave the most flattering reports of the Prince's skill; so did the Groom of the Tennis Court; and as for the Captain of the Guard and Fencing Master, the *valiant* and *veteran* Count KUTASOFF HEDZOFF,* he avowed that since he ran the General of Crim Tartary, the dreadful Grumbuskin,* through the body, he never had encountered so expert a swordsman as Prince Giglio.

I hope you do not imagine that there was any impropriety in the Prince and Princess walking together in the palace garden, and because Giglio kissed Angelica's hand in a polite manner. In the first place they are cousins; next, the Queen is walking in the garden too (you cannot see her, for she happens to be behind that tree), and her Majesty always wished that Angelica and Giglio should marry: so did Giglio: so did Angelica sometimes, for she thought her cousin very handsome, brave, and good-natured: but then you know she was so clever, and knew so many things, and poor Giglio knew nothing, and had no conversation. When they looked at the stars, what did Giglio know of the heavenly bodies? Once, when on a sweet night in a balcony where they were standing, Angelica said, 'There is the Bear.'* 'Where?' says Giglio; 'Don't be afraid, Angelica! if a dozen bears come, I will kill them rather than they shall hurt you.' 'Oh, you silly creature!' says she, 'you are very good, but you are not very wise.' When they looked at the flowers, Giglio was utterly unacquainted with Botany, and had never heard of Linnæus.* When the butterflies passed, Giglio knew nothing about them, being as ignorant of entomology as I am of algebra. So, you see, Angelica, though she liked Giglio pretty well, despised him on account of his ignorance. I think she probably valued *her own learning* rather too much; but to think too well of one's self is the fault of people of all ages and both sexes. Finally, when nobody else was there, Angelica liked her cousin well enough.

King Valoroso was very delicate in health, and withal so fond of good dinners (which were prepared for him by his French cook, Marmitonio),* that it was supposed he could not live long. Now the idea of anything happening to the King struck the artful Prime Minister and the designing old lady-in-waiting with terror. For, thought Glumboso and the Countess, 'when Prince Giglio marries his cousin and comes to the throne, what a pretty position we shall be in, whom he dislikes, and who have always been unkind to him. We shall lose our places in a trice; Gruffanuff will have to give up all the jewels, laces, snuff-boxes, rings, and watches which belonged to the Queen, Giglio's mother; and Glumboso will be forced to refund two hundred and seventeen thousand million, nine hundred and eighty-seven thousand, four hundred and thirty-nine pounds, thirteen shillings, and sixpence halfpenny, money left to Prince Giglio by his poor dear father.' So the Lady of Honour and the Prime Minister hated Giglio because they had done him a wrong; and these unprincipled people invented a hundred cruel stories about poor Giglio, in order to influence the King, Queen, and Princess against him; how he was so ignorant that he could not spell the commonest words, and actually wrote Valoroso Valloroso, and spelled Angelica with two l's; how he drank a great deal too much wine at dinner, and was always idling in the stables with the grooms; how he owed ever so much money at the pastry-cook's and the haberdasher's; how he used to go to sleep at church; how he was fond of playing cards with the pages. So did the Queen like playing cards; so did the King go to sleep at church, and eat and drink too much; and, if Giglio owed a trifle for tarts, who owed him two hundred and seventeen thousand million, nine hundred and eighty-seven thousand, four hundred and thirty-nine pounds, thirteen shillings, and sixpence halfpenny, I should like to know? Detractors and tale-bearers (in my humble opinion) had much better look at *home*. All this backbiting and slandering had effect upon Princess Angelica, who began to look coldly on her cousin, then to laugh at him and scorn him for being so stupid, then to sneer at him for having vulgar associates; and at court balls, dinners, and so forth, to treat him so unkindly that poor Giglio became quite ill, took to his bed, and sent for the doctor.

His Majesty King Valoroso, as we have seen, had his own reasons for disliking his nephew; and, as for those innocent readers who ask why? I beg (with the permission of their dear parents) to refer them to Shakespeare's pages, where they will read why King John disliked Prince Arthur.* With the queen, his royal but weak-minded aunt, when Giglio was out of sight he was out of mind. While she had her whist and her evening parties, she cared for little else.

I dare say *two villains*, who shall be nameless, wished Doctor Pildrafto, the Court Physician, had killed Giglio right out, but he only bled and physicked him so severely that the Prince was kept to his room for several months, and grew as thin as a post.

Whilst he was lying sick in this way, there came to the Court of

Paflagonia a famous painter, whose name was Tomaso Lorenzo,* and who was Painter in Ordinary* to the King of Crim Tartary, Paflagonia's neighbour. Tomas Lorenzo painted all the Court, who were delighted with his works; for even Countess Gruffanuff looked young and Glumboso good-humoured in his pictures. 'He flatters very much,' some people said. 'Nay!' says Princess Angelica, 'I am above flattery, and I think he did not make my picture handsome enough. I can't bear to hear a man of genius unjustly cried down, and I hope my dear papa will make Lorenzo a knight of his Order of the Cucumber.'

The Princess Angelica, although the courtiers vowed Her Royal Highness could draw so *beautifully* that the idea of her taking lessons was absurd, yet chose to have Lorenzo for a teacher, and it was wonderful, *as long as she painted in his studio*, what beautiful pictures she made! Some of the performances were engraved for the Book of Beauty; others were sold for enormous sums at Charity Bazaars. She wrote the *signatures* under the drawings, no doubt, but I think I know who did the pictures—this artful painter, who had come with other designs on Angelica than merely to teach her to draw.

One day Lorenzo showed the Princess a portrait of a young man in armour, with fair hair and the loveliest blue eyes, and an expression at once melancholy and interesting.

'Dear Signor Lorenzo, who is this?' asked the Princess. 'I never saw any one so handsome,' says Countess Gruffanuff (the old humbug).

'That,' said the painter, 'that, madam, is the portrait of my august young master, His Royal Highness Bulbo, Crown Prince of Crim Tartary, Duke of Acroceraunia,* Marquis of Poluphloisboio,* and Knight Grand Gross of the Order of the Pumpkin. That is the Order of the Pumpkin glittering on his manly breast, and received by his Royal Highness from his august father, his Majesty King PADELLA I, for his gallantry at the battle of Rimbombamento, when he slew with his own princely hand the King of Ograria,* and two hundred and eleven giants of the two hundred and eighteen who formed the King's body-guard. The remainder were destroyed by the brave Crim Tartar army after an obstinate combat, in which the Crim Tartars suffered severely.'

What a Prince! thought Angelica; so brave— so calm-looking—so young—what a hero!

'He is as accomplished as he is brave,' continued the Court Painter.

'He knows all languages perfectly; sings deliciously; plays every instrument: composes operas which have been acted a thousand nights running at the Imperial Theatre of Crim Tartary, and danced in a ballet there before the King and Queen; in which he looked so beautiful, that his cousin, the lovely daughter of the King of Circassia,* died for love of him.'

'Why did he not marry the poor Princess?' asked Angelica, with a sigh.

'Because they were *first cousins*, Madam, and the clergy forbid these unions,' said the Painter. 'And, besides, the young Prince had given his royal heart *elsewhere*.'

'And to whom?' asked Her Royal Highness.

'I am not at liberty to mention the Princess's name,' answered the Painter.

'But you may tell me the first letter of it,' gasped out the Princess.

'That your Royal Highness is at liberty to guess,' says Lorenzo.

'Does it begin with a Z?' asked Angelica.

The Painter said it wasn't a Z; then she tried a Y; then an X; then a W, and went so backwards through almost the whole alphabet.

When she came to D, and it wasn't D, she grew very much excited; when she came to C, and it wasn't C, she was still more nervous; when she came to B, *and it wasn't B*, 'O, dearest Gruffanuff,' she said, 'lend me your smelling bottle!' and, hiding her head on the Countess's shoulder, she faintly whispered, 'Ah, Signor, can it be A?'

'It was A; and though I may not, by my Royal Master's orders, tell your Royal Highness the Princess's name, whom he fondly, madly, devotedly, rapturously loves, I may show you her portrait,' says this slyboots: and leading the Princess up to a gilt frame he drew a curtain which was before it.

O goodness, the frame contained A LOOKING GLASS! and Angelica saw her own face!

VII

HOW GIGLIO AND ANGELICA HAD A QUARREL

THE Court Painter of His Majesty the King of Crim Tartary returned to that monarch's dominions, carrying away a number of sketches which he had made in the Paflagonian capital (you know, of course, my dears, that the name of that capital is Blombodinga*); but the most charming of all his pieces was a portrait of the Princess Angelica, which all the Crim Tartar nobles came to see. With this work the King was so delighted, that he decorated the Painter with his Order of the Pumpkin (sixth class), and the artist became Sir Tomaso Lorenzo, K. P., thenceforth.

King Valoroso also sent Sir Tomaso his Order of the Cucumber, besides a handsome order for money, for he painted the King, Queen, and principal nobility while at Blombodinga, and became all the fashion, to the perfect rage of all the artists in Paflagonia, where the King used to point to the portrait of Prince Bulbo, which Sir Tomaso had left behind him, and say, 'Which among you can paint a picture like that?'

It hung in the royal parlour over the royal sideboard, and Princess

Angelica could always look at it as she sat making the tea. Each day it seemed to grow handsomer and handsomer, and the Princess grew so fond of looking at it, that she would often spill the tea over the cloth, at which her father and mother would wink and wag their heads, and say to each other, 'Aha! we see how things are going.'

In the meanwhile poor Giglio lay up stairs very sick in his chamber, though he took all the doctor's horrible medicines like a good young lad; as I hope *you* do, my dears, when you are ill and mamma sends for the medical man. And the only person who visited Giglio (besides his friend the captain of the guard, who was almost always busy on parade), was little Betsinda the housemaid, who used to do his bed-room and sitting-room out, bring him his gruel, and warm his bed.

When the little housemaid came to him in the morning and evening, Prince Giglio used to say, 'Betsinda, Betsinda, how is the Princess Angelica?'

And Betsinda used to answer, 'The Princess is very well, thank you, my Lord.' And Giglio would heave a sigh, and think, if Angelica were sick, I am sure I should not be very well.

Then Giglio would say, 'Betsinda, has the Princess Angelica asked for me to-day?' And Betsinda would answer, 'No, my Lord, not to-day;' or, 'she was very busy practising the piano when I saw her;' or, 'she was writing invitations for an evening party, and did not speak to me:' or make some excuse or other not strictly consonant with the truth: for Betsinda was such a good-natured creature, that she strove to do everything to prevent annoyance to Prince Giglio, and even brought him up roast chicken and jellies from the kitchen (when the doctor allowed them, and Giglio was getting better), saying 'that the Princess had made the jelly or the bread-sauce with her own hands, on purpose for Giglio.'

When Giglio heard this he took heart and began to mend immediately; and gobbled up all the jelly, and picked the last bone of the chicken—drumsticks, merry-thought, sides'-bones, back, pope's nose,* and all—thanking his dear Angelica; and he felt so much better the next day, that he dressed and went down stairs, where, whom should he meet but Angelica going into the drawing-room. All the covers were off the chairs, the chandeliers were taken out of the bags, the damask curtains uncovered, the work and things carried away, and the handsomest albums on the tables. Angelica had her hair in papers; in a word, it was evident there was going to be a party.

'Heavens, Giglio!' cries Angelica; '*you* here in such a dress! What a figure you are!'

'Yes, dear Angelica, I am come down stairs, and feel so well to-day, thanks to the *fowl* and the *jelly*.'

'What do I know about fowls and jellies, that you allude to them in that rude way?' says Angelica.

'Why, didn't—didn't you send them, Angelica dear?' says Giglio.

'I send them indeed! Angelica dear! No, Giglio dear,' says she, mocking him, '*I* was engaged in getting the rooms ready for His Royal Highness the Prince of Crim Tartary, who is coming to pay my papa's Court a visit.'

'The—Prince—of—Crim—Tartary!' Giglio said, aghast.

'Yes, the Prince of Crim Tartary,' says Angelica, mocking him. 'I dare say you never heard of such a country. What *did* you ever hear of? You don't know whether Crim Tartary is on the Red Sea or on the Black Sea,* I dare say.'

'Yes, I do, it's on the Red Sea,' says Giglio, at which the Princess burst out laughing at him, and said, 'O you ninny! You are so ignorant, you are really not fit for society! You know nothing but about horses and dogs, and are only fit to dine in a mess-room with my Royal Father's heaviest dragoons. Don't look so surprised at me, sir; go and put your best clothes on to receive the Prince, and let me get the drawing-room ready.'

Giglio said, 'O, Angelica, Angelica, I didn't think this of you. *This* wasn't your language to me when you gave me this ring, and I gave you mine in the garden, and you gave me that k—'

But what k was we never shall know, for Angelica, in a rage, cried, 'Get out, you saucy, rude creature! How dare you to remind me of your rudeness? As for your little trumpery twopenny ring, there, sir, there!' And she flung it out of the window.

'It was my mother's marriage ring,' cried Giglio.

'*I* don't care whose marriage ring it was,' cries Angelica. 'Marry the person who picks it up if she's a woman: you shan't marry *me*. And give me back *my* ring. I've no patience with people who boast about the things they give away! I know who'll give me much finer things than you ever gave me. A beggarly ring indeed, not worth five shillings!'

Now Angelica little knew that the ring which Giglio had given her was a fairy ring: if a man wore it, it made all the women in love with him; if a woman, all the gentlemen. The Queen, Giglio's mother, quite an ordinary looking person, was admired immensely while she wore this ring, and her husband was frantic when she was ill. But when she called her little Giglio to her, and put the ring on his finger, King Savio did not seem to care for his wife so much anymore, but transferred all his love to little Giglio. So did everybody love him as long as he had the ring, but when, as quite a child, he gave it to Angelica, people began to love and admire *her*; and Giglio, as the saying is, played only second fiddle.

'Yes,' says Angelica, going on in her foolish ungrateful way, '*I* know who'll give me much finer things than your beggarly little pearl nonsense.'

'Very good, Miss! You may take back your ring, too!' says Giglio, his eyes flashing fire at her, and then, as if his eyes had been suddenly opened, he cried out, 'Ha, what does this mean? Is *this* the woman I have been in love with all my life? Have I been such a ninny as to throw away my regard upon *you*? Why—actually—yes—you are a little crooked!'

'O, you wretch!' cries Angelica.

'And, upon my conscience, you—you squint a little.'

'E!' cries Angelica.

'And your hair is red—and you are marked with the small-pox—and what? you have three false teeth—and one leg is shorter than the other!'

'You brute, you brute, you!' Angelica screamed out: and as she seized the ring with one hand, she dealt Giglio one, two, three, smacks on the face, and would have pulled the hair off his head had he not started laughing, and crying,

'O dear me, Angelica, don't pull out *my* hair, it hurts! You might remove a great deal of *your own*, as I perceive, without scissors or pulling at all. O, ho, ho! ha, ha, ha! he, he, he!'

And he nearly choked himself with laughing, and she with rage, when, with a low bow, and dressed in his Court habit, Count Gambabella, the first lord-in-waiting, entered and said, 'Royal Highnesses! Their Majesties expect you in the Pink Throne-room, where they await the arrival of the Prince of CRIM TARTARY.'

VIII

HOW GRUFFANUFF PICKED THE FAIRY RING UP, AND PRINCE BULBO CAME TO COURT

PRINCE BULBO'S arrival had set all the Court in a flutter: everybody was ordered to put his or her best clothes on: the footmen had their gala-liveries; the Lord Chancellor his new wig; the Guards their last new tunics; and Countess Gruffanuff you may be sure was glad of an opportunity of decorating *her* old person with her finest things. She was walking through the court of the Palace on her way to wait upon their Majesties, when she spied something glittering on the pavement, and bade the boy in buttons who was holding up her train, to go and pick up the article shining yonder. He was an ugly little wretch, in some of the late groom-porter's old clothes cut down, and much too tight for him; and yet, when he had taken up the ring (as it turned out to be), and was carrying it to his mistress, she thought he looked like a little Cupid. He gave the ring to her; it was a trumpery little thing enough, but too small for any of her old knuckles, so she put it into her pocket.

'O, mum!' says the boy, looking at her, 'how, how, beyoutiful you do look, mum, to-day, mum!'

'And you, too, Jacky,' she was going to say; but, looking down at him—no, he was no longer good-looking at all—but only the carrotty-haired little Jacky of the morning. However, praise is welcome from the ugliest of men or boys, and Gruffanuff, bidding the boy hold up her train, walked on in high good-humour. The guards saluted her with peculiar respect. Captain Hedzoff, in the ante-room, said, 'My dear madam, you look like an angel to-day.' And so, bowing and smirking, Gruffanuff went in and took her place behind her Royal Master and Mistress, who were in the throne-room, awaiting the Prince of Crim Tartary. Princess Angelica sat at their feet, and behind the King's chair stood Prince Giglio, looking very savage.

The Prince of Crim Tartary made his appearance, attended by Baron Sleibootz, his chamberlain, and followed by a black page, carrying the most beautiful crown you ever saw! He was dressed in his travelling costume, and his hair, as you see, was a little in disorder. 'I have ridden three hundred miles since breakfast,' said he, 'so eager was I to behold the Prin—the Court and august family of

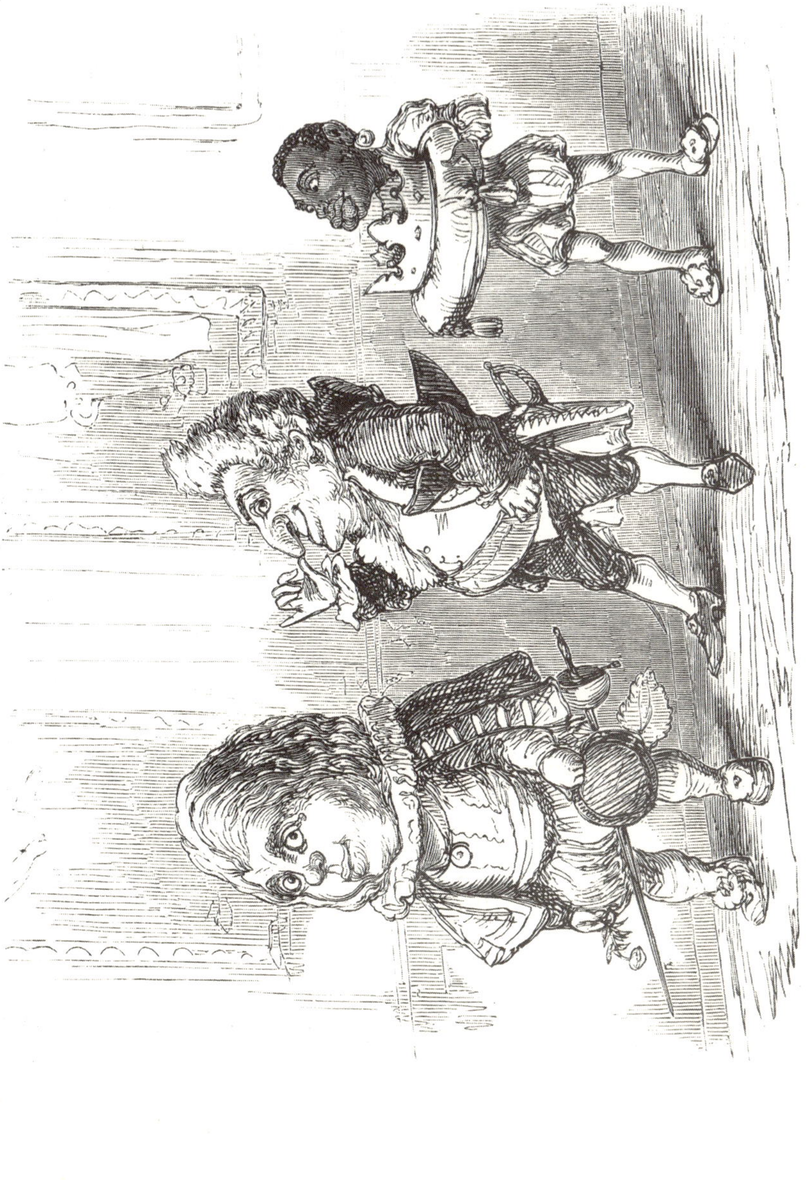

Paflagonia—and I could not wait one minute before appearing in your Majesties' presences.'

Giglio, from behind the throne, burst out into a roar of contemptuous laughter; but all the Royal party, in fact, were so flurried that they did not hear this outbreak. 'Your R. H. is welcome in any dress,' says the King. 'Glumboso, a chair for his Royal Highness.'

'Any dress his Royal Highness wears *is* a Court dress,' says Princess Angelica, smiling graciously.

'Ah! but you should see my other clothes,' said the Prince. 'I should have had them on, but that stupid carrier has not brought them. Who's that laughing?'

It was Giglio laughing. 'I was laughing,' he said, 'because you said just now that you were in such a hurry to see the Princess, that you could not wait to change your dress; and now you say you come in those clothes because you have no others.'

'And who are you?' said Prince Bulbo, very fiercely.

'My father was King of this country, and I am his only son, Prince!' replies Giglio, with equal haughtiness.

'Ha!' said the King and Glumboso, looking very flurried; but the former, collecting himself, said, 'Dear Prince Bulbo, I forgot to introduce to your Royal Highness my dear nephew, his Royal Highness Prince Giglio! Know each other! Embrace each other! Giglio, give his Royal Highness your hand!' and Giglio, giving his hand, squeezed poor Bulbo's until the tears ran out of his eyes. Glumboso now brought a chair for the royal visitor, and placed it on the platform on which the King, Queen, and Prince were seated; but the chair was on the edge of the platform, and as Bulbo sat down, it toppled over, and he with it, rolling over and over, and bellowing like a bull. Giglio roared still louder at this disaster, but it was with laughter; so did all the Court when Prince Bulbo got up, for though when he entered the room he appeared not very ridiculous, as he stood up from his fall for a moment, he looked so exceedingly plain and foolish, that nobody could help laughing at him. When he had entered the room, he was observed to carry a rose in his hand, which fell out of it as he tumbled.

'My rose! my rose!' cried Bulbo; and his chamberlain dashed forward and picked it up, and gave it to the Prince, who put it into his waistcoat. Then people wondered why they had laughed, there was nothing particularly ridiculous in him. He was rather short, rather stout, rather red-haired; but in fine for a Prince not so bad.

So they sat and talked, the personages together, the Crim Tartar officers with those of Paflagonia—Giglio very comfortable with Gruffanuff behind the throne. He looked at her with such tender eyes, that her heart was all in a flutter. 'Oh, dear Prince,' she said, 'how could you speak so haughtily in presence of their Majesties? I protest I thought I should have fainted.'

'I should have caught you in my arms,' said Giglio, looking raptures.

'Why were you so cruel to Prince Bulbo, dear Prince?' says Gruff.

'Because I hate him,' says Gil.

'You are jealous of him, and still love poor Angelica,' cries Gruffanuff, putting her handkerchief to her eyes.

'I did, but I love her no more!' Giglio cried. 'I despise her! Were she heiress to twenty thousand thrones, I would despise her and scorn her. But why speak of thrones? I have lost mine. I am too weak to recover it—I am alone, and have no friend.'

'Oh, say not so, dear Prince!' says Gruffanuff.

'Besides,' says he, 'I am so happy here *behind the throne* that I would not change my place, no, not for the throne of the world!'

'What are you two people chattering about there?' says the Queen, who was rather good-natured, though not overburthened with wisdom. 'It is time to dress for dinner. Giglio, show Prince Bulbo to his room. Prince, if your clothes have not come, we shall be very happy to see you as you are.' But when Prince Bulbo got to his bed-room, his luggage was there and unpacked; and the hairdresser coming in, cut and curled him entirely to his own satisfaction; and when the dinner-bell rang, the royal company had not to wait about five-and-twenty minutes until Bulbo appeared, during which time the King, who could not bear to wait, grew as sulky as possible. As for Giglio, he never left Madam Gruffanuff all this time, but stood with her in the embrasure of a window,* paying her compliments. At length the groom of the chambers announced his Royal Highness the Prince of Crim Tartary! and the noble company went into the royal dining-room. It was quite a small party—only the King and Queen, the Princess, whom Bulbo took out, the two Princes, Countess Gruffanuff, Glumboso, the Prime Minister, and Prince Bulbo's chamberlain. You may be sure they had a very good dinner—let every boy or girl think of what she likes best, and fancy it on the table.[1]

---

[1] Here a very pretty game may be played by all the children saying what they like best for dinner.

The Princess talked incessantly all dinner time to the Prince of Crimea, who ate an immense deal too much, and never took his eyes off his plate, except when Giglio, who was carving a goose, sent a quantity of stuffing and onion sauce into one of them. Giglio only burst out a laughing as the Crimean Prince wiped his shirt-front and face with his scented pocket-handkerchief. He did not make Prince Bulbo an apology. When the Prince looked at him, Giglio would not look that way. When Prince Bulbo said, 'Prince Giglio, may I have the honour of taking a glass of wine with you?' Giglio *wouldn't* answer. All his talk and his eyes were for Countess Gruffanuff, who you may be sure was pleased with Giglio's attentions, the vain old creature! When he was not complimenting her, he was making fun of Prince Bulbo, so loud that Gruffanuff was always tapping him with her fan, and saying, 'O you satirical Prince! O fie, the Prince will hear!' 'Well, I don't mind,' says Giglio, louder still. The King and Queen luckily did not hear; for her Majesty was a little deaf, and the King thought so much about his own dinner, and, besides, made such a dreadful noise, hobgobbling in eating it, that he heard nothing else. After dinner, his Majesty and the Queen went to sleep in their arm-chairs.

This was the time when Giglio began his tricks with Prince Bulbo, plying that young gentleman with port, sherry, madeira, champagne, marsala, cherry-brandy, and pale ale, of all of which Master Bulbo drank without stint. But in plying his guest, Giglio was obliged to drink himself, and, I am sorry to say, took more than was good for him, so that the young men were very noisy, rude, and foolish when they joined the ladies after dinner; and dearly did they pay for that imprudence, as now, my darlings, you shall hear!

Bulbo went and sat by the piano, where Angelica was playing and singing, and he sang out of tune, and he upset the coffee when the footman brought it, and he laughed out of place, and talked absurdly, and fell asleep, and snored horridly. Booh, the nasty pig! But as he lay there stretched on the pink satin sofa, Angelica still persisted in thinking him the most beautiful of human beings. No doubt the magic rose which Bulbo wore caused this infatuation on Angelica's part; but is she the first young woman who has thought a silly fellow charming?

Giglio must go and sit by Gruffanuff, whose old face he too every moment began to find more lovely. He paid the most outrageous compliments to her. There never was such a darling—Older than he was? Fiddle-de-dee! He would marry her—he would have nothing but her!

To marry the heir to the throne! Here was a chance! The artful hussey actually got a sheet of paper, and wrote upon it, 'This is to give notice that I, Giglio, only son of Savio, King of Paflagonia, hereby promise to marry the charming and virtuous Barbara Griselda Countess Gruffanuff, and widow of the late Jenkins Gruffanuff, Esq.'

'What is it you are writing? you charming Gruffy!' says Giglio, who was lolling on the sofa, by the writing-table.

'Only an order for you to sign, dear Prince, for giving coals and blankets to the poor this cold weather. Look! the King and Queen are both asleep, and your Royal Highness's order will do.'

So Giglio, who was very good-natured, as Gruffy well knew, signed the order immediately; and, when she had it in her pocket, you may fancy what airs she gave herself. She was ready to flounce out of the room before the Queen herself, as now she was the wife of the *rightful* King of Paflagonia! She would not speak to Glumboso, whom she thought a brute, for depriving her *dear husband* of the crown! And when candles came, and she had helped to undress the Queen and Princess, she went into her own room, and actually practised, on a sheet of paper, 'Griselda Paflagonia,' 'Barbara Regina,' 'Grizelda Barbara, Paf. Reg.,' and I don't know what signatures besides, against the day when she should be Queen, forsooth!

IX

HOW BETSINDA GOT THE WARMING-PAN

LITTLE BETSINDA came in to put Gruffanuff's hair in papers; and the Countess was so pleased, that, for a wonder, she complimented Betsinda. 'Betsinda!' she said, 'you dressed my hair very nicely to-day; I promised you a little present. Here are five sh—No, here is a pretty little ring that I picked—that I have had some time.' And she gave Betsinda the ring she had picked up in the court. It fitted Betsinda exactly.

'It's like the ring the Princess used to wear,' says the maid.

'No such thing,' says Gruffanuff; 'I have had it this ever so long. There—tuck me up quite comfortable. And now, as it's a very cold night (the snow was beating in at the window), you may go and warm dear Prince Giglio's bed, like a good girl, and then you may unrip my green silk, and then you can just do me up a little cap for the morning, and then you can mend the hole in my silk stocking, and then you can go to bed, Betsinda. Mind, I shall want my cup of tea at five o'clock in the morning.'

'I suppose I had best warm both the young gentlemen's beds, ma'am,' says Betsinda.

Gruffanuff, for reply, said, 'Hau-au-ho!—Grau-haw-hoo!—Honghrho!' In fact, she was snoring sound asleep.

Her room, you know, is next to the King and Queen, and the Princess's is next to them. So pretty Betsinda went away for the coals to the kitchen, and filled the royal warming-pan.

Now, she was a very kind, merry, civil, pretty girl; but there must have been something very captivating about her this evening, for all the women in the servants' hall began to scold and abuse her. The housekeeper said she was a pert, stuck-up thing; the upper housemaid asked how dare she wear such ringlets and ribbons, it was quite improper! The cook (for there was a woman cook as well as a man cook) said to the kitchen-maid that *she* never could see anything in that creetur: but as for the men, every one of them, Coachman, John, Buttons the page, and Monsieur, the Prince of Crim Tartary's valet, started up, and said,

'My eyes!'
'O mussey!'
'O jemmany!'
'O ciel!'*

What a pretty girl Betsinda is.

'Hands off; none of your impertinence, you vulgar, low people!' says Betsinda, walking off with her pan of coals. She heard the young gentlemen playing at billiards as she went up stairs; first to Prince Giglio's bed, which she warmed, and then to Prince Bulbo's room. He came in just as she had done, and as soon as he saw her, 'O! O! O! O! O! O! what a beyou—oo—ootiful creature you are. You angel—you peri—you rose-bud, let me be thy bulbul*—thy Bulbo too! Fly to the desert, fly with me! I never saw a young gazelle to glad me with its dark blue eye that had eyes like thine. Thou nymph of beauty, take, take this young heart. A truer never did itself sustain within a soldier's waistcoat. Be mine! Be mine! Be Princess of Crim Tartary! My Royal father will approve our union: and as for that little carrotty-haired Angelica, I do not care a fig for her any more.'

'Go away, your Royal Highness, and go to bed, please,' said Betsinda, with the warming-pan.

But Bulbo said, 'No, never, till thou swearest to be mine, thou lovely, blushing, chamber-maid divine! Here, at thy feet, the Royal Bulbo lies, the trembling captive of Betsinda's eyes.'

And he went on, making himself so *absurd and ridiculous*, that Betsinda, who was full of fun, gave him a touch with the warming-pan, which, I promise you, made him cry 'O-o-o-o!' in a very different manner.

Prince Bulbo made such a noise that Prince Giglio, who heard him from the next room, came in to see what was the matter. As soon as he saw what was taking place, Giglio, in a fury, rushed on Bulbo, kicked him in the rudest manner up to the ceiling, and went on kicking him till his hair was quite out of curl.

Poor Betsinda did not know whether to laugh or to cry; the kicking certainly must hurt the Prince, but then he looked so droll! When Giglio had done knocking him up and down to the ground, and whilst he went into a corner rubbing himself, what do you think Giglio does? He goes down on his own knees to Betsinda, takes her hand, begs her to accept his heart, and offers to marry her that moment. Fancy Betsinda's condition, who had been in love with the Prince ever since she first saw him in the palace garden, when she was quite a little child.

'Oh, divine Betsinda!' says the Prince, 'how have I lived fifteen years in thy company without seeing thy perfections? What woman in all Europe, Asia, Africa, and America—nay, in Australia, only it is not yet discovered,* can presume to be thy equal? Angelica? Pish! Gruffanuff? Phoo! The Queen? Ha, ha! Thou art my Queen. Thou art the real Angelica, because thou art really angelic.'

'Oh, Prince! I am but a poor chambermaid,' says Betsinda, looking, however, very much pleased.

'Didst thou not tend me in my sickness, when all forsook me?' continues Giglio. 'Did not thy gentle hand smooth my pillow, and bring me jelly and roast chicken?'

'Yes, dear Prince, I did,' says Betsinda, 'and I sewed your Royal Highness's shirt-buttons on too, if you please, your Royal Highness,' cries this artless maiden.

When poor Prince Bulbo, who was now madly in love with Betsinda, heard this declaration, when he saw the unmistakable glances which she flung upon Giglio, Bulbo began to cry bitterly, and tore quantities of hair out of his head, till it all covered the room like so much tow.*

Betsinda had left the warming-pan on the floor while the princes were going on with their conversation, and as they began now to quarrel and be very fierce with one another, she thought proper to run away.

'You great big blubbering booby, tearing your hair in the corner there; of course you will give me satisfaction for insulting Betsinda. *You* dare to kneel down at Princess Giglio's knees and kiss her hand!'

'She's not Princess Giglio!' roars out Bulbo. 'She shall be Princess Bulbo—no other shall be Princess Bulbo.'

'You are engaged to my cousin!' bellows out Giglio.

'I hate your cousin,' says Bulbo.

'You shall give me satisfaction for insulting her!' cries Giglio, in a fury.

'I'll have your life.'

'I'll run you through.'

'I'll cut your throat.'

'I'll blow your brains out.'

'I'll knock your head off.'

'I'll send a friend to you in the morning.'

'I'll send a bullet into you in the afternoon.'

'We'll meet again,' says Giglio, shaking his fist in Bulbo's face; and seizing up the warming-pan, he kissed it because, forsooth, Betsinda had carried it, and rushed down stairs. What should he see on the landing but his Majesty talking to Betsinda, whom he called by all sorts of fond names. His Majesty had heard a row in the building, so he stated, and smelling something burning, had come out to see what the matter was.

'It's the young gentlemen smoking, perhaps, sir,' says Betsinda.

'Charming chambermaid,' says the King (like all the rest of them), 'never mind the young men! Turn thy eyes on a middle-aged autocrat, who has been considered not ill-looking in his time.'

'Oh, sir! what will her Majesty say?' cries Betsinda.

'Her Majesty!' laughs the monarch. 'Her Majesty be hanged! Am I not Autocrat of Paflagonia? Have I not blocks, ropes, axes, hangmen—ha? Runs not a river by my palace wall? Have I not sacks to sew up wives withal? Say but the word, that thou wilt be mine own—your mistress straightway in a sack is sewn, and thou the sharer of my heart and throne.'

When Giglio heard these atrocious sentiments, he forgot the respect usually paid to Royalty, lifted up the warming-pan

and knocked down the King flat as a pancake; after which, Master Giglio took to his heels and ran away, and Betsinda went off screaming, and the Queen, Gruffanuff, and the Princess, all came out of their rooms. Fancy their feelings on beholding their husband, father, sovereign in this posture!

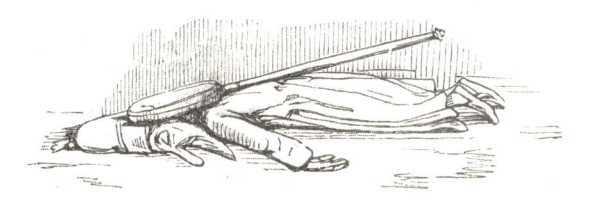

X

HOW KING VALOROSO WAS IN A DREADFUL PASSION

As soon as the coals began to burn him, the King came to himself and stood up. 'Ho! my captain of the guards!' His Majesty exclaimed, stamping his royal feet with rage. O piteous spectacle! the King's nose was bent quite crooked by the blow of Prince Giglio! His Majesty ground his teeth with rage. 'Hedzoff,' he said, taking a death-warrant out of his dressing-gown pocket, 'Hedzoff, good Hedzoff, seize upon the Prince. Thou'lt find him in his chamber two pair up. But now he dared, with sacrilegious hand, to strike the sacred night-cap of a king—Hedzoff, and floor me with a warming-pan! Away, no more demur, the villain dies! See it be done, or else—h'm!—ha!—h'm! mind thine own eyes!' and followed by the ladies, and lifting up the tails of his dressing-gown, the King entered his own apartment.

Captain Hedzoff was very much affected, having a sincere love for Giglio. 'Poor, poor Giglio!' he said, the tears rolling over his manly face and dripping down his moustachios; 'My noble young Prince, is it my hand must lead thee to death?'

'Lead him to fiddlestick, Hedzoff,' said a female voice. It was Gruffanuff who had come out in her dressing-gown when she heard the noise. 'The King said you were to hang the Prince. Well, hang the Prince.'

'I don't understand you,' says Hedzoff, who was not a very clever man.

'You Gaby!* he didn't say *which* Prince,' says Gruffanuff.

'No, he didn't say which, certainly,' said Hedzoff.

'Well then, take Bulbo, and hang *him*!'

When Captain Hedzoff heard this, he began to dance about for joy. 'Obedience is a soldier's honour,' says he. 'Prince Bulbo's head will do capitally;' and he went to arrest the Prince the very first thing next morning.

He knocked at the door. 'Who's there?' says Bulbo. 'Captain Hedzoff? Step in, pray, my good Captain; I'm delighted to see you; I have been expecting you.'

'Have you?' says Hedzoff.

'Sleibootz, my Chamberlain, will act for me,' says the Prince.

'I beg your Royal Highness's pardon, but you will have to act for yourself, and it's a pity to wake Baron Sleibootz.'

The Prince Bulbo still seemed to take the matter very coolly. 'Of course, Captain,' says he, 'you are come about the affair with Prince Giglio?'

'Precisely,' says Hedzoff, 'that affair of Prince Giglio.'

'Is it to be pistols or swords, Captain?' asked Bulbo. 'I'm a pretty good hand with both; and I'll do for Prince Giglio, as sure as my name is my Royal Highness Prince Bulbo.'

'There's some mistake, my Lord,' says the Captain; 'the business is done with *axes* among us.'

'Axes? That's sharp work,' says Bulbo. 'Call my Chamberlain, he'll be my second, and in ten minutes I flatter myself you'll see Master Giglio's head off his impertinent shoulders. I'm hungry for his blood. Hoo-oo, aw!' and he looked as savage as an ogre.

'I beg your pardon, sir, but by this warrant I am to take you prisoner, and hand you over to—to the executioner.'

'Pooh! pooh! my good man!—Stop, I say.—ho!—hulloa!' was all that this luckless prince was enabled to say; for Hedzoff's guards seizing him, tied a handkerchief over his mouth and face, and carried him to the place of execution.

The King, who happened to be talking to Glumboso, saw him pass, and took a pinch of snuff and said, 'So much for Giglio. Now let's go to breakfast.'

The Captain of the Guard handed over his prisoner to the Sheriff, with the fatal order,

'AT SIGHT, CUT OFF THE BEARER'S HEAD.
'VALOROSO XXIV.'

'It's a mistake,' says Bulbo, who did not seem to understand the business in the least.

'Poo—poo—pooh!' says the Sheriff. 'Fetch Jack Ketch* instantly. Jack Ketch!'

And poor Bulbo was led to the scaffold, where an executioner with a block and a tremendous axe was always ready in case he should be wanted.

But we must now revert to Giglio and Betsinda.

XI

WHAT GRUFFANUFF DID TO GIGLIO AND BETSINDA

GRUFFANUFF who had seen what had happened with the King, and knew that Giglio must come to grief, got up very early the next morning, and went to devise some plans for rescuing her darling husband, as the silly old thing insisted on calling him. She found him walking up and down the garden, thinking of a rhyme for Betsinda (*tinder* and *winda* were all he could find), and indeed having forgotten all about the past evening, except that Betsinda was the most lovely of beings.

'Well, dear Giglio,' says Gruff.

'Well, dear Gruffy,' says Giglio, only *he* was quite satirical.

'I have been thinking, darling, what you must do in this scrape. You must fly the country for a while.'

'What scrape?—fly the country? Never, without her I love, Countess,' says Giglio.

'No, she will accompany you, dear Prince,' she says, in her most coaxing accents. 'First we must get the jewels belonging to our royal parents, and those of her and his present Majesty. Here is the key, duck; they are all yours you know by right, for you are the rightful King of Paflagonia, and your wife will be the rightful Queen.'

'Will she?' says Giglio.

'Yes; and, having got the jewels, go to Glumboso's apartment, where, under his bed you will find sacks containing money to the amount of £217,000,000,987,439 13s. 6½d., all belonging to you, for he took it out of your royal father's room on the day of his death. With this we will fly.'

'*We* will fly?' says Giglio.

'Yes, you and your bride—your affianced love—your Gruffy!' says the Countess, with a languishing leer.

'*You*, my bride!' says Giglio. 'You, you hideous old woman!'

'Oh, you, you wretch! didn't you give me this paper, promising marriage?' cries Gruff.

'Get away, you old goose! I love Betsinda, and Betsinda only!' And in a fit of terror he ran from her as quickly as he could.

'He! he! he!' shrieks out Gruff, 'a promise is a promise, if there are laws in Paflagonia! And as for that monster, that wretch, that fiend, that ugly little vixen—as for that upstart, that ingrate, that beast, Betsinda, Master Giglio will have no little difficulty in discovering her whereabouts. He may look very long before finding *her*, I warrant. He little knows that Miss Betsinda is—'

Is—what? Now you shall hear. Poor Betsinda got up at five in a winter morning to bring her cruel mistress her tea; and instead of finding her in a good humour, found Gruffy as cross as two sticks. The Countess boxed Betsinda's ears half-a-dozen times while she was dressing; but as poor little Betsinda was used to this kind of treatment, she did not feel any special alarm. 'And now,' says she, 'when her Majesty rings her bell twice, I'll trouble you, miss, to attend.'

So when the Queen's bell rang twice, Betsinda came to her Majesty and made a pretty little curtsey. The Queen, the Princess, and Gruffanuff were all three in the room. As soon as they saw her they began,

'You wretch!' says the Queen.
'You little vulgar thing!' said the Princess.
'You beast!' says Gruffanuff.
'Get out of my sight!' says the Queen.
'Go away with you, do!' says the Princess.
'Quit the premises!' says Gruffanuff.

Alas! and wo is me! very lamentable events had occurred to Betsinda that morning, and all in consequence of that fatal warming-pan business of the previous night. The King had offered to marry her; of course Her Majesty the Queen was jealous: Bulbo had fallen in love with her; of course Angelica was furious: Giglio was in love with her, and O what a fury Gruffy was in!

'Take off that $\begin{Bmatrix} \text{cap} \\ \text{petticoat} \\ \text{gown} \end{Bmatrix}$ I gave you,' they said, all at once,

and began tearing the clothes off poor Betsinda.

'How dare you flirt with {the King?' Prince Bulbo?' Prince Giglio?'} cried the Queen, the Princess, and Countess.

'Give her the rags she wore when she came into the house, and turn her out of it!' cries the Queen.

'Mind she does not go with *my* shoes on, which I lent her so kindly,' says the Princess; and indeed the Princess's shoes were a great deal too big for Betsinda.

'Come with me, you filthy hussey!' and, taking up the Queen's poker, the cruel Gruffanuff drove Betsinda into her room.

The Countess went to the glass box in which she had kept Betsinda's old cloak and shoe this ever so long, and said, 'Take those rags, you little beggar creature, and strip off everything belonging to honest people, and go about your business;' and she actually tore off the poor little delicate thing's back almost all her things, and told her to be off out of the house.

Poor Betsinda huddled the cloak round her back, on which were embroidered the letters PRIN. . . . ROSAL . . . and then came a great rent.

As for the shoe, what was she to do with one poor little tootsey* sandal? the string was still to it, so she hung it round her neck.

'Won't you give me a pair of shoes to go out in the snow, mum, if you please, mum!' cried the poor child.

'No, you wicked beast!' says Gruffanuff, driving her along with the poker—driving her down the cold stairs—driving her through the cold hall—flinging her out into the cold street, so that the knocker itself shed tears to see her!

But a kind fairy made the soft snow warm for her little feet, and she wrapped herself up in the ermine of her mantle and was gone!

'And now let us think about breakfast,' says the greedy Queen.

'What dress shall I put on, mamma—the pink or the pea-green?' says Angelica. 'Which do you think the dear Prince will like best?'

'Mrs. V.!' sings out the king from his dressing-room, 'Let us have sausages for breakfast! Remember we have Prince Bulbo staying with us!'

And they all went to get ready.

Nine o'clock came, and they were all in the breakfast room, and no Prince Bulbo as yet. The urn was hissing and humming: the muffins were smoking—such a heap of muffins! the eggs were done, there was a pot of raspberry jam, and coffee, and a beautiful chicken and tongue on the side-table. Marmitonio the cook brought in the sausages. O, how nice they smelt!

'Where is Bulbo?' said the King. 'John, where is His Royal Highness?'

John said he had a took hup His Roilighnessesses shaving-water, and his clothes and things, and he wasn't in his room, which he sposed His Royliness was just stepped hout.

'Stepped out before breakfast in the snow! Impossible!' says the King, sticking his fork into a sausage. 'My dear, take one. Angelica won't you have a saveloy?' The Princess took one, being very fond of them; and at this moment Glumboso entered with Captain Hedzoff, both looking very much disturbed. 'I am afraid your Majesty—' cries Glumboso. 'No business before breakfast, Glum!' says the King. 'Breakfast first, business next. Mrs. V., some more sugar!'

'Sire, I am afraid if we wait till after breakfast it will be too late,' says Glumboso. 'He—he—he'll be hanged at half-past nine.'

'Don't talk about hanging and spoil my breakfast, you unkind, vulgar man you,' cries the Princess. 'John, some mustard. Pray who is to be hanged?'

'Sire, it is the Prince,' whispers Glumboso to the King.

'Talk about business after breakfast, I tell you!' says his Majesty, quite sulky.

'We shall have a war, Sire, depend on it,' says the Minister. 'His father, King Padella . . .'

'His father, King *who?*' says the King. 'King Padella is not Giglio's father. My brother, King Savio, was Giglio's father.'

'It's Prince Bulbo they are hanging, Sire, not Prince Giglio,' says the Prime Minister.

'You told me to hang the Prince, and I took the ugly one,' says Hedzoff. 'I didn't, of course, think your Majesty intended to murder your own flesh and blood!'

The King for all reply flung the plate of sausages at Hedzoff's head. The Princess cried out Hee-karee-karee! and fell down in a fainting fit.

'Turn the cock of the urn upon her Royal Highness,' said the King, and the boiling water gradually revived her. His Majesty looked at his watch, compared it by the clock in the parlour, and by that of the church in the square opposite; then he wound it up; then he looked at it again. 'The great question is,' says he, 'am I fast or am I slow? If I'm slow, we may as well go on with breakfast. If I'm fast, why there is just the possibility of saving Prince Bulbo. It's a doosid* awkward mistake, and upon my word, Hedzoff, I have the greatest mind to have you hanged too.'

'Sire, I did but my duty; a soldier has but his orders. I didn't expect after forty-seven years of faithful service that my sovereign would think of putting me to a felon's death!'

'A hundred thousand plagues upon you. Can't you see that while you are talking my Bulbo is being hung!' screamed the Princess.

'By Jove! she's always right, that girl, and I'm so absent,' says the King, looking at his watch again. 'Ha! there go the drums! What a doosid awkward thing though!'

'O Papa, you goose! Write the reprieve, and let me run with it,' cries the Princess—and she got a sheet of paper, and pen and ink, and laid them before the King.

'Confound it! Where are my spectacles?' the Monarch exclaimed. 'Angelica! Go up into my bed-room, look under my pillow, not your mamma's; there you'll see my keys. Bring them down to me, and— Well, well! what impetuous things these girls are!' Angelica was gone, and had run up panting to the bed-room, and found the keys, and was back again before the King had finished a muffin. 'Now love,' says he, 'you must go all the way back for my desk, in which my spectacles are. If you *would* but have heard me out. . . . Be hanged to her. There she is off again. Angelica! ANGELICA!' When His Majesty called in his *loud* voice, she knew she must obey, and came back.

'My dear, when you go out of a room, how often have I told you, *shut the door.* That's a darling. That's all.' At last the keys and the desk and the spectacles were got, and the King mended his pen, and signed his name to a reprieve, and Angelica ran with it as swift as the wind. 'You'd better stay, my love, and finish the muffins. There's no use going. Be sure it's too late. Hand me over that raspberry jam, please,' said the Monarch. 'Bong! Bawong! There goes the half hour. I knew it was.'

Angelica ran, and ran, and ran, and ran. She ran up Fore Street, and down High Street, and through the Market-place, and down to the left, and over the bridge, and up the blind alley, and back again, and round by the Castle, and so along by the Haberdasher's on the right, opposite the lamp-post, and round the square, and she came—she came to the *Execution place*, where she saw Bulbo laying his head on the block!!! The executioner raised his axe, but at that moment the Princess came panting up, and cried Reprieve. 'Reprieve!' screamed the Princess. 'Reprieve!' shouted all the people. Up the scaffold stairs she sprang with the agility of a lighter of lamps, and flinging herself in Bulbo's arms, regardless of all ceremony, she cried out, 'O my Prince! my lord! my love! my Bulbo! Thine Angelica has been in time to save thy precious existence, sweet rosebud; to prevent thy being nipped in thy young bloom! Had aught befallen thee, Angelica too had died, and welcomed death that joined her to her Bulbo.'

'H'm! there's no accounting for tastes,' said Bulbo, looking so very much puzzled and uncomfortable, that the Princess, in tones of tenderest strain, asked the cause of his disquiet.

'I tell you what it is, Angelica,' said he, 'since I came here, yesterday, there has been such a row, and disturbance, and quarrelling, and fighting, and chopping of heads off, and the deuce to pay, that I am inclined to go back to Crim Tartary.'

'But with me as thy bride, my Bulbo! Though wherever thou art is Crim Tartary to me, my bold, my beautiful, my Bulbo!'

'Well, well, I suppose we must be married,' says Bulbo. 'Doctor, you came to read the Funeral Service—read the Marriage Service, will you? What must be, must. That will satisfy Angelica; and then, in the name of peace and quietness, do let us go back to breakfast.'

Bulbo had carried a rose in his mouth all the time of the dismal ceremony. It was a fairy rose, and he was told by his mother that he ought never to part with it; so he had kept it between his teeth, even when he laid his poor head upon the block, hoping vaguely that some chance would turn up in his favour. As he began to speak to Angelica, he forgot about the rose, and of course it dropped out of his mouth. The romantic Princess instantly stooped and seized it. 'Sweet rose!' she exclaimed, 'that bloomed upon my Bulbo's lip, never, never will I part from thee!' and she placed it in her bosom. And you know Bulbo *couldn't* ask her to give the rose back again. And they went to breakfast; and as they walked, it appeared to Bulbo that Angelica became more exquisitely lovely every moment.

He was frantic until they were married; and now, strange to say, it was Angelica who didn't care about him! He knelt down, he kissed her hand, he prayed and begged; he cried with admiration; while she for her part said she really thought they might wait; it seemed to her he was not handsome any more—no, not at all; quite the reverse; and not clever, no, very stupid; and not well bred, like Giglio; no, on the contrary, dreadfully vul—

What, I cannot say, for King Valoroso roared out, '*Pooh!* stuff!' in a terrible voice. 'We will have no more of this shilly-shallying! Call the Archbishop, and let the Prince and Princess be married off-hand!'

So married they were, and I am sure, for my part, I trust they will be happy.

XII

HOW BETSINDA FLED, AND WHAT BECAME OF HER

BETSINDA wandered on and on, till she passed through the town gates, and so on the great Crim Tartary road, the very way on which Giglio too was going. 'Ah!' thought she, as the diligence* passed her, of which the conductor was blowing a delightful tune on his horn, 'how I should like to be on that coach!' But the coach and the jingling horses were very soon gone. She little knew who was in it, though very likely she was thinking of him all the time.

Then came an empty cart, returning from market; and the driver being a kind man, and seeing such a very pretty girl trudging along the road with bare feet, most good-naturedly gave her a seat. He said he lived on the confines of the forest, where his old father was a woodman, and, if she liked, he would take her so far on her road. All roads were the same to little Betsinda, so she very thankfully took this one.

And the carter put a cloth round her bare feet, and gave her some bread and cold bacon, and was very kind to her. For all that she was very cold and melancholy. When after travelling on and on, evening came, and all the black pines were bending with snow, and there, at last, was the comfortable light beaming in the woodman's windows; and so they arrived, and went into his cottage. He was an old man, and had a number of children, who were just at supper, with nice hot bread-and-milk, when their elder brother arrived with the cart. And they jumped and clapped their hands; for they were good children, and he had brought them toys from the town. And when they saw the pretty stranger, they ran to her, and brought her to the fire, and rubbed her poor little feet, and brought her bread-and-milk.

'Look, Father!' they said to the old woodman, 'look at this poor girl, and see what pretty cold feet she has. They are as white as our milk! And look and see what an odd cloak she has, just like the bit of velvet that hangs up in our cupboard, and which you found that day the little cubs were killed by King Padella, in the forest! And look, why, bless us all! she has got round her neck just such another little shoe as that you brought home, and have shown us so often—a little blue velvet shoe!'

'What,' said the old woodman, 'What is all this about a shoe and a cloak?'

And Betsinda explained that she had been left, when quite a little child, at the town with this cloak and this shoe. And the persons who had taken care of her had—had been angry with her for no fault, she hoped, of her own. And they had sent her away with her old clothes—and here, in fact, she was. She remembered having been in a forest, and—perhaps it was a dream—it was so very odd and strange—having lived in a cave with lions there; and, before that, having lived in a very, very fine house, as fine as the King's, in the town.

When the woodman heard this, he was so astonished, it was quite curious to see how astonished he was. He went to his cupboard, and took out of a stocking a five-shilling piece of King Cavolfiore, and vowed it was exactly like the young woman. And then he produced the shoe and piece of velvet which he had kept so long, and compared them with the things which Betsinda wore. In Betsinda's little shoe was written, 'Hopkins, maker to the Royal Family;' so in the other shoe was written, 'Hopkins, maker to the Royal Family.' In the inside of Betsinda's piece of cloak was embroidered, 'PRIN ROSAL;' in the other piece of cloak was embroidered, 'CESS BA. No. 246;' so that, when put together, you read, 'PRINCESS ROSALBA. No. 246.'

On seeing this, the dear old woodman fell down on his knee, saying, 'O my Princess, O my gracious royal lady, O my rightful Queen of Crim Tartary,—I hail thee—I acknowledge thee—I do thee homage!' And in token of his fealty, he rubbed his venerable nose three times on the ground, and put the Princess's foot on his head.

'Why,' said she, 'my good woodman, you must be a nobleman of my royal father's court!' for in her lowly retreat, and under the name of Betsinda, HER MAJESTY, ROSALBA, Queen of Crim Tartary, had read of the customs of all foreign courts and nations.

'Marry, indeed, am I, my gracious liege—the poor Lord Spinachi,* once—the humble woodman these fifteen years syne. Ever since the tyrant Padella (may ruin overtake the treacherous knave!) dismissed me from my post of First Lord.'

'First Lord of the Toothpick and Joint Keeper of the Snuff-box? I mind me! Thou heldest these posts under our royal Sire. They are restored to thee, Lord Spinachi! I make thee knight of the second class of our Order of the Pumpkin (the first class being reserved for crowned heads alone). Rise Marquis of Spinachi!' And with indescribable majesty, the Queen, who had no sword handy, waved the pewter spoon with which she had been taking her bread-and-milk over the bald head of the old nobleman, whose tears absolutely made a puddle on the ground, and whose dear children went to bed that night Lords and Ladies Bartolomeo, Ubaldo, Catarina, and Ottavia degli Spinachi!

The acquaintance HER MAJESTY showed with the history, and *noble families* of her empire, was wonderful. 'The House of Broccoli should remain faithful to us,' she said; 'they were ever welcome at our Court. Have the Articiocchi,* as was their wont, turned to the Rising Sun? The family of Sauerkraut must sure be with us—they were ever welcome in the halls of King Cavolfiore.' And so she went on enumerating quite a list of the nobility and gentry of Crim Tartary, so admirably had her Majesty profited by her studies while in exile.

The old Marquis of Spinachi said he could answer for them all; that the whole country groaned under Padella's tyranny, and longed to return to its rightful sovereign; and late as it was, he sent his children who knew the forest well, to summon this nobleman and that; and when his eldest son, who had been rubbing the horse down and giving him his supper, came into the house for his own, the Marquis told him to put his boots on, and a saddle on the mare, and ride hither and thither to such and such people.

When the young man heard who his companion in the cart had been, he too knelt down and put her royal foot on his head; he too bedewed the ground with his tears; he was frantically in love with her as everybody now was who saw her: so were the young Lords Bartolomeo and Ubaldo, who punched each other's little heads out of jealousy: and so when they came from east and west, at the summons of the Marquis degli Spinachi, were the Crim Tartar Lords who still remained faithful to the House of Cavolfiore. They were such very old gentlemen for the most part, that her Majesty never suspected their absurd passion, and went among them quite unaware of the havoc her beauty was causing, until an old blind Lord who had joined her party, told her what the truth was; after which, for fear of making the people too much in love with her, she always wore a veil. She went about, privately, from one nobleman's castle to another, and they visited amongst themselves again, and had meetings, and composed proclamations and counter-proclamations, and distributed all the best places of the kingdom among one another, and selected who of the opposition party should be executed when the Queen came to her own. And so in about a year they were ready to move.

The party of Fidelity was in truth composed of very feeble old fogies for the most part; they went about the country waving their old swords and flags, and calling 'God save the Queen!' and King Padella happening to be absent upon an invasion, they had their own way for a little, and to be sure the people were very enthusiastic whenever they saw the Queen; otherwise the vulgar took matters very quietly, for they said, as far as they could recollect, they were pretty well as much taxed in Cavolfiore's time, as now in Padella's.

XIII

HOW QUEEN ROSALBA CAME TO THE CASTLE OF THE BOLD COUNT HOGGINARMO*

HER MAJESTY, having indeed nothing else to give, made all her followers, Knights of the Pumpkin, and Marquises, Earls, and Baronets, and they had a little court for her, and made her a little crown of gilt paper; and a robe of cotton velvet; and they quarrelled about the places to be given away in her court, and about rank and precedence and dignities—you can't think how they quarrelled! The poor Queen was very tired of her honours before she had had them a month, and I dare say sighed sometimes even to be a lady's maid again. But we must all do our duty in our respective stations, so the Queen resigned herself to perform hers.

We have said how it happened that none of the Usurper's troops came out to oppose this Army of Fidelity: it pottered along as nimbly as the gout of the principal commanders allowed: it consisted of twice as many officers as soldiers: and at length passed near the estates of one of the most powerful noblemen of the country, who had not declared for the Queen, but of whom her party had hopes, as he was always quarrelling with King Padella.

When they came close to his park gates, this nobleman sent to say he would wait upon Her Majesty; he was a most powerful warrior, and his name was Count Hogginarmo, whose helmet it took two strong negroes to carry. He knelt down before her and said, 'Madam and liege lady! it becomes the great nobles of the Crimean realm to show every outward sign of respect to the wearer of the Crown, whoever that may be. We testify to our own nobility in acknowledging yours. The bold Hogginarmo bends the knee to the first of the aristocracy of his country.'

Rosalba said, 'The bold Count of Hogginarmo was uncommonly kind.' But she felt afraid of him, even while he was kneeling, and his eyes scowled at her from between his whiskers, which grew up to them.

'The first Count of the Empire, madam,' he went on, 'salutes the Sovereign. The Prince addresses himself to the not more noble lady! Madam! my hand is free, and I offer it, and my heart and my sword to your service! My three wives lie buried in my ancestral vaults. The third perished but a year since; and this heart pines for a consort! Deign to be mine, and I swear to bring to your bridal table the head of King Padella, the eyes and nose of his son Prince Bulbo, the right hand and ears of the usurping Sovereign of Paflagonia, which country shall thenceforth be an appanage* to your—to *our* Crown! Say yes; Hogginarmo is not accustomed to be denied. Indeed I cannot contemplate the possibility of a refusal: for frightful will be the result; dreadful the murders; furious the devastations; horrible the tyranny; tremendous the tortures, misery, taxation, which the people of this realm will endure, if Hogginarmo's wrath be aroused! I see consent in your Majesty's lovely eyes—their glances fill my soul with rapture!'

'O, Sir,' Rosalba said, withdrawing her hand in great fright. 'Your Lordship is exceedingly kind; but I am sorry to tell you that I have a prior attachment to a young gentleman by the name of—Prince—Giglio—and never—never can marry any one but him.'

Who can describe Hogginarmo's wrath at this remark? Rising up from the ground, he ground his teeth so that fire flashed out of his mouth, from which at the same time issued remarks and language so *loud, violent, and improper,* that this pen shall never repeat them! 'R-r-r-r-r—Rejected! Fiends and perdition! The bold Hogginarmo rejected! All the world shall hear of my rage; and you, Madam, you above all shall rue it!' And kicking the two negroes before him, he rushed away, his whiskers streaming in the wind.

Her Majesty's Privy Council was in a dreadful panic when they saw Hogginarmo issue from the royal presence in such a towering rage, making footballs of the poor negroes,—a panic which the events justified. They marched off from Hogginarmo's park very crest-fallen; and in another half-hour they were met by that rapacious chieftain with a few of his followers, who cut, slashed, charged, whacked, banged, and pommelled among them, took the Queen prisoner, and drove the Army of Fidelity to I don't know where.

Poor Queen! Hogginarmo, her conqueror, would not condescend to see her. 'Get a horse-van!' he said to his grooms, 'Clap the hussey into it, and send her, with my compliments, to his Majesty King Padella.'

Along with his lovely prisoner, Hogginarmo sent a letter full of servile compliments and loathsome flatteries to King Padella, for whose life and that of his royal family the *hypocritical humbug* pretended to offer the most fulsome prayers. And Hogginarmo promised speedily to pay his humble homage at his august master's throne, of which he begged leave to be counted the most loyal and constant defender. Such a *wary* old *bird* as King Padella was not to be caught by Master Hogginarmo's *chaff*,* and we shall hear presently how the tyrant treated his upstart vassal. No, no; depend on't two such rogues do not trust one another.

So this poor Queen was laid in the straw like Margery Daw,* and driven along in the dark ever so many miles to the Court, where King Padella had now arrived, having vanquished all his enemies, murdered most of them, and brought some of the richest into captivity with him for the purpose of torturing them and finding out where they had hidden their money.

Rosalba heard their shrieks and groans in the dungeon in which she was thrust; a most awful black hole, full of bats, rats, mice, toads, frogs, mosquitoes, bugs, fleas, serpents, and every kind of horror. No light was let into it, otherwise the gaolers might have seen her and fallen in love with her, as an owl that lived up in the roof of the tower did, and a cat you know, who can see in the dark, and having set its green eyes on Rosalba, never would be got to go back to the turnkey's wife to whom it belonged. And the toads in the dungeon came and kissed her feet, and the vipers wound round her neck and arms, and never hurt her, so charming was this poor Princess in the midst of her misfortunes.

At last, after she had been kept in this place *ever so long*, the door of the dungeon opened, and the terrible KING PADELLA came in.

But what he said and did must be reserved for another Chapter, as we must now go back to Prince Giglio.

XIV

WHAT BECAME OF GIGLIO

THE idea of marrying such an old creature as Gruffanuff, frightened Prince Giglio so, that he ran up to his room, packed his trunks, fetched in a couple of porters, and was off to the diligence office in a twinkling.

It was well that he was so quick in his operations, did not dawdle over his luggage, and took the early coach, for as soon as the mistake about Prince Bulbo was found out, that cruel Glumboso sent up a couple of policemen to Prince Giglio's room, with orders that he should be carried to Newgate,* and his head taken off before twelve o'clock. But the coach was out of the Paflagonian dominions before two o'clock; and I daresay the express that was sent after Prince Giglio did not ride very quick, for many people in Paflagonia had a regard for Giglio, as the son of their old sovereign; a Prince, who, with all his weaknesses, was very much better than his brother the reigning, usurping, lazy, careless, passionate, tyrannical, reigning monarch. That Prince busied himself with the balls, fêtes, masquerades, hunting parties, and so forth, which he thought proper to give on occasion of his daughter's marriage to Prince Bulbo; and let us trust was not sorry in his own heart that his brother's son had escaped the scaffold.

It was very cold weather, and the snow was on the ground, and Giglio, who gave his name as simple Mr. Gills, was very glad to get a comfortable place in the coupé* of the diligence, where he sat with the conductor and another gentleman. At the first stage from Blombodinga, as they stopped to change horses, there came up to the diligence a very ordinary, vulgar-looking woman, with a bag under her arm, who asked for a place. All the inside places were taken, and the young woman was informed that if she wished to travel, she must go upon the roof; and the passenger inside with Giglio (a rude person, I should think) put his head out of the window, and said, 'Nice weather for travelling outside! I wish you a pleasant journey, my dear.' The poor woman coughed very much, and Giglio pitied her. 'I will give up my place to her,' says he, 'rather than she should travel in the cold air with that horrid cough.' On which the vulgar traveller said, '*You'd* keep her warm, I am sure, if it's a *muff** she wants.' On which Giglio pulled his nose, boxed his ears, hit him in the eye, and gave this vulgar person a warning never to call him *muff* again.

Then he sprang up gaily on to the roof of the diligence, and made himself very comfortable in the straw. The vulgar traveller got down only at the next station, and Giglio took his place again, and talked to the person next to him. She appeared to be a most agreeable, well-informed, and entertaining female. They travelled together till night, and she gave Giglio all sorts of things out of the bag which she carried, and which indeed seemed to contain the most wonderful collection of articles. He was thirsty—out there came a pint bottle of Bass's pale ale, and a silver mug! Hungry—she took out a cold fowl, some slices of ham, bread, salt, and a most delicious piece of cold plum-pudding, and a little glass of brandy afterwards.

As they travelled, this plain looking, queer woman talked to Giglio on a variety of subjects, in which the poor Prince showed his ignorance as much as she did her capacity. He owned, with many blushes, how ignorant he was; on which the lady said, 'My dear Gigl—my good Mr. Gills, you are a young man, and have plenty of time before you. You have nothing to do but to improve yourself. Who knows but that you may find use for your knowledge some day? When—when you may be wanted at home, as some people may be.'

'Good Heavens, madam!' says he, 'do you know me?'

'I know a number of funny things,' says the lady. 'I have been at some people's christenings, and turned away from other folk's doors. I have seen some people spoilt by good fortune, and others, as I hope, improved by hardship. I advise you to stay at the town where the coach stops for the night. Stay there and study, and remember your old friend to whom you were kind.'

'And who is my old friend?' asked Giglio.

'When you want anything,' says the lady, 'look in this bag, which I leave to you as a present, and be grateful to—'

'To whom, madam?' says he.

'To the Fairy Blackstick,' says the lady, flying out of the window. And when Giglio asked the conductor if he knew where the lady was?

'What lady?' says the man; 'there has been no lady in this coach, except the old woman, who got out at the last stage.' And Giglio thought he had been dreaming. But there was the bag which Blackstick had given him lying on his lap; and when he came to the town he took it in his hand and went into the inn.

They gave him a very bad bed-room, and Giglio, when he woke in the morning, fancying himself in the Royal Palace at home, called, 'John! Charles! Thomas! My chocolate—my dressing-gown—my slippers;' but nobody came. There was no bell, so he went and bawled out for waiter on the top of the stairs.

The landlady came up, looking—looking like this—

'What are you a hollaring and a bellaring for here, young man?' says she.

'There's no warm water—no servants; my boots are not even cleaned.'

'He, he! Clean 'em yourself,' says the landlady. 'You young students give yourselves pretty airs. I never heard such impudence.'

'I'll quit the house this instant,' says Giglio.

'The sooner the better, young man. Pay your bill and be off. All my rooms is wanted for gentlefolks, and not for such as you.'

'You may well keep the Bear Inn,' said Giglio. 'You should have yourself painted as the sign.'

The landlady of the Bear went away *growling*. And Giglio returned to his room, where the first thing he saw was the fairy bag lying on the table, which seemed to give a little hop as he came in. 'I hope it has some breakfast in it,' says Giglio, 'for I have only a very little money left.' But on opening the bag, what do you think was there? A blacking-brush and a pot of Warren's jet,* and on the pot was written,

> 'Poor young men their boots must black.
> Use me, and cork me, and put me back.'

So Giglio laughed and blacked his boots, and put back the brush and the bottle into the bag.

When he had done dressing himself, the bag gave another little hop, and he went to it and took out—

1. A table-cloth and a napkin.
2. A sugar-basin full of the best loaf sugar.
4, 6, 8, 10. Two forks, two teaspoons, two knives, and a pair of sugar-tongs, and a butter-knife, all marked G.
11, 12, 13. A tea-cup, saucer, and slop-basin.
14. A jug full of delicious cream.
15. A canister with black tea and green.
16. A large tea-urn and boiling water.
17. A saucepan, containing three eggs nicely done.
18. A quarter of a pound of best Epping butter.*
19. A brown loaf.

And if he hadn't enough now for a good breakfast, I should like to know who ever had one?

Giglio, having had his breakfast, popped all the things back into the bag, and went out looking for lodgings. I forgot to say that this celebrated university town was called Bosforo.*

He took a modest lodging opposite the Schools, paid his bill at the inn, and went to his apartment with his trunk, carpet bag, and not forgetting, we may be sure, his *other* bag.

*

When he opened his trunk, which the day before he had filled with his best clothes, he found it contained only books. And in the first of them which he opened there was written—

'Clothes for the back, books for the head:
Read, and remember them when they are read.'

And in his bag, when Giglio looked in it, he found a student's cap and gown, a writing-book full of paper, an inkstand, pens, and a Johnson's Dictionary,* which was very useful to him, as his spelling had been sadly neglected.

So he sat down and worked away, very, very hard for a whole year, during which 'Mr. Giles' was quite an example to all the students in the University of Bosforo. He never got into any riots or disturbances. The professors all spoke well of him, and the students liked him too; so that when, at examination, he took all the prizes, viz.,

{	The Spelling Prize The Writing Prize The History Prize The Catechism Prize	{	The French Prize The Arithmetic Prize The Latin Prize The Good Conduct Prize,

all his fellow-students said, 'Hurray! Hurray for Giles! Giles is the boy—the students' joy! Hurray for Giles!' And he brought quite a quantity of medals, crowns, books, and tokens of distinction home to his lodgings.

One day after the examinations, as he was diverting himself at a coffee-house with two friends (did I tell you that in his bag, every Saturday night, he found just enough to pay his bills, with a guinea over, for pocket-money? Didn't I tell you? Well, he did, as sure as twice twenty makes forty-five), he chanced to look in the 'Bosforo Chronicle,' and read off, quite easily (for he could spell, read, and write the longest words now), the following:

'ROMANTIC CIRCUMSTANCE.—One of the most extraordinary adventures that we have ever heard has set the neighbouring country of Crim Tartary in a state of great excitement.

'It will be remembered that when the present revered sovereign of Crim Tartary, his Majesty King *Padella*, took possession of the throne, after having vanquished, in the terrific battle of Blunderbusco, the late King *Cavolfiore*, that Prince's only child, the Princess Rosalba, was not found in the royal palace, of which King Padella took possession, and, it was said, had strayed into the forest (being abandoned by all her attendants), where she had been eaten up by those ferocious lions, the last pair of which were captured some time since, and brought to the Tower, after killing several hundred persons.

'His Majesty King Padella, who has the kindest heart in the world, was grieved at the accident which had occurred to the harmless little Princess, for whom his Majesty's known benevolence would certainly have provided a fitting establishment. But her death seemed to be certain. The mangled remains of a cloak, and a little shoe, were found in the forest, during a hunting party, in which the intrepid sovereign of Crim Tartary slew two of the lions' cubs with his own spear. And these interesting relics of an innocent little creature were carried home and kept by their finder, the Baron Spinachi, formerly an officer in Cavolfiore's household. The Baron was disgraced in consequence of his known legitimist opinions, and has lived for some time in the humble capacity of a wood-cutter, in a forest, on the outskirts of the kingdom of Crim Tartary.

'Last Tuesday week Baron Spinachi and a number of gentlemen attached to the former dynasty, appeared in arms, crying "God save Rosalba, the First Queen of Crim Tartary!" and surrounding a lady whom report describes as *"beautiful exceedingly"*. Her history *may* be authentic, *is* certainly most romantic.

'The personage calling herself Rosalba states that she was brought out of the forest, fifteen years since, by a lady in a car, drawn by dragons (this account is certainly *improbable*), that she was left in the Palace Garden of Blombodinga, where her Royal Highness the Princess Angelica, now married to his Royal Highness Bulbo, Crown Prince of Crim Tartary, found the child, and, with *that elegant benevolence* which has always distinguished the heiress of the throne of Paflagonia, gave the little outcast a *shelter and a home!* Her parentage not being known, and her garb very humble, the foundling was educated in the Palace in a menial capacity, under the name of *Betsinda*.

'She did not give satisfaction, and was dismissed, carrying with her, certainly, part of a mantle and a shoe which she had on when first found. According to her statement she quitted Blombodinga about a year ago, since which time she has been with the Spinachi family. On the very same morning the Prince Giglio, nephew to the King of Paflagonia, a young Prince whose character for *talent* and *order* were, to say truth, *none of the highest*, also quitted Blombodinga, and has not been since heard of!'

'What an extraordinary story!' said Smith and Jones, two young students, Gigilo's especial friends.

'Ha! what is this?' Giglio went on, reading—

'SECOND EDITION, EXPRESS.—We hear that the troop under Baron Spinachi has been surrounded, and utterly routed, by General Count Hogginarmo, and the *soi-disant** Princess is sent a prisoner to the capital.

'UNIVERSITY NEWS.—Yesterday, at the Schools, the distinguished young student, Mr. Giles, read a Latin oration, and was complimented by the Chancellor of Bosforo, Dr. Prugnaro, with the highest University honour—the wooden spoon.'*

'Never mind that stuff,' says *Giles*, greatly disturbed, 'Come home with me, my friends. Gallant Smith! intrepid Jones! friends of my studies—partakers of my academic toils—I have that to tell shall astonish your honest minds.'

'Go it, old boy!' cried the impetuous Smith.

'Talk away, my buck!' says Jones, a lively fellow.

With an air of indescribable dignity, Giglio checked their natural, but no more seemly familiarity. 'Jones, Smith, my good friends,' said the PRINCE, 'disguise is henceforth useless; I am no more the humble student Giles—I am the descendant of a royal line.'

'*Atavis edite regibus*,* I know, old co——,' cried Jones—he was going to say old cock, but a flash from THE ROYAL EYE again awed him.

'Friends,' continued the Prince, 'I am that Giglio—I am, in fact, Paflagonia. Rise, Smith, and kneel not in the public street. Jones, thou true heart! My faithless uncle, when I was a baby, filched from me that brave crown my father left me, bred me all young and careless of my rights, like unto hapless Hamlet, Prince of Denmark;* and had I any thoughts about my wrongs, soothed me with promises of near redress. I should espouse his daughter young Angelica; we two indeed should reign in Paflagonia. His words were false—false as Angelica's heart!—false as Angelica's hair, colour, front teeth! She looked with her skew eyes upon young Bulbo, Crim Tartary's stupid heir, and she preferred him. 'Twas then I turned my eyes upon Betsinda—Rosalba, as she now is. And I saw her in the blushing sum of all perfection; the pink of maiden modesty; the nymph that my fond heart had ever woo'd in dreams,' &c., &c.

(I don't give this speech, which was very fine, but very long; and though Smith and Jones knew nothing about the circumstances, my dear reader does, so I go on.)

The Prince and his young friends hastened home to his apartments, highly excited by the intelligence, as no doubt by the *royal narrator's* admirable manner of recounting it, and they ran up to his room where he had worked so hard at his books.

On his writing-table was his bag, grown so long that the Prince could not help remarking it. He went to it, opened it, and what do you think he found in it?

A splendid long, gold-handled, red-velvet-scabbarded, cut-and-thrust sword, and on the sheath was embroidered 'ROSALBA FOR EVER!'

He drew out the sword, which flashed and illuminated the whole room, and called out 'Rosalba for ever!' Smith and Jones following him, but quite respectfully this time, and taking the time from his Royal Highness.

And now his trunk opened with a sudden pong, and out there came three ostrich feathers in a gold crown, surrounding a beautiful shining steel helmet, a cuirass, a pair of spurs, finally a complete suit of armour.

The books on Giglio's shelves were all gone. Where there had been some great dictionaries, Giglio's friends found two pairs of Jack boots labelled 'Lieutenant Smith,' '—Jones, Esq.,' which fitted them to a nicety. Besides, there were helmets, back and breast plates, swords, &c., just like in Mr. G. P. R. James's novels, and that evening three cavaliers might have been seen issuing from the gates of Bosforo, in whom the porters, proctors,* &c. never thought of recognising the young Prince and his friends.

They got horses at a livery stable-keeper's, and never drew bridle* until they reached the last town on the frontier, before you come to Crim Tartary. Here, as their animals were tired, and the cavaliers hungry, they stopped and refreshed at an hostel. I could make a chapter of this if I were like some writers, but I like to cram my measure tight down, you see, and give you a great deal for your money, and in a word they had some bread and cheese and ale upstairs on the balcony of the Inn. As they were drinking, drums and trumpets sounded nearer and nearer, the market-place was filled with soldiers, and his Royal Highness, looking forth, recognised the Paflagonian banners, and the Paflagonian national air which the bands were playing.

The troops all made for the tavern at once, and as they came up Giglio exclaimed, on beholding their leader, 'Whom do I see? Yes! No! It is, it is! Phoo! No, it can't be! Yes! it is my friend, my gallant faithful veteran, Captain Hedzoff! Ho! Hedzoff! Knowest thou not thy Prince—thy Giglio? Good Corporal, methinks we once were friends. Ha, Sergeant, an my memory serves me right, we have had many a bout at single stick.'

'I'faith, we have a many, good my Lord,' says the Sergeant.

'Tell me, what means this mighty armament,' continued his Royal Highness from the balcony, 'and whither march my Paflagonians?'

Hedzoff's head fell. 'My Lord,' he said, 'we march as the allies of great Padella, Crim Tartary's monarch.'

'Crim Tartary's usurper, gallant Hedzoff! Crim Tartary's grim tyrant, honest Hedzoff!' said the Prince, on the balcony, quite sarcastically.

'A soldier, Prince, must needs obey his orders; mine are to help his Majesty Padella. And also (though alack that I should say it!) to seize, wherever I should light upon him—'

'First catch your hare! ha, Hedzoff!' exclaimed his Royal Highness.

'—On the body of *Giglio*, whilome Prince of Paflagonia,' Hedzoff went on, with indescribable emotion. 'My Prince, give up your sword without ado. Look! we are thirty thousand men to one!'

'Give up my sword! Giglio give up his sword!' cried the Prince; and, stepping well forward on to the balcony, the royal youth, *without preparation*, delivered a speech so magnificent that no report can do justice to it. It was all in blank verse (in which, from this time, he invariably spoke, as more becoming his majestic station.) It lasted for three days and three nights, during which not a single person who heard him was tired, or remarked the difference between daylight and dark, the soldiers only cheering tremendously, when occasionally, once in nine hours, the Prince paused to suck an orange, which Jones took out of the bag. He explained in terms which we say we shall not attempt to convey, the whole history of the previous transaction: and his determination not only not to give up his sword, but to assume his rightful crown: and at the end of this extraordinary, this truly *gigantic* effort, Captain Hedzoff flung up his helmet, and cried, 'Hurray! Hurray! Long live King Giglio!'

Such were the consequences of having employed his time well at College!

When the excitement had ceased, beer was ordered out for the army, and their Sovereign himself did not disdain a little! And now it was with some alarm that Captain Hedzoff told him his division was only the advanced guard of the Paflagonian contingent hastening to King Padella's aid, the main force being a day's march in the rear, under His Royal Highness Prince Bulbo.

'We will wait here, good friend, to beat the Prince,' his Majesty said, 'and *then* will make his royal Father wince.'

XV

WE RETURN TO ROSALBA

KING PADELLA made very similar proposals to Rosalba to those which she had received from the various princes who, as we have seen, had fallen in love with her. His Majesty was a widower, and offered to marry his fair captive that instant, but she declined his invitation in her usual polite manner, stating that Prince Giglio was her love, and that any other union was out of the question. Having tried tears and supplications in vain, this violent-tempered monarch menaced her with threats and tortures; but she declared she would rather suffer all these than accept the hand of her father's murderer, who left her finally, uttering the most awful imprecations, and bidding her prepare for death the following morning.

All night long the King spent in advising how he should get rid of this obdurate young creature. Cutting off her head was much too easy a death for her; hanging was so common in his Majesty's dominions that it no longer afforded him any sport; finally, he bethought himself of a pair of fierce lions which had lately been sent to him as presents, and he determined, with these ferocious brutes, to hunt poor Rosalba down. Adjoining his castle was an amphitheatre, where the Prince indulged in bull-baiting, rat-hunting, and other ferocious sports. The two lions were kept in a cage under this place; their roaring might be heard over the whole city, the inhabitants of which, I am sorry to say, thronged in numbers to see a poor young lady gobbled up by two wild beasts.

The King took his place in the royal box, having the officers of his court around and the Count Hogginarmo by his side, upon whom his Majesty was observed to look very fiercely; the fact is, royal spies had told the monarch of Hogginarmo's behaviour, his proposals to Rosalba, and his offer to fight for the crown. Black as thunder looked King Padella at this proud noble, as they sat in the front seats of the theatre waiting to see the tragedy whereof poor Rosalba was to be the heroine.

At length that princess was brought out in her night-gown, with all her beautiful hair falling down her back, and looking so pretty, that even the beef-eaters* and keepers of the wild animals wept plentifully at seeing her. And she walked with her poor little feet (only luckily the arena was covered with sawdust), and went and leaned up against a great stone in the centre of the amphitheatre, round which the court and the people were seated in boxes with bars before them, for fear of the great, fierce, red-maned, black-throated, long-tailed, roaring, bellowing, rushing lions. And now the gates were opened, and with a wurrawarrurawarar, two great lean, hungry, roaring lions rushed out of their den, where they had been kept for three weeks on nothing but a little toast-and-water, and dashed straight up to the stone where poor Rosalba was waiting. Commend her to your patron saints, all you kind people, for she is in a dreadful state!

There was a hum and a buzz all through the circus, and the fierce King Padella even felt a little compassion. But Count Hogginarmo, seated by his Majesty, roared out, 'Hurray! Now for it! Soo-soo-soo!' that nobleman being uncommonly angry still at Rosalba's refusal of him.

But O strange event! O remarkable circumstance! O extraordinary coincidence, which I am sure none of you could *by any possibility* have divined! When the lions came to Rosalba, instead of devouring her with their great teeth, it was with kisses they gobbled her up! They licked her pretty feet, they nuzzled their noses in her lap, they moo'd, they seemed to say, 'Dear, dear sister, don't you recollect your brothers in the forest?' And she put her pretty white arms round their tawny necks, and kissed them.

King Padella was immensely astonished. The Count Hogginarmo was extremely disgusted. 'Pooh!' the count cried. 'Gammon!' exclaimed his Lordship. 'These lions are tame beasts come from Wombwell's or Astley's.* It is a shame to put people off in this way. I believe they are little boys dressed up in door-mats. They are no lions at all.'

'Ha!' said the King; 'you dare to say "gammon" to your Sovereign, do you? These lions are no lions at all, arn't they? Ho! my beef-eaters! Ho! my body-guard! Take this Count Hogginarmo, and fling him into the circus! Give him a sword and buckler; let him keep his armour on, and his weather-eye out, and fight these lions.'

The haughty Hogginarmo laid down his opera-glass, and looked scowling round at the King and his attendants. 'Touch me not, dogs!' he said, 'or by St. Nicholas the Elder, I will gore you! Your Majesty thinks Hogginarmo is afraid? No, not of a hundred thousand lions! Follow me down into the circus, King Padella, and match thyself against one of yon brutes. Thou darest not. Let them both come on, then!' And opening a grating of the box, he jumped lightly down into the circus.

Wurra wurra wurra wur-aw-aw-aw!!!
In about two minutes
The Count Hogginarmo was
GOBBLED UP
by
those lions,
bones, boots, and all,
and
There was an
End of him.

At this, the King said, 'Serve him right, the rebellious ruffian! And now, as those lions won't eat that young woman—'

'Let her off! let her off!' cried the crowd.

'NO!' roared the King. 'Let the beef-eaters go down and chop her into small pieces. If the lions defend her, let the archers shoot them to death. That hussey shall die in tortures!'

'A-a-ah!' cried the crowd. 'Shame! shame!'

'Who dares cry out shame?' cried the furious potentate (so little can tyrants command their passions). 'Fling any scoundrel who says a word down among the lions!' I warrant you there was a dead silence then, which was broken by a Pang arang pang pangkarangpang, and a Knight and a Herald rode in at the farther end of the circus, the Knight, in full armour, with his vizor up, and bearing a letter on the point of his lance.

'Ha!' exclaimed the King; 'by my fay, 'tis Elephant and Castle,* pursuivant* of my brother of Paflagonia; and the Knight, an my memory serves me, is the gallant Captain Hedzoff. What news from Paflagonia, gallant Hedzoff? Elephant and Castle, beshrew me, thy trumpeting must have made thee thirsty. What will my trusty herald like to drink?'

'Bespeaking first safe conduct from your Lordship,' said Captain Hedzoff, 'before we take a drink of any thing, permit us to deliver our King's message.'

'My Lordship, ha!' said Crim Tartary, frowning terrifically. 'That title soundeth strange in the anointed ears of a crowned King. Straightway speak out your message, Knight and Herald!'

Reining up his charger in a most elegant manner close under the King's balcony, Hedzoff turned to the herald, and bade him begin.

Elephant and Castle, dropping his trumpet over his shoulder, took a large sheet of paper out of his hat, and began to read:

'O Yes! O Yes! O Yes! Know all men by these presents, that we, Giglio, King of Paflagonia, Grand Duke of Cappadocia, Sovereign Prince of Turkey and the Sausage Islands, having assumed our rightful throne and title, long time falsely borne by our usurping Uncle, styling himself King of Paflagonia—'

'Ha!' growled Padella.

'Hereby summon the false traitor, Padella, calling himself King of Crim Tartary,'—

The King's curses were dreadful. 'Go on, Elephant and Castle!' said the intrepid Hedzoff.

'—To release from cowardly imprisonment his liege lady and rightful Sovereign, ROSALBA, Queen of Crim Tartary, and restore her to her royal throne: in default of which, I, Giglio, proclaim the said Padella sneak, traitor, humbug, usurper, and coward. I challenge him to meet me, with fists or with pistols, with battle-axe or sword, with blunderbuss or single-stick, alone or at the head of his army, on foot or on horseback, and will prove my words upon his wicked, ugly body!'

'God save the King!' said Captain Hedzoff, executing a demivolte, two semilunes, and three caracols.*

'Is that all?' said Padella, with the terrific calm of concentrated fury.

'That, sir, is all my royal master's message. Here is his Majesty's letter in autograph, and here is his glove, and if any gentleman of

Crim Tartary chooses to find fault with his Majesty's expressions, I, Tuffskin Hedzoff, Captain of the Guard, am very much at his service,' and he waved his lance, and looked at the assembly all round.

'And what says my good brother of Paflagonia, my dear son's father-in-law to this rubbish?' asked the King.

'The King's uncle hath been deprived of the crown he unjustly wore,' said Hedzoff gravely. 'He and his ex-minister, Glumboso, are now in prison, waiting the sentence of my royal master. After the battle of Bombardaro—'*

'Of what?' asked the surprised Padella.

'Of Bombardaro, where my liege, his present Majesty, would have performed prodigies of valour, but that the whole of his uncle's army came over to our side, with the exception of Prince Bulbo.'

'Ah! my boy, my boy, my Bulbo was no traitor!' cried Padella.

'Prince Bulbo, far from coming over to us, ran away, sir; but I caught him. The Prince is a prisoner in our army, and the most terrific tortures await him if a hair of the Princess Rosalba's head is injured.'

'Do they?' exclaimed the furious Padella, who was now perfectly *livid* with rage. 'Do they, indeed? So much the worse for Bulbo. I've twenty sons as lovely each as Bulbo. Not one but is as fit to reign as Bulbo. Whip, whack, flog, starve, rack, punish, torture Bulbo—break all his bones—roast him or flay him alive—pull all his pretty teeth out one by one! But, justly dear as Bulbo is to me,—Joy of my eyes, fond treasure of my soul! Ha, ha, ha, ha! revenge is dearer still. Ho! torturers, rack-men, executioners—light up the fires and make the pincers hot!* get lots of boiling lead!—Bring out ROSALBA!'

XVI

HOW HEDZOFF RODE BACK AGAIN TO KING GIGLIO

CAPTAIN HEDZOFF rode away when King Padella uttered this cruel command, having done his duty in delivering the message with which his royal master had entrusted him. Of course he was very sorry for Rosalba, but what could he do?

So he returned to King Giglio's camp and found the young monarch in a disturbed state of mind, smoking cigars in the royal tent. His

Majesty's agitation was not appeased by the news that was brought by his ambassador. 'The brutal ruthless ruffian royal wretch!' Giglio exclaimed. 'As England's poesy has well remarked, "The man that lays his hand upon a woman, save in the way of kindness, is a villain."* Ha, Hedzoff?'

'That he is, your Majesty,' said the attendant.

'And did'st thou see her flung into the oil? and didn't the soothing oil—the emollient oil, refuse to boil, good Hedzoff—and to spoil the fairest lady ever eyes did look on?'

'Faith, good my liege, I had no heart to look and see a beauteous lady boiling down; I took your royal message to Padella, and bore his back to you. I told him you would hold Prince Bulbo answerable. He only said that he had twenty sons as good as Bulbo, and forthwith he bade the ruthless executioners proceed.'

'O cruel father—O unhappy son,' cried the King. 'Go, some of you, and bring Prince Bulbo hither.'

Bulbo was brought in chains, looking very uncomfortable. Though a prisoner, he had been tolerably happy, perhaps because his mind was at rest, and all the fighting was over, and he was playing at marbles with his guards, when the King sent for him.

'O, my poor Bulbo,' said his Majesty, with looks of infinite compassion, 'hast thou heard the news (for you see Giglio wanted to break the thing gently to the Prince), thy brutal father has condemned Rosalba—p-p-p-put her to death, P-p-p-prince Bulbo!'

'What! killed Betsinda! Boo-hoo-hoo!' cried out Bulbo, 'Betsinda! pretty Betsinda! dear Betsinda! She was the dearest little girl in the world. I love her better twenty thousand times even than Angelica,' and he went on expressing his grief in so hearty and unaffected a manner, that the King was quite touched by it, and said, shaking Bulbo's hand, that he wished he had known Bulbo sooner.

Bulbo, quite unconsciously, and meaning for the best, offered to come and sit with his majesty, and smoke a cigar with him, and console him. The *royal kindness* supplied Bulbo with a cigar; he had not had one, he said, since he was taken prisoner.

And now think what must have been the feelings of the most *merciful of monarchs*, when he informed his prisoner that, in consequence of King Padella's *cruel and dastardly behaviour* to Rosalba, Prince Bulbo must instantly be executed! The noble Giglio could not restrain his tears, nor could the Grenadiers, nor the officers, nor could Bulbo himself, when the matter was explained to him; and he was brought to understand that his Majesty's promise, of course, was *above every thing*, and Bulbo must submit. So poor Bulbo was led out. Hedzoff trying to console him by pointing out that if he had won the battle of Bombardaro, he might have hanged Prince Giglio. 'Yes! but that is no comfort to me now!' said poor Bulbo; nor indeed was it, poor fellow!

He was told the business would be done the next morning at eight, and was taken back to his dungeon, where every attention was paid to him. The gaoler's wife sent him tea, and the turnkey's daughter begged him to write his name in her album,* where a many gentlemen had wrote it on like occasions! 'Bother your album!' says Bulbo. The Undertaker came and measured him for the handsomest coffin which money could buy—even this didn't console Bulbo. The Cook brought him dishes which he once used to like; but he wouldn't touch them: he sat down and began writing an adieu to Angelica, as the clock kept always ticking, and the hands drawing nearer to next morning. The Barber came in at night, and offered to shave him for the next day. Prince Bulbo kicked him away, and went on writing a few words to Princess Angelica, as the clock kept always ticking, and the hands hopping nearer and nearer to next morning. He got up on the top of a hat-box, on the top of a chair, on the top of his bed, on the top of his table, and looked out to see whether he might escape, as the clock kept always ticking and the hands drawing nearer, and nearer, and nearer.

But looking out of the window was one thing, and jumping another: and the town clock struck seven. So he got into bed for a little sleep, but the gaoler came and woke him, and said, 'Git up, your Royal Ighness, if you please; it's *ten minutes to eight!*'

So poor Bulbo got up: he had gone to bed in his clothes (the lazy boy), and he shook himself, and said he didn't mind about dressing, or having any breakfast, thank you; and he saw the soldiers who had come for him. 'Lead on!' he said; and they led the way, deeply affected; and they came into the court yard, and out into the square, and there was King Giglio come to take leave of him, and his Majesty most kindly shook hands with him, and the *gloomy procession* marched on:—when hark!

Haw—wurraw—wurraw—aworr!

A roar of wild beasts was heard. And who should come riding into the town, frightening away the boys, and even the beadle and policeman, but ROSALBA!

The fact is, that when Captain Hedzoff entered into the court of Snapdragon Castle, and was discoursing with King Padella, the Lions made a dash at the open gate, gobbled up the six beef-eaters in a jiffy, and away they went with Rosalba on the back of one of them, and they carried her, turn and turn about, till they came to the city where Prince Giglio's army was encamped.

When the KING heard of the QUEEN'S arrival, you may think how he rushed out of his breakfast-room to hand her Majesty off her Lion! The Lions were grown as fat as Pigs now, having had Hogginarmo and all those beef-eaters, and were so tame anybody might pat them.

While Giglio knelt (most gracefully) and helped the Princess, Bulbo, for his part, rushed up and kissed the Lion. He flung his arms round the forest monarch; he hugged him, and laughed and cried for joy. 'O you darling old beast, O, how glad I am to see you, and the dear, dear Bets'—that is, Rosalba.

'What, is it you? Poor Bulbo!' said the Queen. 'O, how glad I am to see you;' and she gave him her hand to kiss. King Giglio slapped him most kindly on the back, and said, 'Bulbo, my boy, I am delighted, for your sake, that Her Majesty has arrived.'

'So am I,' said Bulbo, 'and *you know why*.' Captain Hedzoff here came up. 'Sire, it is half-past eight: shall we proceed with the execution?'

'Execution, what for?' asked Bulbo.

'An officer only knows his orders,' replied Captain Hedzoff, showing his warrant, on which His Majesty King Giglio smilingly said, 'Prince Bulbo was reprieved this time,' and most graciously invited him to breakfast.

XVII

HOW A TREMENDOUS BATTLE TOOK PLACE, AND WHO WON IT

As soon as King Padella heard, what we know already, that his victim, the lovely Rosalba, had escaped him, his majesty's fury knew no bounds, and he pitched the Lord Chancellor, Lord Chamberlain, and every officer of the crown whom he could set eyes on, into the cauldron of boiling oil prepared for the Princess. Then he ordered his whole army, horse, foot, and artillery; and set forth at the head of an innumerable host, and I should think twenty thousand drummers, trumpeters, and fifers.

King Giglio's advanced guard, you may be sure, kept that monarch acquainted with the enemy's dealings, and he was in no wise disconcerted. He was much too polite to alarm the Princess, his lovely guest, with any unnecessary rumours of battles impending; on the contrary, he did everything to amuse and divert her; gave her a most elegant breakfast, dinner, lunch, and got up a ball for her that evening, when he danced with her every single dance.

Poor Bulbo was taken into favour again, and allowed to go quite free now. He had new clothes given him, was called 'my good cousin' by his Majesty, and was treated with the greatest distinction by everybody. But it was easy to see he was very melancholy. The fact is, the sight of Betsinda, who looked perfectly lovely in an elegant new dress, set poor Bulbo frantic in love with her again. And he never thought about Angelica, now Princess Bulbo, whom he had left at home, and who, as we know, did not care much about him.

The King, dancing the twenty-fifth polka with Rosalba, remarked with wonder the ring she wore: and then Rosalba told him how she had got it from Gruffanuff, who no doubt had picked it up when Angelica flung it away.

'Yes,' says the Fairy Blackstick, who had come to see the young people, and who had very likely certain plans regarding them. 'That ring I gave the Queen, Giglio's mother, who was not, saving your presence, a very wise woman; it is enchanted, and whoever wears it looks beautiful in the eyes of the world. I made poor Prince Bulbo, when he was christened, the present of a rose which made him look handsome while he had it; but he gave it to Angelica, who instantly looked beautiful again, whilst Bulbo relapsed into his natural plainness.'

'Rosalba needs no ring, I am sure,' says Giglio, with a low bow. 'She is beautiful enough, in my eyes, without any enchanted aid.'

'O, sir!' said Rosalba.

'Take off the ring and try,' said the King, and resolutely drew the ring off her finger. In *his* eyes she looked just as handsome as before!

The King was thinking of throwing the ring away, as it was so dangerous and made all the people so mad about Rosalba; but, being a prince of great humour, and good humour too, he cast his eyes upon a poor youth who happened to be looking on very disconsolately, and said—

'Bulbo, my poor lad! come and try on this ring. The Princess Rosalba makes it a present to you.' The magic properties of this ring were uncommonly strong, for no sooner had Bulbo put it on, but lo and behold, he appeared a personable, agreeable young prince enough—with a fine complexion, fair hair, rather stout, and with bandy legs; but these were encased in such a beautiful pair of yellow morocco boots, that nobody remarked them. And Bulbo's spirits rose up almost immediately after he had looked in the glass, and he talked to their Majesties in the most lively, agreeable manner, and danced opposite the Queen with one of the prettiest maids of honour, and after looking at her Majesty, could not help saying—'How very odd; she is very pretty, but not so *extraordinarily* handsome.' 'Oh no, by no means!' says the Maid of Honour.

'But what care I, dear sir,' says the Queen, who overheard them, 'if *you* think I am good-looking enough?'

His Majesty's glance in reply to this affectionate speech was such that no painter could draw it. And the Fairy Blackstick said, 'Bless you, my darling children! Now you are united and happy; and now you see what I said from the first, that a little misfortune has done you both good. *You*, Giglio, had you been bred in prosperity, would scarcely have learned to read or write—you would have been idle and extravagant, and could not have been a good king as now you will be. You, Rosalba, would have been so flattered, that your little head might have been turned like Angelica's, who thought herself too good for Giglio.'

'As if anybody could be good enough for *him*,' cried Rosalba.

'Oh, you, you darling!' says Giglio. And so she was; and he was just holding out his arms in order to give her a hug before the whole company, when a messenger came rushing in, and said, 'My Lord, the enemy!'

'To arms!' cries Giglio.

'Oh, Mercy!' says Rosalba, and fainted, of course. He snatched one kiss from her lips, and rushed *forth to the field* of battle!

The fairy had provided King Giglio with a suit of armour, which was not only embroidered all over with jewels, and blinding to your eyes to look at, but was water-proof, gun-proof, and sword-proof; so that in the midst of the very hottest battles his Majesty rode about as calmly as if he had been a British Grenadier at Alma.* Were I engaged in fighting for my country, I should like such a suit of armour as

Prince Giglio wore; but, you know, he was a Prince of a fairy tale, and they always have these wonderful things.

Besides the fairy armour, the Prince had a fairy horse, which would gallop at any pace you please; and a fairy sword, which would lengthen, and run through a whole regiment of enemies at once. With such a weapon at command, I wonder, for my part, he thought of ordering his army out, but forth they all came, in magnificent new uniforms; Hedzoff and the Prince's two college friends each commanding a division, and his Majesty prancing in person at the head of them all.

Ah! if I had the pen of a Sir Archibald Alison,* my dear friends, would I not now entertain you with the account of a most tremendous shindy? Should not fine blows be struck? dreadful wounds be delivered? arrows darken the air? cannon balls crash through the battalions? cavalry charge infantry? infantry pitch into cavalry? bugles blow; drums beat; horses neigh; fifes sing; soldiers roar, swear, hurray; officers shout out, 'Forward, my men!' 'This way, lads!' 'Give it 'em, boys. Fight for King Giglio, and the cause of right!' 'King Padella forever!' Would I not describe all this, I say, and in the very finest language, too? But this humble pen does not possess the skill necessary for the description of combats. In a word, the overthrow of King Padella's army was so complete, that if they had been Russians* you could not have wished them to be more utterly smashed and confounded.

As for that usurping monarch, having performed acts of valour much more considerable than could be expected of a royal ruffian and usurper, who had such a bad cause, and who was so cruel to women,— as for King Padella, I say, when his army ran away, the King ran away too, kicking his first general, Prince Punchikoff,* from his saddle, and galloping away on the Prince's horse, having, indeed, had twenty-five or twenty-six of his own shot under him. Hedzoff coming up, and finding Punchikoff down, as you may imagine very speedily disposed of *him*. Meanwhile King Padella was scampering off as hard as his horse could lay legs to ground. Fast as he scampered, I promise you somebody else galloped faster; and that individual, as no doubt you are aware, was the Royal Giglio, who kept bawling out, 'Stay, traitor! Turn, miscreant, and defend thyself! Stand, tyrant, coward, ruffian, royal wretch, till I cut thy ugly head from thy usurping shoulders!' And, with his fairy sword, which elongated itself at will, his Majesty kept poking and prodding Padella in the back, until that wicked monarch roared with anguish.

When he was fairly brought to bay, Padella turned and dealt Prince Giglio a prodigious crack over the sconce with his battle-axe, a most enormous weapon, which had cut down I don't know how many regiments in the course of the afternoon. But, Law bless you!* though the blow fell right down on his Majesty's helmet, it made no more impression than if Padella had struck him with a pat of butter: his battle-axe crumpled up in Padella's hand, and the Royal Giglio laughed for very scorn at the impotent efforts of that atrocious usurper.

At the ill success of his blow the Crim Tartar monarch was justly irritated. 'If,' says he to Giglio, 'you ride a fairy horse, and wear fairy armour, what on earth is the use of my hitting you? I may as well give myself up a prisoner at once. Your Majesty won't, I suppose, be so mean as to strike a poor fellow who can't strike again?'

The justice of Padella's remark struck the magnanimous Giglio. 'Do you yield yourself a prisoner, Padella?' says he.

'Of course I do,' says Padella.

'Do you acknowledge Rosalba as your rightful Queen, and give up the Crown and all your treasures to your rightful mistress?'

'If I must I must,' says Padella, who was naturally very sulky.

By this time King Giglio's aides-de-camp had come up, whom his Majesty ordered to bind the prisoner. And they tied his hands behind him, and bound his legs tight under his horse, having set him with his face to the tail; and in this fashion he was led back to King Giglio's quarters, and thrust into the very dungeon where young Bulbo had been confined.

Padella (who was a very different person in the depth of his distress, to Padella, the proud wearer of the Crim Tartar crown) now most affectionately and earnestly asked to see his son—his dear eldest boy—his darling Bulbo; and that good-natured young man never once reproached his haughty parent for his unkind conduct the day before, when he would have left Bulbo to be shot without any pity, but came to see his father, and spoke to him through the grating of the door, beyond which he was not allowed to go; and brought him some sandwiches from the grand supper which his Majesty was giving above stairs, in honour of the brilliant victory which had just been achieved.

'I cannot stay with you long, sir,' says Bulbo, who was in his best ball dress, as he handed his father in the prog,* 'I am engaged to dance the next quadrille* with her Majesty Queen Rosalba, and I hear the fiddles playing at this very moment.'

So Bulbo went back to the ball-room, and the wretched Padella ate his solitary supper in silence and tears.

All was now joy in King Giglio's circle. Dancing, feasting, fun, illuminations, and jollifications of all sorts ensued. The people through whose villages they passed were ordered to illuminate their cottages at night, and scatter flowers on the roads during the day. They were requested, and I promise you they did not like to refuse, to serve the troops liberally with eatables and wine; besides, the army was enriched by the immense quantity of plunder which was found in King Padella's camp, and taken from his soldiers; who (after they had given up everything), were allowed to fraternise with the conquerors, and the united armies marched back by easy stages toward King Giglio's capital, his royal banner and that of Queen Rosalba being carried in front of the troops. Hedzoff was made a Duke and a Field Marshal. Smith and Jones were promoted to be Earls, the Crim Tartar Order of the Pumpkin and the Paflagonian decoration of the Cucumber were freely distributed by their Majesties to the army. Queen Rosalba wore the Paflagonian Ribbon of the Cucumber across her riding habit, whilst King Giglio never appeared without the grand Cordon of the Pumpkin. How the people cheered them as they rode along side by side! They were pronounced to be the handsomest couple ever seen: that was a matter of course; but they really *were* very handsome, and, had they been otherwise, would have looked so, they were so happy! Their Majesties were never separated during the whole day, but breakfasted, dined, and supped together always, and rode side by side, interchanging elegant compliments, and indulging in the most delightful conversation. At night, Her Majesty's ladies of honour (who had all rallied round her the day after King Padella's defeat), came and conducted her to the apartments prepared for her; whilst King Giglio, surrounded by his gentlemen, withdrew to his own Royal quarters. It was agreed they should be married as soon as they reached the capital, and orders were dispatched to the Archbishop of Blombodinga, to hold himself in readiness to perform the interesting ceremony. Duke Hedzoff carried the message, and gave instructions to have the Royal Castle splendidly refurnished and painted afresh. The duke seized Glumboso, the Ex-Prime Minister, and made him refund that considerable sum of money which the old scoundrel had secreted out of the late King's treasure. He also clapped Valoroso into prison, (who, by the way, had been dethroned for some considerable period past,) and when the Ex-Monarch weakly remonstrated, Hedzoff said, 'A soldier, Sir, knows but his duty; my orders are to lock you up along with the Ex-King Padella, whom I have brought hither a prisoner under guard.' So those two Ex-Royal personages were sent for a year to the House of Correction,* and thereafter were obliged to become monks, of the severest Order of Flagellants,* in which state, by fasting, by vigils, by flogging, (which they administered to one another, humbly but resolutely,) no doubt they exhibited a repentance for their past misdeeds, usurpations, and private and public crimes.

As for Glumboso, that rogue was sent to the galleys, and never had an opportunity to steal any more.

XVIII

HOW THEY ALL JOURNEYED BACK TO THE CAPITAL

THE FAIRY BLACKSTICK, by whose means this young King and Queen had certainly won their respective Crowns back, would come not unfrequently, to pay them a little visit—as they were riding in their triumphal process toward Giglio's Capital—change her wand into a pony, and travel by their Majesties' side, giving them the very best advice. I am not sure that King Giglio did not think the Fairy and her advice rather a bore, fancying it was his own valour and merits which had put him on his throne, and conquered Padella; and, in fine, I fear he rather gave himself airs toward his best friend and patroness. She exhorted him to deal justly by his subjects, to draw mildly on the taxes, never to break his promise when he had once given it—and in all respects, to be a good King.

'A good King, my dear Fairy!' cries Rosalba. 'Of course he will. Break his promise! can you fancy my Giglio would ever do anything so improper, so unlike him? No! never!' And she looked fondly toward Giglio, whom she thought a pattern of perfection.

'Why is Fairy Blackstick always advising me, and telling me how to manage my government, and warning me to keep my word? Does she suppose that I am not a man of sense, and a man of honour?' asks Giglio, testily. 'Methinks she rather presumes upon her position.'

'Hush! dear Giglio,' says Rosalba. 'You know Blackstick has been very kind to us, and we must not offend her.' But the Fairy was not listening to Giglio's testy observations, she had fallen back, and was trotting on her pony now, by Master Bulbo's side, who rode a donkey, and made himself generally beloved in the army by his cheerfulness, kindness, and good humour to everybody. He was eager to see his darling Angelica. He thought there never was such a charming being. Blackstick did not tell him it was the possession of the Magic Rose that made Angelica so lovely in his eyes. She brought him the very best accounts of his little wife, whose misfortunes and humiliations had indeed very greatly improved her, and you see she could whisk off on her wand a hundred miles in a minute, and be back in no time, and so carry polite messages from Bulbo to Angelica, and from Angelica to Bulbo, and comfort that young man upon his journey.

When the Royal party arrived at the last stage before you reach Blombodinga, who should be in waiting, in her carriage there with her lady of honour by her side, but the Princess Angelica. She rushed into her husband's arms, scarcely stopping to make a passing curtsey to the King and Queen. She had no eyes but for Bulbo, who appeared perfectly lovely to her on account of the fairy ring which he wore; while she herself, wearing the magic rose in her bonnet, seemed entirely beautiful to the enraptured Bulbo.

A splendid luncheon was served to the Royal party, of which the Archbishop, the Chancellor, Duke Hedzoff, Countess Gruffanuff, and all our friends partook, the Fairy Blackstick being seated on the left of King Giglio, with Bulbo and Angelica beside her. You could hear the joy-bells ringing in the capital, and the guns which the citizens were firing off in honour of their Majesties.

'What can have induced that hideous old Gruffanuff to dress herself up in such an absurd way? Did you ask her to be your bridesmaid, my dear?' says Giglio to Rosalba. 'What a figure of fun Gruffy is!'

Gruffy was seated opposite their Majesties, between the Archbishop and the Lord Chancellor, and a figure of fun she certainly was, for she was dressed in a low white silk dress, with lace over, a wreath of white roses on her wig, a splendid lace veil, and her yellow old neck was covered with diamonds. She ogled the King in such a manner, that His Majesty burst out laughing.

'Eleven o'clock!' cries Giglio, as the great Cathedral bell of Blombodinga tolled that hour. 'Gentlemen and ladies, we must be starting. Archbishop, you must be at church I think before twelve?'

'We must be at church before twelve,' sighs out Gruffanuff in a languishing voice, hiding her old face behind her fan.

'And then I shall be the happiest man in my dominions,' cries Giglio, with an elegant bow to the blushing Rosalba.

'O, my Giglio! O, my dear Majesty!' exclaims Gruffanuff; 'and can it be that this happy moment at length has arrived—'

'Of course it has arrived,' says the King.

'—And that I am about to become the enraptured bride of my adored Giglio!' continues Gruffanuff. 'Lend me a smelling-bottle, somebody. I certainly shall faint with joy.'

'*You* my bride?' roars out Giglio.

'*You* marry my Prince?' cries poor little Rosalba.

'Pooh! Nonsense! The woman's mad!' exclaims the King. And all the courtiers exhibited by their countenances and expressions marks of surprise, or ridicule, or incredulity, or wonder.

'I should like to know who else is going to be married, if I am not?' shrieks out Gruffanuff. 'I should like to know if King Giglio is a gentleman, and if there is such a thing as justice in Paflagonia? Lord Chancellor! my Lord Archbishop! will your Lordships sit by and see a poor, fond, confiding, tender creature put upon? Has not Prince Giglio promised to marry his Barbara? Is not this Giglio's signature? Does not this paper declare that he is mine, and only mine?' And she handed to his Grace the Archbishop the document which the Prince signed that evening when she wore the magic ring, and Giglio drank so much champagne. And the old Archbishop, taking out his eye-glasses, read, 'This is to give notice, that I, Giglio, only son of Savio, King of Paflagonia, hereby promise to marry the charming Barbara Griselda Countess Gruffanuff and widow of the late Jenkins Gruffanuff, Esq.'

'H'm,' says the Archbishop, 'the document is certainly a— a document.'

'Phoo,' says the Lord Chancellor, 'the signature is not in his Majesty's hand-writing.' Indeed, since his studies at Bosforo, Giglio had made an immense improvement in calligraphy.

'Is it your hand-writing, Giglio?' cries the Fairy Blackstick, with an awful severity of countenance.

'Y—y—y—es,' poor Giglio gasps out, 'I had quite forgotten the confounded paper: she can't mean to hold me by it. You old wretch, what will you take to let me off? Help the Queen, some one,—her Majesty has fainted.'

'Chop her head off!' ⎫ Exclaim the impetuous Hedzoff,
'Smother the old witch!' ⎬ the ardent Smith, and the
'Pitch her into the river!' ⎭ faithful Jones.

But Gruffanuff flung her arms round the Archbishop's neck, and bellowed out, 'Justice, justice, my Lord Chancellor!' so loudly, that her piercing shrieks caused everybody to pause. As for Rosalba, she was borne away lifeless by her ladies; and you may imagine the look of agony which Giglio cast toward that lovely being, as his hope, his joy, his darling, his all in all, was thus removed, and in her place the horrid old Gruffanuff rushed up to his side, and once more shrieked out, 'Justice, justice!'

'Won't you take that sum of money which Glumboso hid?' says Giglio, 'two hundred and eighteen thousand millions, or thereabouts. It's a handsome sum.'

'I will have that and you too!' says Gruffanuff.

'Let us throw the crown jewels into the bargain,' gasps out Giglio.

'I will wear them by my Giglio's side!' says Gruffanuff.

'Will half, three quarters, five sixths, nineteen twentieths of my kingdom do, Countess?' asks the trembling monarch.

'What were all Europe to me without *you*, my Giglio?' cries Gruff, kissing his hand.

'I won't, I can't, I shan't,—I'll resign the crown first,' shouts Giglio, tearing away his hand; but Gruff clung to it.

'I have a competency, my love,' she says, 'and with thee and a cottage thy Barbara will be happy.'

Giglio was half mad with rage by this time. 'I will not marry her,' says he. 'Oh, Fairy, Fairy, give me counsel!' And as he spoke he looked wildly round at the severe face of the Fairy Blackstick.

'"Why is Fairy Blackstick always advising me, and warning me to keep my word? Does she suppose that I am not a man of honour?"' said the Fairy, quoting Giglio's own haughty words. He quailed under the brightness of her eyes; he felt that there was no escape for him from that awful Inquisition.*

'Well Archbishop,' said he in a dreadful voice, that made his Grace start, 'since this Fairy has led me to the height of happiness but to dash me down into the depths of despair, since I am to lose Rosalba, let me at least keep my honour. Get up, Countess, and let us be married; I can keep my word, but I can die afterwards.'

'O dear Giglio,' cries Gruffanuff, skipping up, 'I knew, I knew I could trust thee—I knew that my Prince was the soul of honour. Jump into your carriages, ladies and gentlemen, and let us go to church at once; and as for dying, dear Giglio, no, no:—thou wilt forget that insignificant little chambermaid of a Queen—thou wilt live to be consoled by thy Barbara! She wishes to be a Queen, and not a Queen Dowager, my gracious Lord!' and hanging upon poor Giglio's arm, and leering and grinning in his face in the most disgusting manner, this old wretch tripped off in her white satin shoes, and jumped into the very carriage which had been got ready to convey Giglio and Rosalba to church. The cannons roared again, the bells pealed triple-bobmajors,* the people came out, flinging flowers upon the path of the royal bride and bridegroom, and Gruff looked out of the gilt coach window and bowed and grinned to them. Phoo! the horrid old wretch!

XIX

AND NOW WE COME TO THE LAST SCENE IN THE PANTOMIME

THE many ups and downs of her life had given the Princess Rosalba prodigious strength of mind, and that highly principled young woman presently recovered from her fainting-fit out of which Fairy Blackstick, by a precious essence which the Fairy always carried in her pocket, awakened her. Instead of tearing her hair, crying and bemoaning herself, and fainting again, as many young women would have done, Rosalba remembered that she owed an example of firmness to her subjects, and though she loved Giglio more than her life, was determined, as she told the Fairy, not to interfere between him and justice, or to cause him to break his royal word.

'I cannot marry him, but I shall love him always,' says she to Blackstick; 'I will go and be present at his marriage with the Countess, and sign the book, and wish them happy with all my heart. I will see, when I get home, whether I cannot make the new Queen some handsome presents. The Crim Tartary crown diamonds are uncommonly fine, and I shall never have any use for them. I will live and die unmarried like Queen Elizabeth,* and, of course, I shall leave my crown to Giglio when I quit this world. Let us go and see them married, my dear Fairy, let me say one last farewell to him; and then, if you please, I will return to my own dominions.'

So the Fairy kissed Rosalba with peculiar tenderness, and at once changed her wand into a very comfortable coach-and-four, with a steady coachman, and two respectable footmen behind, and the Fairy and Rosalba got into the coach, while Angelica and Bulbo entered after them. As for honest Bulbo, he was blubbering in the most pathetic manner, quite overcome by Rosalba's misfortune. She was touched by the honest fellow's sympathy, promised to restore to him the confiscated estates of Duke Padella his father, and created him, as he sat there in the coach, Prince, Highness, and First Grandee of the Crim Tartar Empire. The coach moved on, and, being a fairy coach, soon came up with the bridal procession.

Before the ceremony at church it was the custom in Paflagonia, as it is in other countries, for the bride and bridegroom to sign the Contract of Marriage, which was to be witnessed by the Chancellor, Minister, Lord Mayor, and principal officers of state. Now, as the royal palace was being painted and furnished anew, it was not ready for the reception of the King and his bride, who proposed at first to take up their residence at the Prince's palace, that one which Valoroso occupied when Angelica was born, and before he usurped the throne.

So the marriage party drove up to the palace: the dignitaries got out of their carriages and stood aside: poor Rosalba stepped out of her coach, supported by Bulbo, and stood almost fainting up against the railings so as to have a last look of her dear Giglio. As for Blackstick, she, according to her custom, had flown out of the coach window in some inscrutable manner, and was now standing at the palace door.

Giglio came up the steps with his horrible bride on his arm, looking as pale as if he was going to execution. He only frowned at the Fairy Blackstick—he was angry with her, and thought she came to insult his misery.

'Get out of the way, pray,' says Gruffanuff, haughtily. 'I wonder why you are always poking your nose into other people's affairs?'

'Are you determined to make this poor young man unhappy?' says Blackstick.

'To marry him, yes! What business is it of yours? Pray, madam, don't say "you" to a Queen,' cries Gruffanuff.

'You won't take the money he offered you?'

'No.'

'You won't let him off his bargain, though you know you cheated him when you made him sign the paper?'

'Impudence! Policemen, remove this woman!' cries Gruffanuff. And the policemen were rushing forward, but with a wave of her wand the Fairy struck them all like so many statues in their places.

'You won't take anything in exchange for your bond, Mrs. Gruffanuff,' cries the Fairy, with awful severity. 'I speak for the last time.'

'No!' shrieks Gruffanuff, stamping with her foot. 'I'll have my husband—my husband—my husband!'

'You SHALL HAVE YOUR HUSBAND!' the Fairy Blackstick cried; and advancing a step laid her hand upon the nose of the KNOCKER.

As she touched it, the brass nose seemed to elongate, the open mouth opened still wider, and uttered a roar which made everybody start. The eyes rolled wildly, the arms and legs uncurled themselves, writhed about, and seemed to lengthen with each twist; the knocker expanded into a figure in yellow livery, six feet high; the screws by which it was fixed to the door unloosed themselves, and JENKINS GRUFFANUFF once more trod the threshold off which he had been lifted more than twenty years ago!

'Master's not at home,' says Jenkins, just in his old voice; and Mrs. Jenkins, giving a dreadful *youp*, fell down in a fit, in which nobody minded her.

For everybody was shouting, 'Huzzay! huzzay!' 'Hip, hip, hurray!' 'Long live the King and Queen!' 'Were such things ever seen?' 'No, never, never, never!' 'The Fairy Blackstick for ever!'

The bells were ringing double peals, the guns roaring and banging most prodigiously. Bulbo was embracing everybody; the Lord Chancellor was flinging up his wig and shouting like a madman; Hedzoff had got the Archbishop round the waist, and they were dancing a jig for joy; and as for Giglio I leave you to imagine what *he* was doing, and if he kissed Rosalba once, twice—twenty thousand times, I'm sure I don't think he was wrong.

So Gruffanuff opened the hall door with a low bow, just as he had been accustomed to do, and they all went in and signed the book, and then they went to church and were married, and the Fairy Blackstick sailed away on her cane, and was never more heard of in Paflagonia.

AND HERE ENDS THE FIRE-SIDE PANTOMIME.

GEORGE MacDONALD

The Golden Key

There was a boy who used to sit in the twilight and listen to his great-aunt's stories.

She told him that if he could reach the place where the end of the rainbow stands he would find there a golden key.

'And what is the key for?' the boy would ask. 'What is it the key of? What will it open?'

'That nobody knows,' his aunt would reply. 'He has to find that out.'

'I suppose, being gold,' the boy once said, thoughtfully, 'that I could get a good deal of money for it if I sold it.'

'Better never find it than sell it,' returned his aunt.

And then the boy went to bed and dreamed about the golden key.

Now all that his great-aunt told the boy about the golden key would have been nonsense, had it not been that their little house stood on the borders of Fairyland. For it is perfectly well known that out of Fairyland nobody can ever find where the rainbow stands. The creature takes such good care of its golden key, always flitting from place to place, lest anyone should find it! But in Fairyland it is quite different. Things that look real in this country look very thin indeed in Fairyland, while some of the things that here cannot stand still for a moment, will not move there. So it was not in the least absurd of the old lady to tell her nephew such things about the golden key.

'Did you ever know anybody find it?' he asked, one evening.

'Yes. Your father, I believe, found it.'

'And what did he do with it, can you tell me?'

'He never told me.'

'What was it like?'

'He never showed it to me.'

'How does a new key come there always?'

'I don't know. There it is.'

'Perhaps it is the rainbow's egg.'

'Perhaps it is. You will be a happy boy if you find the nest.'
'Perhaps it comes tumbling down the rainbow from the sky.'
'Perhaps it does.'

One evening, in summer, he went into his own room, and stood at the lattice-window, and gazed into the forest which fringed the outskirts of Fairyland. It came close up to his great-aunt's garden, and, indeed, sent some straggling trees into it. The forest lay to the east, and the sun, which was setting behind the cottage, looked straight into the dark wood with his level red eye. The trees were all old, and had few branches below, so that the sun could see a great way into the forest; and the boy, being keen-sighted, could see almost as far as the sun. The trunks stood like rows of red columns in the shine of the red sun, and he could see down aisle after aisle in the vanishing distance. And as he gazed into the forest he began to feel as if the trees were all waiting for him, and had something they could not go on with till he came to them. But he was hungry, and wanted his supper. So he lingered.

Suddenly, far among the trees, as far as the sun could shine, he saw a glorious thing. It was the end of a rainbow, large and brilliant. He could count all the seven colours, and could see shade after shade beyond the violet; while before the red stood a colour he had never seen before. Only the spring of the rainbow-arch was visible. He could see nothing of it above the trees.

'The golden key!' he said to himself, and darted out of the house, and into the wood. He had not gone far before the sun set. But the rainbow only glowed the brighter. For the rainbow of Fairyland is not dependent upon the sun as ours is. The trees welcomed him. The bushes made way for him. The rainbow grew larger and brighter; and at length he found himself within two trees of it.

It was a grand sight, burning away there in silence, with its gorgeous, its lovely, its delicate colours, each distinct, all combining. He could now see a great deal more of it. It rose high into the blue heavens, but bent so little that he could not tell how high the crown of the arch must reach. It was still only a small portion of a huge bow.

He stood gazing at it till he forgot himself with delight—even forgot the key which he had come to seek. And as he stood it grew more wonderful still. For in each of the colours, which was as large as the column of a church, he could faintly see beautiful forms slowly ascending as if by the steps of a winding stair. The forms appeared irregularly—now one, now many, now several, now none—men and women and children—all different, all beautiful.

He drew nearer to the rainbow. It vanished. He started back a step in dismay. It was there again, as beautiful as ever. So he contented himself with standing as near it as he might, and watching the forms that ascended the glorious colours towards the unknown height of the arch, which did not end abruptly, but faded away in the blue air, so gradually that he could not say where it ceased.

When the thought of the golden key returned, the boy very wisely proceeded to mark out in his mind the space covered by the foundation of the rainbow, in order that he might know where to search, should the rainbow disappear. It was based chiefly upon a bed of moss.

Meantime it had grown quite dark in the wood. The rainbow alone was visible by its own light. But the moment the moon rose the rainbow vanished. Nor could any change of place restore the vision to the boy's eyes. So he threw himself down upon the mossy bed, to wait till the sunlight would give him a chance of finding the key. There he fell fast asleep.

When he woke in the morning the sun was looking straight into his eyes. He turned away from it, and the same moment saw a brilliant little thing lying on the moss within a foot of his face. It was the golden key. The pipe of it was of plain gold, as bright as gold could be. The handle was curiously wrought and set with sapphires. In a terror of delight he put out his hand and took it, and had it.

He lay for a while, turning it over and over, and feeding his eyes upon its beauty. Then he jumped to his feet, remembering that the pretty little thing was of no use to him yet. Where was the lock to which the key belonged? It must be somewhere, for how could anybody be so silly as make a key for which there was no lock? Where should he go to look for it? He gazed about him, up into the air, down to the earth, but saw no keyhole in the clouds, in the grass, or in the trees.

Just as he began to grow disconsolate, however, he saw something glimmering in the wood. It was a mere glimmer that he saw, but he took it for a glimmer of a rainbow, and went towards it.—And now I will go back to the borders of the forest.

Not far from the house where the boy had lived, there was another house, the owner of which was a merchant, who was much away from home. He had lost his wife some years before, and had only one child, a little girl, whom he left to the charge of two servants, who were very idle and careless. So she was neglected and left untidy, and was sometimes ill-used besides.

Now it is well known that the little creatures commonly called fairies, though there are many different kinds of fairies in Fairyland, have an exceeding dislike to untidiness.* Indeed, they are quite spiteful to slovenly people. Being used to all the lovely ways of the trees and flowers, and to the neatness of the birds and all woodland creatures, it makes them feel miserable, even in their deep woods and on their grassy carpets, to think that within the same moonlight lies a dirty, uncomfortable, slovenly house. And this makes them angry with the people who live in it, and they would gladly drive them out of the world if they could. They want the whole earth nice and clean. So they pinch the maids black and blue, and play them all manner of uncomfortable tricks.

But this house was quite a shame, and the fairies in the forest could not endure it. They tried everything on the maids without effect, and at last resolved upon making a clean riddance, beginning with the child. They ought to have known that it was not her fault, but they have little principle and much mischief in them, and they thought that if they got rid of her the maids would be sure to be turned away.

So one evening, the poor little girl having been put to bed early, before the sun was down, the servants went off to the village, locking the door behind them. The child did not know she was alone, and lay contentedly looking out of her window towards the forest, of which, however, she could not see much, because of the ivy and other creeping plants which had straggled across her window. All at once she saw an ape making faces at her out of the mirror, and the heads carved upon a great old wardrobe grinning fearfully. Then two old spider-legged chairs came forward into the middle of the room, and began to dance a queer, old-fashioned dance. This set her laughing, and she forgot the ape and the grinning heads. So the fairies saw they had made a mistake, and sent the chairs back to their places. But they knew that she had been reading the story of Silverhair* all day. So the next moment she heard the voices of the three bears upon the stair, big voice, middle voice, and little voice, and she heard their soft, heavy tread, as if they had had stockings over their boots, coming nearer and nearer to the door of her room, till she could bear it no longer. She did just as Silverhair did, and as the fairies wanted her to do: she darted to the window, pulled it open, got upon the ivy, and so scrambled to the ground. She then fled to the forest as fast as she could run.

Now, although she did not know it, this was the very best way she could have gone; for nothing is ever so mischievous in its own place as it is out of it; and besides, these mischievous creatures were only the children of Fairyland, as it were, and there are many other beings there as well; and if a wanderer gets in among them, the good ones will always help him more than the evil ones will be able to hurt him.

The sun was now set, and the darkness coming on, but the child thought of no danger but the bears behind her. If she had looked round, however, she would have seen that she was followed by a very different creature from a bear. It was a curious creature, made like a fish, but covered, instead of scales, with feathers of all colours, sparkling like those of a humming-bird. It had fins, not wings, and swam through the air as a fish does through the water. Its head was like the head of a small owl.

After running a long way, and as the last of the light was disappearing, she passed under a tree with drooping branches. It dropped its branches to the ground all about her, and caught her as in a trap. She struggled to get out, but the branches pressed her closer and closer to the trunk. She was in great terror and distress, when the air-fish, swimming into the thicket of branches, began tearing them with its beak. They loosened their hold at once, and the creature went on attacking them, till at length they let the child go. Then the air-fish came from behind her, and swam on in front, glittering and sparkling all lovely colours; and she followed.

It led her gently along till all at once it swam in at a cottage-door. The child followed still. There was a bright fire in the middle of the floor, upon which stood a pot without a lid, full of water that boiled and bubbled furiously. The air-fish swam straight to the pot and into the boiling water, where it lay quiet. A beautiful woman rose from the opposite side of the fire and came to meet the girl. She took her up in her arms, and said,—

'Ah, you are come at last! I have been looking for you a long time.'

She sat down with her on her lap, and there the girl sat staring at her. She had never seen anything so beautiful. She was tall and strong, with white arms and neck, and a delicate flush on her face. The child could not tell what was the colour of her hair, but could not help thinking it had a tinge of dark green. She had not one ornament upon her, but she looked as if she had just put off quantities of diamonds and emeralds. Yet here she was in the simplest, poorest little cottage, where she was evidently at home. She was dressed in shining green.

The girl looked at the lady, and the lady looked at the girl.

'What is your name?' asked the lady.

'The servants always call me Tangle.'

'Ah, that was because your hair was so untidy. But that was their fault, the naughty women! Still it is a pretty name, and I will call you Tangle too. You must not mind my asking you questions, for you may ask me the same questions, every one of them, and any others that you like. How old are you?'

'Ten,' answered Tangle.

'You don't look like it,' said the lady.

'How old are you, please?' returned Tangle.

'Thousands of years old,' answered the lady.

'You don't look like it,' said Tangle.

'Don't I? I think I do. Don't you see how beautiful I am?'

And her great blue eyes looked down on the little Tangle, as if all the stars in the sky were melted in them to make their brightness.

'Ah! but,' said Tangle, 'when people live long they grow old. At least I always thought so.'

'I have no time to grow old,' said the lady. 'I am too busy for that. It is very idle to grow old.—But I cannot have my little girl so untidy. Do you know I can't find a clean spot on your face to kiss?'

'Perhaps,' suggested Tangle, feeling ashamed, but not too much so to say a word for herself—'perhaps that is because the tree made me cry so.'

'My poor darling!' said the lady, looking now as if the moon were melted in her eyes, and kissing her little face, dirty as it was, 'the naughty tree must suffer for making a girl cry.'

'And what is your name, please?' asked Tangle.

'Grandmother,' answered the lady.

'Is it really?'

'Yes indeed. I never tell stories, even in fun.'

'How good of you!'

'I couldn't if I tried. It would come true if I said it, and then I should be punished enough.'

And she smiled like the sun through a summer-shower.

'But now,' she went on, 'I must get you washed and dressed, and then we shall have some supper.'

'Oh! I had supper long ago,' said Tangle.

'Yes, indeed you had,' answered the lady—'three years ago. You don't know that it is three years since you ran away from the bears. You are thirteen and more now.'

Tangle could only stare. She felt quite sure it was true.

'You will not be afraid of anything I do with you—will you?' said the lady.

'I will try very hard not to be; but I can't be certain, you know,' replied Tangle.

'I like your saying so, and I shall be quite satisfied,' answered the lady.

She took off the girl's night-gown, rose with her in her arms, and going to the wall of the cottage, opened a door. Then Tangle saw a deep tank, the sides of which were filled with green plants, which had flowers of all colours. There was a roof over it like the roof of the cottage. It was filled with beautiful clear water, in which swam a multitude of such fishes as the one that had led her to the cottage. It was the light their colours gave that showed the place in which they were.

The lady spoke some words Tangle could not understand, and threw her into the tank.

The fishes came crowding about her. Two or three of them got under her head and kept it up. The rest of them rubbed themselves all over her, and with their wet feathers washed her quite clean. Then the lady, who had been looking on all the time, spoke again; whereupon some thirty or forty of the fishes rose out of the water underneath Tangle, and so bore her up to the arms the lady held out to take her. She carried her back to the fire, and, having dried her well, opened a chest, and taking out the finest linen garments, smelling of grass and lavender, put them upon her, and over all a green dress, just like her own, shining like hers, and going into just such lovely folds from the waist, where it was tied with a brown cord, to her bare feet.

'Won't you give me a pair of shoes too, grandmother?' said Tangle.

'No, my dear; no shoes. Look here. I wear no shoes.'

So saying she lifted her dress a little, and there were the loveliest white feet, but no shoes. Then Tangle was content to go without shoes too. And the lady sat down with her again, and combed her hair, and brushed it, and then left it to dry while she got the supper.

First she got bread out of one hole in the wall; then milk out of another; then several kinds of fruit out of a third; and then she went to the pot on the fire, and took out the fish, now nicely cooked, and, as soon as she had pulled off its feathered skin, ready to be eaten.

'But,' exclaimed Tangle. And she stared at the fish, and could say no more.

'I know what you mean,' returned the lady. 'You do not like to eat the messenger that brought you home. But it is the kindest return you can make. The creature was afraid to go until it saw me put the pot on, and heard me promise it should be boiled the moment it returned with you. Then it darted out of the door at once. You saw it go into the pot of itself the moment it entered, did you not?'

'I did,' answered Tangle, 'and I thought it very strange; but then I saw you, and forgot all about the fish.'

'In Fairyland,' resumed the lady, as they sat down to the table, 'the ambition of the animals is to be eaten by the people; for that is their highest end in that condition. But they are not therefore destroyed. Out of that pot comes something more than the dead fish, you will see.'

Tangle now remarked that the lid was on the pot. But the lady took no further notice of it till they had eaten the fish, which Tangle found nicer than any fish she had ever tasted before. It was as white as snow, and as delicate as cream. And the moment she had swallowed a mouthful of it, a change she could not describe began to take place in her. She heard a murmuring all about her, which became more and more articulate, and at length, as she went on eating, grew intelligible. By the time she had finished her share, the sounds of all the animals in the forest came crowding through the door to her ears; for the door still stood wide open, though it was pitch-dark outside; and they were no longer sounds only; they were speech, and speech that she could understand. She could tell what the insects in the cottage were saying to each other too. She had even a suspicion that the trees and flowers all about the cottage were holding midnight communications with each other; but what they said she could not hear.

As soon as the fish was eaten, the lady went to the fire and took the lid off the pot. A lovely little creature in human shape, with large white wings, rose out of it, and flew round and round the roof of the cottage; then dropped, fluttering, and nestled in the lap of the lady. She spoke to it some strange words, carried it to the door, and threw it out into the darkness. Tangle heard the flapping of its wings die away in the distance.

'Now have we done the fish any harm?' she said, returning.

'No,' answered Tangle, 'I do not think we have. I should not mind eating one every day.'

'They must wait their time, like you and me too, my little Tangle.'

And she smiled a smile which the sadness in it made more lovely.

'But,' she continued, 'I think we may have one for supper to-morrow.'

So saying she went to the door of the tank, and spoke; and now Tangle understood her perfectly.

'I want one of you,' she said,—'the wisest.'

Thereupon the fishes got together in the middle of the tank, with their heads forming a circle above the water, and their tails a larger circle beneath it. They were holding a council, in which their relative wisdom should be determined. At length one of them flew up into the lady's hand, looking lively and ready.

'You know where the rainbow stands?' she asked.

'Yes, mother, quite well,' answered the fish.

'Bring home a young man you will find there, who does not know where to go.'

The fish was out of the door in a moment. Then the lady told Tangle it was time to go to bed; and, opening another door in the side of the cottage, showed her a little arbour, cool and green, with a bed of purple heath growing in it, upon which she threw a large wrapper made of the feathered skins of the wise fishes, shining gorgeous in the firelight. Tangle was soon lost in the strangest, loveliest dreams. And the beautiful lady was in every one of her dreams.

In the morning she woke to the rustling of leaves over her head, and the sound of running water. But, to her surprise, she could find no door—nothing but the moss-grown wall of the cottage. So she crept through an opening in the arbour, and stood in the forest. Then she bathed in a stream that ran merrily through the trees, and felt happier; for having once been in her grandmother's pond, she must be clean and tidy ever after; and, having put on her green dress, felt like a lady.

She spent that day in the wood, listening to the birds and beasts and creeping things. She understood all that they said, though she could not repeat a word of it; and every kind had a different language, while there was a common though more limited understanding between all the inhabitants of the forest. She saw nothing of the beautiful lady, but she felt that she was near her all the time; and she took care not to go out of sight of the cottage. It was round, like a snow-hut or a wigwam; and she could see neither door nor window in it. The fact was, it had no windows; and though it was full of doors, they all opened from the inside, and could not even be seen from the outside.

She was standing at the foot of a tree in the twilight, listening to a quarrel between a mole and a squirrel, in which the mole told the squirrel that the tail was the best of him, and the squirrel called the mole Spade-fists, when, the darkness having deepened around her, she became aware of something shining in her face, and looking round, saw that the door of the cottage was open, and the red light of the fire flowing from it like a river through the darkness. She left Mole and Squirrel to settle matters as they might, and darted off to the cottage. Entering, she found the pot boiling on the fire, and the grand, lovely lady sitting on the other side of it.

'I've been watching you all day,' said the lady. 'You should have something to eat by-and-by, but we must wait till our supper comes home.'

She took Tangle on her knee, and began to sing to her—such songs as made her wish she could listen to them for ever. But at length in rushed the shining fish, and snuggled down in the pot. It was followed by a youth who had outgrown his worn garments. His face was ruddy with health, and in his hand he carried a little jewel, which sparkled in the firelight.

The first words the lady said were,—

'What is that in your hand, Mossy?'

Now Mossy was the name his companions had given him, because he had a favourite stone covered with moss, on which he used to sit whole days reading; and they said the moss had begun to grow upon him too.

Mossy held out his hand. The moment the lady saw that it was the golden key, she rose from her chair, kissed Mossy on the forehead, made him sit down on her seat, and stood before him like a servant. Mossy could not bear this, and rose at once. But the lady begged him, with tears in her beautiful eyes, to sit, and let her wait on him.

'But you are a great, splendid, beautiful lady,' said Mossy.

'Yes, I am. But I work all day long—that is my pleasure; and you will have to leave me so soon!'

'How do you know that, if you please, madam?' asked Mossy.

'Because you have got the golden key.'

'But I don't know what it is for. I can't find the key-hole. Will you tell me what to do?'

'You must look for the key-hole. That is your work. I cannot help you. I can only tell you that if you look for it you will find it.'

'What kind of box will it open? What is there inside?'

'I do not know. I dream about it, but I know nothing.'

'Must I go at once?'

'You may stop here to-night, and have some of my supper. But you must go in the morning. All I can do for you is to give you clothes. Here is a girl called Tangle, whom you must take with you.'

'That *will* be nice,' said Mossy.

'No, no!' said Tangle. 'I don't want to leave you, please, grandmother.'

'You must go with him, Tangle. I am sorry to lose you, but it will be the best thing for you. Even the fishes, you see, have to go into the pot, and then out into the dark. If you fall in with the Old Man of the Sea, mind you ask him whether he has not got some more fishes ready for me. My tank is getting thin.'

So saying, she took the fish from the pot, and put the lid on as before. They sat down and ate the fish, and then the winged creature rose from the pot, circled the roof, and settled down on the lady's lap. She talked to it, carried it to the door, and threw it out into the dark. They heard the flap of its wings die away in the distance.

The lady then showed Mossy into just such another chamber as that of Tangle; and in the morning he found a suit of clothes laid beside him. He looked very handsome in them. But the wearer of Grandmother's clothes never thinks about how he or she looks, but thinks always how handsome other people are.

Tangle was unwilling to go.

'Why should I leave you? I don't know the young man,' she said to the lady.

'I am never allowed to keep my children long. You need not go with him except you please, but you must go some day; and I should like you to go with him, for he has the golden key. No girl need be afraid to go with a youth that has the golden key. You will take care of her, Mossy, will you not?'

'That I will,' said Mossy.

And Tangle cast a glance at him, and thought she should like to go with him.

'And,' said the lady, 'if you should lose each other as you go through the—the—I never can remember the name of that country,—do not be afraid, but go on and on.'

She kissed Tangle on the mouth and Mossy on the forehead, led them to the door, and waved her hand eastward. Mossy and Tangle took each other's hand and walked away into the depth of the forest. In his right hand Mossy held the golden key.

They wandered thus a long way, with endless amusement from the talk of the animals. They soon learned enough of their language to ask them necessary questions. The squirrels were always friendly, and gave them nuts out of their own hoards; but the bees were selfish and rude, justifying themselves on the ground that Tangle and Mossy were not subjects of their queen, and charity must begin at home, though indeed they had not one drone in their poorhouse at the time. Even the blinking moles would fetch them an earth-nut or a truffle now and then, talking as if their mouths, as well as their eyes and ears, were full of cotton wool, or their own velvety fur. By the time they got out of the forest they were very fond of each other, and Tangle was not the least sorry that her grandmother had sent her away with Mossy.

At length the trees grew smaller, and stood farther apart, and the ground began to rise, and it got more and more steep, till the trees were all left behind, and the two were climbing a narrow path with rocks on each side. Suddenly they came upon a rude doorway, by which they entered a narrow gallery cut in the rock. It grew darker and darker, till it was pitch-dark, and they had to feel their way. At length the light began to return, and at last they came out upon a narrow path on the face of a lofty precipice. This path went winding down the rock to a wide plain, circular in shape, and surrounded on all sides by mountains. Those opposite to them were a great way off, and towered to an awful height, shooting up sharp, blue, ice-enamelled pinnacles. An utter silence reigned where they stood. Not even the sound of water reached them.

Looking down, they could not tell whether the valley below was a grassy plain or a great still lake. They had never seen any space look like it. The way to it was difficult and dangerous, but down the narrow path they went, and reached the bottom in safety. They found it composed of smooth, light-coloured sandstone, undulating in parts,

Mossy and Tangle in the Wood

but mostly level. It was no wonder to them now that they had not been able to tell what it was, for this surface was everywhere crowded with shadows. It was a sea of shadows. The mass was chiefly made up of the shadows of leaves innumerable, of all lovely and imaginative forms, waving to and fro, floating and quivering in the breath of a breeze whose motion was unfelt, whose sound was unheard. No forests clothed the mountain-sides, no trees were anywhere to be seen, and yet the shadows of the leaves, branches, and stems of all various trees covered the valley as far as their eyes could reach. They soon spied the shadows of flowers mingled with those of the leaves, and now and then the shadow of a bird with open beak, and throat distended with song. At times would appear the forms of strange, graceful creatures, running up and down the shadow-boles and along the branches, to disappear in the wind-tossed foliage. As they walked they waded knee-deep in the lovely lake. For the shadows were not merely lying on the surface of the ground, but heaped above it like substantial forms of darkness, as if they had been cast upon a thousand different planes of the air. Tangle and Mossy often lifted their heads and gazed upwards to descry whence the shadows came; but they could see nothing more than a bright mist spread above them, higher than the tops of the mountains, which stood clear against it. No forests, no leaves, no birds were visible.

After a while, they reached more open spaces, where the shadows were thinner; and came even to portions over which shadows only flitted, leaving them clear for such as might follow. Now a wonderful form, half bird-like and half human, would float across on outspread sailing pinions. Anon an exquisite shadow group of gambolling children would be followed by the loveliest female form, and that again by the grand stride of a Titanic shape, each disappearing in the surrounding press of shadowy foliage. Sometimes a profile of unspeakable beauty or grandeur would appear for a moment and vanish. Sometimes they seemed lovers that passed linked arm in arm, sometimes father and son, sometimes brothers in loving contest, sometimes sisters entwined in gracefullest community of complex form. Sometimes wild horses would tear across, free, or bestrode by noble shadows of ruling men. But some of the things which pleased them most they never knew how to describe.

About the middle of the plain they sat down to rest in the heart of a heap of shadows. After sitting for a while, each, looking up, saw the other in tears; they were each longing after the country whence shadows fell.

'We *must* find the country from which the shadows come,' said Mossy.

'We must, dear Mossy,' responded Tangle. 'What if your golden key should be the key to *it*?'

'Ah! that would be grand,' returned Mossy.—'But we must rest here for a little, and then we shall be able to cross the plain before night.'

So he lay down on the ground, and about him on every side, and over his head, was the constant play of the wonderful shadows. He could look through them, and see the one behind the other, till they mixed in a mass of darkness. Tangle, too, lay admiring, and wondering, and longing after the country whence the shadows came. When they were rested they rose and pursued their journey.

How long they were in crossing this plain I cannot tell; but before night Mossy's hair was streaked with grey, and Tangle had got wrinkles on her forehead.

As evening drew on, the shadows fell deeper and rose higher. At length they reached a place where they rose above their heads, and made all dark around them. Then they took hold of each other's hand, and walked on in silence and in some dismay. They felt the gathering darkness, and something strangely solemn besides, and the beauty of the shadows ceased to delight them. All at once Tangle found that she had not hold of Mossy's hand, though when she lost it she could not tell.

'Mossy, Mossy!' she cried aloud in terror.

But no Mossy replied.

A moment after, the shadows sank to her feet, and down under her feet, and the mountains rose before her. She turned towards the gloomy region she had left, and called once more upon Mossy. There the gloom lay tossing and heaving, a dark, stormy, foamless sea of shadows, but no Mossy rose out of it, or came climbing up the hill on which she stood. She threw herself down and wept in despair.

Suddenly she remembered that the beautiful lady had told them, if they lost each other in a country of which she could not remember the name, they were not to be afraid, but to go straight on.

'And besides,' she said to herself, 'Mossy has the golden key, and so no harm will come to him, I do believe.'

She rose from the ground, and went on.

Before long she arrived at a precipice, in the face of which a stair was cut. When she had ascended half-way, the stair ceased, and the path led straight into the mountain. She was afraid to enter, and turning again towards the stair, grew giddy at sight of the depth beneath her, and was forced to throw herself down in the mouth of the cave.

When she opened her eyes, she saw a beautiful little creature with wings standing beside her, waiting.

'I know you,' said Tangle. 'You are my fish.'

'Yes. But I am a fish no longer. I am an aëranth* now.'

'What is that?' asked Tangle.

'What you see I am,' answered the shape. 'And I am come to lead you through the mountain.'

'Oh! thank you, dear fish—aëranth, I mean,' returned Tangle, rising.

Thereupon the aëranth took to his wings, and flew on through the long, narrow passage, reminding Tangle very much of the way he had swum on before her when he was a fish. And the moment his white wings moved, they began to throw off a continuous shower of sparks of all colours, which lighted up the passage before them.—All at once he vanished, and Tangle heard a low, sweet sound, quite different from the rush and crackle of his wings. Before her was an open arch, and through it came light, mixed with the sound of sea-waves.

She hurried out, and fell, tired and happy, upon the yellow sand of the shore. There she lay, half asleep with weariness and rest, listening to the low plash and retreat of the tiny waves, which seemed ever enticing the land to leave off being land, and become sea. And as she lay, her eyes were fixed upon the foot of a great rainbow standing far away against the sky on the other side of the sea. At length she fell fast asleep.

When she awoke, she saw an old man with long white hair down to his shoulders, leaning upon a stick covered with green buds, and so bending over her.

'What do you want here, beautiful woman?' he said.

'Am I beautiful? I am so glad!' answered Tangle, rising. 'My grandmother is beautiful.'

'Yes. But what do you want?' he repeated, kindly.

'I think I want you. Are you not the Old Man of the Sea?'

'I am.'

'Then grandmother says, have you any more fishes ready for her?'

'We will go and see, my dear,' answered the old man, speaking yet more kindly than before. 'And I can do something for you, can I not?'

'Yes—show me the way up to the country from which the shadows fall,' said Tangle.

For there she hoped to find Mossy again.

'Ah! indeed, that would be worth doing,' said the old man. 'But I cannot, for I do not know the way myself. But I will send you to the Old Man of the Earth. Perhaps he can tell you. He is much older than I am.'

Leaning on his staff, he conducted her along the shore to a steep rock, that looked like a petrified ship turned upside down. The door of it was the rudder of a great vessel, ages ago at the bottom of the sea. Immediately within the door was a stair in the rock, down which the old man went, and Tangle followed. At the bottom the old man had his house, and there he lived.

As soon as she entered it, Tangle heard a strange noise, unlike anything she had ever heard before. She soon found that it was the fishes talking. She tried to understand what they said; but their speech was so old-fashioned, and rude, and undefined, that she could not make much of it.

'I will go and see about those fishes for my daughter,' said the Old Man of the Sea.

And moving a slide in the wall of his house, he first looked out, and then tapped upon a thick piece of crystal that filled the round opening. Tangle came up behind him, and peeping through the window into the heart of the deep green ocean, saw the most curious creatures, some very ugly, all very odd, and with especially queer mouths, swimming about everywhere, above and below, but all coming towards the window in answer to the tap of the Old Man of the Sea.* Only a few could get their mouths against the glass; but those who were floating miles away yet turned their heads towards it. The Old Man looked through the whole flock carefully for some minutes, and then turning to Tangle, said,—

'I am sorry I have not got one ready yet. I want more time than she does. But I will send some as soon as I can.'

He then shut the slide.

Presently a great noise arose in the sea. The old man opened the slide again, and tapped on the glass, whereupon the fishes were all as still as sleep.

'They were only talking about you,' he said. 'And they do speak such nonsense!—To-morrow,' he continued, 'I must show you the way to the Old Man of the Earth. He lives a long way from here.'

'Do let me go at once,' said Tangle.

'No. That is not possible. You must come this way first.'

He led her to a hole in the wall, which she had not observed before. It was covered with the green leaves and white blossoms of a creeping plant.

'Only white-blossoming plants can grow under the sea,' said the old man. 'In there you will find a bath, in which you must lie till I call you.'

Tangle went in, and found a smaller room or cave, in the further corner of which was a great basin hollowed out of a rock, and half-full of the clearest sea-water. Little streams were constantly running into it from cracks in the wall of the cavern. It was polished quite smooth inside, and had a carpet of yellow sand in the bottom of it. Large green leaves and white flowers of various plants crowded up and over it, draping and covering it almost entirely.

No sooner was she undressed and lying in the bath, than she began to feel as if the water were sinking into her, and she were receiving all the good of sleep without undergoing its forgetfulness. She felt the good coming all the time. And she grew quite happier and more hopeful than she had been since she lost Mossy. But she could not help thinking how very sad it was for a poor old man to live there all alone, and have to take care of a whole seaful of stupid and riotous fishes.

After about an hour, as she thought, she heard his voice calling her, and rose out of the bath. All the fatigue and aching of her long journey had vanished. She was as whole, and strong, and well as if she had slept for seven days.

Returning to the opening that led into the other part of the house, she started back with amusement, for through it she saw the form of a grand man, with majestic and beautiful face, waiting for her.

'Come,' he said; 'I see you are ready.'

She entered with reverence.

'Where is the Old Man of the Sea?' she asked humbly.

'There is no one here but me,' he answered, smiling. 'Some people call me the Old Man of the Sea. Others have another name for me, and are terribly frightened when they meet me taking a walk by the shore. Therefore I avoid being seen by them, for they are so afraid, that they never see what I really am. You see me now.—But I must show you the way to the Old Man of the Earth.'

He led her into the cave where the bath was, and there she saw, in the opposite corner, a second opening in the rock.

'Go down that stair, and it will bring you to him,' said the Old Man of the Sea.

With humble thanks Tangle took her leave. She went down the winding-stair, till she began to fear there was no end to it. Still down and down it went, rough and broken, with springs of water bursting out of the rocks and running down the steps beside her. It was quite dark about her, and yet she could see. For after being in that bath, people's eyes always give out a light they can see by. There were no creeping things in the way. All was safe and pleasant though so dark and damp and deep.

At last there was not one step more, and she found herself in a glimmering cave. On a stone in the middle of it sat a figure with its back towards her—the figure of an old man bent double with age. From behind she could see his white beard spread out on the rocky floor in front of him. He did not move as she entered, so she passed round that she might stand before him and speak to him. The moment she looked in his face, she saw that he was a youth of marvellous beauty. He sat entranced with the delight of what he beheld in a mirror of something like silver, which lay on the floor at his feet, and which from behind she had taken for his white beard. He sat on, heedless of her presence, pale with the joy of his vision. She stood and watched him. At length, all trembling, she spoke. But her voice made no sound. Yet the youth lifted his head. He showed no surprise, however, at seeing her—only smiled a welcome.

'Are you the Old Man of the Earth?' Tangle had said.

And the youth answered, and Tangle heard him, though not with her ears:—

'I am. What can I do for you?'

'Tell me the way to the country whence the shadows fall.'

'Ah! that I do not know. I only dream about it myself. I see its shadows sometimes in my mirror: the way to it I do not know. But I think the Old Man of the Fire must know. He is much older than I am. He is the oldest man of all.'

'Where does he live?'

'I will show you the way to his place. I never saw him myself.'

So saying, the young man rose, and then stood for a while gazing at Tangle.

'I wish I could see that country too,' he said, 'but I must mind my work.'

He led her to the side of the cave, and told her to lay her ear against the wall.

'What do you hear?' he asked.

'I hear,' answered Tangle, 'the sound of a great water running inside the rock.'

'That river runs down to the dwelling of the oldest man of all—the Old Man of the Fire. I wish I could go to see him. But I must mind my work. That river is the only way to him.'

Then the Old Man of the Earth stooped over the floor of the cave, raised a huge stone from it, and left it leaning. It disclosed a great hole that went plumb-down.

'That is the way,' he said.

'But there are no stairs.'

'You must throw yourself in. There is no other way.'

She turned and looked him full in the face—stood so for a whole minute, as she thought: it was a whole year—then threw herself headlong into the hole.

When she came to herself, she found herself gliding down fast and deep. Her head was under water, but that did not signify, for, when she thought about it, she could not remember that she had breathed once since her bath in the cave of the Old Man of the Sea. When she lifted up her head a sudden and fierce heat struck her, and she sank it again instantly, and went sweeping on.

Gradually the stream grew shallower. At length she could hardly keep her head under. Then the water could carry her no farther. She rose from the channel, and went step for step down the burning descent. The water ceased altogether. The heat was terrible. She felt scorched to the bone, but it did not touch her strength. It grew hotter and hotter. She said, 'I can bear it no longer.' Yet she went on.

At the long last, the stair ended at a rude archway in an all but glowing rock. Through this archway Tangle fell exhausted into a cool mossy cave. The floor and walls were covered with moss—green, soft, and damp. A little stream spouted from a rent in the rock and fell into a basin of moss. She plunged her face into it and drank. Then she lifted her head and looked around. Then she rose and looked again. She saw no one in the cave. But the moment she stood upright she had a marvellous sense that she was in the secret of the earth and all its ways. Everything she had seen, or learned from books; all that her grandmother had said or sung to her; all the talk of the beasts, birds, and fishes; all that had happened to her on her journey with Mossy, and since then in the heart of the earth with the Old man and the Older man—all was plain: she understood it all, and saw that everything meant the same thing, though she could not have put it into words again.

The next moment she descried, in a corner of the cave, a little naked child, sitting on the moss. He was playing with balls of various colours and sizes, which he disposed in strange figures upon the floor beside him. And now Tangle felt that there was something in her knowledge which was not in her understanding. For she knew there must be an infinite meaning in the change and sequence and individual forms of the figures into which the child arranged the balls, as well as in the varied harmonies of their colours, but what it all meant she could not tell.[1] He went on busily, tirelessly, playing his solitary game, without looking up, or seeming to know that there was a stranger in his deep-withdrawn cell. Diligently as a lace-maker shifts her bobbins,* he shifted and arranged his balls. Flashes of meaning would now pass from them to Tangle, and now again all would be not merely obscure, but utterly dark. She stood looking for a long time, for there was fascination in the sight; and the longer she looked, the more an indescribable vague intelligence went on rousing itself in her mind. For seven years she had stood there watching the naked child with his coloured balls, and it seemed to her like seven hours, when all at once the shape the balls took, she knew not why, reminded her of the Valley of Shadows, and she spoke:—

'Where is the Old Man of the Fire?' she said.

'Here I am,' answered the child, rising and leaving his balls on the moss. 'What can I do for you?'

There was such an awfulness of absolute repose on the face of the child that Tangle stood dumb before him. He had no smile, but the love in his large gray eyes was deep as the centre. And with the repose there lay on his face a shimmer as of moonlight, which seemed as if any moment it might break into such a ravishing smile as would cause the beholder to weep himself to death. But the smile never came, and

[1] I think I must be indebted to Novalis* for these geometrical figures.

the moonlight lay there unbroken. For the heart of the child was too deep for any smile to reach from it to his face.

'Are you the oldest man of all?' Tangle at length, although filled with awe, ventured to ask.

'Yes, I am. I am very, very old. I am able to help you, I know. I can help everybody.'

And the child drew near and looked up in her face so that she burst into tears.

'Can you tell me the way to the country the shadows fall from?' she sobbed.

'Yes. I know the way quite well. I go there myself sometimes. But you could not go my way; you are not old enough. I will show you how you can go.'

'Do not send me out into the great heat again,' prayed Tangle.

'I will not,' answered the child.

And he reached up, and put his little cool hand on her heart.

'Now,' he said, 'you can go. The fire will not burn you. Come.'

He led her from the cave, and following him through another archway, she found herself in a vast desert of sand and rock. The sky of it was of rock, lowering over them like solid thunderclouds; and the whole place was so hot that she saw, in bright rivulets, the yellow gold and white silver and red copper trickling molten from the rocks. But the heat never came near her.

When they had gone some distance, the child turned up a great stone, and took something like an egg from under it. He next drew a long curved line in the sand with his finger, and laid the egg in it. He then spoke something Tangle could not understand. The egg broke, a small snake came out, and, lying in the line in the sand, grew and grew till he filled it. The moment he was thus full-grown, he began to glide away, undulating like a sea-wave.

'Follow that serpent,' said the child. 'He will lead you the right way.'

Tangle followed the serpent. But she could not go far without looking back at the marvellous Child. He stood alone in the midst of the glowing desert, beside a fountain of red flame that had burst forth at his feet, his naked whiteness glimmering a pale rosy red in the torrid fire. There he stood, looking after her, till, from the lengthening distance, she could see him no more. The serpent went straight on, turning neither to the right nor left.

Meantime Mossy had got out of the lake of shadows, and, following his mournful, lonely way, had reached the sea-shore. It was a dark, stormy evening. The sun had set. The wind was blowing from the sea. The waves had surrounded the rock within which lay the Old Man's house. A deep water rolled between it and the shore, upon which a majestic figure was walking alone.

Mossy went up to him and said,—

'Will you tell me where to find the Old Man of the Sea?'

'I am the Old Man of the Sea,' the figure answered.

'I see a strong kingly man of middle age,' returned Mossy.

Then the Old Man looked at him more intently, and said,—

'Your sight, young man, is better than that of most who take this way. The night is stormy: come to my house and tell me what I can do for you.'

Mossy followed him. The waves flew from before the footsteps of the Old Man of the Sea, and Mossy followed upon dry sand.

When they had reached the cave, they sat down and gazed at each other.

Now Mossy was an old man by this time. He looked much older than the Old Man of the Sea, and his feet were very weary.

After looking at him for a moment, the Old Man took him by the hand and led him into his inner cave. There he helped him to undress, and laid him in the bath. And he saw that one of his hands Mossy did not open.

'What have you in that hand?' he asked.

Mossy opened his hand, and there lay the golden key.

'Ah!' said the Old Man, 'that accounts for your knowing me. And I know the way you have to go.'

'I want to find the country whence the shadows fall,' said Mossy.

'I dare say you do. So do I. But meantime, one thing is certain.— What is that key for, do you think?'

'For a keyhole somewhere. But I don't know why I keep it. I never could find the keyhole. And I have lived a good while, I believe,' said Mossy, sadly. 'I'm not sure that I'm not old. I know my feet ache.'

'Do they?' said the Old Man, as if he really meant to ask the question; and Mossy, who was still lying in the bath, watched his feet for a moment before he replied.

'No, they do not,' he answered. 'Perhaps I am not old either.'

'Get up and look at yourself in the water.'

He rose and looked at himself in the water, and there was not a gray hair on his head or a wrinkle on his skin.

'You have tasted death now,' said the Old Man. 'Is it good?'

'It is good,' said Mossy. 'It is better than life.'

'No,' said the Old Man: 'it is only more life.—Your feet will make no holes in the water now.'

'What do you mean?'

'I will show you that presently.'

They returned to the outer cave, and sat and talked together for a long time. At length the Old Man of the Sea rose, and said to Mossy,—

'Follow me.'

He led him up the stair again, and opened another door. They stood on the level of the raging sea, looking towards the east. Across the waste of waters, against the bosom of a fierce black cloud, stood the foot of a rainbow, glowing in the dark.

'This indeed is my way,' said Mossy, as soon as he saw the rainbow, and stepped out upon the sea. His feet made no holes in the water. He fought the wind, and clomb the waves, and went on towards the rainbow.

The storm died away. A lovely day and a lovelier night followed. A cool wind blew over the wide plain of the quiet ocean. And still Mossy journeyed eastward. But the rainbow had vanished with the storm.

Day after day he held on, and he thought he had no guide. He did not see how a shining fish under the waters directed his steps. He crossed the sea, and came to a great precipice of rock, up which he could discover but one path. Nor did this lead him farther than half-way up the rock, where it ended on a platform. Here he stood and pondered.—It could not be that the way stopped here, else what was the path for? It was a rough path, not very plain, yet certainly a path.—He examined the face of the rock. It was smooth as glass. But as his eyes kept roving hopelessly over it, something glittered, and he caught sight of a row of small sapphires. They bordered a little hole in the rock.

'The keyhole!' he cried.

He tried the key. It fitted. It turned. A great clang and clash, as of iron bolts on huge brazen caldrons, echoed thunderously within. He drew out the key. The rock in front of him began to fall. He retreated from it as far as the breadth of the platform would allow. A great slab fell at his feet. In front was still the solid rock, with this one slab fallen forward out of it. But the moment he stepped upon it, a second fell, just short of the edge of the first, making the next step of a stair, which thus kept dropping itself before him as he ascended into the heart of the precipice. It led him into a hall fit for such an approach— irregular and rude in formation, but floor, sides, pillars, and vaulted roof, all one mass of shining stones of every colour that light can show. In the centre stood seven columns, ranged from red to violet. And on the pedestal of one of them sat a woman, motionless, with her face bowed upon her knees. Seven years had she sat there waiting. She lifted her head as Mossy drew near. It was Tangle. Her hair had grown to her feet, and was rippled like the windless sea on broad sands. Her face was beautiful, like her grandmother's, and as still and peaceful as that of the Old Man of the Fire. Her form was tall and noble. Yet Mossy knew her at once.

'How beautiful you are, Tangle!' he said, in delight and astonishment.

'Am I?' she returned. 'Oh, I have waited for you so long! But you, you are like the Old Man of the Sea. No. You are like the Old Man of the Earth. No, no. You are like the oldest man of all. You are like them all. And yet you are my own old Mossy! How did you come here? What did you do after I lost you? Did you find the key-hole? Have you got the key still?'

She had a hundred questions to ask him, and he a hundred more to ask her. They told each other all their adventures, and were as happy as man and woman could be. For they were younger and better, and stronger and wiser, than they had ever been before.

It began to grow dark. And they wanted more than ever to reach the country whence the shadows fall. So they looked about them for a way out of the cave. The door by which Mossy entered had closed again, and there was half a mile of rock between them and the sea. Neither could Tangle find the opening in the floor by which the serpent had led her thither. They searched till it grew so dark that they could see nothing, and gave it up.

After a while, however, the cave began to glimmer again. The light came from the moon, but it did not look like moonlight, for it gleamed through those seven pillars in the middle, and filled the place with all colours. And now Mossy saw that there was a pillar beside the red one, which he had not observed before. And it was the same new colour that he had seen in the rainbow when he saw it first in the fairy forest. And on it he saw a sparkle of blue. It was the sapphires round the keyhole.

He took his key. It turned in the lock to the sounds of Æolian music. A door opened upon slow hinges, and disclosed a winding stair within. The key vanished from his fingers. Tangle went up. Mossy followed. The door closed behind them. They climbed out of the earth; and, still climbing, rose above it. They were in the rainbow. Far abroad, over ocean and land, they could see through its transparent walls the earth beneath their feet. Stairs beside stairs wound up together, and beautiful beings of all ages climbed along with them.

They knew that they were going up to the country whence the shadows fall.

And by this time I think they must have got there.

DINAH MULOCK CRAIK

The Little Lame Prince and His Travelling Cloak

A Parable for Young and Old

CHAPTER I

YES, he was the most beautiful Prince that ever was born.

Of course, being a prince, people said this: but it was true besides. When he looked at the candle, his eyes had an expression of earnest inquiry quite startling in a new-born baby. His nose—there was not much of it certainly, but what there was seemed an aquiline shape; his complexion was a charming, healthy purple; he was round and fat, straight-limbed and long—in fact, a splendid baby, and everybody was exceedingly proud of him. Especially his father and mother, the King and Queen of Nomansland, who had waited for him during their happy reign of ten years—now made happier than ever, to themselves and their subjects, by the appearance of a son and heir.

The only person who was not quite happy was the king's brother, the heir-presumptive, who would have been king one day, had the baby not been born. But as his Majesty was very kind to him, and even rather sorry for him—insomuch that at the Queen's request he gave him a dukedom almost as big as a county,—the Crown Prince, as he was called, tried to seem pleased also; and let us hope he succeeded.

The Prince's christening was to be a grand affair. According to the custom of the country, there were chosen for him four-and-twenty godfathers and godmothers, who each had to give him a name, and promise to do their utmost for him. When he came of age, he himself had to choose the name—and the godfather or godmother—that he liked best, for the rest of his days.

Meantime, all was rejoicing. Subscriptions were made among the rich to give pleasure to the poor: dinners in town-halls for the working men; tea-parties in the streets for their wives; and milk and bun feasts for the children in the school-rooms. For Nomansland, though I cannot point it out in any map, or read of it in any history, was, I believe, much like our own or many another country.

As for the Palace—which was no different from other palaces—it was clean 'turned out of the windows,' as people say, with the preparations going on. The only quiet place in it was the room which, though the Prince was six weeks old, his mother the Queen had never quitted. Nobody said she was ill, however; it would have been so inconvenient; and as she said nothing about it herself, but lay pale and placid, giving no trouble to anybody, nobody thought much about her. All the world was absorbed in admiring the baby.

The christening-day came at last, and it was as lovely as the Prince himself. All the people in the palace were lovely too—or thought themselves so, in the elegant new clothes which the Queen, who thought of everybody, had taken care to give them, from the ladies-in-waiting down to the poor little kitchenmaid, who looked at herself in her pink cotton gown, and thought, doubtless, that there never was such a pretty girl as she.

By six in the morning all the royal household had dressed itself in its very best; and then the little Prince was dressed in his best—his magnificent christening-robe; which proceeding his Royal Highness did not like at all, but kicked and screamed like any common baby. When he had a little calmed down, they carried him to be looked at by the Queen his mother, who, though her royal robes had been brought and laid upon the bed, was, as everybody well knew, quite unable to rise and put them on.

She admired her baby very much; kissed and blessed him, and lay looking at him, as she did for hours sometimes, when he was placed beside her fast asleep; then she gave him up with a gentle smile, and saying 'she hoped he would be very good, that it would be a very nice christening, and all the guests would enjoy themselves,' turned peacefully over on her bed, saying nothing more to anybody. She was a very uncomplaining person—the Queen, and her name was Dolorez.*

Everything went on exactly as if she had been present. All, even the King himself, had grown used to her absence, for she was not strong, and for years had not joined in any gaieties. She always did her royal duties, but as to pleasures, they could go on quite well without her, or it seemed so. The company arrived: great and noble persons in this and neighbouring countries; also the four-and-twenty godfathers and godmothers, who had been chosen with care, as the people who would be the most useful to his Royal Highness, should he ever want friends, which did not seem likely. What such want could possibly happen to the heir of the powerful monarch of Nomansland?

They came, walking two and two, with their coronets on their heads—being dukes and duchesses, princes and princesses, or the like; they all kissed the child, and pronounced the name which each had given him. Then the four-and-twenty names were shouted out with great energy by six heralds, one after the other, and afterwards written down, to be preserved in the state records, in readiness for the next time they were wanted, which would be either on his Royal Highness's coronation or his funeral. Soon the ceremony was over, and everybody satisfied; except, perhaps, the little Prince himself, who moaned faintly under his christening robes, which nearly smothered him.

In truth, though very few knew, the Prince in coming to the chapel had met with a slight disaster. His nurse—not his ordinary one, but the state nursemaid, an elegant and fashionable young lady of rank, whose duty it was to carry him to and from the chapel, had been so occupied in arranging her train with one hand, while she held the baby with the other, that she stumbled and let him fall, just at the foot of the marble staircase. To be sure, she contrived to pick him up again the next minute; and the accident was so slight it seemed hardly worth speaking of. Consequently, nobody did speak of it. The baby had turned deadly pale but did not cry, so no person a step or two behind could discover anything wrong; afterwards, even if he had moaned, the silver trumpets were loud enough to drown his voice. It would have been a pity to let anything trouble such a day of felicity.

So, after a minute's pause, the procession had moved on. Such a procession! Heralds in blue and silver; pages in crimson and gold; and a troop of little girls in dazzling white, carrying baskets of flowers, which they strewed all the way before the nurse and child,—finally, the four-and-twenty godfathers and godmothers, as proud as possible, and so splendid to look at that they would have quite extinguished their small godson—merely a heap of lace and muslin with a baby-face inside—had it not been for a canopy of white satin and ostrich feathers, which was held over him wherever he was carried.

Thus, with the sun shining on them through the painted windows, they stood; the King and his train on one side, the Prince and his attendants on the other, as pretty a sight as ever was seen out of fairyland.

'It's just like fairyland,' whispered the eldest little girl to the next eldest, as she shook the last rose out of her basket; 'and I think the only thing the Prince wants now is a fairy godmother.'

'Does he?' said a shrill but soft and not unpleasant voice behind; and there was seen among the group of children somebody—not a child—yet no bigger than a child: somebody whom nobody had seen before, and who certainly had not been invited, for she had no christening clothes on.

She was a little old woman dressed all in grey: grey gown; grey hooded cloak, of a material excessively fine, and a tint that seemed perpetually changing, like the grey of an evening sky. Her hair was grey, and her eyes also; even her complexion had a soft grey shadow over it. But there was nothing unpleasantly old about her, and her smile was as sweet and childlike as the Prince's own, which stole over his pale little face the instant she came near enough to touch him.

'Take care. Don't let the baby fall again.'

The grand young lady nurse started, flushing angrily.

'Who spoke to me? How did anybody know?—I mean, what business has anybody—?' Then, frightened, but still speaking in a much sharper tone than I hope young ladies of rank are in the habit of speaking—'Old woman, you will be kind enough not to say "the baby," but "the Prince." Keep away; his Royal Highness is just going to sleep.'

'Nevertheless, I must kiss him. I am his godmother.'

'You!' cried the elegant lady nurse.

'You!!' repeated all the gentlemen and ladies in waiting.

'You!!!' echoed the heralds and pages—and they began to blow the silver trumpets, in order to stop all further conversation.

The Prince's procession formed itself for returning—the King and his train having already moved off towards the palace—but, on the top-most step of the marble stairs, stood, right in front of all, the little old woman clothed in grey.

She stretched herself on tiptoe by the help of her stick, and gave the little Prince three kisses.

'This is intolerable,' cried the young lady nurse, wiping the kisses off rapidly with her lace handkerchief. 'Such an insult to his Royal Highness. Take yourself out of the way, old woman, or the King shall be informed immediately.'

'The King knows nothing of me, more's the pity,' replied the old woman with an indifferent air, as if she thought the loss was more on his Majesty's side than hers. 'My friend in the palace is the King's wife.'

'Kings' wives are called queens,' said the lady nurse, with a contemptuous air.

'You are right,' replied the old woman. 'Nevertheless, I know her Majesty well, and I love her and her child. And—since you dropped him on the marble stairs' (this she said in a mysterious whisper, which made the young lady tremble in spite of her anger)—'I choose to take him for my own. I am his godmother, ready to help him whenever he wants me.'

'You help him!' cried all the group, breaking into shouts of laughter, to which the little old woman paid not the slightest attention. Her soft grey eyes were fixed on the Prince, who seemed to answer to the look, smiling again and again in causeless, aimless fashion, as babies do smile.

'His Majesty must hear of this,' said a gentleman-in-waiting.

'His Majesty will hear quite enough news in a minute or two,' said the old woman sadly. And again stretching up to the little Prince, she kissed him on the forehead solemnly.

'Be called by a new name which nobody has ever thought of. Be Prince Dolor,* in memory of your mother Dolorez.'

'In memory of!' Everybody started at the ominous phrase, and also at a most terrible breach of etiquette which the old woman had committed. In Nomansland, neither the king nor the queen were supposed to have any Christian name at all. They dropped it on their coronation-day, and it was never mentioned again till it was engraved on their coffins when they died.

'Old woman, you are exceedingly ill-bred,' cried the eldest lady-in-waiting, much horrified. 'How you could know the fact passes my comprehension. But even if you did not know it, how dared you presume to hint that her most gracious Majesty is called Dolorez?'

'*Was* called Dolorez,' said the old woman with a tender solemnity.

The first gentleman, called the Gold-stick-in-waiting, raised it to strike her, and all the rest stretched out their hands to seize her; but the grey mantle melted from between their fingers like air; and, before anybody had time to do anything more, there came a heavy, muffled, startling sound.

The great bell of the palace—the bell which was only heard on the death of some of the Royal family, and for as many times as he or she was years old—began to toll. They listened, mute and horror-stricken. Some one counted: one—two—three—four—up to nine and twenty—just the Queen's age.

It was, indeed, the Queen. Her Majesty was dead! In the midst of the festivities she had slipped away, out of her new happiness and her old sufferings, neither few nor small. Sending away her women to see the sight—at least, they said afterwards, in excuse, that she had done so, and it was very like her to do it—she had turned with her face to the window, whence one could just see the tops of the distant mountains—the Beautiful Mountains, as they were called—where she was born. So gazing, she had quietly died.

When the little Prince was carried back to his mother's room, there was no mother to kiss him. And, though he did not know it, there would be for him no mother's kiss any more.

As for his Godmother—the little old woman in grey who called herself so—whether she melted into air, like her gown when they touched it, or whether she flew out of the chapel window, or slipped through the doorway among the bewildered crowd, nobody knew—nobody ever thought about her.

Only the nurse, the ordinary homely one, coming out of the Prince's nursery in the middle of the night in search of a cordial to quiet his continual moans, saw, sitting in the doorway, something which she would have thought a mere shadow, had she not seen shining out of it two eyes, grey and soft and sweet. She put her hand before her own, screaming loudly. When she took them away, the old woman was gone.

CHAPTER II

EVERYBODY was very kind to the poor little Prince. I think people generally are kind to motherless children, whether princes or peasants. He had a magnificent nursery, and a regular suite of attendants, and was treated with the greatest respect and state. Nobody was allowed to talk to him in silly baby language, or dandle him, or, above all, to kiss him, though, perhaps, some people did it surreptitiously, for he was such a sweet baby that it was difficult to help it.

It could not be said that the Prince missed his mother; children of his age cannot do that; but somehow after she died everything seemed to go wrong with him. From a beautiful baby he became sickly and pale, seeming to have almost ceased growing, especially in his legs, which had been so fat and strong. But after the day of his christening they withered and shrank; he no longer kicked them out either in passion or play, and when, as he got to be nearly a year old, his nurse tried to make him stand upon them, he only tumbled down.

This happened so many times, that at last people began to talk about it. A prince, and not able to stand on his own legs! What a dreadful thing! what a misfortune for the country!

Rather a misfortune to him also, poor little boy! but nobody seemed to think of that. And when, after a while, his health revived, and the old bright look came back to his sweet little face, and his body grew larger and stronger, though still his legs remained the same, people continued to speak of him in whispers, and with grave shakes of the head. Everybody knew, though nobody said it, that something, impossible to guess what, was not quite right with the poor little Prince.

Of course, nobody hinted this to the King his father: it does not do to tell great people anything unpleasant. And besides, his Majesty took very little notice of his son, or of his other affairs, beyond the necessary duties of his kingdom. People had said he would not miss the Queen at all, she having been for so long an invalid: but he did. After her death he never was quite the same. He established himself in her empty rooms, the only rooms in the palace whence one could see the Beautiful Mountains, and was often observed looking at them as if he thought she had flown away thither, and that his longing could bring her back again. And by a curious coincidence, which nobody dared to inquire into, he desired that the Prince might be called, not by any of the four-and-twenty grand names given him by his godfathers and godmothers, but by the identical name mentioned by the little old woman in grey,—Dolor, after his mother Dolorez.

Once a week, according to established state custom, the Prince, dressed in his very best, was brought to the King his father for half-an-hour, but his Majesty was generally too ill and too melancholy to pay much heed to the child.

Only once, when he and the Crown Prince, who was exceedingly attentive to his royal brother, were sitting together, with Prince Dolor playing in a corner of the room, dragging himself about with his arms rather than his legs, and sometimes trying feebly to crawl from one chair to another, it seemed to strike the father that all was not right with his son.

'How old is his Royal Highness?' said he suddenly to the nurse.

'Two years, three months, and five days, please your Majesty.'

'It does not please me,' said the King with a sigh. 'He ought to be far more forward than he is now, ought he not, brother? You, who have so many children, must know. Is there not something wrong about him?'

'Oh, no,' said the Crown Prince, exchanging meaning looks with the nurse, who did not understand at all, but stood frightened and trembling with the tears in her eyes. 'Nothing to make your Majesty at all uneasy. No doubt his Royal Highness will outgrow it in time.'

'Outgrow—what?'

'A slight delicacy—ahem!—in the spine; something inherited, perhaps, from his dear mother.'

'Ah, she was always delicate; but she was the sweetest woman that ever lived. Come here, my little son.'

And as the Prince turned round upon his father a small, sweet, grave face—so like his mother's—his Majesty the King smiled and held out his arms. But when the boy came to him, not running like a boy, but wriggling awkwardly along the floor, the royal countenance clouded over.

'I ought to have been told of this. It is terrible—terrible! And for a prince too! Send for all the doctors in my kingdom immediately.'

They came, and each gave a different opinion, and ordered a different mode of treatment. The only thing they agreed in was what had been pretty well known before: that the prince must have been hurt when he was an infant—let fall, perhaps, so as to injure his spine and lower limbs. Did nobody remember?

No, nobody. Indignantly, all the nurses denied that any such accident had happened, was possible to have happened, until the faithful country nurse recollected that it really had happened, on the day of the christening. For which unluckily good memory, all the others scolded her so severely that she had no peace of her life, and soon after, by the influence of the young lady nurse who had carried the baby that fatal day, and who was a sort of connection of the Crown Prince, being his wife's second cousin once removed, the poor woman was pensioned off, and sent to the Beautiful Mountains, from whence she came, with orders to remain there for the rest of her days.

But of all this the King knew nothing, for, indeed, after the first shock of finding out that his son could not walk, and seemed never likely to walk, he interfered very little concerning him. The whole thing was too painful, and his Majesty had never liked painful things. Sometimes he inquired after Prince Dolor, and they told him his Royal Highness was going on as well as could be expected, which really was the case. For after worrying the poor child and perplexing themselves with one remedy after another, the Crown Prince, not wishing to offend any of the differing doctors, had proposed leaving him to nature; and nature, the safest doctor of all, had come to his help, and done her best. He could not walk, it is true; his limbs were mere useless additions to his body; but the body itself was strong and sound. And his face was the same as ever—just his mother's face, one of the sweetest in the world!

Even the King, indifferent as he was, sometimes looked at the little fellow with sad tenderness, noticing how cleverly he learned to crawl, and swing himself about by his arms, so that in his own awkward way he was as active in motion as most children of his age.

'Poor little man! he does his best, and he is not unhappy; not half so unhappy as I, brother,' addressing the Crown Prince, who was more constant than ever in his attendance upon the sick monarch. 'If anything should befall me, I have appointed you as Regent. In case of my death, you will take care of my poor little boy?'

'Certainly, certainly; but do not let us imagine any such misfortune. I assure your Majesty—everybody will assure you—that it is not in the least likely.'

He knew, however, and everybody knew, that it was likely, and soon after it actually did happen. The King died, as suddenly and quietly as the Queen had done—indeed, in her very room and bed; and Prince Dolor was left without either father or mother—as sad a thing as could happen, even to a Prince.

He was more than that now, though. He was a king. In Nomansland, as in other countries, the people were struck with grief one day and revived the next. 'The King is dead—long live the King!' was the cry that rang through the nation, and almost before his late Majesty had been laid beside the Queen in their splendid mausoleum, crowds came thronging from all parts to the royal palace, eager to see the new monarch.

They did see him—the Prince Regent took care they should—sitting on the floor of the council-chamber, sucking his thumb! And when one of the gentlemen-in-waiting lifted him up and carried him—fancy, carrying a king!—to the chair of state, and put the crown on his head, he shook it off again, it was so heavy and uncomfortable. Sliding down to the foot of the throne, he began playing with the golden lions that supported it, stroking their paws and putting his tiny fingers into their eyes, and laughing—laughing as if he had at last found something to amuse him.

'There's a fine king for you!' said the first lord-in-waiting, a friend of the Prince Regent's (the Crown Prince that used to be, who, in the deepest mourning, stood silently beside the throne of his young nephew. He was a handsome man, very grand and clever looking). 'What a king! who can never stand to receive his subjects, never walk in processions, who, to the last day of his life, will have to be carried about like a baby. Very unfortunate!'

'Exceedingly unfortunate,' repeated the second lord. 'It is always bad for a nation when its king is a child; but such a child—a permanent cripple, if not worse.'

'Let us hope not worse,' said the first lord in a very hopeless tone, and looking towards the Regent, who stood erect and pretended to hear nothing. 'I have heard that these sort of children with very large heads and great broad foreheads and staring eyes, are—well, well, let us hope for the best and be prepared for the worst. In the meantime—'

'I swear,' said the Crown Prince, coming forward and kissing the hilt of his sword—'I swear to perform my duties as regent, to take all care of his Royal Highness—his Majesty, I mean,' with a grand bow to the little child, who laughed innocently back again. 'And I will do my humble best to govern the country. Still, if the country has the slightest objection—'

But the Crown Prince being generalissimo,* and having the whole army at his beck and call, so that he could have begun a civil war in no time; the country had, of course, not the slightest objection.

So the King and Queen slept together in peace, and Prince Dolor reigned over the land—that is, his uncle did; and everybody said what a fortunate thing it was for the poor little Prince to have such a clever uncle to take care of him. All things went on as usual; indeed, after the Regent had brought his wife and her seven sons, and established them in the palace, rather better than usual. For they gave such splendid entertainments and made the capital so lively, that trade revived, and the country was said to be more flourishing than it had been for a century.

Whenever the Regent and his sons appeared, they were received with shouts—'Long live the Crown Prince!' 'Long live the Royal family!' And, in truth, they were very fine children, the whole seven of them, and made a great show when they rode out together on seven beautiful horses, one height above another, down to the youngest, on his tiny black pony, no bigger than a large dog.

As for the other child, his Royal Highness Prince Dolor—for somehow people soon ceased to call him his Majesty, which seemed such a ridiculous title for a poor little fellow, a helpless cripple, with only head and trunk, and no legs to speak of—he was seen very seldom by anybody.

Sometimes, people daring enough to peer over the high wall of the palace garden, noticed there, carried in a footman's arms, or drawn in a chair, or left to play on the grass, often with nobody to mind him, a pretty little boy, with a bright intelligent face, and large melancholy eyes—no, not exactly melancholy, for they were his mother's and she was by no means sad-minded, but thoughtful and dreamy. They rather perplexed people, those childish eyes; they were so exceedingly innocent and yet so penetrating. If anybody did a wrong thing, told a lie for instance, they would turn round with such a grave silent surprise—the child never talked much—that every naughty person in the palace was rather afraid of Prince Dolor.

He could not help it, and perhaps he did not even know it, being no better a child than many other children, but there was something about him that made bad people sorry, and grumbling people ashamed of themselves, and ill-natured people gentle and kind. I suppose, because they were touched to see a poor little fellow who did not in the least know what had befallen him, or what lay before him, living his baby life as happy as the day was long. Thus, whether or not he was good himself, the sight of him and his affliction made other people good, and, above all, made everybody love him. So much so, that his uncle the Regent began to feel a little uncomfortable.

Now, I have nothing to say against uncles in general. They are usually very excellent people and very convenient to little boys and girls. Even the 'cruel uncle' of 'The Babes in the Wood'* I believe to be quite an exceptional character. And this 'cruel uncle' of whom I am telling was, I hope, an exception too.

He did not mean to be cruel. If anybody had called him so, he would have resented it extremely; he would have said that what he did was done entirely for the good of the country. But he was a man who had been always accustomed to consider himself first and foremost, believing that whatever he wanted was sure to be right, and, therefore, he ought to have it. So he tried to get it, and got it too, as people like him very often do. Whether they enjoy it when they have it, is another question.

Therefore, he went one day to the council-chamber, determined on making a speech and informing the ministers and the country at large that the young King was in failing health, and that it would be advisable to send him for a time to the Beautiful Mountains. Whether he really meant to do this; or whether it occurred to him afterwards that there would be an easier way of attaining his great desire, the crown of Nomansland, is a point which I cannot decide.

But soon after, when he had obtained an order in council to send the King away—which was done in great state, with a guard of honour composed of two whole regiments of soldiers—the nation learnt, without much surprise, that the poor little Prince—nobody ever called him king now—had gone a much longer journey than to the Beautiful Mountains.

He had fallen ill on the road and died within a few hours; at least, so declared the physician in attendance, and the nurse who had been sent to take care of him. They brought his coffin back in great state, and buried it in the mausoleum with his parents.

So Prince Dolor was seen no more. The country went into deep mourning for him, and then forgot him, and his uncle reigned in his stead. That illustrious personage accepted his crown with great decorum, and wore it with great dignity, to the last. But whether he enjoyed it or not, there is no evidence to show.

CHAPTER III

And what of the little lame prince, whom everybody seemed so easily to have forgotten?

Not everybody. There were a few kind souls, mothers of families, who had heard his sad story, and some servants about the palace, who had been familiar with his sweet ways—these many a time sighed and said 'Poor Prince Dolor!' Or, looking at the Beautiful Mountains, which were visible all over Nomansland, though few people ever visited them, 'Well, perhaps his Royal Highness is better where he is than even there.'

They did not know—indeed, hardly anybody did know—that beyond the mountains, between them and the sea, lay a tract of country, barren, level, bare, except for short stunted grass, and here and there a patch of tiny flowers. Not a bush—not a tree—not a resting-place for bird or beast was in that dreary plain. In summer, the sunshine fell upon it hour after hour with a blinding glare; in winter, the winds and rains swept over it unhindered, and the snow came down, steadily, noiselessly, covering it from end to end in one great white sheet, which lay for days and weeks unmarked by a single footprint.

Not a pleasant place to live in—and nobody did live there, apparently. The only sign that human creatures had ever been near the spot, was one large round tower which rose up in the centre of the plain, and might be seen all over it—if there had been anybody to see, which there never was.* Rose, right up out of the ground, as if it had grown of itself, like a mushroom. But it was not at all mushroom-like; on the contrary, it was very solidly built. In form, it resembled the Irish round towers,* which have puzzled people for so long, nobody being able to find out when, or by whom, or for what purpose they were made; seemingly for no use at all, like this tower. It was circular, of very firm brickwork, with neither doors nor windows, until near the top, when you could perceive some slits in the wall, through which one might possibly creep in or look out. Its height was nearly a hundred feet high, and it had a battlemented parapet, showing sharp against the sky.

As the plain was quite desolate—almost like a desert, only without sand, and led to nowhere except the still more desolate sea-coast—nobody ever crossed it. Whatever mystery there was about the tower, it and the sky and the plain kept their secret to themselves.

It was a very great secret indeed—a state secret—which none but so clever a man as the present king of Nomansland would ever have thought of. How he carried it out, undiscovered, I cannot tell. People said, long afterwards, that it was by means of a gang of condemned criminals, who were set to work, and executed immediately after they had done, so that nobody knew anything, or in the least suspected the real fact.

And what was the fact? Why, that this tower, which seemed a mere mass of masonry, utterly forsaken and uninhabited, was not so at all. Within twenty feet of the top, some ingenious architect had planned a perfect little house, divided into four rooms—as by drawing a cross within a circle you will see might easily be done. By making skylights, and a few slits in the walls for windows, and raising a peaked roof which was hidden by the parapet, here was a dwelling complete; eighty feet from the ground, and as inaccessible as a rook's nest on the top of a tree.

A charming place to live in! if you once got up there, and never wanted to come down again.

Inside—though nobody could have looked inside except a bird, and hardly even a bird flew past that lonely tower—inside it was furnished with all the comfort and elegance imaginable; with lots of books and toys, and everything that the heart of a child could desire. For its only inhabitant, except a nurse of course, was a poor little solitary child.

One winter night, when all the plain was white with moonlight, there was seen crossing it a great tall black horse, ridden by a man also big and equally black, carrying before him on the saddle a woman and a child. The woman—she had a sad fierce look, and no wonder, for she was a criminal under sentence of death, but her sentence had been changed to almost as severe a punishment. She was to inhabit the lonely tower with the child, and was allowed to live as long as the child lived—no longer. This, in order that she might take the utmost care of him; for those who put him there were equally afraid of his dying and of his living. And yet he was only a little gentle boy, with a sweet sleepy smile—he had been very tired with his long journey— and clinging arms, which held tight to the man's neck, for he was rather frightened, and the face, black as it was, looked kindly at him. And he was very helpless, with his poor small shrivelled legs, which could neither stand nor run away—for the little forlorn boy was Prince Dolor.

He had not been dead at all—or buried either. His grand funeral had been a mere pretence: a wax figure having been put in his place, while he himself was spirited away under charge of these two, the condemned woman and the black man. The latter was deaf and dumb, so could neither tell nor repeat anything.

When they reached the foot of the tower, there was light enough to see a huge chain dangling from the parapet, but dangling only half way. The deaf-mute took from his saddle-wallet a sort of ladder, arranged in pieces like a puzzle, fitted it together and lifted it up to meet the chain. Then he mounted to the top of the tower, and slung from it a sort of chair, in which the woman and the child placed themselves and were drawn up, never to come down again as long as they lived. Leaving them there, the man descended the ladder, took it to pieces again and packed it in his pack, mounted the horse, and disappeared across the plain.

Every month they used to watch for him, appearing like a speck in the distance. He fastened his horse to the foot of the tower and climbed it, as before, laden with provisions and many other things. He always saw the Prince, so as to make sure that the child was alive and well, and then went away until the following month.

While his first childhood lasted, Prince Dolor was happy enough. He had every luxury that even a prince could need, and the one thing wanting—love, never having known, he did not miss. His nurse was very kind to him, though she was a wicked woman. But either she had not been quite so wicked as people said, or she grew better through being shut up continually with a little innocent child, who was dependent upon her for every comfort and pleasure of his life.

It was not an unhappy life. There was nobody to teaze or ill-use him, and he was never ill. He played about from room to room—there were four rooms, parlour, kitchen, his nurse's bed-room, and his own; learnt to crawl like a fly, and to jump like a frog, and to run about on all-fours almost as fast as a puppy. In fact, he was very much like a puppy or a kitten, as thoughtless and as merry—scarcely ever cross, though sometimes a little weary.

As he grew older, he occasionally liked to be quiet for awhile, and then he would sit at the slits of windows, which were, however, much bigger than they looked from the bottom of the tower,—and watch the sky above and the ground below, with the storms sweeping over and the sunshine coming and going, and the shadows of the clouds running races across the blank plain.

By-and-by he began to learn lessons—not that his nurse had been ordered to teach him, but she did it partly to amuse herself. She was not a stupid woman, and Prince Dolor was by no means a stupid boy; so they got on very well, and his continual entreaty 'What can I do? what can you find me to do?' was stopped; at least for an hour or two in the day.

It was a dull life, but he had never known any other; anyhow, he remembered no other; and he did not pity himself at all. Not for a long time, till he grew to be quite a big little boy, and could read easily. Then he suddenly took to books, which the deaf-mute brought him from time to time—books which, not being acquainted with the literature of Nomansland, I cannot describe, but no doubt they were very interesting; and they informed him of everything in the outside world, and filled him with an intense longing to see it.

From this time a change came over the boy. He began to look sad and thin, and to shut himself up for hours without speaking. For his nurse hardly spoke, and whatever questions he asked beyond their ordinary daily life she never answered. She had, indeed, been forbidden, on pain of death, to tell him anything about himself, who he was, or what he might have been. He knew he was Prince Dolor, because she always addressed him as 'my prince,' and 'your royal highness,' but what a prince was he had not the least idea. He had no idea of any thing in the world, except what he found in his books.

He sat one day surrounded by them, having built them up round him like a little castle wall. He had been reading them half the day, but feeling all the while that to read about things which you never can see is like hearing about a beautiful dinner while you are starving. For almost the first time in his life he grew melancholy: his hands fell on his lap; he sat gazing out of the window-slit upon the view outside—the view he had looked at every day of his life, and might look at for endless days more.

Not a very cheerful view—just the plain and the sky—but he liked it. He used to think, if he could only fly out that window, up to the sky or down to the plain, how nice it would be! Perhaps when he died—his nurse had told him once in anger that he would never leave the tower till he died—he might be able to do this. Not that he understood much what dying meant, but it must be a change, and any change seemed to him a blessing.

'And I wish I had somebody to tell me all about it; about that and many other things; somebody that would be fond of me, like my poor white kitten.'

Here the tears came into his eyes, for the boy's one friend, the one interest of his life, had been a little white kitten, which the deaf-mute, kindly smiling, once took out of his pocket and gave him—the only living creature Prince Dolor had ever seen. For four weeks it was his constant plaything and companion, till one moonlight night it took a fancy for wandering, climbed on to the parapet of the tower, dropped over and disappeared. It was not killed, he hoped, for cats have nine lives; indeed, he almost fancied he saw it pick itself up and scamper away, but he never caught sight of it more.

'Yes, I wish I had something better than a kitten—a person, a real live person, who would be fond of me and kind to me. Oh, I want somebody—dreadfully, dreadfully!'

As he spoke, there sounded behind him a slight tap-tap-tap, as of a stick or a cane, and twisting himself round, he saw—what do you think he saw?

Nothing either frightening or ugly, but still exceedingly curious. A little woman, no bigger than he might himself have been, had his legs grown like those of other children, but she was not a child—she was an old woman. Her hair was grey, and her dress was grey, and there was a grey shadow over her wherever she moved. But she had the sweetest smile, the prettiest hands, and when she spoke it was in the softest voice imaginable.

'My dear little boy,'—and dropping her cane, the only bright and rich thing about her, she laid those two tiny hands on his shoulders— 'my own little boy, I could not come to you until you had said you wanted me, but now you do want me, here I am.'

'And you are very welcome, madam,' replied the Prince, trying to speak politely, as princes always did in books; 'and I am exceedingly obliged to you. May I ask who you are? Perhaps my mother?' For he knew that little boys usually had a mother, and had occasionally wondered what had become of his own.

'No,' said the visitor, with a tender, half-sad smile, putting back the hair from his forehead, and looking right into his eyes—'No, I am not your mother, though she was a dear friend of mine; and you are as like her as ever you can be.'

'Will you tell her to come and see me then?'

'She cannot; but I dare say she knows all about you. And she loves you very much—and so do I; and I want to help you all I can, my poor little boy.'

'Why do you call me poor?' asked Prince Dolor in surprise.

The little old woman glanced down on his legs and feet, which he did not know were different from those of other children, and then at his sweet, bright face, which, though he knew not that either, was exceedingly different from many children's faces, which are often so fretful, cross, sullen. Looking at him, instead of sighing, she smiled. 'I beg your pardon, my prince,' said she.

'Yes, I am a prince, and my name is Dolor; will you tell me yours, madam?'

The little old woman laughed like a chime of silver bells.

'I have not got a name—or rather, I have so many names that I don't know which to choose. However, it was I who gave you yours, and you will belong to me all your days. I am your godmother.'

'Hurrah!' cried the little prince; 'I am glad I belong to you, for I like you very much. Will you come and play with me?'

So they sat down together, and played. By-and-by they began to talk.

'Are you very dull here?' asked the little old woman.

'Not particularly, thank you, godmother. I have plenty to eat and drink, and my lessons to do, and my books to read—lots of books.'

'And you want nothing?'

'Nothing. Yes—perhaps—If you please, godmother, could you bring me just one more thing?'

'What sort of thing?'

'A little boy to play with.'

The old woman looked very sad. 'Just the thing, alas, which I cannot give you. My child, I cannot alter your lot in any way, but I can help you to bear it.'

'Thank you. But why do you talk of bearing it? I have nothing to bear.'

'My poor little man!' said the old woman in the very tenderest tone of her tender voice. 'Kiss me!'

'What is kissing?' asked the wondering child.

His godmother took him in her arms and embraced him many times. By-and-by he kissed her back again—at first awkwardly and shyly, then with all the strength of his warm little heart.

The Little Lame Prince and His Travelling Cloak 159

'You are better to cuddle than even my white kitten, I think. Promise me that you will never go away.'

'I must; but I will leave a present behind me—something as good as myself to amuse you—something that will take you wherever you want to go, and show you all that you wish to see.'

'What is it?'

'A travelling-cloak.'

The Prince's countenance fell. 'I don't want a cloak, for I never go out. Sometimes nurse hoists me on to the roof, and carries me round by the parapet; but that is all. I can't walk, you know, as she does.'

'The more reason why you should ride; and besides, this travelling-cloak—'

'Hush!—she's coming.'

There sounded outside the room door a heavy step and a grumpy voice, and a rattle of plates and dishes.

'It's my nurse, and she is bringing me my dinner; but I don't want dinner at all—I only want you. Will her coming drive you away, godmother?'

'Perhaps; but only for a little. Never mind; all the bolts and bars in the world couldn't keep me out. I'd fly in at the window, or down through the chimney. Only wish for me, and I come.'

'Thank you,' said Prince Dolor, but almost in a whisper, for he was very uneasy at what might happen next. His nurse and his godmother—what would they say to one another? how would they look at one another?—two such different faces: one, harsh-lined, sullen, cross, and sad; the other, sweet and bright and calm as a summer evening before the dark begins.

When the door was flung open, Prince Dolor shut his eyes, trembling all over: opening them again, he saw he need fear nothing; his lovely old godmother had melted away just like the rainbow out of the sky, as he had watched it many a time. Nobody but his nurse was in the room.

'What a muddle your Royal Highness is sitting in,' she said sharply. 'Such a heap of untidy books; and what's this rubbish?' kicking a little bundle that lay beside them.

'Oh, nothing, nothing—give it me!' cried the prince, and darting after it, he hid it under his pinafore, and then pushed it quickly into his pocket. Rubbish as it was, it was left in the place where she had sat, and might be something belonging to her—his dear, kind godmother, whom already he loved with all his lonely, tender, passionate heart.

It was, though he did not know this, his wonderful travelling-cloak.

CHAPTER IV

AND what of the travelling-cloak? What sort of cloak was it, and what good did it do the Prince?

Stay, and I'll tell you all about it.

Outside it was the commonest-looking bundle imaginable—shabby and small; and the instant Prince Dolor touched it, it grew smaller still, dwindling down till he could put it in his trousers pocket, like a handkerchief rolled up into a ball. He did this at once, for fear his nurse should see it, and kept it there all day—all night, too. Till after his next morning's lessons he had no opportunity of examining his treasure.

When he did, it seemed no treasure at all; but a mere piece of cloth—circular in form, dark green in colour, that is, if it had any colour at all, being so worn and shabby, though not dirty. It had a split cut to the centre, forming a round hole for the neck—and that was all its shape; the shape, in fact, of those cloaks which in South America are called *ponchos*—very simple, but most graceful and convenient.

Prince Dolor had never seen anything like it. In spite of his disappointment he examined it curiously; spread it out on the floor, then arranged it on his shoulders. It felt very warm and comfortable; but it was so exceedingly shabby—the only shabby thing that the Prince had ever seen in his life.

'And what use will it be to me?' said he sadly. 'I have no need of outdoor clothes, as I never go out. Why was this given me, I wonder? and what in the world am I to do with it? She must be a rather funny person, this dear godmother of mine.'

Nevertheless, because she was his godmother, and had given him the cloak, he folded it carefully and put it away, poor and shabby as it was, hiding it in a safe corner of his toy-cupboard, which his nurse never meddled with. He did not want her to find it, or to laugh at it, or at his godmother—as he felt sure she would, if she knew all.

There it lay, and by-the-by he forgot all about it; nay, I am sorry to say, that, being but a child, and not seeing her again, he almost forgot his sweet old godmother, or thought of her only as he did of the angels or fairies that he read of in his books, and of her visit as if it had been a mere dream of the night.

There were times, certainly, when he recalled her; of early mornings like that morning when she appeared beside him, and late evenings, when the grey twilight reminded him of the colour of her hair and her pretty soft garments; above all, when, waking in the middle of the night, with the stars peering in at his window, or the moonlight shining across his little bed, he would not have been surprised to see her standing beside it, looking at him with those beautiful tender eyes, which seemed to have a pleasantness and comfort in them different from anything he had ever known.

But she never came, and gradually she slipped out of his memory—only a boy's memory, after all; until something happened which made him remember her, and want her as he had never wanted anything before.

Prince Dolor fell ill. He caught—his nurse could not tell how—a complaint common to the people of Nomansland, called the doldrums,* as unpleasant as measles or any other of our complaints; and it made him restless, cross, and disagreeable. Even when a little better, he was too weak to enjoy anything, but lay all day long on his sofa, fidgeting his nurse extremely—while, in her intense terror lest he might die, she fidgeted him still more. At last, seeing he really was getting well, she left him to himself—which he was most glad of, in spite of his dullness and dreariness. There he lay, alone, quite alone.

Now and then an irritable fit came over him, in which he longed to get up and do something, or go somewhere—would have liked to imitate his white kitten—jump down from the tower and run away, taking the chance of whatever might happen.

Only one thing, alas! was likely to happen; for the kitten, he remembered, had four active legs, while he—

'I wonder what my godmother meant when she looked at my legs and sighed so bitterly? I wonder why I can't walk straight and steady like my nurse—only I wouldn't like to have her great, noisy, clumping shoes. Still, it would be very nice to move about quickly—perhaps to fly, like a bird, like that string of birds I saw the other day skimming across the sky—one after the other.'

These were the passage-birds—the only living creatures that ever crossed the lonely plain; and he had been much interested in them, wondering whence they came and whither they were going.

'How nice it must be to be a bird. If legs are no good, why cannot one have wings? People have wings when they die—perhaps: I wish I was dead, that I do. I am so tired, so tired; and nobody cares for me. Nobody ever did care for me, except perhaps my godmother. Godmother, dear, have you quite forsaken me?'

He stretched himself wearily, gathered himself up, and dropped his head upon his hands; as he did so, he felt somebody kiss him at the back of his neck, and turning, found that he was resting, not on the sofa-pillows, but on a warm shoulder—that of the little old woman clothed in grey.

How glad he was to see her! How he looked into her kind eyes, and felt her hands, to see if she were all real and alive! then put both his arms around her neck, and kissed her as if he would never have done kissing!

'Stop, stop!' cried she, pretending to be smothered. 'I see you have not forgotten my teachings. Kissing is a good thing—in moderation. Only, just let me have breath to speak one word.'

'A dozen!' he said.

'Well then, tell me all that has happened to you since I saw you—or rather, since you saw me, which is quite a different thing.'

'Nothing has happened—nothing ever does happen to me,' answered the Prince dolefully.

'And are you very dull, my boy?'

'So dull, that I was just thinking whether I could not jump down to the bottom of the tower like my white kitten.'

'Don't do that, being not a white kitten.'

'I wish I were!—I wish I were anything but what I am!'

'And you can't make yourself any different, nor can I do it either. You must be content to stay just what you are.'

The little old woman said this—very firmly, but gently, too—with her arms round his neck and her lips on his forehead. It was the first time the boy had ever heard anyone talk like this, and he looked up in surprise—but not in pain, for her sweet manner softened the hardness of her words.

'Now, my prince—for you are a prince, and must behave as such—let us see what we can do; how much I can do for you, or show you how to do for yourself. Where is your travelling-cloak?'

Prince Dolor blushed extremely. 'I—I put it away in the cupboard; I suppose it is there still.'

'You have never used it; you dislike it?'

He hesitated, not wishing to be impolite. 'Don't you think it's—just a little old and shabby, for a prince?'

The old woman laughed—long and loud, though very sweetly.

'Prince, indeed! Why, if all the princes in the world craved for it, they couldn't get it, unless I gave it them. Old and shabby! It's the most valuable thing imaginable! Very few ever have it; but I thought I would give it to you, because—because you are different from other people.'

'Am I?' said the Prince, and looked first with curiosity, then with a sort of anxiety, into his godmother's face, which was sad and grave, with slow tears beginning to steal down.

She touched his poor little legs. 'These are not like those of other little boys.'

'Indeed!—my nurse never told me that.'

'Very likely not. But it is time you were told; and I tell you, because I love you.'

'Tell me what, dear godmother?'

'That you will never be able to walk, or run, or jump, or play—that your life will be quite different to most people's lives: but it may be a very happy life for all that. Do not be afraid.'

'I am not afraid,' said the boy; but he turned very pale, and his lips began to quiver, though he did not actually cry—he was too old for that, and, perhaps, too proud.

Though not wholly comprehending, he began dimly to guess what his godmother meant. He had never seen any real live boys, but he had seen pictures of them; running and jumping; which he had admired and tried hard to imitate, but always failed. Now he began to understand why he failed, and that he always should fail—that, in fact, he was not like other little boys; and it was of no use his wishing to do as they did, and play as they played, even if he had had them to play with. His was a separate life, in which he must find out new work and new pleasures for himself.

The sense of *the inevitable*, as grown-up people call it—that we cannot have things as we want them to be, but as they are, and that we must learn to bear them and make the best of them—this lesson, which everybody has to learn soon or late—came, alas! sadly soon, to the poor boy. He fought against it for a while, and then, quite overcome, turned and sobbed bitterly in his godmother's arms.

She comforted him—I do not know how, except that love always comforts; and then she whispered to him, in her sweet, strong, cheerful voice—'Never mind!'

'No, I don't think I do mind—that is, I won't mind,' replied he, catching the courage of her tone and speaking like a man, though he was still such a mere boy.

'That is right, my prince!—that is being like a prince. Now we know exactly where we are; let us put our shoulders to the wheel and—'

'We are in Hopeless Tower' (this was its name, if it had a name), 'and there is no wheel to put our shoulders to,' said the child sadly.

'You little matter-of-fact goose! Well for you that you have a godmother called—'

'What?' he eagerly asked.

'Stuff-and-nonsense.'

'Stuff-and-nonsense! What a funny name!'

'Some people give it me, but they are not my most intimate friends. These call me—never mind what,' added the old woman, with a soft twinkle in her eyes. 'So as you know me, and know me well, you may give me any name you please; it doesn't matter. But I am your godmother, child. I have few godchildren; those I have love me dearly, and find me the greatest blessing in all the world.'

'I can well believe it,' cried the little lame Prince, and forgot his troubles in looking at her—as her figure dilated, her eyes grew lustrous as stars, her very raiment brightened, and the whole room seemed filled with her beautiful and beneficent presence like light.

He could have looked at her for ever—half in love, half in awe; but she suddenly dwindled down into the little old woman all in grey, and with a malicious twinkle in her eyes, asked for the travelling-cloak.

'Bring it out of the rubbish cupboard, and shake the dust off it, quick!' said she to Prince Dolor, who hung his head, rather ashamed. 'Spread it out on the floor, and wait till the split closes and the edges turn up like a rim all round. Then go and open the skylight—mind, I say *open the skylight*—set yourself down in the middle of it, like a frog on a water-lily leaf; say "Abracadabra,* dum dum dum," and—see what will happen!'

The prince burst into a fit of laughing. It all seemed so exceedingly silly; he wondered that a wise old woman like his godmother should talk such nonsense.

'Stuff-and-nonsense, you mean,' said she, answering, to his great alarm, his unspoken thoughts. 'Did I not tell you some people called me by that name? Never mind; it doesn't harm me.'

And she laughed—her merry laugh—as childlike as if she were the prince's age instead of her own, whatever that might be. She certainly was a most extraordinary old woman.

'Believe me or not, it doesn't matter,' said she. 'Here is the cloak: when you want to go travelling on it, say *Abracadabra, dum dum dum*; when you want to come back again, say *Abracadabra, tum tum ti*. That's all; good-bye.'

A puff of pleasant air passing by him, and making him feel for the moment quite strong and well, was all the Prince was conscious of. His most extraordinary godmother was gone.

'Really now, how rosy your Royal Highness's cheeks have grown! You seem to have got well already,' said the nurse, entering the room.

'I think I have,' replied the Prince very gently—he felt kindly and gently even to his grim nurse. 'And now let me have my dinner, and go you to your sewing as usual.'

The instant she was gone, however, taking with her the plates and dishes, which for the first time since his illness he had satisfactorily cleared, Prince Dolor sprang down from his sofa, and with one or two of his frog-like jumps, not graceful but convenient, he reached the cupboard where he kept his toys, and looked everywhere for his travelling-cloak.

Alas! it was not there.

While he was ill of the doldrums, his nurse, thinking it a good opportunity for putting things to rights, had made a grand clearance of all his 'rubbish,' as she considered it: his beloved headless horses, broken carts, sheep without feet, and birds without wings—all the treasures of his baby days, which he could not bear to part with. Though he seldom played with them now, he liked just to feel they were there.

They were all gone! and with them the travelling-cloak. He sat down on the floor, looking at the empty shelves, so beautifully clean and tidy, then burst out sobbing as if his heart would break.

But quietly—always quietly. He never let his nurse hear him cry. She only laughed at him, as he felt she would laugh now.

'And it is all my own fault,' he cried. 'I ought to have taken better care of my godmother's gift. O, godmother, forgive me! I'll never be so careless again. I don't know what the cloak is exactly, but I am sure it is something precious. Help me to find it again. Oh, don't let it be stolen from me—don't, please!'

'Ha, ha, ha!' laughed a silvery voice. 'Why, that travelling-cloak is the one thing in the world which nobody can steal. It is of no use to anybody except the owner. Open your eyes, my prince, and see what you shall see.'

His dear old godmother, he thought, and turned eagerly round. But no; he only beheld, lying in a corner of the room, all dust and cobwebs, his precious travelling-cloak.

Prince Dolor darted towards it, tumbling several times on the way,—as he often did tumble, poor boy! and pick himself up again, never complaining. Snatching it to his breast, he hugged and kissed it, cobwebs and all, as if it had been something alive. Then he began unrolling it, wondering each minute what would happen. But what did happen was so curious that I must leave it for another chapter.

CHAPTER V

IF any reader, big or little, should wonder whether there is a meaning in this story, deeper than that of an ordinary fairy tale, I will own that there is. But I have hidden it so carefully that the smaller people, and many larger folk, will never find it out, and meantime the book may be read straight on, like 'Cinderella,' or 'Blue-Beard,' or 'Hop-o'-my-Thumb,'* for what interest it has, or what amusement it may bring.

Having said this, I return to Prince Dolor, that little lame boy whom many may think so exceedingly to be pitied. But if you had seen him as he sat patiently untying his wonderful cloak, which was done up in a very tight and perplexing parcel, using skilfully his deft little hands, and knitting his brows with firm determination, while his eyes glistened with pleasure, and energy, and eager anticipation—if you had beheld him thus, you might have changed your opinion.

When we see people suffering or unfortunate, we feel very sorry for them; but when we see them bravely bearing their sufferings, and making the best of their misfortunes, it is quite a different feeling. We respect, we admire them. One can respect and admire even a little child.

When Prince Dolor had patiently untied all the knots, a remarkable thing happened. The cloak began to undo itself. Slowly unfolding, it laid itself down on the carpet, as flat as if it had been ironed; the split joined with a little sharp crick-crack, and the rim turned up all round till it was breast-high; for meantime the cloak had grown and grown, and become quite large enough for one person to sit in it, as comfortable as if in a boat.

The Prince watched it rather anxiously; it was such an extraordinary, not to say a frightening thing. However, he was no coward, but a thorough boy, who, if he had been like other boys, would doubtless have grown up daring and adventurous—a soldier, a sailor, or the like. As it was, he could only show his courage morally, not physically, by being afraid of nothing, and by doing boldly all that it was in his narrow powers to do. And I am not sure but that in this way he showed more real valour than if he had had six pairs of proper legs.

He said to himself, 'What a goose I am! As if my dear godmother would ever have given me anything to hurt me. Here goes!'

So, with one of his active leaps, he sprang right into the middle of the cloak, where he squatted down, wrapping his arms tight round his knees, for they shook a little and his heart beat fast. But there he sat, steady and silent, waiting for what might happen next.

Nothing did happen, and he began to think that nothing would, and to feel rather disappointed, when he recollected the words he had been told to repeat—'Abracadabra, dum, dum, dum!'

He repeated them, laughing all the while, they seemed such nonsense. And then—and then—

Now, I don't expect anybody to believe what I am going to relate, though a good many wise people have believed a good many sillier things. And as seeing's believing, and I never saw it, I cannot be expected implicitly to believe it myself, except in a sort of a way; and yet there is truth in it—for some people.

The cloak rose, slowly and steadily, at first only a few inches, then gradually higher and higher, till it nearly touched the skylight. Prince Dolor's head actually bumped against the glass, or would have done so, had he not crouched down, crying 'Oh, please don't hurt me!' in a most melancholy voice.

Then he suddenly remembered his godmother's express command—'Open the skylight!'

Regaining his courage at once, without a moment's delay, he lifted up his head and began searching for the bolt, the cloak meanwhile remaining perfectly still, balanced in air. But the minute the window was opened, out it sailed—right out into the clear fresh air, with nothing between it and the cloudless blue.

Prince Dolor had never felt any such delicious sensation before! I can understand it. Cannot you? Did you ever think, in watching the rooks go home singly or in pairs, oaring their way across the calm evening sky, till they vanish like black dots in the misty grey, how pleasant it must feel to be up there, quite out of the noise and din of the world, able to hear and see everything down below, yet troubled by nothing and teased by no one—all alone, but perfectly content.

Something like this was the happiness of the little lame Prince when he got out of Hopeless Tower, and found himself for the first time in the pure open air, with the sky above him and the earth below.

True, there was nothing but earth and sky; no houses, no trees, no rivers, mountains, seas—not a beast on the ground, or a bird in the air. But to him even the level plain looked beautiful; and then there was the glorious arch of the sky, with a little young moon sitting in the west like a baby queen. And the evening breeze was so sweet and fresh, it kissed him like his godmother's kisses; and by-and-by a few stars came out, first two or three, and then quantities—quantities! so that, when he began to count them, he was utterly bewildered.

By this time, however, the cool breeze had become cold, the mist gathered, and as he had, as he said, no outdoor clothes, poor Prince Dolor was not very comfortable. The dews fell damp on his curls—he began to shiver.

'Perhaps I had better go home,' thought he.

But how?—For in his excitement the other words which his godmother had told him to use had slipped his memory. They were only a little different from the first, but in that slight difference all the importance lay. As he repeated his 'Abracadabra,' trying ever so many other syllables after it, the cloak only went faster and faster, skimming on through the dusky empty air.

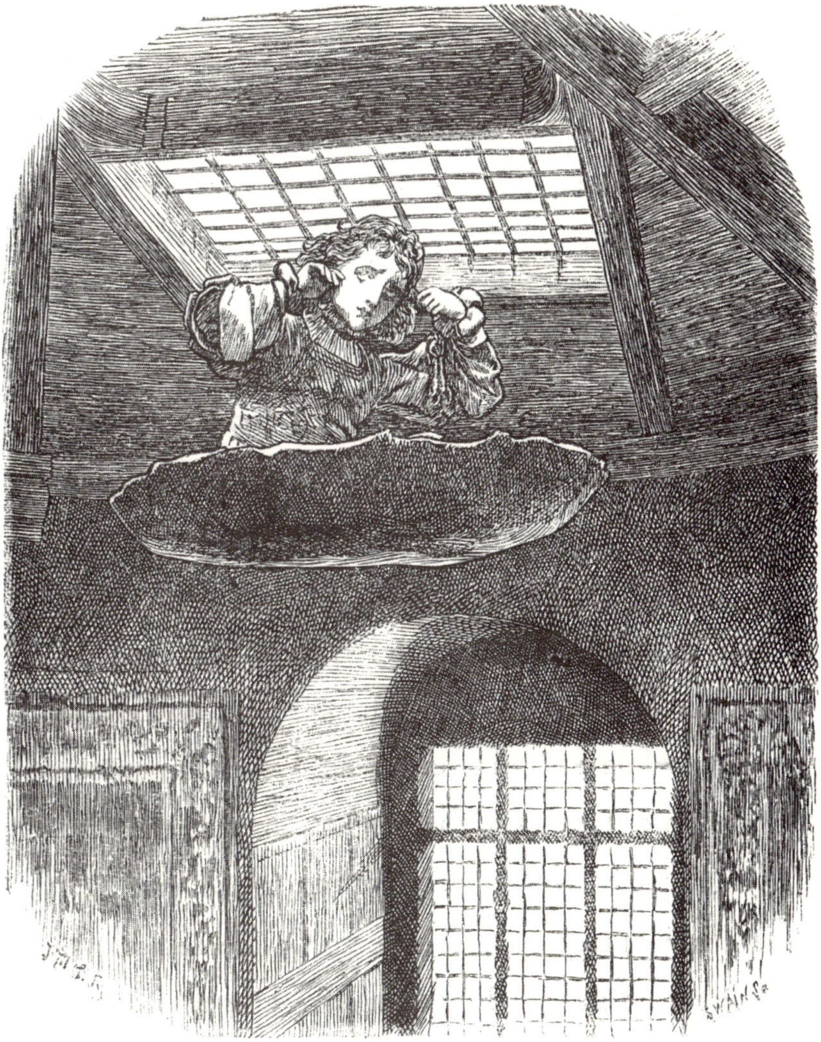

The poor little Prince began to feel frightened. What if his wonderful travelling-cloak should keep on thus travelling, perhaps to the world's end, carrying with it a poor, tired, hungry boy, who, after all, was beginning to think there was something very pleasant in supper and bed?

'Dear godmother,' he cried pitifully, 'do help me! Tell me just this once and I'll never forget again.'

Instantly the words came rushing into his head—'Abracadabra, tum, tum, ti!' Was that it? Ah, yes!—for the cloak began to turn slowly. He repeated the charm again, more distinctly and firmly, when it gave a gentle dip, like a nod of satisfaction, and immediately started back, as fast as ever, in the direction of the tower.

He reached the skylight, which he found exactly as he had left it, and slipped in, cloak and all, as easily as he had got out. He had scarcely reached the floor, and was still sitting in the middle of his travelling-cloak—like a frog on a water-lily leaf, as his godmother had expressed it—when he heard his nurse's voice outside.

'Bless us! what has become of your Royal Highness all this time? To sit stupidly here at the window till it is quite dark, and leave the skylight open too. Prince! what can you be thinking of? You are the silliest boy I ever knew.'

'Am I?' said he absently, and never heeding her crossness; for his only anxiety was lest she might find out anything.

She would have been a very clever person to have done so. The instant Prince Dolor got off it, the cloak folded itself up into the tiniest possible parcel, tied all its own knots, and rolled itself of its own accord into the farthest and darkest corner of the room. If the nurse had seen it, which she didn't, she would have taken it for a mere bundle of rubbish not worth noticing.

Shutting the skylight with an angry bang, she brought in the supper and lit the candles, with her usual unhappy expression of countenance. But Prince Dolor hardly saw it; he only saw, hid in the corner where nobody else would see it, his wonderful travelling-cloak. And though his supper was not particularly nice, he ate it heartily, scarcely hearing a word of his nurse's grumbling, which to-night seemed to have taken the place of her sullen silence.

'Poor woman!' he thought, when he paused a minute to listen and look at her, with those quiet, happy eyes, so like his mother's. 'Poor woman! *she* hasn't got a travelling-cloak!'

And when he was left alone at last, and crept into his little bed, where he lay awake a good while, watching what he called his 'sky-garden,' all planted with stars, like flowers, his chief thought was, 'I must be up very early to-morrow morning and get my lessons done, and then I'll go travelling all over the world on my beautiful cloak.'

So, the next day, he opened his eyes with the sun, and went with a good heart to his lessons. They had hitherto been the chief amusement of his dull life; now, I am afraid, he found them also a little dull. But he tried to be good—I don't say Prince Dolor always was good, but he generally tried to be—and when his mind went wandering after the dark dusty corner where lay his precious treasure, he resolutely called it back again.

'For,' he said, 'how ashamed my godmother would be of me if I grew up a stupid boy.'

But the instant lessons were done, and he was alone in the empty room, he crept across the floor, undid the shabby little bundle, his fingers trembling with eagerness, climbed on the chair, and thence to the table, so as to unbar the skylight—he forgot nothing now—said his magic charm, and was away out of the window as children say, 'in a few minutes less than no time!'

Nobody missed him. He was accustomed to sit so quietly always, that his nurse, though only in the next room, perceived no difference. And besides, she might have gone in and out a dozen times, and it would have been just the same; she never could have found out his absence.

For what do you think the clever godmother did? She took a quantity of moonshine, or some equally convenient material, and made an image, which she set on the window-sill reading, or by the table drawing, where it looked so like Prince Dolor, that any common observer would never have guessed the deception; and even the boy would have been puzzled to know which was the image and which was himself.

And all this while the happy little fellow was away, floating in the air on his magic cloak, and seeing all sorts of wonderful things—or they seemed wonderful to him, who had hitherto seen nothing at all.

First, there were the flowers that grew on the plain, which, whenever the cloak came near enough, he strained his eyes to look at; they were very tiny, but very beautiful—white saxifrage, and yellow lotus, and ground-thistles, purple and bright, with many others the names of which I do not know. No more did Prince Dolor, though he tried to find them out by recalling any pictures he had seen of them. But he was too far off; and though it was pleasant enough to admire them as brilliant patches of colour, still he would have liked to examine them all. He was, as a little girl I know once said of a playfellow, 'a very *examining* boy.'*

'I wonder,' he thought, 'whether I could see better through a pair of glasses like those my nurse reads with, and takes such care of. How I would take care of them too! if only I had a pair.'

Immediately he felt something queer and hard fixing itself onto the bridge of his nose. It was a pair of the prettiest gold spectacles ever seen; and looking downwards, he found that, though ever so high above the ground, he could see every minute blade of grass, every tiny bud and flower—nay, even the insects that walked over them.

'Thank you, thank you!' he cried in a gush of gratitude—to anybody or everybody, but especially to his dear godmother, whom he felt sure had given him this new present. He amused himself with it for ever so long, with his chin pressed on the rim of the cloak, gazing down upon the grass, every square foot of which was a mine of wonders.

Then, just to rest his eyes, he turned them up to the sky—the blue, bright, empty sky, which he had looked at so often and seen nothing.

Now, surely there was something. A long, black, wavy line, moving on in the distance, not by chance, as the clouds move apparently, but deliberately, as if it were alive. He might have seen it before— he almost thought he had; but then he could not tell what it was. Looking at it through his spectacles, he discovered that it really was alive; being a long string of birds, flying one after the other, their wings moving steadily as if each were a little ship, guided invisibly by an unerring helm.

'They must be the passage-birds flying seawards!' cried the boy, who had read a little about them, and had a great talent for putting two and two together and finding out all he could. 'Oh, how I should like to see them quite close, and to know where they come from, and whither they are going! How I wish I knew everything in all the world!'

A silly speech for even an 'examining' little boy to make; because, as we grow older, the more we know, the more we find out there is to know. And Prince Dolor blushed when he had said it, and hoped nobody had heard him.

Apparently somebody had, however; for the cloak gave a sudden bound forward, and presently he found himself high up in air, in that very band of ærial travellers, who had no magic cloak to travel on—nothing except their wings. Yet there they were, making their fearless way through the sky.

Prince Dolor looked at them, as one after the other they glided past him; and they looked at him—those pretty swallows, with their changing necks and bright eyes—as if wondering to meet in mid-air such an extraordinary sort of a bird.

'Oh, I wish I were going with you, you lovely creatures!' cried the boy. 'I'm getting so tired of this dull plain, and the dreary and lonely tower. I do so want to see the world! Pretty swallows, dear swallows! tell me what it looks like—the beautiful, wonderful world!'

But the swallows flew past him—steadily, slowly, pursuing their course as if inside each little head had been a mariner's compass, to guide them safe over land and sea, direct to the place where they desired to go.

The boy looked after them with envy. For a long time he followed with his eyes the faint wavy black line as it floated away, sometimes changing its curves a little, but never deviating from its settled course, till it vanished entirely out of sight.

Then he settled himself down in the centre of the cloak, feeling quite sad and lonely.

'I think I'll go home,' said he, and repeated his 'Abracadabra, tum, tum, ti!' with a rather heavy heart. The more he had, the more he wanted; and it is not always one can have everything one wants—at least, at the exact minute one craves for it; not even though one is a prince, and has a powerful and beneficent godmother.

He did not like to vex her by calling for her, and telling her how unhappy he was, in spite of all her goodness; so he just kept his trouble to himself, went back to his lonely tower, and spent three days in silent melancholy without even attempting another journey on his travelling-cloak.

CHAPTER VI

THE fourth day it happened that the deaf-mute paid his accustomed visit, after which Prince Dolor's spirits rose. They always did, when he got the new books, which, just to relieve his conscience, the King of Nomansland regularly sent to his nephew; with many new toys also, though the latter were disregarded now.

'Toys indeed! when I'm a big boy,' said the Prince with disdain, and would scarcely condescend to mount a rocking-horse, which had come, somehow or other—I can't be expected to explain things very exactly—packed on the back of the other, the great black horse, which stood and fed contentedly at the bottom of the tower.

Prince Dolor leaned over and looked at it, and thought how grand it must be to get upon its back—this grand live steed—and ride away, like the pictures of knights.

'Suppose I was a knight,' he said to himself; 'then I should be obliged to ride out and see the world.'

But he kept all these thoughts to himself, and just sat still, devouring his new books till he had come to the end of them all. It was a repast not unlike the Barmecide's feast which you read of in the 'Arabian Nights,'* which consisted of very elegant but empty dishes, or that supper of Sancho Panza in 'Don Quixote,'* where, the minute the smoking dishes came on the table, the physician waved his hand and they were all taken away.

Thus, almost all the ordinary delights of boy-life had been taken away from, or rather never given to, this poor little Prince.

'I wonder,' he would sometimes think—'I wonder what it feels like to be on the back of a horse, galloping away, or holding the reins in a carriage, and tearing across the country, or jumping a ditch, or running a race, such as I read of or see in pictures. What a lot of things there are that I should like to do! But first, I should like to go and see the world. I'll try.'

Apparently it was his godmother's plan always to let him try, and try hard, before he gained anything. This day the knots that tied up his travelling-cloak were more than usually troublesome, and he was a full half hour before he got out into open air, and found himself floating merrily over the top of the tower.

Hitherto, in all his journeys he had never let himself go out of sight of home, for the dreary building, after all, was home—he remembered no other; but now he felt sick with the very look of his tower, with its round smooth walls and level battlements.

'Off we go!' cried he, when the cloak stirred itself with a slight slow motion, as if waiting his orders. 'Anywhere—anywhere, so that I am away from here, and out into the world.'

As he spoke, the cloak, as if seized suddenly with a new idea, bounded forward and went skimming through the air, faster than the very fastest railway train.

'Gee-up, gee-up!' cried Prince Dolor in great excitement. 'This is as good as riding a race.'

And he patted the cloak as if it had been a horse—that is, in the way he supposed horses ought to be patted; and tossed his head back to meet the fresh breeze, and pulled his coat-collar up and his hat down, as he felt the wind grow keener and colder, colder than anything he had ever known.

'What does it matter though?' said he. 'I'm a boy, and boys ought not to mind anything.'

Still, for all his good-will, by-and-by he began to shiver exceedingly; also, he had come away without his dinner, and he grew frightfully hungry. And to add to everything, the sunshiny day changed into rain, and being high up, in the very midst of the clouds, he got soaked through and through in a very few minutes.

'Shall I turn back?' meditated he. 'Suppose I say "Abracadabra?"'

Here he stopped, for already the cloak gave an obedient lurch, as if it were expecting to be sent home immediately.

'No—I can't—I can't go back! I must go forward and see the world! But oh! if I had but the shabbiest old rug to shelter me from the rain, or the driest morsel of bread and cheese, just to keep me from starving! Still, I don't much mind; I'm a prince, and ought to be able to stand anything. Hold on, cloak, we'll make the best of it.'

It was a most curious circumstance, but no sooner had he said this than he felt stealing over his knees something warm and soft; in fact, a most beautiful bearskin, which folded itself round him quite naturally, and cuddled him up as closely as if he had been the cub of the kind old mother-bear that once owned it. Then feeling in his pocket, which suddenly stuck out in a marvellous way, he found, not exactly bread and cheese, nor even sandwiches, but a packet of the most delicious food he had ever tasted. It was not meat, nor pudding, but a combination of both, and it served him excellently for both. He ate his dinner with the greatest gusto imaginable, till he grew so thirsty he did not know what to do.

'Couldn't I have just one drop of water, if it didn't trouble you too much, kindest of godmothers.'

For he really thought this want was beyond her power to supply.

All the water that supplied Hopeless Tower was pumped up with difficulty, from a deep artesian well—there were such things known in Nomansland—which had been made at the foot of it. But around, for miles upon miles, the desolate plain was perfectly dry. And above it, high in air, how could he expect to find a well, or to get even a drop of water?

He forgot one thing—the rain. While he spoke, it came on in another wild burst, as if the clouds had poured themselves out in a passion of crying, wetting him certainly, but leaving behind, in a large glass vessel which he had never noticed before, enough water to quench the thirst of two or three boys at least. And it was so fresh, so pure—as water from the clouds always is, when it does not catch the soot from city chimneys and other defilements—that he drank it, every drop, with the greatest delight and content.

Also, as soon as it was empty, the rain filled it again, so that he was able to wash his face and hands and refresh himself exceedingly. Then the sun came out and dried him in no time. After that he curled himself up under the bearskin rug, and though he determined to be the most wide-awake boy imaginable, being so exceedingly snug and warm and comfortable, Prince Dolor condescended to shut his eyes, just for one minute. The next minute he was sound asleep.

When he awoke, he found himself floating over a country quite unlike anything he had ever seen before.

Yet it was nothing but what most of you children see every day and never notice it—a pretty country landscape, like England, Scotland, France, or any other land you choose to name. It had no particular features—nothing in it grand or lovely—was simply pretty, nothing more; yet to Prince Dolor, who had never gone beyond his lonely tower and level plain, it appeared the most charming sight imaginable.

First, there was a river. It came tumbling down the hillside, frothing and foaming, playing at hide-and-seek among rocks, then bursting out in noisy fun like a child, to bury itself in deep still pools. Afterwards it went steadily on for a while, like a good grown-up person, till it came to another big rock, where it misbehaved itself extremely. It turned into a cataract and went tumbling over and over, after a fashion that made the Prince—who had never seen water before, except in his bath or his drinking-cup—clap his hands with delight.

'It is so active, so alive! I like things active and alive!' cried he, and watched it shimmering and dancing, whirling and leaping, till, after a few windings and vagaries, it settled into a respectable stream. After that it went along, deep and quiet, but flowing steadily on, till it reached a large lake, into which it slipped, and so ended its course.

All this the boy saw, either with his own naked eye, or through his gold spectacles.

He saw also as in a picture, beautiful but silent, many other things, which struck him with wonder, especially a grove of trees.

Only think, to have lived to his age (which he himself did not know, as he did not know his own birthday) and never to have seen trees! As he floated over these oaks, they seemed to him—trunk, branches, and leaves—the most curious sight imaginable.

'If I could only get nearer, so as to touch them,' said he, and immediately the obedient cloak ducked down; Prince Dolor made a snatch at the topmost twig of the tallest tree, and caught a bunch of leaves in his hand.

Just a bunch of green leaves—such as we see in myriads; watching them bud, grow, fall, and then kicking them along on the ground as if they were worth nothing. Yet, how wonderful they are—every one of them a little different. I don't suppose you could ever find two leaves exactly alike, in form, colour, and size—no more than you could find two faces alike, or two characters exactly the same. The plan of this world is infinite similarity, and yet infinite variety.

Prince Dolor examined his leaves with the greatest curiosity—and also a little caterpillar that he found walking over one of them. He coaxed it to take an additional walk over his finger, which it did with the greatest dignity and decorum, as if it, Mr. Caterpillar, were the most important individual in existence. It amused him for a long time; and when a sudden gust of wind blew it overboard, leaves and all, he felt quite disconsolate.

'Still, there must be many live creatures in the world besides caterpillars. I should like to see a few of them.'

The cloak gave a little dip down, as if to say 'All right, my Prince,' and bore him across the oak forest to a long fertile valley—called in Scotland a strath, and in England a weald—but what they call it in the tongue of Nomansland I do not know. It was made up of cornfields, pasturefields, lanes, hedges, brooks, and ponds. Also, in it were what the Prince had desired to see, a quantity of living creatures, wild and tame. Cows and horses, lambs and sheep, fed in the meadows; pigs and fowls walked about the farmyards; and, in lonelier places, hares scudded, rabbits burrowed, and pheasants and partridges, with many other smaller birds, inhabited the fields and woods.

Through his wonderful spectacles the Prince could see everything; but, as I said, it was a silent picture; he was too high up to catch anything except a faint murmur, which only aroused his anxiety to hear more.

'I have as good as two pairs of eyes,' he thought. 'I wonder if my godmother would give me a second pair of ears.'

Scarcely had he spoken, than he found lying on his lap the most curious little parcel, all done up in silvery paper. And it contained—what do you think? Actually, a pair of silver ears, which, when he tried them on, fitted so exactly over his own, that he hardly felt them, except for the difference they made in his hearing.

There is something which we listen to daily and never notice. I mean the sounds of the visible world, animate and inanimate. Winds blowing, waters flowing, trees stirring, insects whirring (dear me! I am quite unconsciously writing rhyme), with the various cries of birds and beasts—lowing cattle, bleating sheep, grunting pigs, and cackling hens—all the infinite discords that somehow or other make a beautiful harmony.

We hear this, and are so accustomed to it that we think nothing of it; but Prince Dolor, who had lived all his days in the dead silence of Hopeless Tower, heard it for the first time. And oh! if you had seen his face.

He listened, listened, as if he could never have done listening. And he looked and looked, as if he could not gaze enough. Above all, the motion of the animals delighted him: cows walking, horses galloping, little lambs and calves running races across the meadows, were such a treat for him to watch—he that was always so quiet. But, these creatures having four legs, and he only two, the difference did not strike him painfully.

Still, by-and-by, after the fashion of children—and, I fear, of many big people too—he began to want something more than he had, something that would be quite fresh and new.

'Godmother,' he said, having now begun to believe that, whether he saw her or not, he could always speak to her with full confidence that she would hear him—'Godmother, all these creatures I like exceedingly—but I should like better to see a creature like myself. Couldn't you show me just one little boy?'

There was a sigh behind him—it might have been only the wind—

and the cloak remained so long balanced motionless in air, that he was half afraid his godmother had forgotten him, or was offended with him for asking too much. Suddenly, a shrill whistle startled him, even through his silver ears, and looking downwards, he saw start up from behind a bush on a common, something—

Neither a sheep, nor a horse, nor a cow—nothing upon four legs. This creature had only two; but they were long, straight, and strong. And it had a lithe active body, and a curly head of black hair set upon its shoulders. It was a boy, a shepherdboy, about the Prince's own age—but, oh! so different.

Not that he was an ugly boy—though his face was almost as red as his hands, and his shaggy hair matted like the backs of his own sheep. He was rather a nice-looking lad; and seemed so bright, and healthy, and good-tempered—'jolly' would be the word, only I am not sure if they have such an one in the elegant language of Nomansland—that the little Prince watched him with great admiration.

'Might he come and play with me? I would drop down to the ground to him, or fetch him up to me here. Oh, how nice it would be if I only had a little boy to play with me!'

But the cloak, usually so obedient to his wishes, disobeyed him now. There were evidently some things which his godmother either could not or would not give. The cloak hung stationary, high in air, never attempting to descend. The shepherdlad evidently took it for a large bird, and shading his eyes, looked up at it, making the Prince's heart beat fast.

However, nothing ensued. The boy turned round, with a long, loud whistle—seemingly his usual and only way of expressing his feelings. He could not make the thing out exactly—it was a rather mysterious affair, but it did not trouble him much—*he* was not an 'examining' boy.

Then, stretching himself, for he had been evidently half asleep, he began flopping his shoulders with his arms, to wake and warm himself; while his dog, a rough collie, who had been guarding the sheep meanwhile, began to jump upon him, barking with delight.

'Down Snap, down! Stop that, or I'll thrash you,' the Prince heard him say; though with such a rough hard voice and queer pronunciation that it was difficult to make the words out. 'Hollo! Let's warm ourselves by a race.'

They started off together, boy and dog—barking and shouting, till it was doubtful which made the most noise or ran the fastest. A regular steeple-chase* it was: first across the level common, greatly disturbing the quiet sheep; and then tearing away across country, scrambling through hedges, and leaping ditches, and tumbling up and down over ploughed fields. They did not seem to have anything to run for—but as if they did it, both of them, for the mere pleasure of motion.

And what a pleasure that seemed! To the dog of course, but scarcely less so to the boy. How he skimmed along over the ground—his cheeks glowing, and his hair flying, and his legs—oh, what a pair of legs he had!

Prince Dolor watched him with great intentness, and in a state of excitement almost equal to that of the runner himself—for a while. Then the sweet pale face grew a trifle paler, the lips began to quiver and the eyes to fill.

'How nice it must be to run like that!' he said softly, thinking that never—no, never in this world—would he be able to do the same.

Now he understood what his godmother had meant when she gave him his travelling-cloak, and why he had heard that sigh—he was sure it was hers—when he asked to see 'just one little boy.'

'I think I had rather not look at him again,' said the poor little Prince, drawing himself back into the centre of his cloak, and resuming his favourite posture, sitting like a Turk, with his arms wrapped round his feeble, useless legs.

'You're no good to me,' he said, patting them mournfully. 'You never will be any good to me. I wonder why I had you at all; I wonder why I was born at all, since I was not to grow up like other little boys. *Why* not?'

A question, so strange, so sad, yet so often occurring in some form or other, in this world—as you will find, my children, when you are older—that even if he had put it to his mother she could only have answered it, as we have to answer many difficult things, by simply saying 'I don't know.' There is much that we do not know, and cannot understand—we big folks, no more than you little ones. We have to accept it all just as you have to accept anything which your parents may tell you, even though you don't as yet see the reason of it. You may some time, if you do exactly as they tell you, and are content to wait.

Prince Dolor sat a good while thus, or it appeared to him a good while, so many thoughts came and went through his poor young mind—thoughts of great bitterness, which, little though he was, seemed to make him grow years older in a few minutes.

Then he fancied the cloak began to rock gently to and fro, with a soothing kind of motion, as if he were in somebody's arms; somebody who did not speak, but loved him and comforted him without need of words; not by deceiving him with false encouragement or hope, but by making him see the plain hard truth, in all its hardness, and thus letting him quietly face it, till it grew softened down, and did not seem nearly so dreadful after all.

Through the dreary silence and blankness, for he had placed himself so that he could see nothing but the sky, and had taken off his silver ears, as well as his gold spectacles—what was the use of either when he had no legs to walk or run?—up from below there rose a delicious sound.

You have heard it hundreds of times, my children, and so have I. When I was a child I thought there was nothing so sweet; and I think so still. It was just the song of a skylark, mounting higher and higher from the ground, till it came so close that Prince Dolor could distinguish its quivering wings and tiny body, almost too tiny to contain such a gush of music.

'O, you beautiful, beautiful bird!' cried he; 'I should dearly like to take you in and cuddle you. That is, if I could—if I dared.'

But he hesitated. The little brown creature with its loud heavenly voice almost made him afraid. Nevertheless, it also made him happy; and he watched and listened—so absorbed that he forgot all regret and pain, forgot everything in the world except the little lark.

It soared and soared, and he was just wondering if it would soar out of sight, and what in the world he should do when it was gone, when it suddenly closed its wings, as larks do, when they mean to drop to the ground. But, instead of dropping to the ground, it dropped right into the little boy's breast.

What felicity! If it would only stay! A tiny soft thing to fondle and kiss, to sing to him all day long, and be his playfellow and companion, tame and tender, while to the rest of the world it was a wild bird of the air. What a pride, what a delight! To have something that nobody else had—something all his own. As the travelling-cloak travelled on, he little heeded where, and the lark still stayed, nestled down in his bosom, hopped from his hand to his shoulder, and kissed him with its dainty beak, as if it loved him, Prince Dolor forgot all his grief, and was entirely happy.

But when he got in sight of Hopeless Tower, a painful thought struck him.

'My pretty bird, what am I to do with you? If I take you into my room and shut you up there, you, a wild skylark of the air, what will become of you? I am used to this, but you are not. You will be so miserable, and suppose my nurse should find you—she who can't bear the sound of singing? Besides, I remember her once telling me that the nicest thing she ever ate in her life was lark pie!'

The little boy shivered all over at the thought. And, though the merry lark immediately broke into the loudest carol, as if saying derisively that he defied anybody to eat *him*,—still Prince Dolor was very uneasy. In another minute he had made up his mind.

'No, my bird, nothing so dreadful shall happen to you if I can help it; I would rather do without you altogether. Yes, I'll try. Fly away, my darling, my beautiful! Good-bye, my merry, merry bird.'

Opening his two caressing hands, in which, as if for protection, he had folded it, he let the lark go. It lingered a minute, perching on the rim of the cloak, and looking at him with eyes of almost human tenderness; then away it flew, far up into the blue sky. It was only a bird.

But, some time after, when Prince Dolor had eaten his supper— somewhat drearily, except for the thought that he could not possibly sup off lark pie now—and gone quietly to bed, the old familiar little bed, where he was accustomed to sleep, or lie awake contentedly thinking— suddenly he heard outside the window a little faint carol—faint but cheerful—cheerful, even though it was the middle of the night.

The dear little lark! it had not flown away after all. And it was truly the most extraordinary bird, for, unlike ordinary larks, it kept hovering about the tower in the silence and darkness of the night, outside the window or over the roof. Whenever he listened for a moment, he heard it singing still.

He went to sleep as happy as a king.

CHAPTER VII

'HAPPY as a king.' How far kings are happy I cannot say, no more than could Prince Dolor, though he had once been a king himself. But he remembered nothing about it, and there was nobody to tell him, except his nurse, who had been forbidden upon pain of death to let him know anything about his dead parents, or the king his uncle, or, indeed any part of his own history.

Sometimes he speculated about himself, whether he had had a father and mother as other little boys had, what they had been like, and why he had never seen them. But, knowing nothing about them, he did not miss them—only once or twice, reading pretty stories about little children and their mothers, who helped them when they were in difficulty, and comforted them when they were sick, he, feeling ill and dull and lonely, wondered what had become of his mother, and why she never came to see him.

Then, in his history lessons, of course, he read about kings and princes, and the governments of different countries, and the events that happened there. And though he but faintly took in all this, still he did take it in, a little, and worried his young brain about it, and perplexed his nurse with questions, to which she returned sharp and mysterious answers, which only set him thinking the more.

He had plenty of time for thinking. After his last journey in the travelling-cloak, the journey which had given him so much pain, his desire to see the world had somehow faded away. He contented himself with reading his books, and looking out of the tower windows, and listening to his beloved little lark, which had come home with him that day, and never left him again.

True, it kept out of the way; and though his nurse sometimes dimly heard it, and said, 'What is that horrid noise outside?' she never got the faintest chance of making it into a lark pie. Prince Dolor had his pet all to himself, and though he seldom saw it, he knew it was near him, and he caught continually, at odd hours of the day, and even in the night, fragments of its delicious song.

All during the winter—so far as there ever was any difference between summer and winter in Hopeless Tower—the little bird cheered and amused him. He scarcely needed anything more—not even his travelling-cloak, which lay bundled up unnoticed in a corner, tied up in its innumerable knots. Nor did his godmother come near him. It seemed as if she had given these treasures and left him alone—to use them, or lose them, apply them, or misapply them, according to his own choice. That is all we can do with children, when they grow into big children, old enough to distinguish between right and wrong, and too old to be forced to do either.

Prince Dolor was now quite a big boy. Not tall—alas! he never could be that, with his poor little shrunken legs; which were of no use, only an encumbrance. But he was stout and strong, with great sturdy shoulders, and muscular arms, upon which he could swing himself about almost like a monkey. As if in compensation for his useless lower limbs, nature had given to these extra strength and activity. His face, too, was very handsome; thinner, firmer, more manly; but still the sweet face of his childhood—his mother's own face.

How his mother would have liked to look at him! Perhaps she did—who knows!

The boy was not a stupid boy either. He could learn almost anything he chose—and he did choose, which was more than half the battle. He never gave up his lessons till he had learnt them all—never thought it a punishment that he had to work at them, and that they cost him a deal of trouble sometimes.

'But,' thought he, 'men work, and it must be so grand to be a man;—a prince too; and I fancy princes work harder than anybody—except kings. The princes I read about generally turn into kings. I wonder'—the boy was always wondering—'Nurse'—and one day he startled her with a sudden question—'tell me—shall I ever be a king?'

The woman stood, perplexed beyond expression. So long a time had passed by since her crime—if it was a crime—and her sentence, that she now seldom thought of either. Even her punishment—to be shut up for life in Hopeless Tower—she had gradually got used to. Used also to the little lame prince, her charge—whom at first she had hated, though she carefully did everything to keep him alive, since upon him her own life hung. But latterly she had ceased to hate him, and, in a sort of way, almost loved him—at least, enough to be sorry for him—an innocent child, imprisoned here till he grew into an old man—and became a dull, worn-out creature like herself. Sometimes, watching him, she felt more sorry for him than even for herself; and then, seeing she looked a less miserable and ugly woman, he did not shrink from her as usual.

He did not now. 'Nurse—dear nurse,' said he, 'I don't mean to vex you, but tell me—what is a king? shall I ever be one?'

When she began to think less of herself and more of the child, the woman's courage increased. The idea came to her—what harm would it be, even if he did know his own history? Perhaps he ought to know it—for there had been various ups and downs, usurpations, revolutions, and restorations in Nomansland, as in most other countries. Something might happen—who could tell? Changes might occur. Possibly a crown would even yet be set upon those pretty, fair curls—which she began to think prettier than ever when she saw the imaginary coronet upon them.

She sat down, considering whether her oath, never to 'say a word' to Prince Dolor about himself, would be broken, if she were to take a pencil and write what was to be told. A mere quibble—a mean, miserable quibble. But then she was a miserable woman, more to be pitied than scorned.

After long doubt, and with great trepidation, she put her finger to her lips, and taking the Prince's slate—with the sponge tied to it, ready to rub out the writing in a minute—she wrote—

'You are a king.'

Prince Dolor started. His face grew pale, and then flushed all over; his eyes glistened; he held himself erect. Lame as he was, anybody could see he was born to be a king.

'Hush!' said his nurse, as he was beginning to speak. And then, terribly frightened all the while—people who have done wrong always are frightened—she wrote down in a few hurried sentences his history. How his parents had died—his uncle had usurped his throne, and sent him to end his days in this lonely tower.

'I, too,' added she, bursting into tears. 'Unless, indeed, you could get out into the world, and fight for your rights like a man. And fight for me also, my prince, that I may not die in this desolate place.'

'Poor old nurse!' said the boy compassionately. For somehow, boy as he was, when he heard he was born to be a king, he felt like a man—like a king—who could afford to be tender because he was strong.

He scarcely slept that night, and even though he heard his little lark singing in the sunrise, he barely listened to it. Things more serious and important had taken possession of his mind.

'Suppose,' thought he, 'I were to do as she says, and go out into the world, no matter how it hurts me—the world of people, active people, as active as that boy I saw. They might only laugh at me—poor helpless creature that I am; but still I might show them I could do something. At any rate, I might go and see if there was anything for me to do. Godmother, help me!'

It was so long since he had asked for her help, that he was hardly surprised when he got no answer,—only the little lark outside the window sang louder and louder, and the sun rose, flooding the room with light.

Prince Dolor sprang out of bed, and began dressing himself, which was hard work, for he was not used to it—he had always been accustomed to depend upon his nurse for everything.

'But I must now learn to be independent,' thought he. 'Fancy a king being dressed like a baby!'

So he did the best he could—awkwardly but cheerily—and then he leaped to the corner where lay his travelling-cloak, untied it as before, and watched it unrolling itself—which it did rapidly, with a hearty good-will, as if quite tired of idleness. So was Prince Dolor—or felt as if he was. He jumped into the middle of it, said his charm, and was out through the skylight immediately.

'Good-bye, pretty lark!' he shouted, as he passed it on the wing, still warbling its carol to the newly-risen sun. 'You have been my pleasure, my delight; now I must go and work. Sing to old nurse till I come back again. Perhaps she'll hear you—perhaps she won't—but it will do her good all the same. Good-bye!'

But, as the cloak hung irresolute in air, he suddenly remembered that he had not determined where to go—indeed, he did not know, and there was nobody to tell him.

'Godmother,' he cried, in much perplexity, 'you know what I want—at least, I hope you do, for I hardly do myself—take me where I ought to go; show me whatever I ought to see—never mind what I like to see,' as a sudden idea came into his mind that he might see many painful and disagreeable things. But this journey was not for pleasure—as before. He was not a baby now, to do nothing but play—big boys do not always play. Nor men neither—they work. Thus much Prince Dolor knew—though very little more. And as the cloak started off, travelling faster than he had ever known it to do—through sky-land and cloud-land, over freezing mountain-tops, and desolate stretches of forest, and smiling cultivated plains, and great lakes that seemed to him almost as shoreless as the sea—he was often rather frightened. But he crouched down, silent and quiet; what was the use of making a fuss? and, wrapping himself up in his bear-skin, waited for what was to happen.

After some time he heard a murmur in the distance, increasing more and more till it grew like the hum of a gigantic hive of bees. And, stretching his chin over the rim of his cloak, Prince Dolor saw—far, far below him, yet with his gold spectacles and silver ears on, he could distinctly hear and see—What?

Most of us have sometime or other visited a great metropolis—have wandered through its network of streets—lost ourselves in its crowds of people—looked up at its tall rows of houses, its grand public buildings, churches, and squares. Also, perhaps, we have peeped into its miserable little back alleys, where dirty children play in gutters all day and half the night—or where men reel tipsy and women fight—where even young boys go about picking pockets, with nobody to tell them it is wrong, except the policeman; and he simply takes them off to prison. And all this wretchedness is close behind the grandeur—like the two sides of the leaf of a book.

An awful sight is a large city, seen anyhow, from anywhere. But, suppose you were to see it from the upper air; where, with your eyes and ears open, you could take in everything at once? What would it look like? How would you feel about it? I hardly know myself. Do you?

Prince Dolor had need to be a king—that is, a boy with a kingly nature—to be able to stand such a sight without being utterly overcome. But he was very much bewildered—as bewildered as a blind person who is suddenly made to see.

He gazed down on the city below him, and then put his hand over his eyes.

'I can't bear to look at it, it is so beautiful—so dreadful. And I don't understand it—not one bit. There is nobody to tell me about it. I wish I had somebody to speak to.'

'Do you? Then pray speak to me. I was always considered good at conversation.'

The voice that squeaked out this reply was an excellent imitation of the human one, though it came only from a bird. No lark this time, however, but a great black and white creature that flew into the cloak, and began walking round and round on the edge of it with a dignified stride, one foot before the other, like any unfeathered biped you could name.

'I haven't the honour of your acquaintance, sir,' said the boy politely.

'Ma'am, if you please. I am a mother bird, and my name is Mag, and I shall be happy to tell you everything you want to know. For I know a great deal; and I enjoy talking. My family is of great antiquity; we have built in this palace for hundreds—that is to say, dozens of years. I am intimately acquainted with the King, the Queen, and the little princes and princesses—also the maids of honour, and all the inhabitants of the city. I talk a good deal, but I always talk sense, and I dare say I should be exceedingly useful to a poor little ignorant boy like you.'

'I am a prince,' said the other gently.

'All right. And I am a magpie. You will find me a most respectable bird.'

'I have no doubt of it,' was the polite answer—though he thought in his own mind that Mag must have a very good opinion of herself. But she was a lady and a stranger, so, of course, he was civil to her.

She settled herself at his elbow, and began to chatter away, pointing out with one skinny claw while she balanced herself on the other, every object of interest,—evidently believing, as no doubt all its inhabitants did, that there was no capital in the world like the great metropolis of Nomansland.

I have not seen it, and therefore cannot describe it, so we will just take it upon trust, and suppose it to be, like every other fine city, the finest city that ever was built. 'Mag' said so—and of course she knew.

Nevertheless, there were a few things in it which surprised Prince Dolor—and, as he had said, he could not understand them at all. One half the people seemed so happy and busy—hurrying up and down the full streets, or driving lazily along the parks in their grand carriages, while the other half were so wretched and miserable.

'Can't the world be made a little more level? I would try to do it if I were the king.'

'But you're not the king: only a little goose of a boy,' returned the magpie loftily. 'And I'm here not to explain things, only to show them. Shall I show you the royal palace?'

It was a very magnificent palace. It had terraces and gardens, battlements and towers. It extended over acres of ground, and had in it rooms enough to accommodate half the city. Its windows looked in all directions, but none of them had any particular view—except a small one, high up towards the roof, which looked on to the Beautiful Mountains. But since the Queen died there, it had been closed, boarded up, indeed, the magpie said. It was so little and inconvenient, that nobody cared to live in it. Besides, the lower apartments, which had no view, were magnificent—worthy of being inhabited by his Majesty the King.

'I should like to see the King,' said Prince Dolor.

But what followed was so important that I must take another chapter to tell it in.

CHAPTER VIII

WHAT, I wonder, would be most people's idea of a king? What was Prince Dolor's?

Perhaps a very splendid personage, with a crown on his head, and a sceptre in his hand, sitting on a throne, and judging the people. Always doing right, and never wrong—'The king can do no wrong' was a law laid down in olden times. Never cross, or tired, or sick, or suffering; perfectly handsome and well-dressed, calm and good-tempered, ready to see and hear everybody, and discourteous to nobody; all things always going well with him, and nothing unpleasant ever happening.

This, probably, was what Prince Dolor expected to see. And what did he see? But I must tell you how he saw it.

'Ah,' said the magpie, 'no levée* to-day. The King is ill, though his Majesty does not wish it to be generally known—it would be so very inconvenient. He can't see you, but perhaps you might like to go and take a look at him, in a way I often do? It is so very amusing.'

Amusing, indeed!

The Prince was just now too much excited to talk much. Was he not going to see the king his uncle, who had succeeded his father, and dethroned himself; had stepped into all the pleasant things that he, Prince Dolor, ought to have had, and shut him up in a desolate tower? What was he like, this great, bad, clever man? Had he got all the things he wanted, which another ought to have had? And did he enjoy them?

'Nobody knows,' answered the magpie, just as if she had been sitting inside the Prince's heart, instead of on top of his shoulder. 'He is a king, and that's enough. For the rest nobody knows.'

As she spoke Mag flew down on to the palace roof, where the cloak had rested, settling down between the great stacks of chimneys as comfortably as if on the ground. She pecked at the tiles with her beak—truly she was a wonderful bird—and immediately a little hole opened, a sort of door, through which could be seen distinctly the chamber below.

'Now look in, my prince. Make haste, for I must soon shut it up again.'

But the boy hesitated. 'Isn't it rude?—won't they think us—intruding?'

'O dear no! there's a hole like this in every palace; dozens of holes, indeed. Everybody knows it, but nobody speaks of it. Intrusion! Why, though the Royal family are supposed to live shut up behind stone walls ever so thick, all the world knows that they live in a glass house where everybody can see them, and throw a stone at them. Now, pop down on your knees, and take a peep at his Majesty.'

His Majesty!

The Prince gazed eagerly down, into a large room, the largest room he had ever beheld, with furniture and hangings grander than anything he could have ever imagined. A stray sunbeam, coming through a crevice of the darkened windows, struck across the carpet, and it was the loveliest carpet ever woven—just like a bed of flowers to walk over; only nobody walked over it; the room being perfectly empty and silent.

'Where is the King?' asked the puzzled boy.

'There,' said Mag, pointing with one wrinkled claw to a magnificent bed, large enough to contain six people. In the centre of it, just visible under the silken counterpane—quite straight and still—with its head on the lace pillow—lay a small figure, something like waxwork, fast asleep—very fast asleep! There were a quantity of sparkling rings on the tiny yellow hands, that were curled a little, helplessly, like a baby's, outside the coverlet; the eyes were shut, the nose looked sharp and thin, and the long grey beard hid the mouth, and lay over the breast. A sight not ugly, nor frightening, only solemn and quiet. And so very silent—two little flies buzzing about the curtains of the bed, being the only audible sound.

'Is that the King?' whispered Prince Dolor.

'Yes,' replied the bird.

He had been angry—furiously angry; ever since he knew how his uncle had taken the crown, and sent him, a poor little helpless child, to be shut up for life, just as if he had been dead. Many times the boy had felt as if, king as he was, he should like to strike him, this great, strong, wicked man.

Why, you might as well have struck a baby! How helpless he lay! with his eyes shut, and his idle hands folded: they had no more work to do, bad or good.

'What is the matter with him?' asked the Prince again.

'He is dead,' said the Magpie with a croak.

No, there was not the least use in being angry with him now. On the contrary, the Prince felt almost sorry for him, except that he looked so peaceful, with all his cares at rest. And this was being dead? So, even kings died?

'Well, well, he hadn't an easy life, folk say, for all his grandeur. Perhaps he is glad that it is over. Good-bye, your Majesty.'

With another cheerful tap of her beak, Mistress Mag shut down the little door in the tiles, and Prince Dolor's first and last sight of his uncle was ended.

He sat in the centre of his travelling-cloak silent and thoughtful.

'What shall we do now?' said the Magpie. 'There is nothing much more to be done with his Majesty, except a fine funeral, which I shall certainly go and see. All the world will. He interested the world exceedingly when he was alive, and he ought to do it now he's dead—just once more. And since he can't hear me, I may as well say that, on the whole, his Majesty is much better dead than alive—if we can only get somebody in his place. There'll be such a row in the city presently. Suppose we float up again, and see it all. At a safe distance, though. It will be such fun.'

'What will be fun?'

'A revolution.'

Whether anybody except a magpie would have called it 'fun,' I don't know, but it certainly was a remarkable scene.

As soon as the Cathedral bell began to toll, and the minute guns to fire, announcing to the kingdom that it was without a king, the people gathered in crowds, stopping at street corners to talk together. The murmur now and then rose into a shout, and the shout into a roar. When Prince Dolor, quietly floating in upper air, caught the sound of their different and opposite cries, it seemed to him as if the whole city had gone mad together.

'Long live the King!' 'The King is dead—down with the King!' 'Down with the crown, and the King too!' 'Hurrah for the Republic!' 'Hurrah for no Government at all.'

Such were the shouts which travelled up to the travelling-cloak. And then began—oh, what a scene.

When you children are grown men and women—or before—you will hear and read in books about what are called revolutions—earnestly I trust that neither I nor you may ever see one. But they have happened, and may happen again, in other countries beside Nomansland, when wicked kings have helped to make their people wicked too, or out of an unrighteous nation have sprung rulers equally bad; or, without either of these causes, when a restless country has fancied any change better than no change at all.

For me, I don't like changes, unless pretty sure that they are for good. And how good can come out of absolute evil—the horrible evil that went on this night under Prince Dolor's very eyes—soldiers shooting people down by hundreds in the streets, scaffolds erected, and heads dropping off—houses burnt, and women and children murdered—this is more than I can understand.

But all these things you will find in history, and must by-and-by judge for yourselves the right and wrong of them, as far as anybody ever can judge.

Prince Dolor saw it all. Things happened so fast after one another that they quite confused his faculties.

'Oh, let me go home,' he cried at last, stopping his ears and shutting his eyes; 'only let me go home!' for even his lonely tower seemed home, and its dreariness and silence absolute paradise after all this.

'Good-bye, then,' said the magpie, flapping her wings. She had been chatting incessantly all day and all night, for it was actually thus long that Prince Dolor had been hovering over the city, neither eating nor sleeping, with all these terrible things happening under his very eyes. 'You've had enough, I suppose, of seeing the world?'

'Oh, I have—I have!' cried the Prince with a shudder.

'That is, till next time. All right, your Royal Highness. You don't know me, but I know you. We may meet again sometime.'

She looked at him with her clear piercing eyes, sharp enough to see through everything, and it seemed as if they changed from bird's eyes to human eyes, the very eyes of his godmother, whom he had not seen for ever so long. But the minute afterwards she became only a bird, and with a screech and a chatter spread her wings and flew away.

Prince Dolor fell into a kind of swoon, of utter misery, bewilderment, and exhaustion, and when he awoke he found himself in his own room—alone and quiet—with the dawn just breaking, and the long rim of yellow light in the horizon glimmering through the window panes.

CHAPTER IX

WHEN Prince Dolor sat up in bed, trying to remember where he was, whither he had been, and what he had seen the day before, he perceived that his room was empty.

Generally, his nurse rather worried him by breaking his slumbers, coming in and 'setting things to rights,' as she called it. Now, the dust lay thick upon the chairs and tables; there was no harsh voice heard to scold him for not getting up immediately—which, I am sorry to say, this boy did not always do. For he so enjoyed lying still, and thinking lazily, about everything or nothing, that, if he had not tried hard against it, he would certainly have become like those celebrated

>'Two little men
>Who lay in their bed till the clock struck ten.'*

It was striking ten now, and still no nurse was to be seen. He was rather relieved at first, for he felt so tired; and besides, when he stretched out his arm, he found to his dismay that he had gone to bed in his clothes.

Very uncomfortable he felt, of course; and just a little frightened. Especially when he began to call and call again, but nobody answered. Often he used to think how nice it would be to get rid of his nurse and live in this tower all by himself—like a sort of monarch, able to do everything he liked, and leave undone all that he did not want to do; but now that this seemed really to have happened, he did not like it at all.

'Nurse—dear nurse—please come back!' he called out. 'Come back, and I will be the best boy in all the land.'

And when she did not come back, and nothing but silence answered his lamentable call, he very nearly began to cry.

'This won't do,' he said at last, dashing the tears from his eyes. 'It's just like a baby, and I'm a big boy—shall be a man some day. What has happened, I wonder? I'll go and see.'

He sprang out of bed—not to his feet, alas! but to his poor little weak knees, and crawled on them from room to room. All the four chambers were deserted—not forlorn or untidy, for everything seemed to have been done for his comfort—the breakfast and dinner-things were laid, the food spread in order. He might live 'like a prince,' as the proverb is, for several days. But the place was entirely forsaken—there was evidently not a creature but himself in the solitary tower.

A great fear came upon the poor boy. Lonely as his life had been, he had never known what it was to be absolutely alone. A kind of despair seized him—no violent anger or terror, but a sort of patient desolation.

'What in the world am I to do?' thought he, and sat down in the middle of the floor, half inclined to believe that it would be better to give up entirely, lay himself down and die.

This feeling, however, did not last long, for he was young and strong, and I said before, by nature a very courageous boy. There came into his head, somehow or other, a proverb that his nurse had taught him—the people of Nomansland were very fond of proverbs:—

> 'For every evil under the sun
> There is a remedy, or there's none;
> If there is one, try to find it—
> If there isn't, never mind it.'

'I wonder—is there a remedy now, and could I find it?' cried the Prince, jumping up and looking out of the window.

No help there. He only saw the broad bleak sunshiny plain—that is, at first. But, by-and-by, in the circle of mud that surrounded the base of the tower he perceived distinctly the marks of horse's feet, and just in the spot where the deaf-mute was accustomed to tie up his great black charger, while he himself ascended, there lay the remains of a bundle of hay and a feed of corn.

'Yes, that's it. He has come and gone, taking nurse away with him. Poor nurse! how glad she would be to go!'

That was Prince Dolor's first thought. His second—wasn't it natural?—was a passionate indignation at her cruelty—at the cruelty of all the world towards him—a poor little helpless boy. Then he determined—forsaken as he was—to try and hold on to the last, and not to die as long as he could possibly help it.

Anyhow, it would be easier to die here than out in the world, among the terrible doings which he had just beheld. From the midst of which, it suddenly struck him, the deaf-mute had come—contrived somehow to make the nurse understand that the king was dead, and she need have no fear in going back to the capital, where there was a grand revolution, and everything turned upside down. So, of course she had gone.

'I hope she'll enjoy it, miserable woman—if they don't cut off her head too.'

And then a kind of remorse smote him for feeling so bitterly towards her, after all the years she had taken care of him—grudgingly, perhaps, and coldly; still, she had taken care of him, and that even to the last: for, as I have said, all his four rooms were as tidy as possible, and his meals laid out, that he might have no more trouble than could be helped.

'Possibly she did not mean to be cruel. I won't judge her,' said he. And afterwards he was very glad that he had so determined.

For the second time he tried to dress himself, and then to do everything he could for himself—even to sweeping up the hearth and putting on more coals. 'It's a funny thing for a prince to have to do,' said he laughing. 'But my godmother once said princes need never mind doing anything.'

And then he thought a little of his godmother. Not of summoning her, or asking her to help him—she had evidently left him to help himself, and he was determined to try his best to do it, being a very proud and independent boy—but he remembered her, tenderly and regretfully, as if even she had been a little hard upon him—poor, forlorn boy that he was! But he seemed to have seen and learned so much within the last few days, that he scarcely felt like a boy, but a man—until he went to bed at night.

When I was a child, I used often to think how nice it would be to live in a little house all by my own self—a house built high up in a tree, or far away in a forest, or half way up a hillside,—so deliciously alone and independent. Not a lesson to learn—but no! I always liked learning my lessons. Anyhow, to choose the lessons I liked best, to have as many books to read and dolls to play with as ever I wanted: above all, to be free and at rest, with nobody to teaze, or trouble, or scold me, would be charming. For I was a lonely little thing, who liked quietness—as many children do; which other children, and sometimes grown-up people even, cannot always understand. And so I can understand Prince Dolor.

After his first despair, he was not merely comfortable, but actually happy in his solitude, doing everything for himself, and enjoying everything by himself—until bedtime.

Then, he did not like it at all. No more, I suppose, than other children would have liked my imaginary house in a tree, when they had had sufficient of their own company.

But the prince had to bear it—and he did bear it—like a prince: for fully five days. All that time he got up in the morning and went to bed at night, without having spoken to a creature, or, indeed, heard a single sound. For even his little lark was silent: and as for his travelling-cloak, either he never thought about it or else it had been spirited away—for he made no use of it, nor attempted to do so.

A very strange existence it was, those five lonely days. He never entirely forgot it. It threw him back upon himself, and into himself—in a way that all of us have to learn when we grow up, and are the better for it—but it is somewhat hard learning.

On the sixth day, Prince Dolor had a strange composure in his look, but he was very grave, and thin, and white. He had nearly come to the end of his provisions—and what was to happen next? Get out of the tower he could not; the ladder the deaf-mute used was always carried away again; and if it had not been, how could the poor boy have used it? And even if he slung or flung himself down, and by miraculous chance came alive to the foot of the tower, how could he run away?

Fate had been very hard to him, or so it seemed.

He made up his mind to die. Not that he wished to die; on the contrary, there was a great deal that he wished to live to do; but if he must die, he must. Dying did not seem so very dreadful; not even to lie quiet like his uncle, whom he had entirely forgiven now, and neither to be miserable nor naughty any more, and escape all those horrible things that he had seen going on outside the palace, in that awful place which was called 'the world.'

'It's a great deal nicer here,' said the poor little Prince, and collected all his pretty things round him: his favourite pictures, which he thought he should like to have near him when he died; his books and toys—no, he had ceased to care for toys now; he only liked them because he had done so as a child. And there he sat very calm and patient, like a king in his castle, waiting for the end.

'Still, I wish I had done something first—something worth doing, that somebody might remember me by,' thought he. 'Suppose I had grown a man, and had had work to do, and people to care for, and was so useful and busy that they liked me, and perhaps even forgot I was lame. Then, it would have been nice to live, I think.'

A tear came into the little fellow's eyes, and he listened intently through the dead silence for some hopeful sound.

Was there one—was it his little lark, whom he had almost forgotten? No, nothing half so sweet. But it really was something—something which came nearer and nearer, so that there was no mistaking it. It was the sound of a trumpet, one of the great silver trumpets so admired in Nomansland. Not pleasant music, but very bold, grand, and inspiring.

As he listened to it the boy seemed to recall many things which had slipped his memory for years, and to nerve himself for whatever might be going to happen.

What had happened was this.

The Little Lame Prince and His Travelling Cloak

The poor condemned woman had not been such a wicked woman after all. Perhaps her courage was not wholly disinterested, but she had done a very heroic thing. As soon as she heard of the death and burial of the King, and of the changes that were taking place in the country, a daring idea came into her head—to set upon the throne of Nomansland its rightful heir. Thereupon she persuaded the deaf-mute to take her away with him, and they galloped like the wind from city to city, spreading everywhere the news that Prince Dolor's death and burial had been an invention concocted by his wicked uncle—that he was alive and well, and the noblest young Prince that ever was born.

It was a bold stroke, but it succeeded. The country, weary, perhaps, of the late King's harsh rule, and yet glad to save itself from the horrors of the last few days, and the still further horrors of no rule at all, and having no particular interest in the other young princes, jumped at the idea of this Prince, who was the son of their late good King and the beloved Queen Dolorez.

'Hurrah for Prince Dolor! Let Prince Dolor be our sovereign!' rang from end to end of the kingdom. Everybody tried to remember what a dear baby he once was—how like his mother, who had been so sweet and kind, and his father, the finest looking king that ever reigned. Nobody remembered his lameness—or, if they did, they passed it over as a matter of no consequence. They were determined to have him to reign over them, boy as he was—perhaps just because he was a boy, since in that case the great nobles thought they should be able to do as they liked with the country.

Accordingly, with a fickleness not confined to the people of Nomansland, no sooner was the late King laid in his grave than they pronounced him to have been a usurper; turned all his family out of the palace, and left it empty for the reception of the new sovereign, whom they went to fetch with great rejoicing; a select body of lords, gentlemen, and soldiers, travelling night and day in solemn procession through the country, until they reached Hopeless Tower.

There they found the Prince, sitting calmly on the floor—deadly pale indeed, for he expected a quite different end from this, and was resolved if he had to die, to die courageously, like a prince and a king.

But when they hailed him as prince and king, and explained to him how matters stood, and went down on their knees before him, offering the crown (on a velvet cushion, with four golden tassels, each nearly as big as his head)—small though he was and lame, which lameness the courtiers pretended not to notice—there came such a glow into his face, such a dignity into his demeanour, that he became beautiful, king-like.

'Yes,' he said, 'if you desire it, I will be your king. And I will do my best to make my people happy.'

Then there arose, from inside and outside the tower, such a shout as never yet was heard across the lonely plain.

Prince Dolor shrank a little from the deafening sound. 'How shall I be able to rule all these great people? You forget, my lords, that I am only a little boy still.'

'Not so very little,' was the respectful answer. 'We have searched in the records, and found that your Royal Highness—your Majesty, I mean—is precisely fifteen years old.'

'Am I?' said Prince Dolor; and his first thought was a thoroughly childish pleasure that he should now have a birthday, with a whole nation to keep it. Then he remembered that his childish days were done. He was a monarch now. Even his nurse, to whom, the moment he saw her, he had held out his hand, kissed it reverently, and called him ceremoniously 'his Majesty the King.'

'A king must be always a king, I suppose,' said he half sadly, when, the ceremonies over, he had been left to himself for just ten minutes, to put off his boy's clothes and be re-attired in magnificent robes, before he was conveyed away from his tower to the Royal Palace.

He could take nothing with him; indeed, he soon saw that, however politely they spoke, they would not allow him to take anything. If he was to be their king, he must give up his old life for ever. So he looked with tender farewell on his old books, old toys, the furniture he knew so well, and the familiar plain in all its levelness, ugly yet pleasant, simply because it was familiar.

'It will be a new life in a new world,' said he to himself: 'but I'll remember the old things still. And, oh! if before I go, I could but once see my dear old godmother.'

While he spoke, he had laid himself down on the bed for a minute or two, rather tired with his grandeur, and confused by the noise of the trumpets which kept playing incessantly down below. He gazed, half sadly, up to the skylight, whence there came pouring a stream of sun-rays, with innumerable motes floating there, like a bridge thrown between heaven and earth. Sliding down it, as if she had been made of air, came the little old woman in grey.

So beautiful looked she—old as she was—that Prince Dolor was at first quite startled by the apparition. Then he held out his arms in eager delight.

'O, godmother, you have not forsaken me!'

'Not at all, my son. You may not have seen me, but I have seen you, many a time.'

'How?'

'O, never mind. I can turn into anything I please, you know. And I have been a bear-skin rug, and a crystal goblet—and sometimes I have changed from inanimate to animate nature, put on feathers, and made myself very comfortable as a bird.'

'Ha!' laughed the Prince, a new light breaking in upon him, as he caught the inflection of her tone, lively and mischievous. 'Ha, ha! a lark, for instance?'

'Or a magpie,' answered she, with a capital imitation of Mistress Mag's croaky voice. 'Do you suppose I am always sentimental and never funny?—If anything makes you happy, gay, or grave, don't you think it is more than likely to come through your old godmother?'

'I believe that,' said the boy tenderly, holding out his arms. They clasped one another in a close embrace.

Suddenly Prince Dolor looked very anxious. 'You will not leave me now that I am a king? Otherwise, I had rather not be a king at all. Promise never to forsake me?'

The little old woman laughed gaily. 'Forsake you? that is impossible. But it is just possible you may forsake me. Not probable though. Your mother never did, and she was a queen. The sweetest queen in all the world was the lady Dolorez.'

'Tell me about her,' said the boy eagerly. 'As I get older I think I can understand more. Do tell me.'

'Not now. You couldn't hear me for the trumpets and the shouting. But when you are come to the palace, ask for a long-closed upper room, which looks out upon the Beautiful Mountains; open it and take it for your own. Whenever you go there, you will always find me, and we will talk together about all sorts of things.'

'And about my mother?'

The little old woman nodded—and kept nodding and smiling to herself many times, as the boy repeated over and over again the sweet words he had never known or understood—'my mother—my mother.'

'Now I must go,' said she, as the trumpets blared louder and louder, and the shouts of the people showed that they would not endure any delay. 'Good-bye, Good-bye! Open the window and out I fly.'

Prince Dolor repeated gaily the musical rhyme—but all the while tried to hold his godmother fast.

Vain, vain!—for the moment that a knocking was heard at his door, the sun went behind a cloud, the bright stream of dancing motes vanished, and the little old woman with them—he knew not where.

So Prince Dolor quitted his tower—which he had entered so mournfully and ignominiously, as a little helpless baby carried in the deaf-mute's arms—quitted it as the great King of Nomansland.

The only thing he took away with him was something so insignificant, that none of the lords, gentlemen, and soldiers who escorted him with such triumphant splendour, could possibly notice it—a tiny bundle, which he had found lying on the floor just where the bridge of sunbeams had rested. At once he had pounced upon it, and thrust it secretly into his bosom, where it dwindled into such small proportions, that it might have been taken for a mere chest-comforter—a bit of flannel—or an old pocket-handkerchief!

It was his travelling-cloak.

CHAPTER X

DID Prince Dolor become a great king? Was he, though little more than a boy, 'the father of his people,' as all kings ought to be? Did his reign last long—long and happy?—and what were the principal events of it, as chronicled in the history of Nomansland?

Why, if I were to answer all these questions, I should have to write another book. And I'm tired, children, tired—as grown-up people sometimes are; though not always with play. (Besides, I have a small person belonging to me, who, though she likes extremely to listen to the word-of-mouth story of this book, grumbles much at the writing of it, and has run about the house clapping her hands with joy when mamma told her that it was nearly finished. But that is neither here nor there.)

I have related, as well as I could, the history of Prince Dolor, but with the history of Nomansland I am as yet unacquainted. If anybody knows it, perhaps he or she will kindly write it all down in another book. But mine is done.

However, of this I am sure, that Prince Dolor made an excellent king. Nobody ever does anything less well, not even the commonest duty of common daily life, for having such a godmother as the little old woman clothed in grey, whose name is—well, I leave you to guess. Nor, I think, is anybody less good, less capable of both work and enjoyment in after life, for having been a little unhappy in his youth, as the Prince had been.

I cannot take upon myself to say that he was always happy now—who is?—or that he had no cares; just show me the person who is quite free from them! But, whenever people worried and bothered him—as they did sometimes, with state etiquette, state squabbles, and the like, setting up themselves and pulling down their neighbours—he would take refuge in that upper room which looked out on the Beautiful Mountains, and laying his head on his godmother's shoulder, become calm and at rest.

Also, she helped him out of any difficulty which now and then occurred—for there never was such a wise old woman. When the people of Nomansland raised the alarm—as sometimes they did—for what people can exist without a little fault-finding?—and began to cry out, 'Unhappy is the nation whose king is a child,' she would say to him gently, 'You are a child. Accept the fact. Be humble—be teachable. Lean upon the wisdom of others till you have gained your own.'

He did so. He learned how to take advice before attempting to give it, to obey before he could righteously command. He assembled round him all the good and wise of his kingdom—laid all its affairs before them, and was guided by their opinions until he had maturely formed his own.

This he did, sooner than anybody would have imagined, who did not know of his godmother and his travelling-cloak—two secret blessings, which, though many guessed at, nobody quite understood. Nor did they understand why he loved so the little upper room, except that it had been his mother's room, from the window of which, as people remembered now, she had used to sit for hours watching the Beautiful Mountains.

Out of that window he used to fly—not very often; as he grew older, the labours of state prevented the frequent use of his travelling-cloak; still he did use it sometimes. Only now it was less for his own pleasure and amusement than to see something, or investigate something, for the good of the country. But he prized his godmother's gift as dearly as ever. It was a comfort to him in all his vexations; an enhancement of all his joys. It made him almost forget his lameness—which was never cured.

However, the cruel things which had been once foreboded of him did not happen. His misfortune was not such a heavy one after all. It proved to be much less inconvenience, even to himself, than had been feared. A council of eminent surgeons and mechanicians invented for him a wonderful pair of crutches, with the help of which, though he never walked easily or gracefully, he did manage to walk, so as to be quite independent. And such was the love his people bore him, that they never heard the sound of his crutch on the marble palace floors without a leap of the heart, for they knew that good was coming to them whenever he approached them.

Thus, though he never walked in processions, never reviewed his troops mounted on a magnificent charger, nor did any of the things which make a show monarch so much appreciated, he was able for all the duties and a great many of the pleasures of his rank. When he held his levées, not standing, but seated on a throne, ingeniously contrived to hide his infirmity, the people thronged to greet him; when he drove out through the city streets, shouts followed him wherever he went—every countenance brightened as he passed, and his own, perhaps, was the brightest of all.

First, because, accepting his affliction as inevitable, he took it patiently; second, because, being a brave man, he bore it bravely; trying to forget himself, and live out of himself, and in and for other people. Therefore other people grew to love him so well, that I think hundreds of his subjects might have been found who were almost ready to die for their poor lame king.

He never gave them a queen. When they implored him to choose one, he replied that his country was his bride, and he desired no other. But, perhaps, the real reason was that he shrank from any change; and that no wife in all the world would have been found so perfect, so lovable, so tender to him in all his weakness, as his beautiful old godmother.

His four-and-twenty other godfathers and godmothers, or as many of them as were still alive, crowded round him as soon as he ascended the throne. He was very civil to them all, but adopted none of the names they had given him, keeping to the one by which he had been always known, though it had now almost lost its meaning; for King Dolor was one of the happiest and cheerfullest men alive.

He did a good many things, however, unlike most men and most kings, which a little astonished his subjects. First, he pardoned the condemned woman, who had been his nurse, and ordained that from henceforward there should be no such thing as the punishment of death in Nomansland. All capital criminals were to be sent to perpetual imprisonment in Hopeless Tower and the plain round about it, where they could do no harm to anybody, and might in time do a little good, as the woman had done.

Another surprise he shortly afterwards gave the nation. He recalled his uncle's family, who had fled away in terror to another country, and restored them to all their honours in their own. By-and-by he chose the eldest son of his eldest cousin (who had been dead a year), and had him educated in the royal palace, as the heir to the throne. This little prince was a quiet, unobtrusive boy, so that everybody wondered at the King's choosing him, when there were so many more; but as he grew into a fine young fellow, good and brave, they agreed that the King judged more wisely than they.

'Not a lame prince neither,' his Majesty observed one day, watching him affectionately; for he was the best runner, the highest leaper, the keenest and most active sportsman in the country. 'One cannot make oneself, but one can sometimes help a little in the making of somebody else. It is well.'

This was said, not to any of his great lords and ladies, but to a good old woman—his first homely nurse—whom he had sought for far and wide, and at last found, in her cottage among the Beautiful Mountains. He sent for her to visit him once a year, and treated her with great honour until she died. He was equally kind, though somewhat less tender, to his other nurse, who, after receiving her pardon, returned to her native town and grew into a great lady, and I hope a good one. But as she was so grand a personage now, any little faults she had did not show.

Thus King Dolor's reign passed, year after year, long and prosperous. Whether he was happy—'as happy as a king'—is a question no human being can decide. But I think he was, because he had the power of making everybody about him happy, and did it too; also because he was his godmother's godson, and could shut himself up with her whenever he liked, in that quiet little room, in view of the Beautiful Mountains, which nobody else ever saw or cared to see. They were too far off, and the city lay so low. But there they were, all the time. No change ever came to them; and I think, at any day throughout his long reign, the King would sooner have lost his crown than have lost sight of the Beautiful Mountains.

In course of time, when the little prince, his cousin, was grown into a tall young man, capable of all the duties of a man, his Majesty did one of the most extraordinary acts ever known in a sovereign beloved by his people and prosperous in his reign. He announced that he wished to invest his heir with the royal purple—at any rate, for a time, while he himself went away on a distant journey, whither he had long desired to go.

Everybody marvelled, but nobody opposed him. Who could oppose the good King, who was not a young king now? And, besides, the nation had a great admiration for the young Regent—and, possibly, a lurking pleasure in change.

So there was fixed a day, when all the people whom it would hold, assembled in the great square of the capital, to see the young Prince installed solemnly in his new duties, and undertaking his new vows. He was a very fine young fellow; tall and straight as a poplar tree, with a frank handsome face—a great deal handsomer than the King, some people said, but others thought differently. However, as his Majesty sat on his throne, with his grey hair falling from underneath his crown, and a few wrinkles showing in spite of his smile, there was something about his countenance which made his people, even while they shouted, regard him with a tenderness mixed with awe.

He lifted up his thin, slender hand, and there came a silence over the vast crowd immediately. Then he spoke, in his own accustomed way, using no grand words, but saying what he had to say in the simplest fashion, though with a clearness that struck their ears like the first song of a bird in the dusk of the morning.

'My people, I am tired: I want to rest. I have had a long reign, and done much work—at least, as much as I was able to do. Many might have done it better than I—but none with a better will. Now I leave it to others. I am tired, very tired. Let me go home.'

There rose a murmur—of content or discontent none could well tell; then it died down again, and the assembly listened silently once more.

'I am not anxious about you—my people—my children,' continued the King. 'You are prosperous and at peace. I leave you in good hands. The Prince Regent will be a fitter king for you than I.'

'No, no, no!' rose the universal shout—and those who had sometimes found fault with him shouted louder than anybody. But he seemed as if he heard them not.

'Yes, yes,' said he, as soon as the tumult had a little subsided: and his voice sounded firm and clear; and some very old people, who boasted of having seen him as a child, declared that his face took a sudden change, and grew as young and sweet as that of the little Prince Dolor. 'Yes, I must go. It is time for me to go. Remember me sometimes, my people, for I have loved you well. And I am going a long way, and I do not think I shall come back any more.'

He drew a little bundle out of his breast pocket—a bundle that nobody had ever seen before. It was small and shabby-looking, and tied up with many knots, which untied themselves in an instant. With a joyful countenance, he muttered over it a few half-intelligible words. Then, so suddenly that even those nearest to his Majesty could not tell how it came about, the King was away—away—floating right up in the air—upon something, they knew not what, except that it appeared to be as safe and pleasant as the wings of a bird.

And after him sprang a bird—a dear little lark, rising from whence no one could say, since larks do not usually build their nests in the pavement of city squares. But there it was, a real lark, singing far over their heads, louder, and clearer, and more joyful, as it vanished further into the blue sky.

Shading their eyes, and straining their ears, the astonished people stood, until the whole vision disappeared like a speck in the clouds—the rosy clouds that overhung the Beautiful Mountains.

Then they guessed that they should see their beloved king no more. Well-beloved as he was, he had always been somewhat of a mystery to them, and such he remained. But they went home, and, accepting their new monarch, obeyed him faithfully for his cousin's sake.

King Dolor was never again beheld or heard of in his own country. But the good he had done there lasted for years and years; he was long missed and deeply mourned—at least, so far as anybody could mourn one who was gone on such a happy journey.

Whither he went, or who went with him, it is impossible to say. But I myself believe that his godmother took him, on his travelling-cloak, to the Beautiful Mountains. What he did there, or where he is now, who can tell? I cannot. But one thing I am quite sure of, that, wherever he is, he is perfectly happy.

And so, when I think of him, am I.

MARY DE MORGAN

The Wanderings of Arasmon

Long ago there lived a wandering musician and his wife, whose names were Arasmon and Chrysea.* Arasmon played upon a lute to which Chrysea sang, and their music was so beautiful that people followed them in crowds and gave them as much money as they wanted. When Arasmon played all who heard him were silent from wonder and admiration, but when Chrysea sang they could not refrain from weeping, for her voice was more beautiful than anything they had ever heard before.

Both were young and lovely, and were as happy as the day was long, for they loved each other dearly, and liked wandering about seeing new countries and people and making sweet music. They went to all sorts of places, sometimes to big cities, sometimes to little villages, sometimes to lonely cottages by the sea-shore, and sometimes they strolled along the green lanes and fields, singing and playing so exquisitely, that the very birds flew down from the trees to listen to them.

One day they crossed a dark line of hills, and came out on a wild moorland country, where they had never been before. On the side of the hill they saw a little village, and at once turned towards it, but as they drew near Chrysea said,

'What gloomy place is this? See how dark and miserable it looks.'

'Let us try to cheer it with some music,' said Arasmon, and began to play upon his lute, while Chrysea sang. One by one the villagers came out of their cottages and gathered round them to listen, but Chrysea thought she had never before seen such forlorn-looking people. They were thin and bent, their faces were pale and haggard, also their clothes looked old and threadbare, and in some places were worn into holes. But they crowded about Arasmon and Chrysea, and begged them to go on playing and singing, and as they listened the women shed tears, and the men hid their faces and were silent. When they stopped, the people began to feel in their pockets as if to find some coins, but Arasmon cried,

'One by one the villagers came out of their cottages, and gathered round them to listen.'

'Nay, good friends, keep your money for yourselves. You have not too much of it, to judge by your looks. But let us stay with you for to-night, and give us food and lodging, and we shall think ourselves well paid, and will play and sing to you as much as you like.'

'Stay with us as long as you can, stay with us always,' begged the people; and each one entreated to be allowed to receive the strangers and give them the best they had. So Arasmon and Chrysea played and sang to them till they were tired, and at last, when the heavy rain began to fall, they turned towards the village, but as they passed through its narrow streets they thought the place itself looked even sadder than its inmates. The houses were ill-built, and seemed to be almost tumbling down. The streets were uneven and badly kept. In the gardens they saw no flowers, but dank dark weeds. They went into a cottage which the people pointed out to them, and Arasmon lay down by the fire, calling to Chrysea to rest also, as they had walked far, and she must be weary. He soon fell asleep, but Chrysea sat at the door watching the dark clouds as they drifted over the darker houses. Outside the cottage hung a blackbird in a cage, with drooping wings and scanty plumage. It was the only animal they had yet seen in the village, for of cats or dogs or singing-birds there seemed to be none.

When she saw it, Chrysea turned to the woman of the house, who stood beside her, and said,

'Why don't you let it go? It would be much happier flying about in the sunshine.'

'The sun never shines here,' said the woman sadly. 'It could not pierce through the dark clouds which hang over the village. Besides, we do not think of happiness. It is as much as we can do to live.'

'But tell me,' said Chrysea, 'what is it that makes you so sad and your village such a dreary place? I have been to many towns in my life, but to none which looked like this.'

'Don't you know,' said the woman, 'that this place is spell-bound?'

'Spell-bound?' cried Chrysea. 'What do you mean?'

The woman turned and pointed towards the moor. 'Over yonder,' she said, 'dwells a terrible old wizard by whom we are bewitched, and he has a number of little dark elves who are his servants, and these are they who make our village what you see it. You don't know how sad it is to live here. The elves steal our eggs, and milk, and poultry, so that there is never enough for us to eat, and we are half-starved. They pull down our houses, and undo our work as fast as we do it. They steal our corn when it is standing in sheaves, so that we find nothing but empty husks;' and as she ceased speaking the woman sighed heavily.

'But if they do all this harm,' said Chrysea, 'why do not some of you go to the moor and drive them away?'

'It is part of the spell,' said the woman, 'that we can neither hear nor see them. I have heard my grandfather say that in the old time this place was no different to others, but one day this terrible old magician came and offered the villagers a great deal of money if they would let him dwell upon the moor; for before that it was covered with golden gorse and heath, and the country folk held all their merrymakings there, but they were tempted with the gold, and sold it, and from that day the elves have tormented us; and we cannot see them, we cannot get rid of them, but must just bear them as best we may.'

'That is a sad way to speak,' said Chrysea. 'Cannot you find out what the spell really is and break it?'

'It is a song,' said the woman, 'and every night they sing it afresh. It is said that if any one could go to the moor between mid-night and dawn, and could hear them singing it, and then sing through the tune just as they themselves do, the charm would be broken, and we should be free. But it must be some one who has never taken their money, so we cannot do it, for we can neither see nor hear them.'

'But I have not taken their money,' said Chrysea. 'And there is no tune I cannot sing when I have heard it once. So I will go to the moor for you and break the spell.'

'Nay, do not think of such a thing,' cried the woman. 'For the elves are most spiteful, and you don't know what harm they might do to you, even if you set us free.'

Chrysea said no more, but all the evening she thought of what the woman had told her, and still stood looking out into the dismal street. When she went to bed she did not sleep, but lay still till the clock struck one. Then she rose softly, and wrapping herself in a cloak, opened the door and stepped out into the rain. As she passed, she looked up and saw the blackbird crouching in the bottom of its cage. She opened the cage door to let it fly, but still it did not move, so she lifted it out in her hand.

'Poor bird!' said she gently; 'I wish I could give this village its liberty as easily as I can give you yours,' and carrying it with her she walked on towards the moor. It was a large waste piece of land, and looked as though it had been burnt, for the ground was charred and black, and there was no grass or green plant growing on it, but there were some blackened stumps of trees, and to these Chrysea went, and hid herself behind one to wait and see what would come. She watched for a long time without seeing any one, but at last there rose from the ground not far from her a lurid gleam, which spread and spread until it became a large circle of light, in the midst of which she saw small dark figures moving, like ugly little men. The light was now so bright that she could distinguish each one quite plainly, and never before had she seen anything so ugly, for they were black as ink, and their faces were twisted and looked cruel and wicked.

They joined hands, and, forming a ring, danced slowly round, and, as they did so, the ground opened, and there rose up in their centre a tiny village exactly like the spell-bound village, only that the houses were but a few inches high. Round this the elves danced, and then they began to sing. Chrysea listened eagerly to their singing, and no sooner had they done, than she opened her lips and sang the same tune through from beginning to end just as she had heard it.

Her voice rang out loud and clear, and at the sound the little village crumbled and fell away as though it had been made of dust.

The elves stood silent for a moment, and then with a wild cry they all rushed towards Chrysea, and at their head she saw one about three times the size of the others, who appeared to be their chief.

'Come, quickly, let us punish the woman who has dared to thwart us,' he cried. 'What shall we change her to?'

'A frog to croak on the ground,' cried one.

'No, an owl to hoot in the night,' cried another.

'Oh, for pity's sake,' implored Chrysea, 'don't change me to one of these loathsome creatures, so that, if Arasmon finds me, he will spurn me.'

'Hear her,' cried the chief, 'and let her have her will. Let us change her to no bird or beast, but to a bright golden harp, and thus shall she remain, until upon her strings some one shall play our tune, which she has dared to sing.'

'Agreed!' cried the others, and all began to dance round Chrysea and to sing as they had sung around the village. She shrieked and tried to run, but they stopped her on every side. She cried, 'Arasmon! Arasmon!' but no one came, and when the elves' song was done, and they disappeared, all that was left was a little gold harp hanging upon

The Wanderings of Arasmon

the boughs of the tree, and only the blackbird who sat above knew what had come of poor Chrysea.

When morning dawned, and the villagers awoke, all felt that some great change had taken place. The heavy cloud which hung above the village had cleared away; the sun shone brightly, and the sky was blue; streams which had been dry for years, were running clear and fresh: and the people all felt strong, and able to work again; the trees were beginning to bud, and in their branches sang birds, whose voices had not been heard there for many a long year. The villagers looked from one to another and said, 'Surely the spell is broken; surely the elves must have fled;' and they wept for joy.

Arasmon woke with the first beam of the sun, and finding Chrysea was not there, he rose, and went to seek her in the village, calling, 'Chrysea, Chrysea! the sun is up and we must journey on our way;' but no Chrysea answered, so he walked down all the streets, calling 'Chrysea! come, Chrysea!' but no Chrysea came. Then he said, 'She has gone into the fields to look for wild flowers, and will soon be back.' So he waited for her patiently, but the sun rose high, the villagers went to their work, and she did not return. At this Arasmon was frightened, and asked every one he met if they had seen her, but each one shook his head and said 'No, they had seen nothing of her.'

Then he called some of the men together and told them that his wife had wandered away, and he feared lest she might lose herself and go still farther, and he asked them to help him to look for her. So some went one way, and some another, to search, and Arasmon himself walked for miles the whole country round, calling 'Chrysea! Chrysea!' but no answer came.

The sun was beginning to set and twilight to cover the land, when Arasmon came on to the moor where Chrysea had met her fate. That, too, was changed. Flowers and grass were already beginning to grow there, and the children of the village, who till now had never dared to venture near it, were playing about it. Arasmon could hear their voices as he came near the tree against which Chrysea had leaned, and on which now hung the golden harp. In the branches above sat the blackbird singing, and Arasmon stopped and listened to its song, and thought he had never heard a bird sing so sweetly before. For it sang the magic song by which Chrysea had broken the elves' spell, the first tune it had heard since it regained its liberty.

'Dear blackbird,' said Arasmon, looking up to it, 'I wish your singing could tell me where to find my wife Chrysea;' and as he looked up he saw a golden harp hanging upon the branches, and he took it down and ran his fingers over the strings. Never before did harp give forth such music. It was like a woman's voice, and was most beautiful, but so sad that when Arasmon heard it he felt inclined to cry. It seemed to be calling for help, but he could not understand what it said, though each time he touched the strings it cried, 'Arasmon, Arasmon, I am here! It is I, Chrysea;' but though Arasmon listened, and wondered at its tones, yet he did not know what it said.

He examined it carefully. It was a beautiful little harp, made of pure gold, and at the top was a pair of golden hands and arms clasped together.

'I will keep it,' said Arasmon, 'for I never yet heard a harp with such a tone, and when Chrysea comes she shall sing to it.'

But Chrysea was nowhere to be found, and at last the villagers declared she must be lost, or herself have gone away on purpose, and that it was vain to seek her farther. At this Arasmon was angry, and saying that he would seek Chrysea as long as he had life, he left the village to wander over the whole world till he should find her. He went on foot, and took with him the golden harp.

He walked for many, many miles far away from the village and the moor, and when he came to any farmhouses, or met any country people on the road he began to play, and every one thronged round him and stared, in breathless surprise at his beautiful music. When he had done he would ask them, 'Have you seen my wife Chrysea? She is dressed in white and gold, and sings more sweetly than any of the birds of heaven.'

But all shook their heads and said, 'No, she had not been there;' and whenever he came to a strange village, where he had not been before, he called, 'Chrysea, Chrysea, are you here?' but not Chrysea answered, only the harp in his hands cried whenever he touched its strings, 'It is I, Arasmon! It is I, Chrysea!' but though he thought its notes like Chrysea's voice, he never understood them.

He wandered for days and months and years through countries and villages which he had never known before. When night came and he found himself in the fields alone, he would lie down upon his cloak and sleep with his head resting upon the harp, and if by chance one of its golden threads was touched it would cry, 'Arasmon, awake, I am here!' Then he would dream that Chrysea was calling him, and would wake and start up to look for her, thinking she must be close at hand.

One day, towards night, when he had walked far, and was very tired, he came to a little village on a lonely, rocky coast by the sea, and he found that a thick mist had come up, and hung over the village, so that he could barely see the path before him as he walked. But he found his way down on to the beach, and there stood a number of fisherwomen, trying to look through the mist towards the sea, and speaking anxiously.

'What is wrong, and for whom are you watching, good folk?' he asked them.

'We are watching for our husbands,' answered one. 'They went out in their boats fishing in the early morning, when it was quite light, and then arose this dreadful fog, and they should have come back long ago, and we fear lest they may lose their way in the darkness and strike on a rock and be drowned.'

'I too, have lost my wife Chrysea,' cried Arasmon. 'Has she passed by here? She had long golden hair, and her gown was white and gold, and she sang with a voice like an angel's.'

The women all said, 'No, they had not seen her;' but still they strained their eyes towards the sea, and Arasmon also began to watch for the return of the boats.

They waited and waited, but they did not come, and every moment the darkness grew thicker and thicker, so that the women could not see each other's faces, though they stood quite near together.

Then Arasmon took his harp and began to play, and its music floated over the water for miles through the darkness, but the women were weeping so for their husbands, that they did not heed it.

'It is useless to watch,' said one. 'They cannot steer their boats in such a darkness. We shall never see them again.'

'I will wait all night till morning,' said another, 'and all day next day, and next night, till I see some sign of the boats, and know if they be living or dead,' but as she stopped speaking, there rose a cry of 'Here they are,' and two or three fishing-boats were pushed on to the sand close by where they stood, and the women threw their arms round their husbands' necks, and all shouted for joy.

The fishermen asked who it was who had played the harp; 'For,' they said, 'it was that which saved us. We were far from land, and it was so dark that we could not tell whether to go to left or to right, and had no sign to guide us to shore; when of a sudden we heard the most beautiful music, and we followed the sound, and came in quite safely.'

''Twas this good harper who played while we watched,' said the women, and one and all turned to Arasmon, and told him with tears of their gratitude, and asked him what they could do for him, or what they could give him in token of their thankfulness; but Arasmon shook his head and said, 'You can do nothing for me, unless you can tell me where to seek my wife Chrysea. It is to find her I am wandering;' and when the women shook their heads, and said again they knew nothing of her, the harp-strings as he touched them cried again,

'Arasmon! Arasmon! listen to me. It is I, Chrysea;' but again no one understood it, and though all pitied him, no one could help him.

Next morning when the mist had cleared away, and the sun was shining, a little ship set sail for foreign countries, and Arasmon begged the captain to take him in it that he might seek Chrysea still farther.

They sailed and sailed, till at last they came to the country for which they were bound; but they found the whole land in confusion, and war and fighting everywhere, and all the people were leaving their homes and hiding themselves in the towns, for fear of a terrible enemy, who was invading them. But no one hurt Arasmon as he wandered on with his harp in his hand, only no one would stop to answer him, when he asked if Chrysea had been there, for every one was too frightened and hurried to heed him.

At last he came to the chief city where the King dwelt, and here he found all the men building walls and fortresses, and preparing to defend the town, because they knew their enemy was coming to besiege it, but all the soldiers were gloomy and low-spirited.

'It is impossible for us to conquer,' they said, 'for there are three of them to every one of us, and they will take our city and make our King prisoner.'

That night as the watchmen looked over the walls, they saw in the distance an immense army marching towards them, and their swords and helmets glittered in the moonlight.

Then they gave the signal, and the captains gathered together their men to prepare them for fighting; but so sure were they of being beaten that it was with difficulty their officers could bring them to the walls.

'It would be better,' said the soldiers, 'to lay down our arms at once and let the enemy enter, for then we should not lose our lives as well as our city and our wealth.'

When Arasmon heard this he sat upon the walls of the town, and began to play upon his harp, and this time its music was so loud and clear, that it could be heard far and wide, and its sound was so exultant and joyous, that when the soldiers heard it they raised their heads, and their fears vanished, and they started forward, shouting and calling that they would conquer or be killed.

Then the enemy attacked the city, but the soldiers within met them with so much force that they were driven back, and had to fly, and the victorious army followed them and drove them quite out of their country, and Arasmon went with them, playing on his harp, to cheer them as they went.

When they knew the victory was theirs, all the captains wondered what had caused their sudden success, and one of the lieutenants said, 'It was that strange harper who went with us, playing on his harp. When our men heard it, they became as brave as lions.' So the captains sent for Arasmon, but when they came they were astonished to see how worn and thin he looked, and could scarcely believe it was he who had made such wonderful music, for his face had grown thin and pale, and there were gray locks in his hair.

They asked him what he would like to have, saying they would give him whatever he would choose, for the great service he had done them.

Arasmon only shook his head and said,

'There is nothing I want that you can give me. I am seeking the whole world round to find my wife Chrysea. It is many many years since I lost her. We two were as happy as birds on the bough. We wandered over the world singing and playing in the sunshine. But now she is gone, and I care for nothing else.' And the captains looked pityingly at him, for they all thought him mad, and could not understand what the harp said when he played on it again, and it cried,

'Listen, Arasmon! I too am here—I, Chrysea.'

So Arasmon left that city, and started again, and wandered for days and months and years.

He came by many strange places, and met with many strange people, but he found no trace of Chrysea, and each day he looked older and sadder and thinner.

At length he came to a country where the King loved nothing on earth so much as music. So fond of it was he, that he had musicians and singers by the score, always living in his palace, and there was no way of pleasing him so well as by sending a new musician or singer. So when Arasmon came into the country, and the people heard how marvellously he played, they said at once, 'Let us take him to the King. The poor man is mad. Hear how he goes on asking for his wife; but, mad or not, his playing will delight the King. Let us take him at once to the palace.' So, though Arasmon would have resisted them, they dragged him away to the court, and sent a messenger to the King, to say they had found a poor mad wandering harper, who played music the like of which they had never heard before.

The King and Queen, and all the court, sat feasting when the messenger came in saying that the people were bringing a new harper to play before his majesty.

'A new harper!' quoth he. 'That is good hearing. Let him be brought here to play to us at once.'

So Arasmon was led into the hall, and up to the golden thrones on which sat the King and Queen. A wonderful hall it was, made of gold and silver, and crystal and ivory, and the courtiers, dressed in blue and green and gold and diamonds, were a sight to see. Behind the throne were twelve young maids dressed in pure white, who sang most sweetly, and behind them were the musicians who accompanied them on every kind of instrument. Arasmon had never in his life seen such a splendid sight.

'Come here,' cried the King to him, 'and let us hear you play.' And the singers ceased singing, and the musicians smiled scornfully, for they could not believe Arasmon's music could equal theirs. For he looked to be in a most sorry plight. He had walked far, and the dust of the roads was on him. His clothes were worn threadbare, and stained and soiled, while his face was so thin and anxious and sad that it was pitiful to see; but his harp of pure shining gold was undulled, and untarnished. He began to play, and then all smiles ceased, and the women began to weep, and the men sat and stared at him in astonishment. When he had done the King started up, and throwing his arms about his neck, cried, 'Stay with me. You shall be my chief musician. Never before have I heard playing like yours, and whatever you want I will give you.' But when he heard this, Arasmon knelt on one knee and said,

'My gracious lord, I cannot stay. I have lost my wife Chrysea. I must

'He began to play, and then all smiles ceased.'

search all over the world till I find her. Ah! how beautiful she was, and how sweetly she sang; her singing was far sweeter than even the music of my harp.'

'Indeed!' cried the King. 'Then I too would fain hear her. But stay with me, and I will send messengers all over the world to seek her far and near, and they will find her much sooner than you.'

So Arasmon stayed at the court, but he said that if Chrysea did not come soon he must go farther to seek her himself.

The King gave orders that he should be clad in the costliest clothes and have all he could want given to him, and after this he would hear no music but Arasmon's playing, so all the other musicians were jealous, and wished he had never come to the palace. But the strangest thing was that no one but Arasmon could play upon his golden harp. All the King's harpers tried, and the King himself tried also, but when they touched the strings there came from them a strange, melancholy wailing, and no one but Arasmon could bring out its beautiful notes.

But the courtiers and musicians grew more and more angry with Arasmon, till at last they hated him bitterly, and only wanted to do him some harm; for they said,

'Who is he, that our King should love and honour him before us? After all, it is not his playing which is so beautiful; it is chiefly the harp on which he plays, and if that were taken from him he would be no better than the rest of us;' and then they began to consult together as to how they should steal his harp.

One hot summer evening Arasmon went into the palace gardens, and sat down to rest beneath a large beech-tree, when a little way off he saw two courtiers talking together, and heard that they spoke of him, though they did not see him or know he was there.

'The poor man is mad,' said one; 'of that there is little doubt, but, mad or not, as long as he plays on his harp the King will not listen to any one else.'

'The only way is to take the harp from him,' said the other. 'But it is hard to know how to get it away, for he will never let it go out of his hands.'

'We must take it from him when he is sleeping,' said the first.

'Certainly,' said the other; and then Arasmon heard them settle how and when they would go to his room at night to steal his harp.

He sat still till they were gone, and then he rose, and grasping it tenderly, turned from the palace and walked away through the garden gates.

'I have lost Chrysea,' he said, 'and now they would take from me even my harp, the only thing I have to love in all this world, but I will go away, far off where they will never find me,' and when he was out of sight, he ran with all his might, and never rested till he was far away on a lonely hill, with no one near to see him.

The stars were beginning to shine though it was not yet dark. Arasmon sat on a stone and looked at the country far and near. He could hear the sheep bells tinkling around him, and far, far off in the distance he could see the city and the palace he had left.

Then he began to play on his harp, and as he played the sheep stopped browsing and drew near him to listen.

The stars grew brighter and the evening darker, and he saw a woman carrying a child coming up the hill.

She looked pale and tired, but her face was very happy as she sat down not far from Arasmon and listened to his playing, whilst she looked eagerly across the hill as if she watched for some one who was coming. Presently, she turned and said, 'How beautifully you play; I never heard music like it before, but what makes you look so sad? Are you unhappy?'

'Yes,' said Arasmon, 'I am very miserable. I lost my wife Chrysea many years ago, and now I don't know where she can be.'

'It is a year since I have seen my husband,' said the woman. 'He went to the war a year ago, but now there is peace and he is coming back, and to-night he will come over this hill. It was just here we parted, and now I am come to meet him.'

'How happy you must be,' said Arasmon. 'I shall never see Chrysea again,' and as he spoke he struck a chord on the harp, which cried, 'O Arasmon, my husband! why do you not know me? It is I, Chrysea.'

'Do not say that,' continued the woman; 'you will find her some day. Why do you sit here? Was it here you parted from her?'

Then Arasmon told her how they had gone to a strange desolate village and rested there for the night, and in the morning Chrysea was gone, and that he had wandered all over the world looking for her ever since.

'I think you are foolish,' said the woman; 'perhaps your wife has been waiting for you at the village all this time. I would go back to the place where I parted from her if I were you, and wait there till she returns. How could I meet my husband if I did not come to the spot where we last were together? We might both wander on for ever and never find each other; and now, see, here he is coming,' and she gave a cry of joy and ran to meet a soldier who was walking up the hill.

Arasmon watched them as they met and kissed, and saw the father lift the child in his arms, then the three walked over the hill together, and when they were gone he sat down and wept bitterly. 'What was it she said?' he said. 'That I ought to go back to the spot where we parted. She will not be there, but I will go and die at the place where I last saw her.' So again he grasped his harp and started. He travelled many days and weeks by land and sea, till late one day he came in sight of the hill on which stood the little village. But at first he could not believe that he had come to the right place, so changed did all appear. He stopped and looked around him in astonishment. He stood in a shady lane, the arching trees met over his head. The banks were full of spring flowers, and either side of the hedge were fields full of young green corn.

'Can this be the wretched bare road down which we walked together? I would indeed it were, and that she were with me now,' said he. When he looked across to the village, the change seemed greater still. There were many more cottages, and they were trim and well kept, standing in neat gardens full of flowers. He heard the cheerful voices of the peasants and the laughter of the village children. The whole place seemed to be full of life and happiness. He stopped again upon the mound where he and Chrysea had first played and sung.

'It is many, many a long year since I was here,' he said. 'Time has changed all things strangely; but it would be hard to say which is the more altered, this village or I, for then it was sunk in poverty and wretchedness, and now it has gained happiness and wealth, and I, who was so happy and glad, now am broken-down and worn. I have lost my only wealth, my wife Chrysea. It was just here she stood and sang, and now I shall never see her again or hear her singing.'

There came past him a young girl driving some cows, and he turned and spoke to her. 'Tell me, I beg,' he said, 'is not your village much changed of late years? I was here long ago, but I cannot now think it the same place, for this is as bright and flourishing a town as I have ever seen, and I remember it only as a dreary tumble-down village where the grass never grew.'

'Oh!' said the girl, 'then you were here in our bad time, but we do not now like to speak of that, for fear our troubles should return. Folks say we were spell-bound. 'Tis so long ago that I can scarcely remember it, for I was quite a little child then. But a wandering musician and his wife set us free; at least, everything began to mend after they came, and now we think they must have been angels from heaven, for next day they went, and we have never seen them since.'

'It was I and my wife Chrysea,' cried Arasmon. 'Have you seen her? Has she been here? I have sought all over the world ever since, but I cannot find her, and now I fear lest she be dead.'

The girl stared at him in surprise. 'You? you poor old man! Of what are you talking? You must surely be mad to say such things. These musicians were the most beautiful people upon the earth, and they were young and dressed in shining white and gold, and you are old and gray and ragged, and surely you are very ill too, for you seem to be so weak that you can scarcely walk. Come home with me, and I will give you food and rest till you are better.'

Arasmon shook his head. 'I am seeking Chrysea,' he said, 'and I will rest no more till I have found her;' and the girl, seeing that he was determined, left him alone and went on her way driving her cows before her.

When she had gone Arasmon sat by the wayside and wept as though his heart would break. 'It is too true,' he said; 'I am so old and worn that when I find her she will not know me,' and as he again fell a-weeping his hand struck the harp-strings, and they cried, 'I have watched you through all these years, my Arasmon. Take comfort, I am very near,' and his tears ceased, and he was soothed by the voice of the harp, though he knew not why.

Then he rose. 'I will go to the moor,' he said, 'and look for the tree on which I found my harp, and that will be my last resting-place, for surely my strength will carry me no farther.' So he tottered slowly on, calling, as he went, in a weak voice, 'Chrysea, my Chrysea! are you here? I have sought you over the world since you left me, and now that I am old and like to die, I am come to seek you where we parted.'

When he came upon the moor, he wondered again at the change of all the country round. He thought of the charred, blackened waste on which he had stood before, and now he looked with amazement at the golden gorse, the purple heather, so thick that he could scarcely pick his way amongst it.

'It is a beautiful place now,' he said, 'but I liked it better years ago, deserted and desolate though it was, for my Chrysea was here.'

There were so many trees upon the common that he could not tell which was the one on which his harp had hung, but, unable to go any farther, he staggered and sank down beneath a large oak-tree, in whose branches a blackbird was singing most sweetly. The sun was setting just as of yore when he had found his harp, and most of the birds' songs were over, but this one bird still sang sweet and clear, and Arasmon, tired and weak though he was, raised his head and listened.

'I never heard a bird sing like that,' he said. 'What is the tune it sings? I will play it on my harp before I die.' And with what strength remained to him he reached forth his trembling hand, and grasping his harp struck upon it the notes of the bird's song, then he fell back exhausted, and his eyes closed.

At once the harp slid from his hand, and Chrysea stood beside him—Chrysea dressed as of old, in shining white and gold, with bright hair and eyes.

'Arasmon!' she cried, 'see, it is I, Chrysea!' but Arasmon did not move. Then she raised her voice and sang more sweetly than the bird overhead, and Arasmon opened his eyes and looked at her.

'Chrysea!' cried he; 'I have found my wife Chrysea!' and he laid his head on her bosom and died. And when Chrysea saw it her heart broke, and she lay beside him and died without a word.

In the morning when some of the villagers crossed the common they saw Arasmon and Chrysea lying beneath the oak-tree in each other's arms, and drew near them, thinking they were asleep, but when they saw their faces they knew they were dead.

Then an old man stooped and looked at Chrysea, and said,

'Surely it is the woman who came to us and sang long ago, when we were in our troubles; and, though he is sadly changed and worn, it is like her husband who played for her singing.'

Then came the girl who had driven the cows and told them how she had met Arasmon, and all he had said to her.

'He searched everywhere for his wife, he said,' said she. 'I am glad he has found her. Where could she be?'

'Would that we had known it was he,' said they all, 'how we would have greeted him! but see, he looks quite content and as if he wished nothing more, since he has found his wife Chrysea.'

JULIANA HORATIA EWING
The First Wife's Wedding-Ring

MANY years ago, there lived a certain worthy man who was twice married. By his first wife he had a son, who soon after his mother's death resolved to become a soldier, and go to foreign lands. 'When one has seen the world, one values home the more,' said he; 'and if I live I shall return.'

So the father gave him a blessing, and his mother's wedding-ring, saying, 'Keep this ring, and then, however long you stay away, and however changed you may become, by this token I shall know you to be my true son and heir.'

In a short time the father married again, and by this marriage also he had one son.

Years passed by, and the elder brother did not return, and at last every one believed him to be dead. But in reality he was alive, and after a long time he turned his steps homewards. He was so much changed by age and travelling that only his mother would have known him again, but he had the ring tied safe and fast round his neck. One night, however, he was too far from shelter to get a bed, so he slept under a hedge, and when he woke in the morning the string was untied and the ring was gone. He spent a whole day in searching for it, but in vain; and at last he resolved to proceed and explain the matter to his father.

The old man was overjoyed to see him, and fully believed his tale, but with the second wife it was otherwise. She was greatly displeased to think that her child was not now to be the sole heir of his father's goods; and she so pestered and worked upon the old man by artful and malicious speeches, that he consented to send away the new-comer till he should have found the first wife's wedding-ring.

'Is the homestead I have taken such care of,' she cried, 'to go to the first vagrant who comes in with a brown face and a ragged coat, pretending that he is your son?'

So the soldier was sent about his business; but his father followed him to the gate, and slipped some money into his hand, saying, 'God speed you back again with the ring!'

It was Sunday morning, and the bells were ringing for service as he turned sadly away.

'Ding, dong!' rang the bells, 'ding, dong! Why do you not come to church like others? Why are you not dressed in your Sunday clothes, and wherefore do you heave such doleful sighs, whilst we ring merrily? Ding, dong! ding dong!'

'Is there not a cause?' replied the soldier. 'This day I am turned out of home and heritage, though indeed I am the true heir.'

'Nevertheless we shall ring for your return,' said the bells.

As he went, the sun shone on the green fields, and in the soldier's eyes, and said, 'See how brightly I shine! But you, comrade, why is your face so cloudy?'

'Is there not good reason?' replied he. 'This day I am turned out of home and heritage, and yet I am the true heir.'

'Nevertheless I shall shine on your return,' said the sun.

Along the road the hawthorn hedges were white with blossom. 'Heyday!' they cried, 'who is this that comes trimp tramp, with a face as long as a poplar-tree? Cheer up, friend! It is spring! sweet spring! All is now full of hope and joy, and why should you look so sour?'

'May I not be excused?' said the soldier. 'This day I am turned out of home and heritage, and yet I am the true heir.'

'Nevertheless, we shall blossom when you return,' said the hedges.

When he had wandered for three days and three nights, all he had was spent, and there was no shelter to be seen but a dark gloomy forest, which stretched before him. Just then he saw a small, weazened old woman, who was trying to lift a bundle of sticks on to her back.

'That is too heavy for you, good mother,' said the soldier; and he raised and adjusted it for her.

'Have you just come here?' muttered the old crone; 'then the best thanks I can give you is to bid you get away as fast as you can.'

'I never retreated yet, dame,' said the soldier, and on he went.

Presently he met with a giant, who was strolling along by the edge of the wood, knocking the cones off the tops of the fir-trees with his finger-nails. He was an ill-favoured looking monster, but he said, civilly enough, 'You look in want of employment, comrade. Will you take service with me?'

'I must first know two things,' answered the soldier; 'my work and my wages.'

'Your work,' said the giant, 'is to cut a path through this wood to the other side. But then you shall have a year and a day to do it in. If you do it within the time, you will find at the other end a magpie's nest, in which is the ring of which you are in search. The nest also contains the crown jewels which have been stolen, and if you take these to the king, you will need no further reward. But, on the other hand, if the work is not done within the time, you will thenceforth be my servant without wages.'

'It is a hard bargain,' said the soldier, 'but need knows no law, and I agree to the conditions.'

When he came into the giant's abode, he was greatly astonished to see the little weazened old woman. She showed no sign of recognizing him, however, and the soldier observed a like discretion. He soon discovered that she was the giant's wife, and much in dread of her husband, who treated her with great cruelty.

'To-morrow you shall begin to work,' said the giant.

'If you please,' said the soldier, and before he went to bed he carried in water and wood for the old woman.

'There's a kinship in trouble,' said he.

Next morning the giant led him to a certain place on the outskirts of the forest, and giving him an axe, said, 'The sooner you begin, the better, and you may see that it is not difficult.' Saying which, he took hold of one of the trees by the middle, and snapped it off as one might pluck a flower.

'Thus to thee, but how to me?' said the soldier; and when the giant departed he set to work. But although he was so strong, and worked willingly, the trees seemed almost as hard as stone, and he made little progress. When he returned at night the giant asked him how he got on.

'The trees are very hard,' said he.

'So they always say,' replied the giant; 'I have always had idle servants.'

'I will not be called idle a second time,' thought the soldier, and the next day he went early and worked his utmost. But the result was very small. And when he came home, looking weary and disappointed, he could not fail to perceive that this gave great satisfaction to the giant.

Matters had gone on thus for some time, when one morning, as he went to work, he found the little old woman gathering sticks as before.

'Listen,' said she. 'He shall not treat you as he has treated others. Count seventy to the left from where you are working, and begin again. But do not let him know that you have made a fresh start. And do a little at the old place from time to time, as a blind.'

And before he could thank her, the old woman was gone. Without more ado, however, he counted seventy from the old place, and hit the seventieth tree such a blow with his axe, that it came crashing down then and there. And he found that, one after another, the trees yielded to his blows, as if they were touchwood. He did a good day's work, gave a few strokes in the old spot, and came home, taking care to look as gloomy as before.

Day by day he got deeper and deeper into the wood, the trees falling before him like dry elder twigs; and now the hardest part of his work was walking backwards and forwards to the giant's home, for the forest seemed almost interminable. But on the three hundred and sixty-sixth day from his first meeting with the giant, the soldier cut fairly through on to an open plain, and as the light streamed in, a magpie flew away, and on searching her nest, the soldier found his mother's wedding-ring. He also found many precious stones of priceless value, which were evidently the lost crown jewels. And as his term of service with the giant was now ended, he did not trouble himself to return, but with the ring and the jewels in his pocket set off to find his way to the capital.

He soon fell in with a good-humoured fellow who showed him the way, and pointed out everything of interest on the road. As they drew near, one of the royal carriages was driving out of the city gates, in which sat three beautiful ladies who were the king's daughters.

'The two eldest are engaged to marry two neighbouring princes,' said the companion.

'And whom is the youngest to marry?' asked the soldier, 'for she is by far the most beautiful.'

'She will never marry,' answered his companion, 'for she is pledged to the man who shall find the crown jewels, and cut a path through the stone-wood forest that borders the king's domains. And that is much as if she were promised to the man who should fetch down the moon for her to play with. For the jewels are lost beyond recall, and the wood is an enchanted forest.'

'Nevertheless she shall be wed with my mother's ring,' thought the soldier. But he kept his own counsel, and only waited till he had smartened himself up, before he sought an audience of the king.

His claim to the princess was fully proved; the king heaped honours and riches upon him; and he made himself so acceptable to his bride elect, that the wedding was fixed for an early day.

'May I bring my old father, madam?' he asked of the princess.

'That you certainly may,' said she. 'A good son makes a good husband.'

As he entered his native village the hedges were in blossom, the sun shone, and the bells rang for his return.

His stepmother now welcomed him, and was very anxious to go to court also. But her husband said, 'No. You took such good care of the homestead, it is but fit you should look to it whilst I am away.'

As to the giant, when he found that he had been outwitted, he went off, and was never more heard of in those parts. But the soldier took his wife into the city, and cared for her to the day of her death.

OSCAR WILDE

The Selfish Giant

Every afternoon, as they were coming from school, the children used to go and play in the Giant's garden.

It was a large lovely garden, with soft green grass. Here and there over the grass stood beautiful flowers like stars, and there were twelve peach-trees that in the spring-time broke out into delicate blossoms of pink and pearl, and in the autumn bore rich fruit. The birds sat on the trees and sang so sweetly that the children used to stop their games in order to listen to them. 'How happy we are here!' they cried to each other.

One day the Giant came back. He had been to visit his friend the Cornish ogre, and had stayed with him for seven years. After the seven years were over he had said all that he had to say, for his conversation was limited, and he determined to return to his own castle. When he arrived he saw the children playing in the garden.

'What are you doing here?' he cried in a very gruff voice, and the children ran away.

'My own garden is my own garden,' said the Giant; 'any one can understand that, and I will allow nobody to play in it but myself.' So he built a high wall all round it, and put up a notice-board.

> TRESPASSERS
>
> WILL BE
>
> PROSECUTED

He was a very selfish Giant.

The poor children had now nowhere to play. They tried to play on the road, but the road was very dusty and full of hard stones, and they did not like it. They used to wander round the high wall when their lessons were over, and talk about the beautiful garden inside.

'How happy we were there,' they said to each other.

Then the Spring came, and all over the country there were little blossoms and little birds. Only in the garden of the Selfish Giant it was still Winter. The birds did not care to sing in it as there were no children, and the trees forgot to blossom. Once a beautiful flower put its head out from the grass, but when it saw the notice-board it was so sorry for the children that it slipped back into the ground again, and went off to sleep. The only people who were pleased were the Snow and the Frost. 'Spring has forgotten this garden,' they cried, 'so we will live here all the year round.' The Snow covered up all the grass with her great white cloak, and the Frost painted all the trees silver. Then they invited the North Wind to stay with them, and he came. He was wrapped in furs, and he roared all day about the garden, and blew the chimney-pots down. 'This is a delightful spot,' he said, 'we must ask the Hail on a visit.' So the Hail came. Every day for three hours he rattled on the roof of the castle till he broke most of the slates, and then he ran round and round the garden as fast as he could go. He was dressed in grey, and his breath was like ice.

'I cannot understand why the Spring is so late in coming,' said the Selfish Giant, as he sat at the window and looked out at his cold white garden; 'I hope there will be a change in the weather.'

But the Spring never came, nor the Summer. The Autumn gave golden fruit to every garden, but to the Giant's garden she gave none. 'He is too selfish,' she said. So it was always Winter there, and the North Wind, and the Hail, and the Frost, and the Snow danced about through the trees.

One morning the Giant was lying awake in bed when he heard some lovely music. It sounded so sweet to his ears that he thought it must be the King's musicians passing by. It was really only a little linnet singing outside his window, but it was so long since he had heard a bird sing in his garden that it seemed to him to be the most beautiful music in the world. Then the Hail stopped dancing over his head, and the North Wind ceased roaring, and a delicious perfume came to him through the open casement. 'I believe the Spring has come at last,' said the Giant; and he jumped out of bed and looked out.

What did he see?

He saw the most wonderful sight. Through a little hole in the wall the children had crept in, and they were sitting in the branches of the trees. In every tree that he could see there was a little child. And the trees were so glad to have the children back again that they had covered themselves with blossoms, and were waving their arms gently above the children's heads. The birds were flying about and twittering with delight, and the flowers were looking up through the green grass and laughing. It was a lovely scene, only in one corner it was still Winter. It was the farthest corner of the garden, and in it was standing a little boy. He was so small that he could not reach up to the branches of the tree, and he was wandering all round it, crying bitterly. The poor tree was still quite covered with frost and snow, and the North Wind was blowing and roaring above it. 'Climb up! little boy,' said the Tree, and it bent its branches down as low as it could; but the boy was too tiny.

And the Giant's heart melted as he looked out. 'How selfish I have been!' he said; 'now I know why the Spring would not come here. I will put that little boy on the top of the tree, and then I will knock down the wall, and my garden shall be the children's playground for ever and ever.' He was really very sorry for what he had done.

So he crept downstairs and opened the front door quite softly, and went out into the garden. But when the children saw him they were so frightened that they all ran away, and the garden became Winter again. Only the little boy did not run, for his eyes were so full of tears that he did not see the Giant coming. And the Giant stole up behind him and took him gently in his hand, and put him up into the tree. And the tree broke at once into blossom, and the birds came and sang on it, and the little boy stretched out his two arms and flung them round the Giant's neck, and kissed him. And the other children, when they saw that the Giant was not wicked any longer, came running back, and with them came the Spring. 'It is your garden now, little children,' said the Giant, and he took a great axe and knocked down the wall. And when the people were going to market at twelve o'clock they found the Giant playing with the children in the most beautiful garden they had ever seen.

All day long they played, and in the evening they came to the Giant to bid him good-bye.

'But where is your little companion?' he said; 'the boy I put into the tree.' The Giant loved him the best because he had kissed him.

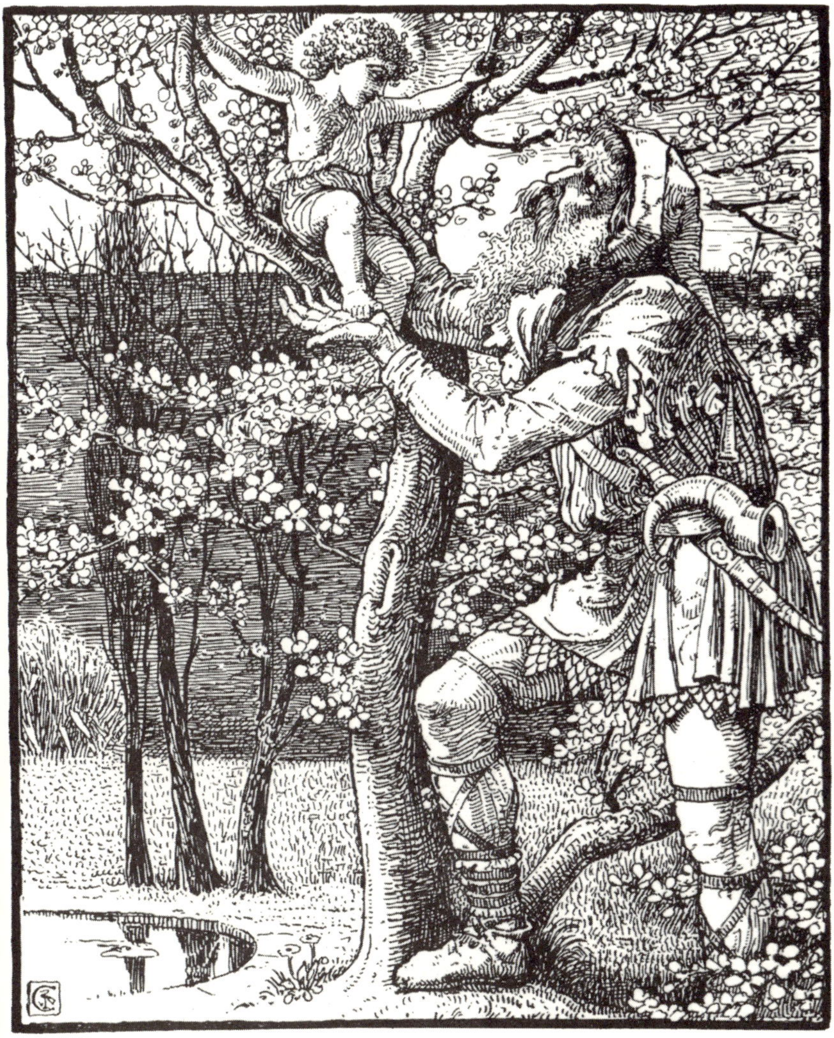

'We don't know,' answered the children; 'he has gone away.'

'You must tell him to be sure and come here to-morrow,' said the Giant. But the children said that they did not know where he lived, and had never seen him before; and the Giant felt very sad.

Every afternoon, when school was over, the children came and played with the Giant. But the little boy whom the Giant loved was never seen again. The Giant was very kind to all the children, yet he longed for his first little friend, and often spoke of him. 'How I would like to see him!' he used to say.

Years went over, and the Giant grew very old and feeble. He could not play about any more, so he sat in a huge armchair, and watched the children at their games, and admired his garden. 'I have many beautiful flowers,' he said; 'but the children are the most beautiful flowers of all.'

One winter morning he looked out of his window as he was dressing. He did not hate the Winter now, for he knew that it was merely the Spring asleep, and that the flowers were resting.

Suddenly he rubbed his eyes in wonder, and looked and looked. It certainly was a marvellous sight. In the farthest corner of the garden was a tree quite covered with lovely white blossoms. Its branches were all golden, and silver fruit hung down from them, and underneath it stood the little boy he had loved.

Downstairs ran the Giant in great joy, and out into the garden. He hastened across the grass, and came near to the child. And when he came quite close his face grew red with anger, and he said, 'Who hath dared to wound thee?' For on the palms of the child's hands were the prints of two nails, and the prints of two nails were on the little feet.

'Who hath dared to wound thee?' cried the Giant; 'tell me, that I may take my big sword and slay him.'

'Nay!' answered the child; 'but these are the wounds of Love.'

'Who art thou?' said the Giant, and a strange awe fell on him, and he knelt before the little child.

And the child smiled on the Giant, and said to him, 'You let me play once in your garden, to-day you shall come with me to my garden, which is Paradise.'

And when the children ran in that afternoon, they found the Giant lying dead under the tree, all covered with white blossoms.

ANDREW LANG

Prince Prigio

CHAPTER I

HOW THE FAIRIES WERE NOT INVITED TO COURT

ONCE upon a time there reigned in Pantouflia* a king and a queen. With almost everything else to make them happy, they wanted one thing: they had no children. This vexed the king even more than the queen, who was very clever and learned, and who had hated dolls when she was a child. However, she, too in spite of all the books she read and all the pictures she painted, would have been glad enough to be the mother of a little prince. The king was anxious to consult the fairies, but the queen would not hear of such a thing. She did not believe in fairies: she said that they had never existed; and that she maintained, though *The History of the Royal Family* was full of chapters about nothing else.

Well, at long and at last they had a little boy, who was generally regarded as the finest baby that had ever been seen. Even her majesty herself remarked that, though she could never believe all the courtiers told her, yet he certainly was a fine child—a very fine child.

Now, the time drew near for the christening party, and the king and queen were sitting at breakfast in their summer parlour talking over it. It was a splendid room, hung with portraits of the royal ancestors. There was Cinderella, the grandmother of the reigning monarch, with her little foot in her glass slipper thrust out before her. There was the Marquis de Carabas, who, as everyone knows, was raised to the throne as prince consort after his marriage with the daughter of the king of the period. On the arm of the throne was seated his celebrated cat, wearing boots. There, too, was a portrait of a beautiful lady, sound asleep: this was Madam La Belle au Bois-dormant,* also an ancestress of the royal family. Many other pictures of celebrated persons were hanging on the walls.

'You have asked all the right people, my dear?' said the king.

'Everyone who should be asked,' answered the queen.

'People are so touchy on these occasions,' said his majesty. 'You have not forgotten any of our aunts?'

'No; the old cats!' replied the queen; for the king's aunts were old-fashioned, and did not approve of her, and she knew it.

'They are very kind old ladies in their way,' said the king; 'and were nice to me when I was a boy.'

Then he waited a little, and remarked:

'The fairies, of course, you have invited? It has always been usual, in our family, on an occasion like this; and I think we have neglected them a little of late.'

'How *can* you be so *absurd*?' cried the queen. 'How often must I tell you that there are *no* fairies? And even if there were—but, no matter; pray let us drop the subject.'

'They are very old friends of our family, my dear, that's all,' said the king timidly. 'Often and often they have been godmothers to us. One, in particular, was most kind and most serviceable to Cinderella I, my own grandmother.'

'Your grandmother!' interrupted her majesty. 'Fiddle-de-dee! If anyone puts such nonsense into the head of my little Prigio*——'

But here the baby was brought in by the nurse, and the queen almost devoured it with kisses. And so the fairies were not invited! It was an extraordinary thing, but none of the nobles could come to the christening party when they learned that the fairies had not been asked. Some were abroad; several were ill; a few were in prison among the Saracens;* others were captives in the dens of ogres. The end of it was that the king and queen had to sit down alone, one at each end of a very long table, arrayed with plates and glasses for a hundred guests—for a hundred guests who never came!

'Any soup, my dear?' shouted the king, through a speaking-trumpet; when, suddenly, the air was filled with a sound like the rustling of the wings of birds. *Flitter, flitter, flutter*, went the noise; and when the queen looked up, lo and behold! on every seat was a lovely fairy, dressed in green, each with a *most interesting-looking parcel* in her hand. Don't you like opening parcels? The king did, and he was most friendly and polite to the fairies. But the queen, though she saw them distinctly, took no notice of them. You see, she did not believe in fairies, nor in her own eyes, when she saw them. So she talked across the fairies to the king, just as if they had not been there; but the king behaved as politely as if they were *real*—which, of course, they were.

When dinner was over, and when the nurse had brought in the baby, all the fairies gave him the most magnificent presents. One offered a purse which could never be empty; and one a pair of seven-leagued boots;* and another a cap of darkness, that nobody might see the prince when he put it on; and another a wishing-cap; and another a carpet, on which, when he sat, he was carried wherever he wished to find himself. Another made him beautiful for ever; and another, brave; and another, lucky: but the last fairy of all, a cross old thing, crept up and said, 'My child, you shall be *too* clever!'

This fairy's gift would have pleased the queen, if she had believed in it, more than anything else, because she was so clever herself. But she took no notice at all; and the fairies went each to her own country, and none of them stayed there at the palace, where nobody believed in them, except the king, a little. But the queen tossed all their nice boots and caps, carpets, purses, swords, and all, away into a dark lumber-room; for, of course, she thought that they were *all nonsense*, and merely old rubbish out of books, or pantomime 'properties.'*

CHAPTER II

PRINCE PRIGIO AND HIS FAMILY

WELL, the little prince grew up. I think I've told you that his name was Prigio—did I not? Well, that *was* his name. You cannot think how clever he was. He argued with his nurse as soon as he could speak, which was very soon. He argued that he did not like to be washed, because the soap got into his eyes. However, when he was told all about the *pores of the skin*, and how they could not be healthy if he was not washed, he at once ceased to resist, for he was very reasonable. He argued with his father that he did not see why there should be kings who were rich, while beggars were poor; and why the king—who was a little greedy—should have poached eggs and plumcake at afternoon tea, while many other persons went without dinner. The king was so surprised and hurt at these remarks that he boxed the prince's ears, saying, 'I'll teach you to be too clever, my lad.' Then he remembered the awful curse of the oldest fairy, and was sorry for the rudeness of the queen. And when the prince, after having his ears boxed, said that 'force was no argument,' the king went away in a rage.

Indeed, I cannot tell you how the prince was hated by all! He would go down into the kitchen, and show the cook how to make soup. He would visit the poor people's cottage, and teach them how to make the beds, and how to make plum-pudding out of turnip-tops, and venison cutlets out of rusty bacon. He showed the fencing-master how to fence, and the professional cricketer how to bowl, and instructed the rat-catcher in breeding terriers. He set sums to the Chancellor of the Exchequer, and assured the Astronomer Royal that the sun does not go round the earth—which, for my part, I believe it does. The young ladies of the Court disliked dancing with him, in spite of his good looks, because he was always asking, 'Have you read this?' and 'Have you read that?'—and when they said they hadn't, he sneered; and when they said they *had*, he found them out.

He found out all his tutors and masters in the same horrid way; correcting the accent of his French teacher, and trying to get his German tutor not to eat peas with his knife. He also endeavoured to teach the queen-dowager, his grandmother,* an art with which she had long been perfectly familiar! In fact, he knew everything better than anybody else; and the worst of it was that he *did*: and he was never in the wrong, and he always said, 'Didn't I tell you so?' And, what was more, he *had!*

As time went on, Prince Prigio had two younger brothers, whom everybody liked. They were not a bit clever, but jolly. Prince Alphonso, the third son, was round, fat, good-humoured, and as brave as a lion. Prince Enrico, the second, was tall, thin, and a little sad, but *never* too clever. Both were in love with two of their own cousins (with the approval of their dear parents); and all the world said, 'What nice, unaffected princes they are!' But Prigio nearly got the country into several wars by being too clever for the foreign ambassadors. Now, as Pantouflia was a rich, lazy country, which hated fighting, this was very unpleasant, and did not make people love Prince Prigio any better.

CHAPTER III

ABOUT THE FIREDRAKE

OF all the people who did not like Prigio, his own dear papa, King Grognio,* disliked him most. For the king knew he was not clever, himself. When he was in the counting-house, counting out his money,* and when he happened to say, 'Sixteen shillings and fourteen and twopence are three pounds, fifteen,' it made him wild to hear Prigio whisper, 'One pound, ten and twopence'—which, of course, it *is*. And the king was afraid that Prigio would conspire, and get made king himself—which was the last thing Prigio really wanted. He much preferred to idle about, and know everything without seeming to take any trouble.

Well, the king thought and thought. How was he to get Prigio out of the way, and make Enrico or Alphonso his successor? He read in books about it; and all the books showed that, if a king sent his three sons to do anything, it was always the youngest who did it, and got the crown. And he wished he had the chance. Well, it arrived at last.

There was a very hot summer! It began to be hot in March. All the rivers were dried up. The grass did not grow. The corn did not grow. The thermometers exploded with heat. The barometers stood at SET FAIR. The people were much distressed, and came and broke the palace windows—as they usually do when things go wrong in Pantouflia.

The king consulted the learned men about the Court, who told him that probably a

FIREDRAKE

was in the neighbourhood.

Now, the Firedrake is a beast, or bird, about the bigness of an elephant. Its body is made of iron, and it is always red-hot. A more terrible and cruel beast cannot be imagined; for, if you go near it, you are at once broiled by the Firedrake.

But the king was not ill-pleased: 'for,' thought he, 'of course my three sons must go after the brute, the eldest first; and, as usual, it will kill the first two, and be beaten by the youngest. It is a little hard on Enrico, poor boy; but *anything* to get rid of that Prigio!'

Then the king went to Prigio, and said that his country was in danger, and that he was determined to leave the crown to whichever of them would bring him the horns (for it has horns) and tail of the Firedrake.

'It is an awkward brute to tackle,' the king said, 'but you are the oldest, my lad; go where glory waits you! Put on your armour, and be off with you!'

This the king said, hoping that either the Firedrake would roast

Prince Prigio alive (which he could easily do, as I have said; for he is all over as hot as a red-hot poker), or that, if the prince succeeded, at least his country would be freed from the monster.

But the prince, who was lying on the sofa doing sums in compound division for fun, said in the politest way:

'Thanks to the education your majesty has given me, I have learned that the Firedrake, like the siren,* the fairy, and so forth, is a fabulous animal which does not exist. But even granting, for the sake of argument, that there is a Firedrake, your majesty is well aware that there is no kind of use in sending *me*. It is always the eldest son who goes out first and comes to grief on these occasions, and it is always the third son that succeeds. Send Alphonso' (this was the youngest brother), 'and *he* will do the trick at once. At least, if he fails, it will be most unusual, and Enrico can try his luck.'

Then he went back to his arithmetic and his slate, and the king had to send for Prince Alphonso and Prince Enrico. They both came in very warm; for they had been whipping tops, and the day was unusually hot.

'Look here,' said the king, 'just you two younger ones look at Prigio! You see how hot it is, and how coolly he takes it, and the country suffering; and all on account of a Firedrake, you know, which has apparently built his nest not far off. Well, I have asked that lout of a brother of yours to kill it, and he says——'

'That he does not believe in Firedrakes,' interrupted Prigio. 'The weather's warm enough without going out hunting!'

'Not believe in Firedrakes!' cried Alphonso. 'I wonder what you *do* believe in! Just let me get at the creature!' for he was as brave as a lion. 'Hi! Page, my chain-armour, helmet, lance, and buckler! *A Molinda! A Molinda!*' which was his *war-cry*.

The page ran to get the armour; but it was *so uncommonly hot* that he dropped it, and put his fingers in his mouth, crying!

'You had better put on flannels, Alphonso, for this kind of work,' said Prigio. 'And if I were you, I'd take a light garden-engine, full of water, to squirt at the enemy.'

'Happy thought!' said Alphonso. 'I will!' And off he went, kissed his dear Molinda, bade her keep a lot of dances for him (there was to be a dance when he had killed the Firedrake), and then he rushed to the field!

But he never came back any more!

Everyone wept bitterly—everyone but Prince Prigio; for he thought it was a practical joke, and said that Alphonso had taken the opportunity to start off on his travels and see the world.

'There is some dreadful mistake, sir,' said Prigio to the king. 'You know as well as I do that the youngest son has always succeeded, up to now. But I entertain great hopes of Enrico!'

And he grinned; for he fancied it was all *nonsense*, and that there were no Firedrakes.

Enrico was present when Prigio was consoling the king in this unfeeling way.

'Enrico, my boy,' said his majesty, 'the task awaits you, and the honour. When *you* come back with the horns and tail of the Firedrake, you shall be crown prince; and Prigio shall be made an usher at the Grammar School—it is all he is fit for.'

Enrico was not quite so confident as Alphonso had been. He insisted on making his will; and he wrote a poem about the pleasures and advantages of dying young. This is part of it:

> *The violet is a blossom sweet,*
> *That droops before the day is done—*
> *Slain by thine overpowering heat,*
> *O Sun!*
>
> *And I, like that sweet purple flower,*
> *May roast, or boil, or broil, or bake,*
> *If burned by thy terrific power,*
> *Firedrake!*

This poem comforted Enrico more or less, and he showed it to Prigio. But the prince only laughed, and said that the second line of the last verse was not very good; for violets do not 'roast, or boil, or broil, or bake.'

Enrico tried to improve it, but could not. So he read it to his cousin, Lady Kathleena, just as it was; and she cried over it (though I don't think she understood it); and Enrico cried a little, too.

However, next day he started, with a spear, a patent refrigerator,* and a lot of the bottles people throw at fires to put them out.

But *he* never came back again!

After shedding torrents of tears, the king summoned Prince Prigio to his presence.

'Dastard!' he said. 'Poltroon! *Your* turn, which should have come first, has arrived at last. Y*ou* must fetch me the horns and the tail of the Firedrake. Probably you will be grilled, thank goodness; but who will give me back Enrico and Alphonso?'

'Indeed, your majesty,' said Prigio, 'you must permit me to correct your policy. Your only reason for dispatching your sons in pursuit of this dangerous but I believe *fabulous* animal, was to ascertain which of us would most worthily succeed to your throne, at the date—long may it be deferred!—of your lamented decease. Now, there can be no further question about the matter. I, unworthy as I am, represent the sole hope of the royal family. Therefore to send me after the Firedrake were[1] both dangerous and unnecessary. Dangerous, because, if he treats me as you say he did my brothers—my unhappy brothers,— the throne of Pantouflia will want an heir. But, if I do come back alive—why, I cannot be more the true heir than I am at present; now *can* I? Ask the Lord Chief Justice, if you don't believe *me*.'

These arguments were so clearly and undeniably correct that the king, unable to answer them, withdrew into a solitary place where he could express himself with freedom, and give rein to his passions.

CHAPTER IV

HOW PRINCE PRIGIO WAS DESERTED BY EVERYBODY

MEANWHILE, Prince Prigio had to suffer many unpleasant things. Though he was the crown prince (and though his arguments were unanswerable), everybody shunned him for a coward. The queen, who did not believe in Firedrakes, alone took his side. He was not only avoided by all, but he had most disagreeable scenes with his own cousins, Lady Molinda and Lady Kathleena. In the garden Lady Molinda met him walking alone, and did not bow to him.

'Dear Molly,' said the prince, who liked her, 'how have I been so unfortunate as to offend you?'

'My name, sir, is Lady Molinda,' she said, very proudly; 'and you have sent your own brother to his grave!'

'Oh, excuse me,' said the prince, 'I am certain he has merely gone off on his travels. He'll come back when he's tired: there *are*

---

[1] Subjunctive mood! He was a great grammarian!

no Firedrakes; a French writer says they are "purement fabuleux," purely fabulous, you know.'

'Prince Alphonso has gone on his travels, and will come back when he is tired! And was he then—tired—of *me?*' cried poor Molinda, bursting into tears, and forgetting her dignity.

'Oh! I beg your pardon, I never noticed; I'm sure I am very sorry,' cried the prince, who, never having been in love himself, never thought of other people. And he tried to take Molinda's hand, but she snatched it from him and ran away through the garden to the palace, leaving Prince Prigio to feel foolish, for once, and ashamed.

As for Lady Kathleena, she swept past him like a queen, without a word. So the prince, for all his cleverness, was not happy.

After several days had gone by, the king returned from the solitary place where he had been speaking his mind. He now felt calmer and better; and so at last he came back to the palace. But on seeing Prince Prigio, who was lolling in a hammock, translating Egyptian hieroglyphs into French poetry for his mother, the king broke out afresh, and made use of the most cruel and impolite expressions.

At last, he gave orders that all the Court should pack up and move to a distant city; and that Prince Prigio should be left alone in the palace by himself. For he was quite unendurable, the king said, and he could not trust his own temper when he thought of him. And he grew so fierce, that even the queen was afraid of him now.

The poor queen cried a good deal; Prigio being her favourite son, on account of his acknowledged ability and talent. But the rest of the courtiers were delighted at leaving Prince Prigio behind. For his part, he, very good-naturedly, showed them the best and shortest road to Falkenstein,* the city where they were going; and easily proved that neither the chief secretary for geography, nor the general of the army, knew anything about the matter—which, indeed, they did not.

The ungrateful courtiers left Prigio with hoots and yells, for they disliked him so much that they forgot he would be king one day. He therefore reminded them of this little fact in future history, which made them feel uncomfortable enough, and then lay down in his hammock and went to sleep.

When he wakened, the air was cold and the day was beginning to grow dark. Prince Prigio thought he would go down and dine at a tavern in the town, for no servants had been left with him. But what was his annoyance when he found that his boots, his sword, his cap, his cloak—all his clothes, in fact, except for those he wore,—had been taken away by the courtiers, merely to spite him! His wardrobe had been ransacked, and everything that had not been carried off had been cut up, burned, and destroyed. Never was such a spectacle of wicked mischief. It was as if hay had been made of everything he possessed. What was worse, he had not a penny in his pocket to buy new things; and his father had stopped his allowance of fifty thousand pounds a month.

Can you imagine anything more cruel and *unjust* than this conduct? for it was not the prince's fault that he was so clever. The cruel fairy had made him so. But, even if the prince had been born clever (as may have happened to you), was he to be blamed for that? The other people were just as much in fault for being born so stupid; but the world, my dear children, can never be induced to remember this. If you are clever, you will find it best not to let people know it—if you want them to like you.*

Well, here was the prince in a pretty plight. Not a pound in his pocket, not a pair of boots to wear, not even a cap to cover his head from the rain; nothing but cold meat to eat, and never a servant to answer the bell.

CHAPTER V

WHAT PRINCE PRIGIO FOUND IN THE GARRET

THE prince walked from room to room of the palace; but, unless he wrapped himself up in a curtain, there was nothing for him to wear when he went out in the rain. At last he climbed up a turret-stair in the very oldest part of the castle, where he had never been before; and at the very top was a little round room, a kind of garret. The prince pushed in the door with some difficulty—not that it was locked, but the handle was rusty, and the wood had swollen with the damp. The room was very dark; only the last grey light of the rainy evening came through a slit of a window, one of those narrow windows that they used to fire arrows out of in old times.

But in the dusk the prince saw a heap of all sorts of things lying on the floor and on the table. There were two caps; he put one on—an old, grey, ugly cap it was, made of felt. There was a pair of boots; and he kicked off his slippers, and got into *them*. They were a good deal worn, but fitted as if they had been made for him. On the table was a purse with just three gold coins—old ones, too—in it; and this, as you may fancy, the prince was very well pleased to put in his pocket. A sword, with a sword-belt, he buckled about his waist; and the rest of the articles, a regular collection of odds and ends, he left just where they were lying. Then he ran downstairs, and walked out of the hall door.

CHAPTER VI

WHAT HAPPENED TO PRINCE PRIGIO IN TOWN

BY this time the prince was very hungry. The town was just three miles off; but he had such a royal appetite, that he did not like to waste it on bad cookery, and the people of the royal town were bad cooks.

'I wish I were in "The Bear," at Gluckstein,'* he said to himself; for he remembered that there was a very good cook there. But, then, the town was twenty-one leagues away—sixty-three long miles!

No sooner had the prince said this, and taken just three steps, than he found himself at the door of the 'Bear Inn' at Gluckstein!

'This is the most extraordinary dream,' said he to himself; for he was far too clever, of course, to believe in seven-league boots. Yet he had a pair on at that very moment, and it was they which had carried him in three strides from the palace to Gluckstein!

The truth is, that the prince, in looking about the palace for clothes, had found his way into that very old lumber-room where the magical gifts of the fairies had been thrown by his clever mother, who did not believe in them. But this, of course, the prince did not know.

Now you should be told that the seven-league boots only take those prodigious steps when you say you *want* to go a long distance. Otherwise they would be very inconvenient—when you only want to cross the room, for example. Perhaps this has not been explained to you by your governess?*

Well, the prince walked into 'The Bear,' and it seemed odd to him that nobody took any notice of him. And yet his face was as well known as that of any man in Pantouflia; for everybody had seen it, at least in pictures. He was so puzzled by not being attended to as usual, that *he quite forgot to take off his cap.* He sat down at a table, however, and shouted '*Kellner!*'* at which all the waiters jumped, and looked around in every direction, but nobody came to him. At first he thought they were too busy, but presently another explanation occurred to him.

'The king,' he said to himself, 'has threatened to execute anybody who speaks to me, or helps me in any way. Well, I don't mean to starve in the midst of plenty, anyhow; here goes!'

The prince rose, and went to the table in the midst of the room, where a huge roast turkey had just been placed. He helped himself to half the breast, some sausages, chestnut stuffing, bread sauce, potatoes, and a bottle of red wine—Burgundy. He then went back to a table in a corner, where he dined very well, nobody taking any notice of him. When he had finished, he sat watching the other people dining, and smoking his cigarette. As he was sitting thus, a very tall man, an officer in the uniform of the Guards, came in, and, walking straight to the prince's table, said: 'Kellner, clean this table, and bring in the bill of fare.'

With these words, the officer sat down suddenly in the prince's lap, as if he did not see him at all. He was a heavy man, and the prince, enraged at the insult, pushed him away and jumped to his feet. As he did so, *his cap dropped off.* The officer fell on his knees at once, crying:

'Pardon, my prince pardon! I never saw you!'

This was more than the prince could be expected to believe.

'Nonsense! Count Frederick von Matterhorn,' he said; 'you must be intoxicated. Sir! you have insulted your prince and your superior officer. Consider yourself under arrest! You shall be sent to a prison to-morrow.'

On this, the poor officer appealed piteously to everybody in the tavern. They all declared that they had not seen the prince, nor even had an idea that he was doing them the honour of being in the neighbourhood of their town.

More and more offended, and convinced that there was a conspiracy to annoy and insult him, the prince shouted for the landlord, called for his bill, threw down his three pieces of gold without asking for change, and went into the street.

'It is a disgraceful conspiracy,' he said. 'The king shall answer for this! I shall write to the newspapers at once!'

He was not put in a better temper by the way in which people hustled him in the street. They ran against him exactly as if they did not see him, and then staggered back in the greatest surprise, looking in every direction for the person they had jostled. In one of these encounters, the prince pushed so hard against a poor old beggar woman that she fell down. As he was usually most kind and polite, he pulled off his cap to beg her pardon, when, behold, the beggar woman gave one dreadful scream, and fainted! A crowd was collecting, and the prince, forgetting that he had thrown down all his money in the tavern, pulled out his purse. Then he remembered what he had done, and expected to find it empty; but, lo, there were three pieces of gold in it! Overcome with surprise, he thrust the money into the woman's hand, and put on his cap again. In a moment the crowd, which had been staring at him, rushed away in every direction, with cries of terror, declaring that there was a magician in the town, and a fellow who could appear and disappear at pleasure!

By this time, you or I, or anyone who was not so extremely clever as Prince Prigio, would have understood what was the matter. He had put on, without knowing it, not only the seven-league boots, but the cap of darkness, and had taken Fortunatus's purse,* which could never be empty, however often you took all the money out. All those and many other delightful wares the fairies had given him at his christening, and the prince had found them in the dark garret. But the prince was so extremely wise, and learned, and scientific, that he did not believe in fairies, nor in fairy gifts.

'It is indigestion,' he said to himself: 'those sausages were not of the best; and that Burgundy was extremely strong. Things are not as they appear.'

Here, as he was arguing with himself, he was nearly run over by a splendid carriage and six, the driver of which never took the slightest notice of him. Annoyed at this, the prince leaped up behind, threw down the two footmen, who made no resistance, and so was carried to the door of a magnificent palace. He was determined to challenge the gentleman who was in the carriage; but, noticing that he had a very beautiful young lady with him, whom he had never seen before, he followed them into the house, not wishing to alarm the girl, and meaning to speak to the gentleman when he found him alone.

A great ball was going on; but, as usual, nobody took any notice of the prince. He walked among the guests, being careful not to jostle them, and listening to their conversation.

It was all about himself! Everyone had heard of his disgrace, and almost everyone cried 'Serve him right!' They said that the airs he gave himself were quite unendurable—that nothing was more rude than to be always in the right—that cleverness might be carried far too far—that it was better even to be born stupid ('Like the rest of you,' thought the prince); and, in fact, nobody had a good word for him.

Yes, one had! It was the pretty lady of the carriage. I never could tell you how pretty she was. She was tall, with cheeks like white roses blushing: she had dark hair, and very large dark-grey eyes, and her face was the kindest in the world! The prince first thought how nice and good she looked, even before he thought how pretty she looked. *She* stood up for Prince Prigio when her partner would speak ill of him. She had never seen the prince, for she was but newly come to Pantouflia; but she declared that it was his *misfortune*, not his fault, to be so clever. 'And then, think how hard they made him work at school! Besides,' said this kind young lady, 'I hear he is extremely handsome, and very brave; and he has a good heart, for he was kind, I have heard, to a poor boy, and did all his examination papers for him, so that the boy passed first in *everything*. And now he is Minister for Education, though he can't do a line of Greek prose!'

The prince blushed at this, for he knew his conduct had not been honourable. But he at once fell over head and ears in love with the young lady, a thing he had never done in his life before, because—he said—'women were so stupid!' You see he was so clever!

Now, at this very moment—when the prince, all of a sudden, was as deep in love as if he had been the stupidest officer in the room—an extraordinary thing happened! Something seemed to give a whirr! in his brain, and in one instant *he knew all about it!* He believed in fairies and fairy gifts, and understood that his cap was the cap of darkness, and his shoes the seven-league boots, and his purse the purse of Fortunatus! He had read about those things in historical books: but now he believed in them.

CHAPTER VII

THE PRINCE FALLS IN LOVE

HE understood all this, and burst out laughing, which nearly frightened an old lady near him out of her wits. Ah! how he wished he was only in evening dress, that he might dance with the charming young lady. But there he was, dressed just as if he were going out to hunt if anyone could have seen him. So, even if he took off his cap of darkness, and became visible, he was no figure for a ball. Once he would not have cared, but now he cared very much indeed.

But the prince was not clever for nothing. He thought for a moment, then went out of the room, and, in three steps of the seven-league boots, was at his empty, dark, cold palace again. He struck a light with a flint and steel, lit a torch, and ran upstairs to the garret. The flaring light of the torch fell on the pile of 'rubbish,' as the queen would have called it, which he turned over with eager hands. Was there—yes, there *was* another cap! There it lay, a handsome green one with a red feather. The prince pulled off the cap of darkness, put on the other, and said:

'*I wish I were dressed in my best suit of white and gold, with the royal Pantouflia diamonds!*'

In one moment there he was in white and gold, the greatest and most magnificent dandy in the whole world, and the handsomest man!

'How about my boots, I wonder,' said the prince; for his seven-league boots were stout riding-boots, not good to dance in, whereas *now* he was in elegant shoes of silk and gold.

He threw down the wishing cap, put on the other—the cap of darkness—and made three strides in the direction of Gluckstein. But he was only three steps nearer it than he had been, and the seven-league boots were standing beside him on the floor!

'No,' said the prince; 'no man can be in two different pairs of boots at one and the same time! That's mathematics!'

He then hunted about in the lumber-room again till he found a small, shabby, old Persian carpet, the size of a hearthrug. He went to his own room, took a portmanteau in his hand, sat down on the carpet, and said:

'I wish I were in Gluckstein.'

In a moment there he found himself; for this was that famous carpet which Prince Hussein bought long ago, in the market at Bisnagar,* and which the fairies had brought, with the other presents, to the christening of Prince Prigio.

When he arrived at the house where the ball was going on, he put the magical carpet in the portmanteau, and left it in the cloak-room, receiving a numbered ticket in exchange. Then he marched in all his glory (and, of course, without the cap of darkness) into the room where they were dancing. Everybody made place for him, bowing down to the ground, and the loyal band struck up *The Prince's March*!

> *Heaven bless our Prince Prigio!*
> *What is there he doesn't know?*
> *Greek, Swiss, German (High and Low),*
> *And the names of the mountains in Mexico,*
> *Heaven bless the prince!*

He used to be very fond of this march, and the words—some people even said he had made them himself. But now, somehow, he didn't much like it. He went straight to the Duke of Stumpfelbahn, the Hereditary Master of the Ceremonies, and asked to be introduced to the beautiful young lady. She was the daughter of the new English Ambassador, and her name was Lady Rosalind. But she nearly fainted when she heard who it was that wished to dance with her, for she was not at all particularly clever; and the prince had such a bad character for snubbing girls, and asking them difficult questions. However, it was impossible to refuse, and so she danced with the prince, and he danced very well. Then they sat out in the conservatory, among the flowers, where nobody came near them; and then they danced again, and then the Prince took her down to supper. And all the time he never once said, 'Have you read *this*?' or 'Have you read *that*?' or, 'What! you never heard of Alexander the Great?' or Julius Cæsar, or Michael Angelo, or whoever it might be—horrid, difficult questions he used to ask. That was the way he *used* to go on: but now he only talked to the young lady about *herself*; and she quite left off being shy or frightened, and asked him all about his own country, and about the Firedrake-shooting, and said how fond she was of hunting herself. And the prince said:

'Oh, if *you* wish it, you shall have the horns and tail of a Firedrake to hang up in your hall, to-morrow evening!'

Then she asked if it was not very dangerous work, Firedrake hunting; and he said it was nothing, when you knew the trick of it: and he asked her if she would but give him a rose out of her bouquet; and, in short, he made himself so agreeable and *unaffected*, that she thought him very nice indeed.

For, even a clever person can be nice when he likes—above all, when he is not thinking about himself. And now the prince was thinking of nothing in the world but the daughter of the English ambassador, and how to please her. He got introduced to her father too, and quite won his heart; and, at last, he was invited to dine next day at the Embassy.

In Pantouflia, it is the custom that a ball must not end while one of the royal family goes on dancing. *This* ball lasted till the light came in, and the birds were singing out of doors, and all the mothers present were sound asleep. Then nothing would satisfy the prince, but that they all should go home singing through the streets; in fact, there never had been so merry a dance in all Pantouflia. The prince had made a point of dancing with almost every girl there: and he had suddenly become the most beloved of the royal family. But everything must end at last; and the prince, putting on the cap of darkness and sitting on the famous carpet, flew back to his lonely castle.

CHAPTER VIII

THE PRINCE IS PUZZLED

PRINCE PRIGIO did not go to bed. It was bright daylight, and he had promised to bring the horns and tail of a Firedrake as a present to a pretty lady. He had said it was easy to do this; but now, as he sat and thought over it, he did not feel so victorious.

'First,' he said, 'where is the Firedrake?'

He reflected for a little, and then ran upstairs to the garret.

'It *should* be here!' he cried, tossing the fairies' gifts about; 'and, by George, here it is!'

Indeed, he had found the spyglass of carved ivory which Prince Ali, in the *Arabian Nights*, bought in the bazaar in Schiraz.* Now, this glass was made so that, by looking through it, you could see anybody or anything you wished, however far away. Prigio's first idea was to look at his lady. 'But she does not expect to be looked at,' he thought; 'and I *won't!*' On the other hand, he determined to look at the Firedrake; for, of course, he had no delicacy about spying on *him*, the brute.

The prince clapped the glass to his eye, stared out the window, and there, sure enough, he saw the Firedrake. He was floating about in a sea of molten lava, on the top of a volcano. There he was, swimming and diving for pleasure, tossing up the flaming waves, and blowing fountains of fire out of his nostrils, like a whale spouting!

The prince did not like the looks of him.

'With all my cap of darkness, and my shoes of swiftness, and my sword of sharpness, I never could get near that beast,' he said; 'and if I *did* stalk him, I could not hurt him. Poor little Alphonso! poor Enrico! what plucky fellows they were! I fancied that there was no such thing as a Firedrake: he's not in the Natural History books; and I thought the boys were only making fun, and would be back soon, safe and sound. How horrid being too clever makes one! And now, what *am* I to do?'

What was he to do, indeed? And what would you have done? Bring the horns and tail he must, or perish in the adventure. Otherwise, how could he meet his lady?—why, she would think him a mere braggart!

The prince sat down, and thought and thought; and the day went on, and it was now high noon.

At last he jumped up and rushed into the library, a room where nobody ever went except himself and the queen. There he turned the books upside down, in his haste, till he found an old one, by a French gentleman, Monsieur Cyrano de Bergerac.* It was an account of a voyage to the moon, in which there is a great deal of information about matters not generally known; for few travellers have been to the moon. In that book, Prince Prigio fancied he would find something he half remembered, and that would be of use to him. And he *did!* So you see that cleverness, and minding your book, have some advantages, after all. For here the prince learned that there is a very rare beast, called a Remora,* which is at least as cold as the Firedrake is hot!

'Now,' thought he, '*if I can only make these two fight*, why the Remora may kill the Firedrake, or take the heat out of him, at least, so that I may have a chance.'

Then he seized the ivory glass, clapped it to his eye, and looked for the Remora. Just the tip of his nose, as white as snow and as smooth as ice, was sticking out of a chink in a frozen mountain, not far from the burning mountain of the Firedrake.

'Hooray!' said the prince softly to himself; and he jumped like mad into the winged shoes of swiftness, stuck on the cap of darkness, girdled himself with the sword of sharpness, and put a good slice of bread, with some cold tongue, in a wallet, which he slung on his back. Never you fight, if you can help it, except with plenty of food to keep you going and in good heart. Then off he flew, and soon he reached the volcano of the Firedrake.

CHAPTER IX

THE PRINCE AND THE FIREDRAKE

IT was dreadfully hot, even high up in the air, where the prince hung invisible. Great burning stones were tossed up by the volcano, and nearly hit him several times. Moreover, the steam and smoke, and the flames which the Firedrake spouted like foam from his nostrils, would have daunted even the bravest man. The sides of the hill, too, were covered with the blackened ashes of his victims, whom he had roasted when they came out to kill him. The garden-engine of poor little Alphonso was lying in the valley, all broken and useless. But the Firedrake, as happy as a wild duck on a lonely loch, was rolling and diving in the liquid flame, all red-hot and full of frolic.

'Hi!' shouted the prince.

The Firedrake rose to the surface, his horns as red as a red crescent-moon, only bigger, and lashing the fire with his hoofs and his blazing tail.

'Who's there?' he said in a hoarse, angry voice. 'Just let me get at you!'

'It's me,' answered the prince. It was the first time he had forgotten his grammar, but he was terribly excited.

'What do you want?' grunted the beast. 'I wish I could see you'; and, horrible to relate, he rose on a pair of wide, flaming wings, and came right at the prince, guided by the sound of his voice.

Now, the prince had never heard that Firedrakes could fly; indeed, he had never believed in them at all, till the night before. For a moment he was numb with terror; then he flew down like a stone to the very bottom of the hill, and shouted:

'Hi!'

'Well,' grunted the Firedrake, 'what's the matter? Why can't you give a civil answer to a civil question?'

'Will you go back to your hole and swear, on your honour as a Firedrake, to listen quietly?'

'On my sacred word of honour,' said the beast, casually scorching an eagle that flew by into ashes. The cinders fell, jingling and crackling, round the prince in a little shower.

Then the Firedrake dived back, with an awful splash of flame, and the mountain roared round him.

The prince now flew high above him, and cried:

'A message from the Remora. He says you are afraid to fight him.'

'Don't know him,' grunted the Firedrake.

'He sends you his glove,' said Prince Prigio, 'as a challenge to mortal combat, till death do you part.'

Then he dropped his own glove into the fiery lake.

'Does he?' yelled the Firedrake. 'Just let me get at him!' and he scrambled out, all red-hot as he was.

'I'll go and tell him you're coming,' said the prince; and with two strides he was over the frozen mountain of the Remora.

CHAPTER X

THE PRINCE AND THE REMORA

IF he had been too warm before, the prince was too cold now. The hill of the Remora was one solid mass of frozen steel, and the cold rushed out of it like the breath of some icy beast, which indeed it *was*. All around were things like marble statues of men in armour: they were the dead bodies of the knights, horses and all, who had gone out of old to fight the Remora, and who had been frosted up by him. The prince felt his blood stand still, and he grew faint; but he took heart, for there was no time to waste. Yet he could nowhere see the Remora.

'Hi!' shouted the prince.

Then, from a narrow chink at the bottom of the smooth, black hill,—a chink no deeper than that under a door, but a mile wide,—stole out a hideous head!

It was as flat as the head of a skate-fish, it was deathly pale, and two chill-blue eyes, dead-coloured like stones, looked out of it.

Then there came a whisper, like the breath of the bitter east wind on a winter day:

'Where are you, and how can I come to you?'

'Here I am!' said the prince from the top of the hill.

Then the flat, white head set itself against the edge of the chink from which it had peeped, and slowly, like the movement of a sheet of ice, it slipped upwards and curled upwards, and up, and up! There seemed no end to it all; and it moved horribly, without feet, holding on by its own frost to the slippery side of the frozen hill. Now all the lower part of the black hill was covered with the horrid white thing coiled about it in smooth, flat, shiny coils; and still the head was higher than the rest; and still the icy cold came nearer and nearer, like Death.

The prince almost fainted: everything seemed to swim; and in one moment more he would have fallen stiff on the mountain-top, and the white head would have crawled over him, and the cold coils would have slipped over him and turned him to stone. And still the thing slipped up, from the chink under the mountain.

But the prince made a great effort; he moved, and in two steps he was far away, down in the valley where it was not so very cold.

'Hi!' he shouted, as soon as his tongue could move within his chattering teeth.

There came a clear, hissing answer, like frozen words dropping round him:

'Wait till I come down. What do you want?'

Then the white folds began to slide, like melting ice, from the black hill.

Prince Prigio felt the air getting warmer behind him, and colder in front of him.

He looked round, and there were the trees beginning to blacken in the heat, and the grass looking like a sea of fire along the plains; for the Firedrake was coming!

The prince just took time to shout, 'The Firedrake is going to pay you a visit!' and then he soared to the top of a neighbouring hill, and looked on at what followed.

CHAPTER XI

THE BATTLE

It was an awful sight to behold! When the Remora heard the name of the Firedrake, his hated enemy, he slipped with wonderful speed from the cleft of the mountain into the valley. On and on and on he poured over rock and tree, as if a frozen river could slide downhill; on and on, till there were miles of him stretching along the valley—miles of the smooth-ribbed, icy creature, crawling and slipping forwards. The green trees dropped their leaves as he advanced; the birds fell down dead from the sky, slain by his frosty breath! But, fast as the Remora stole forward, the Firedrake came quicker yet, flying and clashing his fiery wings. At last they were within striking distance; and the Firedrake, stooping from the air, dashed with his burning horns and flaming feet slap into the body of the Remora.

Then there rose a steam so dreadful, such a white yet fiery vapour of heat, that no one who had not the prince's magic glass could have seen what happened. With horrible grunts and roars the Firedrake tried to burn his way right through the flat body of the Remora, and to chase him to his cleft in the rock. But the Remora, hissing terribly, and visibly melting away in places, yet held his ground; and the prince could see his cold white folds climbing slowly up the hoofs of the Firedrake—up and up, till they reached his knees, and the great burning beast roared like a hundred bulls with the pain. Then up the Firedrake leaped, and hovering over his fiery wings, he lighted in the midst of the Remora's back, and dashed into it with his horns. But the flat, cruel head writhed backwards, and, slowly bending over on itself, the wounded Remora slid greedily to fasten again on the limbs of the Firedrake.

Meanwhile, the prince, safe on his hill, was lunching on the loaf and the cold tongue he had brought with him.

'Go it, Remora! Go it, Firedrake! you're gaining. Give it him, Remora!' he shouted in the wildest excitement.

Nobody had ever seen such a battle; he had it all to himself, and he never enjoyed anything more. He hated the Remora so much, that he almost wished the Firedrake could beat it; for the Firedrake was the more natural beast of the pair. Still, he was alarmed when he saw that the vast flat body of the Remora was now slowly coiling backwards, backwards, into the cleft below the hill; while a thick wet mist showed how cruelly it had suffered. But the Firedrake, too, was in an unhappy way; for his legs were now cold and black, his horns were black also, though his body, especially near the heart, glowed still like red-hot iron.

'Go it, Remora!' cried the prince: 'his legs are giving way; he's groggy on his pins! One more effort, and he won't be able to move!'

Encouraged by this advice, the white, slippery Remora streamed out of his cavern again, more and more of him uncoiling, as if the mountain were quite full of him. He had lost strength, no doubt: for the steam and mist went up from him in clouds, and the hissing of his angry voice grew fainter; but so did the roars of the Firedrake. Presently they sounded more like groans; and at last the Remora slipped up his legs above the knees, and fastened on his very heart of fire. Then the Firedrake stood groaning like a black bull, knee-deep in snow; and still the Remora climbed and climbed.

'Go it now, Firedrake!' shouted the prince; for he knew that if the Remora won, it would be too cold for him to draw near the place, and cut off the Firedrake's head and tail.

'Go it, Drake! he's slackening!' cried the prince again; and the brave Firedrake made one last furious effort, and rising on his wings, dropped just on the spine of his enemy.

The wounded Remora curled back his head again on himself, and again crawled, streaming terribly, towards his enemy. But the struggle was too much for the gallant Remora. The flat, cruel head moved slower; the steam from his thousand wounds grew fiercer; and he gently breathed his last just as the Firedrake, too, fell over and lay exhausted. With one final roar, like the breath of a thousand furnaces, the Firedrake expired.

The prince, watching from the hill-top, could scarcely believe that these two *awful scourges of Nature*, which had so long devastated his country, were actually dead. But when he had looked on for half-an-hour, and only a river ran where the Remora had been, while the body of the Firedrake lay stark and cold, he hurried to the spot.

Drawing the sword of sharpness, he hacked off, at two blows, the iron head and the tail of the Firedrake. They were a weary weight to carry; but in a few strides of the shoes of swiftness he was at his castle, where he threw down his burden, and nearly fainted with excitement and fatigue.

But the castle clock struck half-past seven; dinner was at eight, and the poor prince crawled on hands and knees to the garret. Here he put on the wishing-cap; wished for a pint of champagne, a hot bath, and his best black velvet and diamond suit. In a moment these were provided; he bathed, dressed, drank a glass of wine, packed up the head and tail of the Firedrake, sat down on the flying carpet, and knocked at the door of the English ambassador as the clocks were striking eight in Gluckstein.

Punctuality is the politeness of princes!* and a prince *is* polite, when he is in love!

The prince was received at the door by a stout porter and led into the hall, where *several* butlers met him, and he laid the mortal remains of the Firedrake under the cover of the flying carpet.

Then he was led upstairs; and he made his bow to the pretty lady, who, of course, made him a magnificent courtesy. She seemed prettier and kinder than ever. The prince was so happy, that he never noticed how something went wrong about the dinner. The ambassador looked about, and seemed to miss someone, and spoke in a low voice to one of the servants, who answered also in a low voice, and what he said seemed to displease the ambassador. But the prince was so busy in talking to his lady, and in eating his dinner too, that he never observed anything unusual. He had *never* been at such a pleasant dinner!

CHAPTER XII
A TERRIBLE MISFORTUNE

WHEN the ladies left, and the prince and the other gentlemen were alone, the ambassador appeared more gloomy than ever. At last he took the prince into a corner, on pretence of showing him a rare statue.

'Does your royal highness not know,' he asked, 'that you are in considerable danger?'

'Still?' said the prince, thinking of the Firedrake.

The ambassador did not know what he meant, for *he* had never heard of the fight, but he answered gravely:

'Never more than now.'

Then he showed the prince two proclamations, which had been posted all about the town.

Here is the first:

TO ALL LOYAL SUBJECTS.

Whereas,

Our eldest son, Prince Prigio, hath of late been guilty of several high crimes and misdemeanours.

First: By abandoning the post of danger against the Firedrake, whereby our beloved sons, Prince Alphonso and Prince Enrico, have perished, and been overdone by that monster.

Secondly: By attending an unseemly revel in the town of Gluckstein, where he brawled in the streets.

Thirdly: By trying to seduce away the hearts of our loyal subjects in that city, and to blow up a party against our crown and our peace.

This is to give warning,
That whoever consorts with, comforts, aids, or abets the said Prince Prigio, is thereby a partner in his treason; and

That a reward of FIVE THOUSAND PURSES will be given to whomsoever brings the said prince, alive, to our Castle of Falkenstein.

GROGNIO R.

And here is the second proclamation:

REWARD.
THE FIREDRAKE.

Whereas,
Our dominions have lately been devastated by a Firedrake (the *Salamander Furiosus* of Buffon);*

This is to advise all,
That whosoever brings the horns and tail of the said Firedrake to our Castle of Falkenstein, shall receive FIVE THOUSAND PURSES, the position of Crown Prince, with the usual perquisites, and the hand of the king's niece, the Lady Molinda.

GROGNIO R.

'H'm,' said the prince; 'I did not think his majesty wrote so well;' and he would have *liked* to say, 'Don't you think we might join the ladies.'

'But, sir,' said the ambassador, 'the streets are lined with soldiers; and I know not how you have escaped them. *Here*, under my roof, you are safe for the moment; but a prolonged stay—excuse my inhospitality—could not but strain the harmonious relations which prevail between the Government of Pantouflia and that which I have the honour to represent.'

'We don't want to fight; and no more, I think, do you,' said the prince, smiling.

'Then how does your royal highness mean to treat the proclamations?'

'Why, by winning these ten thousand purses. I can tell you £1,000,000 is worth having,' said the prince. 'I'll deliver up the said prince, alive, at Falkenstein this very night; also the horns and tail of the said Firedrake. But I don't want to marry my Cousin Molly.'

'May I remind your royal highness that Falkenstein is three hundred miles away? Moreover, my head butler, Benson, disappeared from the house before dinner, and I fear he went to warn Captain Kopzoffski* that you are *here!*'

'That is nothing,' said the prince; 'but, my dear Lord Kelso,* may I not have the pleasure of presenting Lady Rosalind with a little gift, a Philippine* which I lost to her last night, merely the head and tail of a Firedrake which I stalked this morning?'

The ambassador was so astonished that he ran straight upstairs, forgetting his manners, and crying:

'Linda! Linda! come down at once; here's a surprise for you!'

Lady Rosalind came sweeping down, with a smile on her kind face. *She* guessed what it was, though the prince had said nothing about it at dinner.

'Lead the way, your royal highness!' cried the ambassador; and the prince, offering Lady Rosalind his arm, went out into the hall, where he saw neither his carpet nor the horns and tail of the Firedrake!

He turned quite pale, and said:

'Will you kindly ask the servants where the little Persian prayer-rug and the parcel which I brought with me have been placed?'

Lord Kelso rang the bell, and in came all the servants, with William, the under-butler, at their head.

'William,' said his lordship, 'where have you put his royal highness's parcel and his carpet?'

'Please, your lordship,' said William, 'we think Benson have took them away with him.'

'And where is Benson?'

'We don't know, your lordship. We think he have been come for!'

'Come for—by whom?'

William stammered, and seemed at a loss for a reply.

'Quick! answer! what do you know about it?'

William said at last, rather as if he were making a speech:

'Your royaliness, and my lords and ladies, it was like this. His royaliness comed in with a rug over his arm, and summat under it. And he lays it down on that there seat, and Thomas shows him into the droring-room. Then Benson says: "Dinner'll be ready in five minutes; how tired I do feel!" Then he takes the libbuty of sitting hisself down on his royaliness's rug, and he says, asking your pardon, "I've had about enough of service here. I'm about tired, and I thinks of bettering myself. I wish I was at the king's court, and butler." But before the words was out of his mouth, off he flies like a shot through the open door, and his royaliness's parcel with him. I run to the door, and there he was, flying right hover the town, in a northerly direction. And that's all I know; for I would not tell a lie, not if it was hever* so. And me, and Thomas—as didn't see it,—and cook, we thinks as how Benson was come for. And cook says as she don't wonder at it, neither; for a grumblinger, more ill-conditioneder——'

'Thank you, William,' said Lord Kelso; 'that will do; you can go, for the present.'

CHAPTER XIII

SURPRISES

THE prince said nothing, the ambassador said nothing, Lady Rosalind said never a word till they were in the drawing-room. It was a lovely warm evening, and the French windows were wide open on the balcony, which looked over the town and away north to the hills. Below them flowed the clear, green water of the Gluckthal. And still nobody said a word.

At last the prince spoke:

'This is a very strange story, Lord Kelso!'

'Very, sir!' said the ambassador.

'But true,' added the prince; 'at least, there is no reason in the nature of things why it shouldn't be true.'

'I can hardly believe, sir, that the conduct of Benson, whom I always found a most respectable man, deserved——'

'That he should be "come for,"' said the prince. 'Oh, no; it was a mere accident, and might have happened to any of us who chanced to sit down on my carpet.'

And then the prince told them, shortly, all about it: how the carpet was one of a number of fairy properties, which had been given him at his christening; and how so long a time had gone by before he discovered them; and how, probably, the carpet had carried the butler where he had said he wanted to go, namely—to the king's Court at Falkenstein.

'It would not matter so much,' added the prince, 'only I had relied on making my peace with his majesty, my father, by aid of those horns and that tail. He was set on getting them; and if the Lady Rosalind had not expressed a wish for them, they would to-day have been in his possession.'

'Oh, sir, you honour us too highly,' murmured Lady Rosalind; and the prince blushed and said:

'Not at all! Impossible!'

Then, of course, the ambassador became quite certain that his daughter was admired by the crown prince, who was on bad terms with the king of the country; and a more uncomfortable position for an ambassador—however, they are used to them.

'What on earth am I to do with the young man?' he thought. 'He can't stay here for ever; and without his carpet he can't get away, for the soldiers have orders to seize him as soon as he appears in the street. And in the meantime Benson will be pretending that *he* killed the Firedrake—for he must have got to Falkenstein by now,—and they will be for marrying him to the king's niece, and making my butler crown prince to the kingdom of Pantouflia! It is dreadful!'

Now all this time the prince was on the balcony, telling Lady Rosalind all about how he got the Firedrake done for, in the most modest way; for, as he said: '*I* didn't kill him: and it is really the Remora, poor fellow, who should marry Molly; but he's dead.'

At this very moment there was a *whizz* in the air; something shot past them, and, through the open window, the king, the queen, Benson, and the mortal remains of the Firedrake were shot into the ambassador's drawing-room!

CHAPTER XIV

THE KING EXPLAINS

THE first who recovered his voice and presence of mind was Benson.

'Did your lordship ring for coffee?' he asked, quietly; and when he was told 'Yes,' he bowed and withdrew, with majestic composure.

When he had gone, the prince threw himself at the king's feet, crying:

'Pardon, pardon, my liege!'

'Don't speak to me, sir!' answered the king, very angrily; and the poor prince threw himself at the feet of the queen.

But she took no notice of him whatever, no more than if he had been a fairy; and the prince heard her murmur, as she pinched her royal arms:

'I shall waken presently; this is nothing out of the way for a dream. Dr. Rumpfino ascribes it to imperfect nutrition.'

All this time, the Lady Rosalind, as pale as a marble statue, was leaning against the side of the open window. The prince thought he could do nothing wiser than go and comfort her, so he induced her to sit down on a chair in the balcony,—for he felt that he was not wanted in the drawing-room;—and soon they were talking happily about the stars, which had begun to appear in the summer night.

Meanwhile, the ambassador had induced the king to take a seat; but there was no use in talking to the queen.

'It would be a miracle,' said she to herself, 'and miracles do not happen; therefore this has not happened. Presently, I shall wake up in my own bed at Falkenstein.'

Now, Benson, William, and Thomas brought in the coffee, but the queen took no notice. When they went away, the rest of the company slipped off quietly, and the king was left alone with the ambassador; for the queen could hardly be said to count.

'You want to know all about it, I suppose?' said his majesty, in a sulky voice. 'Well, you have a right to it, and I shall tell you. We were just sitting down to dinner at Falkenstein, rather late,—hours get later every year, I think—when I heard a row in the premises, and the captain of the guard, Colonel McDougal, came and told us that a man had arrived with the horns and tail of the Firedrake, and was claiming the reward. Her majesty and I rose and went into the outer court, where we found, sitting on that carpet with a glass of beer in his hand, a respectable-looking upper servant, whom I recognised as your butler. He informed us that he had just killed the beast, and showed us the horns and tail, sure enough; there they are! The tail is like the iron handle of a pump, but the horns are genuine. A pair were thrown up by a volcano, in my great-grandfather's time, Giglio I.[1] Excellent coffee this, of yours!'

---

[1] The History of this Prince may be read in a treatise called *The Rose and the Ring*,* by M. A. Titmarsh. London, 1855.

The ambassador bowed.

'Well, we asked him *where* he killed the Firedrake, and he said in a garden near Gluckstein. Then he began to speak about the reward, and the "perkisits,"* as he called them, which it seems he had read about in my proclamation. Rather a neat thing; drew it up myself,' added his majesty.

'Very much to the point,' said the ambassador, wondering what the king was coming to.

'Glad you like it,' said the king, much pleased. 'Well, where was I? Oh, yes; your man said he had killed the creature in a garden, quite near Gluckstein. I didn't much like the whole affair: he is an alien, you see; and then there was my niece, Molinda—poor girl, *she* was certain to give trouble. Her heart is buried, if I may say so, with poor Alphonso. But the queen is a very remarkable woman—very remarkable——'

'Very!' said the Ambassador, with perfect truth.

'"Caitiff!" she cries to your butler;' his majesty went on, '"perjured knave, thou liest in thy throat! Gluckstein is a hundred leagues from here, and how sayest thou that thou slewest the monster, and camest hither in a few hours' space?" This had not occurred to me,—I am a plain king, but I at once saw the force of her majesty's argument. "Yes," said I; "how did you manage it?" But he—your man, I mean—was not a bit put out. "Why, your majesty," says he, "I just sat down on that there bit of carpet, wished I was here, and here I *ham*. And I'd be glad, having had the trouble,—and my time not being my own,—to see the colour of them perkisits, according to the proclamation." On this her majesty grew more indignant, if possible. "Nonsense!" she cried; "a story out of the *Arabian Nights* is not suited for a modern public, and fails to win aesthetic credence." These were her very words.'

'Her majesty's expressions are ever choice and appropriate,' said the Ambassador.

'"Sit down there, on the carpet, knave," she went on; "ourself and consort"—meaning *me*—"will take our places by thy side, and I shall wish us in Gluckstein, at thy master's! When the experiment has failed, thy head shall from thy shoulders be shorn!" So your man merely said, "Very well, mum,—your majesty, I mean," and sat down. The queen took her place at the edge of the carpet; I sat between her and the butler, and she said, "I wish we were in Gluckstein!" Then we rose, flew through the air at an astonishing pace, and here we are! So I suppose the rest of the butler's tale is true, which I regret; but a king's word is sacred, and he shall take the place of that sneak, Prigio. But as we left home before dinner, and as *yours* is over, may I request your lordship to believe that I should be delighted to take something cold?'

The ambassador at once ordered a sumptuous collation, to which the king did full justice; and his majesty was shown to the royal chamber, as he complained of fatigue. The queen accompanied him, remarking that she was sound asleep, but would waken presently. Neither of them said 'Good-night' to the prince. Indeed, they did not see him again, for he was on the balcony with Lady Rosalind. They found a great deal to say to each other, and at last the prince asked her to be his wife; and she said that if the king and her father gave their permission—why, then she would! After this she went to bed; and the prince, who had not slept at all the night before, felt very sleepy also. But he knew that first he had something that must be done. So he went into the drawing-room, took his carpet, and wished to be—now, where do you suppose? Beside the dead body of the Firedrake! There he was in a moment; and dreadful the body looked, lying stark and cold in the white moonshine. Then the prince cut off its four hoofs, put them in his wallet, and with these he flew back in a second, and met the ambassador just as he came from ushering the king to bed. Then the prince was shown his own room, where he locked up the hoofs, the carpet, the cap of darkness, and his other things in an iron box; and so he went to bed and dreamed of his Lady Rosalind.

CHAPTER XV

THE KING'S CHEQUE

WHEN they all wakened next morning, their first ideas were confused. It is often confusing to waken in a strange bed, much more so when you have flown through the air, like the king, the queen, and Benson the butler. For her part, the queen was the most perplexed of all; for she did undeniably wake, and yet she was not at home, where she had expected to be. However, she was a determined woman, and stood to it that nothing unusual was occurring. The butler made up his mind to claim the crown princeship and the hand of the Lady Molinda; because, as he justly remarked to William, here was such a chance to better himself as might not soon come in his way again. As for the king, he was only anxious to get back to Falkenstein, and have the whole business settled in a constitutional manner. The ambassador was not sorry to get rid of the royal party; and it was proposed that they should all sit down on the flying carpet, and wish themselves at home again. But the queen would not hear of it: she said it was childish and impossible; so the carriage was got ready for her, and she started without saying a word of good-bye to anyone. The king, Benson, and the prince were not so particular, and they simply flew back to Falkenstein in the usual way, arriving there at 11.35—a week before her majesty.

The king at once held a Court; the horns and tail of the monster were exhibited amidst general interest, and Benson and the prince were invited to state their claims.

Benson's evidence was taken first. He declined to say exactly where or how he killed the Firedrake. There might be more of them left, he remarked,—young ones, that would take a lot of killing,—and he refused to part with his secret. Only he claimed the reward, which was offered, if you remember, *not* to the man who killed the beast, but to him who brought its horns and tail. This was allowed by the lawyers present to be very sound law; and Benson was cheered by the courtiers, who decidedly preferred him to Prigio, and who, besides, thought he was going to be crown prince. As for Lady Molinda, she was torn by the most painful feelings; for, as much as she hated Prigio, she could not bear the idea of marrying Benson. Yet one or the other choices seemed certain.

Unhappy lady! Perhaps no girl was ever more strangely beset by misfortune!

Prince Prigio was now called on to speak. He admitted that the reward was offered for bringing the horns and tail, not for killing the monster. But were the king's *intentions* to go for nothing? When a subject only *meant* well, of course he had to suffer; but when a king said one thing, was he not to be supposed to have meant another? Any fellow with a wagon could *bring* the horns and tail; the difficult thing was to kill the monster. If Benson's claim was allowed, the royal prerogative of saying one thing and meaning something else was in danger.

On hearing this argument, the king so far forgot himself as to cry, 'Bravo, well said!' and to clap his hands, whereon all the courtiers shouted and threw up their hats.

The prince then said that whoever had killed the monster could, of course, tell where to find him, and could bring his hoofs. He was ready to do this himself. Was Mr. Benson equally ready? On this being interpreted to him—for he did not speak Pantouflian—Benson grew pale with horror, but fell back on the proclamation. He had brought the horns and tail, and so he must have the perquisites, and the Lady Molinda!

The king's mind was so much confused by this time, that he determined to leave it to the Lady Molinda herself.

'Which of them will you have, my dear?' he asked, in a kind voice.

But poor Molinda merely cried. Then his majesty was almost *driven* to say that he would give the reward to whoever produced the hoofs by that day week. But no sooner had he said this than the prince brought them out of his wallet, and displayed them in open Court. This ended the case; and Benson, after being entertained with sherry and sandwiches in the steward's room, was sent back to his master. And I regret to say that his temper was not at all improved by his failure to better himself. On the contrary, he was unusually cross and disagreeable for several days; but we must, perhaps, make some allowance for his disappointment.

But if Benson was irritated, and suffered from the remarks of his fellow-servants, I do not think we can envy Prince Prigio. Here he was, restored to his position indeed, but by no means to *the royal favour*. For the king disliked him as much as ever, and was as angry as ever about the deaths of Enrico and Alphonso. Nay, he was even *more* angry; and, perhaps, not without reason. He called up Prigio before the whole Court, and thereon the courtiers cheered like anything, but the king cried:

'Silence! McDougal, drag the first man that shouts to the serpent-house in the zoological gardens, and lock him up with the rattlesnakes!'

After that the courtiers were very quiet.

'Prince,' said the king, as Prigio bowed before the throne, 'you are restored to your position, because I cannot break my promise. But your base and malevolent nature is even more conspicuously manifest in your selfish success than in your previous dastardly contempt of duty. Why, confound you!' cried the king, dropping the high style in which he had been speaking, and becoming the *father*, not the *monarch*,—'why, if you *could* kill the Firedrake, did you let your poor little brothers go and be b—b—b—broiled? Eh! what do you say, you sneak? "You didn't believe there *were* any Firedrakes?" That just comes of your eternal conceit and arrogance! If you were clever enough to kill the creature—and I admit that—you were clever enough to know that what everybody said must be true. "You have not generally found it so?" Well, you *have* this time, and let it be a lesson to you; not that there is much comfort in that, for it is not likely you will ever have such another chance'—exactly the idea that had occurred to Benson.

Here the king wept, among the tears of the lord chief justice, the poet laureate (who had been awfully frightened when he heard of the rattlesnakes), the maids of honour, the chaplain royal, and everyone but Colonel McDougal, a Scottish soldier of fortune, who maintained a military reserve.

When his majesty had recovered, he said to Prigio (who had not been crying, he was too much absorbed):

'A king's word is his bond. Bring me a pen, somebody, and my cheque-book.'

The royal cheque-book, bound in red morocco, was brought in by eight pages, with ink and a pen. His majesty then filled up and signed the following satisfactory document—(Ah! my children how I wish Mr. Arrowsmith* would do as much for *me!*):

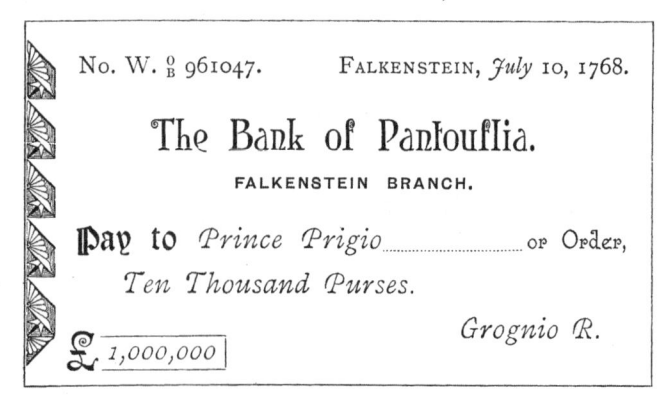

No. W. ^O_B 961047.   FALKENSTEIN, *July* 10, 1768.

The Bank of Pantouflia.

FALKENSTEIN BRANCH.

Pay to *Prince Prigio* _____ or Order,

Ten Thousand Purses.

£ 1,000,000   *Grognio R.*

'There!' said his majesty, crossing his cheque and throwing sand over it, for blotting-paper had not yet been invented; 'there, take *that*, and be off with you!'

Prince Prigio was respectfully but rapidly obeying his royal command, for he thought he had better cash the royal cheque as soon as possible, when his majesty yelled:

'Hi! here! come back! I forgot something; you've got to marry Molinda!'

CHAPTER XVI

A MELANCHOLY CHAPTER

THE prince had gone some way, when the king called after him. How he wished he had the seven-league boots on, or that he had the cap of darkness in his pocket! If he had been so lucky, he would now have got back to Gluckstein, and crossed the border with Lady Rosalind. A million of money may not seem much, but a pair of young people who really love each other could live happily on less than the cheque he had in his pocket. However, the king shouted very loud, as he always did when he meant to be obeyed, and the prince sauntered slowly back again.

'Prigio!' said his majesty, 'where were you off to? Don't you remember that this is your wedding-day? My proclamation offered, not only the money (which you have), but the hand of the Lady Molinda, which the Court chaplain will presently make your own. I congratulate you, sir; Molinda is a dear girl.'

'I have the highest affection and esteem for my cousin, sir,' said the prince, 'but——'

'I'll never marry him!' cried poor Molinda, kneeling at the throne, where her streaming eyes and hair made a pretty and touching picture. 'Never! I despise him!'

'I was about to say, sir,' the prince went on, 'that I cannot possibly have the pleasure of wedding my cousin.'

'The family gibbet, I presume, is in good working order?' asked the king of the family executioner, a tall gaunt man in black and scarlet, who was only employed in the case of members of the blood royal.

'Never better, sire,' said the man, bowing with more courtliness than his profession indicated.

'Very well,' said the king; 'Prince Prigio, you have your choice. *There* is the gallows, *here* is Lady Molinda. My duty is painful, but clear. A king's word cannot be broken. Molly, or the gibbet!'

The prince bowed respectfully to Lady Molinda:

'Madam, my cousin,' said he, 'your clemency will excuse my answer, and you will not misinterpret the apparent discourtesy of my conduct. I am compelled, most unwillingly, to slight your charms, and to select the Extreme Rigour of the Law. Executioner, lead on! Do your duty; for me, *Prigio est prêt*;'*—for this was his motto, and meant that he was ready.

Poor Lady Molinda could not but be hurt by the prince's preference for death over marriage to her, little as she liked him.

'Is life, then, so worthless? and is Molinda so terrible a person that you prefer *those* arms,' and she pointed to the gibbet, 'to *these*?'—here she held out her own, which were very white, round and pretty: for Molinda was a good-hearted girl, she could not bear to see Prigio put to death; and then, perhaps, she reflected that there are worse positions than the queenship of Pantouflia. For Alphonso was gone—crying would not bring him back.

'Ah, Madam!' said the prince, 'you are forgiving——'

'For *you* are brave!' said Molinda, feeling quite a respect for him.

'But neither your heart nor mine is ours to give. Since mine was another's, I understand too well the feeling of *yours! D*o not let us buy life at the price of happiness and honour.'

Then, turning to the king, the prince said:

'Sir, is there no way but by death or marriage? You say you cannot keep half only of your promise; and that, if I accept the reward, I must also unite myself with my unwilling cousin. Cannot the whole proclamation be annulled, and will you consider the bargain void if I tear up this flimsy scroll?'

And here the prince fluttered the cheque for £1,000,000 in the air.

For a moment the king was tempted; but then he said to himself:

'Never mind, it's only an extra penny on the income-tax.' Then, 'Keep your dross,' he shouted, meaning the million; 'but let *me* keep my promise. To chapel at once, or——' and he pointed to the executioner. 'The word of a king of Pantouflia is sacred.'

'And so is that of a crown prince,' answered Prigio; 'and *mine* is pledged to a lady.'

'She shall be a mourning bride,' cried the king savagely, 'unless'—here he paused for a moment—'unless you bring me back Alphonso and Enrico, safe and well!'

The prince thought for the space of a flash of lightning.

'I accept the alternative,' he said, 'if your majesty will grant me my conditions.'

'Name them!' said the king.

'Let me be transported to Gluckstein, left there unguarded, and if, in three days, I do not return with my brothers safe and well, your majesty shall be spared a cruel duty. Prigio of Pantouflia will perish by his own hand.'

The king, whose mind did not work very quickly, took some minutes to think over it. Then he saw that by granting the prince's conditions, he would either recover his dear sons, or, at least, get rid of Prigio, without the unpleasantness of having him executed. For, though some kings have put their eldest sons to death, and most have wished to do so, they have never been better loved by the people for their Roman virtue.

'Honour bright?' said the king at last.

'Honour bright!' answered the prince, and, for the first time in many months, the royal father and son shook hands.

'For you, madam,' said Prigio in a stately way to Lady Molinda, 'in less than a week I trust we shall be taking our vows at the same altar, and that the close of the ceremony which finds us cousins will leave us brother and sister.'

Poor Molinda merely stared; for she could not imagine what he meant. In a moment he was gone; and having taken, by the king's permission, the flying carpet, he was back at the ambassador's house in Gluckstein.

CHAPTER XVII

THE BLACK CAT AND THE BRETHREN!

WHO was glad to see the prince, if it was not Lady Rosalind? The white roses of her cheeks turned to red roses in a moment, and then back to white again, they were so alarmed at the change. So the two went into the gardens together, and talked about a number of things; but at last the prince told her that, before three days were over, all would be well, or all would be over with him. For either he would have brought his brothers back, sound and well, to Falkenstein, or he would not survive his dishonour.

'It is no more than right,' he said; 'for had I gone first, neither of them would have been sent to meet the monster after I had fallen. And I *should* have fallen, dear Rosalind, if I had faced the Firedrake before I knew *you*.'

Then when she asked him why, and what good she had done him, he told her all the story; and how, before he fell in love with her, he didn't believe in fairies, or Firedrakes, or caps of darkness, or anything nice and impossible, but only in horrid useless facts, and chemistry, and geology, and arithmetic, and mathematics, and even political economy. And the Firedrake would have made a mouthful of him, then.

So she was delighted when she heard this, almost as much delighted as she was afraid that he might fail in the most difficult adventure. For it was one thing to egg on a Remora to kill a Firedrake, and quite another to find the princes if they were alive, and restore them if they were dead!

But the prince said he had his plan, and he stayed that night at the ambassador's. Next morning he rose very early, before anyone else was up, that he might not have to say 'Good-bye' to Lady Rosalind. Then he flew in a moment to the old lonely castle, where nobody went for fear of ghosts, ever since the Court retired to Falkenstein.

How still it was, how deserted; not a sign of life, and yet the prince was looking everywhere *for some living thing*. He hunted the castle through in vain, and then went out to the stable-yard; but all the dogs, of course, had been taken away, and the farmers had offered homes to the poultry. At last, stretched at full length in a sunny place, the prince found a very old, half-blind, miserable cat. The poor creature was lean, and its fur had fallen off in patches; it could no longer catch birds, nor even mice, and there was nobody to give it milk. But cats do not look far into the future; and this old black cat—Frank was his name—had got a breakfast somehow, and was happy in the sun. The prince stood and looked at him pityingly, and thought that even a sick old cat was, in some ways, happier than most men.

'Well,' said the prince at last, 'he could not live long anyway, and it must be done. He will feel nothing.'

Then he drew the sword of sharpness, and with one turn of his wrist cut the cat's head clean off.

It did not at once change into a beautiful young lady, as perhaps you expect; no, that was improbable, and, as the prince was in love already, would have been vastly inconvenient. The dead cat lay there, like any common cat.

Then the prince built up a heap of straw, with wood on it; and there he laid poor puss, and set fire to the pile. Very soon there was nothing of old black Frank left but ashes!

Then the prince ran upstairs to the fairy cupboard, his heart beating loudly with excitement. The sun was shining through the arrow-shot window; all the yellow motes were dancing in its rays. The light fell on the strange heaps of fairy things—talismans and spells. The prince hunted about here and there, and at last he discovered six ancient water-vessels of black leather, each with a silver plate on it, and on the plate letters engraved. This was what was written on the plates:

AQVA. DE. FONTE. LEONVM.[1]

'Thank heaven!' said the prince. 'I thought they were sure to have brought it!'

Then he took one of the old black-leather bottles, and ran downstairs again to the place where he had burned the body of the poor old sick cat.

He opened the bottle, and poured a few drops of the water on the ashes and the dying embers.

Up there sprang a tall, white flame of fire, waving like a tongue of light; and forth from the heap jumped the most beautiful, strong, funny, black cat that ever was seen!

It was Frank as he had been in the vigour of his youth; and he knew the prince at once, and rubbed himself against him and purred.

The prince lifted up Frank and kissed his nose for joy; and a bright tear rolled down on Frank's face, and made him rub his nose with his paw in the most comical manner.

Then the prince set him down, and he ran round and round after his tail; and, lastly, cocked his tail up, and marched proudly after the prince into the castle.

'Oh, Frank!' said Prince Prigio, 'no cat since the time of Puss in Boots was ever so well taken care of as you shall be. For, if the fairy water from the Fountain of Lions* can bring *you* back to life—why, there is a chance for Alphonso and Enrico!'

Then Prigio bustled about, got ready some cold luncheon from

---

[1] Water from the Fountain of Lions.

the store-room, took all his fairy things that he was likely to need, sat down with them on the flying carpet, and wished himself at the mountain of the Firedrake.

'I have the king now,' he said; 'for if I can't find the ashes of my brothers, by Jove! I'll!——'

Do you know what he meant to do, if he could not find his brothers? Let every child guess!

Off he flew; and there he was in a second, just beside poor Alphonso's garden-engine. Then Prigio, seeing a little heap of grey ashes beside the engine, watered them with the fairy water; and up jumped Alphonso, as jolly as ever, his sword in his hand.

'Hullo, Prigio!' cried he; 'are you come after the monster too? I've been asleep, and I had a kind of dream that he beat me. But the pair of us will tackle him. How is Molinda?'

'Prettier than ever,' said Prigio, 'but anxious about you. However, the Firedrake's dead and done for; so never mind him. But I left Enrico somewhere about. Just you sit down and wait a minute, till I fetch him.'

The prince said this, because he did not wish Alphonso to know that he and Enrico had not had quite the best of it in the affair with the monster.

'All right, old fellow,' says Alphonso; 'but have you any luncheon with you? Never was so hungry in my life!'

Prince Prigio had thought of this, and he brought out some cold sausage (to which Alphonso was partial) and some bread, with which the younger prince expressed himself satisfied. Then Prigio went up the hill some way, first warning Alphonso *not* to sit on his carpet for fear of *accidents* like that which happened to Benson. In a hollow of the hill, sure enough there was the sword of Enrico, the diamonds of the hilt gleaming in the sun. And there was a little heap of grey ashes.

The prince poured a few drops of the water from the Fountain of Lions on them, and up, of course, jumped Enrico, just as Alphonso had done.

'Sleepy old chap you are, Enrico,' said the prince; 'but come on, Alphonso will have finished the grub unless we look smart.'

So back they came, in time to get their share of what was going; and they drank the Remora's very good health, when Prigio told them about the fight. But neither of them ever knew that they had been dead and done for; because Prigio invented a story that the mountain was enchanted, and that, as long as the Firedrake lived, everyone who came there fell asleep. He did tell him about the flying carpet, however, which of course did not much surprise them, because they had read all about it in the *Arabian Nights* and other historical works.

'And now I'll show you fun!' said Prigio; and he asked them both to take their seats on the carpet, and wished to be in the valley of the Remora.

There they were in a moment, among the old knights whom, if you remember, the Remora had frozen into stone. There was quite a troop of them, in all sorts of armour—Greek and Roman, and Knight Templars like Front de Bœuf and Brian du Bois Gilbert*—all the brave warriors that had tried to fight the Remora since the world began.

Then Prigio gave each of his brothers some of the water in their caps, and told them to go round pouring a drop or two on each frozen knight. And as they did it, lo and behold! each knight came alive, with his horse, and lifted his sword and shouted:

'Long live Prince Prigio!'

in Greek, Latin, Egyptian, French, German, and Spanish,—all of which the prince perfectly understood, and spoke like a native.

So he marshalled them in order, and sent them off to ride to Falkenstein and cry:

'Prince Prigio is coming!'

Off they went, the horses' hoofs clattering, banners flying, sunshine glittering on the spear-points. Off they rode to Falkenstein; and when the king saw them come galloping in, I can tell you he had no more notion of hanging Prigio.

CHAPTER XVIII

THE VERY LAST

THE princes returned to Gluckstein on the carpet, and went to the best inn, where they dined together and slept. Next morning they, and the ambassador, who had been told all the story, and Lady Rosalind, floated comfortably on the carpet back to Falkenstein, where the king wept like anything on the shoulders of Alphonso and Enrico. They could not make out why he cried so, nor why Lady Molinda and Lady Kathleena cried; but soon they were all laughing and happy again. But then—would you believe he could be so mean?—he refused to keep his royal promise, and restore Prigio to his crown-princeship! Kings are like that.

But Prigio, very quietly asking for the head of the Firedrake, said he'd pour the magic water on *that*, and bring the Firedrake back to life again, unless his majesty behaved rightly. This threat properly frightened King Grognio, and he apologised. Then the king shook hands with Prigio in public, and thanked him, and said he was proud of him. As to Lady Rosalind, the old gentleman quite fell in love with her, and he sent at once to the Chaplain Royal to get into his surplice, and marry all the young people off at once, without waiting for wedding-cakes, and milliners, and all the rest of it.

Now, just as they were forming a procession to march into church, who should appear but the queen! Her majesty had been travelling by post all the time, and, luckily, had heard of none of the doings since Prigio, Benson, and the king left Gluckstein. I say *luckily* because if she *had* heard of them, she would not have believed a word of them. But when she saw Alphonso and Enrico, she was much pleased, and said:

'Naughty boys! Where have you been hiding? The king had some absurd story about your having been killed by a fabulous monster. Bah! don't tell *me*. I always said you would come back after a little trip—didn't I, Prigio?'

'Certainly, madam,' said Prigio; 'and I said so, too. Didn't I say so?' And all the courtiers cried: 'Yes, you did;' but some added, to themselves, 'He *always* says, "Didn't I say so?"'

Then the queen was introduced to Lady Rosalind, and she said it was 'rather a short engagement, but she supposed young people understood their own affairs best.' And they do! So the three pairs were married, with the utmost rejoicings; and her majesty never, her whole life long, could be got to believe that anything unusual had occurred.

The honeymoon of Prince Prigio and the Crown Princess Rosalind was passed at the castle, where the prince had been deserted by the Court. But now it was delightfully fitted up; and Master Frank marched about the house with his tail in the air, as if the place belonged to him.

Now, on the second day of their honeymoon, the prince and princess were sitting in the garden together, and the prince said, 'Are you *quite* happy, my dear?' and Rosalind said, 'Yes; *quite*.'

But the prince did not like the tone of her voice, and he said:

'No, there's something; do tell me what it is.'

'Well,' said Rosalind, putting her head on his shoulder, and speaking very low, 'I want everybody to love you as much as I do. No, not quite so very much,—but I want them to like you. Now they *can't*, because they are afraid of you; for you are so awfully clever. Now, couldn't you take the wishing cap, and wish to be no cleverer than other people? Then everybody will like you!'

The prince thought a minute, then he said:

'Your will is law, my dear; anything to please you. Just wait a minute!'

Then he ran upstairs, for the last time, to the fairy garret, and he put on the wishing cap.

'No,' thought he to himself, 'I won't wish *that*. Every man has one secret from his wife, and this shall be mine.'

Then he said aloud: 'I WISH TO SEEM NO CLEVERER THAN OTHER PEOPLE.'

Then he ran downstairs again, and the princess noticed a great difference in him (though, of course, there was really none at all), and so did everyone. For the prince remained as clever as ever he had been; but, as nobody observed it, he became the most popular prince, and finally the best-loved king who had ever sat on the throne of Pantouflia.

But occasionally Rosalind would say, 'I do believe, my dear, that you are really as clever as ever!'

And he *was!*

FORD MADOX FORD

The Queen Who Flew
A Fairy Tale

ONCE upon a time a Queen sat in her garden. She was quite a young, young Queen; but that was a long while ago, so she would be older now. But, for all she was Queen over a great and powerful country, she led a very quiet life, and sat a great deal alone in her garden watching the roses grow, and talking to a bat that hung, head downwards, with its wings folded, for all the world like an umbrella, beneath the shade of a rose tree overhanging her favourite marble seat. She did not know much about the bat, not even that it could fly, for her servants and nurses would never allow her to be out at dusk, and the bat was a great deal too weak-eyed to fly about in the broad daylight.

But, one summer day, it happened that there was a revolution in the land, and the Queen's servants, not knowing who was likely to get the upper hand, left the Queen all alone, and went to look at the fight that was raging.

But you must understand that in those days a revolution was a thing very different from what it would be to-day.

Instead of trying to get rid of the Queen altogether, the great nobles of the kingdom merely fought violently with each other for possession of the Queen's person. Then they would proclaim themselves Regents of the kingdom and would issue bills of attainder against all of their rivals, saying they were traitors against the Queen's Government.

In fact, a revolution in those days was like what is called a change of Ministry now, save for the fact that they were rather fond of indulging themselves by decapitating their rivals when they had the chance, which of course one would never think of doing nowadays.

The Queen and the bat had been talking a good deal that afternoon—about the weather and about the revolution and the colour of cats and the like.

'The raven will have a good time of it for a day or two,' the bat said. But the Queen shuddered. 'Don't be horrid,' she said.

'I wonder who'll get the upper hand?' the bat said.

'I'm sure I don't care a bit,' the Queen retorted. 'It doesn't make any difference to me. They all give me things to sign, and they all say I'm very beautiful.'

'That's because they want to marry you,' the bat said.

And the Queen answered, 'I suppose it is; but I shan't marry them. And I wish *all* my attendants weren't deaf and dumb; it makes it so awfully dull for me.'

'That's so that they shan't abuse the Regent behind his back,' the bat said. 'Well, I shall take a fly.' The truth was, he felt insulted that the Queen should say she was dull when she had him to talk to.

But the Queen was quite frightened when he whizzed past her head and out into the dusky evening, where she could see him flitting about jerkily, and squeaking shrilly to paralyze the flies with fright.

After a while he got over his fit of sulks, and came back again to hang in his accustomed bough.

'Why—you can fly!' the Queen said breathlessly. It gave her a new idea of the importance of the bat.

The bat said, 'I can.' He was flattered by her admiration.

'I wish *I* could fly,' the Queen said. 'It would be so much more exciting than being boxed up here.'

The bat said, 'Why don't you?'

'Because I haven't got wings, I suppose,' the Queen said.

'You shouldn't suppose,' the bat said sharply. 'Half the evils in the world come from people supposing.'

'What are the "evils in the world"?' the Queen said.

And the bat answered, 'What! don't you even know that, you ignorant little thing? The evils in the world are ever so many—strong winds so that one can't fly straight, and cold weather so that the flies die, and rheumatic pains in one's wing-joints, and cats and swallows.'

'I like cats,' the Queen said; 'and swallows are very pretty.'

'That's what *you* think,' the bat said angrily. 'But you're nobody. Now, I hate cats because they always want to eat me; and I hate swallows because they always eat what I want to eat—flies. They are the real evils of the world.'

The Queen saw that he was angry, and she held her peace for a while.

'I'm not nobody, all the same,' she thought to herself. 'I'm the Queen of the "most prosperous and contented nation in the world," though I don't quite understand what it means. But it will never do to offend the bat, it is so dreadfully dull when he won't talk;' so she said, 'Would it be possible for me to fly?' for a great longing had come into her heart to be able to fly away out of the garden with the roses and the marble bench.

'Well, it certainly won't be if you suppose you can't,' the bat said. 'Now, when I was a mouse, I used to suppose I couldn't fly, and so, of course, I couldn't. But, one day, I saved the life of a cockchafer that had got into a beetle-trap, and he told me how it was to be managed.'

'How?' the Queen said eagerly.

'Ah, you like cats,' the bat said, 'and you'd tell them the secret; and then there'd be no peace for me. Ugh!—flying cats!' And the bat shuddered and wrapped his wings round his head.

'Oh, but I promise I won't tell,' the Queen said eagerly; 'indeed I do. Dear bat, you are so wise, and so good, and so handsome, do tell me.'

Now, the bat was rather susceptible to compliments, and so he unshrouded his head, pretending not to have heard, though he had.

'What did you say?' he said.

And the Queen repeated her words.

That pleased him, and he answered, 'Well, there's a certain flower that has two remarkable properties—one, that people who carry it about with them can always fly, and the other, that it will restore the blind to sight.'

'Yes; but I shall have to travel over ever so many mountains and rivers and things before I can find it,' the Queen said dismally.

'How do you know that?' the bat asked sharply.

'I don't know it, I only supposed it; at least I've read it in books.'

'Well, of course, if you go supposing things and reading them in books, I can't do anything for you,' the bat said. 'The only good I can see in books is that they breed bookworms, and the worms turn into flies; but even they aren't very good to eat. When I was a mouse, though, I used to nibble books to pieces, and the bits made rare good nests. So there is *some* good in the most useless of things. But I don't need a nest now that I can fly.'

'How did you come to be able to fly?' the Queen asked.

'Well, after what the cockchafer told me, I just ran out into the garden, and when I found the flower, as I hadn't any pocket to put it in so as to have it always by me, I just ate it up, and from that time forward I have been able to fly ever so well.'

The Queen said, 'Oh, how nice! And is the flower actually here in the garden? Tell me which it is, please do.'

'Well, I'll tell you if you'll bring me a nice piece of raw meat, and a little red flannel for my rheumatism.'

Just at that moment the sound of a great bell sounded out into the garden.

'Oh, how annoying!' the Queen said. 'Just as it was beginning to be interesting! Now I shall have to go in to dinner. But I'll bring you the meat and the flannel to-morrow, and then you'll tell me, won't you?'

The bat said, 'We'll see about it,' and so the Queen arose from her seat, and, stooping to avoid the roses that caught at her, went out towards the palace and up the marble steps into it.

The palace was an enormous hall, all of marble, and very, very cold.

The dining-room itself was a vast hall, as long as an ordinary street, with a table as long and as broad as the roadway thereof, so that the poor little Queen felt rather lonely, sitting at one end of it, with the enormous vessels all of gold, and the great gold candlesticks, and the long line of deaf and dumb domestics that stood and looked on, or presented their dishes kneeling.

Generally the Regent's wife, or, if he hadn't one, his sister or mother, acted as the Queen's governess, and stood behind her chair. But that evening there was no one at all.

'I suppose they've cut her head off,' the Queen said resignedly. 'I wonder what the next one will be like. But I shan't be bothered with her long, if the bat tells me how to fly. I shall just go right off somewhere, and see mountains, and valleys, and rivers, and seas; and hundreds and hundreds of wonderful things out of books. Oh, it will be lovely! And as to the Regents, they can just cut each other's heads off as much as they like.'

And so, having dined, she went to bed, and lay a long time awake thinking how delightful it would be to fly.

The next morning, at breakfast, she found a note to say that the Lord Blackjowl desired an early audience with her on the subject of the Regency.

'I suppose I *must* go,' the Queen said. 'I do hope he won't be much wounded, it's so nasty to look at, and I *did* want to go into the garden to see the bat.'

However, she went down into the audience chamber at once, to get it over. The guard drew back the curtain in the doorway and she went in. A great man with a black beard was awaiting her, and at her entrance sank down on one knee.

'Oh, get up, please,' she said. 'I don't like talking to men when they kneel, it looks so stupid. What is it you want? I suppose it's about the Regency.'

The Lord Blackjowl arose. His eyes were little and sharp; they seemed to look right through the Queen.

'Your Majesty is correct, as so peerless a lady must be,' he said. 'The nobles and people were groaning under the yoke of the late traitor and tyrant who called himself Regent, and so we took the liberty, the great liberty, of——'

'Oh yes, I know what you want,' the Queen interrupted him. 'You want to be pardoned for the unconstitutionality of it. So I suppose I shall have to pardon you. If you give me the paper I'll sign it.'

The Lord Blackjowl handed her one of many papers that he held in his hand.

'If your Majesty will be graciously pleased to sign it here.'

So the Queen sat down at a table and signed the crackling paper 'Eldrida—Queen.'

'I never sign it "Eldrida R.,"'* she said. 'It's ridiculous to sign it in a language that isn't one's own. Now I suppose you want me to sign a paper appointing you Regent?'

The Lord Blackjowl looked at her from under his shaggy eyebrows.

'That was included in the paper your Majesty has been graciously pleased to sign.'

'But I didn't know anything about it,' the Queen said hotly. 'Now that's deceiving, and I shall never be able to trust anything you give me to sign without reading it. I've a good mind to take it back again.'

'I assure your Majesty,' the lord answered, with a low bow, 'I merely wished to save your Majesty the trouble of twice appending your gracious signature when once would suffice.'

'But why didn't you tell me what was in it?' she asked, a little mollified.

'Merely because your Majesty took the words out of my mouth, if I must so say.'

The Queen said, 'Well, and what else do you want me to do?'

'There are sundry traitorous persons of the faction of the late

Regent, whose existence is dangerous to the peace of the realm, and against whom I wish to issue writs of attainder if your Majesty will consent.'

'Yes, I thought so,' the Queen said. 'How many are there?'

'Three thousand nine hundred and forty,' the Regent said, looking at a great scroll.

'Good gracious!' the Queen said. 'Why, that's five times as many as ever there were before.'

The Regent stroked his beard. 'There is a great deal of disaffection in the land,' he said.

'Why, the last Regent said the people were ever so contented,' the Queen answered.

'The last Regent has deceived your Majesty.'

'That's what they all say about the last Regent. Why, it was only the other day that he told me that you were deceitful—and you *are*—and he said that you had thrown your wife into a yard full of hungry dogs, in order that you might marry me.'

'Your Majesty,' the Regent said, flushing with heavy anger, 'the late Regent was a tyrant, and all tyrants are untruthful, as your Majesty's wisdom must tell you. My wife had the misfortune to fall into a bear-pit, and, as for my daring to raise my eyes as high as your Majesty——'

'Why, you're looking at me now,' the Queen said. 'However, it doesn't matter. You can't marry me till I'm twenty-one, and I shan't be that for some time. By-the-by, who's going to be my next governess?'

'Your Majesty is now of an age to need no governess. I think a tutor would be more suitable—with your Majesty's consent.'

'Well, who's to be my tutor, then?' the Queen said.

'I had purposed according that inestimable honour to myself,' the Regent answered.

'Oh, I say! You'll never do!' the Queen remarked. 'You could never darn a pair of stockings, or comb my hair. You'd be so awfully clumsy.'

'Your Majesty has no need to have your royal stockings darned; you can always have a new pair.'

'But that would be so fearfully wasteful!' the Queen said.

'Your Majesty might give the other pairs to the poor.'

'But what *are* "the poor"?'

'The poor are wicked, idle people—too wicked to work and earn the money, and too dirty to wear stockings,' the Regent said.

'But what would be the good of my stockings to them?' the Queen asked.

'It is the usual thing, your Majesty,' the Regent said. 'But will your Majesty be pleased to sign these papers?'

The Queen said, 'Oh yes, I'll sign them, if you'll just go down into the kitchen and ask for a piece of raw meat, about the size of my hand, and a piece of red flannel about large enough to go round a bat. Oh, and what's a good thing for rheumatism?'

The Regent looked a little surprised. 'I—your Majesty, I really don't exactly know.'

'Oh, well, ask the cook or somebody.'

'Well, but—couldn't I send a servant, your Majesty?' the Regent said.

'No, that wouldn't be any good,' the Queen said. 'If you're to take the place of my governess you'll have to do that sort of thing, you know.'

The Regent bowed. 'Of course I shall be only too grateful for your Majesty's commands. I merely thought that your Majesty might need some assistance in signing the papers.'

But the Queen answered, 'Oh no, I can manage that sort of thing well enough myself. I'm quite used to it; so be quick, and remember, a nice juicy piece of raw meat and some red flannel, and—oh, opodeldoc;* that's just the thing. Be quick! I don't want to keep the bat waiting.'

The Regent went backwards out of the room, bowing at every three steps, and, as he was clad in armour from top to toe, he made a clanking noise—quite like a tinker's cart, if you've ever heard one.

So, left to herself, the Queen signed the papers one after the other. They all began—

'BY THE QUEEN, A PROCLAMATION,
E.R.

'*Whereas by Our Proclamation given this 1st day of May*——

But the Queen never read any further than that, because she could never quite understand what it all meant. At the last signature she happened to make a little blot, and somehow or other the ink happened to get into one of her nails, and that annoyed her. It *is* so difficult to get ink out of one's nails.

'I don't care if I never sign another Proclamation,' she said; 'and I hope I never shall. Now, look here,' she continued to the Regent, who at that moment entered. 'If you were a governess I should be able to make you get this ink out; but how can I ask a man to do that?'

'I will make the attempt, if your Majesty pleases,' the Regent said.

'Well, but you haven't got any nail-scissors,' the Queen replied.

'I might use my sword,' the Regent suggested.

But the Queen shivered. 'Ugh! fancy having a great ugly thing like that for it!' she said. 'Oh, well, you've brought the things! Here are your papers. They're all signed; and, if you want anything else, you'll have to come into the garden.'

And she took up the meat and the flannel and the opodeldoc and went into the garden, leaving the Regent with the idea that he had made rather a bad business by becoming the Queen's attendant. But he was a very determined man, and merely set his teeth the firmer.

Under the overhanging rose tree the Queen sat awaiting the bat's awakening.

'It never does to wake him up,' she said. 'It makes him so bad tempered.'

So she sat patiently and watched the rose-petals that every now and then fluttered down on the wind.

It was well on towards the afternoon, after the Queen had had her dinner, before he awoke.

'Oh, you're there?' he said. He had made the same remark every day for the last two years—which made seven hundred and thirty-one times, one of the years having been leap-year.

The Queen said, 'Yes, here I am!'

The bat yawned. 'What's the weather like?' he asked.

The Queen answered, 'Oh, it's very nice, and you promised to tell me the flower that would make me fly.'

'I shan't,' the bat said. 'You'd eat up all the flies—a great thing like you.'

The Queen's eyes filled with tears, it was so disappointing.

'Oh, I promise I won't eat *any* flies,' she said; 'and I'll go right away and leave you in peace.'

The bat said, 'Um! there's something in that.'

'And look,' the Queen continued, 'I've brought you your meat and flannel, and some stuff that's good for rheumatism.'

The bat's eyes twinkled with delight. 'Well, I'll tell you,' he said.

'Only you must promise, first, that you won't tell any one the secret; and secondly, that you won't eat any flies.'

'Oh yes, I'll promise that willingly enough.'

'Well, put the things up here on the top of the seat and I'll tell you.'

The Queen did as she was bidden, and the bat continued—

'The flower you want is at this moment being trodden on by your foot.'

The Queen felt a little startled, but, looking down, saw a delicate white flower that had trailed from a border and was being crushed beneath her small green shoes.

'What! the wind-flower?' she said. 'I always thought it was only a weed.'

'You shouldn't think,' the bat said. 'It's as bad as supposing.'

'Well, and how am I to set about flying?' the Queen asked.

And the bat answered sharply, 'Why, fly. Put the flower somewhere about you, and then go off. Only be careful not to knock against things.'

The Queen thought for a moment, and then plucked a handful and a handful and yet a handful of the wind-flowers, and, having twined them into a carcanet,* wound them into her soft gold-brown hair, beneath her small crown royal.

'Good-bye, dear bat,' she said. She had grown to like the bat, for all his strange appearance and surly speeches.

The bat remarked, 'Good riddance.' He was always a little irritable just after awakening.

So the Queen went out from under the arbour, and made a first essay at flying.

'I'll make just a short flight at first,' she said, and gave a little jump, and in a moment she flew right over a rose bush and came down softly on the turf on its further side, quite like a not too timid pigeon that has to make a little flight from before a horse's feet.

'Oh, come, that was a success,' she said to herself. 'And it really is true. Well, I'll just practise a little before I start to see the world.'

So she flew over several trees, gradually going higher and higher, until at last she caught a glimpse of the red town roofs, and then, in a swift moment's rush, she flew over the high white wall and alighted in the road that bordered it.

'Hullo!' a voice said before she had got used to the new sensation of being out in the world. 'Hullo! where did you drop from?'

'I didn't drop—I flew,' the Queen said severely; and she looked at the man.

He was stretched on the ground, leaning his back against the wall, and basking in the hot sunlight that fell on him. He was very ragged and very dirty, and he had neither shoes nor stockings. By his side was a basket in which, over white paper frills, nodded the heads of young ferns.

'Why, who are you?' the Queen said. And then her eyes fell on his bare feet. They reminded her of what the Regent had said that morning. 'Oh, you must be the poor,' she said, 'and you want my stockings.'

'I don't know about your stockings, lady,' the man said; 'but if you've got any old clothes to spare, I could give you some nice pots of flowers for them.'

The Queen said, 'Why, what good would that do you?'

And the man answered, 'I should sell them and get some money. I'm fearfully hungry.'

'Why don't you have something to eat, then?' the Queen said.

And the man replied, 'Because I haven't got any money to buy it with.'

'Why don't you take it, then?'

'Because it would be stealing, and stealing's wicked; besides, I should be sent to prison for it.'

'I don't understand quite what you mean,' the Queen said. 'But come with me somewhere where we can get some food, and you shall have as much as you like.'

The fern-seller arose with alacrity.

'There's a shop near here where they sell some delicious honey-cakes.'

'I can't make it out,' the Queen said to herself. 'If he's hungry he can't be contented; and yet the Regent said every one was contented in the land, because of his being Regent. He must have been mistaken, or else this man must be one of the traitors.'

And aloud she said, 'Is there a bill of attainder out against you?'

The beggar shook his head. 'I guess not,' he said. 'Tradesmen won't let the likes of me run up bills.'

It was a remark the Queen could not understand at all. They crossed the market-place that lay before the palace door.

'There's no market to-day because the people are all afraid the revolution isn't over yet.'

'Oh, but it is,' the Queen said; 'I made the Lord Blackjowl Regent to-day.'

The beggar looked at her with a strange expression; but the Queen continued—

'I don't see what harm the revolution could do to the market.'

'Why, don't you see,' the beggar said, 'when they get to fighting the arrows fly about all over the place, and the horses would knock the stalls over. Besides, the soldiers steal everything, or set fire to it. Look, there's a house still smouldering.'

And, indeed, one of the market houses was a heap of charred ruins.

'But what was the good of it?' the Queen asked.

And the beggar answered, 'Well, you see, it belonged to one of the opposite party, and he wouldn't surrender and have his head chopped off.'

'I should think not,' the Queen said.

The streets were quite empty, and all the shutters were closed. Here and there an arrow was sticking into the walls or the doors.

'Do people never walk about the streets?' the Queen asked.

'It wouldn't be safe when there's a revolution on,' the beggar answered.

Just at that moment they arrived before the door of a house that, like all the rest, was closely shut up. Over the door was written—

'JAMES GRUBB,
Honey-cake Maker.'

Here the beggar stopped and began to beat violently at the door with his staff.

The sound of the blows echoed along the streets,—and then from within came dismal shouts of 'Murder!' 'Police!' 'Fire!'

But the beggar called back, 'Nonsense, James Grubb; it's only a lady come for some honey-cakes.'

Then, after a long while, there was a clatter of chains behind the door, and it was opened just an inch, so that the Queen could see an old man's face peeping cautiously out at her. The sight seemed to reassure him, for he opened the door and bobbed nervously. At other times he would have bowed suavely.

'Will your ladyship be pleased to enter?' he said. 'I want to shut the door; it is so dangerous to have it open with all these revolutions about.'

The Queen complied with his request, and found herself in a little dark shop, only lighted dimly through the round air-holes in the shutters.

'Give this man some honey-cakes,' she said; and the honey-cake maker seemed only too delighted.

'How many shall I give him, madam?' he said.

'As many as he wants, of course,' the Queen answered sharply.

The beggar proceeded to help himself, and made a clean sweep of all the cakes that were on the counter. There was a big hole in his coat, and into that he thrust them, so that the lining at last was quite full.

The honey-cake maker was extremely pleased at the sight, for he had not expected to sell any cakes that day.

When the cakes had all disappeared there was an awkward pause.

'Now I'll go on again,' the Queen said.

'But you haven't paid,' the honey-cake maker said in some alarm.

'Pay!' said the Queen. 'What do you mean?'

'Paid for the cakes, I mean,' the honey-cake maker said.

'I don't understand you,' she answered. 'I am the Queen; I never pay for what I eat.'

'She *is* the Queen,' the beggar said; 'and if you don't take care she'll have your head off.'

The honey-cake maker jumped back so suddenly that he sat down in a tub of honey and stuck there doubled up with his knees to his chin.

'Oh Lord! Oh Lord!' he said. 'What shall I do? what shall I do?— all my cakes gone, and never to be paid!'

'You won't want to be paid if your head's cut off,' the beggar said.

But the Queen answered, 'Nonsense. No one's going to cut your head off; and I dare say, if you ask them at the palace, they'll pay you, whatever it means. Just pull him out of the tub,' she continued to the beggar, for the unfortunate honey-baker, not being able to move, remained gasping in the tub.

So the beggar pulled him out, and, for all his fright, his business spirit did not desert him.

'Will your Majesty deign to sign an order for payment?' he said.

And the Queen answered, 'Good gracious, no, I won't; the ink always gets into my finger-nails.'

The honey-cake maker bowed lower still. 'At least, your Majesty, deign to give me your signet-ring as a token.'

'Oh, I'll give you that,' the Queen said; and she drew it from her finger.

The honey-cake maker suddenly smote his forehead with his hand, as though an idea had struck him.

'You might carry that ladder out for me,' he said to the beggar, indicating a ladder that lay along the passage wall.

The beggar did as he was asked, and placed it against the house.

'Whatever is he going to do now?' the Queen thought to herself, and, being in the street, awaited the turn of events.

Presently the honey-cake maker came out, carrying a pail of black paint and a large brush, and, thus equipped, ascended the ladder and began to paint, under the

'JAMES GRUBB,
Honey-cake Maker,'
'*to Her Majesty the Queen and the R*——'

But he had got no further than that, when, with tumultuous shouts, a body of soldiers came rushing round a corner, and, seeing the honey-cake maker on the ladder and his door open, they at once tumbled pell-mell into the shop.

No sooner did the unfortunate maker of cakes see this, than, in his haste to descend the ladder, his foot slipped, and he came to the ground, with the paint out of the pot running dismally all over his head.

'Oh dear! oh dear!' the Queen said, and went to pick him up, when, at that moment, the soldiers having found nothing in the shop but a tub of honey and a tub of flour, came out again, not quite as fast as they had entered, until they saw the Queen, when they at once rushed to surround her, and one of them caught at her crown, and another at her bracelets, and another at her lace-handkerchief.

The Queen said, 'Leave me alone, do you hear?'

But the soldiers answered, 'In the Queen's name, surrender.'

'Well, I shouldn't surrender in any name but my own, and I shan't surrender at all. I am the Queen.'

Whereupon the leader of the soldiers, who had not had the fortune to get at any of the Queen's jewellery, said, 'Release the lady;' and, rather crestfallen, the soldiers obeyed him.

'Oh, your Majesty,' the leader said, kneeling, 'we have had such a trouble to find you. The Regent, discovering that your Majesty had left the palace, told us to follow you with all haste to provide for your safety.'

'So you provided for it by trying to rob people's houses,' the Queen said.

And the leader answered, 'Oh no, your Majesty. We feared, knowing that James Grubb is a noted rebel, that he had kidnapped your Majesty, and so were making a domiciliary search.'

'I'm not a noted rebel,' the honey-cake maker gasped. 'I'm only noted for my honey-cakes.'

But no one noticed his little puff.

The Queen said to the soldiers, 'Well, I don't want you. You can go; and don't make any more domiciliary searches.'

The leader, however, answered, 'Oh, but, your Majesty, domiciliary searches are most necessary in the present state of the kingdom.'

'I don't care,' the Queen said; 'I forbid you to make them. So now go away.'

'But, your Majesty,' the leader answered, 'the Regent gave us orders to conduct your Majesty back to the palace. It is not constitutional.'

'I'm sure I don't care,' the Queen answered; 'I'm not going back. Good-bye.'

And she suddenly flew straight up into the air and away over the housetops, and the last sight she had of them showed them, with their faces upturned towards her, gazing in dumb astonishment, the leader still on his knees and the honey-cake maker on his back in the street.

The beggar had long since slunk round a corner and disappeared.

So the Queen rose to quite a great height in the air.

'I shall go right away from the town,' she said. 'The smoke is so choking up here above the roofs. However people can live down there I can't make out.'

So she went right up into the blue sky and made her way towards where, at the skirts of the town, the mountains rose steep and frowning.

Up there, standing on the mountain's crest, she had a glorious view of sea and sky and town and country.

The sea threw back the deep blue of the sky above, and the white wave-horses flecked its surface, and the ships passed silently far out at sea; down below her feet, it beat against the rocky base of the cliff, and in and out amongst the spray the seagulls flew like a white cloud.

The town lay in a narrow valley, broad at the sea face, and running inwards into narrowness between grey, grand hills, right to where it disappeared in the windings of the pass. Down below, in the harbour, she could see the boats getting ready for sea.

'Oh, how wonderful!' the Queen said; 'and it all belongs to me—at least, so they say—though I can't quite see what good it does me, for I can't be everywhere at once. And I can't even make the hills move or the sea heave its breast; so that I can't see that it does me any more good than any one else, because it isn't even constitutional for me to be here. I ought to be down there in the palace garden, seeing nothing at all. However, it's very lovely here, so I mustn't grumble. I wonder how the bat is getting on, and the Regent, and all.'

So for a while she stayed, looking down at the town. Into the streets she could not see, for the houses stood in the way, but she could see the market-place plainly enough and the palace steps.

Presently a number of soldiers came running into the market-place, and up into the palace, and the Queen knew they had come to announce her flight.

And then, a few minutes later, she saw them coming rapidly out of the doors.

'Goodness me!' the Queen said, 'the Regent is kicking them down the steps. I shan't go back there again, or he might take to kicking me.'

So she set out along the hilltops, sometimes walking and sometimes flying over the valleys, so that, by the time the sun was near setting, she found herself in a great stretch of dreary uplands, with nothing like a house for miles around.

'Now, whatever shall I do?' she said. 'It's coming on quite dark, and I don't know where I am. I've a good mind to lie down and go to sleep on the heather; only there might be some sort of wild animals about, and it wouldn't be safe.'

Then the sun sank lower and lower, and the Queen began to feel a little lonely and very nervous. There was not a sound to be heard, save the roar of a brook that ran, gleaming white, among the boulders in the gloom of the valley at her feet.

'If I fly right up in the air again I shall be safe, at any rate,' the Queen said. 'I shan't go tumbling over precipices or getting eaten up by wolves.'

So she flew right up into the upper air where she could see the sun again, and she tried to catch him up, flying fast, fast westwards. But she found that the sun went a great deal faster than she could go—for, you know, the sun goes a great deal more quickly than a train—and gradually he sank below the horizon, and the Queen was left alone with nothing but the stars to keep her company.

As you may imagine, it was not the pleasantest of feelings, that flying through the pitch-dark night, and the Queen felt continually afraid of running against something, though she was really far too high to do any such thing.

But, for all that, she had the dread constantly in her mind, until at last the moon crept silently into being above a hill, seeming like an old friend, and soon all the land below was bathed in white light. The Queen glided on; like a black cloud, she could see her shadow running along the fields below her. She watched till she grew sleepier and sleepier, and found herself nodding, to wake with a start and then fall off to sleep again; till, at last, she fell asleep for good and all, and went sailing quietly along in the white night, whilst the moon gradually mounted up straight overhead, and then sank lower and lower, and the dawn began to wash the world below her with a warmer light.

But the Queen slept softly on; and, indeed, never bed was softer than the air of the summer night.

The sun had been up some little while when she was awakened by just touching on the top of a lofty mountain, that reached up into the sky and stopped her progress; so that, when she was fully awakened, she found herself seated on its peak.

She rubbed her eyes, and in a moment remembered all that had happened before she had dropped off to sleep.

'Goodness me! I feel awfully hungry,' she said to herself, and, standing up, looked around her.

On the one side, the mountain towered above the uplands over which she had passed in the night, but they looked dreary and uninviting; on the other, in a fair plain, stood a town—she could see the smoke rising from the chimneys and the weather-cocks gleaming in the morning sunlight as they veered about in the breeze. So she flew gently down towards it, and the shepherds in the fields and the women at the cottage doors stared in amazement, and came rushing after her as she swept past through the air.

So, by the time she arrived in the town, quite a great crowd had followed her.

At last she alighted just before the town gates, and, as there was no guard to stop her, entered boldly enough, and walked on for a little way until she came to a shop that seemed to be a cake-shop, for one half of its window was full of cakes, and the other of boots and shoes. And, indeed, the owner, an old man with spectacles on, was seated on his doorstep busily working away at his cobbler's bench.

The Queen said, 'I want some cakes, please.'

And the cobbler, looking up from his work, said, 'Then you've come to the right shop.'

The crowd stood round in a ring and whispered.

'Will you give me them, please?' the Queen continued.

And the old cobbler answered, 'I'll sell them to you.'

'But I haven't got any money,' the Queen said.

'Then you've come to the *wrong* shop,' the cobbler said determinedly, and looked down again at his work.

'But I'm the Queen,' she said, remembering her former experience.

The cobbler said, 'Nonsense!' and took a little brass nail from his mouth.

'But I *am* the Queen,' the Queen said angrily.

The cobbler knocked the nail into the shoe. 'King Mark's a widower,' was all he said.

And the crowd laughed until the Queen felt quite uncomfortable. She was not used to being stared at.

'Why, I must have got into another country,' she said to herself; 'and, I suppose, the best thing to do will be to see the King. I dare say he'll give me enough to eat, for he'll tremble at my name.'

So she said aloud, 'Take me to the King.'

And so the crowd showed her the way, some going in front and some following; but all so anxious to see her that they stumbled over each other's legs.

But at last they came to the palace, and the crowd opened to make way for her. To tell the truth, they seemed rather afraid to enter, but the Queen marched in boldly enough till she came to a great hall. Long before she had time to make out what it was like, an enormous voice shouted—

'Who the dickens* are you?'

And, looking at the throne, she could make out an enormous, black-bearded man seated thereon. He was a great deal more ugly than the Regent at home had been, and his red eyes twinkled underneath black, shaggy brows, like rubies in a cavern.

'Who are you?' he shouted.

And whilst his fearful voice echoed down the great dark hall, the Queen answered—

'If you won't tremble, I'll tell you.'

The King gave a tremendous roar of laughter. 'Ho, what a joke!' he said, and, to enforce it, he punched in the ribs the chamberlain who stood at his right hand, and that so violently that the wretched man rolled down the throne steps, taking care to laugh vigorously the whole time, until the King roared, 'Be quiet, you idiot!' when the chamberlain at once grew silent. Then the King said, somewhat more softly, 'I'll try very hard not to tremble; but if I'm very frightened you won't mind, I hope.'

And all the courtiers laughed so loud and long at the King's sarcasm, that the Queen had some difficulty in making herself heard.

Then she said, 'I am Eldrida, by the grace of God Queen of the Narrowlands and all the Isles.'

The King really did seem a little startled.

'What in the world do you want here, then?' he said, and his red eyes glowed again.

'I want something to eat,' the Queen said.

The King seemed lost in thought. 'Your Majesty shall have something if——'

'If what?' the Queen asked.

'If you will marry me,' the King said in a tone that was meant to be sweet; but it rather reminded the Queen of a bull she had once heard grumbling angrily.

She answered decidedly, 'I shan't do anything of the sort.'

The King said, 'Why not?'

'Because you're a great deal too cruel and ugly,' the Queen answered. 'What did you knock that poor man down for? I can't bear that sort of wickedness. And as for ugliness, why, you're worse than the Regent himself, and he's the ugliest man I ever saw.'

The King immediately became so convulsed with rage that he could only roar till the windows shook out of their frames and shattered on the ground; and the Queen stopped her ears with her fingers, perfectly aghast at the storm she had raised.

At last the King regained his powers of speech. 'If you don't marry me this very day,' he said, 'I'll have you beheaded, I'll have you hanged, I'll have you thrown from the top of the highest tower in the town and smash you to pieces.'

'You couldn't do anything of the sort,' the Queen said calmly.

Thereupon the King's rage became quite frightful to see, especially for the courtiers who were nearest him, for he rushed among them and began to kick them so that they flew into the air; indeed, it seemed as if the air was full of them. But, in the middle of it, he suddenly made a dash at the Queen, and, before she could avoid him, had seized her in his fearful grasp.

'I'll show you if I can't dash you to pieces,' he said, and in a minute he had seized her and rushed out into the open air, carrying her like a kitten.

Up to the little door at the foot of the palace tower he went and kicked it open so violently that it banged against the wall and quivered again with the shock, and then round and round and round, and up and up and up, a little dark winding stair, until a sudden burst of light showed that they were at the top.

'Now I'll show you,' he muttered, and, shaking her violently he threw her over the side.

But she only dropped softly a short way, and then hovered up again till she played in the air around the tower.

The astonishment of the King was now even greater than his former rage.

'I told you how it would be,' the Queen said. 'And, if you'll take my advice, you won't lose your temper so fearfully again. It might really make you ill.'

But the King said nothing at all, being a little out of breath at having come so quickly up the tower steps. So the Queen flew gaily off again without saying 'Good-bye.'

But down at the base of the tower the courtiers, discovering that the King was nicely trapped, quietly shut the door and locked it. Then they gave a sigh of relief, and left him till he died. They had been long looking out for such an opportunity.

The Queen, however, knew nothing of that. She flew on for a time, being far too excited to remember her hunger; but at last it came back to her with redoubled force, and she determined to descend at the first house she came to and try to get some food somehow. But, by that time, the country had become sandy and dry, with only a few reeds bristling out over it here and there, and no signs of cultivation or even of houses.

'*Now*, whatever shall I do?' she said to herself, as she flew along so close to the ground that the wind of her flight made the sand flit about in little clouds. 'I'm so awfully hungry and——Why, there is some sort of a building!—at least it looks like one.'

And there, in a hollow among the sand-dunes, stood a funny little black erection, such as you might see upon a beach.

So the Queen alighted and walked towards the house. In front of the door a cat was sitting—a black cat. But not a magnificent creature with a glossy coat that sits on the rug in front of the drawing-room fire and only drinks cream, deeming mice too vulgar. This was a long-limbed, little creature, that looked half-starved and seemed as if its proper occupation would be stealing along, very lanky and grim in the moonlight, over the dunes to catch rabbits.

So the Queen stopped and looked at the cat, and the cat sat and looked at the Queen.*

The black pupils of its yellow eyes dilated and diminished in a most composed manner.

'Poor pussy!' the Queen said, and bent to scratch its neck.

But the cat took no kind of notice, so the Queen lifted the cat in her arms, whereupon it gave vent to an awe-inspiring yell.

The door flew violently open, and the Queen, in alarm, let the cat go, and it dashed into the house behind an old woman, but such an ugly old woman that the Queen was quite startled.

'Well, what do *you* want?' the old woman said.

'Oh, I want something to eat,' the Queen said.

The old woman gave a cunning leer. 'Something to eat, my dear young lady,' she said. 'Why, whatever made you expect to find anything to eat fit for the likes of you in such a place?'

'Oh, I'm not particular,' the Queen said; 'only I'm very hungry.'

'And what will you pay me?' the old woman said.

'I—I can't pay you anything,' the Queen said. 'You see, I haven't got any money.'

The old woman smiled again, in a nasty way. 'Oh well,' she said, 'I'll give you some food, if you'll do a day's work for it.'

'What sort of work?' the Queen said. 'I'm not very clever at work, you know.'

'Oh, quite easy work—just goose-herding.'

The Queen said, 'Oh, I dare say I could do that.'

And the old woman answered, 'Oh, very well; come along in, then.'

And the Queen followed her into a dirty little room, with only a table and a long bench in it.

But there was a fine wood fire crackling on the hearth, and before it a goose was slowly turning on the spit, so that it did not look quite as dismal as otherwise it might have done.

The Queen sat herself down at the table, and the old woman and the cat were engaged in sitting on the hearth watching the fire.

They did not seem at all talkative, and so the Queen held her peace.

At last the old woman gave a grunt, for the goose was done, and so she got up and found a plate and knife and fork, and put them before the Queen, with the goose on a dish and a large hunk of bread.

'There,' she said, 'that's all I can give you.'

And so, although the food was by no means as dainty as what she would have had at home in the palace, the Queen was so remarkably hungry that she made a much larger meal than she ever remembered to have made.

And all the while the cat sat and stared at her, and seemed to grow positively bigger with staring so much, though when the Queen held out a piece of the goose to it, it merely sniffed contemptuously so that the Queen felt quite humiliated.

'Your cat doesn't seem to be very sociable,' she said to the old woman.

And the old woman answered, 'Why should he be?' and took up a large twig broom to sweep the hearth with.

That done, she leant upon it and regarded the Queen malevolently.

'Aren't you ever going to finish?' she said.

The Queen answered, 'Well, I *was* rather hungry, you see; but I've finished now. There's no great hurry, is there?'

'I want *my* dinner,' the old woman said, with such an emphasis on the '*my*' that the Queen was quite amused.

'Why, the goose is there; at least, there's some of it left.'

'But *I* don't like goose,' the old woman said. Her manner was growing more and more peculiar.

'Any one would think you were going to eat *me*,' the Queen said; and the cat licked its jaws.

'So I am,' the old woman said, and her eyes gleamed.

But the Queen said, 'Nonsense!'

'But it's not nonsense,' the old woman said; and the cat began to grow visibly.

'Well, but you didn't say anything about it before,' the Queen said. 'I only agreed to herd your geese.'

'But you won't be able to,' the old woman said.

The Queen said, 'Why not?'

'Because they're wild ones.'

The cat was growing larger and larger, till the Queen grew positively afraid.

'Well, at any rate, I'll have a try,' she said.

And the old woman answered, 'You may as well save yourself the trouble.'

But the Queen insisted, and so they went outside, the old woman carrying her broom, for all the world like a crossing-sweeper.

The great cat rubbed against her skirt and licked its jaws. It was about the size of a lion now.

They came to the back of the house, and there the pen was—a cage covered completely over, and filled with a multitude of geese. The old woman undid the door and threw it wide, and immediately, with a mighty rustle of wings filling the air, the geese swept out of the pen away into the sky.

The old woman chuckled, and the cat crouched itself down as if preparing to spring, lashing its sides with its long tail. But the Queen only smiled, and started off straight into the air, faster even than the geese had gone.

The old woman gave a shriek, and the cat a horrible yell, and then the Queen saw the one mounted upon her broom, and the other without any sort of steed at all, come flying after her.

Then ensued a terrific race. The Queen put up one hand to hold her crown on, and the other to shield her eyes, and then flew as fast as she could, with her hair streaming out upon the wind.

Right through the startled geese she went, and the old woman and the cat followed after; but, fast as she went, they gained upon her, and at last the cat was almost upon her. In despair, she doubled back and almost ran into the old woman, who aimed a furious blow at her with her broom; but the Queen just dodged it, and it lighted full in the face of the cat, and, locked fast together, the cat and the old woman whirled to the ground.

They were both of them too enraged to inquire who was who, and such a furious battle raged that the sand they threw up completely hid the earth from view for miles around.

The Queen, however, after she had recovered her breath, hovered over the spot to see what would happen.

All of a sudden there was a loud explosion, and a column of blue flame shot up.

'Now what has happened?' the Queen thought to herself, and prepared to fly off at full speed. But the cloud of sand sailed quietly off down the wind, and, save for a deep hole, there remained no trace of the old woman and her cat.

Just at that moment the Queen heard a mighty rustling of wings, and, looking up, saw the great herd of wild geese swirling round and round her head.

'Dear me!' the Queen said to herself, 'I wonder if I could talk to them. Perhaps they will understand bat's language.'

Now, it is a rather difficult thing to give you a good idea of what the bat's language is like, because, although one may produce a fairly good imitation by rubbing two corks together, or by blowing through a double button, it doesn't mean any more in bat's language than 'Huckery hickyhoo' would in ours, if any one were foolish enough to produce such sounds.

Suffice it, then, to say that the Queen said in the bat's language, 'Oh, come, that's a good thing!'

And the geese answered, 'Yes isn't it scrumptious?'

You see, geese are rather vulgar kinds of fowls, and so they speak a vulgar language—about as different from the aristocratic bat's as a London costermonger's* is from that of a well-brought-up young person. So that, if you can imagine a gander and a bat proposing each to the lady of his choice, the goose would say, ''Lizer, be my disy;'* whereas the bat would lay one claw upon its velvet coat over its heart and begin, 'Miss Elizabeth,' or 'Miss Vespertilio,'—for that is the bat's surname—'if the devotion of a lifetime can atone for——' and so on, in the most elegant of phrases.

At any rate, the geese understood the Queen, and the Queen understood the geese, which is the main thing.

'Now what shall I do?' the Queen said.

And the geese consulted among themselves. Then an elderly gander spoke up for the rest.

'Ma'am,' he said, or rather hissed, 'you have saved our lives.'

The Queen said, 'I'm sure I'm very glad.'

The poor gander blushed, not being used to speaking in public; but he began again bravely.

'Ma'am, seeing as how you've saved our lives, we've made up our minds to be your faithful servants, and to go where you go, and do what you do.'

'I'm sure it's very good of you,' the Queen said, not knowing exactly whether to be glad or sorry. 'But I don't quite know where I *am* going; though, as it's getting late in the day, I think I'd better be moving on.'

'Why don't you go back to the cottage?' the old gander said. 'There'll be no one there to bother you now.'

'It's rather a good idea,' the Queen said. 'I've a good mind to.'

'Do,' the geese said. 'There's a nice river near by.'

And, although the latter inducement was inconsiderable, the Queen did as she was asked. In their mad career they had come so great a distance that it was close on nightfall before they reached the cottage again.

There everything was quiet and as they had left it, only the fire had almost died away on the hearth.

So the Queen, who rather disliked the darkness, threw one or two turfs on it and blew it up well with the bellows, so that the light glowed and danced cheerfully on the farthest wall of the cottage.

So the Queen sat and looked at the leaping flames, and her shadow danced large upon the walls. But outside, on the dunes before the door, the geese were all asleep, with their heads under their wings. Their shadows did not move in the moonlight. Only the old gander remained as a sentinel, marching up and down before the door. No sentry was ever more perfect in his goose-step.

So, when a fit of nervousness came over the Queen, and she went to look out at the door for fear the old woman and her cat should return, she felt quite reassured.

'It was we who saved the capitol,'* the older gander said; 'so you're quite safe.'

And the remembrance soothed the Queen, so that she went and lay down on the couch of dried fern that served for a bed, and soon was fast asleep.

After all, the geese were some companionship, and it was better to sleep quietly on the bracken-couch than to glide along in a ghostly way under the moon, with no company but one's shadow on the fields far, far down below.

So the Queen slept until morning, and the first sound that awakened her was the quacking of the geese, a really tremendous noise. The sun was just up. The Queen sprang up, too, and dressed herself.

There was a pail in the hut, and, at no great distance, a well. So thither she went, and, drawing a pail of water, washed herself well in it. It was delightfully cold and refreshing.

The geese saluted her with a general chorus of good mornings and good wishes, for which the Queen thanked them.

So, having made herself comfortable, she began to feel not a little hungry, as did the geese. After looking about in the hut, she discovered the cellar door, and, opening it, she went down, not without being a little afraid that it might be full of old women or black cats. She found no trace of either, but merely quite a lot of bread and cheese, and hard biscuits, and a sack of corn, which was evidently intended for the geese.

So she filled a measure with it and threw it to them, and gave them a great pan of water from the well, after which she made a frugal breakfast off a biscuit and an egg which one of the geese had laid.

Then the geese wanted to set forth for the river, and asked the Queen to come with them, which she did willingly enough, after she had tidied the house a little and had made up the fire so that it might not quite go out.

Then gaily they trooped off over the sand-dunes towards the river, the geese marching gravely in line; only the old grey gander went beside the Queen and talked to her.

Just where the river ran was a green meadow with several pools of water in it. And the meadow was perfectly alive with birds; everywhere their wings seemed to be flapping and fluttering and showing the whites underneath them.

They eyed the Queen with something like alarm, but the old grey gander made a speech in which he referred to the Queen as their preserver and friend; and the Queen said that, far from wishing to do them any harm, she was very fond of birds.

And so the flapping of wings went on again, and the sun shone down upon the gay meadow. But the geese led the Queen to the river's edge, and there she sat down on the bank beneath a willow tree, whilst they jumped in and revelled in the clear water.

So the sun rose higher and higher, and the shade of the tree grew more and more grateful to the Queen, and the geese came out of the river and arranged themselves for a nap on the grass around her.

During the sun's height, too, all the other birds were more silent; it was too hot for violent exercise.

So the river gurgled among the rushes, and they rustled and bent their heads, and the willow leaves forgot to tremble for want of a breeze. And the great, placid flow of the river was without a dimple on its face, save when a fish sprang gleaming out after a low-flying midge.

So the Queen felt happy and contented, and she, too, dozed off into a little nap, whilst the woolly clouds slowly sailed across the blue heaven.

But towards evening the birds all woke up; the peewits flew off in a flock to the marshy flats down the river, and the snipe whirred away to the mud-banks, and the geese arose and cropped the greensward with their bills.

And then, towards sunset, they all rose in the air, and the Queen with them, and went whirling round in great clouds of rustling pinions, dyed red in the sunset, geese and peewits, and snipe and herons, all wheeling about in sheer delight of life; until, when the sun was almost down, the geese, with a great cry of farewell, flew off through the gloaming with the Queen towards the hut.

And there she once more blew up the fire for company, whilst the geese outside slept calmly. And so she went to bed again.

Thus it fell about that the Queen remained quite a long time in the hut with the geese for her companions.

The days she spent down where the river whispered to the rushes. When the sun was very hot, she would bathe in the stream and lie among the rushes; and, having cut a pipe, she played upon it in tune with the gurgle of the river.

Then the geese and the gulls and the peewits and the gaunt grey herons would gather round and listen attentively—so attentively that if one of the gulls made a slight rustling in changing legs, he always got a good peck for disturbing them. And the great herons buried their bills in the feathers of their breasts and shut their eyes, and did not move even when the frogs crept out of the water and listened, with their gold-rimmed eyes all agog, and their yellow throats palpitating.

Then when she had finished; the herons snapped their bills; and the gulls cried, 'Kee-ah;' and the peewits, 'Peewit;' and the geese hissed, with their necks stretched out—but that too signified applause.

As for the frogs, they made haste to spring with a plop into the rushes, without any applause at all; but that was because the herons had opened their eyes and were stalking towards them.

So the Queen was very much beloved in the bird-meadow, and the gulls would come out of the shining pools to greet her when she came in the freshness of the morning, and the herons would lay fish at her feet, and the peewits would perch upon her shoulder and fly around her head, and the whirr of wings was everywhere. But the geese were her guard of honour.

One morning before they set out for the bird-meadow, whilst the Queen was engaged in tidying up the hut, the geese suddenly set up a most terrible hissing and quacking.

'Dear me!' the Queen said, 'there'll be a terrible rain-storm soon.'

But at that moment the old grey gander came running excitedly into the hut.

'There's a man—two men—three men coming,' he said, quite out of breath.

The Queen said, 'Good gracious! and my hair in such a state!'

But she went to the door all the same.

There, sure enough, she saw three men coming one after the other. The first two were quite near, but the third was a great way off, though he appeared to hop along over the dunes in a most remarkable manner. He seemed to be habited in a suit of black, and carried a black bag; but he was still a great way off, and the Queen turned her attention to the other two, who were now quite close to her.

The first one was a handsome, very bronzed young man, in a suit of shining armour, that, to the Queen's critical eyes, did not seem to fit him to perfection; whilst the second, a delicate-looking, haughty youth, with very fair skin, was habited in a shepherd's coarse garments, and carried a crook and a sling at his side.

The man in armour bowed a clumsy sort of bow and said—

'Good morning;' whilst the shepherd bowed in a most courteous and elegant manner.

'Good morning, fair madam. Is Mrs. Hexer* at home?'

The Queen said, 'No, there's no one of that name living here.'

'Dear me,' the man in armour said, 'how annoying! I am the—the Prince of Kamschkatka,* and this is a shepherd of Pendleton.'* He said it in a great hurry, just as you might say a newly learned lesson.

But the shepherd of Pendleton said, 'Ah, perhaps Mrs. Hexer does not live here.'

The Queen said, 'No, she doesn't; I live here.'

'What, *alone!*' they both said.

And the Queen answered, 'No; I live with my geese.'

The shepherd said, 'Oh, then perhaps you could tell us where Mrs. Hexer *does* live.'

'I've never heard of her,' the Queen said.

'*What!* never heard of Mrs. Hexer?' they both said.

'The famous witch who has the well of the Elixir of Life,' the prince said.

But the shepherd said, 'Of love.'

The mention of 'witch' brought something to the Queen's mind.

'There used to be a horrible old woman who lived here with a great black cat,' she said. 'Perhaps *she* was Mrs. Hexer; but she disappeared some time ago.'

'That must have been her,' the prince said.

And the shepherd continued, 'Ah, if you would let us sit for a while on the coping of your well, or even give us a draught of its water, we should be infinitely obliged to you.'

The Queen said, 'Oh, you're very welcome,' and turned into the house to get her bucket, when she was astonished to see a coal-black thing with horns and a long tail sitting in the very middle of her fire.

She rubbed her eyes in surprise, and when she looked again there was only a gentleman, clad in an elegant suit of black, with his coal-black hair carefully parted in the middle and falling in sinuous lines on either side of his forehead. He held his hat in one hand, and in the other a black bag and long narrow book.

'Oh, good morning, Mrs. Hexer,' he said. 'You will excuse my liberty; but I saw you were agreeably engaged, and so I took the opportunity of slipping in by the back way.'

'I didn't know there was a back way,' the Queen said.

'The chimney, I should have said, Mrs. Hexer,' the gentleman said.

'But I'm not Mrs. Hexer,' the Queen replied.

'No, indeed,' the gentleman answered. 'The elixir has had a most remarkable success in your case. A photograph of you now would be a most valuable advertisement—before taking and after. I suppose you haven't got one of your former state?'

'But I tell you I'm not Mrs. Hexer,' the Queen said.

Whereupon the gentleman became a shade more serious.

'You have exactly five minutes more life,' he said, after having consulted one of those keyless watches that never seem to have had enough winding. He laid down his hat and bag, and looked carefully in his book. 'Is this not your signature?'

The Queen said, 'Good gracious, no; and I'm not going to sign anything more.'

'You've signed quite enough in this,' the gentleman said.

'But I tell you I never signed it,' the Queen replied.

'Oh, nonsense, Mrs. Hexer,' the gentleman said. 'Come, your time is nearly at hand.'

'It's nothing of the sort,' the Queen said.

And the gentleman bowed. 'You know best, Mrs. Hexer,' he said. 'There's one more minute.'

The Queen waited to see what would happen.

The seconds passed by, and the Queen's heart beat. Then the gentleman tore the page out of his book, at the dotted line, and put the book in the bag.

'By-the-bye,' he said, 'what's become of the cat?'

The Queen said, 'It disappeared with the witch.'

The gentleman looked at his watch. 'Time's up, Mrs. Hexer,' he said, as he put it back in his pocket. 'By virtue of this document, signed by your blood——'

'It isn't my blood,' the Queen said, when, all of a sudden, the hut vanished away over her head, and she found herself standing in the open air among the sand-dunes, amid a large crowd of people; whilst the two men, shepherd and prince, were lying tumbled on the sand, for the well on which they had been seated had disappeared.

But the most astonishing thing was what happened to the gentleman in black, for he suddenly changed into a black demon and advanced roaring towards her, until something seemed to stop him, and he changed just as suddenly back into the gentleman that he had been before.

'I see there has been some mistake,' he said, bowing and placing his hand upon his heart. Then he knelt upon the ground. 'Be mine! be mine!' he said. 'Oh, most adorable maiden, be mine; marry me, and I will reform; I'll give up smoking; I'll never swear; I'll—I'll go to church—only marry me.'

'I can't,' the Queen said. 'Don't be ridiculous and kneel; I never let the Regents kneel.'

'You can marry me—you can,' the gentleman said. 'I can marry while I'm on earth. Of course, down below it's different. But I'll keep regular hours; I'll be most respectable—I will, if you'll only marry me.'

'I tell you I can't,' the Queen said; 'I don't know what I've done to make you go on in this ridiculous way.'

'It's the elixir. You've been drinking it, you know,' the demon gentleman said; 'and so I can't help it. But if you won't marry me, madam, perhaps we can do a little business in my line. I pride myself that my system is the very best—the seven year's purchase system, you know.'

'I don't understand you at all,' the Queen said.

'Why, it's very simple. You give me what I want, and I will re-erect for you the desirable family residence that stood here, with all its advantages—the delightfully secluded spot, the landscape, the well of pure water, and the fowl-house with its stock of geese. Come, let me fill you up a form.'

'Yes, but what do I have to do for it?' the Queen said.

And he answered, 'Oh, a mere trifle—only a formality.'

'But what *is* it?'

'Oh, you only give me your soul—it's nothing at all.'

'*My soul!*' the Queen said. 'Certainly not.'

'But I'll make you rich,' the gentleman said.

'I'm quite rich enough already,' the Queen answered.

'I'll make you powerful—make you a great queen.'

'I'm one already, thanks,' the Queen said.

'I'll give you a broom that you can fly on,' the gentleman remarked.

'I can fly without a broom,' the Queen said.

'I'll let you drink the elixir,' he went on.

'I've had quite enough already,' the Queen said.

The demon gnashed his teeth. 'Then you won't trade?' he said.

'Certainly *not*,' the Queen answered.

'And you won't marry me?'

'*Certainly* not!' the Queen said.

There was blue flame, and a great pillar of sand shot up into the air. The wind carried it slowly away—the gentleman in black had disappeared.

'Come, that's something!' the Queen said, with a sigh of relief, when her eye fell suddenly on the crowd of people that were standing looking at her. They were mostly standing on one leg. 'Why, whoever are you?' she said.

And a grey-haired man answered, 'We are—that is, we were—the geese. I am the oldest of them, and, as such, let me remind you that a ripe man is by far the best one to marry. Oh, maiden, marry *me!*'

But a perfect storm of voices went up. 'No; marry me! I'm——'

But the Queen held up her hand to command silence.

'Don't make such a fearful noise. I can't even hear myself think. I'm not going to marry any of you, though you were very nice, dear geese, and I was very fond of you.'

'No; the lady is going to marry me!' a voice said, and the man in shepherd's clothes stept forth.

'No, marry me!' the man in armour said.

'I'm a prince. I will make you a princess,' the man in shepherd's clothes said.

'I'm a shepherd,' the man dressed like a prince said. 'A shepherd is a far better match for a goose-girl* than a prince is.'

'But why were either of you so deceitful?' the Queen said. 'Because it's so ridiculous. You don't look like a shepherd, prince—your skin is much too fair; and you are much too brawny to be a prince, shepherd.'

'Well, I thought it was not quite respectable for a prince to be seen visiting a witch, and so I changed clothes with the shepherd here.'

'And I changed clothes with the prince because I had seen you from afar, and had loved you; and because I thought a prince would have seemed more splendid than a common shepherd.'

'But you were both wrong to try to deceive me,' the Queen said. 'As for you, prince, I will not marry you to be made a princess, for I am a Queen already; and for you, shepherd, I will not marry you to become a shepherdess, for I am a goose-girl already, though my flock has turned back from its goose-shape again. But how did you become geese, anyhow?' she asked of them.

And he who had been the old grey gander answered, 'The witch turned us into it when we came to ask for the Elixir of Love.'

'Dear me!' the Queen said. 'Does love make such geese of people?'

And the shepherd in prince's clothing said, 'I'm afraid it does.'

'You see, it was as I said,' the old grey gander said; 'those young men are all fools. You had much better marry me.'

He had no sooner said the words than a perfect whirlwind of shouts arose.

'Marry me!' 'No, marry me!' 'Me!' 'Me!' 'Me!'

The Queen put her fingers to her ears. 'If you don't be quiet I'll fly away altogether,' she said.

But it produced no effect at all; the sound of voices went on just like the sound of surf on a pebbly shore.

'Oh, I can't stand it,' the Queen said. 'And to think that it is to go on like this for ever and ever, and all because of this horrible elixir! I shall fly right away from it.'

And she quietly rose and sailed away in the air, and the last she saw of the geese was that they were feebly trying to fly after her, waving their arms frantically as if they had been wings.

The Queen flew straight up into the air, and she had reached a dizzy height before she thought of what she was doing.

To tell the truth, she was a little sorrowful at the thought of leaving the geese; for, with the exception of the old bat, they had been almost her only friends.

'I wish they *could* have flown with me,' she said to herself. 'But, good gracious, how high I am getting! I shall be losing my way. Why, the earth looks quite small and quite like a map.'

And so it did. Then an idea struck the Queen.

'Suppose I were to fly right up to the sun; what fun it would be!'

And, since the idea had come into her head, she determined to make the attempt.

Up, up she flew, higher and even higher, till all the air around was full of strange harmonies, as though ten thousand Æolian harps* were being breathed upon in accord by a great wind. And all around her, too, the planets whirred and spun and the stars gleamed, and now and again she would pass through mists of luminousness and of gleaming hail.

Up, up she went till she came where there was a great bow of iridescent colours, and rising from it a great array of white steps, that ran up, up, so high that it took away her breath to look upon them. At the top was a great glare of light.

The Queen felt tired and a little bewildered; it seemed as if her wings would bear her no longer or, at least, no higher.

Upon the many-coloured road she stood and looked up the great white way. A voice spoke to her like a great rushing of wind.

'Maiden,' it said, 'so far and no further.'

And a feeling akin to fear came over her; but not fear, for she knew not what guilt was.

And the voice spoke again. 'Go down this bow back to the earth, and do the work that is to be done by you. Be of use to your fellows.'

And the Queen turned and went her way down the great road. The air was full of voices, glad voices, such that the Queen had never heard before—full of a joy that made her heart leap to hear.

But she could see no one.

Till at last she came back to the green earth, late in the afternoon.

For a moment, above her, she could see the great span of the rainbow, and then it vanished into the clear air, and the Queen was alone in the little valley. There it was already dusk, though the sky above the long down before her was still golden with the rays of the sun that had sunk behind it.

There was a little rill running along the valley, and the Queen knelt down and drank of its brimfulness, taking the water up in her hand. It was very sweet and cool, and the Queen felt happy to be back on the earth again.

'After all,' she said to herself, as she sat herself down in the soft, cool grass, that tickled her hands—'after all, it's something to have firm ground under one; one feels just a *little* lonely up there, quite away from everything except shooting stars, and the world is a dear old place in the twilight like this.'

Up above the hill-top she saw a man's head appear, together with a pair of horses and a plough. Quite plainly she could hear the bridle trappings' rattle and click, and the heavy breathing of the horses in the evening stillness.

It was all so quiet and natural that she did not feel at all surprised.

Just at the brow of the hill, standing out black against the light, the man halted, and, lifting the plough, turned his team of horses round and set off down the new furrow.

With very little hesitation, the Queen went up the hill towards the spot from which he had disappeared, and in a very short time she had reached the brow and stood looking down the furrows. The western sky was still a blaze of glory, and the yellow light gleamed along the ridge of shining earth that the plough turned up, and on the steel of the ploughshare. The ploughman was singing a song, and his voice came mellowly along over the sunlit stubble that was not yet ploughed up.

'I wonder, now, if it will be safe for me to speak to him, or if he'll fall in love with me as soon as he sees me? because it's really too much of a nuisance.'

However, she went lightly across the stubble towards him. He was just turning the plough as she approached, and he did not seem to notice her.

'Now, lads,' he said to the horses, 'the last lap for this evening.'

And the horses whinnied softly and set their necks to the collar.

'Can I be of any use to you?' the Queen said.

The man stopped his team for a moment, and looked towards her. Against the glow of the sky she could not make out his face; but he seemed to smile.

'No, friend,' he said. 'I have all but finished my day's work; but, if you will lead the horses up the furrow, they may go straighter than I can drive them.'

So the Queen went to the horses' heads, and took one of them by the bridle, and the great beasts stretched to the work. And the Queen felt a new happiness come over her, at the thought that she was of use in the world.

The sun set as they came to the edge of the field. The plougher stretched his arms abroad, and then came to the horses' heads.

'Thank you, friend,' he said to the Queen. He did not look at her, but kept his eyes downcast on the ground with a strangely distant appearance in them. 'Will you not come home and sup with us? It is hardly a hundred yards to the farm, and the nearest place to here is several miles onwards.'

The Queen said, 'Thank you. I should be very glad; but—but—' as the thought struck her, 'I shan't be able to pay you, you know.'

The ploughman laughed. 'Now I see you are a stranger,' he said. 'But yet I have seldom had strangers pass here that offered to help me.'

The Queen said, 'Yes, but it is so nice to be of use to any one;' and seeing that he was engaged in unbuckling the horse from the plough on the right side, she did as much for the one on the left.

The ploughman said, 'Now, can you ride?'

'Well, I've never tried, but I dare say I could if they didn't go *too* fast.'

'No, I don't think they'll go fast,' he said. 'Here, let me lift you on. There, catch hold of the horns of the collar.'

And in a moment the Queen was seated sideways on the great horse. The ploughman made his way to the horse's head and led it down the valley again. The other horse went quietly along by the side of them.

'How delicious everything looks in the owl-light!' the Queen said.

And the ploughman sighed. 'I—I can't see it,' he said. 'I can't see anything. I'm blind.'

The Queen said, 'Blind! Why, I should never have known it. You are as skilful as any one else.'

The ploughman answered, 'Oh yes, I can manage pretty well because I'm used to it, and there are many ways of managing things; but it is an affliction.'

The horses went carefully down the hill, and in a little space they had reached the valley whence the Queen had started. It was now quite dark there, and the harvest moon had not yet arisen, but at no great distance from them the Queen could see a light winking.

So the horses plodded along, stopping now and again to crop a mouthful of grass or drink a draught from the tinkling rill, whose sound had grown loud in the twilight silence. In a very short while they had come to where a little farmhouse lay in the bottom of the valley among trees, that looked black in the starlight.

The ploughman called, 'Mother, I'm bringing a visitor.'

And a little old woman came to the door. 'Welcome!' she said, and added, 'My dear,' when the Queen came into sight in the light that fell through the open door.

The Queen slipped down from the horse and went into the door with the little old woman, whilst the ploughman disappeared with the horses.

'She really is a dear little old woman,' the Queen said to herself—'very different from old Mrs. Hexer.'

And so indeed she was—quite a little woman in comparison with her stalwart son, with white hair and a rosy face and eyes not at all age-dimmed, but blue as the cornflower or as a summer sky, and looking, like a child's, so gentle that a hard word would make them wince.

She put a chair ready for the Queen by the fireside, and then, on the white wood table, set out forks and knives for her.

'You must be tired,' she said kindly; 'but we go to bed soon after supper, and so you will have a good rest.'

The Queen said, 'Yes, I am a little tired; and it is very kind of you to let me stop.'

The little old woman looked at her with an odd, amused look in her gentle eyes.

'Now I see you are a stranger,' she said.

'Yes, I come from a long way off,' the Queen said. 'At least I suppose it is a great way off, for it has taken me a long time to get here.'

At that moment the ploughman came in, with the heavy step of a tired man.

'Mother, mother!' he said gaily; 'I'm hungry.'

'Son, son,' she answered, 'I am glad to hear it. There will be plenty.'

And so the supper was made ready, and heartily glad the Queen was, for she was as hungry as the ploughman.

And they had the whitest of floury potatoes, in the whitest of white wooden bowls, and the sweetest of new milk, and the clearest of honey overrunning the comb, and junket laid on rushes, and plums, and apples, and apricots. And be certain that the Queen enjoyed it.

And, when it was finished, they drew their chairs round the fire, and the ploughman said, addressing the Queen—

'Now, friend, since you have travelled far, tell us something of what may have befallen you on the way, for we are such stay-at-home folk here, that we know little of the world around. But perhaps you are tired and would rather go to bed.'

But the Queen said, 'Oh no, I am very well rested now, and I will gladly tell you my story—only first tell me where I am.'

'This is the farm of Woodward, from which we take our names, my mother and I, and we are some ten miles from the Narrow Seas.'

'But what is the land called, and who rules it?' the Queen said.

The ploughman laughed. 'Why, it is called the land of Happy Folk; and as for who rules it, why, just nobody, because it gets along very well as it is.'

The Queen leant back in the great chair they had given her. She rubbed her chin reflectively and looked at the fire.

'The Regent told me that a country couldn't possibly exist without a King or Queen,' she said.

'Who is the Regent?' the ploughman said. He too kept his face to the fire that he could not see.

'Oh, well, he's just the Regent of my kingdom. But I forgot you didn't know. I am Eldrida, Queen of the Narrowlands and all the Isles.'

The little old woman looked at her interestedly.

And the ploughman said, 'After all, you're not so *very* far from your home; because one can see the coast of it quite plainly on a clear day from our shore, so they say.'

'Why, then you must have quite a number of people from there?' the Queen said.

But the ploughman answered, 'No, hardly ever any one, because the seas run so swiftly through the straights that no boat can live in them—so people would have to come a long way round by land. Besides, they've got everything that we've got, so what could they want here?' the ploughman said, and added slily, 'all except one thing, that is.'

'Why, what is that?' the Queen asked.

And the ploughman answered, 'Why, the Queen, of course; because we have got her.'

But the little old woman held her hand to shield her eyes from the fire's blaze, and looked across at the Queen.

'I shouldn't think it was a very nice country to live in,' she said.

The Queen asked, 'Why?'

'Well, one evening when we were down by the sea, we saw the whole sky lit up over there, and, later, we heard from a traveller, that the people had set fire to the town when they were fighting about who was to be Regent.'

'Yes, I'm afraid they are rather fond of doing that; but I didn't know anything about it.'

'How was that?' the ploughman said.

And in reply, the Queen told them her story, to which they listened very attentively, and hardly interrupted at all to ask questions.

And so, it being finished, the little old woman took the Queen up to bed in a little room under the eaves, and, bidding her a kind good night, left her.

The Queen's window looked out down the valley, and she could, as she undressed, see the moon shining placidly along it, gleaming on the dew mist, and glancing here and there on the waters of the little stream where its zigzag course caught the light.

There was never a sound save the tinkle of the brook or the dull noise of a horse that moved its feet in the stable.

So the Queen fell asleep, and did not awaken till the sun was high in the sky.

She rubbed her eyes and could not quite make out where she was at first. She missed the noise of the geese, to which she had been used to awaken. But gradually it all came back to her, and for a while she lay and watched the roses that were peeping in at the window and nodding in the morning breeze.

'Come, this will never do!' the Queen said to herself. 'Whatever will they think of me?' So she arose from between the warm, clean sheets, and, having dressed herself, went downstairs. There she found the little old woman busy in the kitchen.

'Good morning, my dear,' she said.

And the Queen answered, 'Good morning, mother.'

And the little old woman's eyes smiled her pleasure. 'I didn't wish to wake you,' she said, 'you seemed so tired last night. My son has gone off to his ploughing; but you will see him as you pass the hill, and he will guide you a little on your way, if you have to go further.' The little old woman's eyes looked quite wistful. 'We wish you would stay a little while with us; we should like it so much.'

'Why, of course I will,' the Queen said; 'that is, if I can be of any use to you.'

'Oh yes, you can be of use,' the little old woman said. 'But it is such a pleasure for us to have guests, for we like to talk with them, and we like to please them as much as may be. But here is your breakfast; you must be quite hungry. And afterwards—after to-day, that is—my son will show you all about the farm. Only to-day he wants to finish his ploughing, and I am too old to go very far up the hills.'

'It is wonderful how your son manages to work as he does,' the Queen said.

And the little old woman's eyes looked proud and happy.

'He has lived all his life here, you see. When he was quite a baby a flash of lightning blinded him; but now he knows his way everywhere about, and he can do almost all the farm-work. Sometimes he has a boy to help him; but just now, they're harvesting at our neighbour's, and the boy has gone down to help. But it makes my son rather slow in his ploughing, for he has to guide himself by feeling with his feet the last furrow he has made.'

'Oh, I could lead the horses for him,' the Queen said.

And the mother answered, 'Yes, do, my dear; and you can take your dinner out with you. His dog always fetches this for him.'

So the Queen finished her breakfast, and then set out along the valley towards the ploughing place.

By daylight she could see better how pleasant a place the valley was, very green in the bottom, with here and there a pollard willow by the stream, and here and there linen laid out to bleach on the grass. But the steep hills that shut it in were purple with heather, and brown with bracken, and, now and then, a lonely thorn tree. Behind her was the little white cottage, with a cluster of trees drawn down around it, and with the ducks and turkeys and chickens crowding the valley in front of it. Indeed, every now and then along the valley a lily-white duck would pop its golden-billed head out of the reeds and meadow-sweet of the stream to look at her as she passed along.

So she came to the hill where the valley made a sharp turn, and on the top of which she could see the ploughman. Up it she climbed through the heather, and speedily reached him.

'I've come to lead the horses for you,' she said.

And he looked towards her and smiled.

'That's right,' he said. 'Then you're not going away just yet. It's better here than being shut up in a palace garden, with no one but a bat to talk to.'

'It is,' the Queen said simply.

So, through the autumn day, she led the horses up and down the furrows, whilst he drove the share deep into the ground.

And through the blue sky, up the wind and down the wind, came the crows and starlings to feed on the worms that the plough turned up. So, late in the afternoon, they had come as far as he meant to go.

'Further down the hill,' he said, 'the wheat would catch the north wind. So that's enough for to-day, Queen Eldrida.'

'Don't call me *Queen* Eldrida, because if I am a queen, I'm not your queen. Just call me Eldrida.'

'One name's as good as another,' he said, as he slipped on his coat. 'Now let's go home, and I'll show you a little of the valley behind the house.'

So the Queen stayed for a while with them, and did as they did. And the blind man led her up the hills, and on the hilltops called the sheep, and from all sides they came to his call.

And the Queen halved his work for him, and did those things which his want of sight prevented his doing.

Sometimes she stayed to help the little mother indoors, but, on the whole, she preferred being out in the open air with the blind man.

Then came the beginning of winter, and she went with him up the hillsides, and in among the storms to fold the sheep, and drive the cattle home to the byres.

And then midwinter, when, in the morning, they had to set to work by lanthorn light that cast a luminous yellow circle round them upon the snow, and made their great shadows dance strangely.

Then the snows swept down into the valley and covered everything up beneath the soft white waves, so that, when they wanted to go out, they had to get through one of the roof-windows, for the door was all covered up. Then indeed it was very cold work getting about, and the Queen had always to guide the blind man, because the snow had covered all his familiar landmarks. The snow made it very hard walking, too, and put the Queen quite out of breath, but he sang quite lustily a song—

> ' "Cold hands, warm heart,"
> Then let the wind blow cold
> On our clasped hands who fare across the wold.
>
> ' "Hard lot, hot love,"
> Then let our pathway go
> Through lone, grey lands; knee-deep amid the snow.'

But the Queen was generally too out of breath to be able to sing at all.

At last, however, the snow came right over the roof-tree, and they could not go out of the house at all. So they sat quietly around a great fire, and the little old woman span, and the Queen worked at the loom, and the blind man wove baskets out of osiers. And they told tales.

Said the little old woman, 'I will tell you a tale that I had from my grandmother, and she had it from hers, and so on, a great way back.

'Once upon a time, upon the earth there were no people at all, no men and women, but only little goblin things that covered the whole earth and made it a beautiful green colour. But the sun was a bright flame colour, and the moon very, very white. So the Sun and the Earth took to quarrelling as to which was the more beautiful of the two.

'Said the Earth, "I am the more beautiful; such a lovely green as mine was surely never seen."

'Said the Sun, "But just look at my mantle of flame."

'So, as they could not possibly agree, they submitted the matter to the Moon. Now, the Moon was horribly jealous of the Sun, because he so terribly outshone her; so she gave her verdict for the Earth.

'Then, indeed, the Earth was proud, and gave itself such airs and graces that not only the Sun, but the Moon and all the Stars declared war against it.

'So early one morning the Sun peeped up over the edge of the sea, and sent a great trail of golden warriors over it to attack the Earth-spirits.

'They, for their part, were armed and ready, and all day long they fought and fought, and at last the Sun's warriors had to depart in a long trail over the sea to the Sun again. Then the Earth was more triumphant than ever. But, just as they were lying down to rest, slowly, slowly, the Moon came up and sent a great trail of its warriors over the sea, and the Stars poured down showers of little, little warriors, and the poor Earth-spirits had to begin and fight all through the night. And, although they killed hundreds and hundreds and beat the rest off, no sooner was it done than they had to begin all over again against the Sun.

'This went on—day in, day out; night in, night out—for a long, long time, until the poor Earth-spirits grew wearier and wearier, and their lovely green colour changed into a sickly yellow hue.

'Then in despair they prayed to the spirits of the air and of the great waters to assist them. And the waters arose and covered in the Earth, and the winds of the air brought a mantle of clouds, so that the Earth was shielded from the fury of the Sun and the constellations; but, alas! when the waters receded and the skies grew clear again, it was found that all the poor Earth-spirits were drowned—all save a very few who had taken refuge on the tops of the mountains.

'So these few, having such a lot to eat, gradually grew and grew till they became men. And the dead bodies of the green Earth-spirits grew out of the Earth, too, and became the fruits of the Earth; but the dead bodies of the Sun and Moon warriors became gold and silver, and men dig them out of the Earth.

'But still the quarrel goes on; for gold and silver are man's greatest curse, and the fruits of the Earth his one blessing.'

And so with tales and work they beguiled the time of the waiting for the snow's melting, and at last it came. The valley was filled with the roaring of the brook, grown large with the melting of the snows, and the robin sang from the copses.

So the spring came on, and the earth grew green, and it was the time of sowing, and the Queen had almost forgotten that she was able to fly—indeed, she mostly left her wind-flower crown at home.

But one day her eye fell upon it, and the thought suddenly struck her that the bat had said that the wind-flowers had the power of curing blindness.

'Now, if only I knew how it was to be done, or if I had a few more of them I'd cure *him*. Now, it's not really so very far from here to there. I might just fly over to the palace garden and ask the bat, and be back this very evening'—for it was then the early morning. 'And I won't tell them anything about it, and it'll be delightful.'

And so, without any more hesitation, she just opened the little window and was up among the dawn-clouds that were sweeping up from over the sea. It was a little chilly and very lonely up there, and the silent flights of seagulls that she had caught up and overpassed seemed too alarmed to talk to her. The Queen felt a little lost, as if there was something missing.

'Somehow it doesn't seem half as nice as it used to do,' she said to herself. 'I wonder why it is? I don't think, after I get home—I mean back here—I shall ever go flying again.'

But she folded her hands in her cloak and went silently on over the grey shimmering sea. The sun grew higher and higher, and it was about eight in the morning before she was hovering over the city.

She alighted in a street that seemed somewhat empty, because she disliked the attention that her mode of progression usually excited.

Just in front of her, under a shed formed by the pushing up of the shutters of his shop, a tailor was seated, cross-legged, working away with his head bent down over his work.

'Good morning!' the Queen said. 'Can I be of any use to you?'

The tailor peered up at her through a great pair of horn spectacles. 'Eh?' he said.

'I said, "Can I be of any use to you?"' the Queen replied.

And the tailor regarded her in a dazed way. Suddenly he said—

'Oh yes; marry me, marry me, only marry me!'

The Queen said, 'Oh, nonsense,' because she had just remembered the elixir.

But the tailor answered, 'It isn't nonsense—it really isn't. It's true I'm married already; but I'll knock my wife on the head, and then I'll be free.'

But before the Queen could answer anything at all there began a sudden growling sound that resolved itself into a succession of footsteps coming rapidly down wooden steps, and, in a moment, a door burst open just behind the tailor's back. There was an old woman with a great broom just behind it.

'Ah, would ye now! murder your wife, a respectable married woman, for the sake of a hussy that comes dropping down out of the chimney-tops. I'll teach you.'

And with one sweep of her broom she knocked the poor little tailor off his board, and made a dash at the Queen.

But the Queen took to her heels and ran off.

'Why, she's worse than Mrs. Hexer,' she said to herself. 'But really this elixir is a great nuisance. It makes it impossible to have any peace. But I wonder what all the flags and decorations are about.'

Just at that moment two people, who appeared to be a servant-girl and her mother, came out of a neighbouring house. They were very gay in holiday costume.

'What is to happen to-day?' the Queen asked.

And the mother answered, 'Why, don't you know? The Queen is twenty-one to-day, and she's going to marry the Regent, Lord Blackjowl.'

'Going to marry the Regent!' the Queen said. 'Why, who told you so?'

'Everybody knows it,' the mother answered.

'But how did everybody get to know it?' the Queen asked.

And the mother answered, 'The Regent told them, I suppose.'

And the girl said, 'It's up among the Royal proclamations, on the notice-board at the palace.'

The Queen said, 'Oh! Will you show me the way to the palace?' she continued.

'Why, certainly,' the girl said. 'We were just going that way to see the procession.'

So they set off through the gay streets. As they went along the Queen could see the young men on every side falling in love with her; but she paid no attention to them.

'Are you glad the Queen's going to be married?' she asked her guides.

And the girl answered, 'Oh yes; we get a holiday to go and see the procession.'

'Why, then, I suppose you'd be just as glad if the Queen died, and you could go and see her funeral?'

And the old woman said, 'Of course!'

By that time they had come to the market-place. It was crowded with those who had come to see the sights, and the fountains were running wine instead of water; so, of course, there was rather a scramble to get at the fountains. That left the ground clear for the Queen to get to the notice-board where the Royal Proclamation hung.

There she saw, sure enough, the Regent's proclamation, saying that the Queen would marry him that day. At the end of it there was the signature, '*Eldrida, Queen.*'

'Why, it isn't my signature at all,' the Queen said.

And the mother and daughter looked at her askance.

'Have any of you ever seen the Queen?' she asked.

And the mother answered, 'No; no one has ever seen the Queen but the Regent; but there was a story that a beggar told about a year ago, that she had flown out of the palace and away. And they did say that Grubb the honey-cake maker and some soldiers knew something about it. But the Regent had them all executed, so we never came to know the rights of the story. Anyhow, we've had to pay taxes just the same.'

Now the Queen grew really angry with the Regent Blackjowl.

But she said, 'Thank you,' and 'Good-bye,' to the mother and daughter, and slipped away through the crowd to the side-wall of the palace, where, in the road, she had first commenced her travels.

Here there were very few people about, because there was little chance of seeing the procession from there. She waited until the street was almost empty, and then flew quietly over the palace wall and down into the familiar garden.

There it was, a little more neglected and a little more weed overgrown than ever, but otherwise just the same. Only it seemed to have grown a great deal smaller in the Queen's eyes; but that was because she had grown accustomed to great prospects and wide expanses of country.

The long, thorny arms of the roses had grown so much, that it was quite difficult to get under them into the little seat.

'Now I shall have ever so much trouble to wake him, and he'll be fearfully surly,' the Queen said to herself.

But it is always the unexpected that happens—as you will one day learn—and the Queen found that the rustling that the leaves made at her entrance had awakened the bat.

'Hullo!' he said, 'you there! Glad to see you. Heard from the nightingale that you'd been seen in disreputable company, going about with geese. Well, and what did you think of the world?'

'Oh, it's a very nice place when you're used to it.'

'That's what *you* think,' the bat said. 'Wait till you come to be my age. But now, tell me your adventures.'

'I'd better humour him,' the Queen said to herself, and so she plunged into the recital.

When she had finished the bat said, 'H'm! and so you're going to marry the Regent?'

'I'm not going to do anything of the sort,' the Queen said.

And the bat asked, 'Who are you going to marry, then?'

The Queen answered, 'No one; at least——'

And the bat said, 'Just so.'

And the Queen replied, 'Don't be stupid. Oh, and tell me how one can cure blindness with wind-flowers.'

The bat said, 'Do you know how to make tea?'

'Of course I do,' the Queen answered.

'Well, you make an infusion of dried wind-flowers just like tea, and then you give it to the young scamp to drink.'

'He's not a scamp,' the Queen said; 'but you're a dear good old bat all the same.'

The bat said, 'H'm!'

The Queen rose to her feet. 'Well, I must be off,' she said. 'I've got a lot to do.'

The bat said, 'Wait a minute; I'm coming too;' and he dropped down and hung on to the Queen's shoulder. He was rather a weight, but the Queen suffered it.

'Why, there aren't any wind-flowers left!' the Queen said, surveying the spot where they had grown.

The bat said, 'No; the weeds have choked them all.'

The Queen rubbed her chin and said nothing.

And the bat merely ejaculated, 'H'm!'

So the Queen entered the palace.

All the great halls were silent, and empty of people, and she passed through one after the other, shivering a little at their vastness.

At last she came before the curtain that separated her from the Throne Hall. It was large enough to contain the whole nation.

She pushed the curtain aside and found herself standing behind the great throne. Through the interstices of the carved back she could see everything that was going on. The Great Hall was thronged full of people from end to end. On the throne platform the Regent was waiting, evidently about to begin a speech.

The Queen stopped and peeped; there was a great flourish of trumpets that echoed and echoed along the hall, and the Regent began.

'Ladies noble, my lords, dames commoner, and gentlemen!' His great voice sounded clearly through the silence. 'As you are well aware, our gracious and high-mighty sovereign, the Queen Eldrida, has deigned to favour my unworthy self with the priceless honour of her hand, and that on this auspicious day. Her hand and seal affixed to the weighty document you have seen in the market-place.'

The Queen walked around the opposite side of the throne into the view of the people, who set up a tumultuous cheer. The Regent, however, thought they were cheering him, and went on with his speech.

'I had also announced that it was her Majesty's royal pleasure to reveal herself to her loyal people's eyes on this day.'

The Queen slowly ascended the steps of the throne and seated herself thereon. The great gold crown—it was six feet high, and so heavy that no head could bear its weight—hung above her head by a great gold chain.

The people cheered again, and still the Regent, whose back was to the throne, deemed that they were applauding his speech. He ran his fingers through his black beard and continued—

'It is, however, my painful duty to apprise you that her Majesty has been pleased to alter her design. We shall, therefore, be married in private in the Queen's apartments. The Queen's maiden modesty will not allow her to reveal her charms to the vulgar multitude.'

He paused and watched the effect of his speech, nervously fingering his beard and blinking with his little eyes. The people whispered among themselves, evidently unable to understand what it meant.

Suddenly the Queen's voice rang through the hall.

'My people,' she said, 'it is an infamous lie! I am here.'

The Regent started and turned around; his face grew as pale as death. But from the people a great shout went up at the discomfiture of the hated Regent. It echoed and reverberated through the great hall, and then silence fell again.

The Regent fell on his knees. 'Oh, your Majesty,' he said, 'marry me! marry me! marry me! I adore you! oh, only marry me!'

But the Queen was very pale and stern. 'This man,' she said to the people, 'has concealed my absence, has forged my name, has slandered me. I unmake him; I degrade him; and I banish him from the land!'

Once again the people cheered to see the Regent led off by the guards.

Then one of the nobles spoke. 'Your Majesty,' he said, 'it is for the good of the nation that you should marry. The late Regent was a tyrant, and, as such, unfitted for the inestimable honour; but I am the first noble in the realm. I am beloved by the people; therefore, your Majesty, adding to it the fact that I respectfully adore your Majesty, I beg your Majesty to let these things weigh down the balance of your mind, and marry me.'

But hardly were the words out of his mouth when a tumult arose, the like of which was never heard in any land, for every man of the nation was shouting, 'Marry me! marry me!' till the whole building quivered.

The Queen held up her hand for silence. 'Listen!' she said. 'I shall marry no one of you; and I will not even remain your Queen. For I am quite unfitted for a ruler, and I don't in the least want to be one. Therefore, choose a ruler for yourselves.'

But the people with one voice shouted, 'Be you our ruler!'

The Queen, however, said, 'No; I cannot and will not. It wouldn't be any good at all; besides, all the men would love me a great deal too much, and all the women would hate me a great deal too much, because of their husbands and sweethearts and all. So you must choose a king for yourselves.'

But confusion became doubly confounded, for every man in that vast assembly voted for himself as king.

'Oh, this will never do,' the Queen said; 'because, at this rate, you'll all go on quarrelling for ever, and the kingdom had better have remained under the Regent. Shall I choose a king for you?'

And with one voice the people answered, 'Yes.'

So the Queen said, 'The King I choose is very fit in one way, for he is not likely to be partial, since he is in this vast assembly the only one that is not in love with me. He will be very economical, because he neither needs much food, nor cares for rich robes. Therefore, the taxes will not be heavy; and, even if he is a little weak-eyed, he will not be a bit more blind to your interests, perhaps, than you are yourselves.'

So saying, the Queen arose from the throne and, taking the bat from her shoulder, set him on the vacant seat, where he scuttled about and did not seem particularly comfortable.

The Queen Who Flew

'Now, you're the King,' the Queen said to him.

'H'm!' he said. 'Will they give me some raw meat?'

The Queen said, 'Oh yes; and anything else you like to ask for.'

The bat said, 'H'm! this seat isn't very comfortable. What's that thing up there?'

'That's the crown,' the Queen said.

And the King remarked, 'H'm!' and in a moment he was hanging upside down from the bottom of the crown.

And the people cheered their King.

But the Queen just said, 'Good-bye, your Majesty.'

'Good-bye,' the Bat said. 'I suppose you won't marry *me*?'

'Don't be silly,' the late Queen said; and she slipped behind the curtain and ran through the deserted halls again, and once more out into the garden. And once again she watered her favourite plants, for the last time, and then flew right up into the air and away, away over the troubled seas, to the land that lay low in the horizon.

'How delightful it feels not to be a Queen any longer!' she said to herself. 'I always used to feel afraid, when I sat under that great crown, that it might fall on my head and squash me altogether. But I wonder how the bat got on.'

That the Queen never knew; but this was what happened. The bat took to kingship quite as easily as a duck takes to water, and, for reasons that the Queen gave, made a most popular ruler—even though he *was* strictly just. True, there were only three people in the kingdom who understood him, and they were mouse-trap makers who had learnt the bat language from mice. But, as the King always superintended the carrying out of his own edicts, they did not care to play tricks. And the Bat language was taught in all the schools, so that it became the state tongue. And all the ladies took to wearing brown sealskin cloaks with great puffed sleeves and capes, to as to look as much like bats as possible, and they all pretended to be very weak-sighted and turned night into day, in imitation of the King.

So that altogether the King was a great success from every point of view, as he was very long-lived, the last news that has reached here from the Narrowlands, reported that his Majesty was still hanging head downwards from the great crown, and was still setting the fashion throughout the kingdom, though the news does not tell us that his people have resorted to hanging from the chandeliers by their toes.

But the Narrowlands is very far away from here, so that news does not often reach us from it; there is even no talk of opening the country up, which alone shows how difficult it must be to reach.

* * * * *

In the mean while the Queen had come to the other shore. She flew straight to the little cottage in the valley, and the cock who was standing on the doorsill greeted her with a lusty crow, being glad to see her again.

In the house there was no one to be found.

'The little mother must have gone to her bleaching,' the Queen said to herself, 'and he—oh, he told me he was going to work in the wood to-day, so now I'll see about making the infusion. The kettle's on the boil, and it won't take long.'

She took off the faded wind-flower crown, and looked at it for a moment.

'You poor thing!' she said, 'it seems a shame, but still it can't be helped,' and in a moment she had dropped it into the boiling water, which rapidly assumed the golden straw-colour of a weak cup of tea. This she poured into a drinking-horn, and then set off with it into the wood at the back of the house. It was rather a ticklish task, walking through the low, dusky wood with the horn in her hand, for it was getting on in the day and the light was bad, and the small trees of which the wood was composed were difficult to walk among.

By her side the stream rushed and rustled over its rocky bottom, and her feet crackled too on the flooring of last year's fallen leaves, but the sound that she paused every now and then to listen for she could not hear. There came no sharp ringing of the axe down the valley among the trees.

'He must be binding the faggots together,' she said to herself, and went on until she came to the clearing where he should have been at work; but there he was not.

The light came down the valley duskily through the mist; it gleamed upon the stream and glimmered on the white ends of the newly chopped faggots that were neatly bound together with withies.

'He must have gone further on,' she said to herself, and ran quite swiftly up the steep path that climbed into the heart of the mountains. The falling of the night frightened her a little, and she was anxious to find him.

Up and up the rocky path went, whilst the stream foamed down beside it, and at last she saw him in a slant of light that came down a west-facing valley. He was crossing the stream just above where it thundered over a great boulder.

There was a bridge across the torrent, but it was only a tree-trunk, and he preferred, in his blindness, to cross the stream bottom, over the boulders with the aid of a good staff. The water foamed up to his knees.

She came as close to the water's edge as she could, and called—

'Why, where are you going to?'

In spite of the roaring of the waters he heard her and turned.

'Who are you?' he asked.

And she answered, 'I am Eldrida.'

And in a moment, with a great splashing of the black water, he was at her side.

'I thought you had gone for good,' he said. 'And so I worked as long as I felt able to; but just now it was all so silent and so dreadfully lonely, that I could not stand it, and I was about to set out to search for you through the world.'

'What all alone, and blind?' she said.

And he answered, 'Yes, since you were gone I was alone and blind; but if I had found you I should not have been alone, and hardly blind at all.'

She put the horn into his hand, and said, 'Drink this.'

'Why, what is it?' he asked.

'It is what I went to fetch,' she said; 'drink it and see.'

The light was shining on his face as he raised it to his mouth and drank it off, and suddenly there came into his eyes a look of great joy.

'Why,' he said, 'I can see!' and in a moment he had thrown his arms round her and drew her tightly to him. 'I love you more than all the world!' he said. 'Do you love me?'

She seemed to have forgotten all about the elixir, for instead of saying, 'Don't be ridiculous!' she just said, 'Yes, I love you very much.'

And the stream roared on over the great boulder and whirled back over the rocky shallows, and the shadows in the valleys grew darker and darker; but they both had a great deal to say, though, as a matter of fact, it might most of it have been said with three words and a kiss.

But, you see, they preferred to do it in another way; at least, as far as the speaking went—in my experience, there is only one way of kissing.

'So you see, I shan't be able to fly away any more,' she said, after she had related her story, 'because the poor wind-flower crown is all boiled.'

'Oh well,' he said, 'I dare say you won't want it again, unless you get very tired of me.'

And she said, 'Don't be ridiculous!' but even that had nothing to do with the elixir.

And so they went home down the dark valley to the cottage.

The little mother smiled to see Eldrida.

'I knew you would come back,' she said; 'but my son was in a dreadful state—weren't you, son, son?'

And he only answered, 'Mother, mother, I was. And I am very hungry; and I can see again!'

So there was great rejoicing in the cottage that night, and the little old woman's eyes grew bright with joy-tears.

But next day Eldrida and her love were married, and, from that time forth, they worked together, and went hand in hand up the tranquil valley or in among the storms on the hillcrests, and so lived happily ever after.

LAURENCE HOUSMAN

The Story of the Herons

A LONG time ago there lived a King and a Queen who loved each other dearly. They had both fallen in love at first sight; and as their love began so it went on through all their life. Yet this, which was the cause of all their happiness, was the cause also of all their misfortunes.

In his youth, when he was a beautiful young bachelor, the King had had the ill-luck to attract the heart of a jealous and powerful Fairy; and though he never gave her the least hope or encouragement, when she heard that his love had been won at first sight by a mere mortal, her rage and resentment knew no bounds. She said nothing, however, but bided her time.

After they had been married a year the Queen presented her husband with a little daughter; before she was yet a day old she was the most beautiful object in the world, and life seemed to promise her nothing but fortune and happiness.

The family Fairy came to the blessing of the new-born; and she, looking at it as it lay beautifully asleep in its cradle, and seeing that it had already as much beauty and health as the heart could desire, promised it love as the next best gift it was within her power to offer. The Queen, who knew how much happiness her own love had brought her, was kissing the good Fairy with all the warmth of gratitude, when a black kite came and perched upon the window-sill crying: 'And I will give her love at first sight! The first living thing that she sets eyes on she shall love to distraction, whether it be man or monster, prince or pauper, bird, beast or reptile.' And as the wicked Fairy spoke she clapped her wings, and up through the boards of the floor, and out from under the bed, and in through the window, came a crowd of the ugliest shapes in the world. Thick and fast they came, gathering about the cradle and lifting their heads over the edge of it, waiting for the poor little Princess to wake up and fall in love at first sight with one of them.

Luckily the child was asleep; and the good Fairy, after driving away the black kite and the crowd of beasts it had called to its aid, wrapped the Princess up in a shawl and carried her away to a dark room where no glimmer of light could get in.

She said to the Queen: 'Till I can devise a better way, you must keep her in the dark; and when you take her into the open air you must blindfold her eyes. Some day, when she is of a fit age, I will bring a handsome Prince for her; and only to him shall you unblindfold her at last, and make love safe for her.'

She went, leaving the King and Queen deeply stricken with grief over the harm which had befallen their daughter. They did not dare to present even themselves before her eyes lest love for them, fatal and consuming, should drive her to distraction. In utter darkness the Queen would sit and cherish her daughter, clasping her to her breast, and calling her by all sweet names; but the little face, except by stealth when it was sound asleep, she never dared to see, nor did the baby-Princess know the face of the mother who loved her.

By and by, however, the family Fairy came again, saying: 'Now, I have a plan by which your child may enjoy the delights of seeing, and no ill come of it.' And she caused to be made a large chamber, the whole of one side of which was a mirror.* High up in the opposite wall were windows so screened that from below no one could look out of them, but across on to the mirror came all the sweet sights of the world, glimpses of wood and field, and the sun and the moon and the stars, and of every bird as it flew by. So the little Princess was brought and set in a screened place looking towards the mirror, and there her eyes learned gradually all the beautiful things of the world. Over the screen, in the glass before her, she learned to know her mother's face, and to love it dearly in a gentle child-like fashion; and when she could talk she became very wise, understanding all that was told her about the danger of looking at anything alive, except by its reflection in the glass.

When she went out into the open air for her health, she always wore a bandage over her eyes, lest she should look, and love something too well: but in the chamber of the mirror her eyes were free to see whatever they could. The good Fairy, making herself invisible, came and taught her to read and make music, and draw; so that before she was fifteen she was the most charming and accomplished, as well as the most beautiful Princess of her day.

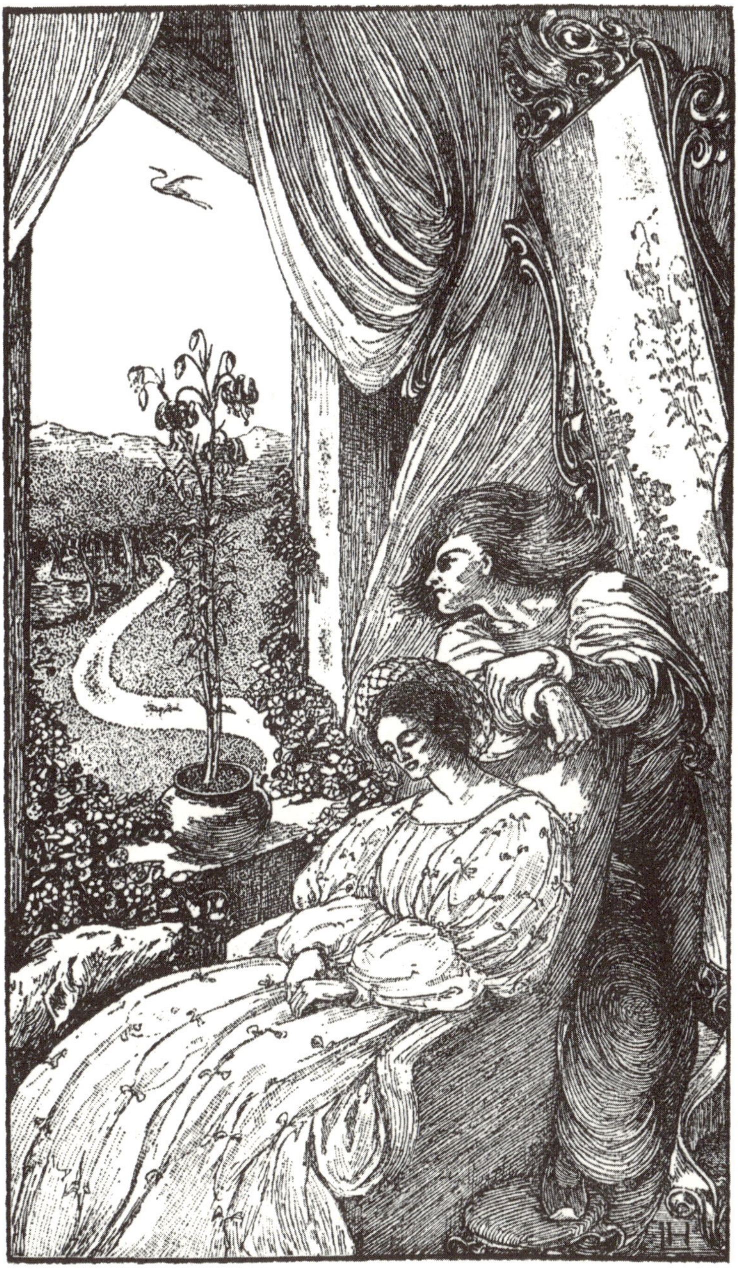

At last the Fairy said that the time was come for her world of reflections to be made real, and she went away to fetch the ideal Prince that the Princess might at first sight fall in love with him.

The very day after she was gone, as the morning was fine, the Princess went out with one of her maids for a walk through the woods. Over her patient eyes she wore a bandage of green silk, through which she felt the sunlight fall pleasantly.

Out of doors the Princess knew most things by their sounds. She passed under rustling leaves, and along by the side of running water; and at last she heard the silence of the water, and knew that she was standing by the great fish-pond in the middle of the wood. Then she said to her waiting-woman, 'Is there not some great bird fishing out there, for I hear the dipping of his bill, and the water falling off it as he draws out the fish?'

And just as she was saying that, the wicked Fairy, who had long bided her time, coming softly up from behind, pushed the waiting-woman off the bank into the deep water of the pond. Then she snatched away the silk bandage, and before the Princess had time to think or close her eyes, she had lost her heart to a great heron, that was standing half-way up to his feathers fishing among the reeds.

The Princess, with her eyes set free, laughed for joy at the sight of him. She stretched out her arms from the bank and cried most musically for the bird to come to her; and he came in grave stately fashion, with trailing legs, and slow sobbing creak of his wings, and settled down on the bank beside her. She drew his slender neck against her white throat, and laughed and cried with her arms round him, loving him so that she forgot all in the world beside. And the heron looked gravely at her with kind eyes, and, bird-like, gave her all the love he could, but not more; and so, presently, casting his grey wings abroad, lifted himself and sailed slowly back to his fishing among the reeds.

The waiting-woman had got herself out of the water, and stood wringing her clothes and her hands beside the Princess. 'O, sweet mistress,' she cried, with lamentation, 'now is all the evil come about which it was our whole aim to avoid! And what, and what will the Queen your mother say?'

But the Princess answered, smiling, 'Foolish girl, I had no thought of what happiness meant till now! See you where my love is gone? and did you notice the bend of his neck, and the exceeding length of his legs, and the stretch of his grey wings as he flew? This pond is his

The Story of the Herons

hall of mirrors, wherein he sees the reflection of all his world. Surely I, from my hall of mirrors, am the true mate for him!'

Her maid, seeing how far the evil had gone, and that no worse could now happen, ran back to the palace and curdled all the court's blood with her news. The King and the Queen and all their nobility rushed down, and there they found the Princess with the heron once more in her arms, kissing and fondling it with all the marks of a sweet and maidenly passion. 'Dear mother,' she said, as soon as she saw the Queen, 'the happiness, which you feared would be sorrow, has come; and it is such happiness I have no name for it! And the evil that you so dreaded, see how sweet it is! And how sweet it is to see all the world with my own eyes and you also at last!' And for the first time in her life she kissed her mother's face in the full light of day.

But her mother hung sobbing upon her neck, 'O, my darling, my beautiful,' she wept, 'does your heart belong for ever to this grey bird?'

Her daughter answered, 'He is more than all the world to me! Is he not goodly to look upon? Have you considered the bend of his neck, the length of his legs, and the waving of his wings; his skill also when he fishes: what imagination, what presence of mind!'

'Alas, alas,' sorrowed the Queen, 'dear daughter, is this all true to you?' 'Mother,' cried the Princess, clinging to her with entreaty, 'is all the world blind but me?'

The heron had become quite fond of the Princess; wherever she went it followed her, and, indeed, without it nowhere would she go. Whenever it was near her, the Princess laughed and sang, and when it was out of her sight she became sad as night. All the courtiers wept to see her in such bondage. 'Ah,' said she, 'your eyes have been worn out with looking at things so long; mine have been kept for me in a mirror.'

When the good family Fairy came (for she was at once sent for by the Queen, and told of all that had happened), she said, 'Dear Madam, there are but two things you can do: either you can wring the heron's neck, and leave the Princess to die of grief; or you can make the Princess happy in her own way, by——' Her voice dropped, and she looked from the King to the Queen before she went on. 'At her birth I gave your daughter love for my gift; now it is her's, will you let her keep it?'

The King and the Queen looked softly at each other. 'Do not take love from her,' said they, 'let her keep it!'

'There is but one way,' answered the Fairy.

'Do not tell me the way,' said the Queen weeping, 'only let the way be!'

So they went with the Fairy down to the great pond, and there sat the Princess, with the grey heron against her heart. She smiled as she saw them come. 'I see good in your hearts toward me!' she cried. 'Dear godmother, give me the thing that I want, that my love may be happy!'

Then the Fairy stroked her but once with her wand, and two grey herons suddenly rose up from the bank, and sailed away to a hiding-place in the reeds.

The Fairy said to the Queen, 'You have made your daughter happy; and still she will have her voice and her human heart, and will remember you with love and gratitude; but her greatest love will be to the grey heron, and her home among the reeds.'

So the changed life of the Princess began; every day her mother went down to the pool and called, and the Princess came rising up out of the reeds, and folded her grey wings over her mother's heart. Every day her mother said, 'Daughter of mine, are you happy?'

And the Princess answered her, 'Yes, for I love and am loved.'

Yet each time the mother heard more and more of a note of sadness come into her daughter's voice; and at last one day she said, 'Answer me truly, as the mother who brought you into the world, whether you be happy in your heart of hearts or no?'

Then the heron-Princess laid her head on the Queen's heart, and said, 'Mother, my heart is breaking with love!'

'For whom, then?' asked the Queen astonished.

'For my grey heron, whom I love, and who loves me so much. And yet it is love that divides us, for I am still troubled with a human heart, and often it aches with sorrow because all the love in it can never be fully understood or shared by my heron; and I have my human voice left, and that gives me a hundred things to say all day; for which there is no word in herons' language, and so he cannot understand them. Therefore these things only make a gulf between him and me. For all the other grey herons in the pools there is happiness, but not for me who have too big a heart between my wings.'

Her mother said softly, 'Wait, wait, little heron-daughter, and it shall be well with you!' Then she went to the Fairy and said, 'My daughter's heart is lonely among the reeds, for the grey heron's love covers but half of it. Give her some companions of her own kind that her hours may become merry again!'

So the Fairy took and turned five of the Princess's lady's-maids into herons, and sent them down to the pool.

The five herons stood each on one leg in the shallows of the pool, and cried all day long; and their tears fell down into the water and frightened away the fish that came their way. For they had human hearts that cried out to be let go. 'O, cruel, cruel,' they wept, whenever the heron-Princess approached, 'see what we suffer because of you, and what they have made of us for your sake!'

The Princess came to her mother and said, 'Dear mother, take them away, for their cry wearies me, and the pool is bitter with their tears! They only awake the human part of my heart that wants to sleep; presently, may be, if it is let alone, it will forget itself.'

Her mother said, 'It is my coming every day also that keeps it awake.' The Princess answered, 'This sorrow belongs to my birthright; you must still come; but for the others, let the Fairy take them away.'

So the Fairy came and released the five lady's-maids whom she had changed into herons. And they came up out of the water, stripping themselves of their grey feather-skins and throwing them back into the pool. The Fairy said, 'You foolish maids, you have thrown away a gift that you should have valued; these skins you could have kept and held as heirlooms in your family.'

The five maids answered, 'We want to forget that there are such things as herons in the world!'

After much thought the Queen said to the Fairy, 'You have changed a Princess into a heron, and five maids into herons and back again; cannot you change one heron into a Prince?' But the Fairy answered sadly, 'Our power has limits; we can bring down, but we cannot bring up, if there be no heart to answer our call. The five maids only followed their hearts, that were human, when I called them back; but a heron has only a heron's heart, and unless his heart has become too great for a bird and he earn a human one, I cannot change him to a higher form.' 'How can he earn a human one?' asked the Queen. 'Only if he love the Princess so well that his love for her becomes stronger than his life,' answered the Fairy. 'Then he will have earned a human body, and then I can give him the form that his heart suits best. There may be a chance, if we wait for it and are patient, for the Princess's love is great and may work miracles.'

A little while after this, the Queen watching, saw that the two herons were making a nest among the reeds. 'What have you there?'

said the mother to her daughter. 'A little hollow place,' answered the heron-Princess, 'and in it the moon lies.' A little while after she said again, 'What have you there, now, little daughter?' And her daughter answered, 'Only a small hollow space; but in it two moons lie.'

The Queen told the family Fairy how in a hollow of the reeds lay two moons. 'Now,' said the Fairy, 'we will wait no longer. If your daughter's love has touched the heron's heart and made it grow larger than a bird's, I can help them both to happiness; but if not, then birds they must remain.'

Among the reeds the heron said in bird language to his wife, 'Go and stretch your wings for a little while over the water; it is weary work to wait here so long in the reeds.' The heron-Princess looked at him with her bird's eyes, and all the human love in her heart strove, like a fountain that could not get free, to make itself known through them; also her tongue was full of the longing to utter sweet words, but she kept them back, knowing they were beyond the heron's power to understand. So she answered merely in heron's language, 'Come with me, and I will come!'

They rose, wing beating beside wing; and the reflection of their grey breasts slid out under them over the mirror of the pool.

Higher they went and higher, passing over the tree tops, and keeping time together as they flew. All at once the wings of the grey heron flagged, then took a deep beat; he cried to the heron-Princess, 'Turn, and come home, yonder there is danger flying to meet us!' Before them hung a brown blot in the air, that winged and grew large. The two herons turned and flew back. 'Rise,' cried the grey heron, 'we must rise!' and the Princess knew what was behind, and struggled with the whole strength of her wings for escape.

The grey heron was beating ahead on stronger wing. 'With me, with me!' he cried. 'If it gets above us, one of us is dead!' But the falcon had fixed his eye on the Princess for his quarry, and flew she fast, or flew she slow, there was little chance for her now. Up and up she strained, but still she was behind her mate, and still the falcon gained.

The heron swung back to her side; she saw the anguish and fear of his downward glance as his head ranged by hers. Past her the falcon went, towering for the final swoop.

The Princess cried in the heron's language, 'Farewell, dear mate, and farewell, two little moons among the reeds!' But the grey heron only kept closer to her side.

Overhead the falcon closed in its wings and fell like a dead weight out of the clouds. 'Drop!' cried the grey heron to his mate.

At his word she dropped; but he stayed, stretching up his wings, and, passing between the descending falcon and its prey, caught in his own body the death-blow from its beak. Drops of his blood fell upon the heron-Princess.

He stricken in body, she in soul, together they fell down to the margin of the pool. The falcon still clung fleshing its beak in the neck of its prey. The heron-Princess threw back her head, and, darting furiously, struck her own sharp bill deep into the falcon's breast. The bird threw out its wing with a hoarse cry and fell back dead, with a little tuft of the grey heron's feathers still upon its beak.

The heron-Princess crouched down, and covered with her wings the dying form of her mate; in her sorrow she spoke to him in her own tongue, forgetting her bird's language. The grey heron lifted his head, and, gazing tenderly, answered her with a human voice:

'Dear wife,' he said, 'at last I have the happiness so long denied to me of giving utterance in the speech that is your own to the love that you have put into my heart. Often I have heard you speak and have not understood; now something has touched my heart, and changed it, so that I can both speak and understand.'

'O, beloved!' She laid her head down by his. 'The ends of the world belong to us now. Lie down, and die gently by my side, and I will die with you, breaking my heart with happiness.'

'No,' said the grey heron, 'do not die yet! Remember the two little moons that lie in the hollow among the reeds.' Then he laid his head down by hers, being too weak to say more.

They folded their wings over each other, and closed their eyes; nor did they know that the Fairy was standing by them, till she stroked them both softly with her wand, saying to each of them the same words:

'Human heart, and human form, come out of the grey heron!'

And out of the grey heron-skins came two human forms; the one was the Princess restored again to her own shape, but the other was a beautiful youth, with a bird-like look about his eyes, and long slender limbs. The Princess, as she gazed on him, found hardly any change, for love remained the same, binding him close to her heart; and, grey heron or beautiful youth, he was all one to her now.

Then came the Queen, weeping for joy, and embracing them both, and after them, the Fairy. 'O, how good an ending,' she cried, 'has come to that terrible dream! Let it never be remembered or mentioned between us more!' And she began to lead the way back to the palace.

But the youth, to whom the Fairy gave the name of Prince Heron, turned and took up the two heron-skins which he and his wife had let fall, and followed, carrying them upon his arm. And as they came past the bed of reeds, the Princess went aside, and, stooping down in a certain place drew out from thence something which she came carrying, softly wrapped in the folds of her gown.

With what rejoicing the Princess and her husband were welcomed by the King and all the Court needs not to be told. For a whole month the festivities continued; and whenever she showed herself, there was the Princess sitting with two eggs in her lap, and her hands over them to keep them warm. The King was impatient. 'Why cannot you send them down to the poultry yard to be hatched?' he said.

But the Princess replied smiling, 'My moons are my own, and I will keep them to myself.'

'Do you hear?' she said one day, at last; and everybody who listened could hear something going 'tap, tap,' inside the shells. Presently the eggs cracked, and out of each, at the same moment, came a little grey heron.

When she saw that they were herons, the Queen wrung her hands. 'O, Fairy,' she cried, 'what a disappointment is this! I had hoped two beautiful babies would have come out of those shells.'

But the Fairy said, 'It is no matter. Half of their hearts are human already; birds' hearts do not beat so. If you wish it, I can change them.' So she stroked them softly with her wand, saying to each, 'Human heart, and human form, come out of the grey heron!'

Yet she had to stroke them three times before they would turn; and she said to the Princess, 'My dear, you were too satisfied with your lot when you laid these eggs. I doubt if more than a quarter of them is human.'

'I was very satisfied,' said the Princess, and she laughed across to her husband.

At last, however, on the third stroke of the wand, the heron's skins dropped off, and they changed into a pair of very small babies, a boy and a girl. But the difference between them and other children was, that instead of hair, their heads were covered with a fluff of downy grey feathers; also they had queer, round, bird-like eyes, and were able to sleep standing.

Now, after this the happiness of the Princess was great; but the Fairy said to her, 'Do not let your husband see the heron-skins again for some while, lest with the memory a longing for his old life should return to him and take him away from you. Only by exchange with another can he ever get back his human form again, if he surrenders it of his own free will. And who is there so poor that he would willingly give up his human form to become a bird?'

So the Princess took the four coats of feather—her own and her husband's and her two children's—and hid them away in a closet of which she alone kept the key. It was a little gold key, and to make it safe she hung it about her neck, and wore it night and day.

The Prince said to her, 'What is that little key that you wear always hung round your neck?'

She answered him, 'It is the key to your happiness and mine. Do not ask more than that!' At that there was a look in his face that made her say, 'You *are* happy, are you not?'

He kissed her, saying, 'Happy indeed! Have I not you to make me so?' Yet, though, indeed, he told no untruth, and was happy whenever she was with him, there were times when a restlessness and a longing for wings took hold of him; for, as yet, the life of a man was new and half strange to him, and a taint of his old life still mixed itself with his blood. But to her he was ashamed to say what might seem a complaint against his great fortune; so when she said 'happiness,' he thought, 'Is it just the turning of that key that I want before my happiness can be perfect?'

Therefore, one night when the early season of spring made his longing strong in him, he took the key from the Princess while she slept, and opened the little closet in which hung the four feather coats. And when he saw his own, all at once he remembered the great pools of water, and how they lay in the shine and shadow of the moonlight, while the fish rose in rings upon their surface. And at that so great a longing came into him to revisit his old haunts that he reached out his hand and took down the heron-skin from its nail and put it over himself; so that immediately his old life took hold of him, and he flew out of the window in the form of a grey heron. In the morning the Princess found the key gone from her neck, and her husband's place empty. She went in haste to the closet, and there stood the door wide with the key in it, and only three heron-skins hanging where four had used to be.

Then she came crying to the family Fairy, 'My husband has taken his heron-skin and is gone! Tell me what I can do!'

The Fairy pitied her with all her heart, but could do nothing. 'Only by exchange,' said she, 'can he get back his human shape; and who is there so poor that he would willingly lose his own form to become a bird? Only your children, who are but half human, can put their heron-skins on and off as they like and when they like.'

In deep grief the Princess went to look for her husband down by the pools in the wood. But now his shame and sorrow at having deceived her were so great that as soon as he heard her voice he hid himself among the reeds, for he knew now that, having put on his heron-skin again, he could not take it off unless some one gave him a human form in exchange.

At last, however, so pitiful was the cry of the Princess for him, that he could bear to hear it no more; but rising up from the reeds came trailing to her sadly over the water. 'Ah, dear love!' she said when he was come to her, 'if I had not distrusted you, you would not have deceived me: thus, for my fault we are punished.' So she sorrowed, and he answered her:

'Nay, dear love, for if I had not deceived you, you would not have distrusted me. I thought I was not happy, yet I feared to tell it you.' Thus they sorrowed together, both laying on themselves the blame and the burden.

Then she said to him: 'Be here for me to-night, for now I must go; but then I shall return.'

She went back to the palace, and told her mother of all that had happened. 'And now,' she said, 'you who know where my happiness lies will not forbid me from following it; for my heart is again with the grey heron.' And the Queen wept, but would not say her no.

So that night the Princess went and kissed her children as they slept standing up in their beds, with their funny feather-pates to one side; and then she took down her skin of feathers and put it on, and became changed once more into a grey heron. And again she went up to the two in their cots, and kissed their birdish heads saying: 'They who can change at will, being but half human, they will come and visit us in the great pool by the wood, and bring back word of us here.'

In the morning the Princess was gone, and the two children when they woke looked at each other and said: 'Did we dream last night?'

They both answered each other, 'Yes, first we dreamed that our mother came and kissed us; and we liked that. And then we dreamed that a grey heron came and kissed us, and we liked that better still!' They waved their arms up and down. 'Why have we not wings?' they kept asking. All day long they did this, playing that they were birds. If a window were opened, it was with the greatest difficulty that they were kept from trying to fly through.

In the Court they were known as the 'Feather-pates'; nothing could they be taught at all. When they were rebuked they would stand on one leg and sigh with their heads to one side; but no one ever saw tears come out of their birdish eyes.

Now at night they would dream that two grey herons came and stood by their bedsides, kissing them; 'And where in the world,' they said when they woke, '*are* our wings?'

One day, wandering about in the palace, they came upon the closet in which hung the two little feather coats. 'O!!!' they cried, and opened hard bright eyes at each other, nodding, for now they knew what they would do. 'If we told, they would be taken off us,' they said; and they waited till it was night. Then they crept back and took the two little coats from their pegs, and, putting them on, were turned into two young herons.

Through the window they flew, away down to the great fish-pond in the wood. Their father and mother saw them coming, and clapped their wings for joy. 'See,' they said, 'our children come to visit us, and our hearts are left to us to love with. What further happiness can we want?' But when they were not looking at each other they sighed.

All night long the two young herons stayed with their parents; they bathed, and fished, and flew, till they were weary. Then the Princess showed them the nest among the reeds, and told them all the story of their lives.

'But it is much nicer to be herons than to be real people,' said the young ones, sadly, and became very sorrowful when dawn drew on, and their mother told them to go back to the palace and hang up the feather coats again, and be as they had been the day before.

Long, long the day now seemed to them; they hardly waited till it was night before they took down their feather-skins, and, putting them on, flew out and away to the fish-pond in the wood.

So every night they went, when all in the palace were asleep; and in the morning came back before anyone was astir, and were found by their nurses lying demurely between the sheets, just as they had been left the night before.

One day the Queen when she went to see her daughter said to her, 'My child, your two children are growing less like human beings and more like birds every day. Nothing will they learn or do, but stand all day flapping their arms up and down, and saying, "Where are our wings, where are our wings?" The idea of one of them ever coming to the throne makes your father's hair stand on end under his crown.'

'Oh, mother,' said the heron-Princess, 'I have made a sad bed for you and my father to lie on!'

One day the two children said to each other, 'Our father and mother are sad, because they want to be real persons again, instead of having wings and catching fish the way we like to do. Let us give up being real persons, which is all so much trouble, and such a want of exercise, and make them exchange with us!' But when the two young herons went down to the pond and proposed it to them, their parents said, 'You are young; you do not know what you would be giving up.' Nor would they consent to it at all.

Now one morning it happened that the Feather-pates were so late in returning to the palace that the Queen, coming into their chamber, found the two beds empty; and just as she had turned away to search for them elsewhere, she heard a noise of wings and saw the two young herons come flying in through the window. Then she saw them take off their feather-skins and hang them up in the closet, and after that go and lie down in their beds so as to look as if they had been there all night.

The Queen struck her hands together with horror at the sight, but she crept away softly, so that they did not know they had been found out. But as soon as they were out of their beds and at play in another part of the palace, the Queen went to the closet, and setting fire to the two heron-skins where they hung, burnt them till not a feather of them was left, and only a heap of grey ashes remained to tell what had become of them.

At night, when the Feather-pates went to their cupboards and found their skins gone, and saw what had become of them, their grief knew no bounds. They trembled with fear and rage, and tears rained out of their eyes as they beheld themselves deprived of their bird bodies and made into real persons for good and all.

'We won't be real persons!' they cried. But for all their crying they knew no way out of it. They made themselves quite ill with grief; and that night, for the first time since they had found their way to the closet, they stayed where their nurses had put them, and did not even stand up in their beds to go to sleep. There they lay with gasping mouth, and big bird-like eyes all languid with grief, and hollow grey cheeks.

Presently their father and mother came seeking for them, wondering why they had not come down to the fish-pond as they were wont. 'Where are you, my children?' cried the heron-Princess, putting her head in through the window.

'Here we are, both at death's door!' they cried. 'Come and see us die! Our wicked granddam has burnt our feather-skins and made us into real persons for ever and ever, Amen. But we will die rather!'

The parent herons, when they heard that, flew in through the window and bent down over the little ones' beds.

The two children reached up their arms. 'Give us your feathers!' they cried. 'We shall die if you don't! We *will* die if you don't! O, do!' But still the parent birds hesitated, nor knew what to do.

'Bend down, and let me whisper something!' said the boy to his father: and 'Bend down, and whisper!' cried the girl to her mother. And father and mother bent down over the faces of their sick children. Then these, both together, caught hold of them, and crying, 'Human heart, and human form, exchange with the grey heron!' pulled off their parents' feather-skins, and put them upon themselves.

And there once more stood Prince Heron and the Princess in human shape, while the two children had turned into herons in their place.

The young herons laughed and shouted and clapped their wings for joy. 'Are you not happy now?' cried they. And when their parents saw the joy, not only in their children's eyes, but in each other's, and felt their hearts growing glad in the bodies they had regained, then they owned that the Feather-pates had been wise in their generation,* and done well according to their lights.

So it came about that the Prince and the Princess lived happily ever after, and the two young herons lived happily also, and were the best-hearted birds the world ever saw.

In course of time the Prince and Princess had other children, who pleased the old King better than the first had done. But the parents loved none better than the two who lived as herons by the great fish-pond in the wood; nor could there be greater love than was found between these and their younger brothers and sisters, whose nature it was to be real persons.

KENNETH GRAHAME

The Reluctant Dragon

OOTPRINTS in the snow have been unfailing provokers of sentiment ever since snow was first a white wonder in this drab-coloured world of ours. In a poetry-book presented to one of us by an aunt, there was a poem by one Wordsworth* in which they stood out strongly—with a picture all to themselves, too—but we didn't think very highly either of the poem or the sentiment. Footprints in the sand, now, were quite another matter, and we grasped Crusoe's attitude of mind* much more easily than Wordsworth's. Excitement and mystery, curiosity and suspense—these were the only sentiments that tracks, whether in sand or in snow, were able to arouse in us.

We had awakened early that winter morning, puzzled at first by the added light that filled the room. Then, when the truth at last fully dawned on us and we knew that snow-balling was no longer a wistful dream, but a solid certainty waiting for us outside, it was a mere brute fight for the necessary clothes, and the lacing of boots seemed a clumsy invention, and the buttoning of coats an unduly tedious form of fastening, with all that snow going to waste at our very door.

When dinner-time came we had to be dragged in by the scruff of our necks. The short armistice over, the combat was resumed; but presently Charlotte and I, a little weary of contests and missiles that ran shudderingly down inside one's clothes, forsook the trampled battle-field of the lawn and went exploring the blank virgin spaces of the white world that lay beyond. It stretched away unbroken on every side of us, this mysterious soft garment under which our familiar world had so suddenly hidden itself. Faint imprints showed where a casual bird had alighted, but of other traffic there was next to no sign; which made these strange tracks all the more puzzling.

We came across them first at the corner of the shrubbery, and pored over them long, our hands on our knees. Experienced trappers that we knew ourselves to be, it was annoying to be brought up suddenly by a beast we could not at once identify.

'Don't you know?' said Charlotte, rather scornfully. 'Thought you knew all the beasts that ever was.'

This put me on my mettle, and I hastily rattled off a string of animal names embracing both the arctic and the tropic zones, but without much real confidence.

'No,' said Charlotte, on consideration; 'they won't any of 'em quite do. Seems like something *lizardly*. Did you say iguanodon?* Might be that, p'raps. But that's not British, and we want a real British beast. I think it's a dragon!'

''Tisn't half big enough,' I objected.

'Well, all dragons must be small to begin with,' said Charlotte: 'like everything else. P'raps this is a little dragon who's got lost. A little dragon would be rather nice to have. He might scratch and spit, but he couldn't *do* anything really. Let's track him down!'

So we set off into the wide snow-clad world, hand in hand, our hearts big with expectation,—complacently confident that by a few smudgy traces in the snow we were in a fair way to capture a half-grown specimen of a fabulous beast.

We ran the monster across the paddock, and along the hedge of the next field, and then he took to the road like any tame civilized tax-payer. Here his tracks became blended with and lost among more ordinary footprints, but imagination and a fixed idea will do a great deal, and we were sure we knew the direction a dragon would naturally take. The traces, too, kept reappearing at intervals—at least Charlotte maintained they did, and as it was *her* dragon I left the following of the slot* to her and trotted along peacefully, feeling that it was an expedition anyhow and something was sure to come out of it.

Charlotte took me across another field or two, and through a copse, and into a fresh road; and I began to feel sure it was only her confounded pride that made her go on pretending to see dragon-tracks instead of owning she was entirely at fault, like a reasonable person. At last she dragged me excitedly through a gap in a hedge of an obviously private character; the waste, open world of field and hedgerow disappeared, and we found ourselves in a garden, well-kept, secluded, most un-dragon-haunted in appearance. Once inside, I knew where we were. This was the garden of my friend the circus-man,* though I had never approached it before by a lawless gap, from this unfamiliar side. And here was the circus-man himself, placidly smoking a pipe as he strolled up and down the walks. I stepped up to him and asked him politely if he had lately seen a Beast.

'May I inquire,' he said, with all civility, 'what particular sort of a Beast you may happen to be looking for?'

'It's a *lizardly* sort of Beast,' I explained. 'Charlotte says it's a dragon, but she doesn't really know much about beasts.'

The circus-man looked round about him slowly. 'I don't *think*,' he said, 'that I've seen a dragon in these parts recently. But if I come across one I'll know it belongs to you, and I'll have him taken round to you at once.'

'Thank you very much,' said Charlotte, 'but don't *trouble* about it, please, 'cos p'raps it isn't a dragon after all. Only I thought I saw his little footprints in the snow, and we followed 'em up, and they seemed to lead right in here, but maybe it's all a mistake, and thank you all the same.'

'Oh, no trouble at all,' said the circus-man, cheerfully. 'I should be only too pleased. But of course, as you say, it *may* be a mistake. And it's getting dark, and he seems to have got away for the present, whatever he is. You'd better come in and have some tea. I'm quite alone, and we'll make a roaring fire, and I've got the biggest Book of Beasts you ever saw. It's got every beast in the world, and all of 'em coloured; and we'll try and find *your* beast in it!'

We were always ready for tea at any time, and especially when combined with beasts. There was marmalade, too, and apricot-jam, brought in expressly for us; and afterwards the beast-book was spread out, and, as the man had truly said, it contained every sort of beast that had ever been in the world.

The striking of six o'clock set the more prudent Charlotte nudging me, and we recalled ourselves with an effort from Beastland, and reluctantly stood up to go.

'Here, I'm coming along with you,' said the circus-man. 'I want another pipe, and a walk'll do me good. You needn't talk to me unless you like.'

Our spirits rose to their wonted level again. The way had seemed so long, the outside world so dark and eerie, after the bright warm room and the highly-coloured beast-book. But a walk with a real Man—why, that was a treat in itself! We set off briskly, the Man in the middle. I looked up at him and wondered whether I should ever live to smoke a big pipe with that careless sort of majesty! But Charlotte, whose young mind was not set on tobacco as a possible goal, made herself heard from the other side.

'Now, then,' she said, 'tell us a story, please won't you?'

The Man sighed heavily and looked about him. 'I knew it,' he groaned. 'I *knew* I should have to tell a story. Oh, why did I leave my pleasant fireside? Well, I *will* tell you a story. Only let me think a minute.'

So he thought a minute, and then he told us this story.

Long ago—might have been hundreds of years ago—in a cottage half-way between this village and yonder shoulder of the Downs* up there, a shepherd lived with his wife and their little son. Now the shepherd spent his days—and at certain times of the year his nights too—up on the wide ocean-bosom of the Downs, with only the sun and the stars and the sheep for company, and the friendly chattering world of men and women far out of sight and hearing. But his little son, when he wasn't helping his father, and often when he was as well, spent much of his time buried in big volumes that he borrowed from the affable gentry and interested parsons of the country round about. And his parents were very fond of him, and rather proud of him too, though they didn't let on in his hearing, so he was left to go his own way and read as much as he liked; and instead of frequently getting a cuff on the side of the head, as might very well have happened to him, he was treated more or less as an equal by his parents, who sensibly thought it a very fair division of labour that they should supply the practical knowledge and he the book-learning. They knew that book-learning often came in useful at a pinch, in spite of what their neighbours said. What the Boy chiefly dabbled in was natural history and fairy-tales, and he just took them as they came, in a sandwichy sort of way, without making any distinctions; and really his course of reading strikes one as rather sensible.

One evening the shepherd, who for some nights past had been disturbed and preoccupied, and off his usual mental balance, came home all of a tremble, and, sitting down at the table where his wife and son were peacefully employed, she with her seam, he in following out the adventures of the Giant with no Heart in his Body,* exclaimed with much agitation:

'It's all up with me, Maria! Never no more can I go up on them there Downs, was it ever so!'

'Now don't you take on like that,' said his wife, who was a *very* sensible woman: 'but tell us all about it first, whatever it is as has given you this shake-up, and then me and you and the son here, between us, we ought to be able to get to the bottom of it!'

'It began some nights ago,' said the shepherd. 'You know that cave up there—I never liked it, somehow, and the sheep never liked it neither, and when sheep don't like a thing there's generally some reason for it. Well, for some time past there's been faint noises coming from that cave—noises like heavy sighings, with grunts mixed up in them; and sometimes a snoring, far away down—*real* snoring, yet somehow not *honest* snoring, like you and me o'nights, you know!'

'*I* know,' remarked the Boy, quietly.

'Of course I was terrible frightened,' the shepherd went on; 'yet somehow I couldn't keep away. So this very evening, before I came down, I took a cast round by the cave quietly. And there—O Lord! there I saw him at last, as plain as I see you!'

'Saw *who?*' said his wife, beginning to share in her husband's nervous terror.

'Why *him*, I'm a telling you!' said the shepherd. 'He was sticking half-way out of the cave, and seemed to be enjoying the cool of the evening in a poetical sort of way. He was as big as four cart-horses, and all covered with shiny scales—deep-blue scales at the top of him, shading off to a tender sort o' green below. As he breathed, there was that sort of flicker over his nostrils that you see over our chalk roads on a baking windless day in summer. He had his chin on his paws, and I should say he was meditating about things. Oh, yes, a peaceable sort o' beast enough, and not ramping or carrying on or doing anything but what was quite right and proper. I admit all that. And yet, what am I to do? *Scales*, you know, and claws, and a tail for certain, though I didn't see that end of him—I ain't *used* to 'em, and I don't *hold* with 'em, and that's a fact!'

The Boy, who had apparently been absorbed in his book during his father's recital, now closed the volume, yawned, clasped his hands behind his head, and said sleepily:

'It's all right, father. Don't you worry. It's only a dragon.'

'Only a dragon?' cried his father. 'What do you mean, sitting there, you and your dragons? *Only* a dragon indeed! And what do *you* know about it?'

"Cos it *is*, and 'cos I *do* know,' replied the Boy, quietly. 'Look here, father, you know we've each of us got our line. *You* know about sheep, and weather, and things; I know about dragons. I always said, you know, that that cave up there was a dragon-cave. I always said it must have belonged to a dragon some time, and ought to belong to a dragon now, if rules count for anything. Well, now you tell me it *has* got a dragon, and so *that's* all right. I'm not half as much surprised as when you told me it *hadn't* got a dragon. Rules always come right if you wait quietly. Now, please, just leave this all to me. And I'll stroll up to-morrow morning—no, in the morning I can't, I've got a whole heap of things to do—well, perhaps in the evening, if I'm quite free, I'll go up and have a talk to him, and you'll find it'll be all right. Only, please, don't you go worrying round there without me. You don't understand 'em a bit, and they're very sensitive, you know!'

'He's quite right, father,' said the sensible mother. 'As he says, dragons is his line and not ours. He's wonderful knowing about book-beasts, as every one allows. And to tell the truth, I'm not half happy in my own mind, thinking of that poor animal lying alone up there, without a bit o' hot supper or anyone to change the news with; and maybe we'll be able to do something for him; and if he ain't quite respectable our Boy'll find it out quick enough. He's got a pleasant sort o' way with him that makes everybody tell him everything.'

Next day, after he'd had his tea, the Boy strolled up the chalky track that led to the summit of the Downs; and there, sure enough, he found the dragon, stretched lazily on the sward in front of his cave. The view from that point was a magnificent one. To the right and left, the bare and billowy leagues of Downs; in front, the vale, with its clustered homesteads, its threads of white roads running through orchards and well-tilled acreage, and, far away, a hint of grey old cities on the horizon. A cool breeze played over the surface of the grass and the silver shoulder of a large moon was showing above distant junipers. No wonder the dragon seemed in a peaceful and contented mood; indeed, as the Boy approached he could hear the beast purring with a happy regularity. 'Well, we live and learn!' he said to himself. 'None of my books ever told me that dragons purred!'

'Hullo, dragon!' said the Boy, quietly, when he had got up to him.

The dragon, on hearing the approaching footsteps, made the beginning of a courteous effort to rise. But when he saw it was a Boy, he set his eyebrows severely.

'Now don't you hit me,' he said; 'or bung stones, or squirt water, or anything. I won't have it, I tell you!'

'Not goin' to hit you,' said the Boy wearily, dropping on the grass beside the beast; 'and don't, for goodness' sake, keep on saying "Don't;" I hear so much of it, and it's monotonous, and makes me tired. I've simply looked in to ask you how you were and all that sort of thing; but if I'm in the way I can easily clear out. I've lots of friends, and no one can say I'm in the habit of shoving myself in where I'm not wanted!'

'No, no, don't go off in a huff,' said the dragon, hastily; 'fact is,— I'm as happy up here as the day's long; never without an occupation, dear fellow, never without an occupation! And yet, between ourselves, it *is* a trifle dull at times.'

The Boy bit off a stalk of grass and chewed it. 'Going to make a long stay here?' he asked, politely.

'Can't hardly say at present,' replied the dragon. 'It seems a nice place enough—but I've only been here a short time, and one must look about and reflect and consider before settling down. It's rather a serious thing, settling down. Besides—now I'm going to tell you something! You'd never guess it if you tried ever so!—fact is, I'm such a confoundedly lazy beggar!'

'You surprise me,' said the Boy, civilly.

'It's the sad truth,' the dragon went on, settling down between his paws and evidently delighted to have found a listener at last: 'and I fancy that's really how I came to be here. You see all the other fellows were so active and *earnest* and all that sort of thing—always rampaging, and skirmishing, and scouring the desert sands, and pacing the margin of the sea, and chasing knights all over the place, and devouring damsels, and going on generally—whereas I liked to get my meals regular and then to prop my back against a bit of rock and snooze a bit, and wake up and think of things going on and how they kept going on just the same, you know! So when it happened I got fairly caught.'

'When *what* happened, please?' asked the Boy.

'That's just what I don't precisely know,' said the dragon. 'I suppose the earth sneezed, or shook itself, or the bottom dropped out of something. Anyhow there was a shake and a roar and a general stramash,* and I found myself miles away underground and wedged in as tight as tight. Well, thank goodness, my wants are few, and at any rate I had peace and quietness and wasn't always being asked to come along and *do* something. And I've got such an active mind—always occupied, I assure you! But time went on, and there was a certain sameness about the life, and at last I began to think it would be fun to work my way upstairs and see what you other fellows were doing. So I scratched and burrowed, and worked this way and that way and at last I came out through this cave here. And I like the country, and the view, and the people—what I've seen of 'em—and on the whole I feel inclined to settle down here.'

'What's your mind always occupied about?' asked the Boy. 'That's what I want to know.'

The dragon coloured slightly and looked away. Presently he said bashfully:

'Did you ever—just for fun—try to make up poetry—verses, you know?'

''Course I have,' said the Boy. 'Heaps of it. And some of it's quite good, I feel sure, only there's no one here cares about it. Mother's very kind and all that, when I read it to her, and so's father for that matter. But somehow they don't seem to—'

'Exactly,' cried the dragon; 'my own case exactly. They don't seem to, and you can't argue with 'em about it. Now you've got culture, you have, I could tell it on you at once, and I should just like your candid opinion about some little things I threw off lightly, when I was down there. I'm awfully pleased to have met you, and I'm hoping the other neighbours will be equally agreeable. There was a very nice old gentleman up here only last night, but he didn't seem to want to intrude.'

'That was my father,' said the Boy, 'and he *is* a nice old gentleman, and I'll introduce you some day if you like.'

'Can't you two come up here and dine or something to-morrow?' asked the dragon eagerly. 'Only, of course, if you've got nothing better to do,' he added politely.

'Thanks awfully,' said the Boy, 'but we don't go out anywhere without my mother, and, to tell you the truth, I'm afraid she mightn't quite approve of you. You see there's no getting over the hard fact that you're a dragon, is there? And when you talk of settling down, and the neighbours, and so on, I can't help feeling that you don't quite realize your position. You're an enemy of the human race, you see!'

'Haven't got an enemy in the world,' said the dragon, cheerfully. 'Too lazy to make 'em, to begin with. And if I *do* read other fellows my poetry, I'm always ready to listen to theirs!'

'Oh, dear!' cried the Boy, 'I wish you'd try and grasp the situation properly. When the other people find you out, they'll come after you with spears and swords and all sorts of things. You'll have to be exterminated, according to their way of looking at it. You're a scourge, and a pest, and a baneful monster!'

'Not a word of truth in it,' said the dragon, wagging his head solemnly. 'Character'll bear the strictest investigation. And now, there's a little sonnet-thing I was working on when you appeared on the scene—'

'Oh, if you *won't* be sensible,' cried the Boy, getting up, 'I'm going off home. No, I can't stop for sonnets; my mother's sitting up. I'll look you up to-morrow, sometime or other, and do for goodness' sake try and realize that you're a pestilential scourge, or you'll find yourself in a most awful fix. Good-night!'

The Boy found it an easy matter to set the mind of his parents at ease about his new friend. They had always left that branch to him, and they took his word without a murmur. The shepherd was formally introduced and many compliments and kind inquiries were exchanged. His wife, however, though expressing her willingness to do anything she could—to mend things, or set the cave to rights, or cook a little something when the dragon had been poring over sonnets and forgotten his meals, as male things *will* do, could not be brought to recognize him formally. The fact that he was a dragon and 'they didn't know who he was' seemed to count for everything with her. She made no objection, however, to her little son spending his evenings with the dragon quietly, so long as he was home by nine o'clock: and many a pleasant night they had, sitting on the sward, while the dragon told stories of old, old times, when dragons were quite plentiful and the world was a livelier place than it is now, and life was full of thrills and jumps and surprises.

What the Boy had feared, however, soon came to pass. The most modest and retiring dragon in the world, if he's as big as four carthorses and covered with blue scales, cannot keep altogether out of the public view. And so in the village tavern of nights the fact that a real live dragon sat brooding in the cave on the Downs was naturally a subject for talk. Though the villagers were extremely frightened, they were rather proud as well. It was a distinction to have a dragon of your own, and it was felt to be a feather in the cap of the village. Still, all were agreed that this sort of thing couldn't be allowed to go on. The dreadful beast must be exterminated, the country-side must be freed from this pest, this terror, this destroying scourge. The fact that not even a hen-roost was the worse for the dragon's arrival wasn't allowed to have anything to do with it. He was a dragon, and he couldn't deny it, and if he didn't choose to behave as such that was his own lookout. But in spite of much valiant talk no hero was found willing to take sword and spear and free the suffering village and win deathless fame; and each night's heated discussion always ended in nothing. Meanwhile the dragon, a happy Bohemian, lolled on the turf, enjoyed the sunsets, told antediluvian anecdotes to the Boy, and polished his old verses while meditating on fresh ones.

One day the Boy, on walking in to the village, found everything wearing a festal appearance which was not to be accounted for in the calendar. Carpets and gay-coloured stuffs were hung out of the windows, the church-bells clamoured noisily, the little street was flower-strewn, and the whole population jostled each other along either side of it, chattering, shoving, and ordering each other to stand back. The Boy saw a friend of his own age in the crowd and hailed him.

'What's up?' he cried. 'Is it the players, or bears, or a circus, or what?'

'It's all right,' his friend hailed back. 'He's a-coming.'

'*Who's* a-coming?' demanded the Boy, thrusting into the throng.

'Why, St. George, of course,' replied his friend. 'He's heard tell of our dragon, and he's comin' on purpose to slay the deadly beast, and free us from his horrid yoke. O my! won't there be a jolly fight!'

Here was news indeed! The Boy felt that he ought to make quite sure for himself, and he wriggled himself in between the legs of his good-natured elders, abusing them all the time for their unmannerly habit of shoving. Once in the front rank, he breathlessly awaited the arrival.

Presently from the far-away end of the line came the sound of cheering. Next, the measured tramp of a great war-horse made his heart beat quicker, and then he found himself cheering with the rest, as, amidst welcoming shouts, shrill cries of women, uplifting of babies and waving of handkerchiefs, St. George paced slowly up the street. The Boy's heart stood still and he breathed with sobs, the beauty and the grace of the hero were so far beyond anything he had yet seen. His fluted armour was inlaid with gold, his plumed helmet hung at his saddle-bow, and his thick fair hair framed a face gracious and gentle beyond expression till you caught the sternness in his eyes. He drew rein in front of the little inn, and the villagers crowded round with greetings and thanks and voluble statements of their wrongs and grievances and oppressions. The Boy heard the grave gentle voice of the Saint, assuring them that all would be well now, and that he would stand by them and see them righted and free them from their foe; then he dismounted and passed through the doorway and the crowd poured in after him. But the Boy made off up the hill as fast as he could lay his legs to the ground.

'It's all up, dragon!' he shouted as soon as he was within sight of the beast. 'He's coming! He's here now! You'll have to pull yourself together and *do* something at last!'

The dragon was licking his scales and rubbing them with a bit of house-flannel the Boy's mother had lent him, till he shone like a great turquoise.

'Don't be *violent*, Boy,' he said without looking round. 'Sit down and get your breath, and try and remember that the noun governs the verb, and then perhaps you'll be good enough to tell me *who's* coming?'

'That's right, take it coolly,' said the Boy. 'Hope you'll be half as cool when I've got through with my news. It's only St. George who's coming, that's all; he rode into the village half-an-hour ago. Of course you can lick him—a great big fellow like you! But I thought I'd warn you, 'cos he's sure to be round early, and he's got the longest, wickedest-looking spear you ever did see!' And the Boy got up and began to jump round in sheer delight at the prospect of the battle.

'O deary, deary me,' moaned the dragon; 'this is too awful. I won't see him, and that's flat. I don't want to know the fellow at all. I'm sure he's not nice. You must tell him to go away at once, please. Say he can write if he likes, but I can't give him an interview. I'm not seeing anybody at present.'

'Now, dragon, dragon,' said the Boy imploringly, 'don't be perverse and wrongheaded. You've *got* to fight him some time or other, you know, 'cos he's St. George and you're the dragon. Better get it over, and then we can go on with the sonnets. And you ought to consider other people a little, too. If it's been dull up here for you, think how dull it's been for me!'

'My dear little man,' said the dragon solemnly, 'just understand, once for all, that I can't fight and I won't fight. I've never fought in my life, and I'm not going to begin now, just to give you a Roman holiday.* In old days I always let the other fellows—the *earnest* fellows—do all the fighting, and no doubt that's why I have the pleasure of being here now.'

'But if you don't fight he'll cut your head off!' gasped the Boy, miserable at the prospect of losing both his fight and his friend.

'Oh, I think not,' said the dragon in his lazy way. 'You'll be able to arrange something. I've every confidence in you, you're such a *manager*. Just run down, there's a dear chap, and make it all right. I leave it entirely to you.'

The Boy made his way back to the village in a state of great despondency. First of all, there wasn't going to be any fight; next, his dear and honoured friend the dragon hadn't shown up in quite such a heroic light as he would have liked; and lastly, whether the dragon was a hero at heart or not, it made no difference, for St. George would most undoubtedly cut his head off. 'Arrange things indeed!' he said bitterly to himself. 'The dragon treats the whole affair as if it was an invitation to tea and croquet.'

The villagers were straggling homewards as he passed up the street, all of them in the highest spirits, and gleefully discussing the splendid fight that was in store. The Boy pursued his way to the inn, and passed into the principal chamber, where St. George now sat alone, musing over the chances of the fight, and the sad stories of rapine and of wrong that had so lately been poured into his sympathetic ears.

'May I come in, St. George?' said the Boy politely, as he paused at the door. 'I want to talk to you about this little matter of the dragon, if you're not tired of it by this time.'

'Yes, come in, Boy,' said the Saint kindly. 'Another tale of misery and wrong, I fear me. Is it a kind parent, then, of whom the tyrant has bereft you? Or some tender sister or brother? Well, it shall soon be avenged.'

'Nothing of the sort,' said the Boy. 'There's a misunderstanding somewhere, and I want to put it right. The fact is, this is a *good* dragon.'

'Exactly,' said St. George, smiling pleasantly, 'I quite understand. A good *dragon*. Believe me, I do not in the least regret that he is an adversary worthy of my steel, and no feeble specimen of his noxious tribe.'

'But he's *not* a noxious tribe,' cried the Boy, distressedly. 'Oh dear, oh dear, how *stupid* men are when they get an idea into their heads! I tell you he's a *good* dragon, and a friend of mine, and tells me the most beautiful stories you ever heard, all about old times and when he was little. And he's been so kind to mother, and mother'd do anything for him. And father likes him too, though father doesn't hold with art and poetry much, and always falls asleep when the dragon starts talking about *style*. But the fact is, nobody can help liking him when once they know him. He's so engaging and so trustful, and as simple as a child!'

'Sit down, and draw your chair up,' said St. George. 'I like a fellow who sticks up for his friends, and I'm sure the dragon has his good points, if he's got a friend like you. But that's not the question. All this evening I've been listening, with grief and anguish unspeakable, to tales of murder, theft, and wrong; rather too highly coloured, perhaps, not always quite convincing, but forming in the main a most serious roll of crime. History teaches us that the greatest rascals often possess all the domestic virtues; and I fear that your cultivated friend, in spite of the qualities which have won (and rightly) your regard, has got to be speedily exterminated.'

'Oh, you've been taking in all the yarns those fellows have been telling you,' said the Boy, impatiently. 'Why, our villagers are the biggest story-tellers in all the country round. It's a known fact. You're a stranger in these parts, or else you'd have heard it already. All they want is a *fight*. They're the most awful beggars for getting up fights—it's meat and drink to them. Dogs, bulls, dragons—anything so long as it's a fight. Why, they've got a poor innocent badger in the stable behind here, at this moment. They were going to have some fun with him to-day, but they're saving him up now till *your* little affair's over. And I've no doubt they've been telling you what a hero you were, and how you were bound to win, in the cause of right and justice, and so on; but let me tell you, I came down the street just now, and they were betting six to four on the dragon freely!'

'Six to four on the dragon!' murmured St. George sadly, resting his cheek on his hand. 'This is an evil world, and sometimes I begin to think that all the wickedness in it is not entirely bottled up inside the dragons. And yet—may not this wily beast have misled you as to his real character, in order that your good report of him may serve as a cloak for his evil deeds? Nay, may there not be, at this very moment, some hapless Princess immured within yonder gloomy cavern?'

The moment he had spoken, St. George was sorry for what he had said, the Boy looked so genuinely distressed.

'I assure you, St. George,' he said earnestly, 'there's nothing of the sort in the cave at all. The dragon's a real gentleman, every inch of him, and I may say that no one would be more shocked and grieved than he would, at hearing you talk in that—that *loose* way about matters on which he has very strong views!'

'Well, perhaps I've been over-credulous,' said St. George. 'Perhaps I've misjudged the animal. But what are we to do? Here are the dragon and I, almost face to face, each supposed to be thirsting for each other's blood. I don't see any way out of it, exactly. What do you suggest? Can't you arrange things, somehow?'

'That's just what the dragon said,' replied the Boy, rather nettled. 'Really, the way you two seem to leave everything to me—I suppose you couldn't be persuaded to go away quietly, could you?'

'Impossible, I fear,' said the Saint. 'Quite against the rules. *You* know that as well as I do.'

'Well, then, look here,' said the Boy, 'it's early yet—would you mind strolling up with me and seeing the dragon and talking it over? It's not far, and any friend of mine will be most welcome.'

'Well, it's *irregular*,' said St. George, rising, 'but really it seems about the most sensible thing to do. You're taking a lot of trouble on your friend's account,' he added, good-naturedly, as they passed out through the door together. 'But cheer up! Perhaps there won't have to be any fight after all.'

'Oh, but I hope there will, though!' replied the little fellow, wistfully.

'I've brought a friend to see you, dragon,' said the Boy, rather loud.

The dragon woke up with a start. 'I was just—er—thinking about things,' he said in his simple way. 'Very pleased to make your acquaintance, sir. Charming weather we're having!'

'This is St. George,' said the Boy, shortly. 'St. George, let me introduce you to the dragon. We've come up to talk things over quietly, dragon, and now for goodness' sake do let us have a little straight common-sense, and come to some practical business-like arrangement, for I'm sick of views and theories of life and personal tendencies, and all that sort of thing. I may perhaps add that my mother's sitting up.'

'So glad to meet you, St. George,' began the dragon rather nervously, 'because you've been a great traveller, I hear, and I've always been rather a stay-at-home. But I can show you many antiquities, many interesting features of our countryside, if you're stopping here any time—'

'I think,' said St. George, in his frank, pleasant way, 'that we'd really better take the advice of our young friend here, and try to come to some understanding, on a business footing, about this little affair of ours. Now don't you think that after all the simplest plan would be just to fight it out, according to the rules, and let the best man win? They're betting on you, I may tell you, down in the village, but I don't mind that!'

'Oh, yes, *do*, dragon,' said the Boy, delightedly; 'it'll save such a lot of bother!'

'My young friend, you shut up,' said the dragon severely. 'Believe me, St. George,' he went on, 'there's nobody in the world I'd sooner oblige than you and this young gentleman here. But the whole thing's nonsense, and conventionality, and popular thick-headedness. There's absolutely nothing to fight about, from beginning to end. And anyhow I'm not going to, so that settles it!'

'But supposing I make you?' said St. George, rather nettled.

'You can't,' said the dragon, triumphantly. 'I should only go into my cave and retire for a time down the hole I came up. You'd soon get heartily sick of sitting outside and waiting for me to come out and fight you. And as soon as you'd really gone away, why, I'd come up again gaily, for I tell you frankly, I like this place, and I'm going to stay here!'

St. George gazed for a while on the fair landscape around them. 'But this would be a beautiful place for a fight,' he began again persuasively. 'These great bare rolling Downs for the arena—and me in my golden armour showing up against your big blue scaly coils! Think what a picture it would make!'

'Now you're trying to get at me through my artistic sensibilities,' said the dragon. 'But it won't work. Not but what it would make a very pretty picture, as you say,' he added, wavering a little.

'We seem to be getting rather nearer to *business*,' put in the Boy. 'You must see, dragon, that there's got to be a fight of some sort, 'cos you can't want to have to go down that dirty old hole again and stop there till goodness knows when.'

The Reluctant Dragon

'It might be arranged,' said St. George, thoughtfully. 'I *must* spear you somewhere, of course, but I'm not bound to hurt you very much. There's such a lot of you that there must be a few *spare* places somewhere. Here, for instance, just behind your foreleg. It couldn't hurt you much, just here!'

'Now you're tickling, George,' said the dragon, coyly. 'No, that place won't do at all. Even if it didn't hurt,—and I'm sure it would, awfully,—it would make me laugh, and that would spoil everything.'

'Let's try somewhere else, then,' said St. George, patiently. 'Under your neck, for instance,—all these folds of thick skin,—if I speared you here you'd never even know I'd done it!'

'Yes, but are you sure you can hit off the right place?' asked the dragon, anxiously.

'Of course I am,' said St. George, with confidence. 'You leave that to me!'

'It's just because I've *got* to leave it to you that I'm asking,' replied the dragon, rather testily. 'No doubt you would deeply regret any error you might make in the hurry of the moment; but you wouldn't regret it half as much as I should! However, I suppose we've got to trust somebody, as we go through life, and your plan seems, on the whole, as good a one as any.'

'Look here, dragon,' interrupted the Boy, a little jealous on behalf of his friend, who seemed to be getting all the worst of the bargain: 'I don't quite see where *you* come in! There's to be a fight, apparently, and you're to be licked; and what I want to know is, what are *you* going to get out of it?'

'St. George,' said the dragon, 'just tell him, please,—what will happen after I'm vanquished in the deadly combat?'

'Well, according to the rules I suppose I shall lead you in triumph down to the market-place or whatever answers to it,' said St. George.

'Precisely,' said the dragon. 'And then—'

'And then there'll be shoutings and speeches and things,' continued St. George. 'And I shall explain that you're converted, and see the error of your ways, and so on.'

'Quite so,' said the dragon. 'And then—?'

'Oh, and then—' said St. George, 'why, and then there will be the usual banquet, I suppose.'

'Exactly,' said the dragon; 'and that's where I come in. Look here,' he continued, addressing the Boy, 'I'm bored to death up here, and no one really appreciates me. I'm going into Society, I am, through the kindly aid of our friend here, who's taking such a lot of trouble on my account; and you'll find I've got all the qualities to endear me to people who entertain! So now that's all settled, and if you don't mind—I'm an old-fashioned fellow—don't want to turn you out, but—'

'Remember, you'll have to do your proper share of the fighting, dragon!' said St. George, as he took the hint and rose to go; 'I mean ramping, and breathing fire, and so on!'

'I can *ramp* all right,' replied the dragon, confidently; 'as to breathing fire, it's surprising how easily one gets out of practice; but I'll do the best I can. Good-night!'

They had descended the hill and were almost back in the village again, when St. George stopped short. '*Knew* I had forgotten something,' he said. 'There ought to be a Princess. Terror-striken and chained to a rock, and all that sort of thing. Boy, can't you arrange a Princess?'

The Boy was in the middle of a tremendous yawn. 'I'm tired to death,' he wailed, 'and I *can't* arrange a Princess, or anything more, at this time of night. And my mother's sitting up, and *do* stop asking me to arrange more things till to-morrow!'

Next morning the people began streaming up to the Downs at quite an early hour, in their Sunday clothes and carrying baskets with bottle-necks sticking out of them, every one intent on securing good places for the combat. This was not exactly a simple matter, for of course it was quite possible that the dragon might win, and in that case even those who had put their money on him felt they could hardly expect him to deal with his backers on a different footing to the rest. Places were chosen, therefore, with circumspection and with a view to a speedy retreat in case of emergency; and the front rank was mostly composed of boys who had escaped from parental control and now sprawled and rolled about on the grass, regardless of the shrill threats and warnings discharged at them by their anxious mothers behind.

The Boy had secured a good front place, well up towards the cave, and was feeling as anxious as a stage-manager on a first night. Could the dragon be depended upon? He might change his mind and vote the whole performance rot; or else, seeing that the affair had been so hastily planned, without even a rehearsal, he might be too nervous to show up. The Boy looked narrowly at the cave, but it showed no sign of life or occupation. Could the dragon have made a moon-light flitting?

The higher portions of the ground were now black with sightseers, and presently a sound of cheering and a waving of handkerchiefs told that something was visible to them which the Boy, far up towards the dragon-end of the line as he was, could not yet see. A minute more and St. George's red plumes topped the hill, as the Saint rode slowly forth on the great level space which stretched up to the grim mouth of the cave. Very gallant and beautiful he looked, on his tall war-horse, his golden armour glancing in the sun, his great spear held erect, the little white pennon, crimson-crossed, fluttering at its point. He drew rein and remained motionless. The lines of spectators began to give back a little, nervously; and even the boys in front stopped pulling hair and cuffing each other, and leaned forward expectant.

'Now then, dragon!' muttered the Boy impatiently, fidgeting where he sat. He need not have distressed himself, had he only known. The dramatic possibilities of the thing had tickled the dragon immensely, and he had been up from an early hour, preparing for his first public appearance with as much heartiness as if the years had run backwards, and he had been again a little dragonlet, playing with his sisters on the floor of their mother's cave, at the game of saints-and-dragons, in which the dragon was bound to win.

A low muttering, mingled with snorts, now made itself heard; rising to a bellowing roar that seemed to fill the plain. Then a cloud of smoke obscured the mouth of the cave, and out of the midst of it the dragon himself, shining, sea-blue, magnificent, pranced splendidly forth; and everybody said, 'Oo-oo-oo!' as if he had been a mighty rocket! His scales were glittering, his long spiky tail lashed his sides, his claws tore up the turf and sent it flying high over his back, and smoke and fire incessantly jetted from his angry nostrils. 'Oh, well done, dragon!' cried the Boy, excitedly. 'Didn't think he had it in him!' he added to himself.

St. George lowered his spear, bent his head, dug his heels into the horse's sides, and came thundering over the turf. The dragon charged with a roar and a squeal—a great blue whirling combination of coils and snorts and clashing jaws and spikes and fire.

'Missed!' yelled the crowd. There was a moment's entanglement of golden armour and blue-green coils, and spiky tail, and then the great horse, tearing at his bit, carried the Saint, his spear swung high in the air, almost up to the mouth of the cave.

The dragon sat down and barked viciously, while St. George with difficulty pulled his horse round into position.

'End of Round One!' thought the Boy. 'How well they managed it! But I hope the Saint won't get excited. I can trust the dragon all right. What a regular play-actor the fellow is!'

St. George had at last prevailed on his horse to stand steady, and was looking round him as he wiped his brow. Catching sight of the Boy, he smiled and nodded, and held up three fingers for an instant.

'It seems to be all planned out,' said the Boy to himself. 'Round Three is to be the finishing one, evidently. Wish it could have lasted a bit longer. Whatever's that old fool of a dragon up to now?'

The dragon was employing the interval in giving a ramping-performance for the benefit of the crowd. Ramping, it should be explained, consists of running round and round in a wide circle, and sending waves and ripples of movement along the whole length of your spine, from your pointed ears right down to the spike at the end of your long tail. When you are covered with blue scales, the effect is particularly pleasing; and the Boy recollected the dragon's recently expressed wish to become a social success.

St. George now gathered up his reins and began to move forward, dropping the point of his spear and settling himself firmly in the saddle.

'Time!' yelled everybody excitedly; and the dragon, leaving off his ramping, sat up on end, and began to leap from one side to the other with huge ungainly bounds, whooping like a Red Indian. This naturally disconcerted the horse, who swerved violently, the Saint only just saving himself by the mane; and as they shot past the dragon delivered a vicious snap at the horse's tail which sent the poor beast careering madly far over the Downs, so that the language of the Saint, who had lost a stirrup, was fortunately inaudible to the general assemblage.

Round Two evoked audible evidence of friendly feeling towards the dragon. The spectators were not slow to appreciate a combatant who could hold his own so well and clearly wanted to show good sport; and many encouraging remarks reached the ears of our friend as he strutted to and fro, his chest thrust out and his tail in the air, hugely enjoying his new popularity.

St. George had dismounted and was tightening his girths, and telling his horse, with quite an Oriental flow of imagery, exactly what he thought of him, and his relations, and his conduct on the present occasion; so the Boy made his way down to the Saint's end of the line, and held his spear for him.

'It's been a jolly fight, St. George!' he said with a sigh. 'Can't you let it last a bit longer?'

'Well, I think I'd better not,' replied the Saint. 'The fact is, your simple-minded old friend's getting conceited, now they've begun cheering him, and he'll forget all about the arrangement and take to playing the fool, and there's no telling where he would stop. I'll just finish him off this round.'

He swung himself into the saddle and took his spear from the Boy. 'Now don't you be afraid,' he added kindly. 'I've marked my spot exactly, and *he's* sure to give me all the assistance in his power, because he knows it's his only chance of being asked to the banquet!'

St. George now shortened his spear, bringing the butt well up under his arm; and, instead of galloping as before, trotted smartly towards the dragon, who crouched at his approach, flicking his tail till it cracked in the air like a great cart-whip. The Saint wheeled as he neared his opponent and circled warily round him, keeping his eye on the spare place; while the dragon, adopting similar tactics, paced with caution round the same circle, occasionally feinting with his head. So the two sparred for an opening, while the spectators maintained a breathless silence.

Though the round lasted for some minutes, the end was so swift that all the boy saw was a lightning movement of the Saint's arm, and then a whirl and a confusion of spines, claws, tail, and flying bits of turf. The dust cleared away, the spectators whooped and ran in cheering, and the Boy made out that the dragon was down, pinned to the earth by the spear, while St. George had dismounted, and stood astride of him.

It all seemed so genuine that the Boy ran in breathlessly, hoping the dear old dragon wasn't really hurt. As he approached, the dragon lifted one large eyelid, winked solemnly, and collapsed again. He was held fast to earth by the neck, but the Saint had hit him in the spare place agreed upon, and it didn't even seem to tickle.

'Bain't you goin' to cut 'is 'ed orf, master?' asked one of the applauding crowd. He had backed the dragon, and naturally felt a trifle sore.

'Well, not *to-day*, I think,' replied St. George, pleasantly. 'You see, that can be done at *any* time. There's no hurry at all. I think we'll all go down to the village first, and have some refreshment, and then I'll give him a good talking-to, and you'll find he'll be a very different dragon!'

At that magic word *refreshment* the whole crowd formed up in procession and silently awaited the signal to start. The time for talking and cheering and betting was past, the hour for action had arrived. St. George, hauling on his spear with both hands, released the dragon, who rose and shook himself and ran his eye over his spikes and scales and things, to see that they were all in order. Then the Saint mounted and led off the procession, the dragon following meekly in the company of the Boy, while the thirsty spectators kept at a respectful interval behind.

There were great doings when they got down to the village again, and had formed up in front of the inn. After refreshment St. George made a speech, in which he informed his audience that he had removed their direful scourge, at a great deal of trouble and inconvenience to himself, and now they weren't to go about grumbling and fancying they'd got grievances, because they hadn't. And they shouldn't be so fond of fights, because next time they might have to do the fighting themselves, which would not be the same thing at all. And there was a certain badger in the inn stables which had got to be released at once, and he'd come and see it done himself. Then he told them that the dragon had been thinking over things, and saw that there were two sides to every question, and he wasn't going to do it any more, and if they were good perhaps he'd stay and settle down there. So they must make friends, and not be prejudiced, and go about fancying they knew everything there was to be known, because they didn't, not by a long way. And he warned them against the sin of romancing, and making up stories and fancying other people would believe them just because they were plausible and highly-coloured. Then he sat down, amidst much repentant cheering, and the dragon nudged the Boy in the ribs and whispered that he couldn't have done it better himself. Then every one went off to get ready for the banquet.

Banquets are always pleasant things, consisting mostly, as they do, of eating and drinking; but the specially nice thing about a banquet is, that it comes when something's over, and there's nothing more to worry about, and tomorrow seems a long way off. St. George was happy because there had been a fight and he hadn't had to kill anybody; for he didn't really like killing, though he generally had to do it. The dragon was happy because there had been a fight, and so far from being hurt in it he had won popularity and a sure footing in society. The Boy was happy because there had been a fight, and in spite of it all his two friends were on the best of terms. And all the others were happy because there had been a fight, and—well, they didn't require any other reasons for their happiness. The dragon exerted himself to say the right thing to everybody, and proved the life and soul of the evening; while the Saint and the Boy, as they looked on, felt that they were only assisting at a feast of which the honour and the glory were entirely the dragon's. But they didn't mind that, being good fellows, and the dragon was not in the least proud or forgetful. On the contrary, every ten minutes or so he leant over towards the Boy and said impressively: 'Look here! you *will* see me home afterwards, won't you?' And the Boy always nodded, though he had promised his mother not to be out late.

At last the banquet was over, the guests had dropped away with many good-nights and congratulations and invitations, and the dragon, who had seen the last of them off the premises, emerged into the street followed by the Boy, wiped his brow, sighed, sat down in the road and gazed at the stars. 'Jolly night it's been!' he murmured. 'Jolly stars! Jolly little place this! Think I shall just stop here. Don't feel like climbing up any beastly hill. Boy's promised to see me home. Boy had better do it then! No responsibility on my part. Responsibility all Boy's!' And his chin sank on his broad chest and he slumbered peacefully.

'Oh, *get* up, dragon,' cried the Boy, piteously. 'You *know* my mother's sitting up, and I'm so tired, and you made me promise to see you home, and I never knew what it meant or I wouldn't have done it!' And the Boy sat down in the road by the side of the sleeping dragon, and cried.

The door behind them opened, a stream of light illumined the road, and St. George, who had come out for a stroll in the cool night-air, caught sight of the two figures sitting there—the great motionless dragon and the tearful little Boy.

'What's the matter, Boy?' he inquired kindly, stepping to his side.

'Oh, it's this great lumbering *pig* of a dragon!' sobbed the Boy. 'First he makes me promise to see him home, and then he says I'd better do it, and goes to sleep! Might as well try to see a *haystack* home! And I'm so tired, and mother's——' here he broke down again.

'Now don't take on,' said St. George. 'I'll stand by you, and we'll *both* see him home. Wake up, dragon!' he said sharply, shaking the beast by the elbow.

The dragon looked up sleepily. 'What a night, George!' he murmured; 'what a—'

'Now look here, dragon,' said the Saint, firmly. 'Here's this little fellow waiting to see you home, and you *know* he ought to have been in bed these two hours, and what his mother'll say *I* don't know, and anybody but a selfish pig would have *made* him go to bed long ago——'

'And he *shall* go to bed!' cried the dragon, starting up. 'Poor little chap, only fancy his being up at this hour! It's a shame, that's what it is, and I don't think, St. George, you've been very considerate—but come along at once, and don't let us have any more arguing or shilly-shallying. You give me hold of your hand, Boy—thank you, George, an arm up the hill is just what I wanted!'

So they set off up the hill arm-in-arm, the Saint, the Dragon, and the Boy. The lights in the little village began to go out; but there were stars and a late moon, as they climbed to the Downs together. And, as they turned the last corner and disappeared from view, snatches of an old song were borne back on the night-breeze. I can't be certain which of them was singing, but I *think* it was the Dragon!

'Here we are at your gate,' said the man, abruptly, laying his hand on it. 'Good-night. Cut along in sharp, or you'll catch it!'

Could it really be our own gate? Yes, there it was, sure enough, with the familiar marks on its bottom bar made by our feet when we swung on it.

'Oh, but wait a minute!' cried Charlotte. 'I want to know a heap of things. Did the dragon really settle down? And did—'

'There isn't any more of that story,' said the man, kindly but firmly. 'At least, not to-night. Now be off! Good-bye!'

'Wonder if it's all true?' said Charlotte, as we hurried up the path. 'Sounded dreadfully like nonsense, in parts!'

'P'raps it's true for all that,' I replied encouragingly.

Charlotte bolted in like a rabbit, out of the cold and the dark; but I lingered a moment in the still, frosty air, for a backward glance at the silent white world without, ere I changed it for the land of fire-light and cushions and laughter. It was the day for choir-practice, and carol-time was at hand, and a belated member was passing homewards down the road, singing as he went:—

> 'Then St. George: ee made rev'rence: in the stable so dim,
> Oo vanquished the dragon: so fearful and grim.
> So-o grim: and so-o fierce: that now may we say
> All peaceful is our wakin': on Chri-istmas Day!'

The singer receded, the carol died away. But I wondered, with my hand on the door-latch, whether that was the song, or something like it, that the dragon sang as he toddled contentedly up the hill.

E. NESBIT

Melisande

or, Long and Short Division

WHEN the Princess Melisande was born, her mother, the Queen, wished to have a christening party, but the King put his foot down and said he would not have it.

'I've seen too much trouble come of christening parties,' said he. 'However carefully you keep your visiting-book, some fairy or other is sure to get left out, and you know what *that* leads to. Why, even in my own family, the most shocking things have occurred. The Fairy Malevola* was not asked to my great-grandmother's christening—and you know all about the spindle and the hundred years' sleep.'

'Perhaps you're right,' said the Queen. 'My own cousin by marriage forgot some stuffy old fairy or other when she was sending out the cards for her daughter's christening, and the old wretch turned up at the last moment, and the girl drops toads out of her mouth to this day.'*

'Just so. And then there was that business of the mouse and the kitchen-maids,'* said the King; 'we'll have no nonsense about it. I'll be her godfather, and you shall be her godmother, and we won't ask a single fairy; then none of them can be offended.'

'Unless they all are,' said the Queen.

And that was exactly what happened. When the King and the Queen and the baby got back from the christening the parlourmaid met them at the door, and said—

'Please, your Majesty, several ladies have called. I told them you were not at home, but they all said they'd wait.'

'Are they in the parlour?' asked the Queen.

'I've shown them into the Throne Room, your Majesty,' said the parlourmaid. 'You see, there are several of them.'

There were about seven hundred. The great Throne Room was crammed with fairies, of all ages and of all degrees of beauty and ugliness—good fairies and bad fairies, flower fairies and moon fairies, fairies like spiders and fairies like butterflies—and as the Queen opened the door and began to say how sorry she was to have kept them waiting, they all cried, with one voice, 'Why didn't you ask *me* to your christening party?'

'I haven't had a party,' said the Queen, and she turned to the King and whispered, 'I told you so.' This was her only consolation.

'You've had a christening,' said the fairies, all together.

'I'm very sorry,' said the poor Queen, but Malevola pushed forward and said, 'Hold your tongue,' most rudely.

Malevola is the oldest, as well as the most wicked, of the fairies. She is deservedly unpopular, and has been left out of more christening parties than all the rest of the fairies put together.

'Don't begin to make excuses,' she said, shaking her finger at the Queen. 'That only makes your conduct worse. You know well enough what happens if a fairy is left out of a christening party. We are all going to give our christening presents *now*. As the fairy of the highest social position, I shall begin. The Princess shall be bald.'

The Queen nearly fainted as Malevola drew back, and another fairy, in a smart bonnet with snakes in it, stepped forward with a rustle of bat's wings. But the King stepped forward too.

'No you don't!' said he. 'I wonder at you, ladies, I do indeed. How can you be so unfairylike? Have none of you been to school—have none of you studied the history of your own race? Surely you don't need a poor, ignorant King like me to tell you that this is *no go*?'

'How dare you?' cried the fairy in the bonnet, and the snakes in it quivered as she tossed her head. 'It is my turn, and I say the Princess shall be—'

The King actually put his hand over her mouth.

'Look here,' he said; 'I won't have it. Listen to reason—or you'll be sorry afterwards. A fairy who breaks the traditions of fairy history goes out—you know she does—like the flame of a candle. And all tradition shows that only *one* bad fairy is ever forgotten at a christening party and the good ones are always invited; so either this is not a christening party, or else you were all invited except one, and, by her own showing, that was Malevola. It nearly always is. Do I make myself clear?'

Several of the better-class fairies who had been led away by Malevola's influence murmured that there was something in what His Majesty said.

'Try it, if you don't believe me,' said the King; 'give your nasty gifts to my innocent child—but as sure as you do, out you go, like a candle-flame. Now, then, will you risk it?'

No one answered, and presently several fairies came up to the Queen and said what a pleasant party it had been, but they really must be going. This example decided the rest. One by one all the fairies said good-bye and thanked the Queen for the delightful afternoon they had spent with her.

'It's been quite too lovely,' said the lady with the snake-bonnet; '*do* ask us again soon, dear Queen. I shall be so *longing* to see you again, and the *dear* baby,' and off she went, with the snake-trimming quivering more than ever.

When the very last fairy was gone the Queen ran to look at the baby—she tore off its Honiton lace cap and burst into tears. For all the baby's downy golden hair came off with the cap, and the Princess Melisande was as bald as an egg.

'Don't cry, my love,' said the King. 'I have a wish lying by, which I've never had occasion to use. My fairy godmother gave it me for a wedding present, but since then I've had nothing to wish for!'

'Thank you, dear,' said the Queen, smiling through her tears.

'I'll keep the wish till baby grows up,' the King went on. 'And then I'll give it to her, and if she likes to wish for hair she can.'

'Oh, won't you wish for it *now*?' said the Queen, dropping mixed tears and kisses on the baby's round, smooth head.

'No, dearest. She may want something else more when she grows up. And besides, her hair may grow by itself.'

But it never did. Princess Melisande grew up as beautiful as the sun and as good as gold, but never a hair grew on that little head of hers. The Queen sewed her little caps of green silk, and the Princess's pink and white face looked out of these like a flower peeping out of its bud. And every day as she grew older she grew dearer, and as she grew dearer she grew better, and as she grew more good she grew more beautiful.

Now, when she was grown up the Queen said to the King—

'My love, our dear daughter is old enough to know what she wants. Let her have the wish.'

So the King wrote to his fairy godmother and sent the letter by a butterfly. He asked if he might hand on to his daughter the wish the fairy had given him for a wedding present.

'I have never had occasion to use it,' said he, 'though it has always made me happy to remember that I had such a thing in the house. The wish is as good as new, and my daughter is now of an age to appreciate so valuable a present.'

To which the fairy replied by return of butterfly:—

'DEAR KING,—Pray do whatever you like with my poor little present. I had quite forgotten it, but I am pleased to think that you have treasured my humble keepsake all these years.

'Your affectionate godmother,
'FORTUNA F.'*

So the King unlocked his gold safe with his seven diamond-handled keys that hung at his girdle, and took out the wish and gave it to his daughter.

And Melisande said: 'Father, I will wish that all your subjects should be quite happy.'

But they were that already, because the King and Queen were so good. So the wish did not go off.

So then she said: 'Then I wish them all to be good.'

But they were that already, because they were happy. So again the wish hung fire.

Then the Queen said: 'Dearest, for my sake, wish what I tell you.'

'Why, of course I will,' said Melisande. The Queen whispered in her ear, and Melisande nodded. Then she said, aloud—

'I wish I had golden hair a yard long, and that it would grow an inch every day, and grow twice as fast every time it was cut, and—'

'Stop,' cried the King. And the wish went off, and the next moment the Princess stood smiling at him through a shower of golden hair.

'Oh, how lovely,' said the Queen. 'What a pity you interrupted her, dear; she hadn't finished.'

'What was the end?' asked the King.

'Oh,' said Melisande, 'I was only going to say, "and twice as thick."'

'It's a very good thing you didn't,' said the King. 'You've done about enough.' For he had a mathematical mind, and could do the sums about the grains of wheat on the chess-board, and the nails in the horse's shoes, in his Royal head without any trouble at all.

'Why, what's the matter?' asked the Queen.

'You'll know soon enough,' said the King. 'Come, let's be happy while we may. Give me a kiss, little Melisande, and then go to nurse and ask her to teach you how to comb your hair.'

'I know,' said Melisande, 'I've often combed mother's.'

'Your mother has beautiful hair,' said the King; 'but I fancy you will find your own less easy to manage.'

And, indeed, it was so. The Princess's hair began by being a yard long, and it grew an inch every night. If you know anything at all about the simplest sums you will see that in about five weeks her hair was about two yards long. This is a very inconvenient length. It trails on the floor and sweeps up all the dust, and though in palaces, of course, it is all gold-dust, still it is not nice to have it in your hair. And the Princess's hair was growing an inch every night. When it was three yards long the Princess could not bear it any longer—it was so heavy and so hot—so she borrowed nurse's cutting-out scissors and cut it all off, and then for a few hours she was comfortable. But the hair went on growing, and now it grew twice as fast as before; so that in thirty-six days it was as long as ever. The poor Princess cried with tiredness; when she couldn't bear it any more she cut her hair and was comfortable for a very little time. For the hair now grew four times as fast as at first, and in eighteen days it was as long as before, and she had to have it cut. Then it grew eight inches a day, and the next time it was cut it grew sixteen inches a day, and then thirty-two inches and sixty-four inches and a hundred and twenty-eight inches a day, and so on, growing twice as fast after each cutting, till the Princess would go to bed at night with her hair clipped short, and wake up in the morning with yards and yards and yards of golden hair flowing all about the room, so that she could not move without pulling her own hair, and nurse had to come and cut the hair off before she could get out of bed.

'I wish I was bald again,' sighed poor Melisande, looking at the little green caps she used to wear, and she cried herself to sleep o' nights between the golden billows of the golden hair. But she never let her mother see her cry, because it was the Queen's fault, and Melisande did not want to seem to reproach her.

When first the Princess's hair grew her mother sent locks of it to all her Royal relations, who had them set in rings and brooches. Later, the Queen was able to send enough for bracelets and girdles. But presently so much hair was cut off that they had to burn it. Then when autumn came all the crops failed; it seemed as though all the gold of harvest had gone into the Princess's hair. And there was a famine. Then Melisande said—

'It seems a pity to waste all my hair; it does grow so very fast. Couldn't we stuff things with it, or something, and sell them, to feed the people?'

So the King called a council of merchants, and they sent out samples of the Princess's hair, and soon orders came pouring in; and the Princess's hair became the staple export of that country. They stuffed pillows with it, and they stuffed beds with it. They made ropes of it for sailors to use, and curtains for hanging in King's palaces. They made hair-cloth of it, for hermits, and other people who wished to be uncomfy. But it was so soft and silky that it only made them happy and warm, which they did not wish to be. So the hermits gave up wearing it, and instead, mothers bought it for their little babies, and all well-born infants wore little shirts of Princess-haircloth.

And still the hair grew and grew. And the people were fed and the famine came to an end.

Then the King said: 'It was all very well while the famine lasted— but now I shall write to my fairy godmother and see if something cannot be done.'

So he wrote and sent the letter by a skylark, and by return of bird came this answer—

'Why not advertise for a competent Prince? Offer the usual reward.'

So the King sent out his heralds all over the world to proclaim that any respectable Prince with proper references should marry the Princess Melisande if he could stop her hair growing.

Then from far and near came trains of Princes anxious to try their luck, and they brought all sorts of nasty things with them in bottles and round wooden boxes. The Princess tried all the remedies, but she did not like any of them, and she did not like any of the Princes, so in her heart she was rather glad that none of the nasty things in bottles and boxes made the least difference to her hair.

The Princess had to sleep in the great Throne Room now, because no other room was big enough to hold her and her hair. When she woke in the morning the long high room would be quite full of her golden hair, packed tight and thick like wool in a barn. And every night when she had had the hair cut close to her head she would sit in her green silk gown by the window and cry, and kiss the little green caps she used to wear, and wish herself bald again.

It was as she sat crying there on Midsummer Eve that she first saw Prince Florizel.*

He had come to the palace that evening, but he would not appear in her presence with the dust of travel on him, and she had retired with her hair borne by twenty pages before he had bathed and changed his garments and entered the reception-room.

Now he was walking in the garden in the moonlight, and he looked up and she looked down, and for the first time Melisande, looking on a Prince, wished that he might have the power to stop her hair from growing. As for the Prince, he wished many things, and the first was granted him. For he said—

'You are Melisande?'

'And you are Florizel?'

'There are many roses round your window,' said he to her, 'and none down here.'

She threw him one of three white roses she held in her hand. Then he said—

'White rose trees are strong. May I climb up to you?'

'Surely,' said the Princess.

So he climbed up to the window.

'Now,' said he, 'if I can do what your father asks, will you marry me?'

'My father has promised that I shall,' said Melisande, playing with the white roses in her hand.

'Dear Princess,' said he, 'your father's promise is nothing to me. I want yours. Will you give it to me?'

'Yes,' said she, and gave him the second rose.

'I want your hand.'

'Yes,' she said.

'And your heart with it.'

'Yes,' said the Princess, and she gave him the third rose.

'And a kiss to seal the promise.'

'Yes,' said she.

'And a kiss to go with the hand.'

'Yes,' she said.

'And a kiss to bring the heart.'

'Yes,' said the Princess, and she gave him the three kisses.

'Now,' said he, when he had given them back to her, 'to-night do not go to bed. Stay by your window, and I will stay down here in the garden and watch. And when your hair has grown to the filling of your room call to me, and then do as I tell you.'

'I will,' said the Princess.

So at dewy sunrise the Prince, lying on the turf beside the sun-dial, heard her voice—

'Florizel! Florizel! My hair has grown so long that it is pushing me out of the window.'

'Get out on to the window-sill,' said he, 'and twist your hair three times round the great iron hook that is there.'

And she did.

Then the Prince climbed up the rose bush with his naked sword in his teeth, and he took the Princess's hair in his hand about a yard from her head and said—

'Jump!'

The Princess jumped, and screamed, for there she was hanging from the hook by a yard and a half of her bright hair; the Prince tightened his grasp of the hair and drew his sword across it.

Then he let her down gently by her hair till her feet were on the grass, and jumped down after her.

They stayed talking in the garden till all the shadows had crept under their proper trees and the sun-dial said it was breakfast time.

Then they went in to breakfast, and all the Court crowded round to wonder and admire. For the Princess's hair had not grown.

'How did you do it?' asked the King, shaking Florizel warmly by the hand.

'The simplest thing in the world,' said Florizel, modestly. 'You have always cut the hair off the Princess. *I* just cut the Princess off the hair.'

'Humph!' said the King, who had a logical mind. And during breakfast he more than once looked anxiously at his daughter. When they got up from breakfast the Princess rose with the rest, but she rose and rose and rose, till it seemed as though there would never be an end of it. The Princess was nine feet high.

'I feared as much,' said the King, sadly. 'I wonder what will be the rate of progression. You see,' he said to poor Florizel, 'when we cut the hair off *it* grows—when we cut the Princess off *she* grows. I wish you had happened to think of that!'

The Princess went on growing. By dinner-time she was so large that she had to have her dinner brought out into the garden because she was too large to get indoors. But she was too unhappy to be able to eat anything. And she cried so much that there was quite a pool in the garden, and several pages were nearly drowned. So she remembered her 'Alice in Wonderland,'* and stopped crying at once. But she did not stop growing. She grew bigger and bigger and bigger, till she had to go outside the palace gardens and sit on the common, and even that was too small to hold her comfortably, for every hour she grew twice as much as she had done the hour before. And nobody knew what to do, nor where the Princess was to sleep. Fortunately, her clothes had grown with her, or she would have been very cold indeed, and now she sat on the common in her green gown, embroidered with gold, looking like a great hill covered with gorse in flower.

You cannot possibly imagine how large the Princess was growing, and her mother stood wringing her hands on the castle tower, and the Prince Florizel looked on broken-hearted to see his Princess snatched from his arms and turned into a lady as big as a mountain.

The King did not weep or look on. He sat down at once and wrote to his fairy godmother, asking her advice. He sent a weasel with the letter, and by return of weasel he got his own letter back again, marked, 'Gone away. Left no address.'

It was now, when the kingdom was plunged into gloom, that a neighbouring King took it into his head to send an invading army against the island where Melisande lived. They came in ships and they landed in great numbers, and Melisande looking down from her height saw alien soldiers marching on the sacred soil of her country.

'I don't mind so much now,' said she, 'if I can really be of some use this size.'

And she picked up the army of the enemy in handfuls and double-handfuls, and put them back into their ships, and gave a little flip to each transport ship with her finger and thumb, which sent the ships off so fast that they never stopped till they reached their own country, and when they arrived there the whole army to a man said it would rather be court-martialled a hundred times over than go near the place again.

Meantime Melisande, sitting on the highest hill on the island, felt the land trembling and shivering under her giant feet.

'I do believe I'm getting too heavy,' she said, and jumped off the island into the sea, which was just up to her ankles. Just then a great fleet of warships and gunboats and torpedo boats came in sight, on their way to attack the island.

Melisande could easily have sunk them all with one kick, but she did not like to do this because it might have drowned the sailors, and besides, it might have swamped the island.

So she simply stooped and picked the island as you would pick a mushroom—for, of course, all islands are supported by a stalk underneath—and carried it away to another part of the world. So that when the warships got to where the island was marked on the map they found nothing but sea, and a very rough sea it was, because the Princess had churned it all up with her ankles as she walked away through it with the island.

When Melisande reached a suitable place, very sunny and warm, and with no sharks in the water, she set down the island; and the people made it fast with anchors, and then every one went to bed, thanking the kind fate which had sent them so great a Princess to help them in their need, and calling her the saviour of her country and the bulwark of the nation.

But it is poor work being the nation's bulwark and your country's saviour when you are miles high, and have no one to talk to, and when all you want is to be your humble right size again and to marry your sweetheart. And when it was dark the Princess came close to the island, and looked down, from far up, at her palace and her tower and cried, and cried, and cried. It does not matter how much you cry into the sea, it hardly makes any difference, however large you may be. Then when everything was quite dark the Princess looked up at the stars.

'I wonder how soon I shall be big enough to knock my head against them,' said she.

And as she stood star-gazing she heard a whisper right in her ear. A very little whisper, but quite plain.

'Cut off your hair!' it said.

Now, everything the Princess was wearing had grown big along with her, so that now there dangled from her golden girdle a pair of scissors as big as the Malay Peninsula, together with a pin-cushion the size of the Isle of Wight, and a yard measure that would have gone round Australia.

And when she heard the little, little voice, she knew it, small as it was, for the dear voice of Prince Florizel, and she whipped out the scissors from her gold case and snip, snip, snipped all her hair off, and it fell into the sea. The coral insects got hold of it at once and set to work on it, and now they have made it into the biggest coral reef in the world; but that has nothing to do with the story.

Then the voice said, 'Get close to the island,' and the Princess did, but she could not get very close because she was so large, and she looked up again at the stars and they seemed to be much farther off.

Then the voice said, 'Be ready to swim,' and she felt something climb out of her ear and clamber down her arm. The stars got farther and farther away, the next moment the Princess found herself swimming in the sea, and Prince Florizel swimming beside her.

'I crept on to your hand when you were carrying the island,' he explained, when their feet touched the sand and they walked in through the shallow water, 'and I got into your ear with an ear-trumpet. You never noticed me because you were so great then.'

'Oh, my dear Prince,' cried Melisande, falling into his arms, 'you have saved me. I am my proper size again.'

So they went home and told the King and Queen. Both were very, very happy, but the King rubbed his chin with his hand, and said—

'You've certainly had some fun for your money, young man, but don't you see that we're just where we were before? Why, the child's hair is growing already.'

And indeed it was.

Then once more the King sent a letter to his godmother. He sent it by a flying-fish, and by return of fish came the answer—

'Just back from my holidays. Sorry for your troubles. Why not try scales?'

And on this message the whole Court pondered for weeks.

But the Prince caused a pair of gold scales to be made, and hung them up in the palace gardens under a big oak tree. And one morning he said to the Princess—

'My darling Melisande, I must really speak seriously to you. We are getting on in life. I am nearly twenty: it is time that we thought of being settled. Will you trust me entirely and get into one of those gold scales?'

So he took her down into the garden, and helped her into the scale, and she curled up in it in her green and gold gown, like a little grass mound with buttercups on it.

'And what is going into the other scale?' asked Melisande.

'Your hair,' said Florizel. 'You see, when your hair is cut off you it grows, and when you are cut off your hair you grow—oh, my heart's delight, I can never forget how you grew, never! But if, when your hair is no more than you, and you are no more than your hair, I snip the scissors between you and it, then neither you nor your hair can possibly decide which ought to go on growing.'

'Suppose *both* did,' said the poor Princess, humbly.

'Impossible,' said the Prince, with a shudder; 'there are limits even to Malevola's malevolence. And, besides, Fortuna said "Scales." Will you try it?'

'I will do whatever you wish,' said the poor Princess, 'but let me kiss my father and mother once, and Nurse, and you, too, my dear, in case I grow large again and can kiss nobody any more.'

So they came one by one and kissed the Princess.

Then the nurse cut off the Princess's hair, and at once it began to grow at a frightful rate.

The King and Queen and nurse busily packed it, as it grew, into the other scale, and gradually the scale went down a little. The Prince stood waiting between the scales with his drawn sword, and just before the two were equal he struck. But during the time his sword took to flash through the air the Princess's hair grew a yard or two, so that at the instant when he struck the balance was true.

'You are a young man of sound judgment,' said the King, embracing him, while the Queen and the nurse ran to help the Princess out of the gold scale.

The scale full of golden hair bumped down on to the ground as the Princess stepped out of the other one, and stood there before those who loved her, laughing and crying with happiness, because she remained her proper size, and her hair was not growing any more.

She kissed her Prince a hundred times, and the very next day they were married. Every one remarked on the beauty of the bride, and it was noticed that her hair was quite short—only five feet five and a quarter inches long—just down to her pretty ankles. Because the scales had been ten feet and ten and a half inches apart, and the Prince, having a straight eye, had cut the golden hair exactly in the middle!

RUDYARD KIPLING

Dymchurch Flit

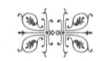

THE BEE BOY'S SONG

Bees! Bees! Hark to your bees!
'Hide from your neighbours as much as you please,
But all that has happened, to *us* you must tell.*
Or else we will give you no honey to sell!'

> A maiden in her glory,
>   Upon her wedding-day,
> Must tell her Bees the story,
>   Or else they'll fly away.
>   Fly away—die away—
>   Dwindle down and leave you!
>   But if you don't deceive your Bees,
>   Your Bees will not deceive you.

> Marriage, birth or buryin',
>   News across the seas,
> All you're sad or merry in,
>   You must tell the Bees.
>   Tell 'em coming in an' out,
>   Where the Fanners fan,*
>   'Cause the Bees are justabout
>   As curious as a man!

> Don't you wait where trees are,
>   When the lightning play;
> Nor don't you hate where Bees are,
>   Or else they'll pine away.
>   Pine away—dwine away—*
>   Anything to leave you!
>   But if you never grieve your Bees,
>   Your Bees 'll never grieve you.

Dymchurch Flit

Just at dusk, a soft September rain began to fall on the hop-pickers. The mothers wheeled the bouncing perambulators out of the gardens; bins were put away, and tally-books made up. The young couples strolled home, two to each umbrella, and the single men walked behind them laughing. Dan and Una, who had been picking after their lessons, marched off to roast potatoes at the oast-house,* where old Hobden, with Blue-eyed Bess, his lurcher dog,* lived all the month through, drying the hops.

They settled themselves, as usual, on the sack-strewn cot in front of the fires, and, when Hobden drew up the shutter, stared, as usual, at the flameless bed of coals spouting its heat up the dark well of the old-fashioned roundel. Slowly he cracked off a few fresh pieces of coal, packed them, with fingers that never flinched, exactly where they would do most good; slowly he reached behind him till Dan tilted the potatoes into his iron scoop of a hand; carefully he arranged them round the fire, and then stood for a moment, black against the glare. As he closed the shutter, the oast-house seemed dark before the day's end, and he lit the candle in the lanthorn. The children liked all these things because they knew them so well.

The Bee Boy, Hobden's son, who is not quite right in his head, though he can do anything with bees, slipped in like a shadow. They only guessed it when Bess's stump-tail wagged against them.

A big voice began singing outside in the drizzle:—

'Old Mother Laidinwool had nigh twelve months been dead,
She heard the hops were doing well, and then popped up her head.'*

'There can't be two people made to holler like that!' cried old Hobden, wheeling round.

'For,' says she, 'The boys I've picked with when I was young and fair,
They're bound to be at hoppin', and I'm——'

A man showed at the doorway.

'Well, well! They do say hoppin'll draw the very deadest, and now I belieft 'em. You, Tom? Tom Shoesmith!' Hobden lowered his lanthorn.

'You're a hem of* a time makin' your mind to it, Ralph!' The stranger strode in—three full inches taller than Hobden, a grey-whiskered, brown-faced giant with clear blue eyes. They shook hands, and the children could hear the hard palms rasp together.

'You ain't lost none o' your grip,' said Hobden. 'Was it thirty or forty year back you broke my head at Peasmarsh Fair?'*

'Only thirty an' no odds 'tween us regardin' heads, neither. You had it back at me with a hop-pole. How did we get home that night? Swimmin'?'

'Same way the pheasant come into Gubbs's pocket—by a little luck an' a deal o' conjurin'.' Old Hobden laughed in his deep chest.

'I see you've not forgot your way about the woods. D'ye do any o' *this* still?' The stranger pretended to look along a gun.

Hobden answered with a quick movement of the hand as though he were pegging down a rabbit-wire.

'No. *That's* all that's left me now. Age she must as Age she can. An' what's your news since all these years?'

> 'Oh, I've bin to Plymouth, I've bin to Dover—*
> I've bin ramblin', boys, the wide world over,'

the man answered cheerily. 'I reckon I know as much of Old England as most.' He turned towards the childen and winked boldly.

'I lay they told you a sight o' lies, then. I've been into England fur as Wiltsheer* once. I was cheated proper over a pair of hedging-gloves,' said Hobden.

'There's fancy-talkin' everywhere. *You*'ve cleaved to your own parts pretty middlin' close, Ralph.'

'Can't shift an old tree 'thout it dyin',' Hobden chuckled. 'An' I be no more anxious to die than you look to be to help me with my hops to-night.'

The great man leaned against the brick-work of the roundel, and swung his arms abroad. 'Hire me!' was all he said, and they stumped upstairs laughing.

The children heard their shovels rasp on the cloth where the yellow hops lie drying above the fires, and all the oast-house filled with the sweet, sleepy smell as they were turned.

'Who is it?' Una whispered to the Bee Boy.

'Dunno, no more'n you—if *you* dunno,' said he, and smiled.

The voices on the drying-floor talked and chuckled together, and the heavy footsteps moved back and forth. Presently a hop-pocket dropped through the press-hole overhead, and stiffened and fattened as they shovelled it full. 'Clank!' went the press, and rammed the loose stuff into tight cake.

'Gently!' they heard Hobden cry. 'You'll bust her crop if you lay on so. You be as careless as Gleason's bull, Tom. Come an' sit by the fires. She'll do now.'

They came down, and as Hobden opened the shutter to see if the potatoes were done Tom Shoesmith said to the children, 'Put a plenty salt on 'em. That'll show you the sort o' man *I* be.'* Again he winked, and again the Bee Boy laughed and Una stared at Dan.

'*I* know what sort o' man you be,' old Hobden grunted, groping for the potatoes round the fire.

'Do ye?' Tom went on behind his back. 'Some of us can't abide Horseshoes, or Church Bells, or Running Water;* an', talkin' o' runnin' water'—he turned to Hobden, who was backing out of the roundel*—'d'you mind the great floods at Robertsbridge,* when the miller's man was drowned in the street?'

'Middlin' well.' Old Hobden let himself down on the coals by the fire door. 'I was courtin' my woman on the Marsh that year. Carter to Mus' Plum I was, gettin' ten shillin's a week. Mine was a Marsh woman.'

'Won'erful odd-gates* place—Romney Marsh,' said Tom Shoesmith. 'I've heard say the world's divided like into Europe, Ashy, Afriky, Ameriky, Austral, an' Romney Marsh.'*

'The Marsh folk think so,' said Hobden. 'I had a hem o' trouble to get my woman to leave it.'

'Where did she come out of? I've forgot, Ralph.'

'Dymchurch under the Wall,' Hobden answered, a potato in his hand.

'Then she'd be a Pett—or a Whitgift, would she?'

'Whitgift.' Hobden broke upon the potato and ate it with the curious neatness of men who make the most of their meals in the blowy open. 'She growed to be quite reasonable-like after livin' in the Weald awhile, but our first twenty year or two she was odd-fashioned, no bounds. And she was a won'erful hand with bees.' He cut away a little piece of potato and threw it out to the door.

'Ah! I've heard say the Whitgifts could see further through a millstone* than most,' said Shoesmith. 'Did she, now?'

'She was honest-innocent of any nigro-mancin',* said Hobden. 'Only she'd read signs and sinnifications out o' birds flyin', stars fallin', bees hivin', and such. An' she'd lie awake—listenin' for calls, she said.'

'That don't prove naught,' said Tom. 'All Marsh folk has been smugglers since time ever-lastin'. 'Twould be in her blood to listen out o' nights.'

'Nature-ally,' old Hobden replied, smiling. 'I mind when there was smugglin' a sight nearer us than the Marsh be. But that wasn't my woman's trouble. 'Twas a passel* o' no-sense talk,' he dropped his voice, 'about Pharisees.'*

'Yes. I've heard Marsh men belieft in 'em.' Tom looked straight at the wide-eyed children beside Bess.

'Pharisees,' cried Una. 'Fairies? Oh, *I* see!'

'People o' the Hills,' said the Bee Boy, throwing half his potato towards the door.

'There you be!' said Hobden, pointing at him. 'My boy, he has her eyes and her out-gate* senses. That's what *she* called 'em!'

'And what did you think of it all?'

'Um—um,' Hobden rumbled. 'A man that uses fields an' shaws after dark as much as I've done, he don't go out of his road excep' for keepers.'

'But settin' that aside?' said Tom, coaxingly. 'I saw ye throw the Good Piece out-at-doors just now. Do ye believe or—*do* ye?'

'There was a great black eye to that tater,' said Hobden, indignantly.

'My liddle eye didn't see un, then. It looked as if you meant it for—for Any One that might need it. But settin' that aside. D'ye believe or—*do* ye?'

'I ain't sayin' nothin', because I've heard naught, an' I've seen naught. But if you was to say there was more things after dark in the shaws than men, or fur, or feather, or fin, I dunno as I'd go far about to call you a liar. Now turnagain, Tom. What's your say?'

'I'm like you. I say nothin'. But I'll tell you a tale, an' you can fit it, *as* how you please.'

'Passel o' no-sense stuff,' growled Hobden, but he filled his pipe.

'The Marsh men they call it Dymchurch Flit,'* Tom went on slowly. 'Hap you have heard it?'

'My woman she've told it me scores o' times. Dunno as I didn't end by belieftin' it—sometimes.'

Hobden crossed over as he spoke, and sucked with his pipe at the yellow lanthorn flame. Tom rested one great elbow on one great knee, where he sat among the coal.

'Have you ever bin in the Marsh?' he said to Dan.

'Only as far as Rye, once,' Dan answered.

'Ah, that's but the edge. Back behind of her there's steeples settin' beside churches,* an' wise women settin' beside their doors, an' the sea settin' above the land, an' ducks herdin' wild in the diks' (he meant ditches). 'The Marsh is justabout riddled with diks an' sluices, an' tide-gates an' water-lets. You can hear 'em bubblin' an' grummelin'* when the tide works in 'em, an' then you hear the sea rangin' left and right-handed all up along the Wall. You've seen how flat she is— the Marsh? You'd think nothin' easier than to walk eend-on acrost her? Ah, but the diks an' the water-lets, they twists the roads about as ravelly as witch-yarn on the spindles.* So ye get all turned round in broad daylight.'

'That's because they've dreened the waters into the diks,' said Hobden. 'When I courted my woman the rushes was green—Eh me! the rushes was green—an' the Bailiff o' the Marshes, he rode up and down as free as the fog.'

'Who was he?' said Dan.

'Why, the Marsh fever an' ague. He've clapped me on the shoulder once or twice till I shook proper. But now the dreenin' off of the waters have done away with the fevers; so they make a joke, like, that the Bailiff o' the Marshes broke his neck in a dik. A won'erful place for bees an' ducks 'tis too.'

'An' old,' Tom went on. 'Flesh an' Blood have been there since Time Everlasin' Beyond. Well, now, speakin' among themselves, the Marsh-men say that from Time Everlasin' Beyond, the Pharisees favoured the Marsh above the rest of Old England. I lay the Marsh men ought to know. They've been out after dark, father an' son, smugglin' some one thing or t'other, since ever wool grew to sheep's backs. They say there was always a middlin' few Pharisees to be seen on the Marsh. Impident as rabbits, they was. They'd dance on the nakid roads in the nakid daytime; they'd flash their liddle green lights along the diks, comin' an' goin', like honest smugglers. Yes, an' times they'd lock the church doors against parson an' clerk of Sundays.'

'That 'ud be smugglers layin' in the lace or the brandy till they could run it out o' the Marsh. I've told my woman so,' said Hobden.

'I'll lay she didn't belieft it, then—not if she was a Whitgift. A won'erful choice place for Pharisees, the Marsh, by all accounts, till Queen Bess's father he come in with his Reformatories.'*

'Would that be a Act o' Parliament like?' Hobden asked.

'Sure-ly. Can't do nothing in Old England without Act, Warrant, an' Summons. He got his Act allowed him, an', they say, Queen Bess's father he used the parish churches something shameful. Justabout tore the gizzards out of I dunnamany.* Some folk in England they held with 'en; but some they saw it different, an' it eended in 'em takin' sides an' burnin' each other no bounds, accordin' which side was top, time bein'. That tarrified the Pharisees: for Good-will among Flesh an' Blood is meat an' drink to 'em, an' ill-will is poison.'

'Same as bees,' said the Bee Boy. 'Bees won't stay by a house where there's hating.'

'True,' said Tom. 'This Reformations tarrified the Pharisees same as the reaper goin' round a last stand o' wheat tarrifies rabbits. They packed into the Marsh from all parts, and they says, "Fair or foul, we must flit out o' this, for Merry England's done with, an' we're reckoned among the Images." '*

'Did they *all* see it that way?' said Hobden.

'All but one that was called Robin*—if you've heard of him. What are you laughing at?' Tom turned to Dan. 'The Phrarisees's trouble didn't tech Robin, because he'd cleaved middlin' close to people like. No more he never meant to go out of Old England—not he; so he was sent messagin' for help among Flesh an' Blood. But Flesh an' Blood must always think of their own concerns, an' Robin couldn't get *through* at 'em, ye see. They thought it was tide-echoes off the Marsh.'

'What did you—what did the fai—Pharisees want?' Una asked.

'A boat, to be sure. Their liddle wings could no more cross Channel than so many tired butterflies. A boat an' a crew they desired to sail 'em over to France, where yet awhile folks hadn't tore down the Images. They couldn't abide cruel Canterbury Bells ringin' to Bulverhithe* for more pore men an' women to be burnded, nor the King's proud messenger ridin' through the land givin' orders to tear down the Images. They couldn't abide it no shape. Nor yet they couldn't get their boat an' crew to flit by without Leave an' Good-will from Flesh an' Blood; an' Flesh an' Blood came an' went about its own business while the Marsh was swarvin' up,* an' swarvin' up with Pharisees from all England over, striving all means to get *through* at Flesh an' Blood to tell 'em their sore need. . . . I don't know as you've ever heard say Pharisees are like chickens?'

'My woman used to say that too,' said Hobden, folding his brown arms.

'They be. You run too many chickens together, an' the ground sickens like, an' you get a squat,* an' your chickens die. 'Same way, you crowd Pharisees all in one place—*they* don't die, but Flesh an' Blood walkin' among 'em is apt to sick up an' pine off. *They* don't mean it, an' Flesh an' Blood don't know it, but that's the truth—as I've heard. The Pharisees through bein' all stenched up* an' frightened, an' tryin' to come *through* with their supplications, they nature-ally, changed the thin airs and humours in Flesh an' Blood. It lay on the Marsh like thunder. Men saw their churches ablaze with the wildfire in the windows after dark; they saw their cattle scatterin' and no man scarin'; their sheep flockin' and no man drivin'; their horses latherin' an' no man leadin'; they saw the liddle low green lights more than ever in the dik-sides; they heard the liddle feet patterin' more than ever round the houses; an' night an' day, day an' night, 'twas all as though they were bein' creeped up on, and hinted at by Some One or other that couldn't rightly shape their trouble. Oh, I lay they sweated! Man an' maid, woman an' child, their Nature done 'em no service all the weeks while the Marsh was swarvin' up with Pharisees. But they was Flesh an' Blood, an' Marsh men before all. They reckoned the signs sinnified trouble for the Marsh. Or that the sea 'ud rear up against Dymchurch Wall* an' they'd be drownded like Old Winchelsea;* or that the Plague was comin'. So they looked for the meanin' in the sea or in the clouds—far an' high up. They never thought to look near an' knee-high, where they could see naught.

'Now there was a poor widow at Dymchurch under the Wall, which, lacking man or property, she had the more time for feeling; and she come to feel there was a Trouble outside her doorstep bigger an' heavier than aught she'd ever carried over it. She had two sons—one born blind, and t'other struck dumb through fallin' off the Wall when he was liddle. They was men grown, but not wage-earnin', an' she worked for 'em, keepin' bees and answerin' Questions.'

'What sort of questions?' said Dan.

'Like where lost things might be found, an' what to put about a crooked baby's neck, an' how to join parted sweethearts. She felt the Trouble on the Marsh same as eels feel thunder. She was a wise woman.'

'My woman was won'erful weather-tender, too,' said Hobden. 'I've seen her brish sparks like off an anvil out of her hair in thunderstorms. But she never laid out to answer Questions.'

'This woman was a Seeker* like, an' Seekers they sometimes find. One night, while she lay abed, hot an' aching, there come a Dream an' tapped at her window, and "Widow Whitgift," it said, "Widow Whitgift!"

'First, by the wings an' the whistling, she thought it was peewits, but last she arose an' dressed herself, an' opened her door to the Marsh, an' she felt the Trouble an' the Groaning all about her, strong as fever an' ague, an' she calls: "What is it? Oh, what is it?"

'Then 'twas all like the frogs in the diks peeping: then 'twas all like the reeds in the diks clip-clapping; an' then the great Tide-wave rummelled* along the Wall, an' she couldn't hear proper.

'Three times she called, an' three times the Tide-wave did her down. But she catched the quiet between, an' she cries out, "What is the Trouble on the Marsh that's been lying down with my heart an' arising with my body this month gone?" She felt a liddle hand lay hold on her gown-hem, an' she stooped to the pull o' that liddle hand.'

Tom Shoesmith spread his huge fist before the fire and smiled at it.

'"Will the sea drown the Marsh?" she says. She was a Marsh-woman first an' foremost.

'"No," says the liddle voice. "Sleep sound for all o' that."

'"Is the Plague comin' to the Marsh?" she says. Them was all the ills she knowed.

'"No. Sleep sound for all o' that," says Robin.

'She turned about, half mindful to go in, but the liddle voices grieved that shrill an' sorrowful she turns back, an' she cries: "If it is not a Trouble of Flesh an' Blood, what can I do?"

'The Pharisees cried out upon her from all round to fetch them a boat to sail to France, an' come back no more.

'"There's a boat on the Wall," she says, "but I can't push it down to the sea, nor sail it when 'tis there."

'"Lend us your sons," says all the Pharisees. "Give 'em Leave an' Good-will to sail it for us, Mother—O Mother!"

'"One's dumb, an' t'other's blind," she says. "But all the dearer me for that; and you'll lose them in the big sea." The voices justabout pierced through her; an' there was children's voices too. She stood out all she could, but she couldn't rightly stand against *that*. So she says: "If you can draw my sons for your job, I'll not hinder 'em. You can't ask no more of a Mother."

'She saw them liddle green lights dance an' cross till she was dizzy; she heard them liddle feet patterin' by the thousand; she heard cruel Canterbury Bells ringing to Bulverhithe, an' she heard the great Tide-wave ranging along the Wall. That was while the Pharisees was workin' a Dream to wake her two sons asleep: an' while she bit on her fingers she saw them two she'd bore come out an' pass her with never a word. She followed 'em, cryin' pitiful, to the old boat on the Wall, an' that they took an' runned down to the Sea.

'When they'd stepped mast an' sail the blind son speaks: "Mother, we're waitin' your Leave an' Good-will to take Them over." '

Tom Shoesmith threw back his head and half shut his eyes.

'Eh, me!' he said. 'She was a fine, valiant woman, the Widow Whitgift. She stood twistin' the eends of her long hair over her fingers, an' she shook like a poplar, makin' up her mind. The Pharisees all about they hushed their children from cryin' an' they waited dumb-still. She was all their dependence. 'Thout her Leave an' Good-will they could not pass; for she was the Mother. So she shook like a aps-tree* makin' up her mind. 'Last she drives the word past her teeth, an' "Go!" she says. "Go with my Leave an' Good-will."

'Then I saw—then, they say, she had to brace back same as if she was wadin' in tide-water; for the Pharisees just about flowed past her—down the beach to the boat, *I* dunnamany of 'em—with their wives an' children an' valooables, all escapin' out of cruel Old England. Silver you could hear clinkin', an' liddle bundles hove down dunt* on the bottom-boards, an' passels o' liddle swords an' shields raklin',* an' liddle fingers an' toes scratchin' on the boatside to board her when the two sons pushed her off. That boat she sunk lower an' lower, but all the Widow could see in it was her boys movin' hampered-like to get at the tackle. Up sail they did, an' away they went, deep as a Rye barge,* away into the off-shore mistes, an' the Widow Whitgift she sat down and eased her grief till mornin' light.'

'I never heard she was *all* alone,' said Hobden.

'I remember now. The one called Robin he stayed with her, they tell. She was all too grievious to listen to his promises.'

'Ah! She should ha' made her bargain before-hand. I allus told my woman so!' Hobden cried.

'No. She loaned her sons for a pure love-loan, bein' as she sensed the Trouble on the Marshes, an' was simple good-willing to ease it.' Tom laughed softly. 'She done that. Yes, she done that! From Hithe to Bulverhithe, fretty man an' petty maid,* ailin' woman an' wailin' child, they took the advantage of the change in the thin airs just about *as* soon as the Pharisees flitted. Folks come out fresh an' shining all over the Marsh like snails after wet. An' that while the Widow Whitgift sat grievin' on the Wall. She might have belieft us—she might have trusted her sons would be sent back! She fussed, no bounds, when their boat come in after three days.'

'And, of course, the sons were both quite cured?' said Una.

'No-o. That would have been out o' Nature. She got 'em back *as* she sent 'em. The blind man he hadn't seen naught of anything, an' the dumb man nature-ally, he couldn't say aught of what he'd seen. I reckon that was why the Pharisees pitched on 'em for the ferrying job.'

'But what did you—what did Robin promise the Widow?' said Dan.

'What *did* he promise, now?' Tom pretended to think. 'Wasn't your woman a Whitgift, Ralph? Didn't she ever say?'

'She told me a passel o' no-sense stuff when he was born.' Hobden pointed at his son. 'There was always to be one of 'em that could see further into a millstone than most.'

'Me! That's me!' said the Bee Boy so suddenly that they all laughed.

'I've got it now!' cried Tom, slapping his knee. 'So long as Whitgift blood lasted, Robin promised there would allers be one o' her stock that—that no Trouble 'ud lie on, no Maid 'ud sigh on, no Night could frighten, no Fright could harm, no Harm could make sin, an' no Woman could make a fool of.'

'Well, ain't that just me?' said the Bee Boy, where he sat in the silver square of the great September moon that was staring into the oast-house door.

'They was the exact words she told me when we first found he wasn't like others. But it beats me how you known 'em,' said Hobden.

'Aha! There's more under my hat besides my hair!' Tom laughed and stretched himself. 'When I've seen these two young folk home, we'll make a night of old days, Ralph, with passin' old tales—eh? An' where might you live?' he said, gravely, to Dan. 'An' do you think your Pa 'ud give me a drink for takin' you there, Missy?'

'They giggled so at this that they had to run out. Tom picked them both up, set one on each broad shoulder, and tramped across the ferny pasture where the cows puffed milky puffs at them in the moonlight.

'Oh, Puck! Puck!* I guessed you right from when you talked about the salt. How could you ever do it?' Una cried, swinging along delighted.

'Do what?' he said, and climbed the stile by the pollard oak.

'Pretend to be Tom Shoesmith,' said Dan, and they ducked to avoid the two little ashes that grow by the bridge over the brook. Tom was almost running.

'Yes. That's my name, Mus' Dan,' he said, hurrying over the silent shining lawn, where a rabbit sat by the big white-thorn near the croquet ground. 'Here you be.' He strode into the old kitchen yard, and slid them down as Ellen came to ask questions.

'I'm helping in Mus' Spray's oast-house,' he said to her. 'No, I'm no foreigner. I knowed this country 'fore your Mother was born; an'—yes, it's dry work oasting, Miss. Thank you.'

Ellen went to get a jug, and the children went in—magicked once more by Oak, Ash, and Thorn!*

A THREE-PART SONG

I'm just in love with all these three,
The Weald and the Marsh and the Down countrie;
Nor I don't know which I love the most,
The Weald or the Marsh or the white chalk coast!

I've buried my heart in a ferny hill,
Twix' a liddle low shaw an' a great high gill.*
Oh hop-bine yaller and woodsmoke blue,
I reckon you'll keep her middling true!

I've loosed my mind for to out and run,
On a Marsh that was old when Kings begun;
Oh Romney level and Brenzett reeds,*
I reckon you know what my mind needs!

I've given my soul to the Southdown grass,
And sheep-bells tinkled where you pass.
Oh Firle an' Ditchlin* an' sails at sea,
I reckon you keep my soul for me!

APPENDIX
WHAT IS A FAIRY TALE?

JOHN RUSKIN

'Introduction' to the Grimm Brothers, *German Popular Stories* (1869)

LONG since, longer ago perhaps than the opening of some fairy tales, I was asked by the publisher who has been rash enough, at my request, to reprint these my favourite old stories in their earliest English form, to set down for him my reasons for preferring them to the more polished legends, moral and satiric, which are now, with rich adornment of every page by very admirable art, presented to the acceptance of the Nursery.

But it seemed to me to matter so little to the majestic independence of the child-public, who, beside themselves, liked, or who disliked, what they pronounced entertaining, that it is only on strict claims of a promise unwarily given that I venture on the impertinence of eulogy; and my reluctance is the greater, because there is in fact nothing very notable in these tales, unless it be their freedom from faults which for some time have been held to be quite the reverse of faults, by the majority of readers.

In the best stories recently written for the young, there is a taint which it is not easy to define, but which inevitably follows on the author's addressing himself to children bred in school-rooms and drawing-rooms, instead of fields and woods—children whose favourite amusements are premature imitations of the vanities of elder people, and whose conceptions of beauty are dependent partly on costliness of dress. The fairies who interfere in the fortunes of these little ones are apt to be resplendent chiefly in millinery and satin slippers, and appalling more by their airs than their enchantments.

The fine satire which, gleaming through every playful word, renders some of these recent stories as attractive to the old as to the young, seems to me no less to unfit them for their proper function. Children should laugh, but not mock; and when they laugh, it should not be at the weaknesses or faults of others. They should be taught, as far as they are permitted to concern themselves with the characters of those around them, to seek faithfully for good, not to lie in wait maliciously to make themselves merry with evil: they should be too painfully sensitive to wrong, to smile at it; and too modest to constitute themselves its judges.

With these minor errors a far graver one is involved. As the simplicity of the sense of beauty has been lost in recent tales for children, so also the simplicity of their conception of love. That word which, in the heart of a child, should represent the most constant and vital part of its being; which ought to be the sign of the most solemn thoughts that inform its awakening soul and, in one wide mystery of pure sunrise, should flood the zenith of its heaven, and gleam on the dew at its feet; this word, which should be consecrated on its lips, together with the Name which it may not take in vain, and whose meaning should soften and animate every emotion through which the inferior things and the feeble creatures, set beneath it in its narrow world, are revealed to its curiosity or companionship;—this word, in modern child-story, is too often restrained and darkened into the hieroglyph of an evil mystery, troubling the sweet peace of youth with premature gleams of uncomprehended passion, and flitting shadows of unrecognized sin.

These grave faults in the spirit of recent child-fiction are connected with a parallel folly of purpose. Parents who are too indolent and self-indulgent to form their children's characters by wholesome discipline, or in their own habits and principles of life are conscious of setting before them no faultless example, vainly endeavour to substitute the persuasive influence of moral precept, intruded in the guise of amusement, for the strength of moral habit compelled by righteous authority:—vainly think to inform the heart of infancy with deliberative wisdom, while they abdicate the guardianship of its unquestioning innocence; and warp into the agonies of an immature philosophy of conscience the once fearless strength of its unsullied and unhesitating virtue.

A child should not need to choose between right and wrong. It should not be capable of wrong; it should not conceive of wrong. Obedient, as bark to helm, not by sudden strain or effort, but in the freedom of its bright course of constant life; true, with an undistinguished, painless, unboastful truth, in a crystalline household world of truth; gentle, through daily entreatings of gentleness, and honourable trusts, and pretty prides of child-fellow-ship in offices of good; strong, not in bitter and doubtful contest with temptation, but in peace of heart, and armour of habitual right, from which temptation falls like thawing hail; self-commanding, not in sick restraint of mean appetites and covetous thoughts, but in vital joy of unluxurious life, and contentment in narrow possession, wisely esteemed.

Children so trained have no need of moral fairy tales; but they will find in the apparently vain and fitful courses of any tradition of old time, honestly delivered to them, a teaching for which no other can be substituted, and of which the power cannot be measured; animating for them the material world with inextinguishable life, fortifying them against the glacial cold of selfish science, and preparing them submissively, and with no bitterness of astonishment, to behold, in later years, the mystery—divinely appointed to remain such to all human thought—of the fates that happen alike to the evil and the good.

And the effect of the endeavour to make stories moral upon the literary merit of the work itself, is as harmful as the motive of the effort is false. For every fairy tale worth recording at all is the remnant of a tradition possessing true historical value;—historical, at least in so far as it has naturally arisen out of the mind of a people under special circumstances, and risen not without meaning, nor removed altogether from their sphere of religious faith. It sustains afterwards natural changes from the sincere action of the fear or fancy of successive generations; it takes new colour from their manner of life, and new form from their changing moral tempers. As long as these changes are natural and effortless, accidental and inevitable, the story remains essentially true, altering its form, indeed, like a flying cloud, but remaining a sign of the sky; a shadowy image, as truly a part of the great firmament of the human mind as the light of reason which it seems to interrupt. But the fair deceit and innocent error of it cannot be interpreted nor restrained by a wilful purpose, and all additions to it by art do but defile, as the shepherd disturbs the flakes of morning mist with smoke from his fire of dead leaves.

There is also a deeper collateral mischief in this indulgence of licentious change and retouching of stories to suit particular tastes, or inculcate favourite doctrines. It directly destroys the child's power of rendering any such belief as it would otherwise have been in his nature to give to an imaginative vision. How far it is expedient to occupy his mind with ideal forms at all may be questionable to many, though not to me; but it is quite beyond question that if we do allow of the fictitious representation, that representation should be calm and complete, possessed to the full, and read down its utmost depth. The little reader's attention should never be confused or disturbed, whether he is possessing himself of fairy tale or history. Let him know his fairy tale accurately, and have perfect joy or awe in the conception of it as if it were real; thus he will always be exercising his power of grasping realities: but a confused, careless, and discrediting tenure of the fiction will lead to as confused and careless reading of fact. Let the circumstances of both be strictly perceived, and long dwelt upon, and let the child's own mind develop fruit of thought from both. It is of the greatest importance early to secure this habit of contemplation, and therefore it is a grave error, either to multiply unnecessarily, or to illustrate them for itself; and, if the intellect is of any real value, there will be a mystery of wonderfulness in its own dreams which would only be thwarted by external illustration. Yet I do not bring forward the text or the etchings in this volume as examples of what either ought to be in works of the kind: they are in many respects common, imperfect, vulgar; but their vulgarity is of a wholesome and harmless kind. It is not, for instance, graceful English, to say that a thought 'popped into Catherine's head;' but it nevertheless is far better, as an initiation into literary style, that a child should be told this than that 'a subject attracted Catherine's attention.' And in genuine forms of minor tradition, a rude and more or less illiterate tone will always be discernible; for all the best fairy tales have owed their birth, and the greater part of their power, to narrowness of social circumstances; they belong properly to districts in which walled cities are surrounded by bright and unblemished country, and in which a healthy and bustling town life, not highly refined, is relieved by, and contrasted with, the calm enchantment of pastoral and woodland scenery, either under humble cultivation by peasant masters, or left in its natural solitude. Under conditions of this kind the imagination is enough excited to invent instinctively, (and rejoice in the invention of) spiritual forms of wildness and beauty, while yet it is restrained and made cheerful by the familiar accidents and relations of town life, mingling always in its fancy humorous and vulgar circumstances with pathetic ones, and never so much impressed with its supernatural phantasies as to be in danger of retaining them as any part of its religious faith. The good spirit descends gradually from an angel into a fairy, and the demon shrinks into a playful grotesque of diminutive malevolence, while yet both keep an accredited and vital influence upon the character and mind. But the language in which such ideas will be usually clothed must necessarily partake of their narrowness; and art is systematically incognizant of them, having only strength under the conditions which awake them to express itself in an irregular and gross grotesque, fit only for external architectural decoration.

The illustrations of this volume* are almost the only exceptions I know to the general rule. They are of quite sterling and admirable art, in a class precisely parallel in elevation to the character of the tales which they illustrate; and the original etchings, as I have before said in the Appendix to my 'Elements of Drawing,'* were unrivalled in masterfulness of touch since Rembrandt;* (in some qualities of delineation unrivalled even by him). These copies have been so carefully executed that at first I was deceived by them, and supposed them to be late impressions from the plates (and what is more, I believe the master himself was deceived by them, and supposed them to be his own); and although, on careful comparison with the first proofs, they will be found no exception to the terrible law that literal repetition of entirely fine work shall be, even to the hand that produced it,—much more to any other,—for ever impossible, they still represent, with sufficient fidelity to be in the highest degree instructive, the harmonious light and shade, the manly simplicity of execution, and the easy, unencumbered fancy, of designs which belonged to the best period of Cruikshank's genius. To make somewhat enlarged copies of them, looking at them through a magnifying-glass, and never putting two lines where Cruikshank has put only one, would be an exercise in decision and severe drawing which would leave afterwards little to be learnt in schools. I would gladly also say much in their praise as imaginative designs; but the power of genuine imaginative work, and its difference from that which is compounded and patched together from borrowed sources, is of all qualities of art the most difficult to explain; and I must be content with the simple assertion of it.

And so I trust the good old book, and the honest work that adorns it, to such favour as they may find with children of open hearts and lowly lives.

JULIANA HORATIA EWING

'Preface' to *Old-Fashioned Fairy Tales* (1888)

> 'Know'st thou not the little path
> That winds about the Ferny brae?
> That is the road to bonnie Elfland,
> Where thou and I this night maun gae.'
>
> THOS. THE RHYMER.*

As the title of this story-book may possibly suggest that the tales are old fairy tales told afresh, it seems well to explain that this is not so.

Except for the use of common 'properties' of Fairy Drama, and a scrupulous endeavour to conform to tradition in local colour and detail, the stories are all new.

They have appeared at intervals during some years past in 'AUNT JUDY'S MAGAZINE FOR YOUNG PEOPLE,'* and were written in conformity to certain theories respecting stories of this kind, with only two of which shall the kindly reader of prefaces be troubled.

First, that there are ideas and types, occurring in the myths of all countries, which are common properties, to use which does not lay the teller of fairy tales open to the charge of plagiarism. Such as the idea of the weak outwitting the strong; the failure of man to choose wisely when he may have his wish; or the desire of sprites to exchange their careless and unfettered existence for the pains and penalties of humanity, if they may thereby share in the hopes of the human soul.

Secondly, that in these household stories (the models for which were originally oral tradition), the thing most to be avoided is a discursive or descriptive style of writing. Brevity and epigram must ever be soul of their wit, and they should be written as tales that are told.

The degree in which, if at all, the following tales fulfil these conditions, nursery critics must decide.

There are older critics before whom fairy tales, as such, need excuse, even if they do not meet with positive disapprobation.

On this score I can only say that, for myself, I believe them to be—beyond all need of defence—most valuable literature for the young. I do not believe that wonder-tales confuse children's ideas of truth. If there are young intellects so imperfect as to be incapable of distinguishing between fancy and falsehood, it is surely most desirable to develop in them the power to do so; but, as a rule, in childhood we appreciate the distinction with a vivacity which, as elders, our care-clogged memories fail to recall.

Moreover fairy tales have positive uses in education, which no cramming of cats,* and no merely domestic fiction can serve.

Like Proverbs and Parables, they deal with first principles under the simplest forms. They convey knowledge of the world, shrewd lessons of virtue and vice, of common sense and sense of humour, of the seemly and the absurd, of pleasure and pain, success and failure, in narratives where the plot moves briskly and dramatically from a beginning to an end. They treat, not of the corner of a nursery or a playground, but of the world at large, and life in perspective; of forces visible and invisible; of Life, Death, and Immortality.

For causes obvious to the student of early myths, they foster sympathy with nature, and no class of child-literature has done so much to inculcate the love of animals.

They cultivate the Imagination, that great gift which time and experience lead one more and more to value—handmaid of Faith, of Hope, and, perhaps most of all, of Charity!

It is true that some of the old fairy tales do not teach the high and useful lessons that most of them do; and that they unquestionably deal now and again with phases of grown-up life, and with crimes and catastrophes, that seem unsuitable for nursery entertainment.

As to the latter question, it must be remembered that the brevity of the narrative—whether it be a love story or a robber story—deprives it of all harm; a point which writers of modern fairy tales do not always realize for their guidance.

The writer of the following tales has endeavoured to bear this principle in mind, and it is hoped that the morals—and it is of the essence of fairy tales to have a moral—of all of them are beyond reproach.

For the rest they are committed to the indulgence of the gentle reader.

Hans Anderssen, perhaps the greatest writer of modern fairy tales, was content to say:

'FAIRY TALE NEVER DIES.'

J. H. E.

GEORGE MACDONALD
'The Fantastic Imagination' (1895)

THAT we have in English no word corresponding to the German *Mährchen*,* drives us to use the word *Fairytale*, regardless of the fact that the tale may have nothing to do with any sort of fairy. The old use of the word *Fairy*, by Spenser* at least, might, however, well be adduced, were justification or excuse necessary where *need must*.

Were I asked, what is a fairytale? I should reply, *Read Undine:* that is a fairytale; then read this and that as well, and you will see what is a fairytale*. Were I further begged to describe the *fairytale*, or define what it is, I would make answer, that I should as soon think of describing the abstract human face, or stating what must go to constitute a human being. A fairytale is just a fairytale, as a face is just a face; and of all fairytales I know, I think *Undine* the most beautiful.

Many a man, however, who would not attempt to define a *man*, might venture to say something as to what a man ought to be: even so much I will not in this place venture with regard to the fairytale, for my long past work in that kind might but poorly instance or illustrate my now more matured judgment. I will but say some things helpful to the reading, in right-minded fashion, of such fairytales as I would wish to write, or care to read.

Some thinkers would feel sorely hampered if at liberty to use no forms but such as existed in nature, or to invent nothing save in accordance with the law of the world of the senses; but it must not therefore be imagined that they desire escape from the region of law. Nothing lawless can show the least reason why it should exist, or could at best have more than an appearance of life.

The natural world has its laws, and no man must interfere with them in the way of presentment any more than in the way of use; but they themselves may suggest laws of other kinds, and man may, if he pleases, invent a little world of his own, with its own laws; for there is that in him which delights in calling up new forms—which is the nearest, perhaps, he can come to creation. When such forms are new embodiments of old truths, we call them products of the Imagination; when they are mere inventions, however lovely, I should call them the work of the Fancy:* in either case, Law has been diligently at work.

His world once invented, the highest law that comes next into play is, that there shall be harmony between the laws by which the new world has begun to exist; and in the process of his creation, the inventor must hold by those laws. The moment he forgets one of them, he makes the story, by its own postulates, incredible. To be able to live a moment in an imagined world, we must see the laws of its existence obeyed. Those broken, we fall out of it. The imagination in us, whose exercise is essential to the most temporary submission to the imagination of another, immediately, with the disappearance of Law, ceases to act. Suppose the gracious creatures of some childlike region of Fairyland talking either cockney or Gascon!* Would not the tale, however lovelily begun, sink at once to the level of the Burlesque—of all forms of literature the least worthy? A man's inventions may be stupid or clever, but if he do not hold by the laws of them, or if he make one law jar with another, he contradicts himself as an inventor, he is no artist. He does not rightly consort his instruments, or he tunes them in different keys. The mind of a man is the product of live Law; it thinks by law, it dwells in the midst of law, it gathers from law its growth; with law, therefore, can it alone work to any result. Inharmonious, unconsorting ideas will come to a man, but if he try to use one of such, his work will grow dull, and he will drop it from mere lack of interest. Law is the soil in which alone beauty will grow; beauty is the only stuff in which Truth can be clothed; and you may, if you will, call Imagination the tailor that cuts her garments to fit her, and Fancy his journeyman that puts the pieces of them together, or perhaps at most embroiders their button-holes. Obeying law, the maker works like his creator; not obeying law, he is such a fool as heaps a pile of stones and calls it a church.

In the moral world it is different: there a man may clothe in new forms, and for this employ his imagination freely, but he must invent nothing. He may not, for any purpose, turn its laws upside down. He must not meddle with the relations of live souls. The laws of the spirit of man must hold, alike in this world and in any world he may invent. It were no offence to suppose a world in which everything repelled instead of attracted the things around it; it would be wicked to write a tale representing a man it called good as always doing bad things, or a man it called bad as always doing good things: the notion itself is absolutely lawless. In physical things a man may invent; in moral things he must obey—and take their laws with him into his invented world as well.

'You write as if a fairytale were a thing of importance: must it have a meaning?'

It cannot help having some meaning; if it have proportion and harmony it has vitality, and vitality is truth. The beauty may be plainer in it than the truth, but without the truth the beauty could not be, and the fairytale would give no delight. Everyone, however, who feels the story, will read its meaning after his own nature and development: one man will read one meaning in it, another will read another.

'If so, how am I to assure myself that I am not reading my own meaning into it, but yours out of it?'

Why should you be so assured? It may be better that you should read your meaning into it. That may be a higher operation of your intellect than the mere reading of mine out of it: your meaning may be superior to mine.

'Suppose my child ask me what the fairytale means, what am I to say?'

If you do not know what it means, what is easier than to say so? If you do see a meaning in it, there it is for you to give him. A genuine work of art must mean many things; the truer its art, the more things it will mean. If my drawing, on the other hand, is so far from being a work of art that it needs THIS IS A HORSE written under it, what can it matter that neither you nor your child should know what it means? It is there not so much to convey a meaning as to wake a meaning. If it do not even wake an interest, throw it aside. A meaning may be there, but it is not for you. If, again, you do not know a horse when you see it, the name written under it will not serve you much. At all events, the business of the painter is not to teach zoology.

But indeed your children are not likely to trouble you about the meaning. They find what they are capable of finding, and more would be too much. For my part, I do not write for children, but for the childlike, whether of five, or fifty, or seventy-five.

A fairytale is not an allegory. There may be allegory in it, but it is not an allegory. He must be an artist indeed who can, in any mode, produce a strict allegory that is not a weariness to the spirit. An allegory must be Mastery or Moor-ditch.*

A fairytale, like a butterfly or a bee, helps itself on all sides, sips at every wholesome flower, and spoils not one. The true fairytale is, to my mind, very like the sonata.* We all know that a sonata means something; and where there is the faculty of talking with suitable vagueness, and choosing metaphor sufficiently loose, mind may approach mind, in the interpretation of a sonata, with the result of a more or less contenting consciousness of sympathy. But if two or three men sat down to write each what the sonata meant to him, what approximation to definite idea would be the result? Little enough—and that little more than needful. We should find it had roused related, if not identical, feelings, but probably not one common thought. Has the sonata therefore failed? Had it undertaken to convey, or ought it to be expected to impart anything defined, anything notionally recognizable?

'But words are not music; words at least are meant and fitted to carry a precise meaning!'

It is very seldom indeed that they carry the exact meaning of any user of them! And if they can be so used as to convey definite meaning, it does not follow that they ought never to carry anything else. Words are live things that may be variously employed to various ends. They can convey a scientific fact, or throw a shadow of her child's dream on the heart of a mother. They are things to put together like the pieces of a dissected map, or to arrange like the notes on a stave. Is the music in them to go for nothing? It can hardly help the definiteness of a meaning: is it therefore to be disregarded? They have length, and breadth, and outline: have they nothing to do with depth? Have they only to describe, never to impress? Has nothing any claim to their use but the definite? The cause of a child's tears may be altogether un-definable: has the mother therefore no antidote for his vague misery? That may be strong in colour which has no evident outlines. A fairytale, a sonata, a gathering storm, a limitless night, seizes you and sweeps you away: do you begin at once to wrestle with it and ask whence its power over you, whither it is carrying you? The law of each is in the mind of its composer; that law makes one man feel this way, another man feel that way. To one the sonata is a world of odour and beauty, to another of soothing only and sweetness. To one, the cloudy rendezvous is a wild dance, with a terror at its heart; to another, a majestic march of heavenly hosts, with Truth in their centre pointing their course, but as yet restraining her voice. The greatest forces lie in the region of the uncomprehended.

I will go farther.—The best thing you can do for your fellow, next to rousing his conscious, is—not to give him things to think about, but to wake things up that are in him; or say, to make him think things for himself. The best Nature does for us is to work in us such moods in which thoughts of high import arise. Does any aspect of Nature wake but one thought? Does she ever suggest only one definite thing? Does she make any two men in the same place at the same moment think the same thing? Is she therefore a failure, because she is not definite? Is it nothing that she rouses the something deeper than the understanding—the power that underlies thoughts? Does she not set feeling, and so thinking at work? Would it be better that she did this after one fashion and not after many fashions? Nature is mood-engendering, thought-provoking: such ought the sonata, such ought the fairytale to be.

'But a man may then imagine in your work what he pleases, what you never meant!'

Not what he pleases, but what he can. If he be not a true man, he will draw evil out of the best; we need not mind how he treats any work of art! If he be a true man, he will imagine true things: what matter whether I meant them or not? They are there none the less that I cannot claim putting them there! One difference between God's work and man's is, that, while God's work cannot mean more than he meant, man's must mean more than he meant. For in everything that God has made, there is layer upon layer of ascending significance; also he expresses the same thought in higher and higher kinds of that thought: it is God's things, his embodied thoughts, which alone a man has to use, modified and adapted to his own purposes, for the expression of his thoughts; therefore he cannot help his words and figures falling into such combinations in the mind of another as he had himself not foreseen, so many are the thoughts allied to every other thought, so many are the relations involved in every figure, so many the facts hinted in every symbol. A man may well himself discover truth in what he wrote; for he was dealing all the time with things that came from thoughts beyond his own.

'But surely you would explain your idea to one who asked you?'

I say again, if I cannot draw a horse, I will not write THIS IS A HORSE under what I foolishly meant for one. Any key to a work of imagination would be nearly, if not quite, as absurd. The tale is there, not to hide, but to show: if it show nothing at your window, do not open your door to it; leave it out in the cold. To ask me to explain, is to say, 'Roses! Boil them, or we won't have them!' My tales may not be roses, but I will not boil them.

So long as I think my dog can bark, I will not sit up to bark for him.

If a writer's aim be logical conviction, he must spare not logical pains, not merely to be understood, but to escape being misunderstood; where his object is to move by suggestion, to cause to imagine, then let him assail the soul of his reader as the wind assails an æolian harp.* If there be music in my reader, I would gladly wake it. Let fairytale of mine go for a firefly that now flashes, now is dark, but may flash again. Caught in a hand which does not love its kind, it will turn to an insignificant, ugly thing, that can neither flash nor fly.

The best way with music, I imagine, is not to bring the forces of our intellect to bear upon it, but to be still and let it work on that part of us for whose sake it exists. We spoil countless precious things by intellectual greed. He who will be a man, and will not be a child, must—he cannot help himself—become a little man, that is, a dwarf. He will, however, need no consolation, for he is sure to think himself a very large creature indeed.

If any strain of my 'broken music'* make a child's eyes flash, or his mother's grow for a moment dim,* my labour will not have been in vain.

LAURENCE HOUSMAN

'Introduction' to *Gammer Grethel's Fairy Tales* (1905)

THE true end and object of a fairy tale—if that can be said to have an object which moves by instinct to its goal—is the expression of the joy of living. There begins and ends the morality of the fairy tale: its value consists in its optimism. So for the true and unpolluted air of fairyland we have to go back to the old and artless tales of a day purer and simpler than our own; purer because so wholly unconcerned with any question of morals, simpler because so wholly unconscious of its simplicity.

Herein lies the superiority of Grimm's Gammer Grethel Tales to any that can be given us by modern writers, even to those of Hans Andersen,* whose morals are always pointed, whose simplicities are always studied to humorous effect. When, in Hans Andersen's 'Fellow Travellers,'* for instance, the poor youth, knocking at the door of the palace, hears the king say, 'Come in!' we know well enough that the author means us to smile; but when in a true folk-tale, like that of the 'Fox's Brush,'* the king causes the apples of his orchard to be counted each night 'lest any of them should be stolen,' we know equally well that the author is making in grim earnest for the development of his tale.

Many years ago Ruskin, in an introduction to Edgar Taylor's translation from Grimm, and Cruikshank's illustrations, drew the distinction between old and new which no literary art can disguise. 'In the best stories recently written for the young there is,' he declares, 'a taint which it is not easy to define, but which inevitably follows from the author addressing himself to children bred in school-rooms and drawing-rooms instead of fields and woods—children whose favourite amusements are premature imitations of the vanities of elder people, and whose conceptions of beauty are dependent partly on costliness of dress. The fairies who interfere in the fortunes of these little ones are apt to be resplendent chiefly in millinery and satin slippers, and appalling more by their airs than by their enchantments.' And he goes on to note how far more congruous in style to the genuine spirit of fairy-tale are Taylor's rough and hearty translation and Cruikshank's illustrations than the more subtle and refined forms produced in the present day.

It is, indeed, the high and singular merit of Cruikshank's designs that they have secured so closely the racy touch of the original, so that his pictures have a sort of guiding influence, telling us what considerations to lay aside and what fond imaginations to revive in order to recover the delights of that out-dated world. I remember when, as a child, I used to think the picture of Snowdrop* in her glass coffin the most beautiful of all imaginable things, and looking at its crude outlines to-day I find no difficulty in recovering the essential charm of its romance. Moreover, I am still heartily of opinion that the gardener's son riding on the fox's brush, and Thumbling the Dwarf straddling on the giant's palm,* are the two best fairy-tale illustrations I have ever seen. And the clear reason is that they are so honestly and unaffectedly at one with the spirit which brought fairy tales to life, and makes all their wonders seem probable, approaching them with that tireless mind of adventurous innocence which does not know better—because it does not know worse.

It is this same atmosphere or attitude of mind which puts to rights even the less admirable elements of the old fairy-tale, whereat timorous moralists now-a-days look askance. Where heads come on and off as easily as saucepan lids, in a world gaily divided between the quite good and the quite bad, a little savagery does no harm; it does but give a tingle of warmth to the blood that ensures good feeding for the brain, and I imagine that the ruthless morals of the fairy-tale have no more made children crueller than they have made them in actual fact braver. But they give quick food—the fresh meat of the hunter—to the imagination, and have helped to make the world of romance become more real at a tender age.

That is the true value of the fairy-tale: it has, for a time at least, in the lives of most of us, put foolish fact in its proper perspective, persuasively voicing the scientific truth, which the routine of experience inclines us to forget, that existence is merely thought. And if the fairy-tale can go on doing that, its value increases rather than diminishes alongside of the harsh and obscuring effects of modern civilisation.

Happy is the man who will still cut the unopened page eager to see again how a fairy-tale that he knows well achieves its end, for it means that he has still the child's delight in a tale that is thrice told; and while he keeps that, his possessions may be small in the eyes of the world, but 'his reward is with him.'*

EXPLANATORY NOTES

JAKOB AND WILHELM GRIMM, *Rumpel-Stilts-kin*

Edgar Taylor's translation of 'Rumpel-Stilts-kin' ('Rumpelstilzchen' in the Grimms' original) appeared in *German Popular Stories, Translated from the Kinder- und Haus Märchen, Collected by M. M. Grimm, From Oral Tradition* (London: Baldwyn, 1823), 213–17. The stories were illustrated by George Cruikshank, one of the greatest graphic artists of the century, known for his caricatures and his illustrations. He collaborated with Pierce Egan (1772–1849) on *Life In London* (1820–1) and illustrated Charles Dickens's (1812–70) *Sketches by Boz* (1836) and *Oliver Twist* (1837–8) and Harriet Beecher Stowe's (1811–96) *Uncle Tom's Cabin* (1853).

Taylor's translation is rather free (for instance, the detail that the king was from the start avaricious is not explicitly stated in the original, and the little man in the German text is by no means 'droll' and never the heroine's 'little friend'). Moreover the English text reads less vividly than the German, at times transposing dialogue into narrative description. Yet Taylor's translation influenced the Grimm brothers themselves, demonstrating that their folk tales might have a popular as well as an academic audience. In the notes to *German Popular Stories* (p. 239), Taylor remarks that 'We remember to have heard a similar story from Ireland in which the song ran,

> "Little does my Lady wot
> That my name is Trit-a-Trot."'

In its essentials the tale is one common to most European countries; it formed the subject for Edward Clodd's *Tom Tit Tot: An Essay on Savage Philosophy in Folk-Tale* (1898) (see Introduction, pp. xiv–xv). In the German original the queen first tries the names 'Kaspar, Melchior, Balzer'; in other words, a version of the names of the three Magi who come bearing gifts to the infant Jesus Christ. The original ends horrifically, not comically, when, in his efforts to pull his leg out of the hole, Rumpelstilzchen tears himself in two.

HANS CHRISTIAN ANDERSEN, *The Princess and the Peas*

The text for this tale comes from Andersen's *A Danish Story-Book* (London: Joseph Cundall, 1846) (there are no page numbers in this volume). Working from German versions of Andersen's text, the story was translated by Charles Boner (1815–70), with 'numerous illustrations by the Count Pocci'. Born in Bath, then in his youth a tutor to the painter John Constable's (1776–1837) children, Boner spent much of his adult life in Germany. Count Franz Graf von Pocci (1807–76) was a court official at the court of King Ludwig I of Bavaria, but also a noted painter, composer, poet, shadow puppeteer, and the author of many fairy-tale plays for children. In Andersen's original version, the princess lies upon a single pea.

ROBERT SOUTHEY, *The Story of the Three Bears*

Robert Southey (1774–1843) was a poet, biographer, and man of letters. A radical in his youth (he planned an abortive utopian 'pantisocratic' society in America with his friend, Samuel Taylor Coleridge), in later life Southey became a high Tory, a supporter of the Established Church, a despiser of industrial progress, and a Poet Laureate happy to sing the praises of the monarchy; as such he was ruthlessly mocked by the younger generation of 'Romantic' poets, most notably Lord Byron. Although his poetry is now almost completely unread, at the time such works as *Thalaba the Destroyer* (1801) and *Madoc* (1805) were influential. (Apparenttly Percy Bysshe Shelley (1792–1822) knew much of *Thalaba* by heart.) Now if Southey is read at all it is as the author of an excellent *Life of Nelson* (1813) and as the man who first wrote down the story of 'The Three Bears'.

The text presented here is from volume iv of Southey's anonymous Shandyesque miscellany *The Doctor* (London: Longman, Rees, Orme, Brown, Green and Longman, 1837), 318–26, where it is presented as coming from 'the Doctor's' illiterate uncle (a 'half-idiot' as the reviewer John Gibson Lockhart (1794–1854) referred to him). The Doctor sets it down with the thought that if a book is to be universal it should be read not only in the library, the boudoir, or the drawing room, but also contain something suitable for the nursery (pp. 315–16). The tale was told to the Doctor as a child, and he has since told it to children himself, and clearly intends his readers to do likewise. Southey's text was the first properly published version of the tale of 'The Three Bears', but the Poet Laureate was not the originator of the story. Despite the origin in childhood presented in *The Doctor* itself, it has been suggested that Southey heard the story in the late summer of 1813 from an acquaintance, the Poor Law reformer George Nicholls (Mark Storey, *Robert Southey, A Life* (Oxford: Oxford University Press, 1997), 225, 326). Nicholls later wrote his own version of the story in rhyming couplets, where, however, he explicitly suggests that 'The Doctor' is the story's 'original Concoctor'. Various independent analogous versions have been discovered, including some where the place of the little old woman is taken by a fox. It was Southey's version that rendered the story popular, and the alterations that entered the tale stem from a reaction to his telling. These changes include replacing the little old woman with a young girl called 'Silver-Hair' (by Joseph Cundall in *The Treasury of Pleasure Books for Young Children* (1849)), the transformation of the three bears into a Father, Mother, and Baby bear (*Mother Goose's Fairy Tales* (1878)), and finally, around 1904, the metamorphosis of the little girl into 'Goldilocks'.

11 *A tale . . . philosophers*: slightly misquoted from George Gascoigne's (c.1534–77) blank-verse satire *The Steele Glas* (1576) (lines 24–5).

13 *bolster*: the firm under-pillow that extends across the top of the bed, on which softer pillows can be laid.

14 *House of Correction*: a building intended for the incarceration and punishment of offenders.

JOHN RUSKIN, *The King of the Golden River*

John Ruskin (1819–1900) stands as one of the great 'sages' of the Victorian period, a man who combined the position of the greatest and most influential art critic of his day with the role of social critic, moral guardian and guide, and dispenser of wisdom on matters of economics, politics, and the relations between men and women. His artistic and political instincts were opposed to Victorian modernity, to industrialism, and to the effects of an unfettered capitalism. In 1848, Ruskin married Euphemia Chalmers Gray, the first reader of *The King of the Golden River*; in 1854, the marriage was annulled on the grounds of non-consumption. In 1858, he became infatuated with the 11-year-old Rose La Touche; in 1866, when she was 18, he proposed marriage to her. She and her father disapproved of Ruskin's religious views (Ruskin having lost his religious faith in midlife), and no marriage took place. In 1875, she died, insane. Ruskin spent much of his last years in the Lake District, at his house, Brantwood, on Coniston Water. There he worked on the unfinished *Praeterita* (1885–9), one of the greatest nineteenth-century autobiographies. From 1875 he endured periodic attacks of madness; his last years were given over to a sombre and dejected silence. Ruskin's most important books of art criticism are *Modern Painters* (5 vols., 1843 and 1860), *The Seven Lamps of Architecture* (1849), and *The Stones of Venice* (3 vols., 1851–3). His works of social criticism include *Unto This Last* (1860), *Sesame and Lilies* (1865), and *The Storm Cloud of the Nineteenth Century* (1884).

In his autobiography, John Ruskin interrupts his account of the writing of *The King of the Golden River* with a somewhat tempered appreciation of Charles Dickens. About the story itself, he says the following:

> The *King of the Golden River* was written to amuse a little girl; and being a fairly good imitation of Grimm and Dickens, mixed with a little true Alpine feeling of my own, has been rightly pleasing to nice children, and good for them. But it is totally valueless, for all that. I can no more write a story than compose a picture. (John Ruskin, *Praeterita*, vol. II, ch. iv, sect. 64 (New York and London: Everyman's Library, 2005), 269)

The young girl in question was the 12-year-old Euphemia ('Effie') Gray, his later wife. Although he was challenged to write the story in 1841, it remained unpublished for another ten years. The story's title recalls the story by the Brothers Grimm, 'Der König vom goldenen Berg' ('The King of the Golden Mountain').

Although he chose never to publish it, in the manuscript Ruskin adds the following epilogue:

> GENTLE READER,—Many and various are the opinions of the old people of the valley respecting the more mysterious of the circumstances above related—every old lady having a particular theory of her own—respecting the texture and price per yard of the King of the Golden River's doublet, which point is sometimes disputed to a late hour on Christmas nights—without arriving at any distinct conclusion,—there being no record

among the haberdashers of the district of having ever had any such stuff in their possession. Nor is the story ever related without many and edifying comments from the mater—with regard to the nature and consequences of the various trials to which the three brothers were exposed, and misty conjectures respecting the probable consequences of their having yielded to the first, second, or third appeals to their pity—which have at different times exercised the acumen of clerks of three several parishes—without the attainment of any absolute result. But the current opinions are, that the King of the Golden River did himself assume the shapes which were seen on their journey by the brothers, that he in each instance assumed shapes more and more calculated to excite their pity—that it was not without three *appeals* of increasing strength, and all useless, that the doom of death was inflicted on the two elder brothers—nor without three *diminishing* in their claims that the full reward was bestowed on Gluck. I have also heard it eagerly maintained by imaginative disputants that had the elder brothers yielded to even the last of the appeals made to them, they would not have perished though their rejection of the first rendered it impossible to receive reward, and that had little Gluck passed even by the *dog* without pity, he would not have succeeded in his design, although his previous charities might have preserved him from death. But respecting all these points—as being still in dispute—you will do well to form your own conclusions. (from *The Works of John Ruskin*, ed. E. T. Cook and Alexander Wedderburn (London: George Allen, 1903), i. 348)

The copy-text of the tale used here is that of the ninth edition (George Allen, 1888). Although the type was reset for this volume, it otherwise reproduces the first edition which, while dated 1851, was in fact published anonymously on 21 December 1850 in London by Smith, Elder & Co., with illustrations by Richard Doyle (1824–83). The book's full title was: *The King of the Golden River; or, The Black Brothers: A Legend of Stiria*. The book was a great success and went into three editions within a year of publication. Dick Doyle was one of the greatest of Victorian illustrators and fairy painters; from 1843 to 1850, he worked regularly for *Punch*; he produced illustrations for such notable classics as Charles Dickens's *The Chimes* (1845), William Makepeace Thackeray's *Rebecca and Rowena* (1850) and *The Newcomes* (1854/5), and Thomas Hughes's *The Scouring of the White Horse* (1859). His great masterpiece is his book of fairy pictures, *In Fairyland* (London: Longman, Green, Reader and Dyer, 1870).

15 *Stiria*: otherwise known as Styria (and written as such on the cover of the first edition), or Steiermark, a small region in south-eastern Austria, bordering now on modern Slovenia.

Schwartz, Hans, and Gluck: all Germanic names, of course, with Schwartz suggesting *Schwarz*, or black, and Gluck perhaps summoning up the German word for 'glug', and therefore the sound of water, as might be thought apt in a tale about a river and thirst. However, Gluck also closely resembles *Glück*, the German word for luck and happiness.

Hans is a common German name that features in several of the Grimms' fairy tales, most notably 'Der gescheite Hans' (Clever Hans) and 'Der starke Hans' (Strong Hans).

17 *four-feet-six . . . three feet long*: that is, the little man is approximately 137 centimetres tall, and his feather is some 91 centimetres long.

a 'swallow-tail': a colloquial term for a dress-coat with tails forked and sometimes tapered like that of a swallow; it first came into fashion in the Regency period.

20 *the string*: as can be seen in the illustration, the roasting mutton is hanging above the fireplace by a string.

25 *Rhenish*: a wine from the Rhine region.

29 *vespers*: the church service of evensong, very likely at this period an act of worship with Roman Catholic overtones.

WILLIAM MAKEPEACE THACKERAY, *The Rose and the Ring*

William Makepeace Thackeray (1811–63) was born in Calcutta, where his father worked as a Collector for the East India Company. He embarked on a legal career, but soon gave it up in order to be a journalist and miscellaneous writer. He published numerous essays, pastiches, stories, sketches, and articles, for such newspapers and periodicals as the *Morning Chronicle*, the *New Monthly Magazine*, *The Times*, and *Punch*. In 1836, Thackeray married Isabella Shawe. They had three daughters, one of whom, Anne Thackeray Ritchie, grew up to be a successful novelist, memoirist, and the author of some volumes of parodic fairy tales. (In her book of essays *Blackstick Papers* (1908), Lady Ritchie adopts the persona of Fairy Blackstick, one of the leading characters in her father's *The Rose and the Ring*.) In 1840, Isabella Thackeray suffered a mental breakdown from which she never recovered. Thackeray is now remembered chiefly as one of the Victorian period's greatest novelists, the author of *Vanity Fair* (1847–8), *Pendennis* (1848–50), and *The History of Henry Esmond* (1852), among others.

The origin of *The Rose and the Ring*, begun during a sojourn in Rome, is described by Anne Thackeray Ritchie:

> We wanted Twelfth Night characters, and we asked my father to draw them. The pictures were to be shaken up in a lottery . . . My father drew the King for us, the Queen, Prince Giglio, the Prime Minister, Madame Gruffanuff. The little painted figures remained lying on the table after the children were gone, and as he came up and looked at them, he began placing them in order and making a story to fit them. (Anne Thackeray Ritchie, 'Biographical Introduction', in *The Works of William Makepeace Thackeray* (London: Smith, Elder & Co., 1899), vol. ix, pp. lv–lvi)

In tandem with *The Newcomes*, Thackeray worked on his fairy tale through July until Wednesday, 1 November 1854, when he finished the text—perhaps completing the drawings at midnight two days later (To Mrs Carmichael-Smyth,

Explanatory Notes

7–8 November 1854, *The Letters and Private Papers of William Makepeace Thackeray*, ed. Gordon Ray (London: Oxford University Press, 1946), iii. 396). The original manuscript of *The Rose and the Ring*, which contains many differences from the published version, is held in the Collection of Literary and Historical Manuscripts at the Morgan Library in New York.

The Rose and the Ring first appeared, with a pink pictorial cover, in December 1854, published by Smith, Elder, & Co., though it was post-dated by one year on the title page as 1855 (a practice that occurred with all Thackeray's Christmas books). The pen name M. A. Titmarsh was, for Thackeray, a long-standing one. It was rapidly reprinted, and the copy-text followed here is that of the 'Second Edition', 1855. The story contains many charming illustrations by Thackeray, of which a selection is included here. While he was working on it in February 1854, he wrote in his diary, 'Drew Fairy Tale', suggesting the primacy in his mind of the pictures—the things which, after all, inspired the text ('Diary for 1854', *Letters*, ed. Ray, iii. 673). Henry James described the text as 'a book of plates, so to speak, "before the letter"' (Henry James, *William Wetmore Story and His Friends* (London: William Blackwood & Sons, 1903), i. 286–7). Thackeray illustrated many of his works, and although the illustrations for his previous Christmas books were redrawn by other hands, it seems likely that in the case of *The Rose and the Ring* he prepared the wood-blocks for the engravings himself: 'I have done a mort of wood-blocks though for Giglio and Bulbo, and am improving in them I think' (To Anne Thackeray, 28 August 1854, *Letters*, ed. Ray, iii. 385; entry for 31 October in 'Diary for 1854', *Letters*, ed. Ray, iii. 677). The running headlines were in the form of rhyming couplets, of which the pair that ran across the first four pages gives a flavour: 'Royal folks at breakfast time. | Awful consequence of crime! | Ah, I fear, King Valoroso, | that your conduct is but so-so!'

38 *in a foreign city . . . English children*: Thackeray began writing *The Rose and the Ring* in Rome, where it was read to a convalescent young girl.

Twelfth-Night characters: this combines the tradition of Mummers' plays with St George, the Turkish Knight (obviously of crucial importance here in a tale written during the Crimean War and set in ancient Turkey), Father Christmas, and others. Given the pantomime context of Thackeray's story, he may also be referring to the standard figures of the imported Italian drama of *commedia dell'arte*, pantomime and harlequinade: the silent Harlequin (Giglio), the clown (Bulbo), and the beloved Columbine (Rosalba).

Piano Nobile: (Italian) literally 'noble storey'; usually the first floor of a house where the reception rooms are.

FIRE-SIDE PANTOMIME: traditionally these were staged each year on the day after Christmas Day. All his life Thackeray was an enthusiast for the Christmas pantomimes, and for pantomime in general—such plays being performed also at other times of the year. Thackeray marks out his text as a pastiche literary fairy tale infused with the ways in which fairy tale operated in pantomime, melding together an ultimately playful

Explanatory Notes 411

melodrama, the harlequinade, a love story, comedy, Christmas festivity, and the presence of a benign supernatural element.

Rodwell Regis: there is no 'Rodwell Regis', but the Dorset villages of Rodwell and Wyke Regis were neighbours. Wyke Regis was then separate from nearby Weymouth, but now forms one of its suburbs. The name 'Rodwell', of course, picks up the disciplinary implications held in the name of the fictional teacher, 'Dr. Birch'; the reader may be reminded of the biblical injunction that 'He that spareth his rod hateth his son; but he that loveth him chasteneth him betimes' (Proverbs, 13: 24).

39 *M. A. TITMARSH*: Thackeray had used this pseudonym before, including for his Christmas book, *Mrs. Perkins's Ball* (1846). Thackeray sometimes jokingly pretended that Mr Titmarsh was someone else altogether (as in a letter to James Hain Friswell, 10 December 1854, *Letters*, ed. Ray, iii. 405).

Valoroso XXIV, King of Paflagonia: *valoroso* means valiant, or brave, in Italian. Paphlagonia (Italian, Paflagonia) was in ancient times the area of north-central Anatolia on the Black Sea coast. In Sir Philip Sidney's *New Arcadia* (1590), Thackeray would have found the story of the 'Paphlagonian unkind king', the source for the 'Gloucester plot' in William Shakespeare's (1564–1616) *King Lear* (*c*.1605). Therefore in addition to its Black Sea links, crucial to the story's oblique engagement with the Crimean War, the use of Paphlagonia is also one of the many ways that *The Rose and the Ring* alludes to Shakespeare's tragedies of usurpation or the wrongful assumption of royal power.

Bulbo . . . Padella: 'Bulbo' may refer in Italian to the fin under the hull of a boat that provides stability, or simply be the word for 'bulb' in the sense of 'tulip bulb'. *A padella* is a pan, specifically a frying pan (Italian).

Crim Tartary: the Crimea, on the north coast of the Black Sea, a region inhabited by the Crimean Tartars. In English culture, the word 'tartar' had accrued connotations of thievery, violence, and vagabondage, but also of strength and power. Thackeray's use of the term here arises most likely as an allusion to the Crimean War (October 1853–February 1856) in which Britain, France, and the Ottoman Empire fought against the Russians, chiefly in the Crimean peninsula.

40 *Angelica*: this ironically contains 'angelic', of course, but may also refer to the common herb of the same name, one often supposed to offer an antidote to poison.

Rimbombamento: in Italian, an archaic or consciously poetic way of saying 'roar'; from the Italian verb *rimbombare*, meaning rumble (as in the rumbling of a storm).

Giglio: the hero's name is the Italian word for 'lily'.

Glumboso: cod Italian, incorporating, of course, the word, 'glum'.

41 *G. P. R. James*: George Payne Rainsford James (1801–60), English novelist, the author of numerous action-packed historical novels written in a thoroughgoing fustian style, such as *Richlieu, A Tale of France* (1829), *Arabella*

Stuart (1844), and *Ticonderoga* (1854). In *Punch's Prize Novelists* (1847), Thackeray chose James (under the name 'Barbazure') as one of the novelists he good-naturedly parodies.

41 *Nantz or Cognac*: Nantz is a brandy produced in the Nantes region of France.

"Uneasy lies the head that wears a crown!": the line famously uttered at the close of his insomniac soliloquy by the usurping Bolingbroke, now King Henry IV, in *Henry IV Part Two*, III.i.31.

blank verse: the unrhymed iambic pentameter verse line, associated in particular with Elizabethan and Jacobean drama, and therefore the plays of Shakespeare.

Savio: wise, conscientious, learned (Italian) (now more usually, *saggio*).

44 *Mangnal's Questions*: a reference to Richmal Mangnall (1769–1820), *Historical and Miscellaneous Questions for the Use of Young People* (1798), a textbook for classroom teaching conducted on the somewhat mechanical principle of set questions and answers. The text was used very widely, and went through many editions and revisions.

Cappadocian, Samothracian: Cappadocia was an ancient kingdom of Asia Minor, in central Anatolia in modern Turkey; Samothrace is an island in the northern Aegean Sea.

Gruffanuff: the name is, of course, a pun on 'gruff enough', and would perhaps have sounded comically Russian to mid-Victorian ears.

45 *necromancer*: that is, a practitioner of 'necromancy', a form of magic that involves the prediction of the future through communication with the dead.

46 *this Princess to sleep . . . vipers and toads from another's*: a reference to Charles Perrault's (1628–1703) fairy tale 'Les Fées' ('The Fairies') from his *Histoires ou Contes du temps passé* (1697), in which (as in *The Rose and the Ring*) the humble are exalted and the haughty are brought low. The tale was often translated as 'Diamonds and Toads'. In the story, a fairy repays one girl for her kindness by causing diamonds, pearls, and roses to drop from her mouth when she speaks; and punishes her older sister for her rudeness by having toads and snakes fall from her mouth whenever she attempts to talk.

Fortunatus's purse: according to the German early-modern legend, Fortunatus's purse is magically replenished every time he draws money from it.

CAVOLFIORE: cauliflower (Italian).

ROSALBA: a portmanteau name, combining *rosa* (Italian for 'rose') and *alba* (the Italian for 'dawn' or 'white').

49 *door hall day*: as in the earlier use of 'hold' for 'old', an attempt to render a 'cockney' accent, which elsewhere in the text involves a generous dropping—as well as the addition—of aitches.

Explanatory Notes 413

53 SQUARETOSO: a pun, of course, on 'square-toes', a phrase used for a strict, narrow-minded, and old-fashioned person.

54 KUTASOFF HEDZOFF: a notably Russian-sounding name, punning (via an English approximation of a strong Italian accent) on 'Cuts off heads off'. Field Marshal Mikhail Illarionovich Golenischev-Kutuzov (1745–1813) was a notable Russian military leader, who fought often in the Crimea during the late eighteenth century's Russo-Turkish wars, though he is most famous for his part in the Napoleonic Wars. (He makes a fictional appearance in Leo Tolstoy's *War and Peace* (1869) and is mentioned in Lord Byron's *Don Juan*, canto viii, stanzas 70–2 (1823).)

Grumbuskin: a portmanteau name merging grim, grump, grumble, and buskin (a boot).

the Bear: she refers to a constellation, either Ursa Major (the Great Bear or Charles's Wain) or Ursa Minor (the Little Bear or Little Dipper).

Linnæus: Carolus Linnaeus, the nom de plume of Carl von Linné (1707–78), botanist, zoologist, and the creator of a system of nomenclature for the classification of flora and fauna.

Marmitonio: a marmiton is a scullion, a kitchen-assistant.

55 *King John disliked Prince Arthur*: an allusion to William Shakespeare's *King John* (*c.*1595). John has grasped the British throne and wishes to retain power despite the better claim of his nephew, Prince Arthur (the son of his deceased older brother); he obliquely orders Hubert, a citizen of Angers, to murder the Prince.

56 *Tomaso Lorenzo*: an Italianate version of Sir Thomas Lawrence (1769–1830), the fashionable portrait painter, favourite of George IV, and president of the Royal Academy.

Painter in Ordinary: in an official, and—in this case—a court, capacity.

Acroceraunia: from Latin *acroceraunius* meaning 'high thunderbolt', sometimes used to refer to a mountain range between Epirus and Macedonia.

Poluphloisboio: from ancient Greek *polyphloisbos*, meaning 'loud-roaring', and used in particular (in Homer) for the sound of water crashing on a beach or against the crest of a ship.

Ograria: a pun on the word 'ogre', suggesting the land of ogres.

57 *Circassia*: a region in the Northern Caucasus, of strategic importance during the Crimean War.

58 *Blombodinga*: possibly a pun on 'plum pudding'.

59 *drumsticks . . . pope's nose*: all parts of a chicken (especially a roast one); the pope's nose, more commonly called the 'parson's nose', refers to the chicken's turned-up rear end.

60 *Red Sea or on the Black Sea*: the Crimean War had begun with the question of the rights of Christians, and especially Orthodox versus Catholic control of sacred sites, in the Holy Land (located on the northern side of the Red Sea), though it quickly became a war centred on the Black Sea.

Explanatory Notes

65 *embrasure of a window*: an embrasure is an interior slanting that makes the inner profile of a window larger than that of its outside.

68 *'O mussey!' 'O jemmany!' 'O ciel!'*: 'mussey' suggests 'missy'; 'jemmany' is more usually spelt 'jeminy', a euphemism for 'Jesus'; and 'O ciel' is 'Oh, heavens' in French.

peri . . . bulbul: originating in Persia, a peri is a female spirit, originally demonic, but later imagined as benevolent and beautiful; a bulbul is a kind of thrush associated with Persia, Arabia, and Turkey, sometimes called the 'nightingale of the East' (with perhaps hints of a small pun on 'bauble').

69 *Australia, only it is not yet discovered*: Australia was discovered by Dutch sailors in 1606; a nice example of this story's happy unconcern regarding anachronism.

70 *tow*: the fibre that makes up flax or hemp.

72 *Gaby*: a fool, a simpleton.

73 *Jack Ketch*: a generic name for a hangman, named after Jack (John) Ketch (Catch), d. 1686.

76 *tootsey*: a playful and flirtatious name for a woman's small foot. The *OED* cites *The Rose and the Ring* as the earliest use of this word.

78 *doosid*: that is, deuced, meaning confounded, devilish—an emphatic expletive.

80 *diligence*: the public stagecoach.

82 *Spinachi*: a comic misspelling for spinach (in Italian, it should be *spinaci*).

Articiocchi: an Italianesque version of 'artichokes' (which would in fact be *carciofi* in Italian).

83 *HOGGINARMO*: a pun on 'hog in armour', and perhaps, at a push, 'hog *en amour*' ('hog in love').

84 *appanage*: either a dependent province, or (already thinking of the children they will have together) a province used for the provision of an inheritance for a younger royal child.

85 *chaff*: husks of corn or grain (furthering the image that Padella is like a pecking bird).

Margery Daw: a nursery rhyme character, as in 'See Saw Margery Daw | Johnny shall have a new master', though Thackeray is more likely to be thinking of this rhyme (from I. Opie and P. Opie, *The Oxford Dictionary of Nursery Rhymes* (1951; 2nd edn., Oxford: Oxford University Press, 1997), 297–8):

> See-saw, Margery Daw,
> Sold her bed and lay on the straw;
> Sold her bed and lay upon hay
> And pisky came and carried her away.
> For wasn't she a dirty slut
> To sell her bed and lie in the dirt?

A 'daw' was a colloquial term for an untidy woman or a slattern; a 'pisky' is a pixie. Fairies were commonly said to dislike untidiness, slovenliness, and dirt.

86 *Newgate*: originally Newgate prison in the City of London, but also, as a consequence of its fame, a generic name for any prison.

87 *coupé*: the front (or rear) compartment of a diligence.

muff: a pun on muff in the sense of a fur covering for the hands, and muff in the sense of a foolish, incompetent, and maladroit person.

89 *A blacking-brush and a pot of Warren's jet*: the black boot and stove polish produced by Warren's Blacking Factory at 30, The Strand, London (where, unknown to Thackeray, his friend and fellow novelist Charles Dickens had worked as a child).

Epping butter: a famously delicious butter produced in the area around the market town of Epping in Essex—though in June 1855, it was reported that 'Lard, dripping and other pleasant substances go up to make that Cockney delectability, "Epping Butter"' (report on 'Mr Scholefield's Adulteration Committee' in *Freeman's Journal* (Dublin), 29 June 1855).

Bosforo: Italian for the Bosphorus, or what were then sometimes called the Straits of Constantinople, the narrow strait between Europe and Asia that connects the Black Sea and the Sea of Marmara (known in classical times as the Propontis). It is also an oblique reference to the fact that etymologically both Oxford and Bosphorus refer to a place where oxen may cross a river.

90 *Johnson's Dictionary*: Samuel Johnson's *A Dictionary of the English Language* (1755).

92 *soi-disant*: self-styled, pretended (French).

the wooden spoon: a booby prize for 'wooden heads' awarded to the lowest-placed person; originally a Cambridge University phrase for the very lowest class of degree.

Atavis edite regibus: Latin for 'descendant of kings' (literally, 'born of monarch ancestors'); a quote from the opening line of Roman poet Horace's Ode I.i, addressed to his patron Gaius Maecenas.

Hamlet, Prince of Denmark: the hero, of course, of the play by William Shakespeare (*c*.1600), and another victim of a usurping uncle.

93 *proctors*: in university terms, an elected officer with administrative and disciplinary duties.

drew bridle: to pull back the reins in order to stop a horse, to call a halt.

96 *beef-eaters*: one of the Yeomen of the Guard in the royal household, and one of the Warders of the Tower of London. Like the earlier reference to Newgate, this is another sign that Thackeray is thinking as much of contemporary London as of ancient Crim Tartary.

Wombwell's or Astley's: Wombwell's was a famous travelling menagerie first founded by George Wombwell (1777–1850) (by the time of his death, he was responsible for three separate menageries under his name); Astley's refers to the circus set up by Philip Astley (1742–1814) and carried on by his son, John Astley (1768–1821). Wombwell's beasts were not as tame as the text implies: in 1821, a lion of his (named Wallace) fought and killed a pack of dogs; and in 1850, the teenage 'Lion Queen' (Ellen Blight) was mauled to death by one of Wombwell's tigers.

98 *Elephant and Castle*: originally the sign of a coaching inn at Newington Butts, south of the River Thames, and by the time of Thackeray's writing, part of London. The inn sign is of an elephant with a castle on its back.

pursuivant: here used in the sense of a royal messenger.

demivolte, two semilunes, and three caracols: a set of artificial motions for a horse learnt in a manège, or riding school: a 'demivolte' is a half-turn made with the forelegs raised; a 'semi-lune' would appear not to be a formal dressage term, but presumably indicates a crescent-shaped movement; while a 'caracol' (or 'caracole') is a half-turn or wheel to the right or left side, originally alternately, making a zigzag movement.

99 *Bombardaro*: from the Italian verb *bombardare*, meaning 'to bombard'.

light up the fires and make the pincers hot: possibly a further reference to Shakespeare's *King John* (c.1595), where Hubert, ordered to murder Prince Arthur, and intending to burn out the boy's eyes, orders his fellow executioners, 'Heat me these irons hot . . .' (IV.i.1).

100 *"The man that lays his hand . . . is a villain"*: unidentified.

101 *her album*: there was a great vogue in the early and mid-nineteenth century for the keeping of autographs, mementoes, and memorial verse in albums.

104 *British Grenadier at Alma*: a 'grenadier' was originally a soldier trained to throw grenades, but by the nineteenth century the term was applied to the best (and most impressive-looking) men brought together in a company within a regiment. Given the context though, Thackeray may be referring to the Grenadier Guards, the most senior regiment of the Guards Division. The Battle of Alma (20 September 1854) was the first major battle of the Crimean War, in which Anglo-French forces under Lord Raglan (1788–1855) and General St Arnaud (1801–54) defeated the Russians, led by General Menshikov (1787–1869). The Grenadier Guards acquitted themselves heroically in the battle (including ignoring an order to retire).

105 *Sir Archibald Alison*: Sir Archibald Alison (1792–1867) was a historian and lawyer, the conservative and reactionary author of the cautionary ten-volume *History of Europe During the French Revolution* (1833–42). Among other works, he also published a *Life of Marlborough* (1847; rev. edn., 1852).

if they had been Russians: again, a patriotic reference to the ongoing Crimean War.

Prince Punchikoff: another Russian-sounding pun.

106 *Law bless you!*: an attempt to represent a cockney version of 'the Lord bless you', but also perhaps (given the political interests of the tale), 'the law bless you (as opposed to tyranny)'.

prog: here used in the sense of provisions, food for a meal.

quadrille: a square dance usually performed by four couples.

108 *House of Correction*: see note to p. 14.

Order of Flagellants: this mention of self-punishing monks may offer a brief moment of anti-Catholic propaganda. In Rome, while preparing *The Rose and the Ring*, Thackeray wrote to his mother: 'I have made acquaintance with a convert, an Oxford man whom I like and who interests me . . . And I am trying to pick my Oxford man's brains, & see from his point of view. But it isn't mine: and old Popery & old Paganism seem to me as dead as the other. Wiseman [that is Cardinal Wiseman . . .] I have heard and think him a tawdry Italian Quack' (To Mrs Carmichael-Smyth, 25–8 January 1854, *Letters*, ed. Ray, iii. 337).

111 *Inquisition*: capitalized as here, likely a glancing reference to the Roman Catholic Church's ecclesiastical tribunal, and therefore again something of an anti-Catholic jibe may be implied.

112 *triple-bobmajors*: a triple bob major is a term from bell-ringing, meaning a peal rung on eight bells.

Queen Elizabeth: a reference to Elizabeth I (1553–1603), the so-called 'Virgin Queen'.

GEORGE MACDONALD, *The Golden Key*

George MacDonald (1824–1905) has strong claims to being Victorian Britain's greatest writer of literary fairy tales. He was born in Huntly, Aberdeenshire; his mother died when he was 7 years old. He studied at King's College, Old Aberdeen, spending his summers in the library of an old castle or mansion. Having received his MA in 1845, he moved to London where he worked as a tutor, before entering Highbury Theological College to train as a Congregational minister. In 1850, he was ordained at a chapel in Arundel, Sussex; in 1851, he married Louisa Powell. In May 1853, due to differences with his congregation, MacDonald resigned his place. He and his family moved to Manchester, where he preached and wrote. He would later leave again for London.

His first published works were in verse (*Within and Without* (1855) and *Poems* (1857)), but in 1858 he published his first truly characteristic book, *Phantastes: A Faerie Romance for Men and Women* (1858), a novel-length fantasy in the spirit of Percy Bysshe Shelley's *Alastor* (1816), Novalis's (1772–1801) *Heinrich von Ofterdingen* (1802), and Friedrich de la Motte Fouqué's (1777–1843) *Undine* (1811). Over the next years, MacDonald lectured and wrote a number of novels, but it is for his children's literature that he is remembered, chiefly *At the Back of the North Wind* (1871), *The Princess and the Goblin* (1872), and *The Princess and Curdie* (1883). His last great fantasy specifically for adults is *Lilith* (1895). In addition to his fictions, MacDonald was a notable Christian apologist, as a disbeliever in the doctrine of eternal punishment; among other things, *Lilith* explores the nature of evil and how in the end it wishes to surrender itself to divine love. MacDonald counted Lewis Carroll, John Ruskin, Robert Browning, Alfred Tennyson, William Morris, Edward Burne-Jones, Mark Twain, and his illustrator Arthur Hughes among his friends. In the twentieth century, MacDonald was a great example and a notable inspiration for such writers as G. K. Chesterton, C. S. Lewis, W. H. Auden, and Madeleine L'Engle.

The copy text for 'The Golden Key' derives from George MacDonald, *Dealings With the Fairies* (London: Alexander Strahan, 1867), 248–308. The book is illustrated by Arthur Hughes, the illustrator in a Pre-Raphaelite style of many other key works from the period, including Lord Tennyson's *Enoch Arden* (1865), an edition of Thomas Hughes's *Tom Brown's Schooldays* (originally published 1857; illustrated by Arthur in 1869), and Christina Rossetti's *Sing Song* (1871). He also illustrated MacDonald's *At The Back of the North Wind* and *The Princess and the Goblin*. 'The Golden Key' is the fifth and last fairy tale in *Dealings With the Fairies*; the others are 'The Light Princess' (MacDonald's other short masterpiece), 'The Giant's Heart', 'The Shadows', and 'Cross Purposes'.

118 *an exceeding dislike to untidiness*: see note to p. 85.

Silverhair: see headnote to Southey, 'The Three Bears', p. 406.

130 *aëranth*: this creature and its name are of MacDonald's invention; both elements in the word derive from ancient Greek, *aër* meaning 'air' and *anth* (deriving from anthos) meaning 'flower'.

131 *peeping through the window into the heart of the deep green ocean . . . in answer to the tap of the Old Man of the Sea*: it may not be fanciful to connect this moment to the recent Victorian craze for the aquarium (originally 'vivarium'), a term popularized in 1854 by the naturalist Philip Henry Gosse in his book *The Aquarium: An Unveiling of the Wonders of the Deep Sea*. The link between the Victorian interest in aquaria and the concern with evolutionary theory, including the hypothesis that life on earth might have originated in the oceans, is perhaps also being brought up here. Only a few years previously, Charles Kingsley's *The Water-Babies* (1863) had made a similar connection.

135 *bobbins*: that part of the spinning wheel or loom around which the thread is wound.

Novalis: pseudonym of Georg Philipp Friedrich Freiherr von Hardenberg (1772–1801), the German Romantic poet and philosopher, and the author of a seminal work of fantasy, the unfinished *Heinrich von Ofterdingen* (1802), a masterpiece of the mythopoeic imagination. Among other German Romantic writers (notably Friedrich de la Motte Fouqué,

Jean Paul (1763–1825), and Johann Wolfgang Goethe (1749–1832)) Novalis was central to MacDonald's literary and philosophical interests; his *Phantastes* (1858) begins with a long epigraph from Novalis about the nature of the fairy tale.

DINAH MULOCK CRAIK, *The Little Lame Prince and his Travelling Cloak*

Dinah Maria Craik (née Mulock) (1826–87) was born in Hartshill, a village in Staffordshire, the eldest child of her Nonconformist minister father and schoolmistress mother. Her father, Thomas, was a difficult and irascible man; for part of her childhood he was detained in a lunatic asylum. In 1839, the family moved to London, where her mother, Jane, ran a school. When her mother died in 1845, her father deserted Dinah and her two younger brothers. Mulock became a writer, scoring early successes with *The Ogilvies* (1849) and *Olive* (1850), a passionate tale of a deformed girl. However, her greatest success came with *John Halifax, Gentleman* (1856), a key novel of the mid-Victorian period and an exemplary text exhibiting Victorian moral standards of Christian behaviour. At the age of 40, she married George Lillie Craik (1837–1905), an accountant at the time, but soon afterwards a partner in Alexander Macmillan's publishing firm. Four years later, in 1869, the couple adopted a foundling child, Dorothy. Dinah Craik kept writing, producing further novels, short stories and tales, travel books, poetry, and essays; she is also the author of some of the finest ghost stories of the mid-century. She died of heart failure during preparations for her daughter's wedding.

The copy text is based on Dinah Craik's *The Little Lame Prince and His Travelling Cloak: A Parable For Young and Old* (copyright edition) (Leipzig: Bernhard Tauchnitz, 1874). Craik's name does not feature on the title page; in its place appears, 'By the Author of "John Halifax, Gentleman"'. The book begins with a dedication: 'Inscribed with deep tenderness, to a dear little boy I know'. The first edition contains twenty-four illustrations by J. McL. Ralston, who also illustrated among other works, the Household Edition of Charles Dickens's *A Child's History of England*. While these have some charm, they are ultimately undistinguished—with one notable exception, that is, the striking picture printed in this volume.

142 *Dolorez*: a name, popular particularly in Spain and Spanish-speaking America, meaning 'sorrows', derived from reference to 'Our Lady of Sorrows', the 'Mater Dolorosa' (Latin). There may be a glancing reference to the heroine of Algernon Charles Swinburne's notorious and blasphemous poem 'Dolores (Notre-Dame des Sept Douleurs)', first published in *Poems and Ballads* (1866), in which case the use of the name might be thought of as reinvesting it with its pious associations.

145 *Dolor*: again a name that suggests suffering, pain, grief.

150 *generalissimo*: the supreme commander (originally Italian).

152 *the 'cruel uncle' of 'The Babes in the Wood'*: a reference to the folk tale

'Babes in the Wood', in which (with variations) a wicked uncle hands over his brother's children to murderers to be killed. The killers fall out, and one murders the other. The repentant murderer leaves the children in the woods, while he goes to fetch provisions—though in fact he never returns. The children wander alone and eventually die, their bodies being covered with leaves by the birds of the wood. The earliest printed version is an anonymous ballad, *The Norfolke Gentleman his last Will and Testament, and how hee committed the keeping of his Children to his owne brother, who dealt most wickedly with them* (London, 1640?). In the nineteenth century, the story proliferated in textual form as a ballad, chapbook, pantomime, burlesque, and harlequinade.

153 *one large round tower which rose . . . which there never was*: Prince Dolor's situation might recall the predicament of Segismundo, a prince imprisoned alone in a tower, in the Spanish playwright Pedro Calderón de la Barca's (1600–81) *La vida es sueño* ('Life is a Dream') (1635?). If Craik was indeed evoking Calderón's play, this would be one of several Spanish references in the tale. In 1853, the poet Edward Fitzgerald (1809–83) published a translation of this play (and five others by Calderón); in the same year a rival translation was published by Denis Florence McCarthy (1817–82). Prince Dolor's imprisonment may likewise recall that of the celebrated Kaspar Hauser (1812–33), a German youth reputedly kept locked in a single room, without human contact, from infancy until to the age of approximately 18. The image of Dolor in his tower also calls to mind the fairy story of Rapunzel, a long-haired young woman confined by a witch to a tower without a door.

Irish round towers: from the early fifteenth century until the mid-seventeenth century, these tower houses were built as a defensive strategy by English settlers in Ireland. There are several thousand scattered across the country.

161 *the doldrums*: this originated in the early nineteenth century as a slang term for depression or a settled melancholy, perhaps derived from 'dold' meaning inert, or from 'dull'.

164 *Abracadabra*: a magical word of occult meaning, perhaps originating in the fourth century AD, and once truly used by cabbalists and practitioners of magic. Various etymologies have been suggested, with origins diversely traced to Hebrew, Aramaic, Latin, or Greek. The word became used by magicians and conjurors (on stage and in literature) as an exclamation designed to unleash magical power.

166 '*Cinderella,' or 'Blue-Beard,' or 'Hop-o'-my-Thumb*': three of the most famous classic fairy tales, all gathered in Charles Perrault (1628–1703), *Histoires ou Contes du temps passé* (1697) (as 'Cendrillon, ou La Petite Pantoufle de verre', 'La Barbe bleue', and 'Le Petit Poucet'). 'Le Petit Poucet' was first known in English as 'Little Poucet', but after *Tabart's Collection of Popular Stories for the Nursery* (1804) (translated and edited

Explanatory Notes 421

either by William Godwin (1756–1836) or Mary Jane Godwin (1768–1841), or both), the tale became known as 'Hop 'o My Thumb'.

172 *'a very examining boy'*: this may possibly be meant to recall the heroine of Juliana Horatia Ewing's 'Amelia and the Dwarfs' (1870), who is several times referred to as a 'very observing child'.

174 *the Barmecide's feast which you read of in the 'Arabian Nights'*: a reference to 'The Story of the Barber's Sixth Brother' from *The Thousand and One Nights*, in which the beggarly hero of the tale is apparently offered a generous meal by the wealthy Barmecide, though each dish turns out to be invisible and purely fictive. The beggar happily plays along with the joke, and for doing so is rewarded with friendship, a genuine feast, and riches. The real Barmecides, or Barmakids, were a powerful family of Buddhist origins living in Baghdad during the Abbasid Caliphate (750–1258). In English, due to the influence of the tale, the word 'Barmecide' became used for a person offering the illusion of comfort, or an unreal good.

that supper of Sancho Panza in 'Don Quixote': Cervantes's *Don Quixote* (1605; 1615), where in chapter 47 of the Second Part (also Book III, ch. xv), a physician presents Sancho Panza, the novel's down-to-earth, pragmatic servant, with a series of exquisite dishes. However, all are snatched from him before he can swallow more than a mouthful. The incident was commemorated in a famous engraving by William Hogarth (1697–1764), entitled *Sancho at the Feast Starved by His Physician*; it had more recently been the subject of a painting exhibited in 1868 by Frederick Yeates Hurlstone (1800–69).

180 *steeple-chase*: originally a cross-country horse race with obstacles to be leapt (fences, hedges, ditches, streams) and with a church steeple as the finishing line and goal.

189 *levée*: from French, and originally simply the act of getting out of bed, but used from the seventeenth century onwards to refer to a morning assembly, especially one conducted by a monarch.

193 *'Two little men | Who lay in their bed till the clock struck ten'*: a reference to the nursery rhyme 'Robin and Richard':

> Robin and Richard were two pretty men,
> They lay in bed till the clock struck ten;
> Then up starts Robin and looks at the sky,
> 'Oh, brother Richard, the sun's very high!
> You go before, with the bottle and bag,
> And I will come after on little Jack Nag.'

MARY DE MORGAN, *The Wanderings of Arasmon*

Mary Augusta De Morgan's father, Augustus De Morgan (1806–71), was a professor of mathematics at University College London; her mother was Sophia Frend (1809–92), a writer (on, among other matters, psychical mediumship).

Mary was born in 1850 in London. She was particularly close to one of her six siblings, William De Morgan (1839–1917), with whom she lived from her father's death in 1871 until his marriage in 1887 at a house in Cheyne Row, Chelsea. William was famous for his stained glass and pottery, and, late in life, for his successful novels. Through her brother, Mary was part of the wider Pre-Raphaelite circle; at a Christmas party in 1873, her first fairy tales were told in person to the Burne-Jones children, to the young Rudyard Kipling, and to William Morris's daughters, Jenny and May. Many years later, the stories in her last book would be told in their turn to Margaret Burne-Jones's (1866–1953) own children, Angela, Denis, and Clare Mackail. Mary De Morgan would be at William Morris's bedside through his last illness. She spent her last years in Egypt, where she had travelled to preserve her failing health. While there, she directed a reformatory for children. She died in 1907 in Helouan.

De Morgan is among the very best of the Victorian fairy-tale writers; her output may have been small, but she nonetheless produced some of the finest tales in the genre, including 'The Seeds of Love', 'A Toy Princess', 'The Necklace of Princess Fiorimonde', 'The Wanderings of Arasmon', 'The Heart of Princess Joan', and 'The Windfairies'. She wrote three books of such tales: *On A Pincushion and Other Fairy Tales* (1877) (illustrated by William De Morgan), *The Necklace of Princess Fiorimonde; and Other Stories* (1880), and *The Windfairies and Other Tales* (1900) (delightfully illustrated by Oliver Cockerell (1869–1910)).

The copy-text followed here comes from the first edition of *The Necklace of Princess Fiorimonde; and Other Stories* (London: Macmillan and Co., 1880), 43–78. It is one of seven stories, and comes second in the book, placed between 'The Necklace of Princess Fiorimonde' and 'The Heart of Princess Joan'. The book includes many fine illustrations and designs by the Arts and Crafts socialist and artist Walter Crane (1845–1915). The story closes with a little design, showing a bird flying over a strung harp that is shaped like a crescent moon. The book begins with the following dedication: 'To | My Six Little Nephews and Nieces | These Stories Are Affectionately Dedicated | By | Their Loving Aunt | Mary De Morgan.'

206 *Arasmon and Chrysea*: I have failed to find any connection with the name 'Arasmon'; however, Chrysea certainly suggests the Greek stem *khrūsós*, meaning 'golden', as seems entirely apt considering the character's self-sacrifice and virtue.

JULIANA HORATIA EWING, *The First Wife's Wedding-Ring*

Juliana Horatia Ewing (1841–85) was born in Ecclesfield, near Sheffield, one of eight children born to Alfred Gatty (1813–1903), a Church of England vicar and author, and Margaret Gatty (1809–73), herself a notable amateur natural historian and writer for children (most famous for her rather didactic fairy tales). (Juliana's unusual middle name is explained by the fact that her maternal grandfather, Alexander John Scott, had been chaplain to Horatio Nelson—and had been with the great man at the moment of his death.) Margaret Gatty also

Explanatory Notes 423

wrote a number of domestic stories for children, many of which focused on the doings of her daughter. The teenage Juliana became the model for the storytelling 'Aunt Judy', the hero of several of her mother's books. Later, Margaret Gatty became the editor of the monthly children's periodical *Aunt Judy's Magazine for Young People*, containing natural history, poems, and stories—including many by Juliana. On her mother's death, Juliana took over the editorship with her sister Horatia (later Horatia Eden) (1846–1945). In 1866 Juliana married Alexander Ewing, a badly paid major in the army pay department. The couple lived for a while in New Brunswick, Canada, where Juliana began writing her old-fashioned fairy tales. After two years, they returned to England, living in Aldershot, Manchester, and York. Her husband was posted to Malta in 1879, but Juliana remained behind, kept in England by poor health (a 'neuralgia of the spine' that was more probably cancer). In 1881 Alexander accepted a new post in Ceylon (now Sri Lanka), but two years later returned to England. With Juliana in very bad health, the couple moved to Taunton, where she died in May 1885.

Ewing's most important works were written for or about children, including *Six to Sixteen* (1872) (a novel about an Anglo-Indian orphan girl that may have influenced Frances Hodgson Burnett's (1849–1924) *The Secret Garden* (1911)) and *The Brownies and Other Tales* (1870) (including 'The Land of Lost Toys', 'Amelia and the Dwarfs', 'Christmas Crackers', and the title story, which inspired Robert Baden-Powell (1857–1941) when forming the Girl Guide movement). In *Old-Fashioned Fairy Tales* (1882), her tales are noticeably plainer and closer in their effect to the folk tales collected by the Brothers Grimm than most stories of the time. A committed Anglican, the moral values that permeate her work are unobtrusive, but unmistakable; her work influenced both Rudyard Kipling and E. Nesbit.

The copy-text is from the first edition of Ewing's *Old-Fashioned Fairy Tales* (London: Society for Promoting Christian Knowledge; New York: Pott, Young & Co., 1882), 155–65. The stories in the volume had all previously appeared in *Aunt Judy's Magazine for Young People*; they include 'The Neck: A Legend of a Lake' and 'The Ogre Courting'. The book has an extraordinary coloured cover by Richard André (1834–1907), with rather spooky fairies, mushrooms and toadstools, a frog, and a disgruntled jester. André specialized in fairy-tale illustrations, making pictures for other books by Ewing, an edition of Grimm's household tales (1890), and versions of *Jack and the Bean Stalk* and *The Three Bears* (both 1888), among many others. Ewing's book also featured illustrations by Alfred Walter Bayes (1831–1909) and Gordon Frederick Browne (1858–1932). Browne was the son of Hablot Knight Browne (1815–82), also known as 'Phiz', one of Charles Dickens's most faithful collaborators; he also illustrated Edith Nesbit's *The Story of the Treasure Seekers* (1899) and Andrew Lang's *Prince Prigio* (1889), among many other works.

OSCAR WILDE, *The Selfish Giant*

Oscar Fingal O'Flahertie Wilde (1854–1900) was a Victorian man of letters— essayist, lecturer, critic, editor, poet, playwright, short-story writer, a one-off novelist, and the creator of some of the finest late nineteenth-century fairy stories. Unlike most men of letters, however, his life itself became a public myth, the record of a man first celebrated and then destroyed by the public he courted. (Indeed elements of Wilde's mythic persona perhaps appear, transformed, in Kenneth Grahame's tale, 'The Reluctant Dragon'.)

Wilde was born in Dublin and educated at Trinity College Dublin, and then at Magdalen College, Oxford. Soon after graduation Wilde became a notorious figure on the London literary and social scene as a wit, a dandy, and an apostle of aestheticism. In 1883, he married Constance Lloyd; they had two children, Cyril (born 1885) and Vivian (later Vyvyan) (born 1886); they were to be an audience for some of Wilde's first fairy tales (though 'The Happy Prince', one of the very best of them, was first told at Cambridge in November 1885, while Cyril was still a baby). In the late 1880s Wilde wrote his first truly excellent works, informed by humour, paradox, anger at injustice, tenderness, and irony: the short stories 'The Canterville Ghost' and 'Lord Arthur Savile's Crime', the poem 'The Harlot's House', a series of brilliant essays, and a collection of fairy stories in the Hans Andersen mode, *The Happy Prince and other Tales* (1888). Through his mother's intervention, at the age of 6 Wilde had been baptized (for a second time) as a Roman Catholic; he maintained throughout his life a stance of mingled fascination with and hostility towards Christianity—though in these fairy tales, as in his last works, his unorthodox Catholic sensibilities are most on display. His socialism, or social conscience, is also palpably present; Wilde sent a copy of the book to Toynbee Hall, a philanthropic institution in Whitechapel, in London's impoverished East End.

In July 1890, Wilde's decadent masterpiece *The Picture of Dorian Gray* appeared in *Lippincott's Magazine*, published the following year in volume form; a second volume of fairy stories, *A House of Pomegranates*, appeared the same year. These later fairy tales forsake the clarity and resonant beauty of those in the first volume for a style complicated and weakened by overwriting and an elaborate pseudo-Orientalism. Each story carries a dedication to a different society hostess; selling at a very expensive 21 shillings per copy, strikingly illustrated in the symbolist style by Charles Ricketts and Charles Shannon, this later volume of fairy stories was clearly meant more as a luxury item for the modish than for use in the nursery. By the time of Wilde's death, the first edition had still not sold out.

From 1892 to 1895, Wilde produced a series of excellent and highly popular comic melodramas, culminating in the pure intellectual farce of *The Importance of Being Earnest*. His imprisonment for homosexual practices ruined him, and he died in poverty in Paris in 1900; he retained his wit and kindness to the end.

The copy-text used here derives from the first book publication of 'The Selfish Giant' in *The Happy Prince and Other Tales* (London: David Nutt, May 1888). It was published in America by Roberts Brothers, of Boston. The book is dedicated to his friend, Carlos Blacker (1859–1928). The book contains five stories: 'The Happy Prince'; 'The Nightingale and the Rose'; 'The Selfish Giant'; 'The Devoted Friend'; and 'The Remarkable Rocket'. Three full-page illustrations by Walter Crane adorn the book. (After Wilde's conviction, Crane would be one of the few to sign a petition asking for clemency.) In addition the book includes drawings and designs by Jacomb Hood (1857–1929). *The Happy Prince* was written for a popular market; it did not, however, find one. The first print run was of 1,000 copies at 5 shillings a copy; in January 1889, a second cheaper edition followed (selling at 3 shillings and sixpence). Yearly sales were around 150 copies (or so Wilde complained to John Lane in a letter of late September 1894). Wilde sent copies of the first edition to Walter Pater (1839–94), John Ruskin, William Gladstone (1809–98), and Florence Stoker (née Balcombe) (1858–1935) (Bram Stoker's (1847–1912) wife and an old flame of Wilde's), among others.

ANDREW LANG, *Prince Prigio*

Andrew Lang (1844–1912) engaged with fairy tales as an imaginative writer, an historian, professional man of letters, an editor, and a collector. Born in Viewfield, Selkirk, he was educated at Selkirk Grammar, the Edinburgh Academy, and the University of St Andrews before moving to Balliol College, Oxford, and then to an Open Fellowship at Merton College. On his marriage to Leonora Blanche Alleyne (1851–1933) in 1875, he abandoned his fellowship and settled to a life of writing in Kensington, London. He first achieved fame as a poet, but soon acquired a reputation as part of the burgeoning study of anthropology, mythology, and folklore. In 1884, he published *Custom and Myth* (a work that imagines a common human psychic unity responsible for the similarity of certain folk tales and motifs across widely different cultures). *Myth, Ritual and Religion* (1887) consolidated this argument, and its corollary that a base substratum of primitive beliefs and images persist as 'survivals' in more sophisticated cultures. He was a founding member of the Folklore Society (1878). The sheer range of Lang's output is staggering, from triolets to treatises, from histories of Scotland to translations of Homer. His impact on the fairy tale at the end of the nineteenth century was a vital and creative one. With his compatriot Robert Louis Stevenson (1850–94), Lang stood for the late nineteenth-century revival of romance—though he brought to that revival a noticeably sceptical spirit. His series of 'coloured' fairy-tale books, from *The Blue Fairy Book* (1889) to *The Lilac Fairy Book* (1910), introduced generations of children to the folklore of the world. At the more scholarly level, he prepared an excellent edition of Charles Perrault's *Popular Tales* (1888), with an extensive and influential introduction. And he wrote himself a series of gently frivolous and imaginatively expansive fairy tales: *The Princess Nobody* (1884); the more serious Scottish, half-historical *The Gold of Fairnilee* (1888); and his two works set in the facetious imaginary kingdom of Pantouflia, *Prince Prigio* (1889) and *Prince Ricardo of Pantouflia: Being the Adventures of Prince Prigio's Son* (1893). In the tale of the impossibly clever Prince Prigio, there may be something of a wistfully ironic self-portrait.

The copy-text is the first book publication of *Prince Prigio* (Bristol: J. Arrowsmith; London: Simpkin, Marshall & Co., 1889) by Andrew Lang (credited as 'Author of "The Mark of Cain," "The Gold of Fairnilee" Etc.'). The book contains twenty-seven illustrations by the prolific and popular artist Gordon (Frederick) Browne (1858–1932). (For more information on Browne, see the headnote above on Juliana Horatia Ewing.) Lang dedicated *Prince Prigio* to 'Alma, Thyra, Edith, Rosalind, Norna, Cecily and Violet'. The text begins with the following preface, a pseudo-scholarly introduction (mocking his own life of scholarship) replete with literary allusions to classics of fantasy (including the Quatermain romances written by his friend and sometime collaborator, H. Rider Haggard (1856–1925)), as though they are anthropological or natural historical works:

> In compiling the following History from the Archives of Pantouflia, the Editor has incurred several obligations to the Learned. The Return of Benson (chapter xii) is the fruit of the research of the late Mr. ALLEN QUATERMAIN, while the final *wish* of Prince Prigio was suggested by the invention or erudition of a Lady.
>
> A study of the *Firedrake* in South Africa—where he is called the *Nana-boulélé*, a difficult word—has been published in French (translated from the Basuto language) by M. PAUL SÉBILLOT, in the *Revue des Traditione Populaires*. For the *Remora*, the Editor is indebted to the *Voyage à la Lune* of M. CYRANO DE BERGÉRAC.

233 *Pantouflia*: the name brings in the French word for slipper, *la pantoufle* (also in German, as *der Pantoffel*). This includes a reference to 'Cinderella' ('Cendrillon, ou La Petite Pantoufle de verre'), and also an ironic allusion to the French verb *pantoufler*, which means both to relax and put one's feet up, but also to talk nonsense, to talk through one's hat.

Cinderella . . . the Marquis de Carabas . . . cat, wearing boots . . . Madam La Belle au Bois-dormant: all tales by Charles Perrault (1628–1703), in his *Histoires ou Contes du temps passé* (1697), which Lang had recently edited as *Perrault's Popular Tales* (Oxford: Clarendon Press, 1888). In addition to Cinderella, he refers to 'Puss In Boots' ('Le Maître chat ou Le Chat botté') and 'Sleeping Beauty'.

234 *Prigio*: our hero's name resembles a vague Italianization of the English word 'prig', in the sense of a fop, a punctilious, self-important, didactic, and superior person.

Saracens: a generic term for the Muslim peoples of North Africa and the Middle East, and hence a way of apparently dating the story in the time of the Crusades, that is between the eleventh and the thirteenth centuries.

235 *seven-leagued boots*: a well-known property in European folklore, which enables the wearer to travel seven leagues with each step. A league varies in length, but can be reckoned as being equivalent to 3 miles (4.82 kilometres). Lang would have encountered this magical footwear most recently in Charles Perrault's 'Le Petit Poucet', where the diminutive hero steals the ogre's 'bottes de septs lieuës' while he sleeps.

pantomime 'properties': for the connection of fairy tales to pantomime see notes to p 38.

236 *to teach the queen-dowager, his grandmother*: in other words, despite the prohibition in the old adage, he has tried to teach his grandmother to suck eggs.

Grognio: another vaguely Italian name, that brings in both the English 'groggy', as in 'intoxicated' or 'unsteady', and also the French *grogner* and *grognon*, as in to grumble or to be a grouse.

237 *counting out his money*: an allusion, of course, to the following lines from the English nursery rhyme 'Sing A Song Of Sixpence':

>The king was in his counting-house
>Counting out his money.

238 *the siren*: a fabulous monster, part woman, part bird, renowned for the beguiling and deceptive sweetness of its singing, and most famous from an episode in Book XII of Homer's *The Odyssey*.

239 *a patent refrigerator*: the refrigerator was an early nineteenth-century invention.

241 *Falkenstein*: literally in German, a falcon stone, and a place name designed to locate the story in a Germanic context. There is a famous ruined Castle Falkenstein in Lower Austria, and a town of the same name in the Harz district in Saxony-Anhalt, Germany.

242 *If you are clever . . . to like you*: perhaps a self-critique on Lang's part, though (in 1889) also likely to provoke thoughts of Oscar Wilde, and perhaps also of William Hazlitt's (1778–1830) essay 'On the Disadvantages of Intellectual Superiority' (first published in the second volume of *Table Talk* (1824)).

243 *Gluckstein*: with the addition of an umlaut, this would mean a happy or lucky stone (see note to p. 15). In the last decades of the nineteenth century, Salmon and Gluckstein was a successful London tobacconist.

by your governess: this may reveal Lang's assumptions about the likely class of the child readers of the book, or perhaps be a joke about such assumptions.

Kellner: a waiter (German), and another indication of a German-Austrian-Swiss setting for a tale that is also so imbued with French language and culture.

245 *Fortunatus's purse*: see note to p. 46.

247 *that famous carpet . . . the market at Bisnagar*: a reference to the magic carpet in the tale of 'The Three Princes and the Princess Nouronnihar', one of the stories in *The Thousand and One Nights*. Like *Prince Prigio*, this tale also deals with three brothers, all of whom wish to marry their cousin, the Princess Nouronnihar. Their father, the Sultan of the Indies, decides that whichever of the brothers brings back the most wonderful object will win the Princess's hand. The eldest brother, Prince Hussain (Houssain,

in Lang's version), travels to Bisnagar (modern day, Vijayanagara) where he buys an ordinary-looking carpet that nonetheless has the magic power to fly anyone who stands on it to anywhere they choose. The tale is one that ends with the cooperation of the brothers, rather than their rivalry; the magic properties found by all three of them are required to save the Princess's life. Lang included the story in *The Blue Fairy Book* (1889) as 'The Story of Prince Ahmed and the Fairy Paribanou'.

249 *the spyglass of carved ivory . . . in the bazaar in Schiraz*: another reference to 'The Story of Prince Ahmed and the Fairy Paribanou' (see note above). In that story, Ali, the middle brother, finds a spyglass that enables him to see whatever in the world he wishes to see, no matter where it is taking place.

250 *Monsieur Cyrano de Bergerac*: Savinien Cyrano de Bergerac (1619–55), a French writer and the author of *L'Autre Monde, ou, Les États et empires de la lune* (1657) (translated into English as *A Voyage to the Moon*) also mentioned in the preface to the book, where Lang playfully takes the work as a non-fiction account. Though Cyrano de Bergerac's title was often popularly transformed to *Le Voyage dans la lune*, it is possible that Lang is confusing the title of Cyrano's text with Jacques Offenbach's (1819–80) *opéra-féerie* (fairy-opera) *Le Voyage dans la lune* (1875), though this adapts Jules Verne's (1828–1905) *De la terre à la lune* (*From the Earth to the Moon*) (1865) rather than Cyrano.

Remora: before Cyrano de Bergerac invented his monster, a remora was (and remains) a slender ray-finned fish famous for attaching itself by a suction disc to the underside of sharks and other large marine animals. In early modern alchemical texts, the remora stands as a symbol of coldness (the real fish was popularly understood to be able to detain ships, or lock them in ice). In Cyrano's text, a cold remora fights a hot salamander.

255 *Punctuality is the politeness of princes!*: a quote (with 'kings' standing in for 'princes') attributed to Louis XVIII (1755–1824) of France.

257 *Salamander Furiosus of Buffon*: in mythology and alchemical lore, the salamander was associated with elemental fire; the real lizard was believed to be born from fire. *Furiosus* means demented, mad, raging (Latin). With the Swedish Carl von Linné (Carolus Linnaeus (1707–78)), Georges-Louis Leclerc, Comte de Buffon (1707–88) is one of the great natural historians of the eighteenth century; Lang's spurious Latin nomenclature forms an element in the story's ongoing joke about the confusion between fairy tale and scholarship (natural historical or anthropological).

258 *Captain Kopzoffski*: a pun that involves a merging of German and Russian, with *Kopf* meaning 'head' in German, and the whole name therefore being Lang's humorous riposte to William Makepeace Thackeray's 'Kutasoff Hedzoff' (see note to p. 54).

Lord Kelso: Kelso is a town in the Scottish borders. Lord Kelso makes a reappearance in Oscar Wilde's *The Picture of Dorian Gray* (1890) as Dorian's grandfather.

a Philippine: it is unclear what Lang means by this word, though a guess might be hazarded that a 'Philippine' is Prigio's joke about the gift of the Firedrake's horns and tail as being a diminutive 'fillip', something of minor importance, a mere trifle.

259 *hever*: another attempt in the tales in this book to render a cockney accent (popularly supposed to involve dropping aitches where they are required, and adding them where they are superfluous). It is a feature of the genre at its most flippant that all servants must be comical cockneys (though the earlier use in this speech of 'summat' for 'something' sounds more Yorkshire than London).

261 *The Rose and the Ring*: see Thackeray's tale above.

262 *"perkisits"*: the butler's mispronunciation of 'perquisites' as set out in the king's proclamation.

266 *Mr. Arrowsmith*: a reference by Lang to the publisher of his tale, James Williams Arrowsmith (1839–1913). Arrowsmith's firm was a leading one in the late nineteenth century; among other works, they published Jerome K. Jerome's (1859–1927) *Three Men in a Boat* (1889), George Grossmith (1847–1912) and Weedon Grossmith's (1854–1919) *The Diary of a Nobody* (1892), and Anthony Hope's (1863–1933) *The Prisoner of Zenda* (1894).

268 *Prigio est prêt*: there are several similar mottoes, including 'Toujours prêt' ('always ready') and 'tout prêt' ('quite ready'), the latter used by the Clan Murray.

271 *Fountain of Lions*: another reference to events in 'The Story of Prince Ahmed and the Fairy Paribanou', included by Lang in *The Blue Fairy Book* (1889). The water has magically healing powers. (There is a real 'Fountain of Lions' at the heart of the Alhambra Palace in Granada, Spain.)

273 *Knight Templars like Front de Bœuf and Brian du Bois Gilbert*: Reginald Front-de-Bœuf (the name literally translates from French as 'ox forehead') and Brian de Bois-Guilbert are both villainous characters from Sir Walter Scott's *Ivanhoe* (1819).

FORD MADOX FORD, *The Queen Who Flew*

Ford Madox Ford (born Ford Hermann Hueffer) (1873–1939) was one of the most talented English novelists of the first half of the twentieth century. He was born into Pre-Raphaelite circles, the grandson of the painter Ford Madox Brown (1821–93) and the nephew of William Michael Rossetti (1829–1919); later in life, he would show a great deal of ambivalence and even hostility to the Victorian milieu that once nurtured his fairy stories. As a youth he was friendly with his Rossetti cousins (the Anarchists Olivia, Helen, and Arthur) and with the literary Garnett family, notably Olive (1871–1958) and Edward (1868–1937), all of whom were intimate with the Russian Anarchist and Nihilist exiles Prince Peter Kropotkin (1842–1921) and 'Stepniak' (Sergey

Mikhailovich Kravchinsky) (1851–95); the radical connections formed here perhaps seep into the politics of *The Queen Who Flew*.

Young Hueffer was a precocious author: by the age of 20, he had published a novel, three long fairy stories (*The Brown Owl*, *The Feather* (both 1892) and *The Queen Who Flew* (1894)), and a volume of poems. In 1894, he eloped with Elsie Martindale; some have seen traces of their relationship in Hueffer's youthful writings—especially *The Queen Who Flew*. Later in the decade Hueffer formed friendships with Joseph Conrad (1857–1924), Henry James (1843–1916), and Stephen Crane (1871–1900) (the so-called 'Literary Impressionists') and H. G. Wells (1866–1946); he collaborated with Conrad on several novels. He wrote one other book for children, *Christina's Fairy Book* (1906), a collection of tales. In the Edwardian period, among other works, he produced a trilogy of historical novels about Catherine Howard, fifth queen of Henry VIII. Ford had an affair with his sister-in-law, Mary, and experienced an agoraphobic 'breakdown'. Later he fell in love with the novelist Violet Hunt (1862–1942); the strains of his marriage fed into Ford's greatest novel— indeed one of the twentieth century's best novels—*The Good Soldier* (1915).

From 1908 to 1910, he was editor of the distinguished literary magazine *English Review*. Always receptive to talent, Hueffer was an ideal editor; among others, he fostered the work of Ezra Pound and 'discovered' D. H. Lawrence. He served as a soldier in the First World War, fighting at the Somme and the Ypres salient; he was nearly killed by a shell, was gassed, and was finally invalided out due to the effects of pneumonia. His Great War experiences were recorded in fictional form in his impressive tetralogy *Parade's End* (1924–8). After the war, Hueffer changed his name to Ford Madox Ford. For a few years he lived in Sussex with a young Australian artist, Stella Bowen (1893–1947); they then went to Paris where, with the aid of Pound, he produced the Modernist periodical *Transatlantic Review*. In the mid-1920s, he had an affair with Jean Rhys. His last years were spent between New York, Paris, and Provence; on 26 June 1939, he died in Deauville.

The copy text of *The Queen Who Flew: A Fairy Tale* comes from its first publication (London: Bliss, Sands & Foster, 1894). The author's name is given as 'Ford Huffer', 'Author of "The Brown Owl" "Shifting of the Fire" etc'. The book begins with a fine frontispiece by Sir Edward Burne-Jones (1833–98), depicting a robed woman leaning over to pour water from a large jug onto flowers. The book also contains a running, elegant, atmospheric design of flying geese among the clouds by Charles Raymond Booth Barrett (1850–1918), military historian and the author and illustrator of *Barrett's Illustrated Guides* to English counties.

The Queen Who Flew begins with the following dedication: 'To | A Princess of the Old Time | Before Us | This Tale | Is Due and Dedicated', and a poem:

> *Over the leas the Princess came,*
> *On the sward of the cliffs that breast the sea,*
> *With her cheek aglow and her hair a flame,*
> *That snared the eyes and blinded them,*
> *And now is but a memory.*

Explanatory Notes 431

> Over the leas, the wind-tossed dream,
> Over the leas above the sea,
> Passed and went to reign supreme.
> —No need of a crown or diadem
> In the kingdom of misty Memory.

280 *"Eldrida R."*: Eldrida is reputedly an Anglo-Saxon name meaning, literally, 'old counsel', and therefore 'wise' or 'sage', but more probably is a Victorian medievalist coinage. 'R.' stands for *Regina*, Latin for 'queen'.

282 *opodeldoc*: a liniment of soap, with camphor and essential oils (often rosemary).

284 *carcanet*: usually a necklace, but also, as here, an ornamental headband.

292 *the dickens*: since the late sixteenth century, a slang word for the Devil (the Deuce) used as an exclamation to express alarm, astonishment, or annoyance.

295 *the cat sat and looked at the Queen*: a reference to the old proverb (dating back at least to the sixteenth century) that 'a cat may look at a king/queen'.

298 *costermonger*: someone who sells fruit in the street; also sometimes taken to mean a poor and worthless person.

"Lizer, be my disy": an attempt to render 'Eliza, be my daisy' in a London, 'cockney' accent.

299 *'It was we who saved the capitol'*: Livy records in his *History of Rome* (Book V, ch. 47) how when the Gauls sacked Rome, they were prevented from taking the Capitol, where the citizens had taken refuge, due to the alarm being raised by cackling geese (kept there because they were sacred to the goddess Juno).

302 *Mrs. Hexer*: *der Hexer* is the German word for a male sorcerer or warlock, suggesting an interesting confusion of genders, since the name might also in this context more usually be thought to derive from *die Hexe*, the German word for a female 'witch'.

Kamschkatka: a slightly garbled version of Kamschatka (with a Germanic cat introduced into the name halfway), the 'North-east Cape of Asia', a peninsula of land in the Russian far east. In the 1890s, the area was noted for being the home of lepers, but is more likely used here as somewhere implausibly remote.

shepherd of Pendleton: possibly a jokey reference to the Pendleton Woolen Mills in Oregon, renowned for the making of wool shirts and blankets. However, more likely, there is also a village of Pendleton in the Ribble Valley in Lancashire, famous for the case of the Pendle witches, when in 1612 nineteen women were accused of witchcraft (and many of them were executed). (The event was immortalized in William Harrison Ainsworth's (1805–82) novel *The Lancashire Witches* (1849).) If some allusion is intended, it may connect to the forthcoming moment in which Eldrida is herself taken to be the witch.

306 *goose-girl*: a reference, perhaps, to the Grimms' fairy tale of the same name. This was one of the Grimms' most famous fairy stories, and exists in many nineteenth-century versions and revisions, including one of the tales gathered in Andrew Lang's first anthology, *The Blue Fairy Book* (1889).

307 *Æolian harps*: originally invented in ancient times, but revived and at a peak of popularity in the Romantic period, this refers to a stringed instrument which produces music when exposed to a current of air. (The adjective derives from Aeolus, the god of the wind.) In poems such as Coleridge's 'The Eolian Harp' (written 1795), the instrument operates as a symbol of the naturally inspired poet.

LAURENCE HOUSMAN, *The Story of the Herons*

Laurence Housman (1865–1959) was both a notable artist and art critic and a writer and playwright. His father, Edward Housman (1831–94), was a county solicitor; his mother, Sarah Jane Williams (1828–71), died when he was 5 years old. One of five boys and with two sisters, he had two particularly gifted siblings. One of these was his older brother, Alfred Edward Housman (1859–1936), professor of Latin at University College London and later at Cambridge, and the poet and author of *A Shropshire Lad* (1896) and *Last Poems* (1922). Like his brother, Laurence was homosexual. Like him, too, he was educated at the Bromsgrove School. On leaving, Laurence attended art schools in London. In the 1880s, aided by a legacy, he and his sister Clemence broke with their oppressive Tory father. Clemence Annie Housman (1861–1955) was his other greatly talented sibling; she was a wood engraver, an illustrator, a talented author, and a notable suffragette (briefly imprisoned for civil disobedience). She and Laurence were close; they lived together in London for much of their adult lives. Laurence himself would write on socialist and feminist themes. In holding his views, he was not afraid of unpopularity: he was a pacifist during the Great War, an early supporter of Indian independence, and a founder member of the Men's League for Women's Suffrage. In the last decades of his life, he became involved with Quakerism, finally in 1952 joining the Society of Friends in Street, Somerset.

Laurence Housman wrote a number of novels, was a prominent playwright, and the author of an entertaining autobiography, *The Unexpected Years* (1937). He illustrated editions of Christina Rossetti's (1830–94) fairy-tale poem *Goblin Market* (first published, 1862; illustrated by Housman in 1893), and George MacDonald's *At The Back of the North Wind* (1871; illustrated 1900) and *The Princess and the Goblin* (1872; illustrated 1900). His own books of fairy tales include *A Farm in Fairyland* (1894), *The House of Joy* (1895), *The Field of Clover* (1898), and *The Blue Moon* (1904), all of a very high quality.

The copy-text here follows the first publication of the story in Laurence Housman, *The House of Joy* (London: Kegan Paul Trench Trubner & Co.,

1895), 51–84. The book contains eight stories, including 'The White King' and 'The Moon-Flower'. 'The Story of the Herons' is the fourth story in the volume. Each tale has its own dedication; 'The Story of the Herons' is dedicated 'To Audrey and Veronica'. Laurence Housman himself illustrated the book with border designs and with pictures in the 'decadent' fashion, somewhere between Edward Burne-Jones's medievalism and Aubrey Beardsley's (1872–98) eroticism.

328 *a mirror*: to Victorian readers, the Princess gazing at the world through a mirror would have recalled the position of 'The Lady of Shalott', in the poem by Alfred, Lord Tennyson (1809–92), first published in *Poems* (1832). The situation of falling in love with someone in a mirror as it appears in Tennyson's poem echoes the way in which Britomart falls in love with Artegall in Sir Edmund Spenser (1552–99), *The Faerie Queene* (1590), Book III, canto ii, stanzas 22 ff.

341 *wise in their generation*: a biblical reference to Luke 16:8: 'And the lord commended the unjust steward, because he had done wisely; for the children of this world are in their generation wiser than the children of light.'

KENNETH GRAHAME, *The Reluctant Dragon*

Kenneth Grahame (1859–1932) was a gentleman banker and the author of three classic books, enjoyed equally by child and adult readers: *The Golden Age* (1895), *Dream Days* (1898), and *The Wind in the Willows* (1908). He was born in Edinburgh, but in 1868 left Scotland for school in Oxford. He moved to London and joined the Bank of England. There for some years he held in tension his bohemian leanings (he wrote for *The Yellow Book*) and the comforts of bourgeois respectability. The title of his first book, *Pagan Papers* (1893), a volume of essays and sketches, indicates his allegiance to a mildly subversive, hedonistic Victorian Hellenism. He achieved enormous success with his next two books. Both *Dream Days*, from which 'The Reluctant Dragon' is taken, and its predecessor, the highly popular *The Golden Age*, detail the adventures of five children, Edward (the eldest), Selina (the eldest girl), Harold (the youngest boy), Charlotte (the youngest girl), and the narrator (whose name we never learn). Critics praised Grahame's boy-narrator for his curious mixture of childlikeness and adulthood. In tandem with his literary career, he was also progressing up the hierarchy at the Band of England. In 1897 Grahame married Elspeth Thomson. They had one child, born in 1900, Alastair ('Mouse') Grahame.

One year after his marriage, in 1898, Grahame was appointed secretary of the Bank of England; this would prove to be the peak of his professional career. The peak of his writing career came ten years later with the publication of *The Wind in the Willows*, one of the funniest and most golden books from the 'Golden Age' of children's literature—although like all of Grahame's work, it has been as much enjoyed by adults as by children. The stories of Mole, Rat,

Badger, and the incorrigible Mr Toad derived from tales told to his young son. Alastair died in 1920, struck by a train on the outskirts of Oxford, in a probable suicide.

The copy-text for 'The Reluctant Dragon' derives from its first appearance in print, as the seventh, and penultimate, chapter of Kenneth Grahame, *Dream Days* (London: John Lane: The Bodley Head, 1898), 177–245. There are no illustrations in this book, but it was illustrated later, rather brilliantly by Maxfield Parrish (1870–1966) in 1902, and then, in 1938, even more brilliantly, in a stand-alone edition of *The Reluctant Dragon* by Ernest Howard Shephard (1879–1976). E. H. Shephard also provided the definitive illustrated edition of *The Wind in the Willows* (1931).

342 *Wordsworth*: the reference is to the poem 'Lucy Gray' by William Wordsworth (1770–1850), one of a group of the so-called 'Lucy poems', stories of a 'child of nature', whose mysterious disappearance and likely death the poet mourns. The poem first appeared in the second edition of *Lyrical Ballads* (1800), and was a work that would have been familiar to most adult and many child readers at the time. Lucy has gone missing and her parents seek her:

> And now they homeward turned, and cried
> 'In Heaven we all shall meet!'
> When in the snow the Mother spied
> The print of Lucy's feet.
>
> (lines 41–4)

They track the 'footmarks small', but these vanish in the middle of a bridge.

Crusoe's attitude of mind: a reference to Daniel Defoe's *Robinson Crusoe* (1719). Following many years of solitude after being shipwrecked on an island, Crusoe comes across a single footprint in the sand, and realizes that he is not altogether alone. Grahame's narrator prefers the adventure and thrill of Defoe's text to the mysterious, possibly mawkish sentiment seen as present in the poem by Wordsworth.

343 *iguanodon*: a herbivorous dinosaur, first named in 1825 by the geologist and pioneer in the study of dinosaurs Gideon Mantell (1790–1852), the name being formed by compounding the lizard name 'iguana' with the Greek word for 'tooth'. Charlotte declares the iguanodon not to be British, but, in a sense, she is quite wrong: Mantell found the fossilized bones and teeth (now thought to come from different genera) in the South Downs, near his home town of Lewes; the Sussex Downs also provide the setting for Grahame's tale.

the slot: here used in the sense of the trail left by an animal.

the circus-man: the narrator and Harold, two of the child-heroes of *Dream Days*, have already encountered this character in an earlier chapter, 'The Magic Ring', in which he asks them if they are bored ('"Or else—let me see; you're not married, are you?"' (*Dream Days*, 101)), and takes them to the circus (the magic ring of the chapter's title being the circus ring).

345 *the Downs*: the range of high chalk hills near the South Coast of England, ranging from the Itchen Valley in Hampshire to Beachy Head in Sussex.

the Giant with no Heart in his Body: originally a Norwegian folk tale, collected by Peter Asbjørnsen (1812–85) and Jørgen Moe (1813–82), and translated into English by Sir George Webbe Dasent (1817–96) in *Popular Tales from the Norse* (1859).

348 *stramash*: an uproar, state of noise and confusion, a smash (*OED*).

353 *Roman holiday*: a merrymaking or day off that involves bloodshed and violence. The phrase alludes to Lord Byron (1788–1824), *Childe Harold's Pilgrimage* (1818), and the description there of a gladiatorial combat: canto iv, stanza 141: 'Butchered to make a Roman holiday!' Earlier in *Dream Days*, in 'The Magic Ring', Harold and the narrator have imagined themselves to be angry cavemen and both felt a similar desire for fighting and carnage: 'For a space we gloated silently over the fair scene our imagination had conjured up. It was *blood* we felt the need of then. We wanted no luxuries, nothing dear-bought nor far-fetched. Just plain blood and nothing else, and plenty of it' (pp. 97–8).

E. NESBIT, *Melisande*

Edith Nesbit (1858–1924) is central to the history of Edwardian children's fiction. After the death of her father, followed by some years abroad, the family settled in Kent. Edith married Hubert Bland in 1880; both she and her husband were founding members of the socialist Fabian Society. Her views were sometimes rigorously 'advanced' and sometimes disappointingly reactionary (she rather looked down on the Suffragettes). Her marriage was, for its time, a highly unconventional one, in which she condoned the feckless Bland's numerous sexual liaisons (even adopting two of his illegitimate children). She wrote poetry and some competent ghost stories and uncanny tales, but found her métier in the writing of books for children. *The Treasure Seekers* (1898) was the first of her books to feature the Bastable children (and is perhaps influenced by Kenneth Grahame's *The Golden Age* (1895)). *The Wouldbegoods* (1901), *The New Treasure Seekers* (1904), and the excellent *The Railway Children* (1906) followed, all set solidly in the sometimes financially precarious world of the turn-of-the-century middle class. However, perhaps her most impressive works are her books that imbue realism with enchantment, mingling a simple humour with a somewhat muted magical delight. Her first tentative forays into the field were the purely fairy-tale *The Book of Dragons* (1900) and *Nine Unlikely Tales for Children* (1901): then came the increasingly engaging series of *Five Children and It* (1902), *The Phoenix and the Carpet* (1904), and *The Story of the Amulet* (1906), tales of wishes and time-travel, followed by *The Enchanted Castle* (1907) and *The Magic City* (1910).

The copy-text follows the story's first book publication, in E. Nesbit, *Nine Unlikely Tales for Children* (London: T. Fisher Unwin, 1901), 159–92. It is the fifth of the 'unlikely tales' in the book; others include the sometimes anthologized 'Fortunatus Rex and Co.'. The book was illustrated by H. R. (Harold Robert) Millar (1869–1940), a prolific and talented Scottish artist, most famous otherwise for his illustrations for many of E. Nesbit's children's books of the 1900s, including *Five Children and It*, *The Story of the Amulet*, and *The Magic City*, as well as for Rudyard Kipling's *Kim* (1901) and *Puck of Pook's Hill* (1906).

366 *Malevola*: like Andrew Lang in *Prince Prigio*, Nesbit begins with a series of allusions to renowned fairy tales, in this case to 'Sleeping Beauty'. Though clearly derived from Latin or French roots meaning 'ill will', the wicked fairy does not have the name 'Malevola' in Perrault's original 'La Belle au bois dormant'; she is similarly nameless in the Grimm Brothers' version of the story, 'Dornröschen'. In the Walt Disney film version (1959), the witch is similarly named 'Maleficent'.

the girl drops toads out of her mouth to this day: a reference to Charles Perrault's (1628–1703) fairy tale 'Les Fées' ('The Fairies'); see note to p. 46.

business of the mouse and the kitchen-maids: this looks back to the preceding story in Nesbit's book, 'The Prince, Two Mice, and Some Kitchen Maids'.

369 '*FORTUNA F.*': 'Fortuna' is the Roman goddess of luck and fortune.

372 *Florizel*: the name suggests the young hero of William Shakespeare's *The Winter's Tale* (*c*.1610–11). Shakespeare perhaps found the name in the popular Spanish romance *Amadis de Grecia* (1535).

374 '*Alice in Wonderland*': in Lewis Carroll's *Alice's Adventures In Wonderland* (1865), the young Alice, having grown to enormous size, weeps copiously and ends up swimming (having shrunk again) in her own pool of tears.

RUDYARD KIPLING, *Dymchurch Flit*

Rudyard Kipling (1865–1936) is one of the most vital of all children's writers, the author of such abiding classics as *The Jungle Book* (1894), *The Second Jungle Book* (1895), *Kim* (1901), *Just So Stories* (1902), *Puck of Pook's Hill* (1906), and *Rewards and Fairies* (1910). Born in Bombay, in 1871 Kipling was sent to England to be educated. His first years there, spent at Southsea with his younger sister, Alice ('Trix'), were marked by terrible unhappiness, largely caused by the abuse carried out by the couple charged with looking after them. He left their care to be educated at the United Service College at Westward Ho!, Bideford in North Devon (the original of the school in his book of linked school-stories, *Stalky & Co.* (1899)). In 1882 he returned to join his family in India. He became a journalist, and soon made a mark as a writer of Anglo-Indian short stories and poems. The stories were collected in a series of books, including *Plain Tales from the Hills* (1888) and *Life's Handicap* (1891); his early verse was published in *Departmental Ditties* (1886) and *Barrack-Room Ballads* (1892). Kipling returned to England in 1889, by now a hugely popular and feted author. In 1892, following the death of his close friend, Wolcott Balestier, Kipling married Wolcott's sister, Caroline. After a globe-trotting honeymoon, the couple moved to Vermont. There their two daughters, Josephine and Elsie, were born. In September 1896, the family returned to England, settling in Rottingdean, East Sussex (also home to Kipling's uncle, the painter Sir Edward Burne-Jones), where Kipling's son John was born in 1897. Kipling was to become devotedly attached to Sussex, which formed the setting for his two books of pageant-like linked fairy tales (or perhaps rather of historical tales with a fairy in them), *Puck of Pook's Hill* and *Rewards and Fairies*. John died at the Battle of Loos in September 1915. Kipling became a member of the Imperial War Graves Commission; among other duties, he wrote a series of moving 'Epitaphs of the War'. After 1914, his writing became less prolific, though its quality remained high.

The copy-text is based on the story's first publication in book form in Rudyard Kipling, *Puck of Pook's Hill* (London: Macmillan and Co., 1906), 253–78. Between January and October 1906, the ten stories in this volume had already been published in the *Strand* magazine, with illustrations by Claude A. Shepperson. 'Dymchurch Flit' appeared in the September issue; it was also published in America in *McClure's Magazine*, in the same month, illustrated by André Castaigne and Frederic Dorr Steele. The book itself was illustrated by H. R. Millar (see headnote to E. Nesbit, 'Melisande', p. 436). As was often Kipling's practice in writing short stories, a short poem introduces and concludes the tale.

378 *to us you must tell*: in folklore, and among select circles of apiarists, it is understood that bees are a highly, indeed mysteriously, intelligent creature. In the preface to Book IV of his translation of Virgil's *Georgics* (1697), John Dryden writes: 'Virgil has taken care to raise the subject of each Georgic . . . and in the last, he singles out the bee, the most sagacious of [animals], for his subject.' Bees are supposed to wish to be informed of what is happening in the houses of their keepers, and particularly of deaths in the family. Kipling might have encountered the idea in Sussex, though it is a common one, as witnessed by the poem 'Telling the Bees' by the American poet John Greenleaf Whittier (1807–92).

the Fanners fan: a 'fanner' bee hovers by the entrance of the hive, fanning it with its wings, in order to keep the hive fresh by helping air circulate through it, drawing out the bad air and blowing in the good. Any honey-bee might do this work of fanning.

dwine away: to pine or waste away, to wither or fade. The use of this perfectly good English word was itself dwining by the end of the nineteenth century, and Kipling's use of it here would, in 1906, have had a rustic, old-fashioned air.

379 *oast-house*: a house for the 'kilning' or drying of hops, for use in the brewing

of beer. The houses have an apparently drooping 'cowl' fixed into the top of a conical roof, designed to help air circulate and keep the weather out. Such houses are a familiar sight in the Kentish countryside.

379 *old Hobden . . . lurcher dog*: throughout both *Puck of Pook's Hill* and *Rewards and Fairies*, to the children Dan and Una, two figures seem immutably present in the landscape: the hobgoblin Puck and the recurring figure of Hobden, the archetypal 'simple' and wise peasant, the genius of the place. A lurcher is a breed of British and Irish dog, somewhere between a greyhound and a terrier. The breed was the poor man's hunting dog, loyal but disreputable, and was associated with poaching.

'Old Mother Laidinwool . . . popped up her head': based on a traditional poem beginning 'Old Mother Nincompoop', adapted by Kipling. The poem refers to the practice, initiated by Charles II in the Burial in Woollen Acts, of the state enforcing the burial of the dead in shrouds made from English wool. The area of Romney Marsh was famous for its sheep. The fourth line ends, 'I'm bound to meet 'em there'. And the first chorus follows:

> Let me up and go
> Back to the work I know, Lord!
> Back to the work I know, Lord!
> For it is dark where I lie down, My Lord!
> An' it's dark where I lie down!

Kipling manages to make a ghostly Sussex pseudo-folk song ring out like a 'Negro spiritual'; he included the full version of the poem in his *Songs from Books* (1912).

380 *hem of*: a great deal of, 'a devil of'.

Peasmarsh Fair: Peasmarsh is a village, not far from the Kent–Sussex border, a few miles from Rye.

Plymouth . . . Dover: a Sussex drinking song; Plymouth and Dover are two southern English ports.

Wiltsheer: that is, the southern English county of Wiltshire.

381 *'Put a plenty salt on 'em . . . man I be'*: it was popularly supposed that fairies disliked salt; they were also believed by some to be compelled to count each grain of spilt salt.

Horseshoes, or Church Bells, or Running Water: all things that are said to deter wicked spirits and fairies (in the case of the horseshoe, in part perhaps because it is made of iron—a metal that bad spirits (and fairies) cannot abide). Witches and vampires are likewise supposed not to be able to cross running water.

roundel: here this refers to the ring-shaped space formed under the oast house's conical roof.

the great floods at Robertsbridge: an English village in Sussex, north of Hastings and south-west of Tunbridge Wells; as it lies on a floodplain, the village is often subject to flooding—so it would be hard to say to which one flood Tom Shoesmith refers.

odd-gates: weird, peculiar.

the world's divided . . . Romney Marsh: Kipling quotes R. H. Barham (1788–1845), *The Ingoldsby Legends* (1840). Barham was a local rector at Snargate, close to Old Romney. Romney Marsh is a sparsely populated wetlands area straddling the Kent and Sussex border.

see further through a millstone: to see clearly into (or through) a dark or difficult matter. (The saying seems to have been particularly popular in nineteenth-century America.)

382 *nigro-mancin'*: that is, 'necromancy'; see note to p. 45. The mispronunciation perhaps brings in the thought that black magic is intended.

a passel: a 'parcel', a small amount.

Pharisees: a malapropism for 'fairies', indirectly associating them with the rigorous Puritans who dismissed them.

out-gate: paranormal, supernatural.

Dymchurch Flit: Dymchurch is an English village, situated on the coast of Kent, south-west of Hythe, on Romney Marsh. A 'flit' is a word of nineteenth-century origin, meaning a moving on, a decamping.

383 *there's steeples settin' beside churches*: in the inland village of Brookland on Romney Marsh, the bell-tower of Brookland church stands adjacent to the main body of the church. In *Rewards and Fairies* (1910), Kipling's poem 'The Brookland Road' closes the story 'The Marklake Witches'.

grummelin': grumbling; to be 'grum' is to be gloomy and morose.

ravelly as witch-yarn on the spindles: when yarn tangled during the process of separation, it was popularly imagined as having been malevolently bewitched.

384 *Queen Bess's father he come in with his Reformatories*: a reference, of course, to the Reformation of the Church, brought in by King Henry VIII (1491–1547), father of Queen Elizabeth I (1533–1603). In Richard Corbett's (1582–1635) poem 'Rewards and Fairies', it is the Reformation—and thereby the end of Roman Catholic England—that drives out the fairies from the country: 'By which we note the fairies | Were of the old profession' (lines 33–4).

I dunnamany: a contraction of 'I don't know how many'.

among the Images: one feature of Protestant zeal was its iconoclasm, the destruction in churches of statues, paintings, carving, and murals, all of which were imagined to be idolatrous.

Robin: that is, Robin Goodfellow, another name for Puck, the fairy character drawn from folklore and from William Shakespeare's *A Midsummer Night's Dream* (1594–6) and central to the stories in both *Puck of Pook's Hill* and *Rewards and Fairies*.

384 *cruel Canterbury Bells ringin' to Bulverhithe*: the bells were rung whenever a heretic was burned. Between Bexhill and St Leonard's, the port of Bulverhithe was swallowed by the sea during the seventeenth century.

swarvin' up: 'swarve' is a Kent and Sussex word meaning to be choked up with silt or sediment.

385 *a squat*: the context suggests this means an infection (perhaps one actually present in the ground itself).

stenched up: packed in, confined.

Dymchurch Wall: since Roman times, the village has had a famous sea wall, designed to protect the land from flooding. The one present when Kipling was writing dated from the thirteenth century.

drownded like Old Winchelsea: in 1287, after decades of eroding storms, the village of Old Winchelsea was washed away by the sea.

386 *a Seeker*: this might be thought to refer to a sect of Protestant dissenters, Puritan but notably tolerant, formed in the 1620s, sometimes seen as forerunners of the Quakers (in so far as both relied on the inner promptings of the spirit). However, the context and date of the story suggest that the woman was a 'seeker' in another sense: a person curious and questioning about life.

rummelled: produced a rumbling sound.

387 *aps-tree*: the Aspen, a tree famous for its tremulous leaves.

hove down dunt: heaved down with a dull-sounding thump.

raklin': rattling.

a Rye barge: river barges left Rye Harbour, by the Sussex coast, taking goods up the River Rother.

388 *Hithe to Bulverhithe, fretty man an' petty maid*: Hythe is a coastal market town on the Kent coast, and Bulverhithe is on the edge of Hastings, on the Sussex coast; 'fretty' and 'petty': fretful and little.

389 *Puck*: see note to p. 384.

Oak, Ash, and Thorn: mentioned in 'Weland's Sword', the first tale of *Puck of Pook's Hill*, where chewing a leaf from an oak, ash, and thorn is supposed to help the children forget the magic they have witnessed. In the following poem, 'A Tree Song', the refrain 'oak, ash and thorn' acts as a burden, evoking the perennial presence of the English countryside:

> Of all the trees that grow so fair,
> Old England to adorn,
> Greater are none beneath the Sun,
> Than Oak, and Ash, and Thorn.

(lines 1–4)

390 *Twix' a liddle low shaw an' a great high gill*: between a low coppice and a high narrow valley.

Explanatory Notes 441

Brenzett reeds: Brenzett is a village inland on the Romney Marsh.

Oh Firle an' Ditchlin: Firle and Ditchling are villages near Lewes in Sussex; nearby Ditchling is Ditchling Beacon, one of the highest points on the range of hills called the South Downs.

APPENDIX

JOHN RUSKIN, 'Introduction' to *German Popular Tales* (1869)

For biographical information on John Ruskin, see headnote to *The King of the Golden River*, p. 407. The copy-text derives from a new edition of Edgar Taylor's translation of the Grimm brothers' *German Popular Stories* (London: John Camden Hotten, 1869), pp. v–xiv. See also headnote for 'Rumpel-Stiltskin', p. 405.

394 *The illustrations of this volume*: John Ruskin had long admired Cruikshank's drawings for the book of the Brothers Grimms' tales. In his autobiography, *Praeterita* (vol. I, ch. iv, sect. 82), he describes how 'I went on amusing myself—partly in writing English doggerel, partly in map drawing, or copying Cruikshank's illustrations to Grimm, which I did with great, and to most people now incredible, exactness, a sheet of them being, by good hap, well preserved, done when I was between ten and eleven' (New York: Everyman's Library, pp. 66–7).

my 'Elements of Drawing': John Ruskin's *The Elements of Drawing, in Three Letters to Beginners* was published in London in 1857 by Smith, Elder & Co.

Rembrandt: Rembrandt Harmenszoon van Rijn (1606–69) was a seventeenth-century Dutch painter and engraver, one of Europe's most profound and humane artists.

JULIANA HORATIA EWING, 'Preface' to *Old-Fashioned Fairy Tales* (1888)

For biographical and further bibliographical information on Juliana Horatia Ewing, see headnote to 'The First Wife's Wedding-Ring', p. 422. The copy-text is that of the first edition of Ewing's *Old-Fashioned Fairy Tales* (London: Society for Promoting Christian Knowledge; New York: Pott, Young & Co., 1882), pp. v–vii.

395 *THOS. THE RHYMER*: Thomas of Erceldoune, a possibly legendary late thirteenth-century poet and prophet, and the subject of a fourteenth-century romance and a border ballad, in both of which he is taken to Elfland by its queen. In *Ministrelsy of the Scottish Border* (3 vols., 1802–3), the ballad was revised and expanded by Sir Walter Scott. Erceldoune is now named Earlston, a market town in Berwickshire, in the Scottish Borders. The quote comes from a moment (lines 41–52) in the poem where the Queen of Elfland points out three paths: the narrow road that

442   *Explanatory Notes*

is 'the path of righteousness'; the 'braid braid road' that is 'the path of wickedness'; and then,

> And see not ye that bonnie road,
> That winds about the fernie brae?
> That is the road to fair Elfland,
> Where thou and I this night maun gae.
>
> (lines 49–52, in Walter Scott's version)

In Scots, a 'brae' is the steep bank of a river, or simply (and as more likely here), a hillside.

395 '*AUNT JUDY'S MAGAZINE FOR YOUNG PEOPLE*': this monthly periodical for children was set up in 1866 by the publisher George Bell (1814–90), with Margaret Gatty (Juliana Horatia Ewing's mother) as its first editor. Gatty had already had success with the children's books *Aunt Judy's Tales* (London: Bell and Daldy, 1861) and *Aunt Judy's Letters* (London: Bell and Daldy, 1862). The magazine featured natural history articles, poetry, and tales (a number of which were written by Juliana Ewing). Charles Lutwidge Dodgson ('Lewis Carroll') was another notable contributor (among other pieces, in 1867 it published his short fairy story 'Bruno's Revenge').

396 *cramming of cats*: from at least the 1740s, 'cram' has been used for the rapid learning of facts for an examination. The verb is also used for the stuffing of poultry in order to fatten them for the table. I am not sure why Ewing uses cats here, unless to suggest the double uselessness of cramming—overfeeding an animal that you cannot actually eat.

GEORGE MacDONALD, 'The Fantastic Imagination' (1895)

For biographical information on George MacDonald, see headnote to 'The Golden Key', p. 417. The copy-text is based on the second enlarged edition of MacDonald's collection of occasional prose *A Dish of Orts: Chiefly Papers on the Imagination, and on Shakespeare* (London: Sampson Low Marston & Company, 1895), 313–22. The book first appeared in 1893. The essay is the last in the book. In the 'Preface', MacDonald remarks of this piece: 'The paper on *The Fantastic Imagination* had its origin in the repeated request of readers for an explanation of things in certain shorter stories I had written. It forms the preface to an American edition of my so-called Fairy Tales' (p. vi). (The edition in question is *The Light Princess and Other Tales* (New York: G. P. Putnam's Sons, 1893).)

397 *Mährchen*: German for a little tale, a folk story, a fairy tale (though one that does not immediately bring in the presence of actual fairies). According to the *OED*, the word was first used in English by Louisa May Alcott in *Little Women* (1869).

Spenser: Sir Edmund Spenser (*c*.1552–99), English poet, and author of the unfinished romantic epic *The Faerie Queene* (Books I–III, published 1590;

Explanatory Notes   443

Books IV–VI, published 1596; two additional 'Cantos of Mutabilitie', published in 1609). This work exerted an enormous influence on later writers and, with Shakespeare's *A Midsummer Night's Dream* and *The Tempest* and John Milton's (1608–74) *Comus*, was decisive in forming a specifically English literary tradition of fairy writing, distinct from the native folk-tale traditions.

Undine: Friedrich Heinrich Karl, Baron de la Motte Fouqué, *Undine* (1811), one of the classic works of German Romanticism. The tale presents the story of Undine, a water-spirit who wishes to marry a human knight and so acquire a soul. By 1818, the tale had already been translated into English; many versions would follow, including that of Sir Edmund Gosse (1849–1928) in 1896. It was one of the most popular romances of the century, and one model for a medievalist, Christianized fantastic.

products of the Imagination . . . the work of the Fancy: here MacDonald draws upon the distinction between the imagination and the fancy set out in Samuel Taylor Coleridge's (1772–1834) *Biographia Literia* (1817). Put briefly, the primary imagination is 'the living power and prime of all human perception'; the secondary imagination is the conscious use of this vital power (in art) to unify, synthesize, harmonize, and reconcile impressions, the internal and the external, nature and the poet's soul; the fancy, however, is of a lesser importance, a mode of memory merely putting together things normally separate in time and space, drawing on—and playing with—the laws of association.

398 *cockney or Gascon*: in late nineteenth-century terms, cockney is, of course, the accent of the indigenous Londoner (it seems to be quite late in the century before the word attached to a style of speaking, as opposed to a type of person), whereas Gascon is the provincial dialect of a region of south-west France. Both kinds of voice may have been thought by MacDonald to be a strongly localized and impure form of their native language. In addition, a Gascon was sometimes used to denote a braggart. (A 'Gasconade' designated a pompous and bombastic boasting speech.)

399 *Mastery or Moor-ditch*: the Moore ditch was a seventeenth-century London sewer between Bishopsgate and Cripplegate, designed to carry waste into the Thames. Moor-ditch was associated with melancholy, as in William Shakespeare, *King Henry IV Part One*, I.ii.76.

the sonata: it is vital to MacDonald's use of the image here that a sonata has both a strongly set form, and that it is an instrumental piece, without words.

401 *æolian harp*: see note to p. 307.

'broken music': an allusion to a Shakespearean piece of wordplay: in *Henry V*, V.ii.240–1, King Henry declares to Katherine: 'Come, your answer in broken music', referring at once to the 'brokenness' of this Frenchwoman's English, and to the technical term used for harmonious

setting of music arranged at once for wind and string instruments. In other words, such music is both broken and unified.

401 *a child's eyes flash, or his mother's grow for a moment dim*: it is possible that W. B. Yeats recalled these words at the end of his poem 'On Being Asked For a War Poem':

> He has had enough of meddling who can please
> A young girl in the indolence of her youth,
> Or an old man upon a winter's night.
>
> (lines 4–6)

LAURENCE HOUSMAN, 'Introduction' to *Gammer Grethel's Fairy Tales* (1905)

For biographical details on Laurence Housman, see headnote to 'The Story of the Herons', p. 432. The copy-text is that of the first edition of *Gammer Grethel's Fairy Tales* (London: Alexander Moring and The De la More Press, 1905), pp. v–viii. The book offers the expanded version of Edgar Taylor's translation, and includes illustrations by George Cruikshank and Ludwig Emil Grimm (1785–1863), the youngest of the Grimm brothers.

402 *Grimm's Gammer Grethel Tales . . . Hans Andersen*: the Brothers Grimms' tales had been published as told by 'Gammer Grethel' since an edition of 1839 for H. Bohn's Illustrated Library. The book reappeared in notable further editions in 1849 and 1864, and again in 1888. 'Gammer' is a form of 'grandma'; 'Grethel' is pronounced with a hard 't', so that it sounds like 'Gretel'. 'Gammer Grethel' stands in for Katharina Dorothea Viehmann (née Pierson) (1755–1816), one of the Grimms' original informants from Hesse-Cassel. Her portrait was drawn by Ludwig Grimm, and used as the frontispiece for a number of the 'Gammer Grethel' editions.

Andersen's 'Fellow Travellers': more usually translated as 'The Travelling Companion', this story appeared under the title 'Rejsekammeraten' in the second collection of *Eventyr* (1835).

the 'Fox's Brush': this tale collected by the Brothers Grimm is more usually known as 'The Golden Bird' ('Der goldene Vogel').

Snowdrop: that is, of course, as she came to be known, Snow White, or 'Sneewitchen'.

the gardener's son . . . fox's brush, and Thumbling the Dwarf . . . giant's palm: the first is from the story 'The Golden Bird', mentioned above; and the latter refers to the tale 'Der junge Riese' or, in English, 'Thumbling the Dwarf and Thumbling the Giant' (sometimes translated as 'The Young Giant').

403 *'his reward is with him'*: from Isaiah 40:10: 'Behold, the Lord GOD will come with strong hand, and his arm shall rule for him: behold, his reward is with him, and his work before him.'